Chocolate Chickens Don't Taste So Good When Mixed Unwillingly in Vanilla Soup

By
Blu Penn

PublishAmerica
Baltimore

First printing

At the specific preference of the author, PublishAmerica allowed this work to remain exactly as the author intended, verbatim, without editorial input.

ISBN: 1-4241-1515-9
PUBLISHED BY PUBLISHAMERICA, LLLP
www.publishamerica.com
Baltimore

Printed in the United States of America

To my Father,
Whose light shines on through me and mine—Forever...
Charles William Penn Sr,
02/22/1946—10/13/2005
I saw you Pop...And I knew that you were there...RIP

-blu

Writing's like going to the gym for me.
All I have to do; is get off my azz—and get there—
And I have a grand time.
blu

When you treat a man as he is, you make him worse than he is. When you treat him as if he is already, what he holds the possibility of being, you make him what he should be.

Ten (1975)

I awoke with a start, short of breath. Once again I found myself swimming in a pool of cold sweat stirred amongst a sea of dirty, crumb-filled linens. Shaking my tiny frame free, with the force and frustration of a little man's life-and-death struggle, I was greeted, once more, by the sticky, pre-spring perspiration of an already hot east coast morning. And once more, I feared I was trapped!

Surrounded...

Wrapped tightly in the un-materialized security of what was (for me, a mere man-child) the ill-fated irony of a divided cluster of very special friends, relatives and downright frightening nemeses, I lay still a second more, dazed and confused as haunting images of so many people floated about me, passing by in dancing frenzies, in and out of my mind's long eye. Each and every one of them, in their own fetid ways, caste me invisible and ignored me completely as they went about the wrecked trivialities of what passed for their own lives. They never saw me. Thus they were entirely incapable, ig'nant or unable to offer a poor, all-but defeated brotha'—the necessity of a willing respite.

And if they could've, I don't think they would've helped anyway.

Sweltering humidity, countered only briefly by the flowing sanctity of the merciful force of a pre-spring, Susquehanna breeze, only scattered more the un-calmable fears jaunting languidly in perpetual, intimidating flutters permeating the terrified caverns of my naïve little mind.

Even now, approaching the early precepts of middle age—when I permit myself to think back on the way we lived—an acrid, chest-burning bile of remembrance lurches upward. It causes the uncomfortable, internal flashback of a heated anguish which still threatens to cloud any sense of the sweetened essence of an expectation of man-hood I've been able to carve out for myself in the present.

The fear—I find... is still here. An ever-slight, torrential foreboding causing the pits of my insides to swell involuntarily, not a thing I've ever been able to completely ward off or control.

The inability to conquer this thing so wholly and seemingly inconsequential was and still is... FRIGHTENING!

The fear is of hunger... of suffering constantly amid abuse. Of painful memories I've forever been unable to stamp out and erase. Of trusting, only to be let down, by callous dream-stealing thieves and twisted, scar faced pimps shallowly aligned with real-to-life thugs who'd cut your heart out for a cent while smiling down at you passively with that rotten-egg'd, sulfur smile while offering,—"Sorry little man. No solid offa' you. But you know bruh'... Da' devil made me do it."

Quickly, they'd slither away in a shuffled hurry. Off to seek out perhaps the calamity and sure-footed swiftness of their next unsuspecting victim; only to find instead, their own under-developed hell-bent demises.

A drunken family line of doped up deviants and sallow cut-throats, coupled with the ever haunting appendages of blightful, familiar molesters frequented my own staggering, personal growth.

For me, a young, salable boy of ten, the possibility of an almost sweltering, all-encompassing extinction was a reaping reality with each new face that materialized, seeking a score, at the door of our tiny apartment in Harrisburg, PA.

But mostly, this fear held something more ultimate.

A dread of abandonment...

The kind of neglect and rejection that is brought about by the production of stupid decisions coupled with abrupt, common carelessness which from birth was forced upon me by way of legacy. In my youth, I found myself obliged on a daily basis to become confronted largely by adult situations I had no business being a part of.

Afraid!

Paranoid wanderings of terrorized thought loomed heavily upon my compassionless belief that things could never-ever change. For me, at ten, nothing else, save strife, was constant.

As far as I'd learned, the way things were, was the way things was gonna' be.

The way they were supposed to be. And that they were exactly that same way for everyone else. I didn't know any better. Had no ROLE MODEL to see me through.

My fear was the twisted silhouette of an ever-looming Boogey-Man. Threatening menacingly—to take my head in one swooping lop if I ever relaxed or permitted myself the increasingly clear breath of rest enough to trust. Naww, man! Could never be caught up—lest I get caught-slippin'.

Ten was overwhelming, immense, and very, very real. It was alive! A living, breathing monstrosity which stifled me and shunted me away from grasping a clue about life's other, more breathe-saving offerings of privilege, self-development, esteem, or personal pride.

Miniscule things...Items such as hope, consistency, warm meals bearing contentment...Security, escaped me initially.

Every day's sun brought new challenge amid turmoiled struggle and ignorance. And, with that came the dark entrapment of terror brought on by my powerlessness of having wisdom enough to know how to fight back. The distress of being so young and ill-equipped to wage war against the demons that, by foul design, so easily materialized, to capitalize on the naivety of the fetid nature encapsulated inside a black child's loneliness—had almost destroyed me.

I was in deed surrounded.

Yet, now, in hindsight, I'm able to take that clearing breath—To stand tall in accepting those formerly frightening, daily challenges prevalent within the damned-up culture of a mangled society. And I can see clearly now as well. Well enough to realize that each one of my friends, family members, and even my still unforgotten nemesis holds a special hand in molding and pushing me forward toward at least a comfortable, personal existence.

Most of these, oft-times had unfortunate, colorful names like: Weezo, Buster, Inez, Ollie Lee, Myrna, Coolie, Gran-MO and Tissy, Mavis Penn and Robert (Bob) White, Mavis and grand-pop Rob. Bem-Bem Johnson, Menissa and Kelvin Braun, Oliviyeh Twist, ("The Motor City TWISTER"). Larry, and Mattie Mea Willems, Dernell McMilland, KiWatta Meisha and

A'maru Lee Willems. auntie Lynnie, uncle Sylver, Slope, Buckey, Tam, Mandy, Landa, Tierra and Kheli Johnston, grand-mom, Mary Anderson, Tammie and Mel Willems, Purskin Jeeters, Alvin and Booby Jetson, Melania Purtiss (Miss Honey), Vonnetta, Miss Dutchess, Miss Midget, my wrestling buddy, Craig, Miss Maula, funky, big butt—Miss Mola, Donnie and Massai Slewson, beautiful, Vette and her rogue husband, Palvador Ubootiya; (She should have married David) then perhaps her sweet behind might have found, as Mama'n always says, "Love Peace & Happiness" the first time around. Miss Gene, Gunny, and Kelvin and Mimmie Eltins also bring fond memories.

My REGGINS…You'all know that—Adversity Forces me to
write…Struggle Forces me to breathe…
Contempt Forces me to fight…
Education Forces me to ACHIEVE!

-blu

There was the Pennsylvania, Boas Street Gang. Ultimate HOMIES, like: Nelly and Puffy Anderson, Rowdy, Steinley and Gus Wilson, Ambria, Peewee and Chip Anderson, Aalston Pryor, Scoottie and Toolie White, Debby Purtiss (Shrimpy) who was Charlie, Kent, Rockie and George Purtiss' little sister. These were joined by Deric Meters, and Byrron and Damion Waleson, whom I doubt, possess the brain power to remember me, but for whom I still hold an unhealthy amount of equal disdain for.

I sometimes wish I could go back.

And…Given the opportunity, before ITSALLSAIDANDDONE…

I probably will.

With hopes of making more than a mediocre attempt at contacting em'—Just to fill them in on the humongous extent to which they've each influenced, with a magnitude of processed energy, the forming of the Person, Husband, Father, Brother, Son, Nephew, Sailor, Citizen—The man, I've become, with their help, today.

Just to let em' know.

How much I appreciate all they've done for me without ever really knowing they'd done anything at all. To take the time to sit for a mere five minutes with each of them to say, "THANK YOU!" I could never have become ME—Without You," would be an excruciatingly pleasureable experience. One I'm not certain I'll ever get.

TWELVE

Produced an entirely new collection of eclectic, sometimes not so wonderful people who'd entered into and crossed through the collage of personality thresholds which became, at times unbearable—Seeming, instead of rendering assistance, to take despicable pleasures themselves in getting caught up in clogging or becoming stumbling blocks to the more positive players standing on the outside in my life—Afraid to reach in to merely take steps to do something about it and bring it all to a surviveable end.

These too assisted in the chore of molding and sculpting my persona. This group embodied a resultant duality—of first, a sudden, ostensibly rushed, cross-country move; the posture of which Toppa, (my brother) and I had initially been led to believe had been the result of Mama'n's culminating, misguided lust for a shiftless, heart-stomping, soldier named, Egbert Rice, whom we traipsed across the entire nation, to Texas, so she could be with him.

The short-lived, torrid affair of course floundered as abruptly as it had begun. Leaving us stranded, destitute and alone in a city where most inhabitants spoke a strange, barren language (Spanish) which none of us had ever even heard. But, true-to-life, it mirrored in its end, with telling alacrity, the fate of most, if not all of Maman's former and future relationships—in a bad way.

We were too young to fully realize it then, but the axiom, "You are as an adult, what you see as a child" almost really fucked both Toppa and me up for good.

...All before we'd even been provided a fightin' prospect at wandering out into the vastness of the awaiting wilderness of adulthood, to be given our own opportunities at our own failures or successes.

This period threatened with impunity, our own determined chances at making or breaking our own resources, of having the courage, morality and commitment to character to one day step out to forge our own moves—permeate our own mistakes, as men.

Egbert Rice was only one of a multitude of Maman's crusty conquests. Only he'd been the one chosen to be used in route to her making a vetted, escaping flight from both her tormentors and from her conscience which all seemed to be centered around the great state of Pennsylvania.

With a corrupting, approachable, almost inspiring flare, backed up by a brightly lit smile which swept easily from one side of his face, clear to the other end, dude was THA' PROMISE MASTER. His charm and slithery wit had easily won Mama'n over completely with a self-serving, slimy grace.

This particular relationship was not unlike most we'd been made to run through. And, like all the others her children frequently endured, it too ended in a scathe. It was additive to placing Toppa and me on the blunt end of losing precariously secured life's-ground—Something he and I had all too frequently grown accustomed to.

Time and Time again—once she and whatever piece of meat she'd been shacking or cohabitating with that week split up, mirrored images of cursing flurries of hateful, verbal blows, adding to flying objects meant to maim, re-repossessions of meaningless furnishings, all coupled with a fat lip here or a sore rib there became the norm.

The injuries were usually hers.

All of this, mixed with, at times, the eye-opening, stark—terror of having to watch in horrific silence, the immensity of real—man-beat'n Maman's ass drama, as physically abusive episodes rang true for my siblings and I on repeated occasions.

She'd always bounce back though.

She was then, as she is now, despite all the shit she's put herself and all of us through, a deftly strong woman.

Gotta' hand that to her. Big—Ups' to Mama'n!

Before whatever fool leaving had trucked all his shit out to whatever raggedy ride he'd putted up to the complex in that day and before he'd spent the next, full length of a waning hour trying every desperate trick he knew to get that muthafucka' started, she'd be back on the market. Copious, hour-long phone calls to fitful town criers and project scandal queens had her all but hooked up for the next party, the next set, next package of goods.

She was like a man-junky... Using and losing men with an affinity. A prevailing grade of a perpetual "F" waiting aimlessly in the wings to reward her repeatedly failed efforts.

Continually she appeared to seek therapeutic ease to whatever drove her to the edge of event-filled, duplicitous concoctions of companionship. Almost as if she sought something which would erase the heaving pangs of a consuming beckoning. I almost felt sorry for her. And I was just a kid. She was plainly an unwilling captive to a wanting call of her own making, as she tried to please her internalized, unforgiving domestic spirits.

Demons inside appeared to goad her incessantly—in an unfortunate yearning to be Loved.

With the deafening climax of each relationship's explosive end, she appeared just that much closer to being thrust toward near-insanity. Time and Time again, she'd profess to have found *tha'realdeal*, only to realize stupidly that all she'd managed to do was place herself, and us back at ground zero—AGAIN! As hind sight, as it always did, set in to the eye-opening reality that she was once more trapped and encased within the filth-riddled hub of her own, unfulfilled, and excruciating torments.

Mama'n was a trip...

She never had to mention a word to Toppa and me. Even at such young ages, we knew. It was plastered all around the ill-fated falter of her every frantic move. To us, she was diaphanous. Not only was she in as much pain, or more, emotionally, as she had unwittingly inflicted upon us. There was something else...

...Something more.

It wasn't hard to identify. All you had to do was know her like we knew her. Just looking at her, you could tell.

Although she tried to put up a strong front, Mama'n was scared too.

Afraid of a lot more n' we knew about or had the knowledge and experience to more clearly understand and see. We were all afraid. But Mama'n, her fears were even more valid than our own.

Sorrowfully, it appeared she'd never learn her lesson. I think now, it would take her a lifetime of anguish, of being used and of using, to realize she was always, somehow, heading down the wrong track toward a looming destruction. Very rarely was she able to find or hold onto a man who would dedicate himself to proffering her the unconditional Love she most likely didn't even realize she was so forlornly seeking.

In truth...that's all she ever really wanted—To be taken care of and Loved.

She came close once—With my little sister, Honey's father, George Purtiss. Just close enough to whet her insatiable appetite for continued episodes of heart-felt frustration and emotional pain.

Instead of finding nirvana and bliss, things she never could have picked out in a crowded closet, even with them staring her right in the face, she only received...more of the same.

Pain!

I wonder.

Every once in a while I recall something out of my seemingly distant past. Some malignant discomfort imparted upon me, by someone I trusted or whom I was supposed to have Loved or been Loved by. This thing culminates as a seedy transgression which bore only hurtful fruits—like sweet nectars of a lifelong, rotting distress. Of malicious affliction, that in a normal childhood, I should never have had to witness or been made a part of—had my early days been as simplistic, and un-encumbering as a careful society of sane guardians would have had me live out.

The utter tragedy of all of this, and the thing placing me at ease, un-fearful at so painstakingly putting my experiences to verse with an abandoned truth (sans regard for Maman's feelings), is not the ultimate fact Mama'n was a sexual glutton, horrible at cultivating and nurturing any kind of relationships whatsoever. Not in relations with her own father, her brothers or sisters, not even with her own children. But, that she passed that shit down, without realizing it. Just handed it off like a ghetto Olympic torch. A flame carried by an aging pro bearing only contempt. With that, she unwittingly enforced an accompanying inability to trust. A sickening incapacity void of a growing excellence we could grasp toward developing and nurturing intimate relationships on our own in the future.

Whether that be a normal, healthy, supportive relationship with another male whom I could lend the long yard of being able to call him my friend, or with the other women who would come to take part in and play different roles in the excitement of life that for me was still to come.

Was it an uncaring mother? A silent brother or an absent father which held me so tightly gripped in the confusion of utter atrocities played out upon me in my youth? At times, I want to disregard the past. Accept only the possibility that it's wholly impracticable for all of these things to have actually happened. The pains so obtuse, as if they had certainly taken place in someone else's life.

Perhaps a character I'd witnessed on a movie screen? A fictitious icon conjured up from inside the bindings of a monumentally awesome book I'd read?

No!

Responsibility demands I not live my life, caught up, now, as a man—twisted within the mangled, abused perceptions of a boy. How far I needed to exorcise distance in order to get away from what I went through, I don't know.

Yet, as a man, I find I must peer at each day anew. Accommodating now the fulfillment inclined in hope matched by the achievement of dreams through the exercise of finally being able to take that clearing breath. Each day I must set my sights on new skies filled with anointing mercies—each day, embracing new thoughts to overcome innovative obstacles which bear developing morality leading to personal character. So that I might face the image of the fool staring back at me squarely in my reflection, with vision, a cleansed heart of healing...And forward thinking confidence which maintains the path before me. One, if nothing else, I ensure now to maintain as a passageway toward healing. A causeway to happiness being my guide to see me through as it's outlined in POSITIVE PERPETUAL MOTION.

To a varied number of young women, due to my own inabilities to trust completely, I've done plenty damage. Some, I'm certain, has been inexcusably permanent. For a very long time, the commodity of being afforded the privilege and companionship of developing close friendships one could rely on, were not to be a reality for me. They were to be shelved, placed far away and out of reach as I refused to engage them internally during the initial period of early manhood.

I sought comfort in being able to rapidly discard them. To place them out of the way as I placated the fear by simply setting my sights on more mundane priorities which helped me keep the uncertainties hidden elsewhere, in total safety. My own selfish concerns would develop instead into unquenchable desires and desperately foolish needs for fulfillment. I wouldn't come to recognize the ultimate destructive forces swirling about such a nature until it was almost too late.

Just like Mama'n.

The smack of a pocked, inebriated emptiness I felt as a friendless, ill-engaged young man had too almost consumed me.

She passed it first, to Toppa. Then to me, like a fucking virus.

Eventually, and even more incriminatingly, she pitched it to her own daughter, my little sister, Miss Honey. A child she herself hadn't even raised. Still…A life of alcoholism, gluttony and waist appears with an alarming stranglehold on even her world as an equally distressing, all-consuming legacy, passed down, as if from the womb, mother to daughter.

Because of this, Toppa and I were completely unable to trust.

I mean…We began to realize that placing the custody of our care in the hands of anyone other than ourselves was a grave, potentially debilitating mistake. We trusted no one. I believe it was during this phase of my life when I began to develop the near fatal and twisted, personal doctrine, of accepting a standard of only a home-run or strike-out in everything I set out to do—No gray areas accepted to this man—Not in this life.

We went about our youth never expecting nor permitting the sanctity and treasures, of placing a stake in the actions, of people…not ourselves, to muddle our lives. Rapidly, through Maman's wary examples, we learned *the hard way*, that PEOPLE…All People…WERE GENERALLY SHIT!

We grew up with a rustic, distrustful awareness…That you could only count on self. Like runaway slaves, too slew-footed to exact a lasting escape, Toppa and I could do nothing more during these times other than TAKE-THE-PAIN, and try desperately to fade away somewhere deep inside ourselves to become lost within the torment of our screaming minds while the immensity of these atrocities played haplessly out. He and I both thought, at times, that she was so upset with her own life, that beating us senselessly, was her the escape she had to assuage her own penitent demons which accosted her and drove her to literally try and kill us daily.

We had no idea... We thought this style of living—was imperceptibly, an admissible principle of accomplished parenting, as normal moms and dads went about their daily chores of correctly rearing children in just the way that she did. We knew no better then. But, believe me, we know infinitely better, not to force our own children to suffer through identical anguishes...now."

This dysfunction malevolently extended even to each other. We literally fought like dire enemies every chance we got.

The one item two brothers need most to make it in this world, unwavering sibling trust, for us was non-existent. We'd never developed a need for or respect of it. And for this reason, we had no real reason to be accommodating of even familiar outsiders. Not family members, who themselves appeared caught up in their own stenches of filth and trickery, while waging their own wayward battles of disgust. Not anyone.

At times it appeared one of us would kill the other. We were two lost souls not knowing where or how to turn for help. As biological brothers he and I had less in common than strangers living thousands of miles apart. There was no way we could ever help each other.

Not even today.

Each day I breathe. At the age of thirty-eight and as a man...when I think how much still, I MISS THE LOVE, CARE, GUIDANCE, AND COMPANIONSHIP, OF HAVING A CLOSER RELATIONSHIP WITH MY BROTHER, I want to yell...Scream out...and cry with a wandering, vengeful anger!

Oh!

Pain...

Only two summers separate us, by birth.

He and I never became friends.

Thanks, Mama'n.

CHOCOLATE CHICKENS DON'T TASTE SO GOOD WHEN MIXED UNWILLINGLY IN VANILLA SOUP

"We were all just little kids in the day, Some happy, some sad, but together—a family,
We peered through eyes of innocence and wonder, Believeing the immensity
of our dreams and that the possibilities of our goals; Could become truth.
Still, together, we can reach for innocence. And develop once more a dependence on reality as a guide; to lift our souls through faith and finally find the joys that escaped our youth"

-blu

At times in my youth, I would delve with a fretful mind to chance furtive, outside glances at the sheer incredibility of our circumstances. As a child, I was forced to serendipitously develop an inner ability to reach for that place within self, wherein lies the personal freedom of being able to relax and breathe freely amid chaos in order to survive. You generally see this in more autistic or literally abusive atmospheres.

I'd retreat far into my own mind's recesses—An uncanny capacity, which has frequently saved me from certain, emasculating doom—for sure.

I'd do this, while maintaining an ever watchful eye on the collusive efforts of a truly unforgiving outside world as it surrounded my slight attempts at struggling to hold onto chaotic fragments of my inner environment.

I think I knew then, what I know now. Just not as completely.

That it was somehow possible to seek out and extrapolate just one good item worth striving toward. A small piece of something—Anything! That could explain my existence as well as to render me final and ultimate, living peace. But I had little clue as to how to go about capturing that one thing securely. No blue print or template had ever been presented to me.

For very long periods, I'd simply sat back, in silence, watching while all the goodness the world had to offer shuffled on by.

And I'd wonder, as a child of eight, nine…ten —and so on, in silence.

"Are we gonna' make it?"

If Mama'n wasn't jacked-up, high on coke, heroin, weed, opium, speed, morphine or sprung on some fool, she was drunk. The ever present, cheap, fifth of vodka was never far from her clutches. Toppa and I were unwilling witnesses to a full slew of swatches in unfamiliar faces forever entering and passing through our lives.

In Harrisburg, Mama'n held a lustful notoriety for her make-the-rent, weed-bale, breakdown parties.

The full outfitting of one of these required only a clandestine score of a bale or two of the city's baddest marijuana, hauled, pushed or rushed in a jittery, paranoid cluster-fucked hurry, down the tiny steps of our basement apartment on 15th Street. She had to be careful, lest the nosey wanderings of the preacher's wife, upstairs, Sister White, get itchy and perhaps catch her up to her no goods in the fit of many, unanswerable questions. Add about ten of her seedy-assed friends all acting as stupefied look-outs. All hunkering down in a humorously vulgar posse equipped with stacks of playing cards, each with one of Maman's treasured collection of funky album covers sat gingerly atop their laps (these items were used to separate the stems and seed from the cronk after the bales were finally broken down and cut up). Completing the preparations were free-flowing finger foods, wine, beer and spirits, mind-altering drugs and sex ta-boot'—and DAG! Mannn…you had yo'self a hellova' party.

I guess she felt herself doing right by Toppa and I under the circumstances. During these periods, we were always banished under the threat of death, if we showed ourselves without first being summonsed, to our rooms, well before the arrival of the first guest. And as even most of the participants knew as well as us, Mama'n had encumbered a reputation. Rarely did any good ever come of seeking to cross her. So, we stayed submissively inside that room, unknowing, unsure, and mostly scared.

The soulful melodies of Isaac Hayes, Smokey Robinson, and the group, War wafted rebellious tones of illegitimate design from the smoke-filled windows of our tiny apartment. From dusk till dawn, during these unlawful tirades, Toppa and I would merely lie in our beds with our pillows clasped tightly over our little heads, in futile attempts at drowning out the deprecating clatter…and we'd pray for death in the boredom of what became a very lonely exile.

We didn't play with one another or talk to each other during these moments. I believe deep inside, he and I both felt the shame of the things we knew to be taking place a thin wall away in our home. And our only solace as youth, as well as into our manhood, was the sanctity of release in having each other to take it out on.

I was as elated as any boy betraying his dedication of Love to his mother could be, when the wonder of the rapidity of the developing magnitude of Maman's business became a frustrating highlight to the narcotics division of the Harrisburg Police Department.

I was glad.

...Because it brought change.

Her horde of ne'er friends, acquaintances, and accomplices, ranged from well-kept ebony princesses, finely outfitted in the latest 70's fashions with swept-up, expensive hair-do's, oversized, suede handbags and huge, roof topping fro's, with Lee press-on nails, Jordache and Gaitano jeans, hyped by slothful, slang and hip talk in identically colorful pedicures, who hung with Mama'n simply for her steady connect with the city's bungling drug cartel—To an assorted compliment of an ever-changing pool of played out ghetto grave robbers, inept thieves and project bandits—All these rounded out by what we called—po'pimps. Every one of them seeking to *Get Over* on the man in the grit and graft of a game they weren't very good at. Not only was it killing them, one by one in the iniquity of the slow, torturous deaths most of them would succumb to. But increasingly, its unmerciful stranglehold on the prosperity of an entire community would brutally rape its youth of their futures, faster than an entire season filled by a hundred occurrences of Hurricane Agnes.

For some reason or other, even though most of them had inherited *THABIZNASS'* as it was handed down, generation-to-generation, and they themselves had been involved in *it'* for most of their lives—and you'd think they'd at least make an attempt to fine tune their efforts to finally excel in *it'*. They weren't very good at it.

You know, perfect their craft of nasty, decay-filled art to prevent themselves from ever getting hemmed-up. To me, that would have been the rightful calling, given their professions.

I recall that they all had criminal catch histories and weren't too shy about recounting them.

We'd always hear of how they'd gotten caught this time or the other by the man while up to no-good deeds.

I blamed it on pure stupidity. What professionals would not practice their craft to perfection looking forward to a continued success, in something they'd chosen to dedicate themselves, their families, their lives to?

It was as if these mutts simply had no real compensatory aim at patience toward learning their game in its entirety, in order to find a way to make it work—FOR THEM, instead of against them?

Just IGNANT'.

A varying crescendo of juggled hues of personalities came and went at all hours of everyday—into and out of our lives. It got so bad; Toppa and I began to make a game of all the characters we were able to pick out and identify and became familiar with who were locked up from time to time. Surreptitiously, we knew, by the festivities of whatever party was being thrown, who was just released, who was scheduled to get out or who had just been caught and was celebrating their last days before finally going in.

Sorrowfully, in this way, our influences began to grow steadily, day by day.

His, a more enamoring, at times violent embrace of the game—Mine, more pushing away from it with a divergent need to break and run as far and as fast away as my wits and my feet could carry me.

How she'd permitted these particular vermin to latch onto her was puzzling? She was still coarsely fine, at twenty-nine, after having two kids by the age of seventeen. Sharply ambitious and beautiful, her naïve attempts at becoming a willing participant into cons only fools played with any realistic expectation of becoming successful in, kept her from realizing her true worth and potential as a Scholar, mother, sister, and Wife.

Looking back, following an epiphany of clarity, I'm almost certain, with a sweeping flair of regret, she's now able to hold her own personified vision of what was a twisted, life-mangling past. And, in it, I can peer at her and tell…She does see that back then—She was sick.

The truth is inescapable. Even though she was unable to realize true fact back then, these despicable characters actually meant her more harm than they ever offered her any supportive good.

Before long, she had no choice, but to see. Soon realizing, that no matter the intrigue of the guile they briefly permeated, she herself was trapped. Snared like a sweet, helpless lightning bug. Mesmerized instantly by the beckoning trance of a searing flame, hers, and our fate sealed. The iniquitous fire of the unforgiving streets called her name incessantly—Almost a time too many.

Soon, her head began to swell with the pain and reality of the resultant negativity of things she herself had designed. And, as a complimentary offering, void of a steeped, saving, common sense, and seemingly a lack of motherly compassion, she forced her children to suffer with her as well.

Because of the decisions she refused to correctly seek out and make—AS A MOTHER, Toppa, Miss Honey and I endured countless abuses and neglects in place of what was supposed to have been our youth.

To Mama'n, it appeared that no matter the ferocity of preparation she'd dedicate to her clandestine efforts, she never came out on top. Her efforts appeared consistently doomed to failure.

Just like most who seek to delve in the illusive prosperity of trafficking in illicit drugs, she never made or saved a shining dime. Why is it that most drug dealers fail to prosper? It seems, all the effort they go through to score, prepare, present and safeguard their product that the majority of them would be living lavishly amid the splendor and

pomposity of opulent mansions, and be ferried about by stoic chauffeurs inside gleaming rides. But, as you know, this is not the even the case of a minority among them.

Why Time and Time again, she allowed herself to fall for the Oopty-Doop'. Her part in this game wasn't supposed to have been projected to last very long.

SIKE! In my many experiences, I've never known an old drug dealer who's actually prospered and survived.

Obsolescence due to the narcotics trade would actually permeate throughout her existence—For a lifetime.

She'd failed once more, to read the signs—Nobody wins this game. EVER!

Everybody loses... All the time.

These smooth talking shysters held illusions of putting Mama'n on their client-vendor, Ho'strolls. Thank GOD, she was actually too smart to be led down the slaughter of that path to completely fall victim to such destiny.

She was a player. Not a *mark*—Their equal, not their prey. They failed to realize she too was as at times as wolfish as even they could be themselves.

Forever plotting...Working out some saving angle or plotting scheme dipped in wickedry.

Even with her own lengthy list of naiveté's, she prided herself on being able to fully matching the slime those within her circles slopped about, step for step.

Eventually, the slicksters and *SMOOV* talkers tried even her patience, finally gettin' on her nerves for the last umpteenth time.

With their hollow gifts and worthlessness, unfulfilled words of tribute, their pushy demands and empty promises, they began to alienate her. They called themselves, runnin' game. Conning a mark they'd selected for manipulation—A very basic scam, no matter the twist.

They'd simply mark a sucker for taking—An ancient craft, centuries old, not new. Find a way into their inner sanctuaries; attach themselves like blood-sucking leeches, then, squeeze with a pseudo-expertise which never really seemed to come off right. The privilege of becoming a mark extended to both friends and unknown victims alike. Some attempted such seriousness about their ways, they even went so far as to refer to their marks, as businessmen would their clients, as customers.

Nothing and nobody was held sacred. No honor existed among this band of ruthless thieves. Not family members, close friends, nor acquaintances. Anybody was capable of becoming a mark and being bled bone dry of anything of value—not to mention all earnings they foolishly made the mistake of permitting to become accessible.

Thank GOD! Mama'n wasn't putting up with it for it too long.

Still, although she was smart enough to recognize the period when that shadowy line between mark and friendship had somehow become clouded and crossed, she continued to tolerate them much longer than I think she should have.

For unexplained reasons, she placed a fair amount of misguided worth and trusts in the mediocre encumbrances her relationships with these thugs routinely produced. Almost as she would a useless piece of an ever-changing puzzle she had no intention of ever finishing as a child. Yet for other reasons, as an adult, she was wholly unable to give up on and completely forsake the unfinished masterpiece her street life very rapidly developed to be.

These folks were worthless. But, they still held value for her...in a sick, macabre, unexplainable, sort of way.

It used to kill me to watch as she took the most vagrant slime-ball and placed him atop the most precious pedestal with ease.

I guess, in a way, that was Maman's gift. She knew these people were shit! Yet she still permitted them presence and entry into a centered, very personal part of every facet of her life.

"WHY?"

Thugs weren't the only life and death suckers who drew from Maman's never-ending energies. There was also a medley of motley squares. Unwanted bunches of part-time, wannabe' bandits who had attached themselves to her as co-workers at the job she barely attended with the state. Those who'd caught wind of her underhanded lifestyle, and consequently had placed her on a pedestal of their own making, looking up to her in efforts to live out their own maniacal fantasies, in vicarious adoration, peering at her moves with misguided awe. They were lost souls who were fascinated with her penchant for boisterous outbursts against establishment. They looked to her as more than just another clerk typist. Benignly, they sought to just be near the immensity of strength radiating from her. For them, she was the image of a ghetto-hooded, fist-waving portrayal of the activist, Angela Davis.

Most of these participants were white or of a mixture of a mutt of cultures.

And most of them were men.

Sprinkled throughout this ungrounded group, of course, was a sparsely arranged clique of likewise, white, fluttery females, trying desperately to find themselves, through the illicit use of a colorful array of stimulants and depressants, lustful sex and the escape offered while hanging out with Mama'n.

That was one of the things about Mama'n. She was generally a better friend to men than she was to women. And she forever appeared to treat these *friends* better than she treated us or herself.

But she would eventually pay and pay well. Her focus on the wrong priority would come to very nearly cost her one of the grossly used nine lives she stretched so insistently toward their ends.

Unknown to Miss—"They'll never catch me because I'm too hip," select members of Harrisburg's Police department had also infiltrated the most trusted influences of her increasingly numbered acquaintances.

Hence, the second facet of the true reason Mama'n had been seeking a lofty flight away and out of the great state of Pennsylvania. She just needed a way to bring it off in a manner in which she'd secure an escaping freedom from the fiery edge of the sweeping blade of a judicial reaper which was drawing dangerously close, threatening to fell her, with an increasingly looming and lengthy term, if not life, behind bars.

In the back of her mind, she also sought to pull it off in the light of making a better life for us, her children, the ones whom through all her trials and tribulations, suffered the daily neglect of a mother aimlessly addicted to negativities, turmoil and strife.

At least she had the right idea—at heart.

Not that she had much of a choice...

Her shit was hot!

She'd received a merciful alert from a friend on the inside indicating she was a sparse number sixteen on a statewide dragnet roster that amassed more than a hundred soon-to-be felons the state authorities had been maintaining a watchful surveillance on for some time. The intent had been to coral this horde of known and newly identified drug-dealing, aberrant residents of the state, as a single, widely-cast net to free society of their terrorizing activities with an all-inclusive, inducing expediency.

Her savior had soulfully materialized through the rarity of a true friendship. It had come by way of an old high school girlfriend, who'd been shocked to catch glimpse of Maman's name highlighted as a suspect during a meeting with her counterparts in the city's District Attorney's office. Maman's surreptitious aspirations of becoming a big money player in the East coast drug trade had become flagged by the state's attorney for warrant, arrest, prosecution and subsequent conviction. They had all but outfitted, deloused, bunked, and bucked-up ole' Mama'n—out to da' big house.

The 'WEEZ' was in trouble, about to be taken down.

She was only twenty-seven. Yet, she had already expended a lifetime of dread and excitement inside a mini underworld which threatened to cancel her family out like a worthlessly used, priceless stamp.

It sort of tickles me now to picture my Mama'n then, at a youthful twenty-seven. Her worn, tattered mug shot adorning the top left corner of some task force, office cork board, ala' John Gotti. Or better yet, Toni, or Uncle Junior, of "Soprano" fame.

Turns out, one of her most staunch drug cohorts and graft companions, was a infiltrating, Puerto-Rican, pretty boy, known only as Juan.

Mama'n was taken to Juan like a fly to a backyard barbeque. For a time, Juan had been all-too-delicious.

All that!...And a bag of chips.

Light of color, lean and svelte with strapping muscles held up on great looks, he played himself off as expertly prenticed to what young, hetero—female drug dealers still to this day enjoy most; Juan spent just about every day plying trade, with-and-to Mama'n. So dedicated was he to his first, true, Love of craft—the law, that he even went so far as to actually get caught up in "using" product with her on a regular basis. It was nothing for Toppa and I to come in from school on a regular basis to find the motley duo, barely outfitted in more than a pair of silk, polka-dotted boxers and a sweat-soaked, disheveled camisole, twisted outta' their gourds, lying exhausted amid an apartment filled with acrid smoke as they huddled in a spent, kama-sutra heap on our living room floor.

But, we were well trained...Good little puppies who knew the wrath of extension-cord obedience training. Facing this almost daily, after our hour long ride from Middletown where we attended the Middletown Christian School, we'd simply enter using one of our keys we both had extended by shoe strings around our necks, and we'd slip quietly and respectfully passed their sticky, satiated forms, to enter the tiny room he and I shared at the back of the dwelling. Once there, we'd attack that day's homework with muted, hate-filled silence, without as much as a mention of the carnal image we'd just strode past.

With Juan as silent partner, Mama'n thought her ship had finally come in. His freely provided connections brought in almost four times her normal volume. Quickly, she fell in Love with the heaping amounts of added opportunity the increased cash flow produced. She found herself enamored in more late night, romantic dinners at the city's finest restaurants. She bathed in an assortment of lavishly presented gifts he showered upon her frequently, as well as in all the other, ill-gotten amenities she'd previously been unable to invent while dealing product on her own. He opened pathways toward success she'd never even suspected existed for her.

He fed her misguided drive for higher achievement in the clandestine aspect of her worldly dealings. While keeping Toppa and me up nights, working the hell outta' some bedsprings, hittin' it for ever seeming never to an end. Her lust-filled bellows were almost impossible to sleep through. And they always seemed to last well into the wee hours of what seemed to roll into every captive moment of a fitful morning.

How many of ya'll know all of this wasn't for free?

Mama'n thought she was in heaven. I'll say she was far from it. Blessed for certain, but heaven was still a long way off in coming.

Surely she, and the three of us, paid a heavy price for her previous indulgence.

Another life of her nine irresponsibly expended. She found out early on that she would soon be forced to mask a witting escape away from her ill fated labors. Or be forced to face the finite throng of retribution attendant in the unmerciful hammering of a judge's gavel.

Turns out, Juan, *was the man.*

Wisely, she secured a clean break away from him, (a task executed with experienced ease, pulled off with the rapid skill of having been through it so many times before with so many different figures of her past)

Soon after, she met Egbert Rice.

Egbert was a nice enough guy—to us kids. With a dark chocolate complexion, he was well-muscled and all-too conniving in an intelligent sort of way. He held a crystalline, trustworthy smile which gleamed to stretch from the Pennsylvania Turnpike, clear up through the southern tips of Maine with ease. It didn't take long at all for Mama'n to throw the hooks on him and ride his coattails in a whirlwind courtship spanning the full stretch of an entire nation.

He lazed in our tiny apartment all of a week. Again the howling, again no sleep, again another new variable entered into our meager thought processing. Her brief infatuation with Egbert would cause her to decide to pull up chocks and engineer an eventful trek, which would change Toppa's, Miss Honey's and my own life forever.

This trip began in Pennsylvania and ended in a new beginning, in El Paso Texas.

As a child, I often attributed Maman's wretched sense of reversed fortune with men—on the men. It was natural, she was Mama'n and I Loved her. It couldn't, as I am still finding in my dealings with her today—have been her fault.

Of course not, CHILE' P-a-leeeze!

Just as my thoughts and utter belief in her, back then, as a young, frightened, unaware and impressionable boy seared through all she put us through, I can't help now Loving and caring for her completely, and even more now as well.

Yet, as a man, I've taken on a more realistic explanation and personal view of factual processing which permits me to look back with vigor to see those poor guys, *her victims*, in a totally new and entirely different light. They'd never stood a chance. For them, Mama'n was more like a striking praying mantis lying in wait than a conquest. Once she'd leapt on them, she'd use them then spit them back out bitterly following her own unfulfillable, gratification. Their lives warped and twisted to all get out…never again matching what they'd been before running into her.

Sort of like our own…

It was eerie, the manipulative, bullying effect she seemed to successfully ply on everyone she met. I've come into contact with quite a few women in my own time since Mama'n, who portrayed traits very similar to hers. They were incapable of truly creating or ever receiving Love.

They chose instead to carve out a path of denigration and angst for themselves—Selfishly taking, instead of willingly giving, at every turn, the wary, embattled cry of their forte. They could never be made to feel good, contented or satisfied, no matter the lengths extended in attempts at trying to please them. They were perpetually unhappy and could place trust in no one—without first assuring a domineering role in the relationship; even if it meant finding themselves forever embroiled in the totality of argumentative abandon that infused domestic confrontation could play out to be.

Mayhem was their only solace. They were unable to become aroused unless they were in control and arguing or fighting over some mundane cause which eventually fed into the wanton requirements of their desires.

At first inkling of these discontented personalities, guys much smarter and more astute than me wisely tend to light out for higher ground.

Toppa and I, up to this point, had never known what real, classic security was. We'd never known that there were certain things you were supposed to be able to claim from devoted, loving parents. Solidities such as doting, palpable expectations like dependable, hard-working fathers and loving, compassionate mothers—both in the same home... Who Loved each other under the same roof, with the same ideas in mind, working hard toward the same, wholesome, productively proffered goals. This, filled with solid values passed down one generation to the next—was a prospect held foreign to us.

He and I held no clue.

We were unaware that things such as the basic necessities—food on a constant basis, heat, and the type not turned off on more and more frequent occasion, or other things... Like, it wasn't really normal to have to pick up and move every time the rent was due. Things like effective discipline, (which did not include being stripped butt-naked and being forced to stuff your little arms and hands into the opening separating the seat cushion and the backboard of one of the kitchen chairs, while Mama'n filleted your ass bloody with an extension cord) which wasn't supposed to open you up so profusely at times there was no chance you were going to school the following full two-weeks because she feared the authorities, should someone notice the healing scabs of our torn skin as it splayed in crisscrossed patterns and swelter amid the whelps and bruises of her handiwork.

Like runaway slaves, too slew footed to exact a lasting escape, Toppa and I could do nothing more during these times than TAKE THE PAIN, and try desperately to fade away somewhere inside of ourselves to become lost within the torment of our screaming minds while these abuses played out.

We thought, at times, that she was actually so upset with her own life that while beating us, she was attempting to assuage the penitent demons accosting her by trying to literally kill us. We didn't know. We felt this style of living was imperceptibly, the acceptable principle of practiced, loving parents as they went about the daily chore of correctly rearing children just like she did. We knew no better then.

But believe me, we know infinitely better...now

We had no idea we'd been subjected to the ravings of a depressed, criminally incensed, abusive monster, known as Mama'n.

Thinking back now, I could have taken the shoe to the other foot a million times over. And very easily in my little blood-raked mind, I could have killed my mother...

Just strangled her and left her body for strangers to find. Or just beat her over the head, whacking her good, with her own cast-iron skillet, time and time again as she sat before me, her back to me, watching television.

To return to that time and to have been offered a chance to stop the pain then, of things she did to me and forced my brother and me to suffer through, and are still suffering through today, as adult men—I don't even have to think.

Would I have gone through with the caper....given another chance?

You bet I would.

Given the chance, I would have splattered her brains all over the prized four-finger bag of her best weed and thought nothing of it as I kept right on steppin'.

We had no idea what it meant to be nurtured and Loved completely. For us, life was spelled S-T-R-U-G-G-L-E, as taught to us so vehemently by our own Mama'n.

Eventually, and it didn't take long—Believe me.

Mama'n was on point in carrying out her mission of fleeing Pennsylvania.

Turns out, the wonder warrior with the pretty skin, ready package and alluring smile had only been passing through our shady green, peaceful town of Harrisburg. He'd been on furlough from the Army; en-route to his ultimate duty station, at Fort Bliss, in El Paso. And, like any young strapping stallion of any era, what he first thought he was getting himself into (A fine young sista' with twinkling eyes, pretty hair and a body to melt in yo' mouth) was far, from what he found himself holding onto, trying desperately to break free and run from, in the end.

I can empathize with the brotha' now, as a man. He'd merely been looking for a good time, not a wistful piece of ass. Whether that meant spending time with his brother, Dickie, a long-haul trucker who'd been shackin' with one of Maman's acquaintances in our complex on a "Baby, I'm in town, can I drop by for a week or two' basis," or accepting an invitation of respite, intrigue and the provocative allure of knocking off a piece of some strange tail offered him as it was presented in the form of my Mama'n during his stay.

My uncle was always so fond of saying, "WHOWOULDA'THUNKIT?
Her plan worked to perfection!
Almost...

It was only after setting out, with what meager shit we'd packed and hand-carried during the sweat and gruel of the four-days it took us, packed like sardines, in an un-vented, Greyhound bus to cross the United States, that finally...right about the time when Toppa and I felt we could stand no more of being cooped-up under Maman's piercingly strict and watchful eye, the developing ball of a blazing, Texas sun poured out over the front of our bus to swoon in and bring the opaque vastness of the El Paso desert as it greeted us harshly.

I remember steeling a glance over at Toppa. The stark, horrified, disbelieving immensity staring back, facing us outside that bus was unsettling. Trying desperately, (I knew better than to let Mama'n catch me rolling my eyes atop, disrespectfully pursed lips) I indicated to him swiftly, "Somebody's crazy!" This couldn't be it? Where were the oak trees, the green grass, the four seasons...? Where were my squirrels that sprung effortlessly, from tree to tree along Boas Street as I'd watched them in the rain? Where were all of our cousins', our friends, uncles' and aunties' we'd become accustomed to so easily relying upon in the past? How I longed for one of my grand mom, Mavis' *Hot Wheel,* racing track whoopin's...

If we thought things were rough in *THA*-BURG, what we were about to go through was really lost on us as we became enveloped in facing the poverty and listlessness that we were about to enter in Texas.

It was only an hour or two of being forced to showcase good manners while we sat waiting, aimlessly (banished for what seemed an eternity to the hard, plastic chairs of El Paso's Greyhound station) for the fool to come retrieve us, before I first had the thought, "We're in trouble!"

When the morning sun appeared for the second time from behind the cascading expanse of beauty that is the span of the Franklin Mountains, I remember waking to a conglomeration of transplanted horror—filled and excited emotions. Two things pecked away at me incessantly. One, I had the persistent urge to take a never-ending pee. A pestering desire which threatened not to meet the timeline of me getting up to race the short distance it would take for me to reach the station's public restroom. The other, of fear and stark amazement at the unbelievable realization that.... We'd just spent the night in the cool interior of a rustic, hundred year old building that was El Paso's Greyhound bus station.

Vagrants!...To say the least. Four terrified souls (Mama'n included, although I gathered she was more pissed than scared) drift-less, in a strange town that had an odd, very peculiar odor about it. I remember equating it to the dry, clogging, dirt smell of grand mom Mavis' attic.

Me, with the bad sinuses.

We had spent the evening, hungry and disheveled, splayed limply atop the hardest chairs GOD had ever created (necks literally pained from trying with all our might to break them as they'd fallen from side to side, a thousand times during the night, with our futile attempts at finding an infinitesimal slice of comfort). Afraid and unsure of what was to come next, while wiping drool amid crusts of sleep from the sides of our faces and outta' our eyes. Toppa and I awoke to a cluster of excitement as we quickly flung sleep aside to witness with inviting interest, the serious frolic of about ten Border Patrol agents scampering all over the station, as they chased and apprehended about a million illegal aliens who'd arrived and spent the night there as well, just like us, waiting to be picked up. I remember counting them as they flashed by.

That was then, and still is now, my *thing*—to keep my mind busy in times when I was just frightened or had nothing better to do.

COUNTING!

I counted anything and everything. The number of stairs I went up and came down. The amount of broken white lines I could catch as the bus hurled its way down deserted, two lane highways in route to our ultimate destination. I even went so far as to the count the mini grid lines on people's faces, breaking them up evenly into individual quadrants of fours, a trait I never knew possible, but which I passed on in a transfer of genes to my own daughter, Ashle'.

Although we were even more terrified following the event, amid the entire ruckus, we were able to use the encounter to rap our fears up in quiet solitude, for a moment. To just for a second push past the previous cares of mounting hunger pangs swilling inside us. I wondered who had it worse, the scrambling illegals or us? The increasing uncertainty of feeling that we'd been left behind, loomed greatly for what seemed like an eternity.

Suddenly wide-eyed, we had only each other to look to, seeking answers.

Mama'n was there, of course. But she was completely unavailable in offering us support.

Sure... The full level of expressions and indications she caste toward the three of us, of her own frustrations at our predicament, didn't warrant the bravery necessary to approach even a whisper of a countering question. We knew better. And, we weren't about to set a record. One that would blatantly afford the dubious distinction of taking the award for being the only boys to take an ass-whuppin', in two different states, at opposite ends of the country in a span of a briefly entered week, for the mere reason of—being born, or rather, for being alive that very second as constant reminders of her continued failures.

Like all other things when it came to Mama'n—We just endured.

We'd been stuck in that Greyhound station for more than twenty hours, waiting for our BETTER life to begin.

Egbert Rice finally came. But he arrived with an evident, distrustful reluctance which screamed, that he was fully unprepared and unwilling to embrace our wayward family as his own. The disappointment he fostered with that, hit home when he deposited the four of us (Mama'n, Toppa, Miss Honey, who was only three, and me) in our new home on Skylark Way.

From the bus station, during the entire twenty minute ride to our new house, not a one of us murmured a single word. Egbert attempted a half-ass patronizing try at making an apology, while attempting weakly to paw at and plant slobbery kisses Mama'n's way as a measure of seeking forgiveness for his obtuse and disrespectful tardiness.

"Aww...Damn, daahhlin'. I swear fo' Gawd! I thought you'ns tole' me yawl' wasn't cummin' in till tomorrow eebenin'. I been callin' and callin' yawl's number back in da' BURG, try'n ta' track you'ns down. But I keept' on gett'n dis' ree-co'ding, which tole me dat' da' numba' was disco'neck-tid." His smile widened more pervasively each time he tried to explain, while continuing to shake his head stupidly from side to side with a feigned frustration.

Didn't this fool realize we had just spent an entire, hunger-filled, sleepless day and restless night in a fuckin' Greyhound station? With cut throats and mean-looking illegal aliens to boot. And where'd he get that drawl from? I thought he was supposed to have been from New York. Rochester, if I recalled correctly. I never remembered him being such a yokel when he'd taken over our living room so completely back at *home.* This fool could talk no better than the stammering clods that'd frequented Maman's former drug den, right after we'd witnessed them sit on an arm and pump dangerous amounts of coke or heroin into what was left of an unsuspecting vein.

I remember revisiting the horror of thinking, *If we had to depend on this character*, our goose might as well have been cooked—FOR GOOD!

It wasn't long after we'd been firmly dropped-off at the new house he had rented for Mama'n, (one completely void of anything resembling furniture—that place was as empty on the first night we all entered it, as it was, for the entirety of the almost year-long period we inhabited it, before the rent came due—late, one too many times, and we were finally and efficiently evicted) that Toppa and I began to attend Zach White Elementary school.

It wasn't the first time I truly began to respect and adore school as a welcoming haven. I'd long peered at the halls and stairways of Middle Town Christian Academy as more than just bastion of a saving sanctity. To me, it had become the only grace a young brotha' had in life.

Each morning, we'd traipse, in two year's past clothes, along the streets with a neighborhood of newfound friends. Most, who were, unlike those we'd grown accustomed to, in P.A., mostly White, Indian, or Mexican, to enter the safety of the school's campus to be met by the utter immensity of the steaming aromas of hot meals at both breakfast and lunch as it was provided free to us as a direct result of Maman's lack of employment.

I Loved it!

The state of Texas really had a thing for expecting a general standard from its institutions of learning. And it was there, at a very young age, that I first began to appreciate the gift I had for writing. Even in the paucity of all we had, I'd begun to develop a Love for being offered the freedom of being able to hoard any piece of paper bearing space where I could put down my every feeling. And, through a saddened prose of mostly sick and twisted poetic verse, I sought an escape which I discovered no one and no body was capable of taking away from me.

For me, writing became a life's blood event. It was my bastion of saving sanctity and grace when ripped so complete a distance away from the ones I had learned to count on back home. It was how I fought off the monstrosity of frustrations which threatened increasingly to overwhelm me every day.

It didn't take long before both Mama'n and us kids finally figured Egbert's azz' out for good.

For us, the truth became clearly apparent that the fool already had a family stashed in another, more affluent part of the city—Complete with baby biologicals. And for those too, just like for us, he was doing a piss-poor job of caring for as well. I don't really judge the brotha' too harshly. Although responsible for his actions, he was young. And, with youth comes simple-mindedness, an inability to focus on things not relating to urges and the clouded certainty which generally led to hurtful stupidity. It happens to all of us. He wasn't exempt. No way was he prepared to step up to take on the ire of troubles Mama'n and her brood of omni-needy children brought with them in tow.

For Mama'n, except the part about engineering a better result than what she'd already been able to eek out back in Pennsylvania, her plan for an absolute and rapid escape had all but worked, *for her*, to perfection.

She'd escaped the humiliation of being incarcerated. And what she had engineered had maintained the circle of her struggling family.

But maintained it—Toward what?

Pipe dreams are pipe dreams. Lusts are followed by fools. And...fools will always be fools—Forever following the illustrious fissures hidden within half-truthful promises coaxed to belief by the selfishness of minor organs.

Hunger pangs are for real.

Damn...Somebody bring on tha' Love!

Now names like Egbert Rice, Harold Breen, Gorge Purtiss, siblings, (One toe) Rimmy, Jimmy, and Taura, sexy assed Miss Bartha, Aunt Dee-Dee, Rhris and Lippy, two Toms—Barton, and another ultimate HOMIE, Walstein, Mavid Wynn, J.P. Bales, Kelvin and Lucille, Skoesh, T-man, Little Harry, Robbie and Sike Jackson became the influences at the forefront of my life.

Most of these people engaged me during a time replete with abject instability. I mean: I had no idea things could have actually gotten worse.

But they did!

Periods earmarked by hunger I'd never before known existed, and by abuse that almost soured me so much that I had no positive beliefs, only misgivings, of ever being afforded an opportunity of developing into a smart, productive man, engulfed me. Loneliness, resentment, homelessness, hatred and internal, life perpetuating strife caused me to steel myself even further against the hard knocks, non-wavering pathway which could only promise personal-foundation building, achievement and success—or complete, and utter doom on the flip-side.

There had to be goodness... Somewhere. There was no way we'd go through all of this only to come out in the bitter end, still helpless and pitiful like the damned.

Somewhere deep inside, I didn't know how I'd do it, but I knew, I'd never stoop to having to live my life like those of my own mother and father's. I wouldn't abandon, beat, abuse, corrupt or berate my own children or my wife. I would never use or deal in illegal drugs.

Even if it meant getting up to open McDonald's at four-thirty each morning, picking up aluminum cans in route—for recycling, and closing it again, as a toilet swabby, at ten—P.M. later that evening

This was all in my own personal dedication toward supporting the successes of what I yearned for most as a kid.

A real family.

The kind I saw on T.V. after school at a friend's house. Cause' after our move to Texas, we never had one. All of our belongings had been sold at auction, after Egbert's brother, the long-haul trucker had *gotten us tha' killer deal* through Allied Van Lines, promising that they'd move our entire apartment, Pennsylvania to El Paso, free of charge, all on the propensity of his good-standing within the company.

How many out there realize that it wasn't for free?

Upon reaching Texas, our belongings were boxed into a holding storage until Mama'n could come up with the fourteen-hundred dollars it would cost for us to reclaim things like bicycles, birth certificates, and beds. We never saw any of that stuff again.

Toppa and I generally attempted to spend as little time as possible inside our own house. Staring at empty rooms and barren walls only mocked what we too had taken on as our embarrassing failure. These, matched with endlessly vacant, teasing cupboards were no way for two energy-filled ruffians to spend each waking moment in any kind of peace.

You see, that's the thing. As a young boy, it seemed as if my own parents cared less about the successes they so ill-prepared me for, in achieving tangible accessions in life, than they did about appearing to bend over backwards in anomaly toward their own circus performances of extending themselves in fucking-up their own lives so completely. As if I was conceived of seed and egg, shot down the birth canal, and spat out onto a dirty, virus infected birthing room floor to fend for myself from the very start.

Off and away from bare necessities like motherly-Love and parental nurturing, which I'd already grown accustomed to never getting, I was wise enough, even at that young age, to have a very brief idea what I needed to make my way minimally. I needed to develop and perfect an art, on my own, for getting the things required most by life. This was the only way I could begin taking responsibility I'd never been taught for myself. The only way I would be able to correct the atrocities played out against me previously and begin to call my own shots.

I began searching for a way out. One by which I'd be able to learn new, more inviting skills I could use to ensure the turn around of the awful negativity lingering threateningly to taint my existence forever.

So, one day after baseball practice, (Which, unlike today's athletic events was absolutely free) while walking down Railroad Drive, I made a life altering turn at Borsberry Construction Company, just to wander and see if I could escape the crisp Texas heat for just a breath and perhaps get a drink of cool water.

Once inside, I engaged first, the receptionist. A young, strikingly beautiful, white girl, outfitted in the expected short-short, Calvin Klein skirt, and a crisply starched-white blouse, topped off with thigh-high black boots, the leather of which looked so soft and supple it appeared well-kept enough to eat off. After asking if I could take a drink from their fountain, I plied my best, although weak trade and asked off the cuff, "Ummm, Say? You guys hiring today?" Smiling at the inadequacy of my meager attempts to mix flirtatious wit with obvious desperation and need, she apparently took pity on my presence, I'm sure, and ushered me in with an empathetic smile (I must've looked a mess) to speak with the owner, John.

Believe you me...I walked outta' that piece, at almost fourteen, a man—BEAMING...WITHAJOB!

THIRTEEN-FOURTEEN

...Opened a new world of possibilities along with a totally new type of hurt and emotional anguish for me. While the job, which eventually entailed painting the interior and outer buildings of the entire company, did a lot to expand my world of influence as a poor teen, not afraid of back-breaking, hard work, it was all I could do to maintain a workable schedule.

Mr. Borsberry had initially told me I was too young to hire. "Against Texas state law fer' me ta' giveya' work kid," he'd drawled. He countered that immediately, drawing closer to me with an internal, piercing scrutiny, looking directly into my eyes, not wavering for a second. "Guess if ya' show some moxie, I might be able ta' come up wit' a matta' or two ya' might can take on and handle roun' dese' parts. I could feel the swell of pride and excitement beginning to welter inside of me.

Imagine! I'd be able to buy food for Miss Honey and Toppa on a more regular basis, instead of ripping the local Circle—K blind for mediocre necessities like eggs, cheese, and cigarettes for Mama'n, and my favorite, Nestle's chocolate milk. Word is mine, we stole any and everything, with Mama'n generally turning a blind eye of justification, (times were a' changin') prior to me getting that job, just to survive.

He went on, "Pay ain't much, mindya' but pay is pay, Junior." I didn't care.

"But," He sidled almost uncomfortably closer, I almost choked on the cutting scent of his *High-Karate* cologne, as if he was trying to take a stronger whiff of just what it was I was made of. "If ya think yer comin' round' these parts loafin' yo' sef on de' job and all ta quit school and that mount ta' mess, ya can fergit' da job and scanty on outta' here back whereya' tuckered in from." Still holding me in that gripping, uneasy glare, he challenged, "How old are you, anyhoo's, boy?"

"I.... I, ummmm...I'm sixteen." I lied.

"Good!" He sneered, with an all-too-knowing, conspirational gleam. "We can use some new heart roun' these parts." And, peering down into my arms at the tattered rag of the glove I held, he gestured with, "And tha' same goes fer' ball too." I looked back at him, with question, not quite understanding.

Thrusting an elongated digit forcefully out at me, he bellowed, "NO QUITTIN! I mean," as he tried to compose his own excitement at having possibly discovered an endearing protégé, "just cause' o' the work n' all." And he snorted twice, turned his back on me and left me standing there in the foyer, dazed, without another word.

My heart leapt completely! It turned wild flips of wonder-filled somersaults inside the now-pounding cavity of my hairless chest. I was struck dumb by Mr. Borsberry's gruff of kindness towards me. Never before had any middle-aged, successful, white man so readily extended himself to me. But, he had, and I suddenly felt like a TRUMP APPRENTICE as I just as readily accepted the sparse terms of gaining my very first employment.

After giving the sexy receptionist girl my information while extolling her many virtues (letting me into the door leading to an opportunity not hardly the least) I gained a promise from her that she would entice the ole' man to contact Mama'n, some way, the following day (We were once again—in between phone companies at the time, so he couldn't place a call to her) I stepped outta' Borsberry Construction Company with a skip to my step and a resounding leap toward manhood.

I painted that place with meticulous perfection for months on end. I think the old man had taken a liking to me from the start. When I'd finish painting what seemed like the last thing on the entire yard that needed a re-coat, he always found other, more challenging tasks for me, to learn and to complete.

I Loved that old guy.

This time was also marked by my first attempt, and failure, at reaching for first Love. A mysterious, chocolate hottie (swarthy of hip and sway...WAY too well—skilled naturally for my Love-naïve behind) entered my nuances and *swept me* off my feet.

She was sixteen. And she sampled my heart in one hungry chew, and...as well, spat me back out, following an extended probationary period of lustful huffing, like a pesky nuisance.

Her eventual rejection banished me back toward an ill-confidenced exile, as if scolding me to, "Get back across that fence. Stay on the little kid's side of the playground. You know where you belong."

-Couldn't really blame her. It had taken her almost an entire summer to train and mold me into a willing toy that could actually handle her speculative experience. It wasn't long, before I even had to admit to myself that I truly was ill equipped, outta' my league, both physically and emotionally, and had little business, if any, licking and tickling her X—rated wares at fourteen, from the git-go'.

Annny-Waayz'!

Neither my heart nor my rep had developed manly-enough scrapes and bruises enough to keep the beast lurking between those thighs expertly in check. Yet, even still, once I had my first hit, my nose couldn't have been wider, with want and need for that girl.

TALK ABOUT SPRUNG...

At sixteen, she was a stunning, brick-shit-house-beauty! Already a woman, and exquisite in every sense of the word. Petite,—yet pretentiously thick, that girl was just bootie and titties—titties wit' more bootie, jumpin' out everywhere! GREAT Goog-a mungas! I could barely stand to be near her without finding myself swollen and slick You know, for a very brief time, I thought I'd died and finally been rewarded entry into a realm of scarce pussy-gettin' paradise.

Before discarding me with a swoosh of a curtly flung hand, and moving on to *REAL MEN*, she rubbed me right more preciously than any I'd ever experienced before that. And she taught me things.

Things of joy, which I still find myself expert at and still unable to do without

for too long this day.

Her name was, Rolanda Howse.

Our THANG' lasted but for a minute. It was a fleeting, torrential downpour of a quickly—gasped, very special breath. And it ended just as abruptly as it had begun.

I remember wondering if the break up had anything to do with what I hadn't learned about Love, from Mama'n. But I very quickly quelled such defeating notions as rapidly as they appeared.

Had to.

They had no substance... Yet!

I'd begun to realize that I had to get out from under the shadow of negativities her experiences had trigger-stamped on my life. It was imperative in order to exercise growth on my own, as an all too impressionable young man. As well, it didn't take very long before I eventually began to actively put a stop to trying to attach blame to her, for events beginning to unfold along my own winding path in life.

Rolanda had simply outgrown me and quickly moved on to an older, more-hip brotha—Harry. That's all there was to it. She'd grown weary of teaching and sought instead to be taught, and I couldn't help her.

He was much older. Something like, twenty-two. One of those brothas' who had no bid-nazz' tappin' a sweet young sister like her. Needless to say, there's no way I was competing. He'd far surpassed my level of expertise at successfully plying and properly caring for the supple, young tenderness of her kitty, which was a living, breathing fiend just discovering itself—and consequently, had no intention of ever slowing down to be controlled. Throughout the brief development of our time together, that thang' metamorphosed... It took on altering stages of overpowering life all its own when approaching a sweating maturity. Increasingly, its demands to be constantly stroked and fed were incessant. Sleep? Rest! Ha'... what was that? Of course a brotha' couldn't compete. I didn't know how.

FIFTEEN

...Produced my first clumsy attempt at chasing the elusive meanderings of a real relationship. Can't say I'd learned any kind of lesson from allowing myself to open up to being squashed like a pussy bug during my dealings with Miss Howse. But this time, I had a different game. I wasn't awe-stricken by the sweet, tangy stench of warming moisture the perfect girl could pretend to sweetly possess. This time...instead, materialized a slender goddess in the form of an almond eyed, sweet-delicacy of a gentle, honey-colored princess named, Sarita Valeria Vanitta Barks. Val, although she genuinely never meant to, came into my life, bearing true to course run-ins and life-threatening dramas which, in shrieking silence, like a bad fucking dream, never appeared to end.

Events surrounding this girl were always somehow pseudo-lethal. Encounters with people like Bucket Barks, her egg-head, wanna' be thug, brother. (Not a wonder the fool went by the moniker, BUCKET). That's perhaps where most of his brains had been flung following conception. Also, Katy Klumpers, Val's ever-present, always signifying girl friend. She was a girl possessing a straight up porn star handle. Yet, to match that, she offered a nauseatingly, pimply face, which, if leased out, could be used to stop runaway freight.

Though her name might conjure up certain lustful images, Katy also had an ass literally shaped like a swollen ostrich egg, (that thing must've extended a good two and a half feet out from the plane of her back) and she couldn't get laid, by any single guy, not certifiably retarded, if she took off every stitch of clothing, bent over bucket naked, grabbed both ankles securely and sent out an availability broadcast transmitting, "Free Pussy" in front of every conjugal trailer at San Quentin on hoe-down Sundays.

Then there was Nailaya Smith. A hot-hottie of Thai-Black mix, she'd actually all but accosted me one early morning even before the fat Mexican ladies doling out free breakfasts had raised their aluminum blinds to usher in the pushin' and shovin' sea of pubescent, black muttons—all standing around, hungrily seeking that morning's high school gruel.

Apparently, she'd seen me enter the cafeteria that morning and had been waiting for me to finish and return. Not taking note of her, I'd almost passed her by, lost in thought of trying to make it to my day's first classes on time. Reaching out to me ever-so-slightly, she was so pretty, her touch froze me in step at an instant. Peering deeply into me with such yummy conviction, (my heart, among other organs, melted instantly as she pulled me deeper toward the wicked temptation of promise lying untapped beneath a knee-buckling, succulent smile) without a word, she thrust a piece of crisply folded paper into my palm, so smooth it appeared she'd ironed it. Then, she just turned, with..."I'm expecting my answer befo' the end of the day too..."

And she smiled tartly and sachet'd that sexy ass away and down the hall, as if she'd never seen me.

Once again, I found myself instantly dumbfounded. Her actions had caught me completely off guard. I stood there, glued in one spot for a long time, like an idiot, not knowing at first what to do or think. It usually takes a dull second for me to make up my mind that I want to head in a specific direction; no matter how detrimental those first steps might prove to be.

I'd peeped her before. But I'd always figured she was outta' a brotha's league...My flair with Rolanda cautioned me against moving once more toward the wrong course. She'd always hung out with more, hard-core players. Dudes with fast, cherried-out rides. The kind of whips, no law-abiding youngster, like me, could ever keep up or dream of affording. And too, the pimply, wanna-be gangsta's with fists full of ready cash scored from complex heists and drug deals were more her type than me. These fools had ice, and gold teeth, long before the term bling-bling ever matriculated to main stream. These were the type niccas' a girl like Mizz Smith held a reputation for generally not being able to do without. Her type usually had a hunkering for the spice and adventure that crowd readily provided. Baby sharks in training had more morals than half of those brothas'. And they had every vice with which to feed and support girls like her's slithery whims.

I wasn't ready fo' none o' dat. The water was way too warm down at her end of the pool.

I knew it!

Still...Curiosity killed me more deeply every tickling second. I was aching to find out...

WHATDIDSHEWANTWITHME?

There was sumpin' about a brotha' she obviously felt interested in.

It wasn't the first time, and surely wouldn't be the last, that mediocre but sharp looks, grinding wit, and a wholesome stick of charm coupled with an almost stupid sense of guts would get me over.

The note, meticulously scripted in that squirrelly, scented girlish prose (all the cute ones seemed to have) bore just four simple words. Each formed a phrase to build a heated, tightly wound, open-ended question. Making sure I was by myself before settling in to look into it further, (Couldn't have one of the fella's nearby to peep what I was playin'-he'd tell the whole gawdoggit' world...of course) and if it was funky or mushy and messed up or something like that, I'd be a laughing stock. Punked till the punkin'd never seemed to stop.

Her note read: "YOU LIKE IT HOT?"

WHAT!

Needless to say, I spent a lot of time over that girl's house!

After we'd established a brief stretch of necessary ground rules between us, things took off like an unstoppable wildfire. These were self predicatory things she offered and demanded.

Like, she had a man.

A real one.

One she had no intentions of giving up or leaving just because she was starting to dib-n'-dab with me. And she could care less if I had a girl. She never wanted to see her or ever have her thrown up into her face. Didn't even wanna' hear about her. Her man was twenty-two, to her tender, young sixteen, (turning seventeen in just three more weeks) and he was in the Army, stationed just up Railroad Drive at Fort Bliss.

And I could expect ta' get *KILT'* if he ever found out she was fuccin' wit' me, a mere high school punk, actually carrying books and doing real homework and shit like that.

She'd actually chuckled solemnly to herself while angling her head slightly, offering a pursed, but sweet smirk, toying with me. I didn't know what she was thinking, as if she herself wasn't really sure—whether he'd actually believe it, if he ever did find out.

There were other stipulations as well, if I really wanted to take a shot at saying nice things to the awaiting kitty. Like, she didn't have time to be waitin' on me or sneaking around with me. If I wanted ta' hit', it would have to be before school started when it jumped off, no other time. Her man picked her up everyday, at the park, down the street from her crib when school let out, like clockwork.

Who was she kiddin'?

I set my alarm almost two hours early on our rendezvous days, just to get ready for her.

It took everything I had, while standing in front of her, not to give away my excitement of anticipation of what plying into her would feel like. I gripped with all I had just to remain calm, maintain my cool, while the two of us discussed this over the phone one night before the festivities actually kicked off.

This hunny had some energy!

I had no problems easily meeting her demands—TO A-"T".

I soon found myself, not only meeting with her early mornings, I got bold. Skipping morning classes at least twice a week, I'd get into her hood early. Wait around the corner till her mom's car passed by on her way to work. Then, I'd creep into the house to find her there expecting me. Waiting in anticipation, and already wet with mounting desire, she'd greet me, still in her pretty pink, see-through teddy, and nothing else.

Our game always played out the same. For a long time, neither of us grew tired of it. I'd squeeze, lick, suck and pound away at her perfect body, like a stark-raving, hungry, mad-man craving manna, for hours. Our youth refused to let each other up for air all morning long during those sessions. And sometimes chancing it, we'd even chance cutting it close, deep-breathing on into the approaching later hours of afternoon. Or at least until I was so spent and raw, it pained me to even touch myself when I went to take a pee.

WHEW…!

This not so subtle arrangement lasted a full, tenth grade year and on into a vast part of the ensuing summer. My partners at this time all thought I was nuts. They each had girlfriends. But wasn't none of dem' gittin' what they knew (because I schooled them how I was hittin') what I was gittin'. In reality, they were each looming a bit wary albeit envious of my carnal exploits.

Scared and a bit panicky about their own, newly found sexualities, Mickey Rodrigo, a towering Puerto-Rican of little words, would just as soon take on a full accompaniment of a rival school's football team in one of our regular, Friday night haunts, as he would eat a bowl of his favorite Cheerios (no milk, no sugar.) with hulking crunches of opened mouth gulps, than be forced to come face-to-face with a real, live—breathing, naked honey.

He hit me with...

"Whatt' "R" chew gowing' do, if that sexy lee-tle' Skeez goes and geets' here-self preggo, huh, Blu?"

"B.A.", Bennie Azudo, a spittin' image of the eighties nerd, before the term computer geek was even cultivated, was the type kid who sported high-water, faded jeans, the daily, striped, IZOD shirt—complete with pocket protector which held only a comb, which he drove us all crazy with, as he used it incessantly in a desperate fight against an unruly wave of sweeping hair. Somehow he'd constructed and trained this thing, like a pet above his brow, into one cantankerous, super bang. He put it to use in covering up an entire left or right side of his face, depending on the severity of that day's outbreak of acne. His conspicuous attempts to hide a face so pocked with spoiling zits only added to his social discomfort and relational atrophy. This caused him such embarrassment when it came to approaching girls, that the running joke (only members of our group could ever hope to get away with in chiding him) was that he was the last of the late-great Latino, virgin, Lovers left alive in the entire state of Texas.

He spat back toward Mickey, so lithely beneath his breath that barely any of us heard him.

"She ain't get there by herself. Sides'...Least Blu's gittin' sumpin'. More-N' I can say for the rest of us." He shirked, peering at the others with fatherly disdain. I shook my head stupidly. I knew he was feeling down and referring mostly to himself. Rounding us off, was tiny, Mike-Mike Pauluto—the first M&M, (A self-administered handle). Although at fifteen, he didn't really have a neck, and the rippling strain of both his legs resembled striated masses of purely cured oak, to match the pines that were his arms and torso, he was the smallest Samoan any of us had ever laid eyes on.

Quick and speedy, he was the group's pretty boy, and the team's star running back. His stoic swagger belied his abridged stature. And, the sharply-hewn detail of his "Playgirl-like" features had set us all up, on more than one occasion, for wicked fights we generally won against a full slew of jilted, hopelessly jealous boyfriends. His sly, unassuming outlook was only a mask for his stone-cold sense of self-confident nature.

He spat back in reply at "B.A."

"Who cares if Blu's tappin' that azz'? Somebody else's strangling that piece at the same time. She gets knocked up, blame it on the otha' fool and carry on, soldier—call it a fuc'n day," was his offering.

That's what I liked about M&M. He had so many ladies; he was carefree and unworried about letting any one of them get at him enough to bring him down in any way. He was fortunate. Females simply never frustrated him, like they did for most others. He instead, feasted—on them. I figured his attitude toward fessin' up to responsibility for a baby would last about as long as it took for science to market the first swiftly administered paternity test or DNA test, which was still a ways off in becoming popular.

While I was tappin' Nailaya, my "PLAY" with Val went on. While…not actually, "GOING-ON". Cause' although she and I did partake of some very heavy, unfulfilled, groping or petting sessions, we never got increasingly close enough to mix body fluids and actually do-tha' do. It wasn't that I hadn't been trying. She just wasn't the type to be give it up.

BIGUPS, VAL.

It wasn't until returning from a summer trip to Virginia, following the death of my last living grand father, Ollie, with twenty—five fat pounds added to my weight, that she and I stopped seeing each other altogether.

I'd spent a great deal of time in Flint—Hill, Virginia, Rapahannock County to be exact. While there, I worked harder than I ever had before helping my second cousin, George Burk, build a cinderblock garage on the edge of his property. Don't know how I gained so much weight over such a short period of time. I mean he worked me and his son, Marvelle, like dogs, I should have returned emaciated and sparse. We toiled so hard, at times, literally, from dust till dawn, that I was havin' ole'-time slave flashbacks and finding myself hummin' well-known Negro spirituals while making plans for mys's…s-scape' back ta' Texas away from de' massa's hand up at da' big house.

Must've been a testament to Cousin George's wife, Emma's, wonderful cooking over those three months. I mean, I really packed it on while I was down there. But not only did Cousin George see to it I was well-fed while under his care, his down-right Nazi demands forced upon Marvelle and me while building that garage added wealth in the beginnings of an established, life-long, work ethic that would come to support me well into all my future endeavors.

Although I gave him my best in working my butt off for that man, also, like the animal I was, I repaid his familiar hospitality and mentorship, with a multitude of integral acts of lasciviousness. These found me securely and hastily run out of town on a proverbial rail (or Greyhound bus, depending how you look at it) as soon as his truck could cart me. Marvelle and I had both found ourselves culpable by way of swift and immediate judgment (cousin George's) after being caught doing way-too nasty things to my delightfully willing, female cousins, Rona and Amanda.

Of course, it wasn't my fault. Rolanda and Nailaya had spoiled and ruined me forever.

Returning to El Paso, I found Val had done some growing all her own over the course of those summer days. While I'd been gone, she'd ripped a page right from Nailaya's book and had fallen in love with a thug. And a real, Gerry-Curl drippin' Straightoutta' Compton fool ta'-boot.

Baby, the name he went by, was a squat, powerfully built, five nine, two-fitty'. And he'd shown up on-scene with his rep securely in-tact, as a tattooed, bullet-scar riddled gangster known to literally be in training by the local, junior-mafia, drug-running set to break heads and take lives without the slightest inkling of remorse. His idea of seventeen meant the number of rounds in the clip and the chamber of a little girl named NINA'-his *GAT*. Homey was, at such a young age, a bonifide, stone-cold killa' and he'd taken my girl.

Tha' fool was supposed to've been graduated two years ago. He had ta' be twenty, and sported a full beard and drove a straight—dope, LLAC' which he parked in the school principal's spot anytime he chose, daring the man to even approach him, inviting drama.

I'd already had enough of that type shit in my life. She wasn't worth revisiting the pangs of memories I'd almost completely been able to bury deeply enough inside of myself in order to be able to close my eyes restfully each night to sleep soundly while keeping thoughts of beasts like him out. She wasn't worth my life.

I was out of business. And all but for good—as far as she was concerned.

Her surreptitiously stolen affections were no longer my concern. I wisely left her alone.

Hell…

I planned on outlivin' dat nicca'. And those plans had nothing to do with giving him the chance to play the part of grim reaper.

EARLY SIXTEEN

Through just the paltry experiences I'd already had, though not much, by comparison to today's youth, I began to consider myself a little better prepared to enter deeper toward manhood. Yet I was still going through life with my everything based solely upon sexual gratification as was taught to me very early in the near misses of my own victimized, childhood molestations and their resultant, adult relationships. Most of these which I'd thus far cultivated very poorly. I began to reconsider females.

To look at them with an entirely different eye.

The women roving in and out of my life up to that point, from Mama'n to aunties, cousins, supposed friends, and sexual partners began to be looked upon with more of an apprehensive understanding. No matter how they came at me, nor how I approached them as I began to play with much older women than myself, each in the end would begin to become demons to me, no matter how sweet. In the fucc'd-up convoluted torture my mind demanded to be swathed in, each of them sought something or other from me instead of engaging me with a genuine sense of common decency amid real, heart-felt emotion.

Pressing me...Pawing at me, with little couth or tact, to do for them, to pay that bill, pick their kids up from football practice, buy their food...For some pussy. Who you kiddin'?

Unrealized by me, some actually were sincere in their intentions of wanting to take something from me. Something I'd earned, internally. In a way, even they tormented me. Some tried taking away my pain. As if they were righteous enough to soothe that part of me which drove me on in a reckless stupor.

Get real! I was like a rebellious smoker, accustomed the hack and cough of strife. These ones, I really pushed away with quickness.

How dare they think enough or care enough about me to place themselves on the chopping block of vulnerability—in attempts to help me out?

SHIT! Take care of your own worries! Leave me in peace-to wallow in mine.

I didn't care that much at all—about myself.

I began considering slowing down…Just a little—For a minute.

Believe that if you wanna'.

Up to this point, I'd engaged in three frighteningly unfulfilling relationships with little girls only masquerading as women. I went on, following these to experiment with a slew of frenzied freaks and coquettish damsels. Looking back, I'm freely able to laugh at myself with endless, mind-clearing clarity. The image I view of myself, portrayed correctly, as the stumbling, bumbling idiot; foolishly going about my life, thinking I was already in fact, a man, looms ridiculous to me in the present.

Who was I kidding? I was far from being a man. I was still a little boy.

I was a clone. The tormented, spitting image of a social minion of a legacy set forth by my mother.

And let me tell it truthfully as it is. To young men everywhere, struttin' about so naievly with supposed bravery…

'Thinking you've got what it takes to grab life by the balls and swing it around till *IT'* gives in. Surely and simply, whenever the wind blows unexpectedly, your wee-wees swell upon demand, this length or another, and this is not necessarily a thing of such great importance. That's what they were engineered by GOD—to do in support of procreation toward re-making HIMSELF—An occurrence as uneventful as a ball retracing its motion back up in a sweeping arc after being bounced. Consider this: If it were such a magnanimous occurrence, why does the identical thing happen to little-little boys at morning and week old—tiny babies at changing? Because the penis is just a tool.

Nothing else…

A tool that comes with the responsibilities and boundaries of truth. Stop placing such emphasis on its work. Used wisely, you will be able to recall and count on your fingers the times you're afforded the splendor of opportunity and pleasing allure of utilizing it correctly, with one you Love and are joined with in holy union toward its properly intended purpose. The more frequently you use it incorrectly, or with anger or malice, you can consider yourself looked upon as a pawn piece, mere fodder in a cruel, ritualistic game—of a devious life or premature death. You choose. In choosing incorrectly, you embrace a diversion away from the all-encompassing beauty capable of being created upon choosing to enter the game appropriately. Spawn fury for such an explanation, you play hand to becoming the fool as you're made to become insignificant and ultimately extinct by an all-knowing, master gamer—GOD. THE ONE, who knew completely, when he engineered truth at its start, that this instrument had the ability to bear confusion and ultimately be materialized on so many occasions as the commencement of either unceremonious flow, from which nothing good easily follows, or sweet, fruit-bearing harmony through which joy and happiness are possible.

That is....

We have become all but incapable of properly and ultimately looking at it for anything other than what it all too truly is.

And that, if continued to be spread around in an ever-present application of irresponsibility, the efficaciously proffered curse of strictly—promised doom invites the un-welcomed invocation of digression, until we are properly—mentally, emotionally, and financially equipped to wield such power that is enmeshed in finally and fully bearing responsibility for being a man; as each of us is correctly called to be.

Until you reach a point of a multi-tasked, self-control and management, where you're able to discern and exercise a heightened maturity, misuse of the penis will be like living in Arizona. Great in the winter...but feeling like you're living seven inches from the sun, each day a living hell of its own, during summer.

You're not a man.

Not for the entire length of time during which this maturation piece of your own life is missing from your scrambled puzzle. And for some of us, a full grip upon manhood comes early. There are a select few who actually benefit from having happy, healthy mothers and fathers in functionally sound homes who do mature early, becoming men at seventeen, eighteen, or even younger. But, for most, me included, it takes a long, long time before we can cultivate enough sense of worthwhile experiences to finally be able to call ourselves rightfully—men."

My primary engagement to sex at thirteen was not my first, actual, sexual encounter. That came at the hands of a lecherous pig of a molesting auntie, at the age of only seven.

-Believe it or not.

Looking back now, at my mature exploits, I can honestly say I dodged a serious bullet while being ushered into an extremely fertile flutter of a hot, very explicit, sexual experimentation. Yet, retrospectively, as a consequence of my poignant ignorance with Rolanda, Nailaya, the girl cousins and a few others, I could well have, at thirty-eight, had a child today who would be twenty-five or twenty-six on their very next birthday.

WHAT THE HELL WAS I THINKING?

That's just it.

Like so many others out there playing, I wasn't thinking.

I was trying my best to be made a pawn and be offered up as fodder toward self—destruction and ultimately social extinction.

The things those young girls and I did, from my thirteen to fifteen were at the time, feeling wa.aay too good…Too good to know enough about or entertain and accept judgments for failing to place measurements on those judgments which could very well one day extend our lives. We all but turned the blind eye of stupidity to the way our actions were hurting us and holding us back with a skilled, time tested discipline, which threatened to prevent all of us further, responsible development.

And definitely too good for us to be smart enough to halt the strength and force of the speeding, runaway train our passions had misguidedly suckered our hearts into believing we had to have for each other.

Heck, we were in—Love. Couldn't NOBODY tell us nothin'

DAMN! Hindsight is so compelling. A thing I wish I could give my own children freely, from birth.

But, I know better.

I feel fortunate to have survived those tumultuous experiences; blessed to have persevered with my ability to Love, and to be able to discern truth, for real, still in tact.

This experience surely didn't exclude my initial incorporation into a fraternal frequency of heart-wrenching fellowship within a brood-hood of anxiety, prevalent in the irresponsible participation in unprotected coital interactions. Nine times out of ten, in the beginnings, middles, and ends of every teenaged sexual frolic, my own notwithstanding, plies the evilly concocted, inevitability of the slithering head of the unwittingly developed realization—that somebody's either gonna' get pregnant, is pregnant, or was pregnant.

I was by far not exempt. I began to falter beneath the weight of frustrations that began to bombard me almost from every side amidst a medley of sequences bringing on unprepared, teen-pregnancy scares every time I turned around.

Whew! I wouldn't want to go back to revisiting that period of angst and uncertain illegitimacy…For nothing!

That VISION thang is a real trip!

During this period Mr. and Mrs. "P." (Nooten and Ieena), (More O' dem' slave names) Kammy, Lucinda and Rathan Pall, Willie and Candy Green, twins—Lonny and Johnny Williams, Gerwin Williams, Truby and Auzelia Cale, and Fab (FABEOUS) and Right (ALL RIGHT) Marley; (The four of them, Truby, Auzelia, Fabe and Right, actually had another, little brother, named STUPENDOUS…at home…I give up!) all entered my life.

Why parents did such things to helpless, unsuspecting kids as paste them with those field-hand monikers was beyond me. Boy, we all felt for them whenever we thought about it. The first time I was introduced to these characters, it took a long time before I could fully believe or actually come to call them by their given names.

Go Figure.

Other accomplices included again Garv Emanuelles, Dave and Pamela Burstow.

Pamela still holds the dubious distinction of having the worst breath I've ever smelled emanating from any one female. Only my former boss, Operations Officer on a ship I'd served on outta' Point Loma, California, prior to going to Constellation, Boo-Boo-Breath, Brazington (A brotha', and an academy grad, no less) matched her rancid oral intensity so easily at the other end of a darkly blown, putrid whisper.

But, feel me though….

Both had "ZACTLY" breath—their breath smelled "ZACTLY" like the crack of their azzzz....... Chauntre' Cay, Devonee Lupre, Tirra Hallis, Albey Muniga and Dave Gables rounded out the bunch.

Boy!

What are they teaching those suckers at the service academies anyway? It definitely wasn't how to brush.

Was I ever far off from holding a garnered knowledge of being able to coral things in my life? Or would I ever come to being able to coral things saturated by both physical and emotional turmoil, which my involvement with this unseasonably bizarre lot seemed to perpetually bring? As fate would have it, I was in store for more than an education. One intrigued by folly and wholly mismanaged maneuverings, which, from inception, I would feel myself reeling, tumbling, and seemingly falling backward in a spiral—perpetually reaching to catch myself and break my fall—no matter how hard my efforts to stay afloat were re-numerated.

Little did I know, the *Real Deal* was ju-uust about to begin.

An almost unmerciful slap—fronting the face of reality, shook me with abridged abandon. This caused my already confused state to become further shaken by the Love, grief, despondency and unquenchable insecurities of others' surrounding my rapidly spinning, quickly deteriorating world as it began to materialize further.

It was all applied, as if those embedded within my inner circle, constantly went out of their ways to rain down havoc in a heavy, choking sandstorm upon me. Although I had begun to break out just slightly, of my former protective shell of not being able to fully trust, I reserved the right internally, of rapidly thrusting myself back toward this stifling sentiment should putting up with the chores of just managing the idiosyncrasies and challenges my new friends presented become too challenging.

It became harder as I attempted a sparse grasp at maturity. Scratching with a real desperation, I sought to find a balance within my own existence while the new frenzies they each threw towards me tried with skilled determination to trip up my each following step.

A true friend and an even wiser and more-valuable mentor once relayed to me:

"VISION HAS BEEN DEFINED AS FORESIGHT WITH INSIGHT, BASED UPON HINDSIGHT".

Also, All thanks to GOD ALMIGHTY, I began to learn how to apply diplomacy to most things I did.

In this, I very rapidly began to make changes to how I accepted the actions of others as they applied to the sanity and sanctity of my own life. Toward this, for me, I learned to permit the definition of the word DIPLOMACY to mean: The art of permitting someone else, with a determined tenacity—to have things—"MY" way.

SIXTEEN

I'd either left or been asked to vacate the premises—IMMEDIATELY! The cozy remnant belying normalcy, within what was then the battlefield of our family home, was to be my resting place no longer. (Details are inexplicably sketchy, depending on whether you're inclined to believe me, my brother, Toppa, who was eighteen at the time, or our Mama'n and her husband). My recollection of events followed an all too serious, physical altercation between the aligned combatants of my brother and me versus that same almost hapless, far outpaced, yet still-useful stepfather, Garvin Emanuelles.

I quit my job at TACO BELL where I'd been toiling since old man Borsberry sent me on my way, mid eleventh grade year and, with Maman's blessing, I enlisted in the Delayed Entry Program of the United States Navy.

Ever heard the old-adage, GOD puts people in your life for specific, pre-determined reason? In all reality and with hindsight, I owe my initial success within the Navy to the very man whom immaturely, at sixteen, I felt was the assessed cause of the final, separating break up of our highly—dysfunctional family.

Originally, I'd had no thoughts of enlisting at such a young age.

Heck, I was going to college!

Didn't know how. Nor to which one. Or who or what it was going to take in getting' me there. But I was still goin' just the same.

Heck....What did he know?

He was ONLY a flunky. A NON-COM in Uncle's underused Army. Thereby affording him little or no insight into the special, highfalutin plans I'd already professed to have worked out for my life. These, mind you, were plans for which outwardly, I espoused total prefatory knowledge and detail for making them become a reality. Factors of which the range and scope still escape me now.

I knew what I was going to do with my life. He couldn't tell me nothin'.

In actuality, I had nothing whatsoever in the form of a profitable internal scheme for what direction my life was to be headed.

"GREAT-GOOGALOO, Junior!" He was always so fond of saying... What da sam-hill you goin' do wit' your life?"

"You'll see, fool." I'd answer back with a smirking, almost whispered disrespect.

"Leave me alone, George," I'd warn him emptily. "I got plans." I'd say. Shaking my head as if I was the only one in the know *and he was the idiot*.

With Love, he'd smirk back knowingly and settle further into his chair. In reply, he'd tilt his head mockingly to one side to showcase a long, squarely set jaw line pasted with infected, razor nicked bumps. The slight inkling of a wizened, prideful smile would enter to spread across the contour of his coal black face.

"Weeelll.... I don't see no dog-gone plans jumpin' off sittin' round here on your butt—Doin' nuffin'—Do you? Heck! Da chicken had plans ta get up ta' cross dee' road too.—Dats' jus fore' da wolf in da' weeds waitin' for em' ate em'," he laughed himself back into the solitude of his and Maman's bedroom.

I didn't need to hear all this.

This particular conversation took place and the outcome occurred as a result of him returning home one day and completely out of character for him, he was nice to me. The atmosphere inside our house on Nike Lane was generally one of contemptuous complaint, deceitful underhandedness and one-upmanship. An asphixious envelope of counter-counter movements, where anger relaxed among us freely while milk cartons were marked with measuring lines, cereal boxes were hoarded in the safety of closets in Garv's and Maman's bedroom to keep us from gobbling them up in a breath. And rarely, even in the case of outbreak of fire, or greater catastrophe, did anyone in the house successfully communicate with any familiar care on any sort of regular basis.

He offered me one of his precious OLD ENGLISH 800's .—A thick, tar-like, fetid malt liquor, the flavor of which I can only compare to ear wax, to which I still attach the dubious moniker of being, distilled, LIQUID CRACK and have thankfully, since outgrown today.

And he challenged me! In a ruse of offering a simple, fifty dollar bet.

"Junior? I bet you ain't got da' balls ta' get off your duff, get on dat' dere' phone,' he directed with a finger longer than Arsenio's, 'and call a Marine recruiter to come out ta' talk at ya..."

There was that tilt of the head again. And that damned smirk. I was sure I couldn't trust him. Wished with all of me that I could knock that smirk from the face of his six foot four frame with one punch.

"And GET-IT-STARTED!" He'd topped off.

"Get what started?" I countered, trying my best to block his presence out and ignore him.

"Yo' life!" He parried back. The whites of his eyes so widely extended, they actually appeared to encircle his brows instead of lie beneath them.

SEVENTEEN

Garv, at the time, was an E-6 in the Army. He was stationed at Fort Bliss, in El Paso, when Mama'n and he'd first met. It wasn't until I'd frolicked my own number of years in the Navy that I fully understood his reasoning behind not suggesting I call an Army recruiter. Grass is always greener in somebody else's yard while water is more brackish from the rusting pipes of your own spigot. And every man has his own demons driving him through life toward achievement no matter how slight. I called the Marines and believe it or leave it.

Thank GOD! They never showed!

As I sit now. A MUSTANG Lieutenant, waiting for the results of a Lieutenant Commander's promotion board, a full—twenty years after, that bet's been almost long forgotten. This manuscript was begun while still aboard "America's Flagship," the USS Constellation CV64, in route to join operations off the coast of IRAQ, during her final voyage. And it was begun with my uncle, Big Bem Bem Johnson and my cousin, Amaru' Leen Willems fighting at the front on the ground there—in theater, during the first week of "Operation Iraqi Freedom."

Ole' Garv, seems more and more a veritable genius...NOW! Rather than the buffoon and inconsequential illiterate so many of us tried so painstakingly pin on him back then. His care and concern for what I did with my life steered me closer to accomplishment and led me toward a direction commanding respect and common decency. I never thought to present him the smallest credit in return back when he was giving so much of himself in an attempt to lead our fledgling household, which refused to be led out and away from confusion toward success.

More capable now of thinking clearly, He was a great influence on my life.

Thank you, Homey!

EIGHTEEN

Anywaaayzzz'... Was the major stupidity of my thought patterns of the time.

Man! If we could just bring our children to recognize, without pain, the wisdom present in the words we offer them presently during youth...

I'd been an entire, two years thrust into the world of making my own ducats and paying what small portion of my own way I was capable of pulling off via my little TACO BELL gig. And although this seemed important to me at the time, it was fully inconsequential to him. For a man of his caliber to have cared so much for me, an unruly, smart-assed kid, not even his own, was outstanding.

Garv had never given up that day.

After we'd sat waiting for the Marine recruiter, well into the middle of a full two hours. "Call the dag-gone Navy!" He exacted, almost too forcefully with his next words.

And boy! Am I ever grateful?

Although it still didn't prevent me from falling on my head from the top bunk of life, on frequent occasion, thinking I was Superman, even while in the Navy, it provided a pristine start a great majority of American men of African descent cannot even imagine for themselves.

It was this year, still new to the military that I would really begin to believe with strength of conviction in my own developing manhood. Having had no real, consistent paternal influence for such an extended period of time, (Mama'n and Garv eventually split up too, well before I actually left for basic training)—though not attempting to use this as any kind of excuse, I was so far behind. And it took a while, decades even, of forcibly willing myself to hone in with tenacity on correcting the particular deficiencies holding me back in my every action.

Even though eighteen and on my own now, I found myself faced, repeatedly with situations brightly honing home the fact, reminding me over and over again, that I didn't know how to carry myself as a man should when out alone in a very unforgiving world. Because of this fact, it was then that I began to make a medley of almost overwhelming and costly personal mistakes as a supposedly mature (Sounding like my grand mother, Inez pronounces it—sounding a lot like manure, as if spelled matoo-or) adult.

Some of these things, I'm certain…I am still paying for today.

It was during this tumultuous stage of circumspect, that I hurled headlong into adulthood. It became an initiation of sorts…And instead of taking the proper steps to fall in with a grouping of successful individuals, what I'd gained was an un-welcomed entry into a colloquial quagmire of collectively miserable people.

I didn't know. No one had been there to show me the way.

Some, were unable to help their antics of placing the heavy on others. But, more, for selfish reasons, others just seemed hell-bent on destroying as many dreams and people as possible as they hurled impetuously toward their own damaged endings, sweeping bodies up in mass along their paths. This almost included me, as I quickly became twisted within the volatile machinations of destructive paths constructed amid friend-born hatreds which to that point I'd never experienced with such clarity as they were distributed with dexterity, like Raid, by close acquaintances and strangers alike.

These folks tended to work seamlessly, in groups. But the best of them perfected their skills of completing the demoralization of lives on their own. Outwardly, these were the types who assessed blame for their own despicable situations and actions covered in negativity with ignorance, upon others. And they generally did this as a matter of daily course, while overlooking in their own accepting' blindness the splendor of available internal abilities they too possessed in being able to formulate plans of achievement and personal successes within their own lives.

Looking back now, it's hard to believe I'd become so easily manipulated and enamored, just as Mama'n had, back in her day.

The vicious cyclic theory of the sins of the parents being revisited upon the children had caught up with me.

And…

In reality, ain't shit changed…but the dot and the range. Everybody's hopes are targeted.

I found myself plagued in the same way, in my own, naive involvement with such people as Stephanie, Antawn, Kammy and Lieza Pall, Dee Dee Plout, Big-Dog and Shirmey, Baby Boy and Bonita Faxton, Ronald Thames, Cyril and Danita Lofmon, Cee-BO, Ernie Blanks, and an even shadier lot. To include, George, the not-so-real, cracked-out homey who worked in my ship's radio room, Simp-Daddy (Marvis Billups) and his sidekick, Lil'-Dog, as well as with all the other suffering souls of character such as Goldie Jenkins, Skosh Amerie and Alfie Browning.

It was also at eighteen that I first traded in my fraternal status as son, brother, student, athlete, and veteran—for the addition, (Depending on how you look at it) of becoming a husband.

What was a husband?

Who's husband?

Hell, I didn't know!

I was just doing like I'd done on every other occasion whenever I was taking whatever steps held out before me called for me to do. And just like all the times before this one, I leapt headlong into an unbalanced, thought void of thinking myself manly.

I was WINGIN' IT!

What did husbands do?

I had no bidd-nazz' being no-body's huzzzbin'…

In the past, I'd always held a restrained, disdainful snicker for these type guys whenever I'd seen them in a public setting.

And…I had a wondering amount of curiosity and RESPECT for them too. How'd they do what it was they were counted on or were supposed to do, for wives and for their families when becoming husbands?

AWW…-Shit!

I'd stepped into it firmly, A*G*A*I*N.

These fellas' were the ones you always saw at the mall, carrying momma's purse while they waited at the outskirts of "Claire's", while queen ameba was inside shucking out ducats for trinkets neither of them could afford. All the while wishing he could just abandon the baby stroller and just go over for a second of personal peace to check out the new JORDAN's up the row of shops at FOOT LOCKER. Or, they were the healthy, hustly-bustly types you always see jogging behind those immense, colorful baby carriages as they ran each morning, baby in tow, while momma got the rest of her sleep soundly back at home.

If I'd had any clue what the heck I was doing that day when I hauled myself up to approach Mr. P. asking to become one *of them,* I would have certainly opted for running for the hills to take on a life of celibacy, should someone have painted a picture of what life was going to be like (The things I would go through) following the uttering of those two little words, "I—DO".

Mr. P was an affable, slight, *REAL* man who always appeared to be available to me, like a POP, at any and all different times of any day. I'm here to tell it... The man, to this day, still looms more of what a father and husband should be, toward his family than many I've witnessed since. Just retired from the ARMY, and more than a little bit removed from the things his teenaged daughters were up to, he was forever reserved and soft-spoken as he'd attempt to lend whoever was engaging him, his full attention, and he'd slyly contemplate thought while shifting or twirling an almost always-present tooth-pick from side to side about the interior of his tightly held mouth.

A brotha' of more complete responsibility, solidity of character and sounder repose I've never met.

The Palls were our neighbors. They lived right next door, just a wall's hop away. That day, I'd either peeked up over the wall of our yard into theirs (He was always working, doing something or other, just toiling, to maintain his house or his yard in impeccable condition) with hopes of catching Mr. P. out back. The Pall's had the baddest' house on the block—both inside and out. Perhaps I simply hopped across the waist-high rock wall separating our two homes. I had grown over a period of about three years to attach myself, warmly to the entire Pall family and because of this; I'd hopped that wall and just walked into their household with only a perfunctory and familiar knock, unannounced about a million times. It was nothing for Mrs. P. to come from round' a corner to find me sprawled in the immense interior of her den, watching T.V. to instruct me, "Blu. Go out back and bring that load of boxes out to tha' front and put them in Mr. P's truck so's he can take them to the dump."

And, I knew with an inward smile, that later that day I'd be on my way to the dump to help the beloved, Mr. P. with whatever chores his queen had assigned us.

The two of them were special. Who knew the torrid affair of their story's beginning? All I focused in on was they were so completely in Love and compatible now. Almost as if they appeared to be the same person. They were a wonderful example of what Love and marriage could be—if given the proper chance.

They had it like that man! And I wanted it, with their daughter.

Who knew the daughter would fall so far from the trunk of the tree of both the mother and the father? I mean, I reveled in the purity and foundation of what Mr. and Mrs. P. had. Those two could mime with the simple nod of a head or send telepathically atop a raised brow, thoughts—important, life-altering ones, to one another in a splendid display of perfected communication, without ever cracking a sound.

In them, I sought and found a mere portion of sanity and completeness. Something I knew I wanted to one day emulate in my own family.

And, I think they saw something in me as well.

In that house, I felt such LOVE. For a time, Mrs. P., would even set an extra plate at dinner, daily, just for me, in case I was again gonna' weasel my way into another of her awesome, home-cooked meals. (Mama'n never cooked—besides, we rarely had enough food in our fridge to put together any semblance of a fine meal).

Did I know?

Hell no!

Once more in life, I was operating without a savoring clue.

All I knew was—If what the two of them had could be developed, with hard work and determination and was truly workable, over time, I was in.

Sign me up!

Plus, like an idiot of the most high order, I had years before, fallen (I mean DIRTY-DRAWS crazy) in Love with Kammy, their youngest daughter. If such a thing truly exists and I know it does because the very same thing hit me again, later on in life. I fell for Kammy, like I fell for my Ree, on first site.

Seemed a safe bet at the time.

I'd been home on leave, freshly returning, after proudly completing my

NAVY basic training and initial electronics curriculum. I remember fondly the swell of accomp-lishment swooning inside me as I waited for the Palls to retrieve me from the El Paso airport. Maman's car just happened to be acting up again when it was time for me to need a ride home following my flight and Garv had been long gone for months.

I'd greeted them sporting the command of an impressive, single chevron topped by the menacingly perched, bust of a white "crow"ing eagle sewn securely atop my left sleeve. These denoted me a newly promoted—Third Class Petty Officer.

Wheew! A brotha' had it all goin'-on! The promotion had been awarded before I'd departed Great Lakes, Illinois for home.

While in Great Lakes, I'd pal'd around with the likes of Robert (Bolo—From

L.A.) and my ultra Homey, Pike Holmes, (He used to always joke that he was John Holmes, the nefarious porn star's, brother) also from California. Pike was my road dog. He and I were so close. We hit the gym and swapped outlandish boasts together daily. So close, he used to come into my barracks room or I would go to his, any time, night or day, and using the keys we'd provided one another, we'd help ourselves to the other's stash of ready cash whenever we found ourselves in a fiscal bind. And we never mentioned these loans. But they were always repaid in full on timely order. That's how close we were. He and I collaborated on many trips of leisure to Milwaukee, where we partied like carefree idiots in clubs like Pappagaios, and the Safe House. At the time, the drinking age in Wisconsin was only seventeen. He and I were just above the wire.

Another included in the saga of motley bandits who ultimately offered droves of experience in shaping the primary period of my military service, was a crusty, middle-aged character known only as Papa Smurf.

Back at home, on leave, I remember being in my room, sitting on the edge of my single bunk, discussing with Kammy, her thoughts on us taking the plunge toward marriage. It was weird. It wasn't like a true confessional proposal or conversation. It was kinda' surreal. Not one in which both parties offered their own invited views of good and bad opinions on the subject at hand. It had gone something like this:

Benignly, peering into the glimmer of her sparkling eyes, I offered her something stupidly, like, "Whaddaya say? Wanna' get married?"

She smiled shyly. I know she didn't think I was being for real. She was seventeen and still in high school. And as experience would come to tell, the girl was no real genius.

She said softly, tossing the tuft of a newly styled jerry-curl to one side, and she pursed those STRAWBERRY tinted lips I hungered so much for, with a singular shrug, "Sure."

And that was that....

How awful!

As my uncle Larry used to so fondly say whenever he had cause to even think of me, after the nuptials were cemented, "BOY! YOU BIG STUPID!"

All I know. Is...I recall getting up off that bed, walking straight out the front door of Maman's house, and after sighting in on Mr. P. as he stood in his front yard, expertly pruning roses, I remember him cocking that toothpick lazily to the other side of his mouth as I approached and he greeted me with a slight smile as if he'd already known and had patiently been expecting exactly what I was there for.

He started first, while continuing to trim, appearing untouched by the immensity of the stark terror coursing through my veins like warm ice water.

He staved me off with, "What's on your mind, Blu?"

I recall stuttering forward with something utterly life-changing, like...

"Uhhhh...Mr. P, Sir?" My feet shuffled aimlessly in stationary space screaming indecision from side to side.

"Ummmmm...Uhhh...mmmmm." Shuffle, shuffle, shuffle...

Finally, reaching inside to pull up that shit every man needs when finding himself lost in the terror of Love's tattered battlefield," Sir, uu.mmm, Kam and ummm...Kam and I—wanna' get married."

I couldn't quite pick it out fully at the moment, but I swear I remember him looking at me with a quickly paved-over glean of sudden, teary-eyed sadness. Almost as if, warding me away from sure and certain pending doom. This appeared to be accompanied by a slight reservation showcasing pity in his eyes too as he shifted his shears with deft patience, one hand to the other, and extended his arm, palm up, toward the front of the house directing me to start *movin' it* in that direction.

"Looks like we need ta' ummm...' Reaching for the more and more graying stubble covering the point of his dusty chin,—'go inside. And talk these kinda' things out."

He knew... Ya' know...

I was sure of it.

But, at that very moment, no matter how much he wanted to ward me off or step forward to reach out and thrust me away from seemingly assured self-destruction, he was her father, he couldn't.

His reaction somewhat shocked me catching me off guard for a second. It was akin to the helpless sigh of a father feeling trapped when looking across an institution visiting room table, through thick, tic-tacked, bullet-proofed security glass—at the broken image of his only son.

A son who's just been forced to accept the stark realization that he was about to spend the next fifty-two years to life, trapped behind bars for a crime his father had continually warned him about—cautioned against and taught him to beware of, time and time again, even before he could fully even spell his own name. His crime... Being born prideful, hard-headed, ambitious—without a guided direction, and without possessing more than the three strikes a merciless government would provide him as his common pleas and seemingly invisible attempts at begging a judge not to hold it against him the fact he'd been birthed... BLACK, fell on deaf ears.

Again, following the almost nervous, tooth-pick play he finally brought the well-worn stub to rest along the left side of his face.

Bringing his gaze lower to almost call out my uncertainty, following each of my shuffling feet almost comically, he added, cocking his head lightly at an angle to one side.

"And... uhhh. You're sure this is what you wanna do, Blu?"

I mean, all the signs were there. The man cared so much for me he was all but screaming out to me, "BLU! Run, RUN, RuN!"

Did I listen? Did I even see one of the signs he was so Lovingly thrusting my way?

You know the answer. No way.

And thus it began.

At eighteen, I had a new (blessed by the Justice of the Peace) wife—Herself, a mere seventeen. And, for the first, six months following my marriage to Kammy, I quickly became skeptical of every person in the world who'd ever indicated marriage was a two-way street, fair and good, nice and pleasant thing, all-for-one-one-for-all endeavor. With her, I soon realized they, were all contemptuous liars—True prevaricators of the worst caliber; worthy only of the most excruciating pain of being impaled on a flaming iron skewer for their despicable, emblazoned efforts. Marriage for me, after this, became an acrid stench of putrid bile in back of my mouth.

This timeframe also saw the re-inclusion in my life of my cousins Dernell, Meinsha, and Amaru' Leen, auntie Mattie Mae, Leboy Plight—Da' Real Live Navy Chief Petty Officer and now born-again Christian, and his baseball bat wielding wife Hesther. There was also, Nay Williams and his wife, Glorietta. (Herself, a notorious half of what was to become nefariously known among our pack of struggling misfits, as "The package deal") A term not so respectably placed albeit justifiably based on she and a girlfriend's penchant for forming a sleazy, tag-team duo—down for double teaming a brotha' and his whole crew, no matter who was present, in a minute, working out every kink of a body that happened to be home—completely, plying sexual favors of every position and kind without any suggestive hint at a marital remorse. Then there was sorry-azz Meeche, matched by the funky-azz personage of a weak-minded, sorry character referred to only by the name—Skippet.

NINETEEN

By miraculous occurrence, (Don't ask me to recall how I did it) but, at this young age, I achieved the rank of E-5 and was thoroughly enthralled in the splendor of my very first overseas deployment. This took place aboard the guided missile cruiser, USS England CG-22.

Didn't take long to foresee this, ehh, Mr. P? But, Kammy and I had been dis-affectionately separated, and had all but called our marriage quits for a full half of the entire year we'd been married and during the entire time I was to be deployed. When I was in port and home for long periods, we'd seemed to accept each other just fine. Little did I know, like most points in our Love, this too turned out to be a farce-filled lie and long-played out charade. She, at eighteen found the increasing struggle of imperceptive patience required to fight through the interrupted phases of coital calibration that materialized whenever I'd be gone at sea for lengthy stretches to be unbearable. Kam was one hunny who craved steady dickmatick.

Her pussy was like a living, breathing deity—One which was strict in its demands, even when I was not home, of being fed continuously, in unbroken abandon.

And serviced Miss Kammy would be. Never to be denied. Only thing is, she was continually being seated by the wrong maitre D'.

The girl had never quite figured me out. If she had, we might still be Husband and Wife today. I wanted one woman to fulfill my every need...Not a woman who wanted a hundred men to fill her one.

It was following this that the shape of my life began to become more permanently marred by a myriad of bad moves. All made in and out of the company of a few, select, and very beautiful women. Some crossed, intertwined and co-mingled amidst a shadow of smoothly hewn, fluttery faces, coupled with a smorgasbord of spectacularly curved figures, others just a haze of memory among the many.

You see, following Kam, I'd mistakenly regressed into thinking that that was what life was all about. Hit and Run. Run or be hit.

Look back at history. King David, Marc Antony, Sampson, even the President, William Jefferson Clinton, the most looked—upon moguls among us, all powerful icons of society in their eras, all fell short in their abilities to ward off assured doom in their discarded sentry of a maintained couth and decorum as they each found themselves faced with the choice of walking away and living out dreams of a lifetime or the alluring possibility of perhaps playing up in some mighty moist and wet for just a few minutes in somebody else's yard.

I know I don't need to point out how poorly things developed for each of them.

Do I?

It was after that initial deployment, that my eyes were opened more precisely toward discarding a large portion of the naiveté I'd departed homeport waters with just six months before. After experiencing a bit more of the world in the guise of ruse evident in places like Hawaii, the Philippine Islands, Japan, Singapore, Korea, and Australia, I returned to San Diego with Kam firmly in place, back at her parent's home in El Paso, on Nike Lane. I was then freed up to begin to toy with the feigned beauty of a hustling, thickly built sweetie named Carlyn Hite.

Caryln was the epitomy of what the fella's called a HOOD-RAT. Some felt better suited to referring to her type as Foot Draggers. Skillfully adept at latching on to a sailor's (Any Sailor's) steady source of continuing income, they never relinquishing their hold on the poor unsuspecting momma's boy from BAMA' till his paycheck was attached, extended, or garnished in two ways more than one, while his credit was increasingly maxed-out as he struggled each pay period to cover all the installments she'd busta'd his azz into, toward furnishing her entire, HUD subsidized, section-eight villa, just prior to showing him the door for good—with simplistic reasoning, "I tole' you before you got attached that my Boo, Pookie was getting out tha' pen in two monfths'."

Caryln, rarely ever went anywhere alone. She traveled; carrying an all-too-seriously depleted hope-chest of emotional, physical, and smothering familiarity of weight that, at times, could prove to be life-threatening, lethal baggage. There were her mother and stepfather, her sisters, Ferrari and Daisy, her brother, Stoop, who was a young thug, both renowned and notorious the same for his gang affiliations within the Bloods, Crips, Pyroos or Sumpin'—An aspiring drug dealer all the same who stupidly and explicitly plied trade in his hood, killing his own peeps'.

Keep in mind, Caryln was twenty-four when I met her at THE DEVIL DOG, one of the hottest clubs located aboard the Marine Corps Recruiting Depot station in San Diego. I was a wide-eyed, nineteen.

The very first time I'd gone to pick her up for a date and dinner, at her parent's house, where (although upon our first meeting, she'd professed to having her own place where she lived with her daughter while attending law school at Western University) she actually lived while accepting public assistance for her four year-old daughter, Veronique, I was greeted with the bizarre sight of Stoop crouched like a khaki-clad China-man as he knelt over what seemed to be hundreds of individual pieces of a completely field-stripped MAC-10, machine pistol. When I'd driven up, he'd been engaged in cleaning it, right there in the front of their house, with parts and pieces strewn everywhere.

Looking up briefly breaking concentration away from his work, he greeted me for the first time ever, with a welcoming bid of a sharply nodded gesture, his chin seeming to reach the height of his picked-out fro and back down again, in ultra cool, slow motion.

With searing eyes that had already seen way too much life…and death, he bore into my soul at an instant.

"WHAASSSUP…Homey?" He gestured down toward the mess scattered about his feet, "Ever clear a-10 into a crowded set?"

Trying to give off at least a pseudo-hard appearance, I replied back, "Naaw-Playa'. I role wit' Nina (Nine-millimeters)," I faded with desperation.

Who was I kiddin'? I was three thousand miles away from being any kind of hard.

It would be easier for me to take a job herding cats than to comfortably fit in and excel as a *playa'* among the likes of Stoop and his gang.

I remember hoping beyond hope that he wouldn't engage me further on my feigned, variable knowledge of street gats. A knowledge I think both he and I knew full well I didn't possess. He didn't press me. Getting back to his work, he seemed instantly to forget that I'd even driven up.

Thank GOD!

He dismissed me with, "Carol's in da' crib, *mark*."

I must have been inside the house for ten minutes before she and I finally departed on our date. Miraculously, when the two of us exited the front door, we were met by the picture of Stoop firmly fondling the completely restored weapon. He smiled a crooked grin up at us, cradling it, like a beloved child, turning it over, side to side with awe-inspiring gleam, in, what was it…adoration, as the life-taker hung its glistening sheen of oiled perfection within his deadly grasp.

Caryln's cousin Tanny, a sweet, likeable young lady who never seemed to have very much to offer by contrast to Caryln's sham at maintaining an outwardly portrayed, boisterous life stride, was forever a hanger-on. Always there, hanging out to a point, that I found myself on more than one occasion, tasked with hooking her up with whatever available BUSTA' I came across on the ship while readying myself for my own evening's expensive misery with Carlyn.

One of the contributing factors to my finally being able to extricate myself from Caryln and her family came one Sunday afternoon after the two of us had been seeing each other for about six months. We had just returned to her parent's house after a Sunday beach outing.

There we were a house full of her people. Her old man and I were in the living room taking in the end of yet another sorry attempt by the Chargers to stave off yet another losing season when suddenly off in the distance, the phone rang. Next thing I knew, all hell began to break loose instantly, throughout the entire household around me.

"Momma! Moooommmm—a!" Camc the bone-chilling shrill of Daisy, Caryln's mouthy, ill-considerate, teen sister.

"Stoop's down at 'TURDIE THURD—fight'-in'…", Daisy bellowed with an intensive, life-ending shatter.

I'd never seen a household so negatively transformed at such a rapid pace in all my days. I stepped back as closets materialized as ammunition and hardware lockers. Cupboards became feed bins and mini armories, as shotguns, pistols and illegally possessed assault rifles were tossed, hand-over-hand, in an assembly line of expectant combatants led by an exasperated trail from each room in the house, toward the front door where daddy already had the van idling. Bandoleers and machetes appeared from beneath previously comfortable couch cushions. I remember having to lightly pass a large Bowie knife to one of the sisters from its hiding spot against a wall at the back of a love-seat closest to me.

Watching it all develop, in pure, inexperienced shock, I tried to curl up into an unaccountable ball of invisibility in a safely held corner of a tattered couch along a wall. I'd never seen any shit like this all my life!

After all the hardware had been securely loaded, Caryln's pop stopped back in the living room briefly in route to the door. And, as if conducting one final survey to make sure no cannons had been negligently left behind, he turned his gaze to me. Almost as if I was the one thing he had forgotten and had come back to retrieve. He threw a nod my way with a twisted, furrowed brow bearing down on him with indecision. Setting his head in a hardened stupor, he asked directly, "Blu? You comin'?"

Gesturing, he made an attempt at shooing me along the fated pathway toward the front door. A journey his entire family had just taken, one by one.

I think both of us knew I had zero intentions of following him and his broad of hood-rats towards doom. I'd just met them. There was nothing they were after, on Turdie-Thurd street or there in that home, for that matter, that I felt worth protecting.

With my heart pounding a thundering drum inside my chest, my mind screamed in incessant, silent frustration. I'd found myself once again, back in that tiny projects bathroom with a toilet full of everyone else's shit, my nose barely able to stomach the funk of Mama'n not being able to pay the water bill for the past three months—Seeking aimlessly, an acceptable way out, while I closed my eyes and with clenched teeth, stole myself, unable to do anything else, atop the last person's mess, with added futility.

"Naaah…

I'mmmm….Umm. Think I'm aaaahh…sit this one out. Ya-Know. Stick round n' hole' things down here. Don't worry…I'll lock up on my way out," I offered him almost too pleasantly.

No way was I getting mucked in with the normalcies of that crowd.

As soon as I felt it was safe, I left that house and I never went back. In fact, I never took Caryln to the movies ever again.

Following Caryln, entered the gifted, smart beyond her years, Yvette Rhosea. For me, Yvette was the "shorty", JUST SEVENTEEN, the lyrically gifted 'Musiq'-The Love-Child, sang of, in his tune about a girl, too young to be mixed up in the genres of a game she actually played too well.

Yvette was a sweetie. I broke her heart.

And still, I regret with abundant sorrow, the way I treated her. If I ever see her again, I'd only have two words of friendship to offer her in passing.

"I'm sorry."

TWENTY

Brought the realization that fairy tales do not in fact exist. Dreams can not be plucked from trees. And, without a doubt, drama would forever continue to swirl around my head with a stifling, fetid breeze.

But too, it was during this period when I began to develop ways of softening each blow of unexpected occurrence that came my way with negative swagger. I knew things could be much better in life than I'd previously experienced. I had faith there was a way out. I began to dump culpability for all the terrorizing shit my childhood had woefully saddled upon me. Instead, I began to formulate plans for reclaiming my adulthood. I started to actually pay heed to critical teachings of instructions learned from the trials of the past. I began to pick up on the relative importance of factors such as dependability and accountability as the two were pliable to valuable commodities reaching towards long life and affluence in one's youth.

"A man who wishes to make a profession of goodness in everything must necessarily come to grief among so many who are not good. Therefore it is necessary for a prince, who wishes to maintain himself, to learn how not to be good, and to use this knowledge and not use it, according to the necessity of the case."

-CHAPTER XV, "OF THE THINGS WHICH MEN, ESPECIALLY PRINCES, ARE PRAISED OR BLAMED,"

THE PRINCE, NICCOLO' MACCIAVELLI

I think this was the period when I first began to engineer and adhere to that personal life-shaping theory professing belief in nothing less than A HOME RUN OR A STRIKE OUT in all my dealings. As I stated previously, no other result would be warranted, considered nor accepted. No gray areas permitted. A philosophy for which I would take on and lose many lopsided battles, not to mention a full bushel of friends and relatives, who simply became fed up with the alienating nature that my quest for personal perfection, (as it began to take a toll of scraping against beliefs inherent within their own lives) would become.

And although I came up on the losing end of many of life's-experience battles, still, I pride myself on having stepped forward. Like a man, to let a story be told as it should be told—with vigor...

To let it be known, THAT I WAS IN FACT—IN THE FIGHT! I hadn't given up. I didn't want to suffer the same, like my Great grand father's, grandfather's, my uncles, and my father, and step-father before me.

I was flat out refusing to give in to the pressures of things preventing me from realizing the full greatness GOD meant for me as he pushed and pulled me over and through the stumbles and valleys of trials, not of a wicked society, but of my own making, which were preventing me from becoming a man.

Someone very special to me, still today, is forever chiding me, trying continually to sway my view of this world with words to the effect of: "Honey, why do you always have to look at everything like it's some sort of battle? Everything's not contestable."

Because to me, by more indications than one—It is all... Just that—a BATTLE!

A war waged only within self. Not a mêlée for an African/Nigger/ Colored/Porch-Monkey, Spear-Chucker/Black Sambo/Negro/African American/CITIZEN of today's America society. Sadly, in truth, if not approached, at least internally, as such, I fear I run the risk of falling prey to re—opening and permitting an endangering outlook to seep lazily back into a place scantily tucked away in my history, wherein I might once again, as our culture has in the past, begin to pin my problems on a perceptively uncertain and still robust, American racism.

Does racism still exist in the United States today?

HELL-YEAH!!! Of course it does.

Does it possess the same frightening power it once had?

No! It doesn't have to. Not if attacked swiftly and correctly, with the acuminous adherence to education sought after with a determined resolve to banish ignorance.

Please don't pretend shock. From as far back as the Pilgrims, with their mad, psychotic grab for territory, to the welcomed words of a venom-spewing Willie Lynch, to the recently re-opened case of Emmit Till, add in Watergate, the Iran Contra scam, to the alleged, government sponsorship of offing a sitting President, the Rodney King debacle, to O.J. getting off, (but not gettin' off) to Susan Smith's disrespectful proffering of a claim entirely acceptable by a maddened society, that a black men had hi-jacked her car, with her two, helpless infant boys inside—when it was she herself who was the culprit. Sending those two precious soles, strapped securely in the back seat of her car, to a suffocating depth of a nearby river deep (who woulda' thought—a mother?). To the almost identical claims of another criminal, yet affluent, white man, who claimed a gang of young black men had shot his pregnant wife, and himself beneath a secluded city overpass, when he was in fact the homicidal shooter. Add in the crazed culinary practices of Jeffrey Dalmer, eating humans, to priests inside the Catholic Church, raping young, defenseless parishioners, to present, which rings in the treachery and ineptitude of the Clinton presidency, the Whitewater scandal…Monica? Throw in both Bush's, OPERATIONS DESERT STORM, RESTORE HOPE, PROVIDE COMFORT, DESERT SHIELD, and IRAQI FREEDOM. To the additive spectacle of an unseemly realization of craziness which perpetuates fact that black people do commit approaching atrocities on a grand scale such as these themselves as well; the Wayne Bertram Williams, Atlanta Child murders, Kobe Bryant and Michael Jackson sexual misconduct scandals, the idiot who barricaded himself and nine members of his family, women, children (most of them his, he'd fathered with his own daughters) and reportedly shot-gunned them all to death in an instant, preceding a lengthy police stand-off, which culminated with him the only survivor.

Through all of this, it was fast becoming vitally important for me to find a place within the assurance of a disciplined, inner position inside myself. A place of solemn peace and GOD given joy, where I'd be able to hold everything which battered the rims of my exterior, threatening outrage, contempt and failure, outside and at bay, while securing an affordably earned, (Had to be earned—not given), opportunity of gaining the promise of knowledge both professional and personal—leading to triumphs. I had to find and do things which brought about a realization of goals. The presentations of which, I'd just recently begun to be able to see clearly amidst the dissipating fog of an always present chaos that seemed to forever saturate my life before.

Dipped in chocolate...Enamored of grace...
Sprinkled with beauty...
Good LORD...She is a BLACK WOMAN!

As if finally hearing my prayers of loneliness', God sent me Miss Marie Antoinette Taylor.

"NETTIE".

Nett, to her many brothers and sisters.

"Maria" to her Mama, Miss Carrie.

Her mother's story was that she had originally meant to name her Maria Antoinette after a Catholic nun, sister Maria, who had shown her a fair modicum of parity and kindness during the birth of what was then her third daughter, and the ninth of her twelve children. But the correct spelling and meaning of her name never made it onto the official documentation recording the event of her birth.

Mama, Baby-Doll, Sweetie, Honey Bun, and Boo-Ba, are all other names she's heard me call her by, during the lifetime of good experiences we've shared with one another. As well as a whole slew of an entire arsenal of other, explicative, not-so-spiritual handles I've addressed her by, during the oftentimes, tumultuous circumstances we've survived—together and too were ingrained in our Love spanning almost twenty years of marriage.

I first met her in 1986. It was Yvette's turn in the barrel. And I think I was approaching boredom with her ever-present acquiescence. And, without fully realizing it, I found myself seeking a woman offering more challenge, coupled with a greater opportunity for drama and ultimate achievement.

Boy! Again I could hear uncle Larry's—"*BIG-STUPID*!"

Why'd I have to go looking for that?

CAREFUL WHAT YOU WISH FOR...JUST MIGHT GET IT.

In Nettie, I got all that...And ten buckets more! She came with a doting, but stern mother, whom I still suspect Loves her third daughter so fiercely, because she reminds her so much of herself, in her own youth. There were a total of fourteen brothers and sisters. Eight from her mother and father, and six more from two separate legs or branches of familial relationships developed between her parents and others over the years. Also, there was, of course, an irresponsiblly estranged Baby's Daddy, an absent, un-caring father and a kooky, loveable Stepfather, Malvin. And a full slew of wonderful nieces and nephews to supply hugs, tickles, kisses and laughter to on a daily basis. These were all accompanied by a colorful selection of both seedy as well as otherwise wholesome, brothers and sisters—in laws and other friends.

"NETTIE" came as a package not fully blooming. And with a degree of challenge I had yet to experience from the females I'd toyed with up to that point. Just like with Kam, I'd known the second I'd seen her. Call me a romanticist, a sucker for Love, an idiot.

I fell for her instantly.

It didn't matter I was about to jump head-first AGAIN into a situation I found myself completely unprepared for. Heck, I didn't have (as Mama'n woulda' put it so eloquently) a pot ta' piss in. And no hopes of even stealing one come high noon.

But, this young woman held hidden qualities of stature and assured prosperity that screamed out plainly, evidently, only to me. She was piece of coal waiting to broken out into the full-fledged splendor of an awe-glistening, priceless yet productive Diamond.

Before knowing all the facts, the freight train of Love's drama had chugged forward, sweeping me up in its whirlwind, almost knocking me from my feet. I was to take so many emotional HITS—on account of her in the future.

But I didn't care.

Instantly, I Loved Miss "NETTIE".

For me, my feelings of infatuation for this one woman became almost magical. If she was willing, I was game.

CHOCOLATE CHICKENS DON'T TASTE SO GOOD WHEN MIXED UNWILLINGLY IN VANILLA SOUP

My life changed at an instant, uncertainly...forever—upon meeting her. My heart raced incessantly with just the thought of her. Just the essence of *HER*...It hit me with an overwhelming force which can only be described as the weight of a billion bricks suddenly stranding me to pay heed to her every whim. I began to find that whenever I was near her, the wells of my palms perspired slightly with a sort of heated anticipation of things to come—in life.

Of what?...Man, I had no idea. All I knew was; the previous period of peace and tranquility I'd almost forcefully enjoyed following Caryln, and with Yvette, were instantly flung through a still closed window meeting a fate of never-ending, see ya—fo'ever' when it came to me and "NETTIE".

The shakeup in my life caused by just meeting "NETTIE", still, even—to—this—ay, causes me to find myself fully braced against better judgments from time to time. Instantly, I became at times wickedly addicted to her.

I'd fallen into perhaps the strongest Love I've ever experienced to date.

GOD had sent me—My soul-mate.

But, what he didn't do...was, assure me that holding my newfound Love dear to me was going to be easy, always simple and gratifying.

We were both the same age. She a bit more experienced than I. Yet still not more mature or more responsible in the areas of personal reliability, the poor girl was barely able to care for herself completely.

We'd met in a Portland, Oregon nightclub, called Pinocchio's. I was part of a contingency of sailors visiting the city during its annual Rose Festival event. She, by chance, was there to join her family in a celebration commemorating the return of one of her many brothers', Tony, who'd just returned from completing his military service in Germany.

Our meeting came at a time in which I was becoming more and more frustrated with my efforts with Yvette. I still maintained my contact with her, albeit on a long tether. But rapidly mounting frustration with her had begun to mount to a point where, I knew she was on her way out of my life as I began to develop and finally see her questionable commitment to our relationship.

I'd already had enough of such treatments in dealing with Kammy. I was very skeptical about permitting any female to put me through the mess I'd put up with in my first marriage to her.

Because of this, Yvette, was never given Kammy's numerous, second chances.

Repeatedly, prior to "NETTIE", I'd find myself returning to the ship after a night of partying or of being out toying with Yvette. Only to find myself lying, staring up listlessly at a brightly lit rack light on the ship alone—thinking.

There's got to be more to life than this.

I'd lie there, staring up at the seemed nothingness that was life for me. I'd pray for restlessly gained sleep to quell my destructive emptiness.

And, inside, I'd fret knowingly. Yvette just wasn't the girl for me.

Though I didn't really know it then, this frustration began to metamorphous into the form of a rather nagging, relentless internal pressure—to start a family.

So, in adherence to my formerly stated, battlefield policy—OPORD 101—"Home Run or Strike Out..."

I went out during that trip to Portland with intentions to build, latch onto, create or borrow one.

A Family...

I went out and. I found her. I desired her. I wanted her.

I cared so much about my lack of genuine trust from Yvette that fifteen minutes after meeting "NETTIE", I stole away out to the front of the club, phoned Yvette and dumped her, compliments of MA BELL.

There was no comparison between the two. "NETTIE" had Yvette beat, hands down.

I got her.

But it wasn't entirely Marie who'd finally captured me and solidified the case for causing me to settle down. Honestly, I have to relate. She was surely beautiful, in a roughly hewn, under-cultivated sort of way. And after spending just a moment in the discord and disorder of what was her every day ordinary life, these things only added challenge and intrigue to the purely sexual allure emanating from her to me whenever she just looked at me.

Never once did the immensity of the problems she had cause her beauty to pale in my base assessment and I never entertained briefly even a second thought of her needing more work than I had skills and effort to offer.

A diamond in-the-rough, per se', she was.

She was worthy, and had seemed to be just waiting for a guy like me; not scary of taking on the challenges we'd soon carve out in a lifetime as we faced the universe together. We became for each other, the ones who wouldn't bolt whenever we each needed support the most. After getting to know her during the few short hours of the five days I'd spent in Portland, I was more than willing to eek through the pains and testaments of waiting for her to fully develop into the beautiful WOMAN, WIFE, SISTER, MOTHER, and FRIEND she is today.

I know..., *BIG STUPID!*

But I wasn't fearful. I was young enough to still think of myself as invincible, unwary to the dangers that could befall such an unseemly union. In the years that followed,—together, we would both grow immensely. Collectively, we would learn to support one another and stretch out completely to reach for a Love that would spring us forward towards the maturity it would take to ultimately bring, not just her, but an entire family to shine pricelessly.

And, though no one knew it then, not doubtful family members, such as signifying uncles, nor worrisome mothers, through challenging and counting on one another, she and I would eventually beat the odds.

But still, in the beginning...

The girl had more problems than a Harvard remedial math book.

I was soon to find out that she had another side attached to her, literally at the hip. And that little surprise became the beginnings of the family I'd lain in that rack back at the ship and longed for and envisioned so illusively without satisfaction.

This attachment presented itself in the sweet, cherubic form of a golden-haired baby girl of about five months old. It was after the very first time that I bent low to sweep her pudgy little form up Lovingly into my arms to nuzzle the soft, puffy bulbs of her tiny cheeks that I completely discarded any and all doubts that I might have had as I began to permit myself to open up and float completely toward Loving her—forever.

Her name was Brittney!

Britty-Boo, Britt-Britt, Knucklehead, Nanna's Wunkins, her mother's pet name for her, BMTP, an acronym, pronounced, Boom—i-ta-puh', short for Brittney Marie Taylor Penn, RittBritt or SPAZZ to her thousands of e-mail friends. And...Nerd, the name I Lovingly call her whenever she does something attributed to bone-headed lapses of teen aged judgment. I Loved that Baby just as I had her mother, from first sight. For many years we've been blessed to watch her sprout and grow into the wonderful and beautiful young woman she's materialized into today.

Under two sets of very watchful, overly-protective eyes, Britty, continues to flourish and surprise us with her achievements.

Our first meeting took place as I'd exited the third city bus I had taken that summer day. Beginning at the wharf downtown where my ship was birthed, I'd set out with plans for meeting Marie at her mother's house for an early date. I'd trekked across the city, completely uncertain of my eventual destination. If I ever got there, she and I were on our way to take in a movie.

Our first meeting was the result of an almost tentative scheduling, secured while I'd been delegated the privilege, while still at the club, seated next to her, of massaging the freshly danced out dogs of her dainty, and tired feet. *Those puppies had no clue the life-distances that they were being prepared by me to travel.*

"NETTIE," had hinted that she might have problems finding a baby sitter. In fact I even got to witness her paltry efforts of attempting to convince her younger sister, Min (short for Mynthia), by way of a couple of rolls of pennies, to look after Nanna's, while we were gone. But, Min, in her re-directive nature of feisty outspokenness, a manner she still maintains Lovingly today—wa'n't haaavin' it.

So, after her attempts to convince another sister failed, I suggested we simply tag the sweet little bunion along with us to the theater. And we've been doing just that now, for more than eighteen years.

It seemed this one little girl lit up the entire arena of the movie house with her golden brown skin and almost blond hair as soon as our trio had entered. I was struck dumb by her. I had never seen a black baby with naturally blond hair before—Picture that. She was definitely something special.

Bright-eyed and precious, she easily captured the full attention of everyone in whatever room she was being passed around in. For a bunch of people, she was more than enough reason for them to get up each morning and just go right on living. I'd never seen anything like it.

Neither had I ever been surrounded by so many individuals of the same family who all hung so tightly together offering a total interior structure and support to one another. "NETTIE'S" family, for me, was a curious anomaly.

Still today, not many of my brothers and sisters in Law live far from the stable dependability and safety of Miss Carrie's house.

I was smitten by Brittney though. I'd been around babies before. But never one, who at such a young age, easily and intelligently exhibited such attention and charisma.

Muscular in her tiny, sculpted, almost perfect form, an obvious intellect radiated from her like twinkling stars of perceptive brilliance. This little girl was active and smart. She was perhaps the happiest baby I'd ever seen. She'd giggle lightly, wrapped lithely in the protected strongholds of a caring auntie or uncle's arms, and was forever contented to be bounced jovially around the house—at her whim. It was very easy to envision caring for and raising her as my Daughter.

I was shocked and startled the first time I witnessed her point a stubby little finger at different objects inside her grand mother's house, as she was carted around and as they swept through her field of view.

As they passed by, she seemed as if she actually took the time to comment on each item with seriousness. In a juicy-mouthed stammer, the tiny wrinkles of her baby brow would furrow and with a dogged determination, she'd continue to point, then turn to her benefactor holding her securely and ask, "Whasssat? Whassat"?

I think I almost dropped her the first time I heard the words come from her so clearly as they rolled from her five month old mouth.

And did it take long for her to cast her little web of a Loving spell in becoming a light for me as well?

Two Seconds...

And although I knew that I didn't have much that was tangible I could offer her, for me, life had just begun, and as well, had gotten' infinitely better. I had nothing from my own past which prepared me to step forward and do all I could to make this sweet little girl's journey through time impervious to such things as danger, contempt, prejudice, abandonment and disappointment.

Sorta' like...I was meant to be her Daddy.

But, I knew I'd die trying in an attempt to ensure she didn't as much as step on a thorn and hurt her little foot for as long, and longer, that I held the title—in her eyes—of being, *HERDADDY*.

The three of us saw Alice Walker's, "THE COLOR PURPLE". I believe it was probably the first time "NETIE" had actually lost her patience and gotten mad with me. I kept slippin' Britty little bits of popcorn here and there whenever I thought her mommy wasn't looking. Brit Loved it. She played right along with me, stealing furtive little glances of expectation my way, whenever she thought mommy was concentrating on the huge, brightly lit movie screen, waiting for the next kernel. Net thought I was a nutcase. Plying such a young baby with salty, messy popcorn! "*WHAT if she choked?*" Unable to really eat what she pawed and grabbed at from the super-sized bucket I'd purchased, I was completely focused on her. It was more fun watching the fervor of her unchecked effort to slobber up a fistful than watching the movie itself.

I remember thinking, only my second day in Oregon, as I sat on my soon to be mother-in-law's couch, *Yvette was history*—All but already forgotten.

Once my heart had opened to Brittney, I quickly formulated the decision that from that little house in Portland, I would establish a legacy. I'd do it with that young Woman, Marie. And never entertaining the slightest thought that she was not biologically my daughter, I'd begin with that child, Brittney.

I was a goner...Dude!—Stick a fork in me.

The ship was only there in Portland for a total of five days. It was during the final day, prior to the ship pulling out, that I first approached the idea with Marie of the possibility of the two of us carrying our new relationship to a higher level of seriousness than either of us had originally expected.

Immediately, she knew exactly what I meant. And...she was now certain, that I was some kinda' nut. Pure-D crazy, for real!

Thinkin' I wanted to marry her after knowing her only four days. We'd met on my second day in Oregon. Actually I'd gotten arrested the first night, after coming out of a local strip joint, where I'd had way too much to drink. Me and another partner had been picked up for harassing an available hooker, who'd just happened to be holding up the nearest light post as the two of us had come out of the overly packed club. Turns out, *our hooker* was in fact an undercover vice cop. So, we spent the rest of the night in the slammer, until the daily Shore Patrol visits snagged us up the next morning. After ensuring we'd been charged with nothing, they returned our I.D. cards and re-deposited us along a righted trail.

Once you think about it, Portland is not the place a cunning sailor needs to solicit...Lovin'. For us, the entire city was a lustful variety of freely offered, feminine gluttony.

I know for a fact, her entire family thought we'd both fallen off the deep end.

Heck, a new flood of sailors visit Portland every year to participate in and lend military support to the Rose Festival. A million girls and two or three hundred guys come together in all manner of twisted ways. Along that pathway, a fleet's-worth of whimsical promises are both made and just as quickly broken, at times in the same breath.

That's how it felt, at least, from the Sailor's side.

An entire metropolis of these small "white" lies was almost intentionally offered with no true objective of ever being kept. And generally, both sides held this understanding from the start. The normal expectation of the visit, which turned out year after year as a veritable smorgasbord for an entirely willing lot of horny sailors and very giving young womenN, was just that, one gigantic and humongous *BOOTY CALL*.

The whole thing was perplexing if you were, like I was, looking for something a bit more permanent. All a sailor had to do was toss a dixie-cup, white hat to an unsuspecting honey who'd made the trip to the waterfront seeking excitement, and she'd side up to him with a feigned honestly, as if saying, "O.K. sweetie, Go ahead. Lie to me." Seemingly, in an instant, she'd become his five day play-thang' for as long as *he* could stomach her.

It was suddenly Australia all over again for a brotha'.

Why wouldn't they think *we* were crazy?

She was a fruitcake for gambling on hers and her little girl's lives and placing trust in me. Believing I actually meant all that I'd said. After only four days...Why should she place faith in me telling her I Loved her?...And that I wanted her to be my wife forever? And me...Who was I? To them, I was a simp. They didn't know me from Adam. What was my history? What kind of past did I have or what immense total amount of palling baggage was I threatening to unload upon them as I purported to become part of their wonderful family?

Totally crazy for having the balls to even let the words of such a supposition escape my unworthy lips. Thinking I'd met the girl of my dreams so quickly. Assuring her that I was gonna' make good on the promises of staying in touch, supporting the relationship, and eventually sending for her or return to get her and make the fairy tale true for she and her precious baby girl?

Was I some kinda' nut? Had I lost it? How was I going to ever stand up to covering all the lies I'd just told this sweet and Lovely young girl? Simply peering into her eyes for a second, I could tell that I had captured her. And once more, I didn't have the slightest idea how I was going to get out of this one or how I was going to pull it all off.

But I know now.

THAREALDEAL I sought so evidently on previous occasion, and which I was fully unaware of, at the moment, was suddenly staring me in the face with a fury.

Although in the back of all their minds, every one of them, all the brothers and sisters in consortium, Mamma' included, secretly held out what they feared was an unrealistic confidence that I *was* in fact the one and that I was for real. I could feel their hope as they bore into me with an unspoken, questioning uncertainty.

"NETTIE" was in need of some good luck. They stifled their compassionate optimism as they'd watched my every move surreptitiously. They were like a band of protective angels, each one witness to her determined efforts of trying to right herself amid a myriad of fledgling, personal searches yearning for oneness. They were pulling for her all right. She was due somebody to bring a reasonable measure of sunshine and stability into her life. She too needed a light.

-A black, knight on a white stallion all her own.

...One that would lend himself to the vulnerability and sacrifice which accompanied the pain of patiently striding and striving with her till the end. One destined to eventually see her through the rough edges of her own humanity's struggle, motivating her to Love and do good things for herself, and others, while doing right by her beautiful baby.

Someone had to finally step forward for that girl and treat her with the respect and dignity so many other fools had mistakenly taken for granted as they'd used and discarded her so aimlessly over a shallow past already filled, at the age of twenty, with disappointment.

Still, they remained wary. Everybody in the Taylor household held back their *I-tole'-you-so* sighs as they began to consider our many grandiose plans and high-falutin' goals for a life together on our own, not really believing in us, at first.

What they didn't know... Was that I knew all about pain. My own life was one of seeing through strife born of patient determination.

Damn! I was pretty weary myself. I knew I'd thrown down an irretrievable gauntlet, letting myself in for yet another life-challenging encounter.

I had no clue what I'd stepped into. Nor any clue how to make everybody's dreams come true, including my own.

I was still a boy, playing dangerously close to losing again at a man's game.

Was I thinking straight? People just didn't generally take on and fare well in what we were threatening to embark on. We *were* living in a fantasyland.

Fools!

Was what so many family members on both sides felt (and they held no qualms about openly expressing their thoughts)—albeit unsolicited, something the two of us might a—shoulda'-woulda' heeded?

"Ignorance is the curse of GOD, knowledge, the wing upon which we fly to Heaven". That's what it was going to take if I was to set all the things I'd promised in motion. I had very little time to prepare.

First.

A gang of knowledge about the conceptions of a wholly unfamiliar world, in which I had to totally begin to separate thoughts centering solely on self, was the only saving grace which was going to assist my successes in this endeavor. No longer would I be involved in relationships wherein only another single person and I were considered. I was hurtling headlong toward an approach which greatly stripped any points which I could easily, in excuse or explanation, cover any formerly played reliance upon ignorance.

What was I thinking? Although I was young, I'd known better, no matter how sweet the feelings, to caution myself sternly against again entering into the monstrosity that marriage tended to evolve into. As well, that caution brought with it the sobering reality that I had a whirlwind of work to do, on me first, before approaching a moment where I could honestly entertain the idea of once more taking that plunge of caring for and being responsible for another.

I wasn't that same boy who had naively soared over that rock fence to sheepishly beg Mr. Pall for Kammy's unfaithful, palsied hand. I had become wiser, in a way…smarter, shrewder, and at the same time, harder.

Without first putting myself through a personal dedication of fully reforming to a more altruistic way of looking at relationships and at women, the new feelings I had for "NETTIE", and for Brittney, would be short-lived, lost forever, and doomed to a failure plaguing the men of the Penn generations for as far back as anyone could remember.

If I was going to have second thoughts, now was the time.

It's a shame that I cannot recall one extended family unit among my many relatives, with the exception of both mine and Toppa's, where a leading father and a supportive mother were still together in healthy relationships which gave their own children the opportunity and example of wedded happiness and a hope filled success. In our clan, marriage had become that expendable irritation that was dispensed with first before going about solving whatever other problems you felt you had.

Consequently, I'd witnessed and been taught the worst about marriage. It was something, for most of us that just wasn't done anymore. It was an expendable quantity, most of us felt we need not take part in.

What for? All you had to do to get what you wanted and needed, on occasion, was shack-up.

…And *Forever Hold Your PEACE.*

"He that has truth on his side is a coward and a craven idiot as well as a fool, if he is apprehensive about owning it because of the prevalence or masses of men's opinion' "

Up to that point in life, I really didn't have much. No mansion, no million dollars. No adolescent misgivings of having to patiently wait for that one, true and special Love. I hadn't hailed from the greatest circumstance of family—couldn't depend faithfully on any documented, well-trusted lineage. I could count on one hand the number of times I'd seen my own father during my then minimal, twenty-year existence.

All I had was a rapidly developing belief in a system. A newly embraced structure thrust before me in the form of the United States Navy. An organization in which a poor, young black man could actually set things in motion to make it at least look (You know—Fake it till you make it) as if he were being afforded the same opportunities as his white counterparts who were suddenly surrounding him seeming to appear from every angle.

It was a great time to be in the Navy. War was far off; at least an exciting eight more years away. The government was making great strides in attempting to right itself with its self challenges of extricating itself from the soiled nature of its former doctrine to mandating a newly developed quality by denouncing the niggardly acts of a still clandestine past. The immorality and underhandedness of a motionless, sorely felt era requiring the reshaping and re-designation of its intentions caused racism within its ranks, for the most part, to fall way to a more inclusive, equalizing and secure placement of Americans of African descent and other minorities within leadership positions among its ranks.

While in the military of this great nation, I was presented with what I felt was an almost fair shot at learning and mastering communicative skills, a progressive culture and success-driven mannerisms supportive of developing, cutting edge technologies which placed me in the stronghold of a privileged company of America's best, young white technicians. While soaking up leadership techniques and stress coping principles, I began to notice and take on a new reality. Almost reluctantly, and despite myself, inside, I was becoming privy to the novel possibilities of these things taking me a long way toward being able to realize a professional success which had never before been achieved by any other male or female member of my entire family.

I believe despondently, because of my willingness to become enthralled in a greater part of American society, (As well as a still lingering inability to trust) I had very few, (maybe one or two—to count em') close friends who were American men of African heritage within my own profession whom were near my own age.

Perhaps the overlying reasoning behind this was that a slim minority was in college. A greater majority were imprisoned. Many had already fallen and were dead. Grossly due to the wayward schemes of an uncivilized, genocidal plot, thought to have been the brain child of a mad, former Director of the nation's Federal Bureau of Investigations, in his purely uncivilized plot to capitalize on the ignorance of an entire culture by engineering their demise through the known, yet covert support and supply of bloody gang and drug wars which spread across our nation internally, like an unchecked wildfire. Or, they were in the service.

In 1986 there still weren't many twenty-year-old, Second Class Petty Officers (E-5's) leading groups of other young men of varying cultures and who was indirectly responsible for a twenty million dollar, electronic fire-control system, aboard a guided missile cruiser in the World's greatest Navy.

My career in the navy has been at times plagued with the vindictive sorcery of young brotha's unable to permit themselves to initially place faith in and relate to me as well. But this was for differing reasons and away from simple trust issues. Earlier than most, (Even young, white men), I held positions of higher rank and openly assumed more accountable responsibility at a younger age than most felt possible.

The brotha's perpetually maintained an arm's length of dysfunctional distance. For *SAFETY's* sake, they mistakenly chose to look at me as some figure synonymous with their historical, institutional oppressors. To them, I might as well have been the enemy—An establishment flunky, only out to make the man another dollar on the backs of the plighted many.

But, that wasn't my motive at all. It wasn't then. It's never been. And it still isn't now.

On the flip side, my white counterparts didn't confide in me very much either. To them, I was an anomaly, a freak to be studied and dissected. Most had never spent much time in the world I'd come up in. What shocked them most was the fact that I didn't quite fit the mold taught to them that American men of African descent were supposed to be. *I never fetched—or—stepped it.* I was never a butt shark. Always worked hard... Which meant arriving early and staying late. I knew my craft better than most. And I was known, from the start, to exercise not only indignation, but an outraged intelligence, whenever I was treaded upon unjustly. They couldn't quite put their finger on what it was that made me tick. I think they half-heartedly continue, even at times today, to expect me to implode and show the true *COLOR* of the *Porch-Monkey* their upbringings lumped me into being at the onset of any professional or private tragedy which befell us while living so closely together and at sea.

I had my own, internalized problems dealing with them as well. At least some of the brotha's could assimilate a fair consideration of what I was going through, due to the proximity of most of our similar beginnings. But, walk, talk or struggle in the tattered and weary shoes and life experiences of the *normal*, American man of African descent? Of a division of forty, where I was the only one of my culture, there was no single individual who placed emphasis on coming close to trying to understand the things I was genuinely made of. What really made me tick?

And being the man that I was, I sort of preferred it that way, at first. It took a lot for me to get close to or permit anyone else to befriend me as a true confidante. Of course, some tested me. There was Anthony Eberhard, a devout Christian and man of grace, who just knew he was going to break down my solemnly placed walls of solitude using faith. Also, Rastess, (Jack) Feltman. A down to earth, Texas boy, who knew everything about every hustle and scam, and whom also taught me a lot about guts and survival in a mean, mean world. Others tested as well, more negatively of course.

But, because I understood them more insightfully than they did me, they were fully dumbfounded in their attempts to peer at me with stereotypical molds of the icons they themselves attempted to shape me into. I refused to let them corral me into stifling corners of mediocre conventions in order to benefit their own familiar traditions of prejudice steeped in intolerance and discord.

It hurt me greatly that I was unable to form better relationships with the young Brotha's my age. This fact always made me feel as if I was missing out on something of vital importance. Although I sought the benefits of holding the skills necessary to reach out and take advantage of all that a functional society could offer me, through assimilation I very easily transformed to embrace *their* educational standards to fit in. Inside, I was still Blu Penn, still held on tightly to inner self. While walking a different walk, talking a more corrected talk inside, I was still ghetto, ever rebellious, while on the outside, one of *THEM.*

I determined further to stick to an original plan. My own were not accepting of me. Others more tolerated me, because policy required that of them. Even though I felt ostracized at both ends of the spectrum, I was able to focus on more positive and more important things to achieve what I needed. I couldn't sulk in the circumstances of my minor surroundings. I had bigger fish to fry. Plans to engineer and complete. I had a journey before me. One which would cause my every dream to become a reality and therefore benefit me in the largest way, if I could successfully get this NAVY thing down, while not permitting too extravagant a change in my original character.

No matter how hard I tried, many, (On both sides) professed not to understand my speak, my language, my mannerisms, my lack of historic claim to a rooted element within a valued component of our precious nation. I reveled in some of their thwarting efforts of trying to gain an angle on figuring me out. At times it became a thwarting game of ill-fated one-upsmanship between us. It intrigued me that it seemed an entire vessel and division of men would dedicate themselves solely, on a daily basis, to attempting to wrap their minds around the workings of thoughts that were my own. It was if they came to work each day with the determination of figuring me out by the later hours of each afternoon. The confounded frustration among them was wide-ranging. It stemmed from the lowest seaman to the highest-ranking position on my ship, the Captain.

The more junior Brotha's held me at bay with their inabilities to offer me the trust of working inside their personal confidences thereby laying the ground work for friendship. The more senior, non-Brotha's, attempted to exclude me further, and although not realizing it, enabled me to achieve more easily, through their underestimation of my intelligence and abilities to function just as productively and skillfully in the same shipboard technical environments that they were operating in.

I began not to care. It was I who had very easily figured *them* out. Their system was cake. I saw this, realizing that all I had to do was apply myself doggedly, study, work hard, *DON'T REACT!* Success in this way was looming largely before me—for the taking, without so called, friends. It was an easy decision for me. Give up my search for that which I had never had; close acquaintances and familiar relationships with others, in order to make that success real. Or permit myself to be pulled down into the trickery of the destruction meant for me by those who wouldn't offer me membership at either venue in the first place.

Formerly, the Navy had only to permit itself to consider roles for men of African American Descent in menial ratings. These previous occupations had never been canvassed by requirements for placing trust in us by assigning identical, TOP SECRET security clearances or admitting us to structured programs such as the Personnel Reliability Program, (Which afforded recipients access to the more *SPECIAL* weapons systems needed during cold war times in the protection of the country) like they did for themselves.

For the American men of African heritage, in the Navy, jobs of technical requirement and merit had been, for decades, non-existent. But hold on. Suddenly, things were looking like the beginnings of change were finally taking root, at least for the crew of the guided missile cruiser, USS ENGLAND CG-22.

As I began to rapidly gain rank, all at once regulations theoretically smelted in stone began to become thoroughly enforced to squash "*COLORFUL*" jokes still prevalent, yet hidden in today's service. Open prejudices outwardly became thought provoking discussion sessions. And stereotypical mannerisms became the scorn of a division of men who, on that ship, depended heavily on one another and were taught, in a collective lot, by me, to take pride in being the technical prima donnas they were. Instead of wasting energies in other opaque shenanigans, my blatant, shoot from the hip style of "HOME-RUN-OR-STRIKE-OUT, didn't letting any of them off the hook easily.

No way...

It's amazing what even an American man of African Descent is capable of when he is rewarded for taking the time to learn and comprehend the rules of a system that almost reveres, as well, the efforts of learning to break the same, but correctly.

That was how the system worked.

The rank gave me presence. Culminated with knowledge and experience, the presence commanded respect. I refused to allow anyone to peer through me, disregarding my commitment and eventual achievements as if I was still, to them, *invisible*. I engineered settings in which others had no choice but to engage me directly, almost forced to look me squarely in the eye when conversing. If there were those who just couldn't bring themselves to face me, I focused even more intently on them. I challenged with my own personal, technical and professional questions. Never being fully satisfied, seeking answers and countering their jokes with hard work. I shot down prejudices firmly through the use of wise, countering intelligence. I refused to permit them to count me imperceptible any longer. Knowledge became my closest friend. Sensible lessons my only comfort. Belying falsehoods of what the heritage of American history for those of African descent at that point had come to be was my guide. The malicious narrative in which I was expected to *act out* in an anti-assimilated depiction of lackluster labors, minimal successes and denigrated existences was not the path I had chosen to showcase my efforts. I'd joined the Navy complete with a fresh sense of determination to do one thing and one thing only.

—To *ACHIEVE!*

Scholarship within the Navy soon became enough for me to dispel the distrusting ravings of my like brothers.

Some quietly and some more outwardly referred to me of course, as "Uncle Tom" "Bitch-Made" or "Sell-Out".

Of course, I only let this bother me a little. For me, the registration of care for their feelings about me didn't fit with the attainment of my objectives. In other words, I didn't allow myself to become responsible for their errant, negative emotions. They were the ones collared in the toil of painting the ship, cleaning heads (restrooms) and serving others; while I got to rack my brain interrogating the complex schematics of billion dollar satellite guidance systems, all stark consequence of purely individual efforts resulting from personal assertions or slothful failures.

Therefore I rarely internalized their scathing attacks and never took them seriously.

I still wonder... Why does my ability to make and keep friends I can identify with in a realm of my own have to fall prey in ignorance to the wisdom I so desperately reach toward in causing myself to have a life better than that which was originally expected of me?

Torrid shadows of the twisted faces of masses who had held out hope for me, casting proudly from hollow glances trapped inside a thousand grizzly black ghettos of history was my strength. From behind the stains of dingy curtains and in pissy hallways of incarcerating slums, from a million dingy, American jail cells, after four hundred years of transparency, materialized my encouragement. I couldn't permit anyone, no matter race or color to use me in their own perverse maneuvers to get me to refuse to claim my rights to contribution and triumph, or my people, as my own. It mattered very little that some, because of my successes had problems looking upon and claiming me as still one of their own. How do you disassociate a person associated with identical heritage and race from birth?

A blessed sense of positive motion accompanied by real visions of tangible grandeur began to become realized as I focused on attainable, productive achievements garnered via hard work.

My belief both in faith and miracles steeled my resolve in causing me to believe I could actually pull it off. All I had to do was move slowly; bask in the creation of only wise, calculated decisions.

But, you know what they say?

The best and most well laid battle plans go to shit as soon as the enemy is encountered.

For me, the enemy here was not so much naivete any longer as much as it was inexperience. I couldn't wave any banners high professing knowledge in the Love arena.

My brief entanglement with Kammy didn't count.

I knew what counted. My name would forever be mud, if I let that sweet girl, her baby and all her family members down. Not to mention she had an ARMY of brothers, each of them military veterans who could easily go on the prowl if they chose, in a protracted manhunt reminiscent of the "Hatfields and Mccoys"—A deadly, interstate raid of revenge ending in my demise payment for stringing along their Lovely little sister.

I didn't need those type of problems!

Now, as my ship returned to San Diego, I had a whole new list of got-to-doos' picking and plaguing at me profusely. My priorities had changed instantaneously.

Had to get rid of Yvctte!

Get off that ship and find a place to live!

Buy a car!

Had to...How had Garv put it? "*GET IT STARTED*"!

This period was one of the most exhilarating times of my life so far! I had new goals. I had discovered a purpose and some semblance of a plan.

But first…

Not only Yvette.

Officially, I still had to get rid of Kammy?

Man! In all the new excitement of thinking about Brit and Nettie, I'd all but forgotten about what little responsibilities I stilled owed to her. Although she and I had eternally parted ways months and months prior to my life-changing trip to Portland, we had never responsibly made the separation legal nor sought to be fully divorced.

Here I was, proposing to another woman. And I was still married to my first. I don't mind saying, things were beginning to get a bit scary.

I had no clue where Kam was, or how to even locate her. Although I was in all actuality the wronged party in the relationship, her parents had taken her side in shutting me out after our troubles. All Mammas and Pappas tend to side with their offspring no matter the terms at the end of a relationship. I held no grudges. I knew my long established status with Mr. and Mrs. P was long past its original pristine nurture.

Time and time again I made calls asking to be put in touch with her?

They didn't budge. But, you know…

GOD is good…All the time!

Turns out, Mr. and Mrs. P. were just as anxious, even more so than me,

to step forward and clean up the disorder Kam had made of her life and of our fledgling matrimonial mess. After all the feelings of anguish and apprehension I'd felt at having to bring myself to contact them, trying to find her finally materialized into becoming pretty much a mute point. They took care of getting her signature on the requisite papers as well as ensuring they were mailed back promptly to the courts in San Diego. The entire ordeal of securing the divorce became as simple as filing the paperwork, waiting the mandatory cooling period and having the papers FEDEX'd to the Pall home in Texas upon finality.

It was another time of amazement for me proving that at times the most harrowing obstacles in life can be overcome quickly with just the slightest nudge of Positive Perpetual Forward Motion and prayer. Sit on your haunches and the train of prosperity rushes right on by and you're stuck right back where you originated from—At Jump Street.

More and more, I was finding and believing that prayer was the key to the kingdom with faith unlocking the door.

"He has the right to criticize who has the heart to help"
-Abraham Lincoln

I returned to Oregon once more before Nettie and I got married. It was in the fall leading into 1987. I had taken leave to spend Christmas with her and Nanna's Wunkins. At the time she had moved out of her mother's house and was sharing an apartment with another girl, Rheanne and her boyfriend, Elvis.

Rheanne and Elvis were two unfortunate souls. She, a stringy haired, seemingly forever soiled, white girl and he, a snuff dipping, rebellious malcontent whom always appeared about six haircuts short of attitude and membership reticent of the local Aryan brotherhood chapter. His favored disrespect of Rheanne was to douse her completely in the contents of his spittle cup when the two of them charged headlong into a heated argument.

Something about me told him to be careful about the times he chose to treat her in this way. Although none of my business at the time, and I remained stoically aloof, he never did any shit like that while I was there. Ole' boy would've been force-feedin' his face through a sip-straw had I witnessed him do something so hideous.

I spent a full two weeks with Net and Britty. Guess you could call that our official courtship and engagement period. Everything went well for the duration of the first week. It was during the culmination of week two that I began to think more along the lines of running. Stupidly, I remained. I should have run; and kept on running—and running. . .and running!

It was during this timeframe when I was first introduced to the grand issue greatly looming to plague the initiation of our future together. I'd been lounging in the front room of the tiny, two-bedroom apartment when a girlfriend of hers *just happened* to stop by. The two of them retreated into the privacy of her bedroom toward the apartment's rear.

At first, I thought nothing of it. It was only after about another hour, lying by myself in the living room, that I got off the couch and took steps that changed my thoughts of her forever. As I entered Netties bedroom, I took notice of her girlfriend sitting comfortably on one edge of her bed. There, she sort of babied a slim, glass tube about six inches in length as she held it just inches from her awaiting lips. The girl gave me little notice as she stared at the tube with a deep, almost lustful commitment. Raising it to fit securely into her mouth, she lit what appeared to be a mini-torch. A slight, piercing, crackling sound could be heard as the flame leapt forward to heat up the tiny, rock-like crystal lying atop a screen at the tubes opening.

Offering nothing at first, "NETTIE" closed the door behind me. I moved further into the room. My gaze locked in on the girl making out with the tube ahead of me. After closing the door, Nett, all but ignored me as she moved closer to the Woman and took her place as she sat down beside her friend to wait her turn on the bed.

At first, inside, I really didn't want to know what to think. I knew enough to know they were doing some sort of drugs. I wasn't entirely a doofous. The hair began to stand up at the nape of my worrisome neck. *WHAT HAD I GOTTEN' MYSELF IN TO?*

Thus far, drugs had played an all too luminous part in my life. Stark, horrific memories of watching my mother and a house full of people all sit around breaking up brick after brick of moist, pungent, sticky weed using playing cards atop album covers, right in our front room came trembling back in a flood of shameful condemnation. Stems, seeds and rocks went one way. While buds, leaves and fill went another. Plastic baggies strewn everywhere, scales atop paraphernalia filled tables and the instability of easily purveyed cash were always present.

I knew even then that the frequent *PARTIES* parading powdered cocaine, heroin, morphine pills melted down and sucked up into syringes with dirty needles were nothing nice. Especially for a kid whose mother, on one hand, scuffled to send him to a private, Christian school, with hypocritical hopes of teaching him (Oftentimes all too graphically) manners, polite ethics and a studious labor as the only ways securing a measurable success. Kissing my head and whipping me into behavioral acquiescence at the same time, two fingers crossed securely behind her back in seclusion, as she shoo'd me and my brother into back rooms, thinking that we held no clue as to what was actually going on.

But this was no longer the seventies or early eighties.

This was 1986 leading fast into 1987.

I had separated myself from all of that. And I'd done such a good job at almost forgetting all that shit even existed. And the Navy, and its fast-approaching demand for zero tolerance toward illegal drug use, was on-point in aiding me as I determined to immerse myself fully into a set of productive ideals by which to live my life by, following such dreadful beginnings.

Due to my past, I could very easily count myself knowledgeable in a wide-sweeping array of the areas of unlawful procurement, preparation and distribution of illicit narcotic substances. So the appearance of it now in the midst of "NETTIE's" bedroom didn't hit me completely unaware.

But it sure slapped me squarely in the face…and went a long way toward bearing down on me with a debilitating contempt. This caused me to quickly re-think my former thoughts of fairy tale living amid realistically promised dreams.

It also began to piss me the fuck off!

No way! I wasn't going to let her cause *Us* to succumb to such mediocre circumstances. My mind clicked in to sweep me up in a whirlwind of clearing, de-fogging motion.

I wouldn't permit myself, or them, to continue to be numbered among the uncounted.

Standing there completely ignored. I was becoming more and more irate.

What the heck was she doing? Didn't she know that shit could ruin your life—(our lives)? Not to mention fuck up your brain! What about *OUR CHANCES*?

I remember leaving the room, slamming the door behind me forcefully, for gathering effect in my wake. I can now imagine "NETTIE's" thoughts as she realized I'd exited the room—none all too glad.

"GET UP GO AFTER HIM! CALM HIM DOWN—FIND A WAY…SAY ANYTHING! EXPLAIN IT ALL TO HIM…

HELL NO! IT'S MY TURN—NO FUCKIN WAY THIS BITCH IS GONNA SUCK UP MY DAMN HIT!

When she finally did come out to join me in the living room, her eyes bugged—out atop a brow covered with a thousand, tiny beads of nervous sweat, her friend shuffled by, almost unnoticed, as she exited through the front door without a GOOD BYE.

My own thoughts became a kaleidoscope of torn indecision. Caught up in a suffocating mist of confusion, between bolting, as intuition had prodded me to grasp at previously, and what I knew the repercussions of her drug habit would mean for the two us, if I didn't turn my back on her and Brittney now for good and fall back to my former, personal methods of operating—Of only caring for or worrying about myself. Suddenly, once again, I found myself torn and lost.

Had no clue what I was gonna' do. I never felt so helpless and I didn't like it one bit. There wasn't anything or anyone to tell me how I should handle all that had been so egregiously tossed into my lap by this sometimes, more-than-beautiful young Woman.

I stared at her with scathing conviction. There was nothing seemingly that she could do to quell the range ignited inside of me, by her deceit. And, for both of us, just as we've found ourselves amid daunting challenges in most situations today, we just stood there—*TOGETHER,* Miss Marie Antoinette—And Me, relying solely on ourselves.

There was no way out! I did what I always tend to, whenever I find myself boxed into the painted corner of a collapsing gray—area. Fearful and helpless, I lashed out!

Pointing a critical finger at her and moving toward her direction, I accosted her.

"What the hell was that you n' ole girl were in there doin'?

Attempting to wish herself smaller, trying desperately to escape the demeaning splendor of my mounting, wickedly strewn wrath, she at first cowered away from me, seeking refuge in a corner of the edge of the pillows thrown atop the tattered old couch.

Half-whispering, in a cracked, sore-throat, piped-out offering, she threw back only,

"CR.... AAACK... "

"Crack!" I dove even closer to stringing her up with the noose of her own guilty plea in ever increasingly furious and accountable verdict.

"CRACK? I was shocked.

My desire to reach out and to strike her became all too weakening, threatening aimlessly, with impunity, to shut down my mental re-activeness. I'd never seen anything like it. I'd never felt such hurt, not even from Mama'n. I felt as if all the air had just been jolted outta' my body forcefully, by a heaping kick, right-square-in the nuts.

Reaching inside to coax myself into concentrating on nothing more than mere breathing, a creeping, savior swept forward at the nape of my already pounding head and gently wrapped me in cautious, level-headed sense. Regaining composure slightly, I began taking baby steps of thought-provoking guidance from that point on.

Just the smell of the whole situation told me I didn't belong there any more. Saving premonitions fostering more deceit and greater advances of waste began to also impart, that I should begin to be very…very wary.

She stood aloof from me offering nothing at first.

I peered across at her. The full sweep of her hair spread matted in disheveled clumps of knotted sponge across the front, rear and sides of her once majestically softened face. The previous sieve of shining perspiration that had been slowly trickling down one side of her face now danced uncontrolled concertos of beaded droplets as they cris-crossed the full sweep of her highly-set jaw line, not just the top of her brow as they had before. She goggled at me, wide-eyed, captured in her own, helpless sorrow.

Her unspoken words became internal incantations of grave attempts to reach out and touch my heart, willing me, desperately, in silence, to—"*Just—PLEASE*!

"Stay."

I didn't know what I'd do.

But I did know one thing. I didn't want no' doped up, drug dealing, girl friend, fiancée…for a what?

A—WIFE. *AREYOUKIDDIN'ME?*

Hell! I didn't need to become involved in this type of shit. I had run from this very lifestyle as far and as fast as I could in the past. The exact same thing, so many years of wasted breaths before had attempted to entrap me in a lifetime of bitterness amid never-redeemable iniquities, early deaths and assured penal shortcomings.

I didn't have to take it. Besides, I had plenty of willing, *CLEAN,*

WOMEN I could make a selection from back in the beach-filled glamour of San Diego. All sorts of delectable morsels I could *get* with.... Who didn't do drugs, didn't live with funky, white girls and their racist, spit spewing boyfriends. Who didn't have no fuckin' kids!

I didn't need this shit. No, I didn't need it at all.

And I all but told her exactly that, albeit inside my head.

Holding up my hands while backing away from her as I began to gather my things together into cluttered heaps, I half-heartedly offered, "I'm just gonna back out."

"Back out? What do you mean? Back out?"

"You know what I mean. Back-the-fuck-out! Out of your crazy life with your twenty million brothers and sisters, your crazy fuckin' baby's—Daddy, drama problems, your livin' wit' yo' Mamma, living here wit' these stupid malcontents, doing your fuckin' drugs in the back of your room, BACK THE FUCK OUT—Back out. That's what I mean: back out"

She folded her arms across the front of her chest in a frustrated, pouting stupor. Suddenly she began to react and appear a little bit more sober.

This girl was a mystery. Was I fooling myself, thinking I knew her?

"You can't back out," she almost whispered, drawing nearer.

"I sure as fuck can!" I'd just finished slipping on my shoes and had begun to reach for my jacket.

Yvette, who I had dumped months before, was beginning to look better and better all the time in those surroundings.

"Watch me."

I sensed a subtle shift in her body language. Her arms had come unfolded. She now stood, cradling an elbow in one hand while she seemed to stare past me while still appearing to look at me. She began...

Sucking her thumb, while gently, rocking rhythmically from one side, back and forth, to the other.

She had a glazed over gape which appeared to no longer be with me. The forceful negativity of the situation had become too much for her drug-infested mind to keep up with. She couldn't cope and had simply checked out, while rocking away, side-to-side, in a peaceful, serenity of unified motion.

It was a depiction of the most absolute helplessness I'd ever seen take over another human being.

Plans for making my next move swarmed dauntingly, all mixed up, inside my head. The horror of the things I'd just experienced waved incessantly at me from both near and from afar.

I still had my return trip, plane ticket. I'd call a taxi to take me to the airport. Once there, I'd exchange the ticket for an earlier flight, and be back on my way toward the girls and the sun of San Diego in just a couple of hours. The maniacal backdrops completely forgotten, tossed languidly behind me, as if it had all been a bad dream, rightfully suppressed there forever.

A very doable plan...

...Even easier for me to consider now, given the circumstances.

Everything I'd ever been taught, sifting through grown-up, adult, supposedly more mature, drug—vilifying, family member's shit had prepared me for making the right decision that very moment. I knew enough to seek more positive experiences.

People's lives change...I'm not so certain about People though.

Not only had my own mother been an addict, but also divorced and an *outsider* among society's general expectations of its average citizens. Her mother and father and her step mother's and step fathers, virtually all of her brothers and sisters, and almost every one of her acquaintances (Wanna' call them accomplices) as well, had either been hooked on something—a bottle, a pipe, a pack, a needle or worse, or had lent themselves as shining examples of jumping into and out of relationships and marriages—to the detriment of the hordes of unruly, under-educated passels of kids they left behind in their spoiled, guilt-ridden wakes. Or, they found a way to end it all young. Most never married, because they were unable to nurture and caress or truly care for anyone other than themselves.

It was an epidemic among us.

Most never reached the age of 65, but were dead and gone before ever having the privilege of collecting their first stipend from Social Security, as if a great many of them ever worked a hard day's work in their lives at all.

The disease and decay of slothful lives shackled them to existences replete with overindulgence and backward commitments to the sure-footed demise of the streets, all but assuring a slippery trail towards early graves.

My uncle Larry once intimated to me. And he was serious…

"*BOY! Wives are temporary. Family is forever.* Don't ya' fucc'in forget *IT.*"

In an unpolished sense of crudely passing on his loftful teachings, he once imparted, *"I am your uncle, BOY! Believe me, all of your uncles, and great uncles, and grandfathers, and greatgrandfathers…where just like me!!!!! Me, uncle Twist, uncle Slyver, uncle Dan, your grandfather, Ollie, great grandfather, Wade Willems, were just like YOU! We had the same freakisms, and the same desires. That is what binds us…and Toppa Penn Junior, and Amaru, and…Blu Junior…same freak!!! Shame huh?*

The only one that I don't remember is your great—great grandfather. His name was Wade…and he was my grandfather…I don't know if I ever met him or if he ever seen me. But he was murdered by some white guys…if I was mad, I would say klansmen or rednecks…but we don't know. This was my father's Dad. They threw him into a snake pit. It is said that he had a lot of drinks, his son…my dad had a lot of drinks. Me, I have lots of drinks…but due to the military…I had a late start, and it seems that my son…has drinks. Nephew…something is going to get us: pussy, money, drugs, greed, alcohol, prescription drugs, screaming spouses! But something is going to get us all!"

I didn't want to ever completely buy into uncle's words. Why? I can't really say. I always listened, sifting through the thicket, separating the suffocating weed from the chaff, but I always wondered what it was, in his life that had taken such a toll in completely souring him? I remained steady, just holding out an inkling of a hope, praying…That just perhaps—he was wrong.

I didn't want to live my life beneath the seemingly futile umbrella of such cynical counsel. That wasn't what I wanted or had envisioned for myself at all.

I wanted Love…

I wanted it all!

I sought Love as a passion for oneness,—An intimacy and desire to know and be known. I figured there was no way I'd find what I was seeking in this girl.

I was walkin', Man!

I'd never put that plan into motion.

I still to this day can't put a finger on what held me steady during the following minutes, in the center of that tiny living room, after our confrontation. (I think it was actually weakness) Still, I didn't budge. Didn't make a move toward the phone to call no taxis or exchange any tickets or take any flights scampering from Portland as fast as my ticket would carry me back to Diego.

I remained put.

Before I knew it, things seemed to have calmed down and "NETTIE" was in my arms. The two of us held on tightly for—forever. We lent each other support and protection, each worthy and serialized by our own life's desperation. I believe we were trying not to let go of something both of us knew, from that moment on, we would never be able to do without.

I stayed the rest of the week. And during that time, there weren't any more clashes—No more upsetting, friendly-visits and no more drugs. Just the occasional brother or sister dropping by to see Nett and the baby and the occasional knock of Cliff, *the diaper guy* who made his living going from door to door peddling, for pennies on the dollar, HUGGIES and PAMPERS he'd boosted from Portland's major outlet chain, Fred Myer.

Unc, also told me good things. He was an epiphany of knowledgeable contrasts. He once imparted an ancient African tale of a wise imam who lived atop a mighty mountain.

I don't know what it was he felt I needed during the day of the telling of this particular offering, but I thought his offering to me then to be extremely profound.

He said, "*One day, a young warrior approached the imam and asked of him, "Imam, I am told you can show me the way to contentment and to never-ending prosperity. Please imam; I would do anything to have such knowledge." The imam remained stooped in his haunches appearing to just stare at the young man lazily. After a brief period, without offering a word, the imam got up and with the young warrior following, he began to walk off down a pathway winding around towards the bottom of the mountain. Their journey ended with the two of them standing before the ocean. Without looking back, the imam broached the water's edge and he walked steadily into the on-rushing waves spread out in front of him. A bit hesitantly, the young warrior, true to form, followed. As the imam continued on, the water rose above the level of first, his knees. He kept going. The water rose to cover his chest. He kept going. Finally, the level of water had risen to fully cover his entire body, engulfing him, seeming to sweep him under and away completely. And... Keeping with his prior behavior, the young warrior's movements matched those of the wise man, determined to show his relentless seriousness of character in gaining what he'd come for. The imam, seeing that the young man had followed, waited for the warrior to approach. When he was within reach, the imam reached out and grasped the young man savagely about the shoulders. With the strength of ten men, he held him beneath the waters, not letting him above the surface until the young, strapping man's struggles had almost appeared at an end. The imam finally released him and when the imam had exited the water and was once again standing on shore next to the water's edge. He spoke to the beleaguered warrior for the very first time.*

Reaching for the warrior ever so gently, placing a steadying hand of paternal comfort upon the small of the now exhausted man's back, he said, "My son. Tell me? What was the only thought racing through your mind the entire time you were under the water?"

"You stupid old man!" The warrior bellowed back with disrespectful retort, shaking sinewy vines of slimy seaweed off glistening, muscles of steel. "What do you mean? My only thoughts were of breathing!"

The imam sighed slightly while slowly shaking his head with confidence. Turning to take his leave of the mighty warrior, he started his long journey back up the side of the mountain, departing with...

"When you seek what you are looking to find with the same determination in which you sought to breathe air while you were trapped under water—Then and only then shall you be successful in gaining that which shall truly be yours forever."

YOU MUST NEVER BE AFRAID TO DO WHAT IS RIGHT!

EVEN IF YOU HAVE TO DO IT ALONE YOU MUST STRIVE—FOR YOURSELF—IN ALL THINGS—TO DO THEM—WITH STRENGTH...AND WITH HONOR!

The usefulness of the story Unc had told me knocked me off my haunches as its relevance charged forward into the reality of the answer I relayed to many friends and family members, acquaintances and foes, who all wondered why I'd stuck around and placed such awesome faith in this one, troublesome young Woman for so long.

To them, she was a throw-backable, worthless non—commodity. Barely vibrant and laudable enough in her inebriated condition to be worthy of the immense amounts of time I already expended upon her. They didn't know. They were wholly under aware of the fact that, because of her turmoil, (the things she'd already seen and been through, in such a very short amount of time, to live through them and still come out so dog-gon'ed beautiful, as no doubt, she was; because of these things) *I* counted her worthy.

To me, that's all that mattered. She represented the possibilities of workable craftsmanship—a *diamond in the rough*—whose strength, beauty, poise and potential appeared evidently crystal-clear with streaming light to me.

I wanted to help her fix whatever problem she was experiencing in life that was holding her back. I wanted to make a life for and with her and Brittney. The need I felt for assisting her along this path was much more than symbolic to me.

I wanted to help her with such magnitude that it felt at times, a desire *more* than breathe itself. Perhaps it was because I was able to envision our successes. Through eyes of dream-filled wonder and optimistic possibility I was able to picture the sweet-smelling garden of flourishing roses our life together would be.

I just had never factored in the thorns. *You know what they say...*

The two of us made plans, via phone for her and *my* baby to leave Portland and fly to a new life with the three of us together in San Diego. I mailed her $500.00 to put to use in getting her affairs in order. Pay off some bills—purchase a small amount of luggage and perhaps an outfit or two for her and the baby.

And we promised steadfast Love to one another.

And we waited...

While we endured the duration of our self-imposed separation, I had to move fast in order to complete the preparations necessary for the two of them to finally come down. My plans were encumbered by an inevitability of ever decreasing slim choices. We either stayed a while with my uncle Larry and his wife, auntie Mattie Mea, who at the time lived in Military Housing in the Tierra Santa community of "Murphy Canyon" until we were able to find an apartment that suited us, or I got off my duff (I heard ya', Garv) and found an apartment fast!

But not any ole' apartment—It couldn't be in the slums, couldn't cost an arm and a leg, and couldn't be too far as driving distance goes from the Naval base, a scant fifteen miles from Murphy Canyon. I wasn't quite sure how trustworthy the little Honda Accord I'd purchased only a month before would be. I was determined not to ever subject them to an environment more morose and unseemly than the one they'd come from, and I wasn't going to give them anything less than my best in providing for them.

Inanely, I always operate in exactly the same mode of execution. I was, and still am very often at times thwarted by a penchant for *Letting go—and Letting GOD.* My ability to conceive for the mere fact that I believed has lifted and carried me further than any man has ever deserved.

Astutely, I am forever diving in head-first, without a prudence of concern for where that dive might lead. I always figured I'd either come up smelling roses, or prune and weed those suckers till an exacting life of splendid wonder developed from them, the product of the effects of good will and determined tenacity through hard work.

I found the perfect little spot, situated over a Lovely little pool in a tree-lined complex thirty-five miles from the base in the city of Oceanside. I was so enamored with this accomplishment. Our first apartment waited with me with joyous expectation of our special arrivals. I had the car, the place, and the Love. The only things missing were the two of them.

Nett and I spent hours on lengthy long-distance calls, excitedly mapping out the lofty visions of the life we were preparing to embark upon together. We discussed plans for finding her a good vocational or business school to attend. So she too could begin to build something all her own that she could bring to and offer our budding relationship.

While I went each day to 32nd Street Naval base to work aboard the USS England CG22, she'd hone the brilliance of her sharply keen mind to learn a valued skill that would prepare her for acquiring a good job with a solid future.

On the day she and *Britty* were scheduled to arrive, I'd spoken with her in Portland by phone prior to her departure for the airport. To me, she'd seemed still a bit hesitant and unsure. But I felt inside, that she was as ready and as excited to come, almost as anxious to begin our new life together, as I was.

Her flight, instead of landing in San Diego, was actually scheduled to touch down at the Long Beach airport. Giving myself precisely enough flexibility to arrive at the airport a full hour prior to her arrival, I drove the full, two-hour distance, San Diego to Long Beach, in record time. Once there, on or about the hour her flight was supposed to get in, the plane pulled up to the gate. Endless enchantments of bouncing butterflies danced glibly in driving spasms of scattered flurries inside my nerve wracked gut. I could barely stand to wait there any longer for her and Britt to disembark. I'd missed and longed for the two of them so much.

After watching face after unfamiliar face roll by me as they exited the plane, entered the terminal, and eventually met up with their awaiting parties to depart the terminal for a litany of scattered destinations, I began to take on a foreboding feeling that something wasn't exactly right. Slumping ever-so-slightly, I finally became conscious with a distressing reality that she and the little girl who would grow up to call me Daddy forever were never going to walk down that gangway through those doors to embrace me.

The butterflies were dead.

They weren't on the flight!

She'd killed them!

Following a brief investigation at the counter back dropping the terminal, I determined that my fears were in fact true. The desk attendant, after kindly re-checking the passenger manifest, sadly informed me that she was not listed there and had never boarded the plane to make the flight.

A hardened heart of confused sadness I never believed was possible. I stopped in my tracks and slowly murmured a clearing breath of prayer that she and Miss Brittney were both O.K. and all right. Collecting myself as completely as I could, I started off in search of the nearest pay phone.

From my position before a phone tree inside the airport, I found out through a call to her mother's house in Portland, that she'd never even gone to the airport to catch the flight. She couldn't have. She'd never even purchased a ticket.

Instead, she had spent every last dime of the money I had originally sent her—*ON DRUGS!*

I didn't know what to do. Not right away anyway. I was unable to come up with a plausible answer for the kind of craziness it took for her to glumly throw away our life together like she had, all for a minutes worth of false euphoria as the deceitful high of synthetic drugs almost candidly appear to be.

The moment of indecision and the lack of control and regimented direction my life had suddenly become intrigued me with a stunning persistence.

I didn't like that feeling at all. I could barely even breathe. In a heart's beat, something and someone had affected my life to such a degree of proliferating power that I stood there, stupefied, once more waiting for Mama'n, that belt, and with that increasingly shrinking hole in the center of that kitchen chair, expecting doom.

I asked her mother if I could speak to her. Reluctantly at first, (I'm still not certain which of the two of us she was actually protecting, trying to look out for—Marie or Me) I still hold the inkling, it was me. She sent out a holler, steeped in disgust and eventually put her on the line.

I had no clue what I was going to say to her. When she came online, all I could begin with was, "Are you O.K.?"

Instantly, she began to weep. Her cries were gripping, sobbing, wails of pent-up anguish and searing pain as they began to leap from her body in escaping, lurching jolts. She began to pour out her soul into that phone, seemingly from the other side of the universe, all at once.

I didn't understand.

Cutting through the mutterings of her inarticulate stammer, I could barely push back and hide demeaning thoughts of being forced, time and time again, to revisit my own agony of just how badly I had wanted to see she and that little girl get off that plane.

How much faith and resolve I had used up in attempting to bring a more solid lifestyle to both her and that sweet little bunyion. I was beginning to be unable to envisioned waiting for them any longer; the solemn, impending emptiness of my opened, outstretched arms never reaching them completely.

When she had calmed down enough for the two of us to talk, she really didn't have to say much for me to figure out what had happened.

And... Within a millisecond of stubbornness, I didn't even care.

No way was I letting anything short of GOD himself stand in front of our eventual happiness.

"Do you Love me?" I asked her. Shuffling my feet insipidly, not completely certain that I was really ready for her answer.

"Ye.... Yessssss..." Came her softly spoken reply.

"You still wanna' come?"

I held my breath.

I could almost feel the sweeping flow of a smile as brightly lit as a single ray of sunshine, begin to become implanted, spreading soothingly all throughout her chest to once again pierce her heart completely, providing her hope.

Man! How I Loved me some "NETTIE"

"You still want me to come?" She answered my question—with a question.

Even today, it drives me bananas when she does this. As if apprehensive and afraid to chance putting a thought of her own on the table.

"Of course I do, baby," I offered thoughtfully in reply.

She met my answer with an extended silence on the other end of the line.

I didn't mind. She was most likely offering a somber prayer of thanksgiving to GOD. I hoped.

I put the silence to rapid use. Instantly, I sprung into action with the reasoned formulation of yet another plan, all in the optimism of seeking happiness.

"I'll go downstairs to the airline's ticket counter and buy you guys another ticket. All you have to do is pack whatever you want to bring. Don't worry too much about the stuff you leave behind. We'll buy more. Pick up the ticket at the counter at the airport on your end; and get your pretty behind on that plane."

I wasn't about to send her any more cash. I Loved her immensely. But my trust had fallen victim to the experience of feeling like I'd been had.

"For real!"

I too began to feel the sweep of frustration begin to dissipate as it began to be replaced by a sense of welcomed relief that our story hadn't abruptly ended before fully starting. What I wasn't sure of, was how much more of this shit I was man enough to stand up to and take.

There was definitely more to come.

"For real sweetie—Just gather your things and go to the airport and get on that plane...And hey...?"

"Yes, baby?"

"I Love you, "NETTIE."

"Love you too."

Inside, I truly believed she did.

My marriage to Kammy came to a definitive end on the 25th of February, 1987.

Net and I were married that same day in a quaint little wedding chapel, on Pennsylvania Avenue, in Hillcrest, a charming, cottage-filled community of San Diego.

The following week, I re-enlisted for another six-year hitch and received a $30,000.00 bonus. Amazing, the timing and perpetual—puzzle piecing the events of that era in our lives evolved into. The bonus made it possible to make all the things happen I had originally focused on and had forecasted, when briefly building a plan for the three of us to begin life together back in June of the previous year.

I'd done it!

After all I'd been through; my efforts culminated to form a sweetly gained success.

I'd been able to find a way to push previously held anxieties, ones steeped in the negativities of defeating thoughts—almost routinely, out of my way.

Man.... I had a family!

"...For she is more profitable than silver and yields better returns than gold...she is more precious than rubies; nothing you desire can compare to her...Long life is in her right hand; in her left hand are riches and honor."

Proverbs 3:14-16

Chapter One

WEEZO'

Audrey Louise Willems is my Mama'n. Born in March of 1948, as a youngster, she was a highly intelligent, American beauty of African descent. Petite and pretty, with a sweeping flow of long jet-black hair, she was raised by her father, my grandfather, Ollie Lee Willems. Originally, from the township of Rappahanock, Virginia, a small, rural community, that at the time of his birth, in 1922, had no streetlights, as was still the case, in 1937, when he left to eek out a life for himself in Pennsylvania. Rumor had it that the Rappahanock of his day was so backwards and oppressive that even the cows were searching for ways out. Once settled in Harrisburg, Pennsylvania, he made his living as a part-time mason, full-time cabby and, due to a lifetime of breathtaking disappointments leading to a final definitive breaking of his spirit, developed completely, in his later years, to becoming a fully committed—and miserable drunk.

It was he who had given Mama'n the nickname "Weezo".

Throughout her formative years, Ollie was most revered and affectionately remembered as a stern task—master. Strict beyond design, yet Loving, the severity of his strictness often materialized without reason. He was habitually a burden upon friends, a terror to his many wives and girlfriends, and a pestilent nightmare to many of his children. Inside their home, shouted demands of never—ending beratement and corrective direction shrieked as his bellowing voice rattled windows and unearthed plaster with frequent tirades of his insensitive raving.

"Weeee-ZO'! My other good shoe. Where's it at?

Weee-ZO'!

Get in here, girl…n' get these dishes messed up.

Weee-ZO', Right now!

Sit up straight. Achhhtt!... Weez'—Knock off that talk at this here table!"

He had a more sensitive, Loving grand pappy side as well.

"Weee-ZO', Daddy Loves ya' little girl...."

Despite his brusque, sometimes cruel and oppressive nature, he had a special, radiating spot in his hard-edged heart of hearts for what would eventually be the first of his five daughters.

His efforts of creating a World in which his little girl could dwell safely were always far off from becoming reality amid the clashes and turmoil that shadowed his every day, very brief lifetime. Though positive results (of what some would call, the torment he subjected her to on a daily basis—in order to better prepare her for what she would come to face in her own life) were plainly evident in his traditions, some would say, Mama'n, as a youth, experienced a simmering slice of living hell putting up with him.

Not merely pretty, petite and respectful (almost to a fault) Wee-ZO', was a determined, and outstanding student. She excelled in all her studies while amassing multiple personal and academic achievements. Moreover, she even went on to become the first marching band majorette of African descent in the entire state of Pennsylvania.

Ollie, even in all his gruffness and almost fear-filled Love, although he never knew it, had been on to something grand.

My initial recollection of him was of a robust, hearty man—light skinned, with

good, wavy hair all his own. The kind of personality women swooned over at first sight and consequently, other men immediately resented.

The Loves of his life included, primarily—his little girl. A bushel full of an assortment of very often, loose women—fishing, hunting and lazy evenings picking away at his favorite guitar while reeling after his many leisure's.

His tumultuous expectations of Mama'n, and later of me, of continual, respectful manners and pristine, articulate speech structured towards producing flawless, lady-like etiquette often approached the extreme. With hindsight, today, albeit tough and unforgiving, I hold the compensity of his emboldened actions to be nothing short of being ingeniously constructive. She was required to address him directly by nothing other than Daddy or Yes, Sir. She was never to challenge or disagree with him. An episode of this occurring would produce a horrific invective of both mental and assured physical abuse fueled by wrath.

No elbows on the table. Pretty dresses were cleaned, pressed and worn daily.

...And, if he was perhaps wrong. It was to be plainly disregarded and immediately overlooked—without question.

To Ollie, his own and any one else's children were here to be seen and never to be heard, and he meant it!

I knew him only as grand pappy. My memories of him encased within joyous moments of happy, boisterous outbursts, along with steeped, opinionated clamor—matched only by the pain of scruffy whiskers and the hearty bellow of inviting laughter as he swept you up mercilessly in steel tempered arms chiseled by years of, tough, manual work and he hugged you almost to death—while scratching up the soft tenderness of the side of one of your cheeks, yelling all the while, "OWW-UCH!-OUCH-OUCH-OUCH-OUCH"—as he was Lovingly smattering your entire face in moist, sloppy, heart-felt kisses.... And all that could be seen of you during those times would be your tiny little legs dancing futilely, in their attempts of trying to extricate themselves far, and away from him, as the burn that those whiskers produced scruffed away any indisputable care of meaningful, grandfatherly concern he genuinely intended.

You almost had to understand *him*, to fully grasp the reasons behind Mama'n being the way she is today.

Sadly, life in the streets soon caught up to grand pappy. He met his end, at the age of fifty-nine, in the tomb of his own bedroom inside the tiny apartment he rented on Baumbaugh Street, in Harrisburg. His ultimate demise, the resultant blend of failing to take proper care of himself, as well as the primary consequence of a severe blow he had taken to the head during a barroom fight just two weeks prior to his eventually succumbing.

I was just fourteen, about to turn fifteen when he died. This became the reason I'd found myself in Virginia, building cousin Book's outdoor garage and getting in trouble *playin'* with cousins following his funeral in Harrisburg about a month before.

I still remember his funeral. We buried him in Steelton, a tiny, smelt encrusted town on Harrisburg's outer edge. Major Wynfield attended to him. He was infamous for handling most end-of-life family matters for my people, as well as for extending himself greatly towards trying his best to skin whoever was funding the occasion, by bilking and overcharging relatives of his customers exorbitantly. Family members from all over the World came out of the woodwork to pay grand pappy their respects. For me, it was all very overwhelming and emotionally astounding. I never knew we even had so many close kin before squeezing in among them all, trying desperately to get to my OWWUCH-OUCH for the very last time. Where'd they all come from so suddenly? During his everyday life, whenever he was in need, none of them had ever been around to step forward to lend him even the most sparse offering of a piece of sage, supportive advice. Yet there they all were, dolled up in pricey, peacock colors and widely-brimmed, expansive, suede hats. Each one *Puttin'-on-aires'*, as if they'd just lost the best friend any one of them had ever had in life.

I've never had the inkling to be white. Yet, there were some things endearing to me with regard to the solidity of familial situations ingrained within the American white culture. I'm perfectly content and happy with what and who I am ethnically. I simply choose to embrace the concept of an encouraging foundation which begins with an infinitesimal spark of the hopes and dreams of perhaps a single person. A thing which eventually engulfs the thoughts of millions, with pragmatic expediency, to be carried out to bring positive, sweeping changes which uplift the hearts, minds and efforts of an entire nation toward development—amid the utter chaos these ideas create—all on the mere forethought of a civilly agreed upon idea.

Americans of African descent unquestionably lack the roots upon which such an accommodating foundation is cemented. This was largely due to the interruption of families and familial traditions as these very important staples of *their* former communities became violently shattered during the quad-llenium which upheld the atrocious misgivings of a purely genocidal slavery trade. A great majority of us just never got it—because, *IT* had never been a part of our lives, or of our parent's lives, or of their parent's—parent's lives.

Up to that time, at fourteen, it appeared that most of my family members remained explicitly aloof. You weren't getting much in the way of support from any one of them during your dire times of need. I loathed this then—and still do despise this fact about us today. Jim Crow and the outright racism of segregation played a large part in culminating to erode the chances of so many—at their starts. But toward their ends, I believe there was an attempt by past majorities of generations of Americans of African descent, my family members included, to escape familiarity with a blatant shirking of responsibility. This invaded to routinely set each of us apart from the perpetuated stability of generation after generation of our American white counterparts.

...A doctrine of almost ultra extropersonalism played out to fan through us like a defeating tornado, biting its way through our entire clan, family to helpless family. If you were a member of the Willems/Penn extension, *WATCH-OUT!*...Because you were steadfastly doomed, immediately upon being hatched. Expect to be pushed off the end of that damned tree branch in the very same instant of the day you drew your first breathe—And BABY! You'd better have wings that work. Cause' if they don't flap and you don't catch that wind just right to assist you in helping yourself; you were destined to wind up at the bottom of the cesspool, flapping around in the disgusting stench of an all encompassing SPLAT! You were never taught or ever *cultured* how to *FLY*. On the pavement—dead—just two feet below, would be your only destiny—a mere helping nudge of support would have been all it would have taken to save you.

A simple caring nudge to make you stronger—in finally being able to develop strengths which would eventually lift *you* up, thereby offering support in sustaining the entire clan was too much for any of them to rate.

It's still today, twenty-five years later, hard to believe grand pappy's actually gone. It seemed life owed him so much more. As a black man in that day's America, all he'd been given were hard times, strife and disappointment amid twenty lifetimes of broken promises. He never got to see the culminating fruits of his labors. No opportunity to beam prideful as his fourth great grandson was born to be named after him. No bouncing baby great *grands* on his knee, driving them crazy with a legacy storm of scratchy OWW-OUCH OUCHES.

Mama'n had all but broken his heart when she'd become pregnant with my brother, Toppa, at the innocent age of just fifteen. It was for him, a final nail in a lifelong journey sealing his destiny of direction toward one of Marshall

Wynfield's faux-lined velvet coffins. It was all it took to push him over the edge toward giving in completely to an escape of guile and drink, which therefore led to his all too early death.

We were in Texas at the time of grand pappy's death. Mama'n had latched onto and conned Garv into marrying her. And although we were living ten times better than our former experiences had proven for us, we were disrespectful, selfish and hardly realized that, through his efforts, we actually had it pretty good. Through his ARMY benefits, things formerly unable to be expected, like regular check-ups, dental exams, and commissary privileges became common. Our rent was never late. We stopped moving every month. And we were eventually presented military dependent I.D.'s which opened an entirely different set of circumstances which supported each one of us in ways we'd never known were possible.

Yet, we gave him very little credit. Instead, we berated and talked about him (all of us, Mama'n included) behind his back, and we went varying distances in our attempts to annoy him at every juncture of the short time we all lived together in the quaint little house on Nike Lane.

Grand pappy threw Mama'n out solidly on her own when he found out she was pregnant with Toppa. She butter flied around, staying with friends and family, until my grand mom, Mavis, (my father's mom) took her in and began to school her in the art of becoming a MOTHER and a WOMAN. My parents were married in Baltimore, Maryland just previous to Toppa's birth. He was a confused seventeen, and she a very naïve fifteen. My father was a cruel, seemingly uncaring man. During the full tenure of their very brief marriage, he exhibited his Love for Mama'n by beating and abusing her in a multitude of physical ways, almost daily. He even beat up grand pappy a couple times when Ollie would attempt to reclaim the fatherly rights he had previously discarded by throwing Mama'n in the streets to be tended to by the wolves.

With grand mom Mavis, Mama'n made her way through the tyranny of my father's rule, day in and day out, never knowing when the time would come when his violent beatings would finally cripple or kill her. I recall the telling of a frightening situation where he actually hefted Maman's sewing machine as if it were as light as a thimble and hurled it at her, hitting her in the side of the head. The results of that episode bear their mark on her to this very day by way of a debilitating scar on the cornea of her left eye. For Mama'n, the horror of her captivity with my father would never completely end; the physical scar upon her body, results of his actions, for her, would serve as a daily reminder of his un-Loving brutality for more than thirty-five determined years.

Still sweet and mostly innocent, Mama'n hid behind grand mom Mavis' skirt tails for almost two years. There were many occasions where only grand mom could keep my father off of Mama'n. No matter the furor of his rages, she, grand mom, was the one person in this life my father could never bring himself to cross. She was a petite Woman with sharply structured, Indian features. A brightly red colored complexion with a softened, tender demeanor instantly metamorphosed into steaming, blood curdling fury coupled with a tenacious bearing of defensive determination whenever she found herself backed up to a kitchen cupboard, the assuring length of a sturdy broom handle wielded expertly in her tiny, work-hardened hands as she beat back my father's advances upon Mama'n with a definitive clarity in saying, "Leave *my* daughter and *my* grand babies alone—*RIGHTNOW-Y*ou fucc'n brute!"

This was the beginning of Mama'n finding a niche toward survival as a young hapless damsel caught up in the realities of life and its at times unmerciful carnage. We finally moved out of the huge house on Kelker Street and moved into the Harrisburg Park apartments off of Fifteenth Street on Harrisburg's growing South side. It was there that Mama'n truly began to shine in causing her life to become even more confused and twisted with a myriad of self-inflicted miseries she would engineer as the years tolled forward.

But nephew...you, and only you can keep me on track....because black man....I have had it, with this country and this world. I know why my father drank; I know why your father drinks, I know why I drank. It is hard being black, and married to a black woman, in this cold, cold—white world....-UNCLE LARRY

Chapter Two
'BUSTER'

My pops went by the name, Charles William Penn Sr.

Buster, to his Mama, and to his pop, whose only claim to fame was as partner and one-time cellmate of the nefarious leg-peddler, Iceberg Slim. His name was Robert White, called Bob, by his many acquaintances. Himself a despicable pimp and not-so-successful street smut hustler. He passed on the worst of *his* best to my father. For Mr. White's first of many sons, Buster, *TROUBLE* would become his contribution to friends, *TERROR* his promise of purpose to even more enemies. Born in February, 1946, he was, for a long time the only child of my grand mom, Mavis Juanita Penn.

All I can recall of my paternal grandfather—insidiously, was his funeral. A wickedly ruthless and yet contrarily, a dotingly generous man all the same, he'd met his end following a wicked shotgun blast he'd taken to his abdomen. An adversary had caught him slippin' and had punched his ticket, thereby canceling Christmas for him everlasting on a day he surely should have remained in bed.

There were numerous accounts remembered where he'd provided for my Mama'n and for us lavishly, during times when things like food, water, and general health were scarce or during one of the many occasions my pops found himself languishing in one or the other of the county's various jails.

The ceremony celebrating his life, or his death depending which part of the city you settled on, was held in a huge, cabaret ballroom when I was only six. The reverence of his demise holds pictures in my brain of the very first images I've ever had of meeting my father.

He'd been escorted into the hall after everyone else had settled into their seats and had already begun the lascivious chore of counting heads and whispering in gossiping tones of comment on so-and-so's outfit or on remembered accounts of the acts that played out to cover grand pop Bob's young life.

Chaperoned by four, white and burly Pennsylvania State Troopers, he took up a hulking position, standing pensively at the rear of the familiar gathering. The chilling clanging and tin of shackles and chains bound his hands and feet as he shuffled from time

to time, sending pangs of both anger and frustration seething through my tiny, questioning frame.

That couldn't be my daddy. That man was a bad man! Hemmed up and all restrained by the white policemen standing silently, almost peacefully on each of his firmly girded sides. My daddy would never have been presented in such a crude damning circumstance! How had he come to this?

I remember Mama'n repeatedly scolding me for constantly stealing conspicuously awestricken glances back to the area of the packed room where they held him. *That was my daddy?* A zoo of cages couldn't have caused me to remain silent and sit stoically in my seat. After each minute's gaze, I'd turn to Mama'n, searching her face for recognition and relief of the millions of questions bombarding my little mind feverishly. There was now way for her to evade me. No getting away or escaping my inquisitive demands. Finally fed up, and with no kitchen chairs with damning holes in their centers for her to use to beat me senseless, she whispered forcefully, the full, unspoken determination to kill me at first chance when we were back at home, plainly evident.

"Turn a-round'—Blu...*DAMNIT!*

Yes, boy!

That's your daddy." She offered almost meekly. The embarrassing flood of a tirade of heartbroken tears rushed to swell deeply within both her eyes—today, I completely understand the pain that moment held for Mama'n.

That was my daddy...?

But why was he back there? And not up there in the front, honoring his own father and sittin' with us like he should have been?

It took a long time, many years, before I realized what had actually caused

Mama'n to cry that day. Like her father before her, she had envisioned for herself, a better life.... And she'd wanted the same for both Toppa and I. What mother in her right mind could have taken pride in introducing her husband to his eight and six year old sons, for what they'd forever be able to recall their very first time, like that? It shamed her, for my father to have greeted his sons under such conditions. But, today, I disregard any preference for considering his feelings about the situation.

He had a family which he'd beaten up on heartlessly and had all but thrown away with his actions. It was his fault entirely that he was made to stand, almost at a slouching attention at the back of that room, watched like the dangerous animal that he had become, by the uncaring eyes of the dusky white troopers whose only thoughts were how they would professionally maintain strict lanes of fire, so as not to kill the relatives should he attempt an escape- While those of us who did not break the law and kill and maim our friends were afforded the *FREEDOM* of conducting ourselves appropriately at *HIS* father's funeral.

Even at six, and not knowing him fully, as is still the case today, I Loved him. He was undeniably a small part of me...and I, an even greater part of him.

Up to that point, inside Mama'n, there still shimmered an infinitesimal spark of no longer Love, but hope for my father. This was merely for the sake of her boys, I'm certain. But there was no longer any actual Love simmering for him inside of her. He'd beaten and abused her for far too long and killed all of that, not an inkling capable of surviving. For her, nothing approaching anything other than a languished contempt and a platonic well-wishing towards him sat flourishing, disdainfully, protecting her, her children, and, her heart.

Some scientists insist babies hold recollections of events occurring outside the womb prior to their day of birth. I can't attest to this completely. Yet, I can relate that almost subliminally—stark visions of terror, at the age of one or two (subconscious flashes of invasion and dread, in which my Mama'n would be screaming horrifically for mercy, scrambling desperately on scabbed-up knees, scraping—seeking escape, while protecting us, beneath a barrage of fists, kicks and flurries of knuckles reigning down upon her, as he attempted, time after time, again and again, to stomp the life and beauty from her entirely)—scar my memories of the beginnings of life with him forever.

...And there he was in the flesh. The very same Buster, who'd, held a butcher-knife to my neck when I was just a toddler, threatening to slice my throat cleanly in his angered accusations that Mama'n had been screwing around and that I was therefore somebody else's baby. Not none O' his. His weak attempts at denial were merely a stall tactic-an approach upon coping with finally beginning to *smell* himself, thereby increasing his sense of feeling once again, cornered. Trapped by a life in which he had no way of creating and holding the successes of a productive vision of his own. He tried vociferously to give the indication that the extents of his economic and mental frustrations were the results of Mama'n somehow betraying him while he was up river and his stressors, at that instance, were most easily culminated by forming the fact, for him, that I was not his kid.

Even the streets knew this to be a wholly preposterous claim. If you were ever to be in the same room with the two of us together, the likeness I share with him would be convincing and truthfully uncanny. Not to mention the fact I have these little nubs on the sides of each of my baby fingers. As does he! Remnants of actual extra fingers we've both had since birth.

The nubs have always perplexed me in making me different from every other kid I knew growing up. I don't think I was ever really able to feel at peace with them, until years and years later when I witnessed their harmlessness on the fingers of my own children, as they held the same additional digits at birth. They weren't useable fingers per say. Hospital personnel were indifferent to them and had simply tied silk thread around them, cutting off the blood circulation, causing the tiny, grape-like appendages to die and eventually fall off. Just miniscule nubs of raised skin now, irrefutably tying me to him as a product of his spoiled loins.

Short of DNA, these nubs, my exacting features, and my now disciplined willingness to kill or be killed when facing certain situations bear paternal proof and make me without question what I am today—Buster's Boy...

Buster was born during a time in America when intelligent Men of African descent were shunned, routinely mutilated and scorned by a society deftly afraid of what they held the possibility of offering. They were beaten unmercifully, lynched and murdered without culpable reason or proper adjudication of productive justice. For the more militant, troublesome characters among them, such as himself, there were only two definable fates. Outright extermination at the hands of a gun-toting *Good-Ole'-Boy*, and the other, a lifelong, stifling exile of incarceration, in one of many state and federal institutions built seemingly to house the entire race of unworthy nonconformists that the Americans of African descent were increasingly materializing to be. These squalid foundations of ill-reputed rehabilitation, our own government's initially wicked investment in attempting to quell an ever growing cultural awareness among the youth of an entire era of fifties and sixties America only matched with fear and complacency—the faltering ignorance and entrapment evident in the teachings of a speech given almost two hundred—thirty four years prior to Buster's birth, to a gathering of Virginia plantation owners of 1712. The words of that speech are those delivered by a hateful, Dutch slave owner, named Willie Lynch. The exposition of the speech surrounded the concerns the slave owners of the day had for how to keep their slaves divided, thereby defeating and canceling out any hope the captives, through collective efforts, might have been able to develop toward becoming knowledgeable and organized. A veritable disconnection from society through culpable twisting and warehousing of souls was the nature of the program from which Mr. Lynch spoke of and had advocated that day. He began his speech with:

"Gentlemen:...In my bag here, I have a fool-proof method for controlling your black slaves. I guarantee every one of you that if installed correctly it will control the slaves for at least three hundred years. My method is simple, any member of your family or any overseer can use it.

I have outlined a number of differences among the slaves, and I take these differences and make them bigger. I use fear, distrust, and envy for control purposes. These methods have worked on my modest plantation in the West Indies, and it will work here, throughout the South. Take this simple little list of differences and think about them. Atop the list is the slave's age. But it is there only for its propensity for beginning with the letter "A"; the second degree of difference being "Color" or shade of darkness; there's also "intelligence", the spread of your plantation size, attitude of the owners, whether the slaves live in the valley, on a hill, East, West, North, South, have fine or coarse hair, or are tall or short.

Now that I have provided the list of differences, I shall give you an outline of action—-but before that, I shall assure you that distrust is stronger than trust, envy stronger than adulation, respect or admiration. The black slave, after receiving this indoctrination, shall carry on and will become self-refueling and self-generating for hundreds of years, maybe even thousands.

Don't forget, you must pitch the old black versus the young black males, and the young black male against the old black male. You must use the dark slave versus the light skinned slaves, and the light skinned slave versus the dark skinned slaves. You must use the female versus the male, and the male versus the female. You must also have your servants and overseers distrust all blacks, but it is necessary that your slaves trust and depend on us. They must Love, respect and trust only us. Gentlemen, these kits are your keys to control, use them. Have your wives and children use them. Never miss an opportunity. My plan is guaranteed, and the good thing about this plan is that if used intensely for one year, the slaves will remain perpetually distrustful."

THEY WILL REMAIN PERPETUALLY DISTRUSTFUL....

He also went on to extol the practice of actually making a slave. His retort called for taking a pregnant nigger woman and her baby nigger boy and using the identical principles used in breaking horses, reducing them from their innate states of natural ability and capacity for caring for their own needs and the needs of their offspring; thereby breaking the expected string of independence from them, creating a dependency whereby the slave owners are able to get from them an entirely useful production supportive of both business and personal pleasures. He called for breaking both the nigger and the horse in exactly the same ways. Long-range, comprehensive economic planning was his justification for calling on all slave owners to rapidly perfect his wickedly spewn arts.

His evil dissertation edified the importance of cross-breeding in order to produce a varying division of labor. His words called for employing all the principles he taught together, for the good of the nation. Routinely, in his speech, he grouped both the wild, natural nigger and the wild horse in the same categories of danger once captured. Rightfully, he espoused the warning that both will have the tendency to seek their *customary* freedom and, in doing so, might kill their owners while they lay deeply engulfed in sleep. His principal was simple, and still plays out to engulf communities of Americans of African descent in the present.

"Keep the body and take the mind. Break the will to resist.

Break first the female. She will in turn, break the youth during its early developmental years, thereby producing productive service from generation after generation of broken, will suppressant dependents. Then break the nigger male by stepping up the pressure to completely reverse the workings of his mind. Take the meanest and most restless nigger, strip him of his clothes in front of the remaining niggers, the female, the infants, and tar and feather him, tie each leg to a different horse faced in opposite directions, set him afire and beat both horses to pull him apart in front of the on looking niggers. Next, beat the rest of the nigger males to the point of death in front of the female and infant children. Don't kill him, but only put the fear of GOD in him, because he can be used for breeding in the future.

Submit the female to a series of tests. Test her in every way to determine if she will submit to your desires willingly. If she exhibits any signs of resistance, do not hesitate to use the bull whip on her to extract that last bit of bitch out of her. Be careful; not to kill her. For if you do this, you spoil any chance of using her toward an accepted sense of continued economics.

With the bull whipping of the one nigger and the pulling apart of the other, she will be left dependently alone with an absurd urge to protect her male offspring on her own. Her natural dependence on the uncivilized male disconnected, she will therefore now have a limited protective dependency toward her male offspring and would raise female offspring to be like her. She is now trapped into a frozen independence state. She will now raise both her female and male offspring in reversed roles. She will fear for the young male's life and she will train him, psychologically, to be mentally weak, but physically strong, like the horse. She will train the female offspring to become psychologically independent in a way as well.

What have we got?

We have the nigger woman out in front. The nigger man behind, and scared. This is the perfect circumstance that will be guaranteed to produce sound sleep and hearty economics. We are able to sleep soundly, unafraid of the nigger male due to the frozen fear of the female as she watches over us, never permitting him to get past her early, infant captivity molding process.

He is a productive tool ready to be shackled to a horse in the field by the tender age of sixteen, soundly broken, ready for a long life of efficient and sound service. This orbiting chain relies only upon itself. The woman's frozen psychological state prepares generations of a good labor force. By constantly breaking the uncivilized niggers and by taking away the protective image of the nigger male slave, the cycle churns on its own axis forever, should you never permit the re-shifting of the importance of the nigger male slave to become regenerated. And by continuing to maintain the nigger male slave in a submissive, dependent mind, mating and interbreeding him, the cycle continues indefinitely.

A most important part of training the nigger male in such a way, just like with the mule, is the controlling of every aspect of his daily life. You must completely eradicate any semblance of his former religion and mother tongue while instituting new verbal communication techniques using a new language.

The ability to communicate speaks to the soul of people. The more a person not from their current habitat knows about the language of their new surroundings, the more easily they will be able to move through all levels of those surroundings and operate productively. But, keep in mind, you absolutely cannot teach him to the extent that he is able to fully grasp and understand the complete body of that close language, for then, the nation will become vulnerable to attack. He will learn the immensity of all your secrets and he is then no longer your slave; because you will be unable to fool him any longer...And, having them fools is the key ingredient to the making of a successful system of slavery."

Buster, through the un-thwarting futility of his own engineering, soon found that he was surrounded—Brandished a fool.

Like a slave, he was soon kept, overseen and maintained, until such time as he no longer portrayed himself as an uncivilized danger to society. A society fully unwilling, his crimes notwithstanding, to look at and offer him, even if he were an upstanding citizen, a fair amount of equality amid a place among them where he could proudly build upon something he could one day call his own. He'd permitted the legacy of Willie Lynch to cause him to play out a lifetime of staring dazed into that *frozen* psychological state, stamping his own destiny and hopes toward attainable dreams a complete failure.

Pride filled and at times amassing that super human strength and physical power, so many of the slaves of Lynch's era possessed, this frustrated Buster. Instead of marching forward to buy into and embrace the attainable successes, no matter how slight, so many others whose circumstances mirrored his own were able to exact in developing ways of overcoming, he chose instead to take the road most trampled and doused his troubles within the fuel of enraged, drunken failure. And once drunk, he would vent those frustrations with misguided vengeance, on those he held such an all-consuming, ruthless reign over.

Mama'n, Toppa, and myself.

Grand mom, Mavis, used to tell stories of sending him to the store for soup when he was a kid. When he'd returned home, she'd find that each of the cans she'd sent him for would be all bent up and battered. Upon questioning him, she'd find that he'd used them to bash boys he'd come to blows with in the streets in his path toward returning feverishly back home. Evidently, something had been rather wrong with him from his start.

My uncles' Larry, and Oliviyeh Twist, used to throw their heads back in haunted laughter at their own memories of Buster. Almost relieved senses, and quieted mutterings of thanks that the fool was no longer around, plainly indicative of their still recalled fear of him would overcome their storytelling now, even in their middle ages. Reaching back to another era they'd almost pensively relay tales of how Buster was revered for his toughness in the neighborhood of their youth. Their stories related, almost as easily as if they'd been speaking of the vicious depravity of their most favored, very deadly, pit-bull dog.

"Boy.... All I had to do was tell them niggas, I was gonna sic Buster on em' and they'd leave me alone immediately," smiled uncle Larry. "Yeah, man....Ole' Bus-Bus wa'nt no joke, a pure junkyard dog was that mu'fucca'," uncle Twist would then chime in—tossing his head slyly, beneath the twisted cluster of an almost toothlessly crooked smile. Reaching a cigarette stained hand up languidly to smooth the prickly edges of his dirty goatee sharply, he'd allow himself to wander backward through time, peering almost longingly to a place where he'd actually felt privileged to be related to my father in the past.

Mama'n used to recant stories of how the two of them had first met.

They'd been in the fifth grade, attending Hamilton Elementary School uptown, in Harrisburg. She said, he was the most handsome boy goin' but still, because of his attitude, at first, she couldn't stand him. He used to pull her pigtails and tease her incessantly. But as the years went on, her feelings for him grew like a sweeping, air-sucking fire.

His infatuation with her would eventually turn ugly, toward a twisted, more sinister sense of something—bordering on personal ownership.

It wasn't long after she'd finally given in to his advances that Toppa came along. And...22 months later, came me soon thereafter.

He was nineteen and she seventeen. With two kids, their anguish appeared only to increase. Grand pappy had physically fought with Buster on numerous occasions over what he felt was the spoiled virtue of his precious "Weez". But, even in the former glory of his youth, he was no real match for Buster's swollen, plying might.

The finale resulted in Mama'n being put out into the streets. This was how our stay with grand mom Mavis, originally began. Mama'n Loved this arrangement. Grand mom seemed the only person able to handle Buster, even during one of his drunken periods of terror filled rage. She was able to do more with my father on these occasions than a full squad of Pennsylvania domestic troopers as it once took six of them to tackle and finally trap him into the steel bracelets he would wear on his many trips back and forth to jail. She was the only one capable of commanding a complete authority over his overpowering persona, always there to stop him in his tracks. Like a mini general, exerting only a hundred pound frame and a lengthy, broken, broom stick complete with a fervid confidence that Buster wasn't already crazy enough to sink to a level of raising a hand in anger to his own mother as he frequently tried to lunge for Mama'n in anger.

For a time, Buster promised not to beat her any more. He even got a job and slowed his drinking just a bit. The four of us went forward, briefly, attempting to carve out everyday life as a united, albeit, functionally frightened, family.

But this was to be short-lived. I'm not certain if it was the boil of blood supplied him by his own, pimp hustling, silver-tongued father, or simply the addictive lure of the many troubled streets of which he was independently crowned King. But Buster was fully incapable of gettin' his shit together long enough to find a way to make it work and keep it all together for his young family.

There was just no explanation for what it was that made him tic so violently.

Both intelligent and articulate beyond his years, he was an instant ass-hole. Just add alcohol to bring the façade complete.

This all came to a head one fateful evening when Buster and one of his faithful, road dogs, Dusty, were holding court in an uptown bar. Mama'n was at home with Toppa and me. By that time, we'd moved out of grand mom's place and had our own tiny little house located at 313 Hamilton Street. It wasn't until grand mom had called her, plainly upset and crying hysterically, that Mama'n began to piece together exactly what had taken place in the unruly life of the lackluster King of the streets earlier that fateful evening.

By accounts of others present that night, Buster had been inside the bar, drinking shots of liquor with his road dog, partner and friend, Dusty. It had been Dusty's turn to buy the next round of drinks. After paying for and downing two drinks each, Dusty and Buster's calculations of whose turn it was to pick up the next volley began to become murky. This sparked up what was originally thought to be a friendly banter between them. No one could recall what it was that had set these two friends, previously thick as thieves, so firmly against one another that evening. It was said it couldn't have been the meager bickering over the drinks. It had been a Friday and both men had just been paid following a day of work at a local construction quarry prevalent for hiring their types—down and out, two time losers and convicts. But the broo-ha suddenly turned sinister, and caused such a stir of commotion with what became a veritable wrestling match which swept all of the bar top items, drinks included, suddenly sailing from the counter to the floor that the barkeep demanded they leave the bar and... *TAKE THAT SHIT OUTSIDE!*

Incredulously, they did.

They began to pummel and pound upon each other like bitter enemies instead of the lifelong friends everyone knew them to be.

I can almost relate to the chilling scene as it played out both inside the establishment and on the pavement outside that uptown bar that evening. I've borne witness to Buster's polarized shifts of calmed haze—quickly turning life threatening in a vicious sweeping of neck-snapping, pent-up rage. During grand pappy's wake held at cousin Mandy's, he'd first appeared happy and excited to see Toppa and I, after having already missed out on so much of our lives up to that point. Then, playing lightly, I remember him pushing Toppa, the situation changing at an instant, his personality shifting so very quickly, like a three-hundred pound chameleon adapting effortlessly without aide.

I remember him bellowing. "Ya'll think ya' big enough ta take on the ole' man huh?

.... Do ya?"

It was right about that time I began to become on edge silently, and I inched confidently a second's step closer toward the safety of cousin Mandy's back screen door.

That was right before he laid Toppa (a full, inexperienced, sixteen at the time) out completely with a critically applied, thunder-raining, single, unfatherly punch.

In his quarrel with his friend, Dusty, something inside of Buster finally snapped to a point of becoming murderous. Deciding to end the fracas completely, he drew a lengthy knife from his pocket, snapped it open fully and attempted to slash his unwitting opponent with a deadly swipe trying to cut him cleanly. In the fog of the fight's frustration, it soon became clear that his blade had found its intended mark.

And when the caper of play cleared for the crowd, there stood Buster, knife still firmly of hand—BLOODY! The prone figure of what used to be his young friend lying on the ground at his feet—dying. The rush of life sustaining blood pumped endlessly to cover Buster's shoes, staining and scarring his existence forever. His efforts had opened a gaping wound from ear to ear largely about Dusty's neck.

There wasn't one witness present who hadn't seen Buster take his friend's life. Buster was nineteen. Toppa was two. I was still a newborn.

When I was two, Mama'n had all but exhausted hope of extricating her marital connections with him for good. She tried numerous times to secure a divorce from him while he was still inside. He'd spent more than twenty-five years in and out of various Pennsylvania State and Federal prisons. At the time, Pennsylvania State had a law that it would grant no marital judgments of divorce against inmates while the injured party, the inmate, was warehoused in Federal institutions nor against those deemed crazy.

Buster hit both of these categories head-on.

Mama'n had to wait.

We visited him once or twice. We'd go with grand mom or someone else, but never with Mama'n. I barely remember those occasions growing up. I think I've chosen to repress most of these memories. I do recall he always had the brightest smile each time he'd come through the loudly slamming doors followed by the clinging and clanging of

the numerous, heavy-duty locks he went through to get to us. And he'd always be securely chained. Like that time I'd first seen him, during his father, Bob White's funeral.

It perplexed me, at first. Why was *my daddy* one of the very few that had to remain shackled during our very infrequent visits? Many other visitors were permitted to reach for and hug their inmate relatives, but not us.

I realized later that the State of Pennsylvania knew what it was doing in its handling of Buster. They knew that particular man wasn't nothin' nice—and that he was incapable of playing nicely when mixed among civilized society or when offered unfettered *FREEDOM*.

One occasion, he was fat and seemingly very unhealthy. On another, he'd be thin as a rail, a mere shadow of his former self.

As the years moved on, we stopped going to see him and we eventually moved to El Paso, which canceled any chance we had of continuing our visits. The loss of opportunity to see him and be given the chance to bond with him, if that was ever possible, was transparent to me. From my recollection, he'd never really been a father, per say, to me; only a person, relative to my existence in some unexplained, still unproven way, whom we took a pretty cool road trip to see behind bars once or twice.

We'd barely known each other and I soon went about my life, seemingly able to push feelings about him from my conscious thoughts forever. I forgot about him.

Toppa sure didn't forget him. He refused to permit himself such peace. Still today, he holds a deep, very dark grudge of hatred for our father. Buster's actions toward his first born son had culminated to be anything other than Loving.

I don't hate him. But I don't hold a cherished respect for or reverence for him like I think a son should hold for a father worthy of the same.

Having my own family whose everyday problems and needs I have under my own charge causes me to have no clue how Buster could have thrown away something so precious. How he could *make the choices he did*—disregarding his overall responsibility to my Mama'n, to us—to society? How could seeking temporary faith of things never to be, as they were evident in a pipe dream brought about through a haze induced stupor found inside a bottle become so all important and take the place of being—my father?

Know how society says alcoholism is inheritable? I believe it. Yet still, I disbelieve it. Based on the many experiences I've lived in my own life thus far. I believe that if you see one or both of your parents drunk and drinking every day that this becomes the normalcy of a set environmental stimulus for you and begins to become faithfully a degree of your own meager essence—that which forms to make you who or what you will be. I look at smoking cigarettes and doing drugs just the same.

I believe it's entirely possible for this to be made your own reality—given a choice. I do not believe that just because Ollie and Buster were alcoholics, that Blu Penn, Larry, Amaru' and KiWatta Willems were doomed as well to existences of alcoholism, lost to living useless lives as malcontents and bums.

I just cannot believe this.

Some, a very educated majority, hold beliefs alcoholism is indeed a sickness.

A significant disease that holds a place all its own among other well-known maladies such as Cancer, SARS, and AIDS as they would also have us believe.

I can buy that. Up to a point....

I'm no doctor. But it appears clearly, using common sense, that a period in which the alcoholic refuses to take stock honestly can be attributed to a sickness. In becoming lost within their own denials, refusal to face the alcoholism, their own ailing health and their own inability to face and accept life on life's terms begins to permeate, overtaking their souls vehemently. They become incapable of standing firmly to meet a responsibility those around them expect of them routinely. They soon develop into barely being able to be responsible for themselves. Yet their charge of bracing and meeting that responsibility is never relieved of them.

That's where the decaying stench of rotting, personable disease takes place. It is a very personal and irresponsible decision to discard lives of others simply because they, the alcoholic, are too weak, too lazy, or too rebellious to step up to the plate and *BE A MAN OR BE A WOMAN.* Overall, they're selfishness and immaturity points to their uncaring concern for whom or what they destroy in their own destructive paths reaching towards death.

Today, Buster's made a full turn. Out of prison close to fourteen years, he lives in the very same housing project, Johnson Licht Homes, now converted to house an aging generation of the city's poor, that he had first moved Mama'n into almost forty years before. The last real contact I had with him was years ago, about 1988. He called me out of the nowhere following grand mom Mavis' death.

His motive for contacting me was: Years ago, grand mom had taken out one of those "Gerber" child insurance policies on both Toppa and me when we were first born. And, he was requesting both Toppa's and my social security numbers "*SO I COULD* GO HEAD' AND GET YA'LL BACK ALL THE MONEY MOM PUT IN," I remember him saying.

"Hole-up! What do you mean insurance policy?" I countered him all at once.

"Yeah, that's right. mom had a policy on you guys and I wanted to get the money—Uhhh...*For y'all.*"

My immediate reaction was not to trust him any further than quickly cutting off the conversation. My own personal ability to trust him had fallen prey to lifelong experiences of others who had made the mistake of placing faith in this man. Mama'n comes to mind the most. If ever one person was responsible for ruining the dreams, chances and life of another, this individual on the other end of the phone had killed my mother, just as assuredly as if the shimmer of his blade had glistened with the thinning paste of her flowing blood, causing her to fall every step of her way and canceling out hope, felling her among a variety of unhelpful witnesses as it had Dusty. I told him I'd call him back.

I then called grand mom's husband, my uncle Bem-Bem's dad, Rob Johnson.

"Grand pop? It's Blu. How you doin?"

"Abraham! (A pet nickname he'd taken to calling me since I was very little)

How you been boy? You know, I was jussthinkin' bout' you and Toppa juss' the otha' day."

I shrugged it off, staying my course completely. Rob was that type. Always—*Jussthinkin'* bout' you although he never thought to pick up a phone to let you know he was still alive or had a need.

I asked him whether he knew about the validity of this so-called policy grand mom had held on both my brother and me. He corroborated Buster's claims that a policy did in fact exist. And he gave me the company's name. I quickly crossed the name to a phone number via the internet and found the underwriting company very easily.

After placing the call and speaking with a company representative, I found out that there was in fact a valid policy. The cash value of which amounted to a grand total of sixty-five dollars.

What a rip off?

I felt immediately sad for grand mom. Only GOD, she and the rip-off artist company representatives knew how much of her hard earned money she'd plugged into that policy over the course of more than twenty years. Buster saved me the uneasiness of having to call him back. He called me almost everyday. I kept putting him off. I'd been waiting for the insurance company to get back with me with more information.

"Blu?"

"Yeah…? I'm here."

"You gonna' give me the social security numbers so I can call the company and get the money…or what?" His tone had suddenly changed. I could envision the shift in his eyes that very second, as he flexed his knuckles, open and closed…Open and closed, as he permitted the metamorphosis to phase over him in one big, bi-polar shift.

Had I been standing before him that very second, I would have been backing away slightly, out of reach in my concern for him snapping forward to rip my throat out.

I didn't know. Since his first call, which had been the first time I'd spoken with him since I was fourteen, and he'd visited cousin Mandy's house, where we were having the wake for grand pappy, Ollie, I'd been doing some real hard thinking. And the more I thought about Buster and the kind of person he was, the kind he had been, and unknowingly to me, had become... There was no way I wanted him walking around the earth in possession of something as personal as my social security number.

Who knew? Besides, I still figure today—He was my biological father. If he'd a'-been anything worth that weight as a father, he should have known my social security number outright.

I have three children. And I can produce each of their social security numbers, right here, right now!—Upon demand.

"Why do you need my social security number to get at this money?" I took a brief pleasure in toying with him. A little payback for all he had never done for me.

"Whattaya' mean? Why do I need the numbers? You know.

So I can get the money—For you, like I said before. Quit playin' games, godammit, Blu!"

"Have you got any idea how much money we're talking about here?"

I knew. Seeing how I'd already spoken with the representative from the company holding the policies.

"Whattaya' mean?" He asked

"You know what I mean. You have any idea how much money we're talkin' about with this thing? How much the policies are worth?"

"I don't like the tone of your voice. What are you tryin' ta' do?"

"My tone, what are you talking about, my tone?"

I laughed openly with an incredulous stupor. I could almost feel the rage building on the other side of the phone threatening at any moment to explode. But that was all right. He was in P.A. and I was in California. I wouldn't have to shoot my father dead that day to keep him off me, unless he took the *CONCORDE* seeking the sixty-five dollars *he* didn't know he was really after.

"Why don't you just give me the name of the company and a contact there? I'll call em' up and get the money and... I tell you what—I'll split whatever it is with you," I continued to test him. For all he could gather, I was try'n ta' cut in on *his million-dollar find.*

I believe I wanted all along to think that my father hadn't really picked up the phone to call me, his son, after all these years, just to get his hands on sixty-five bucks.

"Why should I do that?" A long pause interrupted his thoughts and our conversation. "What have you done for me lately?"

His response almost felled me. It came close to sweeping me off my feet and sucking away my very next breath.

"I can't believe this shit. What are you talking about? Do you know how old I am? Man! I'm twenty-three years old. What have I done for you lately?" I could feel the beginnings of years of *His* neglect and anti-personal irresponsibility welling up inside the swell of *my* now heaving chest.

My reaction to what he had just said scared me. Was I bi-polar like him, just the same? I think I am. There have been plenty instances in my own life, when I've just appeared to *SNAP!*...For no explainable reason. I think that was one of the reasons I chose the military as my first, great career. Because of my knowledge of this disease boiling inside me, because of Maman's lifestyle as well, I somehow sought to overcompensate, in canceling out the defeating effects the power of such feelings held over my goals of reaching toward life's successes. The military provided that bi-polarism with structure and a commanded discipline and control in keeping the inherited flaws of my inner personality in check.

"I can't believe you'd even have the balls to approach me like that." I remember taking a full second trying futilely to gather a useful grip upon a savory control as I went forward, continuing to engage him.

"Where's my new shoes when all I had to wear were ones with holes in em'—tips flappin', toes hangin' out? Were you anywhere nearby, where I could call you when the holes in my pants had me so cold from being exposed that I had no desire to play with the other, warmer-little kids? Where's my baseball glove? Or my Green Machine? My Big Wheel? Where's my Christmas presents and bedtime stories? Where's all that shit...*YOU* were supposed to be for me all those years in my past?

Where were you when Toppa and I were forced to fend for ourselves—fatherless?"

It took an increasing moment before I realized "NETTIE" was standing beside me. She began to soothe me, lightly stroking the back of one of my hands. A clearly evident, caring concern spread to cover her features as the Lovely outline of her face showed the anguish of the heart-wrenching ebb and flow of a lifetime of feelings she felt pour out of me into that phone all at once. It also didn't dawn at me at first that the phone line on the other end—had gone dead.

He'd hung up.... And got away again—The punk!

And that's the last real contact I've had with Buster since.

For me, it wasn't the matter of the amount, just sixty-five dollars, which held the most importance. I think my ultimate motive had been to not permit him a gained access to my life by way of freely giving up my social security number. Plus, I think I wanted to condemn him, finally, and cause him to meet me now, on my terns, as a grown man. It appears kind of selfish on my part, now. I wanted to cause him to take responsibility, in

at least admitting his failures as both a father so many years ago and in all that he could possibly offer me, if he wanted—as a friend now.

As it turns out, I again phoned the gentleman from the insurance company. After providing him the proper endorsements of identification, I gave him Buster's information and his address and told him to mail him the check for sixty-five dollars and fourteen cents. I didn't particularly need or want the money.

I needed a father.

Long live the King!

"In the End, we will remember not the utterances of our enemies, but instead—the still silence—of our friends."

Chapter Three
'EKSEDES'

With Buster firmly enthroned in serving what was to be, for all intents and purposes, a life-sentence, Mama'n finally began to regain a chance at blossoming. She got us the little apartment in the city's South Side. I still remember our address, 1415 South 15th Street in the Harrisburg Park Apartments. Although she hadn't completed high school and had dropped out in her tenth grade year (Pregnant with Toppa) she'd always been a very smart, intelligent young girl. She was hired on with the state as a clerk typist.

Her wage wasn't much. But it was enough to just barely keep a roof over our heads, buy our food, and lead her into a lifestyle of parties, people and purveyance.

Mama'n had what you'd call an inviting personality. She could make friends with the devil himself sittin' on an iceberg if given the chance. And for her, and us, at times it appeared that's exactly what she did.

Our tiny apartment had two whole bedrooms. A separate, very small kitchen, a single bathroom, and even a living room big enough to house her entire collection of popular albums (At one time, she must have had about a thousand).

I remember an initial period of peace living there. For a brief time, Toppa and I shared a room with Mama'n, while a young, Nigerian student, named Ba-Ba Femmie, rented out the additional bedroom. Femmie was a great guy. He helped Mama'n as much as he could. But he was in our lives only a short time. My recollection of him is one of a very soft-spoken, peace filled Brotha' out only to complete his studies and take his education and accomplishments back to Africa to make a life for himself with a family all his own.

Within the apartments, we very quickly became surrounded in the shroud of an entirely new assembly of what became a protective, pseudo family. There was Sister and Elder White. He was pastor of his own church. She was his first lady and my baby sitter. She lived upstairs on the second floor and she watched over me while Toppa went to first grade at Foose Elementary and Mama'n was off at work. I recall Sister White's patience with clarity. During one incident, it amazed me, she didn't even bat a lash or appear upset, when as a teeming four year old, after awaking from a fitful nap, I'd pee'd all over the top of her new coffee table.

And....

To top that off, had attempted to cover my tracks by slyly using the throw pillows from her couch to wipe up my mess.

That's some patience, boy.

I woulda' killed me! Mama'n would have come home from work to one—dead little—pissy boy.

There was Maman's friend, Miss Judy Preske and her two daughters, Snoopy and Shirley. Miss Judy was a hard working redhead, who had only two things in life she really cared for. Her girls was one...and an unbeatable jones and magnetism for being mistreated by a full, unworthy hoard of no-good, black men, the other. Then there was Miss Mola, her husband, Donnie Lawson and their little girl, Massai. Don was a no good, cheatin' dog of a weak man. Miss Mola, was a huge, rotund, very outspoken freak. She was so huge and he so little, I wouldn't put it past her to actually have been *beatin' his ass* from time to time. Maman's road dogs and close friends, sisters, Miss Midget and Miss Dutchess were two points of caring light who could always be counted on with genuine Love for each of us to make certain things didn't get *too* far out of hand. They were the next best thing approaching a support system Mama'n had.

We became friends with Yvette Jones. An extremely shy, teenaged beauty, who's street-running, very illusive Daddy held an apartment in the same complex. She always seemed to be introverted and alone. Mama'n being Mama'n, she quickly took Vette in and placed her, with Love, under her wing. So strongly, that for a long time thereafter, she was never again alone. She'd been drafted into the family for good. Still today, we consider Vette a sister. We hold a very special place in our hearts for her. Much the same way as we hold Love for Shanelle, almost thirty years later. "Nelle" was another of Maman's urchins. The lady had a knack for picking up lost, unwanted, betrayed—stray heartbeats along the way of her own, varied troubles. She'd take them in and provide what she could offer in the way of Love and what guidance she herself could bring them in tow. And she never asked anything of them, always giving freely of herself. Her only goal, in ironic parody, of keeping the world's pains from mercilessly reaching others and hurting them in the way she herself had been hurt.

It just seemed she never applied those forms of life-saving mercy she gave so freely to others, to her own children.

Particularly—Not to me.

Although the full theme of Maman's life had begun to change for the better; she no longer had to put up with the oppressive tyranny she experienced under Buster's rule, she still gave off the image of being extremely stressed—All the time. She never really appeared to be capable of getting a firm footing upon completely entrenching hers and our lives firmly on the right track.

Toppa and I were both soon enrolled in the wonderful splendor of private education at the Middletown Christian School. We took a bus to Middletown, about thirty miles away, past Steelton, each morning. We were the only two little black kids there. And at that time, the school's Loving faculty completely overlooked that fact in making us feel at home and special. This would not be the first time we'd found ourselves in that situation. Not always with as comfortable a circumstance or results. I still Love that place. It was a school run by the efficient husband and wife team of Mr. and Mrs. Brown. And for the first time in a long while, mixed in with the torrid uncertainties parading through our young lives at home, it held stability and a firm assurance for the two of us. I met my first white friend, David Kobus. And it was there that I first began to develop coping skills for stepping forward to overcome challenge.

This came mostly in the form of a skinny little girl, with the silkiest, long, blond hair and piercing blue eyes, named Jenna Mauldin. Jenna was verifiably the smartest kid in the whole school.

Although I don't think she knows it, she became my role model for studying and achieving high marks on daily worksheets and follow on tests.

No matter the subject, whether on quizzes, in-class work, or on tests, I quickly developed an inner fire to do only one thing on a daily basis—that was get a better grade than Jenna Mauldin on every exam. She was a whiz. She mastered me on more occasions than I won. But for me, shadowing her footsteps sparked me to look forward to developing a hearty work-ethic which is still prevalent in my life today.

Thank You, Jenna!

If I ever become filthy rich and the school is still around, they get the largest grant or endowment I can possibly provide them to continue working the magic they so easily spun for me so many years ago. It was there that a comely old lady, Mrs. Carpenter, my kindergarten teacher, first taught me to read and write. I recall. I was the first kindergartner in her class that year that learned to really read. She rewarded my accomplishments with a very special, blue ribbon.

As well, as I moved up grade levels, I began pulling closer and closer to matching Jenna's marks and achievements, but I never quite caught her. At each year's end of school banquet, she forever received the coveted gold coin of academic excellence. I always got the silver.

Now days I capture the grey-area within that fact with thoughts of; *the early bird always gets the worm—But the second rat always gets the cheese.*

And I didn't mind so much taking second. I was still much better at my studies than all but one of the institution's thousand other students.

Maman's job seemed enough to keep us all in spidey-roos and peanut butter for a time. And her Love life began to blossom as well. A full assortment of different men came and went into and out of our lives, their faces changing sometimes seemingly on a nightly basis, breeding confusion. Toppa and I were still too young to fully keep up.

And still, she never seemed to be fully content. She was always somehow—*RESTLESSLY*... One step behind.

It seemed happiness had all but escaped her inner psyche. No matter what it was she did so desperately trying to secure success, it was not something she could easily have.

And... She took out her frustrations—On Me!

Mama'n had inherited her style (Or lack there of) for child-rearing from her own father, grand pappy, Ollie. But she, in fact, was at times, a hundred percent worse than he. Toppa and I were ultra polite, bow-tie wearing, little, gentlemen. Every Sunday, she packed the two of us out front—rain, sleet or snow, to be picked up by the local church van and she'd watch that van pull away each week, safely, then turn back around, her joint solidly lit as she would never accompany us, choosing instead to forego her own journey toward salvation, substituting instead, the fleeting comforts of whatever bum's arms she'd spent the previous night in to keep her warm. We'd trudge sleepily off to church as they'd made it hard for us the night before to rest, after wading through a minefield of bombardment the passionate throes of their raucous Love-making generally played out to be.

With hypocritical abandon, she held some misguided idea that the two of us were always going to be polite, demure and church-taught, urchins. Initially, she refused to entertain the idea of permitting us to fight back against the many, wild, young boys in our neighborhood who challenged us, and *her* lessons incessantly on a daily basis. Instead, she taught us to be warming, syrupy polite, offering almost—To turn the other cheek and just be accepting of the ass whuppins' we took during our many battles.

"Don't start fights and be nice and play with all the boys without causing trouble."

We were held back years in our natural development and consequently became not only hers but a full horde of neighborhood bully's punching bags. Toppa and I were two, well-dressed, extremely articulate, bitch-made punks. The neighborhood thugs, nemesis and the tag-team duo of maniacal brothers, Byron and Damion Waleson held punch-out parties terrorizing us so much that Toppa and I would rather do chores and housework than take the chance of running into one of our overseers outside while playing.

Butt whuppin's at the hands of Byron and Damion quickly became a daily occurrence. Anytime they caught us together, without the security of adult supervision, they'd run us down, kick and hit us unmercifully. Our torture continued, till we were either bloodied—always terrorized, or the saving grace of someone walking by found them on top us, pummeling away, and only that would cause them to jump up off us and run for home. This would save us briefly. Till the next time they caught us running to the store with 50 cents in our pocket—for cigarettes—for a mother who seemed not to really care.

This infuriated me. While I wanted to lend credence of respect to the wisdoms being forced upon me by Mama'n, I was still plagued with Buster's genes, his build, his thought-patterns, *aaaa-and*. . .his temper. I vehemently sought my chance to lash out and strike back at my tormentors with a vengeance.

Even then, at that young age of eight, nine and ten, my analytical prowess caused me to wonder—Why doesn't mommy Love us? Why didn't she Love me? Why'd she keep sending us out like that, for her cigarettes, unarmed, forbidding us to fight, even when she knew we'd be beaten senseless before being able to completely make the trip safely back to our home?

We just kept quiet and went right on taking those beatings, from her, and from them as well.

From time to time, I'd just get fed up and come out and ask her. This usually took place before the unhappy preparation of her beginning to beat the shit outta' me once again. I'd be made to strip butt naked. Place both my little hands securely in the little hole between the high-back and seat cushion of one of our dining room chairs, and she'd just wail away at me for literally hours—beating me sometimes senseless. I think she abused me so with hopes that her own frustrations would be assuaged and decide to depart her as she attempted to pass them on to me. She pounded me so profusely at times that I could no longer feel the raining down of the blows from her heavily wielded leather strap.

Instead of fighting back against the cold, continuing slash and slice of her belt across the smoothness of my tender, five to eight-year-old backside, I'd be offered an almost calming mercy as it would settle over me in the form of my ability to simply float away, my body still there enduring the cruelty of her labors, but my mind safely tucked away in the corner of a far off, happier place, dancing silently, somewhere deep inside myself. Although I didn't know it at the time, what I was doing, was refusing to allow her to take my mind, while destroying my body. Even after the viciousness of her brutality began to become almost unbearable, my will to resist remained firmly in tact.

While stooped there naked, with her hulking over me looking as if she hated me, shaking, fear stricken, I'd look back at her briefly between breaths, gigantic, crocodile tears of misunderstanding rolling imperviously down my upturned face. I'd look to her and simply ask…

"Mommy…. Don't you Love me?"

And more than once, I remember that simple question drew me what I'd like to think was a compassionate clemency. A stay for a high crime of perhaps—breaking one

of my toys. Or for drinking the last bit of milk or (I was then and still today am—a rat) eating the last piece of cheese.

Don't you Love me mommy?

I'm sorry—mommy? Mommy…I'm Sorry! Don't you Lov…?

It generally tended to cause her to pull up and stop, dead in her tracks.

Just stop fucc'n hitting me! Was what I really wanted to scream at her, exactly what I felt at that time.

Toppa got it too, although his turns *ON THE RACK* were far less numbered than my own. He was asthmatic, and had quickly learned the saving grace of being able to bring on the instant occurrence of an Asthma-attack to efficiently protect him from her furious tirades. But, I recall her beating him once with an extension chord. I felt so helpless. There was no way for me to help him. I just stood there, watching, like all the rest of the slaves, as she almost killed my brother, his backside torn and bloodied from blow after blow of her horrific maltreatment. I remember when it was over, thinking he looked like one of those animals, penned down and not yet really slaughtered, but dying all the same, from the gunshot wound it had just taken to the head. Snot ran unchecked from each of his heaving nostrils. Bile and bowel movement covered him as he lay still, too weak to get up or move initially.

My own body still bears the scars of those beatings. There were times I wasn't permitted to go to school. Out of fear someone, perhaps a curious, school nurse or counselor would stumble across my residual pangs or see a welt or scar still healing, I was kept home until at least the scabs began to smooth over and could better be blamed on my own childhood clumsiness while outside at play. And I hated this, because for me, school was somewhat of a refuge. I trusted those people working there and with every bone in my body, I wanted to run up to any one of them and scream, "Help Me, Please! My mommy's trying to kill me."

I'm a firm believer that I will most probably never completely recover from that period in my life. And even now, writing this, it brings tears to my eyes and anguish to my heart—That I Loved her so then and still Love her so much now, even though she caused me so much pain and never ending—emotional strife.

Thinking back now...and while I'm not trying to make any excuses for her behavior, I do believe more inherently, that I caught so much hell from her because I reminded her so much of my father. And that terrorized her. She meant, in her own way to dissuade my mannerisms, temper, and drive which were much then and still are today, identical to his.

But, I'm now and always have been different from him. I've been able to learn from his mistakes and from his crimes committed a previous millennium ago. She didn't have to take out on me what she'd permitted him to do to her. Since I could think for myself, I have made choices for my own life, which have set me far and apart from things he has not left for me by way of a success-driven legacy. I've never killed anyone, or pummeled my wife to within an inch of her life.

That's not what I am about as a man.

I don't permit my problems with the bottle to ruin the lives of the members of my family. I've never been arrested or carted off to jail. I've never held a knife to my precious baby's neck, threatening to castigate the child for presumed sins of its mother.

And I wish I could go back then and reinforce for her that it didn't take killing me—*out of love*—for me to come close to being able to embrace these clearly evident conclusions today as a man.

Such treatments for me went unchecked from about the ages of five until about eight and a half to nine. Then, there was a short break in the terror and mistreatment. Only to be replaced by a whole new set of neglectful abuses, as the twisted, instability of her life burrowed on.

Can you imagine? Two sweet, little boys, eight and ten, each day shuffled off outside irresponsibly. To be, as my uncle Bem-Bem used to say, "*MURD-A-LIZED,*" by the likes of local hoodlums whose only real life turn-on's were in getting away with preying on us viciously while our own mother's inability to concern herself with things other than staying laid-up and high—

sentenced us to horrendous childhoods. The two of us were firmly placed out of sight and pushed from her mind habitually. We became invisible until we'd return home after each day's tactics and plans of having to fend for ourselves evading marauders in the streets. Rarely were we able to find peace enough on a single day at play to let down our guard of being serious little foot-soldiers as we trudged along our ways building upon roles of being—the already defeated men—as Maman's neglectful acts were shaping us up to be.

We kept watchful eyes out for each other as we sought to take routes which kept us off the paths of bullies, only to enter a house following that play where a scornful, heavy handed beast lurked, angling lethally in wait, to criticize, pummel and dissect the compositions of our every move.

Ever feel like you're being followed? At times I do. I had this feeling when I was very young and still trapped within the abuse when the torment of being Maman's offspring was at its heightened greatness.

...And GOD sent me an angel. I still feel that angel's presence from time to time whenever I'm in danger or about to make a bone-headed move threatening my life.

I first began to feel the angel's presence about the time of the birth of my little sister. They called her Miss Honey. Her actual name is Melania Yannice Purtiss, and I feel GOD heard my cries, and knew my plight and frustrations. Through my little sister, I believe a gate was opened to send an angel to protect me. Born when I was six, she was the result of the entry into our lives of a man named, Mr. George Evan Purtiss.

Mr. George, as Toppa and I called him, was an invigorating breath of fresh air for the two of us. Mama'n had met him at a party. She had at first been interested in one of his brothers, Charlie, a handsome, very articulate, strappingly built young man easily likeable by any family... We all Loved Charlie. Toppa and I were fortunate to have been able to openly welcome him into our lives. Turns out though, Charlie, wasn't exactly what you'd call a young man interested only in the ladies. He was gay. But, being the great guy that he was, that fact was simply overlooked, and he instead kindly introduced Mama'n to his older brother, George.

Mr. George was in the Army at the time of their meeting. A paratrooper in Vietnam, he was a man of cutting edge character. Following the completion of his tour, he all but inserted himself into our lives and once encased there, he took firmly over.

"THANK YOU, GOD!"

Mr. George brought to the picture, a battlefield of foundation—buildable knowledge, steeped with the necessities which held the possibility of supporting, for us, a positive agenda. These were coupled with personal convictions of spirit strong enough not to be afraid to cause what we needed most—the saving sweetness of a sweeping change to become a reality.

He moved in. And, for a time, life became real darned good, almost normal.

Suddenly, instead of Toppa and I running outside to play, only with each other, he pushed us past the barriers of our own Mama'n inflicted obstructions to venture further. He encouraged us to wander off the stoop, prodded us to inch out and away from the relative safety of the home front—to seek out and make new friends and to search for more precarious adventure than we had previously become accustomed to.

Initially, we had no idea how to let him in on our previously held fears stemming from of our losing battles with Byrron, Damion and a whole slew of others who'd so deftly made our lives miserable as they held us tightly captive within the clutching grips of their rancorous talons.

But, he was no fool. It didn't take him long to soon figure it all out.

Thereafter, he began to instruct us, with prideful determination, in the kinds of things young boys needed most from the experiences and teachings of a doting father. Maman's previous edicts against fighting were gloriously discarded.

Toppa and I were shocked, but grateful all the same. We had never seen Mama'n permit one of her many conquests to take such an even-handed interest in providing us guidance—and seemingly against her formerly compelling wills.

It was like suddenly we actually mattered. Someone other than she began to care for and about us. And he had a genuine Love for us, *his* boys...

It was just what we needed. I have no clue what kind of man I'd be today, had it not been for the introduction into my life of that man, Mr. George Purtiss.

I remember the day he came home with two brand new pairs of boxing gloves. After our initial reluctance to take part in the pain of learning how to use them properly, we learned a different kind of step and dance. Except this one, we both embraced. With a hungering tenacity, we soaked up every lesson he provided in teaching us to finally be able to walk outside our apartment, infinitely prepared to protect ourselves. We learned cunning and deceit, the importance of proper footwork, and things like bobbing and weaving, jabbing and feinting.

I became an avid study. All he taught us would very soon become very handy. After learning our newly hewn skills, we not only used them against the bullies whom thereafter we almost hunted—every chance we got—but, for us, entering the mean streets each day began to take on a whole new meaning as we sought a lifetime of long overdue payback.

Amazing what just having a responsible male figure in the home does for the self-esteem and confidence of young men…

Soaring with invigorated stamina, Toppa and I were finally afforded the beginnings of the necessary steps of taking on challenge and accepting the achievements that came with the almost holistic releasing of our formerly held fears.

We learned courage. He taught us to face our doubts and to confront them closely, instead of fleeing from them like babies at every turn. We learned how to develop strengths for being able to take pain while steadying our wills. We began to develop walls of stabilizing maturity which swept us upward with tantalizing force toward growth. We learned how to overcome—and how to fight back as young men.

He also instructed us in the very important facets of facing and overcoming failure.

Without the dexterity of being able to pick ourselves up previously and without the ability to take conclusive stock of our manageable abilities, Toppa, and me, as young men would never have mastered the art of coping under Maman's care. Developmental skills bearing a sense of self confidence would have escaped us forever and he and I would never have experienced the joys and qualities of becoming the newest gladiators to encircle the formerly panic-stricken surroundings of arenas we shied away from in our childhoods.

. . .Struggle, young man. . .Struggle!

Byrron and Damion soon became terror-filled, former worries. And very rapidly it became known, throughout the entire hood that something with the Penn boys had suddenly changed.

While we did continue to adhere to former teachings of never being the ones to start the fights, we fought a lot, for a short time. We boldly took on all comers. We fought on the playground. We fought at school. We fought in church. Almost as if we were making up for lost time, reclaiming atrocities of being forced to fulfill roles as punching bag, exploitable *PUSSIES.* At times, we were even known to tag-team a few customers completely should they be so unlucky to cross us. As we matured, we fought even more viciously, and were both dreaded and revered for our commitments to fighting till our opponents were either beaten to succumbing pulps or lain out in the releasing comforts of unresponsive stupors.

It wasn't long after we first began our journey into the lion's den of fighting that we began to be able to travel into just about any outlying neighborhood surrounding the Park Apartments, no longer fearful, instead, others a bit apprehensive about approaching the two of us in perhaps the wrong way.

Soon, we began to look at things like shiners as veritable badges of necessary battle, fat lips, show-cased ribbons, detailing our willingness to mix it up—get in and throw with the best of the hooligans, whose clubs we never really after that, permitted *ourselves* to become a part of. Then the fighting stopped—Till we got to Texas.

I believe, through Mr. George's mentorship, that I began to attack life's challenges squarely, taking them on, with an exacting theme of demanding: *A HOME RUN OR A STRIKE OUT.* It was his fault thereafter that I overtaxed myself on so many occasions in search of a personal, internalized and overtly proffered perfection in every task.

Also, through his tutelage, I discovered a ceaseless, compellingly satisfying Love for almost every kind of sport. The man was a sports fanatic! An endearing ailment I soon took on and still possess today. He and I could always be counted on to be in our places, flopped about the living room, me hugged up as closely to him, tucked beneath his warm, endearing frame as I could possibly be (He never complained or pushed me away). We watched re-run after re-run of Ali-Frazier, or Lew Alcindor, (Kareem) doing his thing for UCLA. Football season was perhaps our favorite. I remember him carting mounds and mounds of every variety of sports equipment into our tiny apartment all the time—just for me.

Toppa wasn't as much of a natural sports enthusiast as me. His asthma pretty much kept him sidelined and prevented him from gaining a real Love for or respect of the joys offered in competitive sports.

I tried out for city league football. I was selected to play on the *CARDINALS* and to my wonder; we won the all-city championships in our age group. I still credit Mr. George for honing the skills within me which afforded me my first, honest-ta'-goodness real trophy! I was more than proud of that thing as I set it atop the dresser I'd had since the days of Buster's reign and I cherished it as a striking reminder that I could in fact accomplish anything in life that I set my body and my mind to completely.

I recall when spring came around and it was time for baseball tryouts. Everyday after work, he could barely contain his zeal and excitement for taking me on the side of our apartment building, sticking a bat in my hand, and hurling at times, painful hardballs at me in an attempt to better instruct me in hitting. On many evenings, we'd return to the house with me all bruised up from his wildly thrown pitches. His aim and control wasn't all that great. But he significantly dissipated my fear of that ball which went a long way toward me realizing the Love I've had for the game even today.

And...Because of him, I have, with identical excitement, gladly imparted the same Love and respect of sports to my own son, Boomer.

I remember my very first baseball coach, Mr. Perkins. About three weeks after tryouts, he came put-puttin' around the neighborhood in a nearly broken-down, no longer white, station wagon. When he pulled into the driveway of our apartments, he pulled the suffering ride to one side of a group of us boys and stopped the engine with a continuing hack and coughing and sputter—before the thing finally came to a choking end. Slanting his badly chewed cigar to a secure spot at one side of his jaw, he shuffled through a disheveled heap of wrinkled and tattered papers that he had scattered across the face of a battered clipboard. Finally looking up at the crowd of kids shuffling in around me, he zeroed in on me, calling out, with a beckon.

"Hey, kid? You know a boy by the name of uhhh...," checking his list once more, "Uhhhh...Blu Penn?"

My heart leapt!

We'd all witnessed him driving around slowly, making his rounds through other blocks, finding other boys and giving *them* their team uniforms. Now, I prepared myself to receive mine.

Right There! *Infronta' GAWWWD and everybody!*

It was a time of excitement for me. One in which, for a very brief moment, I was the intended star. I just stood there, beaming for a second, playing out my part of the unlikely town hero.

"Uhhhmmm... Yes, Sir." I answered. "Tha... Th... That's me!"

"Good...." He retorted, reaching for and wiping the sweat from his brow on the back of dingy handkerchief clipped atop the remaining names on his list.

He then turned around to reach for something inside the back seat of the car. Coming back around to his front to face us once again at his side, he checked a mark off on the wrinkled paper and he pitched a long, narrow, white box, reminiscent of the type a dozen roses comes in, at me. The whole welcomed package landed in a clouded puff of dirt and kicked-up gravel at my feet, as it beamed up at me from the street. He'd never left his car.

I at first stared at him, incredibly stumped in my tracks, lost in wonder.

"Go head' boy." He pointed a stubby finger, the kind and shape of which were slightly knurled and pudgy, akin to those of my grand pappy. "That ere's your uniform." Smiling brightly to show the tarnished stains of severely tobacco affected teeth, he topped that off with, " Ya' made the team kid."

Turning back around, his smile had disappeared as he departed grand pappy mode to reenter his former, intimidating persona, as coach. He reached for the key in the ignition, and he putted off into the wind in search of his next hometown champion. My insides threatened to burst suddenly with a swelling sense of joy, laughter and achievement. I knew that not every boy that tried out for baseball in the seventies made the team. And there I was, my first time up, having the coach come looking for me—to personally deliver *my* uniform.

I swept that box up from the ground in one fell swoop. And was about to stand a little bit taller among all my friends gathered there as I gloated. He brought the experience to an end, looking back over his shoulder, inching away my fantasy, with, "Be at the ball field at 4:30 sharp—For practice, startin' Wednes-dee'."

Even with the mini respite Mr. George provided, rather than viewing us as the breathing, Loving, endearing little boys his efforts instilled in us daily, Mama'n still looked at Toppa and me as nothing more than a pesky brood of never-intended chattel. Our development still remained secondary to her as she fully missed out on a slew of very special changes taking place inside of us. With her continued dedication to refusing to begin to view the two of us differently, the precious gifts of our progress were lost on her completely.

She still made attempts at trying to place us under the thumb of her irresponsible, absolutely unreasonable rigor. She did this by continuing to foster images of us as completely needy cells incapable of offering anything other than respectful, robotic replies of-*"Yes, Ma'am,"* or *"No, Ma'aaa...m,"* to her mundane questions, motives and overbearing suggestions. We suffered internally in silence with her still holding out hope of molding us into clones of her and grand pappy Ollie. And still, up to this point, even though the Yes Ma'am's far outnumbered the No's, even she had to begin to realize that he and I soon, would be reclaiming our bodies as well as stepping forward toward exercising a more fiercely offered *FREEDOM* of our growing, rapidly cultivating minds.

We were wisely still wary and careful of cutting too closely against the roughened grind of her rapidly changing moods and edges though. You just never thought to bring the wrath of Maman's ire down on you by appearing to be in too total a disagreement with her. But it wouldn't be long before even that would begin to change all around us—for good.

The good times of having food in our fridge, more than we could possibly eat, of having a perpetually clean apartment (Mr. George hated an untidy house) and someone who talked to you as if your thoughts and feelings really mattered, instead of just opening their mouths to yell at and scold you were soon to turn out to be short-lived.

Mr. George had finally come to the realization that Mama'n would never fully conform to meeting his standard of living. That she would always refuse to be held up to being the perfect model of the mother and *help-meet* he was seeking with whom he could share his life. He'd all but given up hope of trying to reform her.

He'd arrived just too late. Had he caught her during the pre-Buster era, she might have stood a wifely chance of being finely sculpted and subsequently not so combative. Then and only then would she not have been already soiled, thereby more willing to make him happy. But, her own near life and death experiences in the midst of a madman had somehow tainted her. They'd caused her to look at life and its struggles differently from the way normal; otherwise, sweet, impressionable, and healthy women peered at it a long time before the two of them had ever met.

She was stubborn. Tough beyond her years, the hardened edge of her wiser upbringing could not stand up to soften, even a wedge, to gently permit herself to embrace the things he was presenting her. He had dreams that he'd initially wanted her to share. But for her, a vision was only a pretend dream, something you heard about at a frightful séance setting.

I was almost ten. Our lives, once again.... began to fall apart.

Following his departure, Mama'n very rapidly digressed to beginning to associate herself with people she had all but shunned and shut out of her life completely during the *happy* year or two that Mr. George had held our shit confidently together.

Only this time, it appeared she hit uncontrollable depravity even harder.

Suddenly guys like Juan, a pretty boy, Puerto-Rican and Muddy and Treyball, began to spend more and more time cluttering up the minimal spaces of our quickly clouding conscience. The weed, coke, morphine and heroin made a rapid, gut wrenching return. And as long as those things were available like running water at that location, the floods of people moving in and out of our existences became once again a variable blur. Life reentered a phase of becoming frighteningly eerie. It was almost as if a call had gone out at the local jail cells, bars and brothels—that *WEEZO* was back in business.

And back in business she was...

I recall, during a particularly *heavy* paraphernaliac party, the screech of a record scratched a terrifying melody as that evening's party ended abruptly in a pathway of coagulated bodies, all trying to depart our apartment in one panicked, shrieking stream.

Toppa and I always held out worry for our Mama'n in the midst of so many devils and demons (Again—We weren't stupid. We knew exactly what was going on) rushing feverishly about taking over our tiny living room. He and I both maintained a watchful ear, tracking Maman's movements throughout the apartment, by sound and by feel of her scent, her steps. We waited. We worried…and as we remained banished inside the confines of our tiny, cupboard size room we both learned—and we watched.

Usually her parties went on till the wee hours of a weekend evening and they tended to approach the next day's dawn. But on this particular occasion, the quiet storm of abruptly entertained silence that swept through the dwelling without warning told us that something had most definitely gone dreadfully wrong. Upon ensuring each other that it was safe to venture out, we became faced with, what I felt at the time, would be the most ghastly sight I'd ever see in connection with my Mama'n. I thought this one thing would be the capping factor of a terror which threatened to haunt my soul forever.

I was wrong. It wouldn't be the most awful.

The living room area was of course empty. The only people left were our grown cousin, Landa Johnston, cousin Mandy's daughter, and her boyfriend, Skip. The two of them all but ignored us as they made speedy trips, back and forth, between the bathroom and the little freezer in our kitchen.

Cousin Landa was Maman's age, maybe a year or two younger. The two of them had grown up together. As thick as two of Ali Baba's thieves, they were inseparable partners in reaching for lives ingrained with crime and malice. If either of them were to ever run for political office, they would immediately be unsuccessful, unless they bumped off the other, the dirt they held on one another so immense and compellingly corrupt; their opponent would easily enjoy a landslide victory once rumor of their capers caught the wind.

Of the two forms jetting about our apartment, Cousin Landa appeared to be the one in charge. She barked orders and fevered demands at Skip like *she* was Mama'n. He dutifully mirrored her actions and followed her every command without a scornful word. Very soon thereafter, Toppa and I began to inch our way toward the bathroom where their trips appeared to end and begin…begin and end. We could tell that their focus played out with terrorizing concern as they tended to something or someone who was in deep trouble there.

Having only each other for steadies, and totally unsure of ourselves, our only thoughts were: *Where's our Mama'n?*

Skip and Cousin Landa, like everyone else at first, disregarded us, not paying particular attention to our movements as we edged closer to the bathroom door. We were able to gain enough of a fleeting angle to peek quickly inside to see what was taking place there, before Cousin Landa reached out and attempted to backhand swoosh the both of us in an attempt to shoo us back toward the feigned brainlessness of the stuffy tomb inside our tiny room. .

We'd found her.

TV dinners and mini-steaks.

She was naked. Blood seemed to be everywhere as Cousin Landa purposefully sat on the tub's edge, attempting to arrange a medley of different items, ice cubes, cold-packs and other frozen goods beneath her arm pits, onto the back of her neck and between her pasty-looking thighs. All the while, Cousin Landa implored in an almost desperately whispered repeated-ramble, gibbering for Mama'n to somehow reach down and pull out life as her baby Cousin fought for her, begging her to find the will to live.

Toppa and I stood there for what seemed an eternity, stricken with what we'd seen of what was left lying there of our Mama'n, we were barely able to move to take shortened steps away, as Skip came over to gently guide us both out into the front room.

We had no inkling what was going on. For all we knew, we were soon to bcome orphans for real, having the *RAISED BY WOLVES* mantra Mama'n had always pasted upon us become a haunting reality as we were in danger of losing the only parental figure we had left. If Mama'n died, who would take us in? There were three of us now—Toppa, Miss Honey, and me. Even though we'd all suffered so grievously under her hand, she was all we ever knew. The only figurehead we had grown accustomed to in at least a sparing way that we held the slimmest chance of being able to count on.

It didn't look good for Mama'n under the livid state of her present set of circumstances. From what we'd been able to see during our very brief peak, she was lying spread eagle, completely naked, the full weight of her body splayed out, like a dead fish, completely covering the inside of the tub. Her eyes cracked open slightly, all you could see of them were the whites as the remaining portions rolled back to be completely hidden in the upper regions of their lids. Her hair, formerly glistening, always sweet-smelling, jet black and beautiful was matted all over the fronts and sides of her now puffy face as it clumped in matted heaps, falling everywhere to make her look as if she was a fallen beast, already dead, a prize to be dressed and carted off—instead of the mother Toppa and I held out a fleeting chance of hope for within the light of our starkly whispered, heart-beating prayers.

Even so young, church had already taught us a thing or two about relying upon faith.

Spattering streaks formulating illuminated trails of Maman's blood covered each corner of the bathroom walls. It was the crimson stains running in storming peaks and clouded valleys that attacked my eyes most, filling my head with mind-numbing terror holding me captive during the original moments I stood before that door. It was as if our apartment had suddenly developed into the ghastly roped off corridor of a demon-filled, homicidal crime scene. I expected at any minute to be overrun by a swoon of cops, paramedics and news crews as the life of the Woman I called Mama'n slipped imperviously away with an ironic peace, the sifting varnish of a heroin vapor the last offering she'd ever present us.

She lay in that tub, packed completely in ice for more than four hours. I recall Cousin Landa suddenly turning on Skip cursing him out for an apparent bout of sheepishness. She was more infuriated with him than I had ever seen her upset with anyone before. He had vehemently refused to take a huge syringe Mama'n had kept securely wrapped at the back of the freezer, expressly for such an occasion, which Landa had thawed and prepared, as she tried to coax the man to take the hypodermic and plunge its contents deeply into Maman's chest to revive her awaiting heart and save her life heroically.

No matter what she did or what she called and cajoled him, there was no way Skip was taking the chance of sticking that ten inch needle into Maman's torso. With the calming strength of five Skips, Cousin Landa took matters into her own hands. Piercing the breast plate in a single, brutally thrusted plunge, she injected her favorite cousin with what she felt was a billion cc's of quick reacting adrenaline

Once again, GOD played a cruel, almost sadistic joke.

Mama'n survived...

Signs of her returning to consciousness began to make their ways to warm and encircle us. Needless to say, after what we'd all been through together, the four of us were instantly relieved.

All of us except Skip that is. Upon realizing that Mama'n was going to be all right, he jumped up quickly, grabbed his leather jacket, and with Cousin Landa screaming at his heels, cursing his cowardice nature once again, she had no need to kick him out of our apartment. He all but fled the surroundings, streaking a bee's line for the door with a vitality which caused his heels to skip steps, three at-a-time as he placed distance between himself, Mama'n, Landa—all of us.

I never saw him again. But, I thank him for sticking around giving all he had to give for as long as he had. It was more than most men had done for Mama'n.

This would be only one of a multitude of near misses she would come to endure over the course of an event filled, extremely traumatic life. The overdose causing Mama'n to languish for four hours as Landa desperately tried to embolden Skip to help her held her rapidly close to an approaching, early death. It caused her to take a brief step back to circumspectly review her actions and to slow down a bit, to reconsider things she was permitting to affect us negatively. As well, it forced her to take stock in what she was doing to her herself.

She was forever indebted to Cousin Landa. Had she not been there and known precisely what to do when she was needed most? She never refused her angel of a Cousin her most complicated wish following that day.

Who knows how life would have turned out differently for Toppa, Miss Honey and me?

Hmmmmm....

Yeah... Who knows?

Toppa and I were both kinda' mad at Mama'n during the seeming weeks it took for her to fully recover. I don't think we completely knew why it was we were so furious at her. We just knew for a fact that we should be.

Following her total recovery, he and I went to great lengths to never be caught alone with her or even to have cause to speak

to her other than a respectful *Good-Morning, Hello, or Good-Bye*. Like the good little soldiers we had become good at faking to be, we got along by doing as we were told and like little cockroaches, we silently scampered out from beneath her weakened clutches, shying away from her mediocre attempts to make betta' all she had sent us through irresponsibly.

Toppa and I sat many nights going over, re-hashing and playing back the events that took place that night. We came to the conclusion that all the blood had come from her tampon. Cousin Landa had been forced to remove it when she had removed her clothes to pack even her vagina with the heart-slowing cubes of frozen ice.

How it had gotten flung about to paint the walls like it had, we had no clue? Perhaps it was just a little smatter which loomed infinitely large in our little eyes as they'd attempted to process so many thoughts of all we had been through.

All in all, I believe the sentiment scoring the highest for me, with regard to Mama'n, was the feeling of loss for her in the bone-chilling embarrassment I knew she would suffer once the word got out in-the-streets, that she had O.D.'d and had had to be pierced in the heart to be revived, with a dope-fiend's level of adrenaline to bring her back. I was embarrassed for her, wishing Skip had not been there, in a way, even though, in my eyes, he had done nothing but the decent thing, sticking by Cousin Landa's side till the very end.

I don't know…

It was my first time witnessing the horrors of overdose.

Mama'n didn't use drugs for a long while following that. Life began to take on more of a forming normalcy for us. She thrust most of her time into work and her family. She had a lot of brothers and sisters, and cousins. Most who lived within driving distance in the same city of Harrisburg. We spent time with grand mom, Myrna, the third of grand pappy's ex-wives. And with Tammy and Me'lady, Mama'n's little sisters. We began to become immersed in the care and Love of family, more along the lines of how things should have been from the start, had she not expended so much energy *chasing the fast fizzle—instead of embracing a more invitingly slower, extremely powerful burn*. It was a nice period of rest for us.

We spent more time with our Aunt Lanny and our uncle, Sylver (Short for Sylvester). He was always the coolest cat on whatever block he happened to squat on for any given length of time. It was during this period when I began to develop a relationship with my buddy, Kelin Eltins.

Kelin was a year or two older than I was. I'd met his sister, Mimmie first, out behind the main building of our apartments. She was just a tiny little bug of a thing. When I'd come upon her, she was trying her best to get up and jump on a huge Pogo stick almost three times her size. She was perhaps the blackest little girl I'd ever set eyes upon at that time. I recall sidling up to her and asking if I could take a turn at jumping. She told me I'd have to ask her brother.

"Where's he at?" I replied back to her.

With pretty, oval shaped eyes, their whites as wide as canyons, she never replied, initially, only gestured with her head and a sly, crooked little smile of perfection as she directed me toward her big brother's whereabouts.

Turning gaily toward the thirty—five foot oak trees lining the entire wash behind the complex and separating our buildings from the Hall Manor projects, she pointed toward the sky.

"Up there..."

"Whatta' ya mean? Up there?"

"Up there, in that tree." She drew my attention in closer to focus on a haunting figure sitting peacefully, cross-legged, watching us on the ground below him as he sat on a thin branch about twenty feet up in one of the trees you could see covering the marsh-like setting of the woods.

He was... Just sitting there, watching us.

"That's your brother?"

"Yyyup...!" She smiled a shy little banter, as if the two of them had just completed playing a sly little trick on me. The butt of their little joke held unearthed, only for their pleasures.

Shrugging it off, I countered, never taking my gaze off the figure who'd begun to move stealthily from branch to branch, tree to tree. "What's his name?" I whispered. The figure had somehow... What? Disappeared!

I swore I had never taking my eyes off him, but still the same, he was gone.

"S'... name's, Kelin." She giggled. I then looked at her incredulously.

Looking back up, I'd already formed the words to ask Kelin if it was all right if Mimmie let me take a stab at using his Pogo stick when I confirmed for a fact he was no longer there.

He was now, to my amazement, staring a full head down at me, standing beside his little sister, no longer in the spot of the tree, twenty feet up, where he'd been just two minutes before. I turned to greet him, almost in shock.

I offered him a twisted, "How'd you…?" Pointing off toward the tree he'd been sitting in.

"How'd I what?" He toyed with me. Smiling that same brightly lit shimmer of a smile I'd seen his giggly little sister play out just moments before.

He stuck out his hand and offered, "Kelin Eltins. Whaassup?"

"Blu.

Blu Penn," I offered in return.

"This here's my lil' sis, Mimmie," he shot back.

"I know." Turning now to give little Miss Mimm my best, evil eye ever, I offered, "We already met."

The three off us took off and headed in the direction of the front of our complex.

"Wanna' try out the Pogo?" He then asked in a sort of peace offering.

Following that initial meeting, it didn't take long before he and I became lifelong friends. I introduced Mama'n to his mother, Miss Ilene, a nurse, and his father Bunny, a Marine who always seemed to be away and never at home. They were from Pittsburgh. Kelin and I and our two families shared everything for a period of about three years.

Following this, I guess things got too good for Mama'n as she began to feel antsy once again, leaning toward giving in to that invitingly familiar, illicit itch.

STUPID!

This carried with it my own internal feelings that for us trouble was soon on its way to rearin' its ugly head again.

This was when Mama'n first met Egbert Rice, a smooth talking, thickly built man of cocoa colored complexion. It wasn't long before Egbert had her all hot and bothered, infatuated and eating out of the palm of his hand for good. He was as sweet as a ripened mango. He catered to Mama'n *like nobody's business*. Doting on her and fawning over her with an almost syrupy devotion.

Only problem was, his affections and devotions only extended realistically as far as Maman's fully engaging bedroom. She was so tired at such a young age of being broken down and beaten at the hands and minds of men who'd promised to sweep her up and whisk her away to a better life for her and her children that she was ripe for just about anything. Even those who presented only havoc and ever-increasing decay with their tumultuous wakes of clamoring disorder received an audience with the queen.

Failing to heed the lessons of her past, she was very rapidly overtaken by the smooth flowing words coming from yet another *homeboy* shyster.

For another month or so, life in our tiny apartment again became livable. It was nothing approaching the steady productivity of having Mr. George return. But still, there were additional stocks of food following numerous shopping trips necessary to support both Egbert and his brother, *Uncle* Richard—a long-haul driver for Allied Van Lines, who had suddenly materialized soon after Egbert, had arrived to set up shop on the scene as well.

The two of them had a good thing going, for a while.

Maman's former all-night parties returned but shifted into a lower, more bearable gear. The presence of a hoard of single men was cut down largely to merely include a few girlfriends and Richard, Egbert and their mini casts. And she held herself back, maintaining a thoughtful distance from any drug other than marijuana.

These boys were out of Rochester, New York. All we knew of them was that they resembled unsuccessful nomads both with no place in particular they had to go.

Richard, whose humongous rig seemed to have been stationed on the side street of our apartments, not moving to make any money by hauling precious freight, for more than two full months of lounging in our front room on the couch, was the worst of the two. That Brotha's feet smelled like a pound of fish in a garbage bin after it has been locked up inside a' Baskin Robbins fridge' with no power for a week

Egbert was either currently on his way to or fully operating out of an Army base in Texas—El Paso to be exact. He said he was a sergeant in uncle's under-used Army and apparently was either AWOL (Absent without Leave) or on a very-extended period of furlough during which time he lazed and laid up in the confines of our cozy little apartment unchecked.

These people so effectively *moved in* to take over such a huge portion of our lives, over a very short period of time, that even their sister, *Auntie* Rosie, and her children paid us a visit in Harrisburg, in route from Rochester, to their own home, across country, in Hobbs, New Mexico. Although Egbert's presence in our home did a lot to calm and slow Maman's motives down, her prior pathways which were leading her toward self destruction rolled on unceremoniously, threatening her continued well being and personal freedom now as well. While she was enjoying her newly discovered *Love* for Egbert, other maneuverings were not only forming, but were almost fully cultivated bearing burning embers of pinning her down in a trap of deceit, betrayal and immaculate conspiracy.

While Mama'n had thought herself a bigger turkey in the design of things than she'd brought forward to the shoot, in shocking hindsight and reality, she was no more than a small-time city girl seeking illegitimate adventures. She had no idea how far over her head her primary quests of and involvement in formerly devious dealings had caused her to become, thereby placing both she, and us at risk.

Turns out, the *pretty boy, Puerto-Rican,* Juan, upon rediscovering his own reality as an undercover Narco-cop, closed out his secure pass into her inner circle, and delivered his dossier of names, places, faces and transactions to his superiors.

But Mama'n had been just one step ahead of his ass too.

After receiving the alarm spelling out his treachery, and upon delving deeper, retracing the steps she'd taken (And forgotten to take) the anxiety of a trap which would snare she and a bunch of others (some close to her—like cousin Landa) encapsulated her. This ambush had already been put into irreversible motion. A heavy indictment detailing an assortment of varying, extremely serious charges where, if snagged, she would spend the next twenty years washing out *BIG BERTHA's* draws, was soon to be dropped squarely into her lap.

Panicking and feeling overwhelmed, she knew she had to think of something...And fast.

It wasn't long after coming to her new revelations of discovery that she began to plant and kick around the saving idea of *escaping* to Texas with Egbert, once he departed to return there just a week or two away.

Mama'n being Mama'n, she formulated a quick diagram centered around her inevitable goals of making a clean, life consuming get away with increasing haste.

She and Egbert would leave for Texas immediately. They would all pack into *uncle Richard's* Allied rig and light out for the figuratively greener, freer pastures across the interstate toward El Paso. Toppa, Miss Honey and I were to be left behind, in the apartment, under the care of one of Maman's drugged—out, crony girlfriends, Miss Vetta, along with one of which ever worthless boyfriends she had on hand with her that minute.

Mama'n gave Ms Vetta fifty dollars cash and a pittance amount of food stamps to take care of her compensation for watching over us.

What kind of great peyote were they all smoking? Fifty bucks and a fist full of coupons? What idiot in their right mind thought that would stretch far enough to feed five increasingly hungry mouths?

Mama'n jetted! Leaving behind only empty promises of the life she was reaching out for, she vanished, assuring Vetta that she'd be back for us all within a week.

This arrangement was obviously fright full of asinine indecision plagued by a sub natural immaturity pointing desperately to Maman's lack of a steady mind. Hadn't she learned *NUFFIN'* after all she'd been through? She should have been settling down, perhaps taking the rightful sense of responsibility for everything she'd let herself get caught up in.

...And perhaps given us a chance at happiness and the search for productivity in our lives.

Instead, she only hurled herself forward headlong once again towards failure.

Her plan had all but fallen before it had been recklessly thrown into place. Vetta was a sadistic, mean, self-centered, *bitch.* She treated the three of us like unworthy pariah. She banished us to our bedroom, (We were used to that) forbidding us access to the entire front area of *our* apartment. She routinely slapped us in the backs of our heads and pinched us in passing as we ventured out to eat or pee, almost tiptoeing. We stopped going to school.

She and that day's lucky pussy-participant too tired to set an alarm clock and get us up to the corner on Fourteenth Street to catch the bus. She terrorized us with her mean spirit and her funky breathe as she forced new complexities upon us with unreasonable demands steeped in her displeasure at Mama'n for *sticking* her with her three hungry brats.

She didn't know. Although her abuse was steady, there wasn't nothin' that she could do to us—that our own mother hadn't already attempted to cause us to endure. He and I were champs. Our only concern was for protecting our little sister, Miss Honey, from the robust pains of Vetta's daily harangues.

In a matter of days, the food stamps quickly ran out. The food Mama'n had Egbert stock in our refrigerator prior to leaving was gone too. It was completely empty due to the vast amounts of *visitors* she'd allowed carte blanche to freely roam in and out of our home.

We never benefited a lick from the fifty dollars Mama'n had given her. It too was long gone. Spent up, on drugs almost before Egbert, *Uncle* Richard and Mama'n had even made it across the Pennsylvania state line.

Out of frustration, hunger and indignation, Toppa and I began to put our heads together to try to see what it was we still had available to us that we could use in support of an even more-meager existence than we'd become accustomed to living with Mama'n.

Let me tell you...Looking around, we felt helpless. An abusive, absent mother who fancied herself a mini kingpin, all mixed up in the depravity of a drug induced world—on the proverbial lam now, in a state none of us knew seeking novel beginnings.

We were Christian school cherubs whose only escapes were things like reciting bible verses and reading cute, endearing little children's books about characters whose lives were far different from our own.

Being watchful understudies of the acts of our mother for so long hadn't gone untended. We both had what it took to be forced to grow up very suddenly; finally realizing that with Mama'n away, we had to come up with something to somehow get rid of the vicious bitch, Vetta before she killed us all with her neglectful ways.

But we had no plan at first. Nothing we could put our heads together for making our wishes of vaporizing that bitch come true.

So, instead, we waited for Vetta and numb-nuts to go to sleep one evening. We snuck into the front room and dialed the only number that we were sure would rain down a shit-storm of wrath and fury on both their heads in an instant.

We dialed the number both of us knew—by heart.

We called our grand mom, Mavis.

Grandmom didn't have a driver's license. She'd never been known to pilot any type of vehicle. And her own relationship with her husband, grandpop, Rob, who did drive was always just a knife's throw or teargas pistol short of a vengeful dissolution.

But, she materialized as if she'd been waiting around the corner, and all hell broke out there in an instant.

Suddenly, her petite little frame of fire had all but kicked in our apartment door. The amount of commotion and havoc she caused with her entrance stirred up all our neighbors abruptly. Lights appeared on swiftly, in every apartment, on all three, fully-stocked floors. Neighbors peered from behind drawn curtains and ventured at their own peep holes with a wondering amazement at what was going on over at Maman's place?

Grandmom arrived like an active hurricane just picking up to enter full gale force. Spouting commands and instructions over her shoulder to grandpop Rob, to gather a couple days clothing for each of us *grans*, she headed for Maman's bedroom. Once there, she struck the juggler of Maman's previous stupidity a firm and lethal blow.

Within seconds, I remember her dragging Vetta's screaming, pleading form securely outta' Maman's bed, by her hair. Doofous, Vetta's friend for the evening tried desperately to retrieve his fallen belongings as grand mom's presence had scattered them profusely all about the tiny room with her attempts to get at Vetta and punch her ticket—for good. Soon thereafter, all that was left of them was a depleted trail of trash and disorder leading out the front door.

Toppa, Miss Honey and I, tucked safely within the shield of her freshly laundered smock, Loved her more that very minute, if that were possible, than we ever had before. Our grand mom had saved the day. She'd rescued us.

Grandpop scooped up Miss Honey into his Loving arms. Grandmom locked up using the apartment keys she'd beaten out of Vetta, and the three of us, an hour or two later, were tucked snugly beneath chilled, sweet smelling covers of new beds at her home out on the hill on Boas Street.

Why do the sheets at a grandmother's house always seem so inviting? Their crisp, coolness and softening fabric reaching up for you wrapping your entire body in the security of a familiar comfort which is fully unobtainable anywhere else in the entire world.

Feeling the sunrise as it swept up to cover my face from behind the rickety railing of the balcony on the back porch leading off grand mom's guest bedroom the next day never soothed life's aches so doggoned good as it did that first morning when Top and I woke up to realize our nightmares might be over and our dreams come true forever. We were really back in P.A.!

We moved about excitedly, like liberated prisoners, just back from life's war—waking to take in the releasing splendor of our first moments free from captivity. Once we'd brushed our teeth, bathed (scrubbing behind our ears what must have been ten times—grand mom's thang') and eaten our individual shares of an entire box of *Rice Cryspies*, we ventured out onto the relative haven of safety present upon grand mom's front porch.

For me, my memory of that porch has got to be one of relaxing within the grips of the most cherished spot on GOD's green earth. My eased recollection of spring torrential downpours passing me by as I lounged atop a cushioned rocker sofa or swing, bring back a simplistic tranquility as I used to just let go and watch peacefully as the rain covered so heavily, taking over to mask with a clearing serenity all the many torments of my purely exhausted, child's mind.

I think that is the period where I first fell in Love with the rain. I could sit there forever without movement, watching playful families of squirrels dart in sputtered dances, jumping with ease from branch to branch of the many oak trees lining the entire block.

I would always try to be the first up. Just to sit out on that porch alone, rocking away in the veranda swing, listening to the calls of the birds and putters of squirrels, tucked safely in the sanctuary grand mom's house had come to provide.

It wouldn't be long after I'd been sitting there, before one of the many friends we'd made during one or two of the millions of times we'd visited, would come up to the banister to join in my stillness trying to renew their former acquaintances.

Perhaps it would be Bucky, with his older sister, Tam, in tow to keep his mischievous behind out of trouble? He had to have been borderline retarded. He was always doing stupid stuff like starting fires in abandoned houses and starting fights with people he barely even knew, for simple reasons. Or, it might have been the brothers, Scootie and Toomie White, or our neighborhood senior and ring-leader, Coolie Williams?

For what seemed an eternity more, we lived with grand mom and we did things like play uncle Bem-Bem's electric football game on the front stoop. A full collection of bristling boys waiting anxiously for their turns, all with plastic baggies filled with individually crafted, plastic competitors they'd hand painted an assortment of pseudo-*NFL* colors matching their favorite teams themselves. Or we chased each other playfully bearing homemade sling shots from which we launched acorns and acorn shells at one another in heated battles winding in and out of parked cars along the lengthy street.

I have no clue how not one of us ever lost an eye.

Man! Those were good times...

That crowd of kids surrounding us on Boas Street lent us their hands in a Love they had no idea they were actually providing. Perhaps it was common knowledge, the disparity of our previous home-life situation, but none of them ever made mention of it.

None, that is, except uncle Bem, who was born on the same day, just two years before me. At the age of thirteen, Bem, was an incorrigibly spoiled brat. One of his favorite caches of ammunition in our many heated pseudo-sibling bouts was to spit vehement accusations at Mama'n to us, detailing for us her inability to make good as a solid provider and nurturing mother, based upon her drug abuse and loose behaviors.

He was right. But we ignored him. We knew what he was saying was true. The boy was singing to a choir about events Toppa and I had been there to live through.

It's a shame the grandeur of things your friends and family will spit at you, hitting you squarely in the back while your head is turned, to your front, on the look out for your enemies.

It took a long time, well into adulthood, for me to be able to extend my now Loving uncle a forgiveness for his ravings back then.

We stayed with grand mom for a while waiting for Maman's return from Texas. No one had heard from or had seen her, since she'd departed with Egbert so many days before. While there, we discovered things both about ourselves and about others who lent a swatch of differences to the newly painted settings surrounding us.

I learned that our presence was putting an even heavier strain on grand mom's and grandpop Rob's already tenuous relationship.

I learned that I held a stoically maintained inner strength—A living, breathing thing which I would later learn to cultivate and draw on for many, many years of turmoil to come. I learned my little sister; Miss Honey, could climb trees and scramble over fences almost as good as me, just like a little brother. During the entire period of our internment there, rarely did she ever leave my side or my sight for more than a few very antsy seconds. I was determined that it was my overall responsibility to do nothing else but keep her safe until Maman's return.

I also learned something else about her. For the very first time, in our minds, this revelation made her somehow different from both Toppa and me. That was, that she had a healthier base of a strengthened support system than we did.

This materialized in the form of her father, Mr. George, and his family. These included Debbie, her auntie, and a strikingly beautiful, blossoming teen they all called *SHRIMPY.* Toppa and I both fell in Love with her at first sight. She was our secret crush for a multitude of little boy years.

But this was to be short lived. Shrimpy would eventually succumb to a way too early death. The effects of Lupus wrenched away from her a lifetime of certain achievements and history that she would never be given the opportunity to have.

They'd routinely come to pick up Miss Honey and while with them, she'd be wrapped snugly in a shroud of showered Love and care in their attempts at salving the wounds inflicted by a wayward mother whose whereabouts no one could point out.

Also there was Mr. George's mother, Miss Carolyn, and his grand mother, Mamma Lil'. There was her husband, Georgie, and Miss Carolyn's husband Sunny. All these people stepped forward for her to try to ensure with all she'd been through that her continued wealth of being and gradual health remained in tact.

They were nice to Toppa and me too, up to a point. We were just little kids and they were cordial. But, still, we weren't blood kin, part of the family and we were therefore, for the most part—left out.

Either Mr. George or one of his brothers, Charlie, Kent or Rocky, would faithfully be at the front of grand mom's house each week, to pick Miss Honey up. They'd whisk her away back to their Love around her other family, which stretched all over the city, from uptown and out on the hill, to the rolling hills of the Edgemont suburbs. Toppa and I got to go too, once or twice.

We pined away our days and held our breaths the entire time she was gone. We Loved her so much and her leaving to spend the day with her father, Mr. George, was just another example of things we'd come to steel ourselves against to bear and expect, even though we were to be denied. We greeted each occasion they'd bring her back as special cause to celebrate. And we'd both be at grand mom's front door to greet her and swallow her up with smeared, wet kisses. The three of us back together. Finally able to relax and breathe again once more.

Mr. George finally had had enough of visiting his only child at grand mom's weekly, and demanded that Miss Honey come live with him. This broke our hearts, even more-so than being virtually abandoned by our mother. But there was no curtailing him. He had his parental rights and grand mom Mavis was doing all she could not to struggle in keeping us three boys in check. Honey moving to her father's was just a small break she needed and deserved to relieve her of some of the daunting pressures of raising her child's children—all on a budget that never appeared to increase.

Towards the start of the coming school year, Toppa and I were supposed to enter the fifth grade. He'd failed the fourth once, which placed us now, a tag-team, in sometimes the same classes. Grandmom had busied herself making hasty preparations to enroll us at Woodward Elementary just a stone's throw and across the street from the front door of her house. She sent off to *SEARS* via mail order, buying us both warm corduroy pants suits with matching jackets, shirts and undergarments, complete with the same *sporty* tube sock collections grandpop Rob, bought frequently for uncle Bem-Bem.

I'll tell you boy-o... We were stylin'! We were all very excited as we waited anxiously for the new semester to start.

Suddenly one evening, as the three of us boys has just been scolded for wrestling around on the carpet following a *Flip Wilson* re-run on the TV, the phone rang hauntingly. I was sitting there munching on the last of what was left of my plastic baggie's contents which had originally been filled with *CHARLES CHIPS*. I took note of how grand mom had quickly turned away and had exited the room, immediately after answering it.

I wondered... waiting patiently, to see if something would develop. I was the one always on Mama'n watch. Dreaming frequently, of seeing her at a bus stop or of her standing at the foot of my bed, appearing magically, coming to reclaim us, all our fears and worries no longer of concern, to a beautiful home located in a happiness filled—wherever. Trying hard to listen to the conversation grand mom was having in the kitchen, it wasn't long before a figment of my dreams would soon come true.

"Toppa... A-ree!" Went screeching out grand mom's familiar call.

She always called me by my given name, Avery, refusing to call me by my nickname, just a fantasy approaching a color—Blu. And she never just called one of us. She forever grouped us together, whether we were in trouble or in her strengths of a productive life's worth of an apportionment of Love that she gave so well.

If she bought for one, she bought for the other. Usually, when she took off after us, with an orange hot-wheel track, to discipline us, it was usually the two of us getting the spanking, not just one of us—and Bem-Bem got his fair share too.

That Woman had more Love in her and we could see it daily, even when we broke her heart by stressing her out with our shenanigans of mischievous clamor.

When we were both standing in front of her, she handed the phone first, to Toppa. I could see the beginnings of a fateful tear begin to slide its way down the side of her face as the inevitability of change began to make its way for her out and away from her kitchen.

"It's your mother," she almost choked in a whisper. She walked out of the room, her reaction to Mama'n calling a confusing surprise to us.

Instead of being elated, as we eventually were, her feelings mounted more along the lines of a poorly hidden, maternal disgust of impatience. The kind a hopeful father experiences just following his son's third try at having dropped out of college.

Toppa and I lit up like two little chocolate Christmas trees. All visions of our memories and thoughts of former abuses teemed with our recent abandonment were very fickly instantly swept from our minds and forgotten.

I danced around beside him, barely able to conceal my bursting excitement of waiting for my turn. When that time finally came, I took a steadying breathe and sent her only four words.

"Mama'n? Where are you?"

She told me she was in town. But that we couldn't tell anyone until she was actually there, at grand mom's house to pick us up.

"Mama'n? When will you be here?" I engaged her further.

"Soon, Boy—Damn it!" Came her frustrated reply.

I could tell that I had somehow already pissed her off and sought to hunker away from continuing our conversation. Passing the phone back to grand mom, I quickly left the room. My former excitement and happiness completely canceled, my former elation now developing into a cry.

She'd hurt my feelings by swearing at me. *Me!*

It had be me who'd gotten into countless fights, with even life-long friends, like Deric Meters, who'd caused me to display my Buster tendencies as I beat him from one end of Boas Street to the other, for making the slightest suggestion of blemish to her honor and her character. Me who'd held out hope, day in and day out, of her returning, while Toppa never indicated any emotion whatsoever concerning her and Miss Honey was lost, off living the good life with her father.

I didn't understand her.

Grandmom gathered the two of us up, packed what little bit of stuff she'd bought us, and we all waited for Mama'n to make an appearance.

When she did finally arrive, she entered grand mom's house as if everything in all our lives was and had been just hunky dory. Not a hint at having been gone for such an extended length of time, leaving only fifty dollars cash and a handful of food stamp vouchers to ensure the welfare of *her* three children. No mom, "Thank you for being there for me once again. I'm an irresponsible lout for leaving my kids with a mad woman." No—nothin'.

I was having a hard time figuring out who was worse? Audrey or Buster?

Toppa and I, when you think about it, couldn't win for losing with either one of them. The only consolation, Audrey, (Mama'n) hadn't yet taken anyone's life.

Or hadn't she?

It sure felt like she was attempting to kill us kids slowly with all her unsteady tomfoolery she was pulling off. She'd subjected us to things we should never even have known about, let alone have experienced, in our young, pliable boyhood existences.

I can say all of that. She was my Mama'n. It was safe for me to talk bad about her. But I'd still gouge out the eyeballs of anyone else alluding, albeit correctly, to the fact that she wasn't anything other than perfect, the not so well hidden facts plainly evident in our lifestyle just the same.

Before we all knew it, we were safely passing Pittsburgh and then Cincinnati on a rickety, smelly old Greyhound bus. It was on the outskirts of St. Louis that we all thought we were going to die. Turns out, our bus driver had been stealing himself nips of liquor and in his inebriated stupor, he hit an approaching car at an exorbitant rate of speed. I remember contemplating an approaching dusk while watching out my window, as the poor victim, a lady, and her car shot sweepingly across the freeway in full view upon crushing impact.

We were held up for hours, while the Missouri State Troopers sorted out the particulars trying to piece together what had actually taken place.

After handcuffing and carting the driver off to pay penance for his irresponsible act, we waited an additional four hours for the Greyhound home office to provide us with an additional, more suitable replacement.

We spent four full captive days in the tomb of that bus. It seemed Greyhound stopped in every nook of every cranny of every po-dunk town along the way. On more than one occasion, I'd become restless and had suffered the wrath of Mama'n pinching me and twisting the pinch so painfully in the upper, interior soft-skin of my bicep that today, I still have the mark.

Very quickly, it was beginning to feel like old times...

When we finally arrived at our destination of El Paso, Texas, Toppa and I stood in shock as sweltering waves of choking heat hit us squarely in our faces as we disembarked the bus at the downtown terminal. It was almost fall and still the place was so hot you could literally see the heat. Coming from the cool, humid breezes of Pennsylvania, we could barely believe it was all real.

He and I knew things could be worse. What we didn't know—could kill us.

His actions suggested, "We'd a' been better off staying back at grand mom's."

But she was our Mama'n. We were her children. And we belonged with her, no matter the circumstance or situation.

Mama'n didn't talk much to us during our trip about where we would eventually be staying. Her previous confident thoughts and demeanor were replaced with the discomforting appearance of a circumspect, nervous tic, complete with solemn rocking to match the darkening color of the rings beneath her eyes in varying rows. Stealing quick looks in her direction, she appeared to be lost in the safety of an all-consuming trance. I wasn't sure if it was contentment and a final settling of ease or the rabid consequence of depression and depravity I was witnessing as it appeared take hold of my worried mother.

We were deposited on Skylark Way. Egbert, for some reason hadn't wanted to drive us directly up to the front door and instead dropped us all off about a block away from our new home. As we made our way through the streets, houses more beautiful and different than any we'd ever seen before began to surround us on a narrowly spaced, almost drastically clean avenue. They were all one-story dwellings. Their yards manicured, sculpted and immaculate in ways we'd never known was even possible. Nice, new Mercedes and Cadillac's could be seen all around. In some driveways, two of the same or an assortment of other high-end vehicles lingered.

Toppa and I held our breaths, playfully plucked each other, as we jutted forward just to make sure what we were seeing was in fact real. We smiled at each other. Mama'n had hit the jackpot! Were we suddenly somehow—*RICH!*

When we'd entered the front of our own new house, the two of us were ecstatic. I remember running through the long hallways taking time to stop each trip to count then re-count each of the bedrooms (There were three of them)! I kept a guarded eye out for Mama'n, unsure of being brought to paying penance for such purely naïve abandon.

Unsure of being happy, still I flew through the swinging doors, into the huge kitchen, chasing and high-five'ng Toppa. It was, for a very brief moment, a time for the two of us to be free spirits. For a millisecond, we were just little boys, instead of soldierous men, no longer charged with finding ways of fending off enemy after enemy threatening impressionably to massacre us.

Our happiness at being returned to at least a facade of a simpler promise of normalcy overshadowed the fact that the entire house was bare-bones empty. Not a stick of furniture sat awaiting use in any of the rooms on the interior.

When we finally did calm down to take notice, Mama'n told us *Uncle* Richard had all of our stuff—*at the warehouse*. And he would be bringing it by to us before long with increasing haste.

Of course, we believed her. That's the wonder of being young and a kid. No matter the amount of disappointments, you always had that inane ability to trust and trust again those whom you Loved no matter how they'd hurt you and let you down so errantly in the past. Optimism is a wonderful gift of strength GOD bestows upon little children. Had he not, none of them would ever survive, to tell their own lies and build up their own piles of disappointments for their children.

The four of us slept that first evening, huddled together on a single mattress as we were plagued by fits of utter freezing cold. El Paso can be unbearable in the winter evenings without heat. Amid a swath of thinly threaded blankets and sheets, we tried desperately to bundle up and to focus on the positives of being there together in our new home.

I began to silently wonder where Egbert was. Where had he been at the time it came to pick us up down at the station? Why hadn't he made certain the heat was on? What about our furniture—Our bicycles and our beds? Something didn't sit right with what Mama'n had told us.

These things didn't hold a candle to the worst of what would soon become our newest worries.

FOOD!

While the house was nice and all, pristine and clean with a beautifully landscaped, sculpted yard, just like the others around it, the truth finally came out. All of our belongings were being held at an Allied Van Lines warehouse—For ransom. It would cost more than fourteen-hundred bucks, money that Mama'n obviously didn't have, to reclaim it all and for the four of us to once again lay our heads down in comfort on our own beds.

Seems *Uncle* Richard, hadn't cut her such a golden *deal* after all.

We kissed all of our stuff, a fully loaded tractor-trailer, *GOODBYE*. We never saw a speck of any of it again. No leather couch, Mr. George had bought to replace the beaten cloth furniture Mama'n had had since the days of Ollie and Buster. No bunk beds, the tops of which I'd stood upon, with a red cape tied lightly about my neck, at five playing *SUPERMAN*, just before I launched off, leaping in a hunch to be met by the tile floor at Toppa's shuffling feet below rewarding me with my very first concussion.

Mama'n was infuriated. She had to call Mr. George to come up from his mother's house to rush me to Harrisburg Polyclinic Hospital for x-rays.

The last time I'd been there was during birth. No baptismal or birth certificates even. Every facet of our former lives lost, completely stuffed inside the dark interior of that warehoused van.

Toppa, Miss Honey and me soon began to share single peanut butter and jelly sandwiches, once a day, for sustenance.

Egbert had duped Mama'n. Although he smiled a lot, drove a nice, new car and talked a smooth, suckering game, she'd been hipped to his game, by of all people, his own, younger sister, Marilyn. Not only was he unprepared for us, in providing the normal things expected of a ready-made family, the fact that the bum was already married and kept wife and kids in a comfort different than the squalor of our own on the West side (The good part) of town, caused Mama'n to almost bust a blood vessel.

She was shocked, instantly frightened and furious!

What had she expected? Her cake, a...aand' icing too?

She'd just met the dude. He'd used her. She'd used him. Call it a wash and move on making your day bearable...Shit!

Get over it—face facts.

And face them, she did. But I'm not so sure if she was ever really able to get over the disappointment and heartbreak of having been so easily deceived. It's most difficult for the most selfish to easily swallow receipt of the same treatment in return.

For Toppa and me, school again became our saving factor. It was our first experience intermingling among a predominantly Mexican or Latino majority. The daily *manna'* we received there, more than we'd seen in weeks. Rapidly developing pack rat skills by this time, we inconspicuously stole away choice items into our backpacks. Sometimes waiting for other kids to wantonly discard uneaten apples, fruit cups of applesauce, vegetables—YUCK! We'd store each item, stealing the briefest of brief comparisons from time to time, like candy received during Halloween Trick-or-Treating, to cart it all home, so that Honey and Mama'n would also be able to eat.

On weekends, he and I pilfered every kind of items from the local Circle K in order to eat. We became master thieves. We were soon so adept at being able to look a helpless store clerk firmly in the eye, while lifting things—that we brought home essential items like, bread, milk, bologna, cheese, even cigarettes for Mama'n, and disposable diapers for Honey, all under the attendant's watchful gaze.

For two, former Christian school urchins, we sure didn't stop to think on or feel guilty about the actions we were undertaking. It was natural for us to so easily be capable of resorting to such extremes. When you're desperate and hungry, all formerly recited proverbs of memorized versus are tossed uselessly out the window. We utilized the soft deceitful and believable images our faces offered up as well as our developing techniques of graft to keep ourselves strong and nimble.

Mama'n continued to wallow unproductively in her own, self-inflicted mess.

And it began to get to her. It became so conflicting for her, that believe it or not, she actually began to spend less time with the three of us at home. Suddenly our home life structure became Toppa, at thirteen, Miss Honey at five and me all of eleven. And we were left alone for lengthy stretches, at times twenty-four to ninety-eight hours at a stretch.

All terrors of her former heavy-handed discipline ceased. She could no longer bring herself to scold and teach us, for and about things that she would have tried to kill us for previously.

We never questioned her—At first.

Initially, we'd figured she was spending her time during the day doing the right thing, out looking for a job. But, she wasn't.

What she'd actually been doing, was hanging out in a downtown hotel, *The Continental*, with a new guy she'd just met who called himself *Baltimore and sometimes Dirty Red.* His real name was Charles Cantrelle. He rented a room there, and appeared to be in hiding from a life, which if it ever caught up with him completely, threatened to sink him with canceling annihilation, as he was assuredly stalked by the wickedness of his own past. He was as shady a character as you could possibly see. A dirty half-stocking covered naturally red, kinky hair, cut short, but processed and laid back like a woman's perm. Dimpled specks of red splotches shot lightly to cover in spurts the entire front of his face. Dude had freckles! The sockets of his eyes jutted out at you, holding deep, yellow balls of terror. And he always seemed to be reaching into the furthest recesses of your soul, never registering the slightest surprise with those peepers. You would just shiver in death in his presence as it shrouded, surrounding him completely.

Because of that dirty stocking he always seemed to have half-on-half-off his head, my mind now, as it did then, always wants to refer to him as *DIRTY* instead of his former name, *BALTIMORE—RED.*

Eventually, when her conscience got the best of her, she'd come to retrieve us to take us in tow to visit with him. Mr. Cantrelle was so macabre, that after the first time meeting him, none of us ever wanted to return to the hotel with her during the many trips she made there, stuck in the interior of that suffocatingly tiny room ever again. We were content to stay in our furniture-less house, with no lights and padlocked running water. Mama'n hadn't paid the bill since we moved in.

We only had each other, once more.

Soon the eviction notice came. Egbert had at least paid the first couple month's rent. But that had quickly become a mute point, as the tattered pages of an unstoppable calendar swiveled forward without fortune in a rotating quiver. It was time for her to get her shit together and make plans for her next, eventual move.

It was about this time that I first began to develop an explanation for friends of why I attended so many schools throughout the years.

Our next foray landed us in the John Taylor project homes. They were located off Railroad and Hondo Pass. Brand new, they came complete with a huge backyard, two bedrooms, and a beautiful, park-like setting where a community pool and gymnasium were co-located. While we were no longer in the luxury of Skylark Way, we still had a roof over our heads and a little bit of furniture donated by a local church.

But, we still had very little food. And the food we did have had to be consumed right away and couldn't be kept.

After our first two months of living there, Mama'n had let the electricity bill lapse. This turned our fridge into an enormous space-swallowing paperweight, there only to hold down the linoleum. We were once again in the dark. The water bill payment followed quickly in identical failure. Candles and borrowed water became our daily flavors.

Our only solace during that time was the company of a family of friends including (One Toe) Rimmy, called that because he only had one toe, the big one, on each of his feet—and that was it!. The result of a careless baby sitter who'd placed him in a scalding tub of water in preparation for bathing him without first gauging its temperature after she'd drawn it. There was his little brother, Jimmy, and his older sister, and my pre-teen infatuation, Taura.

Our parents hung together. Instead of working jobs and paying bills, like normal folks, these citizens drank, smoked weed and partied all night playing bid-whist, tunk, or spades, gambling scoops of pennies better spent taking care of their children.

The four of us boys all attended Mary I. Stanton Elementary. We were serious partners, down for each other through thick and thin in whatever ways were possible.

We actually burglarized the public pool together.

It was easy. We pulled it off without much planning and without a technical thieving, hitch.

Without fully realizing it, I'd noticed one day that at the end of each session, the lifeguards at the pool would only haphazardly check the individual stalls in the bathrooms to ensure all the little kids were on their ways home and didn't get locked up inside, left alone in the bewildering darkness.

Just so happens, we got into the pool for free during its summer sessions. And I always made certain to do my number two's there, just prior to closing. The filth and stench of our toilet at home was so inundating with disease and nausea, due to no running water but bowels that were still being relieved there, I'd make my way to the cold, smelly public toilets of the pool to carry out my business and remain fresh.

I plotted out and relayed a quickly put together plan to the fella's.

"Anybody in there…Heeell-oooo? Is there any bo-deeee in there?"

The four of us stood in our high top jeepers behind stall doors atop the seats of the toilets. Nobody came in to make a thorough check. Waiting a little while longer for the last lifeguard to make his departure, we made our move.

And, we were home-free.

After boosting little Jimmy up to place hands on the cash box teeming with perhaps a week's take, we crept through the rear doors leading to the outside, where we hurled an entire roll of tickets into the pool. Why we did that, I have no clue.

I do know. It was a boneheaded move. We were four incorrigibles. Unaware that those thousands of tickets were going to clog up the pool's filter and consequently keep us in the house, weeks on end, while expensive repairs were made to the pump during an extensive period in which the pool was out of commission.

But, while we had no pool to swim in to knock the edge off an unmerciful summer's heat, we were in good spirits still. Having committed our first, real crime together, without the slightest hitch, we were on cloud nine. It had been a synch.

Then, we ran off to the nearest Whattaburger, a favorite hamburger joint which none of us ever got to go to—cause' our parents never had any money. Once there, our quartet of ghetto pool bandits feasted joyously on what ever it was we had cause or want for to order.

Our full take that day amounted to rolls and rolls of quarters totaling more than one hundred-twenty dollars.

By that time in our lives, we were so tainted that we even boldly ordered bags of food to go, for all our parents and siblings. We carted them back home with our bellies full and smiles on our faces, in triumph.

Walking into the house with our booty caused very little alarm for Mama'n. She merely accepted her cut and warned us not to bump into the newly erected shrine she'd put up in her newfound worship of Buddha as we sidled by.

She'd found a new anomaly to include in her life.... Supposedly the little statue of the fat guy supplied her strength through chanting.

After finishing my third milkshake and eating till I felt I was gonna' burst, I found there was no getting around being bombarded by the slumbering stench of that bathroom. In all the excitement of pulling off our caper, I'd forgotten to include my daily constitutional relief as part of our plans back at the pool.

I was now about to split a gut in frustration.

I'd just have to carry on and take care of business. Then, meander outside to see if the neighbors would let me fill up a bucket with water from their outside spigot to bring back into the house to wash the heaps of mine and others' defecate down completely.

This was our status for about six months. It got so bad that the unseemly things we became forced to live with and accept in our daily lives began to appear to us to us be plainly normal. It was nobody else's business what kinds of things were taking place inside the four corners holding up the walls of our integrally unblessed home.

Or so Mama'n repeatedly told us...

It wasn't long after this that she had finally visited a place inside her own head which screamed in stark raving, bloody horror, that her children were unkempt, and suffering silently from borderline malnutrition, as they lived in putrid squalor.

Finally giving up...

She sought solace in the one place she'd always been taught by her own father as a youth that she could trust.

She sought out a *helping hand*...from the church.

"A man who refuses to stand for something that he truly believes in will eventually fall for anything"

Chapter Four
'SLAPBOXING'

Towards the end of our stay in the Taylor projects, a different type of people began to surface in our lives. Suddenly Mama'n was coaxing us to get into our Sunday best more often. She'd even finally discarded that little box shrine to Buddha, who had seemingly brought us little help. I was glad to see that thing poking its cagey head out the top of our garbage outside. I was more than tired of her and Rimmy's moms being on their knees chanting without much grace, their fitful, *NUM-YAHOLL-HO'-REN-GAY-KEEO's*... When they'd finished, the two of them kicking back on the only two pieces of furniture we had, a couple of chairs in the living room area we'd salvaged from a dumpster, finished worshipping, but now passing a joint between them.

The sweet, acrid stench of subtle escape mixed in among them both to take the place of relief Buddha had yet to send them in offering reply.

Those clothes for some reason made me ache. I hated this. Toppa's shoes no longer fit. And my butt was threatening with each movement to come bursting out through a pair of polyester pants which were a perfect fit just a year and a half before.

For a short while, she even began to slack off on the amount of weed she was smoking on a daily basis. We'd be trudged along with her, sometimes her pulling and pushing us beside her with earnest.

We must've visited what felt like, a hundred different churches, seeking help.

First the Catholic churches. With their stodgy services, all pent up and hollow, there was no way they were for us. Besides, they weren't really looking to help nobody no-way. Then the Lutherans and the

Presbyterians... These we found just a bit off center. Not fully able to place much trust in the folks we encountered there, their concern always

seemed to fly in the face of—smiling at you endearingly, shaking your hand, pushing you along, while making certain to keep you fully, at an arms length away unless you were donating.

Shoot! We needed some good ole' down home embracin' that was gonna' get us through. We kept on, Sunday after Sunday, keeping up our journey.

The suffering continued.

We even tried the Baptists. She thinking, surely they'd help us. That was the religion she'd been raised up in. There was no way they wouldn't bend over backwards to see that she and her children were provided relief.

She was mistaken once again. All they wanted to do was explain to her, how it was more GOD-like and humane to consider one or the other, more forsaken actions.

"*Simply permit us to help you separate the children for a short time—and place them each in the loving care and guidance of good, Christian homes. While you work on yourself, child, and then are better able to withstand the things life has placed upon you.*"

Sage advice, if you ask me. But Mama'n wasn't buying in to their unhelpful themes.

When we'd been introduced to the Church of GOD in Christ, we felt our prayers heard and the magnificence of the end of our torture at hand. The people there were of a predominantly American of African descent majority.

Had to call them that. Over a long period of time, we had gracefully transitioned through the point of being called *Coloreds or Blacks.* The new name now society had penned for us was... *AFRICAN AMERICANS.*

Sound better? Just barely...

Today, I'm just an American. Leaving every little square box on any type of application or form blank beside the *Black/Negro* column, I always write in, just a simple—*AMERICAN.* I do this refusing to be left out of the splendor and glory of the greatness of this nation's *Constitution*—All because the majority of the idiots who had originally conceived, generated and signed it—owned slaves, whom they were too ignorant at the time to include in the meanings of the part which declared: "*We hold these truths to be self-evident that all men are created equal.*"

Somebody lied!

American or if it must be defined, American of African descent is just fine—for me.

These folks provided our tattered and exhausted family a warm and hearthy welcome. They fed us and clothed us. Some even welcomed us into their homes. They even promised to do whatever it was they could, about that ole' rent, lights, gas and water bill problem Mama'n gave the appearance she'd been fighting with so profusely.

They sent teams of people over to our house. They blessed our home and us with it in cheerful joy and even scared up some inviting laughter. But we still remained distant. We were bound. Unable to fully choose to settle our full trust in them, we remained detached.

That is, until the lights did come back on. The fridge began to take on a whole new meaning as it actually began to be put back into service, with food in it for a fair amount of time. The toilet flushed and Mama'n even began to again make us home-cooked meals from time to time.

We Loved this! It was almost how most of our friends on the West side had lived. Although she hadn't done it in a long while, Mama'n was the best cook we've had the privilege of sampling, even in my fatness to date.

For a short while, things were good.

Mama'n still had no work. Heck, during that entire time we had nothing, I can't ever recall her really going out to look for a job.

And she'd never really given up her almost daily, dangerous liaison with the heart-wrenching, *Dirty Red.*

Mr. Cantrelle, for all his scary, outward appearances, was good to Mama'n in a way. I wasn't privy to the full extent of their confusing relationship. But he always provided her snippets of cash and for us, candies or pastries, when she left him to return home hoping the three of us were still alive.

As history would have it, although not confirmed the same person, there exists an excerpt in the back of my head concerning a character, known only as Baltimore Red. This one was a running mate to a young, *Detroit Red,* along with one, *ST. Louis Red,* 'back in the day'.

Detroit Red had been a nefarious thief, pimp, gambler and hustler. A preacher's son, who's father had created the Universal Negro Improvement Association (UNIA) and who was ultimately murdered sticking to the dedications of his beliefs at the hands of hateful racists, he was contrarily known for his own ruthless nature and was held to be black hearted and rotten beyond all contrition.

And then there was St. Louis Red, a reputed cohort of both Detroit's, and Baltimore's. But this Red had chosen a different path. Seeking, instead of crime and racketeering, to become a classy, charismatic, but gruff comedian, he more assisted people to experience joy in their lives by bringing them to knee-buckling laughter.

Detroit Red went a long way towards committing himself to change in transforming his life as well. He discovered while in prison, a place of refuge in the teachings of the Honorable Elijah Muhammad. He offered himself as a Nation of Islam convert. And through the mastery of *his* struggles and strengths of knowledge he learned therein, he took on an entirely new, name-changing persona. He went on to become, in leaps and bounds, a viable, number-one threat to that day's fearful, American society with his mantra of demanding equality for Americans of African descent, "*BY ANY MEANS NECESSARY*".

The enamoring substance of his words began to draw Americans of African descent closer to his principles as he threatened to frightfully lead a nation of oppressed peoples, out of slave confrontation steeped of ignorant mentalities, into a rapidly recognized freedom, uplifting Black Nationalism.

It was following this, after a fateful pilgrimage to the holy city of Mecca, that he again made a sweeping change and began to renounce the fervor and malice of his former teachings. His eyes had indeed been opened in Mecca. No longer was every white man to be referred to as a blue-eyed demon. He'd supped and met with many sharing the same faith bearing white skin while visiting during his trip.

He'd also began to discover disheartening truths about the roles and acts of the man, formerly known as Elijah Poole, who now referred to himself, following conversion, as Elijah Muhammad.

Rumor had reached him that it appeared Muhammad was hypocritical in his treatment of vows of fidelity as he wallowed in the blemished chastity of a number of faithful young girls residing among the leader's congregation. Muhammad and Red extended the fury of their disagreements when Muhammad censured him, forbidding him to continue to speak out or to teach in the temple. He met his end both prematurely and abruptly, at the hands of other American men who in conspirational assassination, took his life, with his young family watching as he spoke.

And through this, he has materialized, in today's American history, as an icon of vigorous demand for equality and racial harmony among the masses.

I never thought Mr. Baltimore Red, ever held a candle to standing up in the footsteps of his former associates. From his appearance of unhealthy circumstance when I knew him, it indicated he had chosen the way of so many young dealers and gangsters who never evolved to feel the rush of happiness evident in being able to watch grandchildren play as they themselves approached old age. And even then, he was a dying ember of his former self. He held on to Mama'n for a while. Eventually, he expired in that hotel, victim of a heroin overdose.

The Church of GOD and Christ members soon became frustrated with Mama'n and her continued lack of efforts. They became overwhelmed in their own attempts of saving us while expecting much more of a fight from her than she put up in matching them. It wasn't long before the exhaustive measure of their tempered patience soon began to reach their definitive limits.

They retreated and pulled up camp to move out.

And, suddenly, and even more rapidly than it seemed before, things slew back in a crippling direction, to the former nature of our promising demise.

Toppa and I once again, picked ourselves up and prepared for re-entering things that would ultimately support us with a pallid determination our own Mama'n could never muster. We prowled and scavenged the more, well—heeled neighborhoods surrounding our own.

In one day's catch, I remember the four of us (Rimmy and Jimmy were never far behind) walking through a particularly affluent area. No one ever called the cops on us back then. After all, we were just four harmless little boys, instead of the gang who'd just robbed you blind, while the entire family had been out at a graduation dinner.

As we passed a particular house we upped our level of boldness. We could plainly see the inhabitants, having breakfast on the screened porch of a comfortable

veranda. They were all there, Mamma, Papa, little Tommy and Susie. Heck, there may even have been a grandma or grandpa—an entire, fully functioning family sitting idly while being unscrupulously ripped them off.

The compelling meaning and nature of this meant nothing to the four of us.

Our only focus was on the awaiting images of the four, brand new bicycles parked, during more normal times, *for them*, securely beneath the opened window screen directly in sight of the family's gathering cluster. And the money we could get for them once we sold them to a Mexican guy we all knew who dealt with such matters without remorse.

Rimmy and I took the lead. Toppa and Jimmy acted as lookouts. Heeding primitive hand signals we'd each come to understand as an anterior sort of complex code in our endeavors, he and I inched forward, hunched on the ground beneath the window. When the signal was given—to GO! We both inch-wormed our ways to being within inches directly beneath the window. Upon Rimmy's determination that it was safe to continue, we pulled up and darted for the bikes. Hopping aboard one, and grabbing the handlebars of the others, we pedaled slowly away, with the confidence and quiet experienced of ice-cold, cat burglars.

We were four boys definitely headed for bids in the big house, given time to further develop.

With Toppa and Jimmy riding now as well, all four bikes were in our possession. I remember peering back to cover a venturing glance on my *"six"* only to find the continued peace and tranquility of a still sleeping nation, as the family went on with breakfast, not yet unaware of our treachery in tow.

Normally, we would have pedaled directly to our fence's house. But, this time, we allowed ourselves a detour. Either Toppa or Rimmy had begun to complain in exasperated tones that they had to go Boo-Boo. "And they had to do it now!" They'd said.

Giving in to the emergency of their complaints, we made a rapid turn and ended up along the connecting streets of our own neighborhood.

As we drew up to the front of our house, we could see Mama'n standing there, saying much of nothing, wrapped up in conversation with their mother, Miss Sarah.

Toppa and Jimmy threw each other a telling look.

Both of our mothers were extremely high.

My only thoughts were, *"Where'd they get the money to continually keep themselves in such hazed—over intoxication?"*

Looking at the two of them, still straddling that stolen bike, I felt unexplainably cheated.

For a long time after that, I kicked myself figuratively. I should have caused the four of us to either ditch the bikes and wait out the pleading bowels of the member who'd brought us to this, or merely continued on, to a ravine at the side of our complex, where he could have taken a shit with peace, using what was left of his already crusty underwear—to wipe his butt when he was done. We could have then returned to the house on foot where we would get in touch with Jose', our fence, and be on our ways to perhaps even more of a take than our public pool event had yielded us.

We stupidly steered the bikes, smiling like idiots, attempting to think fast how we would cover our tracks, right up to the front of the house.

And...

To her credit, Mama'n suddenly pulled out an exhibited edge of her former self.

Watching us ride up, as if we sat atop two-wheeled vehicles she herself had purchased, with smiles on our faces, totally disrespecting her as we sought replete disregard once again for our actions, she began.

"Ohhhhh....*HEELLL-NO!* No you little Nigga's didn't just go and rip off somebody's bikes and ride em' right up here in my face, right in front of my house!" She flailed her arms and shuffled her hair atop her head with displeasure.

Toppa, Rimmy and Jimmy, all looked over to the end of our straddling line, at me.

WHAT!

Why me? What did I do—Force em' to get on the bikes and ride away with me into the sunset?

Wasn't my fault some-body couldn't hold their got-doggit' bowels!

Pulling our collective gazes back to Mama'n, we all witnessed her now sitting, with her legs folded beneath her, with her head bowed lightly, held in both hands, in the exact spot she'd stood in when she first began to yell at us. She only sat there on the curb and cried. The immediate rage of her welcoming lecture, a mere sputter of the reaction we could have expected just a year before.

She was a beaten Woman.

Finally looking up, she gestured toward the house.

"Blu...?"

Keeping to firmly ingrained instructions of habits of old, I answered...not sure at first and cautiously

"Yes, Ma'am"?

She peered at me. Offering at first only silence. Then, shaking her head slowly, from side to side, she accosted me with, "Where'd you get those got'-dammed bikes?"

Turning about, seeking to enlist some silent sense of help from my accomplices, she yelled at me, while flinging her tiny frame towards me, stepping closer in a threatening huff.

"BOY! Don-chew' look at them. I didn't ask none o' them."

"Yes, Ma'am." I lowered my head slightly in respectful cower.

"I'm asking *you*!"

My only thoughts were *NEVER TELL ON YOURSELF! NEVER TELL ON YOURSELF, NEVER...*

"We, ummm.... Weee'...found em'—in the ravine." A lie, I felt, couldn't get me in anymore trouble. I knew...My goose was already cooked.

Mama'n began to cry harder. She'd all but given up hope.

I was certain, and I actually remember thinking this that very moment—that she thought she could envision the futures of her two sons as they were well on their way, to mirroring the shackled footsteps of their absentee, very abusive father.

Her head back in her hands, she instructed me, crazily. "Blu, go inside and call the police."

You should have seen four pairs of pre-teenage eyes light up with all-consuming fear.

Even Rimmy and Jimmy's moms stepped forward to begin to question her intentions.

"Weezo? Wait a minute now." Her hands placed firmly on her hips, in preparation for protecting her own. "What chew gone' do?" Came her next pursed expression.

Of course, I did as I was told. In my mind, I equated Maman's loss of marbles in telling me to call the cops to her being explicitly mad at me for ruining hers and Miss Sarah's high so abruptly.

When the squad car arrived, Mama'n informed the officers something like—her boys had found four bikes, lying in the ditch of a ravine as they were returning home from choir practice. Course they never believed her for a second, I'm sure. The two sarcastic patrolmen hefted the bikes into the backseat and trunk of their unit and they drove off leaving behind unconfirmed promises that if anyone didn't come forward to claim the bikes, within ninety days, they'd return them to us, and they'd be ours for good—for keeps.

We rightly held out very little hope of that ever happening. We never heard back from them and we never saw those bikes again.

Through it all, looking back, I remember cocking my head slightly to one side, holding Maman's gaze. She shook her head slowly, up and down, while rolling her eyes at me, matching that with the pursing of her lips. I chanced a smile at her with a careful uncertainty. She refused to return my gesture. In this way she could tell herself that she'd done the right thing and hadn't chosen to offer us any more of a misguided sense of approval for our failed adventure.

I wished she had known at the time just how proud of her—her actions brought me to be.

She'd done *THE RIGHT* thing. It had been a very long time since we had witnessed that from her.

It also told me that she hadn't entirely given up hope for us, and for herself, completely.

I just stood there, still perplexed why she had singled me out as the group's spokesman and eventual fall-guy-leader.

Back then, I didn't know.

Today, I'm solidly certain why.

I was the un-appointed leader in everything the group had ever undertaken.

And, to her, I was therefore the one responsible. The person she knew she could *always* hold accountable. Or hold on to.

It was during this period, directly following the bicycling incident that our stay in the Taylor homes began to come to an end. Mama'n had begun to wither even more in her determination to keep our fledgling family upright. She'd begun to become felled by the rigors of what she'd seen us be forced to struggle through thus far. Her ability to counter the many obstacles she'd previously found ways of ducking or leaping over, began to falter. It was the very first time I'd ever witnessed her—begin to give in to the fight.

Unexpectedly the people from the Baptist church were back. But, this time, they brought with them, hoards of capricious social workers armed with orders from demanding, absentee judges. Mama'n all but tossed up her hands under the weight of the newest, rolling thunder.

Keeping with their original plan, Toppa, Miss Honey and I were to be sliced up and diced up. Separated! To be carted off toward different homes of strange families. For Mama'n, if they had had their ways, her fate was jail and further prosecution—For neglect and child—endangerment in a grand way.

But, Mama'n being Mama'n, she somehow stretched out with the esteemed vapor of a nimbly designed final breath seeking escape.

After pleading with and finally convincing the invaders to at least give her another day or two before yanking away her babies, she went next door to the neighbor's and she placed two, collect calls back to Pennsylvania. The first was to Mr. George, Miss Honey's father.

The second....

To grand mom, Mavis.

The sun hadn't set over the completion of the first day they had allowed her, before Mr. George had shown up in the Taylor projects, rapping gently at our front door to claim his child. Bundling Honey up, along with the miniscule pile of her possessions, he whisked her away, to what Toppa and I thankfully felt for her would be a better life. He left us there, only the uncertainty of quivering, apprehensive—agitation our destinies to endure.

It wasn't long after, that Mama'n said goodbye to us for a short while as well. She didn't have the money to transport us back to the Burg. We went to stay with a nice lady from that Baptist church. They hadn't split the two of us up after all. All I remember of that woman, was, that she was real kind to Toppa and I. And she had a teenage daughter of half-Japanese, half-black descent. She was a beautiful girl, who paid us very little attention. As well, the lady had the worst case of diabetes I have ever seen, even since.

She mostly moved about the comforting interior of her modest home by wheelchair on her bad days. But when she felt well, she'd be up, cooking and cleaning and doing our laundry. Only then would the extreme results of the progression of her disease be plainly evident. A mass of overblown swelling had converted both her legs to bloated, puss-bags of pain-filled tragedy. It was such an advanced stage of stinking decay that her spoiled limbs frightened us whenever we saw them. The skin of the full length of each extremity had split to peeling and cracking like the knuckled texture of an alligator's back, from

knee to bloody, swollen toe. They reminded you of the body of the comic character, Brock, of "*THE FANTASTIC FOUR*".

The fact that this poor Woman had taken us in had appeased the hungered pack of Baptist wolves seeking Maman's head. And I'm certain—secured a place that she wasn't long to see, in heaven.

For a period of about three months, Mama'n was away from us. Doing whatever it was she'd been able to busy herself with. She visited us as much as the lady would permit her to.

During those gatherings, the three of us chose, in unspoken agreement to steer around and off the issue of the status of *our lost*, Miss Honey.

And it wasn't long before Mama'n and the lady (With the entrance of assurances provided via phone with grand-mom, Mavis) had come to agreement of concocting a plan to get Toppa and I out from under the divisive hands of the church for good. The gist of their ultimate arrangement would soon find us back in the familiar surroundings of that Lovely little house with the lining oak trees outside it. We had exited Texas and were headed for Harrisburg, Pennsylvania once more.

Under the cover of darkness, one evening, a light knock was heard on the lady's front door. After being granted access, Mama'n was suddenly there, in the middle of a clouded secrecy, exhorting Toppa and I to, "Hurry up chile! Get da' rest o' yer' things. Let's go!

No! You can't take that....Don't belong ta' you. "

After an exasperated sigh, "Ain't you learned nothing being round' these church people for so long?"

And Toppa and I were on our way back to the Burg. We took an airplane this trip. It was all pretty exciting, our first time taking flight.

We arrived at the Harrisburg Municipal airport. grand-mom, Mavis, and grand-pop Rob met us there, waiting for our hurried return. The two of them together, in crisis, were a funny sight. She gave the orders. He followed them strictly, in silence, while

scrounging up his nose to register displeasure he'd never allow to come out, when the two of them were engaged in something, they truly deemed important.

Toppa and I were once again welcomed into grand-mom's fold. Bem-Bem greeted us excitedly. Happy to have his *PARTNERS IN CRIME* returned to him. We must have slept forever over the course of the next two days. Grand-mom had given stern orders to everyone in the house. "To leave her grandbabies alone for a while....N' let em' rest!

No! ToppaAree can-not come out to play...They are restin'" She'd tell all our friends who ambled by, up to the front porch inquiring how long it would be before they'd again get a crack at us.

She quickly enrolled us in Melrose Middle school. The only city institution with room enough for us that would take us after the start of an already active semester. It was there that I met perhaps the most interesting white man I had ever come across in the harrowing chapters of my very short life.

His name was Allen Woodell. He was my history teacher. About twenty-four, twenty-five years old, he was tall and slim, with greater American features (Blond-Blond hair and the bluest of piercingly blue eyes) and he offered good-hearted attempts at *Real-Honest-to-GOD* teaching. His chiseled, good ole' American boy looks were lost on us.

To us, during the tenure of our lives thus far, white people were people. We hadn't suffered so much yet to become hateful or tempered toward racism like so many others.

He'd entered teaching as a personal calling, following a very eventful, two-year tour in Africa, as a volunteer in the Peace Corps.

Mr. Woodell had a heart of gold! He didn't only teach history. He had a knack about him for calming the scattered reactions of hormone infested pre-pubescent boys and girls both. He went out of his way to instruct us on other, more life necessifying things.

He taught us how to begin to attend to our personal hygiene, how to grasp power over our management of internal angers, and how to conduct ourselves properly when demanding the consideration of—a lady.... as well as other more important items slipping away from our communities, such as self-control.

Mr. Woodell, for me, was a GOD-send.

While I'd always been more than just a good student, I didn't have the best rapport with faculty. This behavior caused me to become enamored in the worst way with the paddle of an all too willing principal Edwards.

I think Mr. Woodell's most intriguing skill was in drawing a bead on the diamonds lying beneath the roughly scarred exteriors of many of his students who would present lesser teachers the complexities of an all-too-unwelcomed challenge.

He could pick us out of a crowd with dexterity. There was Titus. A tall, thickly built boy, with the definitive nature of a big ole' gentle teddy-bear. He had a crush on my cousin, Monique, who also attended the school. Also in our group, was Lem. He was virtually a genius. A stuttering fool once he got excited. So much so, it would take him a full fifteen minutes of sputtering gasps and cut-off breaths just to make a single solitary point. But the boy could sure handle his figures. He could piece together groupings of numbers to come up with six-figured answers to questions it took the rest of us pencils, calculators and a full class period to follow up with.

I would almost miss my bus as a daily occurrence, and sometimes would be forced to trek the full four and a half-mile distance home. All because the three of us would find ourselves, at the end of the day, lost in putting together our collective efforts in a quizzical caper, as we tried desperately to figure out one of Mr. Woodell's educational riddles.

Among other things, I began playing baseball again. That year, I played both pitcher and catcher. More catcher though. I was way too wild for the coach to be able to rely on me for anything other than beaning a kid in the helmet on every other throw.

It was that winter that I first learned to do many things. Such as shoot dice and make even more lethal slingshots out of cutoff two by fours, industrial rubber bands, nails and spring-loaded pins used to hang clothes. Our ammo though remained the near-harmless and plentiful acorn. We played spin the bottle on grand-mom's front porch. There'd be Coolie, a young boy of fifteen, and the unspoken leader of our group of inner-city tag team bandits, his sisters, Gran-MO and Tissy. Then factor in Puffy Anderson, other boys named Rowdy, Steinley, Gus, and Scoottie and Toolie White.

Then there were the other girls, Nelly, Ambria, and Peewee Anderson, and also my distant cousin, Kimmie Peavey. We spent many evenings slobbering and poking at one another, at first on grand-mom's porch, then, when things became more heated and personal, as the games progressed, lying down next to each other on the cold alleyway concrete, the consuming silence of the darkness hiding the fact that our pants were down around our ankles, with our butts moving rhythmically, our cover.

It was also during spring of that year that I first began to discover ways of reaching identical pleasures without having the necessity of having to have one of the girls present.

I was almost thirteen when I first discovered masturbation. Puberty was right around the corner.

Believe it or not, I had been initially introduced to the dastardly deed by a friend and baseball teammate of mine, Aalston Pryor.

Aalston's father was our team's coach. I began spending a lot of time at his house. Grand-mom placed no tether at all on our movements throughout the many blocks surrounding our city neighborhood. Just as long as we checked in from time to time, stayed out of trouble and didn't make too much racket when we finally did return home each day, she had to haul her tired self outta' bed daily, at four-thirty A.M. to catch the five o' clock bus, uptown where she worked as a cook in a retirement home community.

I was upstairs at Aalston's sitting in a fat chair in his den, watching cartoons or something or other, when he threw me for a loop by suggesting he had a cure for what we called our *cockiness* back in the day. He alluded to the fact that what he had in mind would settle us down and assist us in our play—for the better—before that day's game.

At first, I had no clue what he was talking about. Suddenly, with an ill-consuming quickness, he produced an industrial size jar of Vaseline that he'd made materialize from outta' nowhere,. It seemed to have come from beneath the cover of the chair where he'd been sitting. In his anxiousness to usher me in to the depravity of this, his despicable fold, he then whipped out his scrawny little teeter, and after covering it with a well-oiled lather, he began to plainly *JACK AWAY*...

I was dumbfounded and even felt like hitting him.

I knew immediately, right then and there (Didn't take me a second's worth of worried thought) that Aalston Pryor, wasn't a boy I'd be spending too much more time with any more.

I wasn't all that skilled or schooled sexually. But I did know what it meant to *BEAT OFF*. And I also knew that it wasn't something that you ever shared with your best buddy, like a jacket or a drag on a cigarette butt.

But, when I was alone, a million times thereafter, I tried it.

Aalston had planted a seed, *figuratively*.

I also began to do other things, more constructive that year. Bem, Toppa and I got our first real jobs, almost. We worked for a crippled—old man, who always seemed to have dried, encrusted, yellow puss gathering thickly about the corners of both sockets of his watery eyes.

We sold newspapers he provided. Knocking door to door, we traveled after school, until far into the night throughout a project-acreage, known as the Smith homes. It wasn't long before the many dimes we collected for each paper soon became *not enough*; in payment, for the toils of our foot aching labors.

The old man soon shifted us to becoming solicitors. Still moving door to door, this time we sought individual subscriptions. This paid us a good deal more, .50 cents per signature. All we had to do was convince the subscriber to accompany their first month's three-dollar deposit with their signature. And we were paid in cash, at the end of every single night.

But even that wasn't enough for us. We were mere, disrespectful little jackals, caught up in the mediocrity of impoverished, simplistic patterns of thought. Instead of being grateful and simply continuing to work hard for the old man, we devised ways in which we could rip him off completely. We knew when and where his wire-wrapped stacks of papers were dropped off at the beginnings of each new day's morning. We'd be there, sometimes at two and three o'clock in the morning, freezing our behinds off, lying in wait, staking out our booty. The news trucks would toss bundle after bundle before the outsides of still closed stores around our mini community.

We'd abscond away with twenty or thirty bushels. We worked like determined ants. Sometimes making forty and fifty trips pedaling our bikes between the three of us (Bem, Toppa and I) to store what seemed like a thousand or more papers in the safe dry confines of an old abandoned garage we'd found previously during another caper. Once we'd gathered them all there, we'd cut the banding and quickly roll each paper into a .10 cent roll of prosperity.

We'd then work other project homes, the Cooper and Broderick developments.

It was my bright idea to lower our demands for each paper to just a nickel. To garner more of a market share for our ill-gotten products—that got us into trouble.

Soon the old man's subscription seekers, who were still fanning out to work the same hoods we were operating out of, began to be questioned by their consumers. People were suddenly wondering why they were trying to sign folks up for subscriptions to papers pairing out to cost more than the nickel per piece they were able to get them for from us. It wasn't long before the word reached back to the old man.

One day following, when we'd staked out our positions to wait for the delivery trucks, GOD was watching out for us again. We noticed the clamor of a group of thugs hanging out in front of *our* store drops waiting for us. The old man had had enough of us dipping into his accounts. Neither toughened, nor ready for a fight, we naively backed off, allowing our former venture fold. We permitted it to melt away without a fuss.

Setting back to take stock of our apparent near misfortune, we became aware that that was no ordinary, crippled old man that we'd attempted to deceive. That dude had been a racketeer. He had his hands in everything from the newspaper delivery scheme, to the vengeful labors of drug trafficking. He had scores of hoodlums on his payroll. And he could have easily shelled out enough ducats to deal us some broken bones, or worse, had that Angel not been watching over us.

The three of us were effectively scared straight. We suspended all operations infused with graft and began to take on more civil chores. Things like shoveling snow, raking leaves and helping little old ladies cross the street. Not to mention buying and selling, at an exorbitantly marked up price, various candies, to all the other kids running around the block. Due to the abrupt cancellation of our previous endeavors, the three of us quickly adapted to becoming the pushers of an assortment of sugar'd, and easily replaceable, tooth decay causing goods and delicacies. We were the ice cream man walking around.

It didn't matter. To us, in more ways than one, *Enterprise* had solidly become the implanted order of the hour. It had replaced our former airs of dependence. We were sick and tired of leaving our fate to folks who gave every indication they were wholly unprepared or unwilling to *care* for us. And we were beginning to develop a fading patience for those incapable of leading, as well.

For a long while, we just stuck to our candy and chip business. I'd also gone into a side business sweeping up and clearing leaves from outside the local corner store which was nothing more than a converted section of a family home, set up to engross a variety of items prevalent in meeting the needs of those families inhabiting about twenty blocks.

I'd do whatever they needed. Sweep up, clear away leaves and arrange stock. Plus it aided our sweets business. We began to gain our own stock, at a way cheaper price. We also expanded our clientele to include our classmates at Melrose Middle. One of the three of us worked daily shifts. Each morning we'd set up shop above a set of stairs located at one side of the school. We'd dole out taffy, chips, powdered Kool-aid strips, and gum before the start of each day's busy classes. When our day's inventory was sold, we'd make our way to lessons ourselves, our pockets jangling, packed full with a weighted assortment of dimes, nickels and quarters of the day's take-all to be split evenly, three ways, when we got home.

Most days, we were bussed to school each morning. It was no easy accomplishment, getting there. Not only did you have to be up on-time. You had to slip into the freshly ironed clothes grand-mom had set out for us prior to catching that 5 A.M. bus to work herself. There was making sure there was always enough time to choke down a bowl of cold cereal.... Couldn't forget any books, while reminding ourselves in suspension over the final flight of stairs, to be sure not to forget to lock the front door, in route to the bus stop.

Once there, we'd then stand around for at times a seemed eternity, waiting for the bus to slowly poke its nose around the bend of a salted up, snow-plowed corner.

And that hour wasn't always undertaken in the most humane of comforting conditions for us neither. We faced rain, sleet, and slippery patches of ice, sometimes the results of melted, six-foot snowdrifts. That was just to make it there. We fought off rock-packed snowball atrocities, pencil-snapping games, which very often led to real, physical, fistfights and the pressures of having to showcase cool, in every situation, no matter what.

Cause' pretty girls, who attended the school as well, also rode the buses and hung out in gingerly scatters around our stop.

A new development which captivated my interest as the three of us rounded the fence leading up to our stop one day was the appearance of a small crowd of boys, they seemed to be moving about in a swarm, thronging about in a shuffle of energetic shifts.

Their movements followed the activities of two other boys, both of them appearing to be locked up in the bustle of a fist-to-cuffs clatter. They seemed to be lost in a flutter of blows as they attacked each other in a hail of testosterone and fists of a bravado'd, utter stupidity.

We held back, at first, away from the center of the slowly angling crowd. Looking over to my uncle, Bem, I shrugged my shoulders while shaking my head with uncaring confusion.

I didn't have time for little boy games. There was money to be made at that stop and their commotion might cut into my action.

"They slapboxin', " Bem supplied.

I was even more confused. I'd never seen anything like it. I'd never witnessed two people approach one another in such a way, without actually going for each other's throats. I watched the combatants more intently now for a second. For a reason I couldn't admit, what they were doing became more and more attractive to me as the minutes of battle ticked on.

I studied how first one boy would go on the offensive, pouring floods of scattering fists in the direction of his parrying, ducking opponent. The other boy, noting that an offensive was underway, would side step quickly, while trying rapidly to unleash a fusillade of his own, before attempting a hapless feint, then a bob, and a fluttering jaunt, jutting back and forth, seeming to move his entire upper body out of harms way with an experienced lethality which intrigued me all at once.

I thought what they were doing to be very interesting. Heck, I thought that shit was *major* cool! I could do that. And be good at it. I knew I could.

Bem and Toppa goaded me slightly in the direction of *our* spot. You see, everything and every place to everybody, in the overcrowded interior of the mean streets of 1977's city, was territorial. Certain crews had staked out particular spots where only they, their friends or those calling themselves their girlfriends that week were allowed to

inhabit. Encroach upon havened territories without having been invited and a storm of perhaps *getting' jumped* could ultimately become your fate.

I allowed myself to be led in the direction providing a bastion of safety of our own.

But I found it almost impossible to drag my gaze from the battle as the flurries of loudly placed thumps and bopping whacks moved on. Once there, we were met by Coolie, Deric Meters, Purskin Jeeters, Alvin and Booby Jetson, Coolie's sisters, Gran-Mo and Tissy, Steinley Grimes, of course Scootie and Toomlie, and my cousins, Kimmie Peavey and her brother, Gus. So we had most of the *light work* taken care of, if it came to bustin' up some fools if they wanted to start stirrin' up a fuss.

But you know…

You were forever faced with the antics of that one, village idiot—the sucker who always wanted to test the waters of an extremely fast moving train to seal *his* fate. And that fool always came woofin', without the full law of gross tonnage supporting him.

That day's victim's name became Pudgy Watkins.

Pudgy was a robust, kindly boy. Powerfully built, he towered over most of us. But ole' Pudge wasn't exactly what you'd call, the smartest banana on the tray. Known for an innate ability to write checks his ass couldn't cash, he'd spared no lengths to do stupid things which sometimes brought thunder to rain down on most of his buddies, who were all but sworn, by association, to jump in, and protect him, should it come to that.

For reasons still unknown to me, Pudgy zeroed in on me that morning. Making the fateful mistake of abandoning the sanctuary of his group's cobblestone island, I looked up to find him staring into my face, standing over me, with an air of faux, practiced contempt.

I turned my head slowly to look to Bem, and then to Toppa. They each stepped forward in preparation for what they felt was sure to be the next direction.

His movement to block me could have meant anything, to anyone else in any other part of the World. To me, it only meant one thing. He was pissed at me for something that had been relayed to him or perhaps about what someone else had heard me say, about maybe his ugly momma, or about his little sister's unsightly cleft-lip.

Or, Pudgy was just being Pudgy, maybe he'd eaten too much sugar on that morning's *CORNFLAKES*, and was merely seeking release, in stupidity by joking around instead of meaning to actually stir up trouble.

Trouble got my vote.

I stood there. No fear in my heart—just confusion.

I had no clue what I could have done to the big, lummox of a boy to roust his anger that winter's morning.

I shrugged. Appearing bored, not in the least bit enamored. Suggesting to Pudgy…

"WHATYOUWANNA DO FAGGOT?"

I was no stranger to scrappin'. At times I suffered the possession of a temper matching ten boys my age—and the hands, footwork and determination to back that all up with speed and ferocity, if need be.

Tactically, I attempted to pass off my bag full of candies and the day's other products with surreptitious movement, to Toppa. Witnessing his chance to make his move at producing a reason for me to be forced to have to fight, Pudgy intercepted the bag with a lightning swift movement which belied his overgrown size. He stood for a moment, holding his captured prize with raised triumph above his head as he tiptoed around at a canter for all those interested to see.

After he'd gained everyone's attention with his actions, then began the wolfin'.

"Yeeeaaah…. What now, lil Nicca'? What now?" Looking back to the rest of his posse, most seemingly to bolster his own convictions, I took note that not all of them fully realized what had just happened.

I shifted my weight stealthily in the quickened force of heated contemplation.

He danced around me. His movements matched the lumbering clumsiness, one foot to another, of a big, sallow galloping bear. He taunted me with my own bag—shaking it at me, while taking the time to push and paw at me with increasingly upsetting vigor.

I lowered my head and my eyes briefly, thinking. *I can't believe I gotta' fight this fool to take back some shit that's rightfully, already mine!*

At that time, we didn't fight very often in the streets of the hill in the Burg. Whenever we beef'd. Specifically, in this instance when it was with somebody not even a resident of our block (Two-hundred kids from a whole lot of blocks used that one corner of Boas and Eighth Streets for jump off points for school busses) you usually settled things by setting up a meeting. One at which you tried your best to bust up and maim your opponents, on the field of play, battling in a football game—Over in the huge grassy field of the National Guard armory, located just across Herr Street.

In convoluted wonder, generally, if we did fight, we fought one another—Rarely ever against other kids outside of our immediate living area.

It didn't appear Pudgy had a sports competition in mind. It wasn't until the best of his gluttony got the better of him and he could no longer fend of urges to reach inside *my* bag, did I make my plans to react decisively.

I wasn't about to let him snatch a whole day's profit away from me without a fight. Besides, this was my house. He'd come into our area, to eat off our plates of misery. Taking in Coolie's, Scootie's and the immediate reactions of the others around me, I knew they all expected me to swallow the responsibility of making this stupid fucca' pay for ever having disrespected our clique in such a way.

I moved in sleekly. Slow playing images of what I was gonna' bring down on him began to pour out in infinite, filtered projections streaming across my mind at the front of my head.

I could tell he'd sensed my shift. Looking back to the other members of his own crew, almost seeking resolve, I pinpointed what loomed a sudden fear as it overtook him in realizing;

Once again, his mouth had been cashing champagne checks, based entirely on a beer salary.

I almost feel sorry for him now. Looking back, on an occurrence which took place in the life of a person totally different from the one writing this piece today.

I had other motives. And I had no nerves. They'd all been burned out, back in Texas, with Mama'n.

I set out not only to get my bag back and to reclaim the dignity he'd taken from my block brothers; I had intentions of hurting him badly, right there in front of all those people.

He didn't know me...

I was just a kid he'd picked out of a crowd. Because *he thought* he was bigger n' me. He had no clue the enormity of his unlucky blunder.

Looking around with nervousness, recognizing he'd already passed the point of no return, he centered before me squarely. He tried to pass *my bag* off over his shoulder to one of the friends siding with *his* crowd. Coolie stepped in, between them, to intercept it. Another member of his group offered a feigned indignation. Coolie easily quelled this as he stepped towards the offending party offering an additional challenge.

At fifteen, he was even bigger than Pudgy. But his stature was a chiseled, well-muscled proportion by comparison. There wasn't one fool among them stupid enough to want to have to deal with him.

"*SLAP-BOX! SLAP-BOX! SLAP-BOX!*" Began the chant played out among the gathering crowd.

Without waiting for invitation, I was on him with the escalating force of a very unlikely style. My homeys had faith in me. I was certain. They did know me. They knew I'd box till somebody either fell in finality or a melee broke out with everyone caught up in battle, only blood or death stopping us altogether.

Pa-Lease'...Come-On!

I was Buster's kid...The legend of my father held a well-known street folklore around those parts. They'd all had his story passed down furtively to them by their own fathers, during more private, quiet, father-Son moments.

Heck—I had faith in myself. I didn't need their endorsement or co-signing to be successful.

All the years Top and I had been dropped off over grand-mom's, they'd never seen me back away from even the things I should well have better considered.

But, in my mind, I wasn't slap boxing. My hands never stopped moving as I hurled myself at him, dodging at first the girth of his slumbering body, striking blow after blow, my fists securely closed with intent on causing everyone around me to look at me differently from that moment, forever more.

I didn't know how to slap box. All of the fights in my life had been for real. Nothing these chumps could wing at me could even come close to matching the terror and determination it took to breathe on, during battles of scuffling for scraps of food, and hoping beyond hope for even the most miniscule speck of motherly attention from Mama'n.

It was during the malevolence of those encounters that I'd learned how to be and had already been crowned a champion.

I knew pain and could accept it. Mama'n had taught me well—to feel the pain, and the joy, of a mature man never presented the opportunity of being a boy. Through it all, I'd never had time to play boys' games pretending to be a man. By all rights, at almost thirteen, I was a man.

I'd fed and clothed myself without the help of others. Through various efforts, I'd maintained a roof over my head. Only on the outside was I was thirteen. Inside, I churned a nefarious forty-five.

I didn't even toy with him, like so many in my group later professed they'd wished I had done.

Shoot! *It was too cold out there in them streets to get caught-up messing around.* And the temperatures weren't all that cozy either.

After bloodying his nose quickly, it began to dawn on his posse members that I wasn't exactly playing fair, along the lines of their rules of slap box combat etiology.

WHAT!

LIFE WASN'T FAIR…It was time for me to pull them out completely from beneath the hem of all their momma's skirts.

With not as much feverish rhetoric as before, they registered heaps of heated concerns in beginning to protest my already condemning movements. I could sense the sides of both crowds beginning to ease in on me as the gathering seconds moved an inch or two more toward becoming a fully blown row.

Coolie shot me a confidenced nod. I knew he was there to take care of me should things turn ugly and we all wound up trying our best to kill one another that morning in the melting drifts of Pennsylvania snow. With the ruckus this created, I sensed my opponent's compulsory, silent insistence on breaking, to perhaps plead out his case among a wandering jury which itself began to worry for its own well being.

That's when I moved in to apply my worst.

Stepping reticently to one side, I raised then quickly brought down the heel of my boot to savagely land on the side of one of his meaty thighs. I'd caught him just above his left knee. I could feel the thing give with a loud, popping sound like a rubber band snapping in beaten protest. He crumbled before me instantly. Great gasps of air mixed in foam splattered spittle smeared across his mouth, bellowing an exhausted froth of chilled, blood splashing fog. He attempted to look up at me as he regained his feet, favoring that left leg unevenly. I felt his unspoken appeal for mercy come crashing down upon my utterly deaf ears. A tear beginning to well in one of his eyes, and his expression pleaded ominously to me—"*PLEASE! Take back the searing pain!*"

This was soon followed by inflicted sobs of pure unadulterated anguish. He had no clue what I'd already done to him. All he knew was…it wasn't right.

I wan't havin' it.

I swooped in. Setting the edge of the palm on my right hand, I feinted slightly and brought it to slam viciously, with direct contact to his throat. He began to fall backward as I moved in even closer, looming over him in a trance.

Suddenly the earth's rotation slowed to a creeping, partitioned, stillness. He just lay there, sucking in frustration, gasping even harder for air. A slow, long, drawn out moan whined from his motionless form on the ground beneath me in the snow. His windpipe traumatized, he attempted feverishly to regain its flow.

Pulling myself back to time of present, I noticed I had begun to quiver. Unleashed dams of surreal, pulsating adrenaline surged violently unchecked throughout my veins. My breathing was the steady pace of a panting, maniacally raging bull. When they had finally decided amongst themselves that they weren't really ready to take the fight a notch higher, the entire fold of teens seemed to all stop abruptly, frozen in their tracks.

Having stood in horror to witness the results of the damage I'd just enacted, not more than a few seconds before upon their friend Pudge, It brought them to suddenly begin to question their own abilities to carry the tussle on even further.

Then, came realizations of trying to assess their own, self-righteously formulated blame.

Looking around, panning to realize recognition of horror stained gazes, a sea of searing faces spread out to gander appallingly before me. They scowled at me. The girls choked back tears, hiding them amid the palms of their mittens they now held in front of their faces as they shook their heads, peering at me, as if I was some kind of sick, sadistic, twisted animal.

SHIT!

It wasn't my fault. It was their fucc'ing game.

They'd drug me into it. This was *their* game.

They'd just had no clue as to how I'd play.

Reclaiming my thoughts, I again began to approach Pudgy's now supine form. Looking down on him, still writhing and moaning at my feet, I took a second to further capture the crowd. I then pulled back my strong leg, excruciatingly slow, for a gathering effect. And…as he lay there, still gasping for air. I sent a decadent kick to his groin area, causing him to bellow out in a frightened and continual, whooping yelp of diffusive pain—Like the sound a little dog makes when it gets hit by a speeding car.

At almost thirteen, I wasn't nuttin' nice.

Not tall by any measure, but solidly built—and thick. With a calculating mind, bordering on the genius, I was all too serious about my own matters. I'd been robbed of a fleeting childhood. Had become forced to face harrowing realities of becoming a man

All too soon. Even my own homeys, like Coolie, Scootie and Alvin n' them began to distance themselves, pushing away distrustfully, to become leery of being around me following what they'd witnessed me do to Pudgy, the ogre.

But Toppa, and Bem, they knew me. They stuck by my side.

FAMILY...

The three of us soon began to stake out an area of our own to wait by ourselves for the bus.

None of them fools ever messed with any of us again. Not even whenever we saw them thereafter, when each of us had finally reached maturity as grown men.

SLAPBOXING had gained me my own reputation that day. Pudgy survived. His parents scooped him up off that pavement and then sent him, for his own safety, to live with his grandmother up in Washington State.

Mr. Woodell held me up one day in the halls at Melrose Middle. He enlightened me how he'd heard about my encounter with Pudgy.

.and how disappointed in me he was that I had so viciously stooped to hurt another human being in such a way.

I have to admit. Standing before him then, just the two of us in that passageway, it upset me immensely to have let him down so un-righteously. He had put so much into assuring my mental, spiritual, and physical health.

But who was I to deserve so heavy a helping of his mentoring ways?

I was just a boy, an American of African descent.

I didn't matter...Not even to myself.

"NO" means—Numerous Opportunities...In another explanation,—a three letter word which begins with the letter "Y" (why) and ends with the letter "S" (esssss....)

Chapter Five
'VIBRATIONS'

Where there is evil, there is confusion…

So there must've been a lot of evil in me. Cause' at thirteen, I was as confused as any man-child could be. We could tell that although she felt an obligation, grand mom was beginning to welter beneath the weight of the overwhelming responsibility of tasks it took to keep us all together.

There was never any hallucination of peace residing in her house. Either we, the three boys, were bickering and fighting each other over the most mundane, materialistic, and trifling things. Or Buster and Rob were driving her crazy. The first, from whatever cell he was in at that moment, with his increasingly, unrealistic demands, the other, his unpredictable nature, fraught with solicitous, outlandish womanizing and near-death excursions while trippin' through a night spent boozin' or on his tibbit; running with fear, when grand mom finally figured out and caught wind of him tip-toeing after Miss Pearline (Who lived just cross' the street) and she took after him, with a butcher knife in her hand, meaning to filet up some damaged goods.

Suddenly she was sick all the time and had renewed her passion for smoking cigarettes. A habit she'd given up some months before. The addition of the weight her stopping had added to her tiny frame had looked good on her. So much so, from time to time that even the porch pirates sent her flattering catcalls as she passed them by on her way to the corner store.

She began to spend more and more time away from us. Choosing instead to linger in her housecoat inside her bedroom, not raising holy hell with the three of us, something we always stammered about, but looked forward to on at least a daily basis.

To me, our time with grand mom seemed very short. When we were old and wise enough to finally recognize her value, just like grand pappy, Ollie, she'd done passed on to Jesus in her sleep.

But not before she'd seen us safely back into the care of our own mother.

Well, I don't know for sure, if that's what you would have called it...safe.

She'd shown up like a leaf blown in on an wayward wind. And just like before, I'd felt like I'd been dreaming about her, standing at the foot of my bed in the back room with the porch on top where you could always feel the heating rays of a new day's sun.

And there she was.

Of course Mama'n never showed up in the middle of the day when the sky was still perky. She always whisked in like a subtle bandit, reclaiming her worldly possessions and jetting back out again in the same breath. Her movements had always leaned toward being a little nocturnal.

But she came back for us, had to credit her for that. Another four or five-day Greyhound ride—this time, soaring into the night, sleepy as all get out, wondering back to how much we'd miss Bem, off once again to try to begin our future.

The ride that time back to Texas was uneventful. Watching her closely, I could tell she had changed a whole lot. She had an air of confidence that we hadn't seen flutter about her for a very long time. She no longer felt the need to lash out at us. A casing of internal peace had replaced her previous angers which appeared to permit her to think more sharply while breathing more clearly.

The only part of her plan that didn't come off quite how she'd planned it was her inability to convince Mr. George to relinquish the stranglehold he'd placed protectively over Miss Honey. There was no ever getting her back now. She was a goner, almost seemingly, for sure.

We'd talk to her from time to time, by phone, as we each grew up. But it still wasn't the same. Her being raised by her father, and us continuing to be on the wild, challenging precipices and stereotypes routinely as she, Toppa and me began to develop differently.

She would be brought up with a timid air of hesitation and a detailed sense of unsurety. Toppa and I would come to project nothing weaker than a fervent stride of convicted strength, sometimes dipped in malice. She would go on to attend the best private Catholic schools. And was an only child, wanting for nothing for a very long time.

I didn't begrudge her these things. Nor was I hatin' on the fact that her father knew how to get out of his bed, after turning off his alarm, and that he took his ass to work to provide for her very well.

Toppa and I still had each other. But we never knew it.

And if we went to school—on the days we did choose to go, or the reverse (Because Mama'n never really bothered herself with such things too much any more), then we did.

It would be more than twenty-one years, besides summer visits, barely continuing past her age of ten, before the three of us would come to be reunited. She'd be a grown Woman with a daughter of her own. Toppa and I would be grown as well.

We'd each have our own families, and still be worrying about Mama'n.

Grandmom held on for another eleven more years. She'd end each infrequent phone conversation with scary, fatalistic ramblings like, "ToppaAree... YoooKnow grand mom hasn't been feeling so well lately. N' you know she ain't gooin' be around for much longer now."

We'd always placate her.

To us, she had always seemed invincible. She couldn't die. It was something approaching the unthinkable.

...She did.

We returned to Texas to find Mama'n had done the unthinkable as well. She had been holding down a job, supposedly cut back on her drug use (Now she mainly drank Vodka and toked only a little weed) and to top it all off with incredulous reality, she actually had a man she'd kept, for more than about a month.

His name was Harold Breen. He weighed all of about ninety-eight pounds. I mean, Dude! The man...was emaciatedly, skinny! He was an Army Lifer meaning he'd spent the best part of more than ten years in the service. And he dealt the best and most coppable weed from El Paso to Las Cruces, directly out of what was to become our house.

Here we go again...

It wasn't that bad though.

The two of them had a good gig going. Both had jobs. Mama'n held down a piece as a transcriptionist at the local El Paso Doctor's hospital. His forte was primarily dealing, the military thing a mere distraction, for cover.

To Toppa and I, the apartment was a veritable palace. It had real carpet, two bedrooms, a real live, working TV, complete with the little black and brown, push-button cable box amenity and a dishwasher. An appliance neither one of us had ever really seen. We shared a bedroom and a bed.

The really exciting thing about the place was that it was completely furnished with the latest contemporary items. The two of them had paid a little extra and had moved into it that way.

We attended Morehead Junior High School, located a stone's throw away winding around our street on *Fiesta Way*. And we were once again, the only two black kids to cross the daily rolls there.

But we didn't care, cause' baby, we were home!

For us this wasn't an extreme problem. It was only after the shock of witnessing a few of the less deeply, implanted Mexicans and other more ignorant white boys begin to find simplistic pleasures in throwin' around their Daddy's favorite word, that he and I quickly began to roll out the ass-whippins' as we not only began to truly exemplify the term—*NIGGER,* we began to charge tax, in blood, for its every bane occurrence.

We quickly reestablished reputations for making the utterance of that expression become costly at all times, almost too expensive for those insisting on embracing and perpetuating it to keep up.

With an uncultured futility, he and I resembled *tha 'wurd—NIGGER* crusaders, bashing and breaking heads just for the sake of it.

Wish I'd a known then, what I know now, *(That it holds no power, possesses no grip upon me—MEANS NOTHING)* I could have saved myself a mountains amount of worry and inner contempt.

I continued to do well with my studies. I pulled out all the stops in my struggles to make it through the daily turmoil plaguing my life at home. I did this while striving to develop other more productive skills in support of assimilation within what I was originally taught was the interior workings of a scornful society. I learned quickly with such a mindset that I was well on my way to failure. Catching it quickly though, I turned it all around and instead set out to begin the task of learning all I could about the lifestyles and families of surrounding cultures. I spent lavish evenings with friends on weekends, intermingling in many luxurious homes of Mexican, as well as many white, families, as a guest.

Heck, it was much better than remaining to flounder in the inebriated sallow of my own home. I took it all in. Storing away with detail, pictures and images of the finer things I saw as I envisioned for myself and my own family a much better future than I had previously been taught to expect. I began to formulate a visualization of finding a way to reach toward such emulated metaphors of success.

I won the city-wide, Spanish as a second language spelling Bee and Spanish poetry competitions. My mentor, Mr. Ytturalde, a short, squat, former boxer and Navy man was a gifted teacher only rivaled by another previously, Mr. Woodell.

Ironically, the Principal and Vice Principal of our school would grow right along with us. They would both hold identical positions of authority at one or another of the many high schools we would attend, but not graduate from, almost five years into the future. It was there at Morehead that I first met Rhriss and Lippy and their mother, Miss Bartha Edmunds.

They were the next two Brothas' to *infiltrate* Morehead's white-washed, impeccably clean hall ways. Rhriss, the oldest, had a lopsided afro-sheen fro' and a twisted grille which caused him to hide every smile whenever he smirked with elated frustration, in the open. He was a strong-head, just like me. I'd met him on the basketball court down at the school one day on a sweltering weekend.

The two of us hit it off immediately.

On more than one occasion we would stay on that court, beating the shit out of one another as we leaned into sweat drenched games of twenty-one, almost daily till it started getting dark.

Rhriss and Lippy's mom, Miss Bartha, was a self-edifying, sultry woman at the time, of about thirty. She, along with Miss Daphnee, (An accent wielding beauty from Jamaica) caused me unwarranted carnal frustrations (In thought) anytime I was around them. Most of my not-so-charming fantasies and acts of self-gratification were increasingly completed with the two of them lustfully in mind. These feelings began to advance. At times I'd conjure up the two of them, together, and they'd wait on me hand-and-foot, me, the delirious king, giving in to being pampered by their desirous aches to only please me and receive the ceremonious flow of my teen-aged yearnings.

Miss Bartha was a curvaceous, succulently sweet talking, chocolate honey. Adept at holding her own when it came to cat-like purring whenever she felt like tossing the embers of a voluptuous eye wickedly at any man. She had high thought herself plainly deserving of the fortune of a long line of worthwhile prey to select from in placating her lofty sexual needs.

She was a purchasing agent for a national marketing company—A good job for any Woman no matter the hue of her skin or dynamics of her race at the time.

She was supposedly a friend to Mama'n. Yet somehow, she could never bring herself to quell her sweetly braggadocios nature to completely solidify this.

The reason for this was she continually held herself...and her boys—with the permanence and air of an upturned nose to be better than Mama'n, Toppa and myself.

Eventually, we would both ultra-exceed the two of them even more so now, as we are all grown Men, approaching mid-life and on our own.

Rhriss turned out to cause his mother the most troubling heartache and grief.

How ironic...He'd always been the one she'd held up so high as being ultimately gifted. She went out of her way to dote upon and highlight his every falsified accomplishment, gloating over him to no end.

He eventually ended up taking revolving trips, back and forth between his father's house, in Waco, (Because his mother could no longer handle him) and whatever jail he'd find himself in after being nabbed for his less than scholarly efforts. The guy was no

saint. For the most part, he was even inept at pulling off the pettiest of crimes. I lost touch with him just prior to departing Texas for the Navy.

Lippy, on the other hand, was an entirely different story altogether. His was a tale spiraling with showcased aplomb which eventually blossomed into a genuine success. He'd always been a frail, disenfranchised little boy. Shy and introverted beyond healthiness. He'd always held back, taking his every lead from an overbearing and impatient Rhiss. Even his own mother treated Lip differently. I doubt she'd admit it, but she fawned over and fondled at him just like he was a pretty little girl.

He had one true Love, his music. Lip was the only little man of American of African descent that I'd ever seen to cart a violin case, back and forth to school, and pretty much wherever he went on a daily basis. He had the prodigious dedication of a naturally budding master and we never knew it—till later

This type of effort was seen in other boys, white ones or from others of a minority affluence. To reach for the angles of perhaps making a success of yourself in the music industry, specially with a dog-gonn'ed violin, for us was a laughable mirage.

Lippy was always sick. I think he had asthma or perpetual bronchitis or something. Perhaps that was a major reason his mother expressed such fondness for fawning all over him and handling his every movement for him as if he was a tiny little baby.

But I'll say one thing for Lip. I've never seen him speak or lash out in anger towards another living soul. And I didn't witness his eventual transformation up close. I had already left the state when this had taken place. But homey could play the hell outta' that violin.

There's a café' called *Bassam's* in the gas lamp district of downtown San Diego. They provide a menagerie of yodeling hopefuls a free setting to present a sampling of their competing wares to the public every Tuesday night, without fail. Nettie and I had gone there one evening to listen to a friend of hers (Her hairdresser, Leslie) sing.

Leslie has a beautiful voice. Not to mention two of the most beautiful little girls, Khatora and Kharastin, both miniature clones of their momma.

After Les did her piece, another group, a duet, made their way to the stage to begin to bring their offering.

A young American of African descent stroked the violin sweetly and his *partner,* a cross-eyed, white dude, nimbly petted the ivories of a mini-electric keyboard as the two of them made music together, the presentation of which was nothing short of angelic.

A symphony of professionals, together thirty-five years, couldn't have done a better job of entertaining us or have even held a candle to them.

When their gig was over I approached them. Choosing my words carefully (Not wanting to come off as a total idiot out in public) I offered....

"Thank you so much for your rendition. Your music and your style are so completely dynamic!"

The two of them together bust forward in broad, bubbly, almost coquettishly pleased laughter. Obviously my unsolicited praise of their musical mastery had touched a cord in peaking both their joining egos.

The ice had been broken.

"You guys have a CD I can purchase?" I asked.

"SURE!" The familiar looking violinist exclaimed excitedly. I could tell he was hoping my enthusiasm while positioned there would ignite other patrons to take notice and cause a purchasing frenzy of wanting the CD as well.

He produced a professionally wrapped package at once.

Taking it from his grasp, I was watching him and I noticed something about his face. A flashing memory which made me pause a millisecond, sweeping me up in a fleeting sense of delusional déjà vu.

I'd seen this joker somewhere before. I engaged him further. We'd completed our transaction for the CD.

I wondered.

"You know? When I was a kid, I had this friend, named Lippy, who played the violin as well. And he was pretty damned good at it too." Pocketing my change, I began to turn about to resume my search for "NETTIE" and Les.

Caught in mid stride of my turn, I felt this fella' reach out to me and grab me by the arm. I was immediately astounded at first. Although I had taken on the memory for a brief second, I hadn't given two thoughts more to delving into it further to bring it complete. Right then, it didn't really matter where I had seen the violinist before. I reflexed and stiffened my arm instantly. Wheeling about, I was standing to face him squarely once more in turn. I peered into his eyes with question.

I could tell I had startled him. He repelled a step backward, retreating away from me, his breath suddenly catching in shortened gasps of startled spurts. He stood there holding his arms across his chest, resembling a frustrated Woman.

Regaining his former conviction, he returned my gaze, looking me questioningly in the eye.

We stood there. I was like, *"WHAT!"*

He bent slightly at the knee and called out in a sass, while limply throwing just one hand forward in a *go- 'head, stop kiddin'* wavy-style, "Avery?"

I peered back at him more deeply. Finally drawing full recognition, I answered back, "Lippy?"

He sided up (Almost too close) to me in a rush and corrected, hiding an overly conspicuous whisper behind a lightly held hand. I could see the beginnings of grey reaching through his strictly groomed mustache and I could tell, from the curvature of his teeth, that hadn't ever really beaten that thumb sucking problem even in manhood.

"It's Liiiiffoord now," he threw back over a sachet'd shoulder thrown in a hoity-toity splash of feminine gesture.

Stepping back a pace for *posterior's* sake, the past swept back to take hold of me and I disregarded his overblown antics, and fully embraced him with an optimistic familiarity.

"For Reeeaaal?" I had to bend a bit myself to look at him closer. "No SHIT!"

Peering at him more deeply, I tried to reconcile the face of the frail, cherubic, little boy I'd known in my youth; to the fully gay spectacle of the man I now saw standing before me. I couldn't believe it.

"It's me in the flesh." He tapped a carelessly placed toe before him, while holding both hands, palms up, out to his sides. Turning back to his keyboard player, he then presented, "Let me introduce you to my husband." His gesture was accomplished with such syruppy tenderness that it caused me to become obviously caught up in and immediately stifled by an uncontrollable shiver.

It was now my turn to choke on my breath. Barely able to maintain my composure, I shook *his man's* hand.

"Pleased to meet you."

I was at a loss for what to say next. Did I call him Mr. ummm...Lifford's last name, uhh...Edmunds? Or was *MYBOY*, Lippy, *bouncin'* around, the receiver, with ole' boy's moniker tatooed on the back side of his...?

How'd that work?...Never mind.

We all got through it.

After introducing him and his husband to "NETTIE" and to her girl, we exchanged information, dapped a bit and promised to keep in touch. I even invited the two of them to a barbecue I was having that following weekend.

Course', they never showed. I wish they had. And they never called either. I don't know why. I'm not homophobic. I Loved Lippy. He and I had been like brothers...to a point.

Guess they figured I wasn't their kinda' crowd. I think they'd both registered my initial sense of embarrassment followed by an uneducated apprehension as it had taken me a full moment to squash my stereotypic indignation and accepted the fact that my former little friend, Lippy, had grown up to Love Men.

I never did hear from Lip again.

I wish him well.

Maman's new beau, Harold Breen, never permitted himself to become too intimately acquainted with us. He maintained an arms-length presence while assuring us, from time to time, on what side of our bread *he* provided the butter.

We didn't mind.

Topp and I pretty much kept busy with our schoolwork, down at the complex pool, ogling young girls, or out of habit of old, fighting over whom was watching what on the colored TV. Each tidbit of these items, for us, was an extremely luxurious pleasure. These were things the two of us had never dreamed we'd see in a lifetime of our own.

Harold was her thang'. As long as she was happy, we left the fool alone. That is, until he began to develop the abusive persona of a traitorously diminutive Napoleon Bonaparte.

Towards this, subtle hints began to materialize that things were not quite cake and fat-free cookies between the walls that separated them from us at night. Not as perfectly matched as we had at first gleaned.

Then again, what ever is?

While the same, raucous sounds of heated Lovemaking could be heard through those paper-thin walls almost nightly, a different materialization began to suddenly take form. It began to become more evident that Mama'n was in fact no longer entirely happy within their unprincipled arrangement.

Always out of our view, he'd begun to push her around and approach her with an ever increasing heavy-handed style. Did he think Toppa and I were fools? I still have no clue why he ever thought something like that (With both of us eatin' more than him at every setting) would last. Actually slapping and punching her whenever he felt he could get away with it, the appearances of dark bruises and unsightly welts began to alert us as they took form to cover the sides of her high-yella' arms and along the inner edges of her thighs.

In my mind, it was as if she was being held up in a relationship against her better judgment, with dreams of making something positive stick, just for the sake of us boys'. We were kind of held silent by this, not knowing what to do at first as he and I discussed between ourselves what it was we thought we should do. We were both shocked that she was not the Mama'n of old, no longer captivator of her own destiny, the creative master of her own soul.

In her mind's eye, she could suffer this. She'd been through and had succeeded when faced with worse. She only wanted a continuation of the perpetuation of being the simple American family, without trouble, the weed and salacious sales of it notwithstanding.

We weren't prepared intelligently enough to continue on with perpetuating the hoax.

Toppa and I, at thirteen and fifteen, were no little boys of pocket-sized stature. Both of us wore larger draws and wider shoes than skinny-assed Harold. And I think he realized with a recurring frustration, that we'd take his ass out, within the slick of a Pennsylvania-sized, buffalo headed nickel if need be.

Just as he had no hesitation relaying to us who it was that bought all the food, we began to make no qualms about imparting our intentions of certifying this fact to him equally, as well.

I remember standing beside him one morning, mixing up some toast before school. He'd come in after a shower and was preparing his bag for that day's work. As we were accustomed, neither of us really acknowledged the others presence, initially, just kept right on doing what we had to do, barely staying out of each other's way, with the goal of getting out of there, free of drama with no follow on regrets.

As he reached across me with not even the slightest appearance of manhood respect, to grab something (—I don't know, the bread, the bologna—something...) he brushed up against me, and gave the slightest disrespectful push to go along with it.

I did nothing.

I had a present day premonition of where this encounter was heading should I make quick mention of his infraction, out loud, and encase it in too much boyish vigor.

All I did was offer him three words, at first.

Squaring up to looking at him directly, my gaze a full six inches or so over the top of his own, I intimated in a slightly negative head shake that there was no mistaking, with bone-chilling seriousness, "I'm not Mama'n!"

He knew what I meant. And being the punk that he was, he scrambled to immediately gather up his fixings and light out of the apartment, not slowing to huff and puff in all his usual banter, till the pane of the front door had him almost safely on his way to work.

That fool knew I'd given him fair warning. My words hinted at the fact that his time for openly abusing my mother was quickly drawing to an end.

One sleepy evening as the four of us prepared to end our day, the two sides equally separated in our perspective rooms, for no reason, Toppa suddenly bolted outta' bed and began to quickly search around, for his shoes.

"Where tha' hell you goin'?" I whispered to him as I brushed the last wink of the sleep I'd get that evening crustily from my eyes.

Looking back at me with that tired, impatient look of pure—D' grim he always held reserved, just for *me*, "Maman's crying!" He bolted. "Get your ass up, and come on…"

We were both tired. Tired of sitting idly by to watch Mama'n permit herself to accept such inhumane treatment at the hands of a ninety-eight pound *pussy* who got his kicks holding it over her head that *HEWASTHA'—man.* Guess he felt that this gave him the right to abuse her anytime he felt the urge was at hand.

We were about to hip him to something different.

Outraged and fed up with his shit, it wouldn't take us long to easily cast off Maman's attempts at dissuading us from killing Harold and burying his body in a million available places nobody would ever think to begin to look—(In the desert along the outlying acres) surrounding our unhappy home.

But we didn't cause the trick to draw his last breath that evening. Only a few teeth, whatever dignity he'd brought home with him from that days work, and the full heftiness of his valued marijuana stash, which we held like captured booty, even after the two of them began talking once more, this time, he from a phone at his new apartment, and Mama'n from the divided safety of our own.

We burst into their bedroom and chased after Harold with a vengeance. He let out a shrieking squeal—just like a little girl. The images darting back and forth crazily inside his head shrieked of just a twinge of the fully throbbing pain that awaited him as a result of our unmerciful intentions of exacting atonement. This had him scrambling his scrawny frame out of the bed trying pointlessness to make an escape.

There were no words to be spoken. No need for em'...Everybody there knew exactly our reasons. There was no questioning precisely why we had come. We pulled him off the bed, sliding his scuttling figure off the bed by his legs. Bouncing his head on the edge of the cold wooden floor surface, we then backed him into a curve, the one with the tiny window above it as we quickly caged him in to the crook of a non-escapable corner like a captured cat.

We beat him savagely.

Maman's only recourse was to stand there in stark terror, thinking to scream but only able to whimper in teary eyed silence as she watched. Our frustrations of hearing the bumps and thuds of her closely held, nightly screams were relieved as we pounded penance into his azz with an exacting retaliation. She finally found voice in being able to rave, screaming, bloody—murder, finally coming to appreciate the impeccable saltiness of our work with horror, as the two of us handled *ourbidd-nazz* like homicidally, unruly men.

Initially, Toppa hit him high. I had taken low. We beat him like a rag-doll bully, our hunger for retribution for what *we* felt he'd done to our mother for far too long, not fully assuaged by the phalanx of stark-raving, raw enormity and power covering the ferocity of our first hammering blows.

Finally heeding Maman's screams, following the first volley, we let him up to sway uneasily before us as he attempted to regain control for a brief second upon weary, disloyal legs. Gathering himself succinctly, he made a last-chance dash for the kitchen. Once there, with us hot on his heels, he grasped the greasy handle of a skinny little steak knife which he thrust out swinging and jabbing at us with it in desperation, trying gravely to make his way toward the safety of the apartment's front door.

Topp and I glanced uneasily at each other, because we knew. If we continued forward from that point on, somebody was getting killed there that night for sure. In solemn commitment to Buster's legacy, he and I both realized—that that somebody wouldn't be me, or him.

Mama'n knew it too. Taking stock of her vision of seeing Harold lying lifelessly at her feet with his throat cut out and the not-so-subtle caretaker of a thousand holes, she actually pushed past us to cause herself to be placed between us and him. In doing so, she presented the beaten man time to gather his Chuck Taylor's, his last, freshly laundered fatigues, (Still starched and wrapped in the plastic bag from the cleaners) and he slipped aimlessly out of our lives, almost bolting out the front door with a sculpting sense of personally exercised relief.

The next time we saw ole' Harold, a full six or eight months had gone by. After long nights of courting, and attempts to accompany each other on real, honest-ta'-goodness dates, *ta' get their heads together*, they'd said, he and Mama'n had almost rekindled their sick exasperation for one another—almost to the point of him being back at the point of once again calling himself her man.

What's wrong with these women?

The two of them never fully regained the completeness of their former relationship.

Thank GOD!

He decided that the morose nature of the azz-whippin' he'd suffered at our hands was too much to ever be forced to revisit in humiliated memory. Had I been in his shoes, I wouldn't have wanted to have to face the same either on a daily basis.

Mama'n was worn out. Barely able to exhibit strength enough to keep us in check or forge on to reenter the devices under which he had meted her such despicable abuse. Plus, she knew she would be unable to extend herself further in being able to protect him completely from us.

What this inevitably meant for us as well, was the fact that after he'd left, *the rent came due.* And we moved. We relocated into the same complex where Miss Bartha, Rhris and Lippy lived, just down the street. Mama'n, in normal reactive form, quickly began to lend her time to another baby-faced, wayward soldier, a naive character, more suited to playing jacks and hopscotch than bedroom games, named David.

David was about six feet tall and lanky. He gave the impression of not being entirely ready for the things a relationship with Mama'n would present him. He fumbled about our new apartment, certainly unprepared for the running of the gauntlet of jilted Love and artillery, he'd soon come to wither under as the two of them scornfully began their matter of playing house together.

Drawing a long story up short, the last time we saw Harold, or David, was when; Harold, who still considered himself Maman's man, by defaulted proxy, had chased David, who'd been lounging lazily on our couch watching television when Harold had driven up and rapped unannounced at our front door.

David, after fully realizing who it was at the stoop, lit out, bolting like a yellow-jaded *pussy* in a non-fire retardant jacket, and he leapt through the wire-mesh screen of the opened, sliding glass door to beat a hastened exit toward the rear of the house.

Harold, who had never even made it inside the house, lighted out after him with an expressed determination.

In all the excitement, Toppa and I ran after them to see what would eventually take place. Mama'n slowly brought up our rear, huffing and puffing violently, herself wholly unaware of exactly what had just gone down. When we'd caught up with the two of them, we held off smartly at a distance. We cautiously watched as we took in the image of skinny-azz'd Harold standing over the now prostrated form of the extremely larger punk, David. Harold had appeared to change his tactics since last we'd seen him.

He towered over a now crying, panicked David, who scooched heavily along the blacktop exterior of an adjoining complex parking lot with frantic urgency, trying desperately to shade his pummeled features while scrambling frantically out of reach of Harold's fiercely thrown blows.

"*Aww...iightt! Aww...ight! Damn, man! I got-cheew!*" David pleaded, reaching out for an un-present mercy like an already defeated, billowing *bitch.*

Harold wasn't hearing him.

Toppa and I stood dumbfounded. We didn't understand at first. David stood at least a full five inches taller than Harold. And he had at least fifty pounds, and not to mention youth on him as well.

It wasn't until the searing glare of a cold—morning's, Texas sun flashed the glimmer of a waving, machine-edged smoothness of something Harold held in his hand, that we began to realize, with compensatory intelligence, the reason behind David's preservatory, herky-jerky, non-combative reactions. We knew then exactly why he'd run.

Harold continued, unchecked to bring the full swing of an exacting penance to rain down on him as he beat him senseless, to a bloody stupor, with the butt and barrel of a 357 magnum he'd had on him the entire time.

David paid that day, for nothing else other than being in the wrong place at the wrong time—with the wrong woman.

Guess ole' Harold felt none too safe round' those parts anymore without packin' the confidence-building heftiness of his iron.

COULD YOU BLAME IM'?

After the tortuous event of the convoluted gunplay, Mama'n finally got rid of scrawny-azz'd Harold.

She continued to dib and dab her fair share with a motley gathering of an ostensibly manlier cast of misfortunate characters. Of the hundreds she *dated*, there wasn't to be found a single, solitary inner peace for her in the entire slew of the whole heaping lot. She didn't have a steady, live-in for a while after. But that never cautioned them to keep them away, or thwarted her efforts as she sure never gave up trying.

It seemed the wild natures of her past had soured and tainted her. She could never find True-Love anywhere.

We lived in that particular location for almost a year.

Then…

You got it—Rent came due…

We moved this time, into a house. It was on DeLeon Street, a bit deeper into the city's increasingly affluent, west side. Our new digs set us up near a more sober setting of prospering, single-story homes. This house had three bedrooms, and was an older model with a huge backyard where we kept our prized Siberian Husky, Sabu'.

We'd always had a dog, even inside the stuffy interiors of whatever apartment we lived. Poor dog…no room to run and play, but to us that never mattered. All of us, the dog included, somehow found a way to live in the stench and filth infested surroundings, as we allowed carpet after carpet of a handful of interiors to become ruined, all in our penchant for keeping and cooping up a four-legged (shittin' all over the place) creature to inhabit the sanctity of all the places we called home.

There were more than a few landlords that literally hated us.

We'd had Pee-Pee and Butch, our German Sheppard, and Keplit, the little black runt I'd gotten from a friend and had lied to Mama'n, telling her,—"Some boys were beating it up, kicking it around in the streets. So *I* bravely stopped them—and I '*KEPT IT*' and brought him to safety—on home." Hence the name…

For us, little Sabu' took the cake. From the second we got her as a tiny puppy, Mama'n always professed, "*that she was gonna' breed her and make a gazillion dollars sellin' off her puppies to the neighbors round' there.*" She made good on her word too, in a way.

She saw an advertisement in the newspaper seeking an AKC partner for a male stud version of Sabu'.

You see, Mama'n frequently went to lengths such as this. Paying scant attention to other, more insistent priorities of everyday responsibilities, she'd spent a grip on Sabu'. AKC registration, lengthy trips, back and forth to the Vet, for shots, the most highly touted, expensively canned dog kibbles, while the cavernous pits of our own cupboards and the shelves of our own fridge' remained excruciatingly bare.

She'd said she was making an investment. After coming so profusely outta' pocket on that dog, she did finally breed her.

Sabu' birthed nine puppies. One was even born with the ends of its intestines extending outside its little body as it struggled, just like us, for survival. Surprisingly, after they were born and Mama'n had begun to realize that the neighbors weren't all beating a lined up path to our door to purchase them, she somehow never had enough money to get that particular little pup to the vet. So the poor thing just suffered in yelping pain each time it used the bathroom.

We kept every one of those dogs until such time as they grew big enough to jump the fence and make their way into a neighbor's yard where they cornered, killed and devoured about thirty of his chickens. They'd had an exemplary feast, Sabu' taking charge, in the lead. I still remember going to court with Mama'n to answer charges for their audaciously culinary acts.

She escaped judgment again and got off. The neighbor man was deemed at fault. The judge said he was in error for having so many fowl cooped up in one space inside the purview of the city's limits.

We sold nary-a one of those dogs. Not a single, pissy, howling mutt. They either ran away or were given away prior to yet another month's rent coming due.

It was about this time that Rolanda Howse, a darkly complected, sexy young lady with a keen, almost criminally sharp mind abruptly entered our lives. She was fifteen when she and her brother, Daniel, moved into the neighborhood with their mother and her new and crazy, Nigerian native husband—a dude named Bobotu' Okwnonde. They resided in an apartment complex just up the street from our house.

I'd first eyed her at school long before coming to realize she'd moved in so close to us up the block.

That made it six Americans of African descent students now attending.

She was sitting in the lunchroom and she pretended at first not to notice me as I strolled on past her in my best, feigned, self-assurant show of confidence.

Before I'd even moved in—to check her out, all of the *white* boys had approached me, fawning all over this yummy little girl as they extolled all about the protruding dilectabilities of her peaks, valleys and curves.

"*Duuuude! Wait till you see this chick!*" My football buds, David Mavyn, Tom Barton and Tom Walstein spilled all over themselves.

"Dude... She's like a freakin' African Princess and WHATNOT!"

"I'm tellin' ya Blu. She's some sorta' KICKASS!

BITCHIN', man."

I'd remained silent. What else was I gonna' do? Get all excited over some girl new to the school that I hadn't even seen yet? Besides, even in my short lifetime, I'd seen literally thousands of beautiful, African Princesses who were also very "*KICKASS" and "Bitchin'*" too as Tom had so eloquently put it. I held off initially, not wanting *their* excitement to overshadow my first encounter with her.

When I finally did muster up comfort enough to approach her, standing there now, gawking at her from the side of the table where she sat, I found their descriptions of her to be compounded within the culmination of efforts which caused my palms to sweat and my heartbeat to quicken. Words escaped me as I fell prey to an increasingly encumbering inability not to be taken aback by the severe sense of this girl's raw beauty. I found myself completely unable to stop staring at her.

They were right...

Baby *was* hella-fine't!

She held a dark, dark...shiny complexion. The radiance of her color so brightly captured me with its opaquely hewn tinge that baby's skin appeared to burnish in an opulently rare and perfectly refined attractiveness. This was matched by the whitest, most clearly sparkling eyes I'd ever seen. She played them about, scattering your emotions fancily, a whimsical literacy pushing past her perfectly whitened teeth to engage you as she peered into you deeply seeking to be seen. She had many different angles of causing you to react in ways you never had any intentions of portraying there in the lunchroom, in front of her and all the rest of the school's patrons and faculty as well to see.

She wore a simple pair of navy slacks. The arches and bulges of her body all but tugged at your senses as they attacked beneath the infinitely sculpted curves of a smooth, enticing devilishness completely filled out beneath the press of her extremely starched white blouse. Her skin loomed up at me, smooth and baby oil soft. The evidence of a full, mounting breast poked its way across her cleavage, with mouth-watering contempt, stammering out at me from buttons not fully braced, no matter the position she sat or stood before me now.

This girl couldn't have been for real!

DAMN!

Seeing me coming, she stood tall to shuck off the blue wool of a jacket which had a "Little Red Riding Hood" flap in the back. As if she'd known I was trying my damnedest to check out all that booty with a single, clandestined glance, she bent over slyly to slowly retrieve a pencil she'd toyed at dropping, just seconds before I made my presence known.

She sat back down briefly. I could tell she'd been still composing herself, lying in wait, like a vicious snake, preparing her debilitating venom for prey that had suddenly stumbled upon her hole.

I walked up and sat down beside her as if the two of us had been introduced friends forever. I think this shocked her. She opened her mouth sweetly as if to register a sudden, protesting surprise. I turned to her looking directly into her eyes.

"So...."

"So...*what?"* She countered, folding her gum, over and over again with the skill of her tongue, popping it loudly each time thereafter.

"So, you're the fine honey's got all tha' white boys gawkin' and cummin' all over they'selves, like fools huh?"

Cocking her head slightly to one side, I gazed deeply into the inviting area of her (sexy, *beggin' me ta kiss and suck on it)* neck, her gum-popping suddenly becoming more heated and rapid. She shifted her weight to one side, crossing her legs to showcase the grand smoothness of an exceedingly supple hip.

Rolling her eyes atop her head, she continued her attempts at trying to look pensively bored. Instead of appearing to give me the impression that she was in the least bit interested in anything I had to say, she began to stare off at a fixed, glazed over location at something on the other side of the room.

"You cummin' too?"

She lowered her head slightly, still popping away at that gum, not yet looking at me, the beginnings of a devilish smirk beginning to play lightly about the corners of the Lovely slanting edge of her mouth. Calming a bit more now, she peered up at me sweetly from her perch on the lunch room table bench. Her gaze then zeroed in, and threateningly challenged, as she leered directly at the swollen predictability of my peaking pelvic area.

"*Hmph...*"

This girl *was BAD!*

I turned away slightly, feigning a retreat to try and hide the betrayal of my lascivious excitement. Spreading my legs wide in a slightly braced balance, I returned to stand before her.

Tha wind had blown. There was no helping it. I gave in—nothing else to do.

I stood there with the full, protruding form of my hormonally-engorged erection, plain for her to see.

She lowered her eyes, appearing to arrogantly embrace it with a welcoming stare of sly, telling depravity.

I had the feeling she actually yearned to reach out and touch it. Could all but see the visions dancing about inside her head of wrapping her fingers tightly around me as I gave in to her and the two of us went further together, seeking the satiation we each were bursting at during our first moments alone.

But she was an ice-princess in a hot, hot house sense of the words.

Showing very little reaction, she unexpectedly lost her grasp on her former feistiness, for a second. The gum popping stopped all at once. Her sass instantly dissolved leaving her demeanor coquettish, vanishing into thin air. With an apparent deathly calm, she'd become still, silent and serious, still staring with an entranced interest at the still bulging front of my pants.

"Hmph..." She finally offered again on her own.

"Nice." She tossed her back, licked her lips like a bawdy harlot and rested her head again to one side.

"I can see it moving."

"What?" I queried back, uncertain at first what she'd meant.

She nodded, then looked around as if to make a sweeping take on security. She gestured toward it.

"Your *thingie."* Nudging the tip of her nose at *it*.

"I can see the pulsing it makes when you stand there in front of me like that."

Reaching up with gentle hands, she placed them both on the sides of each of my hips, and, looking deeply up into my eyes, she smiled. With an unspoken promise, she pushed at me forcing me to turn away from her with a disquieting whisper.

"Get that thing outta' my face. Fore' I bite it."

I remained turned away for a second more. With every ounce of willing strength, I implored myself to quickly regain some amount of physical control over my body's functions. I hoped to spend more time confronting and getting to know this wonderful girl before the two of us had to chance missing pending opportunities, by having to take off and fitfully return to our afternoon classes.

"Promise?" I threw back at her.

Not really wanting to break off the already evident, sexual tension flowing so heavily between us. I tried to silently appeal for her to linger with me longer. She and I had in some way really hit it off. We'd captured each other's intrigue, without seemingly even trying to.

And suddenly she was up and walking away slowly. She turned and gazed at me while stepping carefully backward. Turning about again, she threw back her head and confined me once again with that smile.

"Yupp…

Promise," she lilted out

She then sassed, tossing a freshly unwrapped, red blow-pop into her awaiting mouth and she faded off into the outer hallway in route to her next class.

I just stood there. Nimble yet fully unable to move or respond. I'd been waylaid.

That girl had just completely blown my mind—fo'sho'.

And…She'd done it so tough. Leaving me there all bothered and extended to fend for myself—hoping nobody else would take notice of the traitorous knot of the outline of my deeply disappointed, thirteen year-old boner before I was able to suppress it completely, sweeping it securely back under a well-hiddened out-of-sight control.

With her at fifteen, and myself, almost fourteen, I got first option to see all of that body, in its completely nekkid', pliable splendor, about a month after the moment of our first meeting. She'd been held back twice during her years of a more formal education.

THANK GOD.

And she became *MY GURL'* the very second she'd gotten up off that lunch bench and sachet'd away so haughtily.

As I've recounted previously, she wasn't my first sexual encounter. I guess you could say I'd been willingly molested at the age of seven, by a teenaged auntie who visited us from Detroit. But infinitely now, that experience didn't matter and was barely held onto in the routine basis of not permitting it to even count. All it did was place me inside of a vagina for the very first time.

That occurrence then, was kind of confusing for me and not at all at my own behest. She was fourteen at the time. My mother, her sister, had left Toppa and me alone in her care while she ran the streets, and auntie made proverbial use of the time. She did everything, from performing for us first, then instructing us as best she could, in the tangy, face-scratching complexities of an entirely strange obsession we didn't really enjoy at the time, called—oral sex.

I never thought the little node of skin tying my tongue to the inside of my mouth would ever return to its original state. At seven, this scared me. It was so sore following that, for seemingly a week thereafter. And the scratchy, scraping grain of her pubic hair had wreaked havoc on the softening flex of my seven-year-old facial skin, as she'd ground her hips like a mad-Woman into my face, as she'd become lost in the pleasures of having her miniature nephews service her completely. She forced us, one after the other to, "Take your time. Try ta' get tha' hang of it and do auntie a good job, just like she just did for you."

Ole' auntie's urges had been ravenous. She rode and was ridden by the both of us, for extended lengths of time during her stay, any time she was able to con Mama'n into leaving us with her during the culmination of many of her lengthy absences.

He and I weren't yet 'shooting' shit. But every time Mama'n would be getting ready to go out with her partying friends while auntie was still there with us, *tha wind would blow* and we'd both be prepared to 'strap on' tha' wood when she finally walked out that front door.

We knew what time it was.

I think she got away with it all these years, without Mama'n ever finding out what she'd done to Top and I as little impressionable boys because we feared the wrath of our wholly unconventional mother, should she find out, more than we were actually bothered by the tepid, steamy wetness of her acts as they settled down to hover over us for almost three months, going on to providing the warmth of ill-gotten pleasures for years more whenever she happened by.

We weren't tellin'. Heeeck' no! We both understood that auntie wasn't *wrapped-too-tight* upstairs. And we also feared and figured that we ourselves were old enough to know a little bit about better thinking out what we were continually doing.

At that age...as long as she was openin' those legs on a daily basis, sadly, the two of us were continuing to dive.

Shame!

Although a pretty mischievous lot at seven and nine, all the same, we weren't supposed to have been subjected or have been placed in such a position of having to turn away or provide acceptance of such obvious antics of familiar molestation.

Some say Revenge is a dish better served—cold

Rolanda and I first made Love about two weeks after her and her brother, Daniel, came to live with us at Maman's house, on De Leon. This came about on an unusually rainy night following a hauntingly eerie knock one Saturday evening at our front door.

First, it rarely rains there, specially the kind of down pouring storm it appeared to be without end that entire day. Second, Mama'n never got up to answer the door or the phone (When we had one). She considered herself and her time too valuable to waste in chasing after unanswerable calls that were rarely for her from the start.

Something about this particular knock that night had compelled her to wave me off as I'd headed forward to open the door. Upon reaching it, her heart almost leapt from her chest, as she opened it to find herself staring crudely into the ruddy faces of two of El Paso's finest.

THA' PO-LICE!

I know her mind raced rabidly, trying to initially figure out what she or one of us had done warranting their presence there, as they stared back at her at first glumly, standing outside the house. Any occasion the cops had for coming to even being within the vicinity of our home, for us, things ceased to become completely normal.

She always had weed strewn about all over the place. And if you looked hard enough, any amounts of other illegal drugs and other illicit substances could be found as well. That is, if she wasn't caught in the middle of one of her parties, the ritual of which, she'd resurrected in Texas, even after the episode years before in the bloody tub of the bathroom with cousin Landa, back in our apartment in Pennsylvania.

Playing it off like the true champ she was, Mama'n merely smoothed the front of her blouse and greeted the officers warmly, like they were long, lost relatives or something just returning from the movies to the house.

"Why, hello gentlemen. How may I be of service to you on this terrifically rainy evening?"

I could tell she was nervous. She kept scratching at the nape of her neck beneath the cascading length of her thickly splayed hair. The chalk-board resonance of her motions drove even the patrolman crazy as she continued to do this with the length of just one obtrusively long, red pinky nail.

Moving past this, they informed Mama'n that they had Rolanda Howse and her brother, Daniel, outside in the back seat of their cruiser. They'd been told by the two of them that they knew us and felt they'd be easily welcomed into our home. Mama'n indicated that this was, in fact true.

"Yes, of course...Dan and Rolanda are over here all the time. They know they're always welcomed here in my home," Mama'n laid on the sweet motherly charm a bit thickly.

By that time, I was already, in my house shoes, standing out in the rain with the cruiser car door open, with Rolanda securely in a slump, inside the protective warmth of my arms.

Dan exited the car appearing to be in shock, extremely overwhelmed as he faltered beneath the weightiness of what the two of them had been through earlier in the torrent of that evening. Mama'n accepted the one, thinly stuffed, plastic bag containing a scant amount of their belongings from one of the policemen and hauled it with her into the house.

I was still in the dark as to why they were there. I hadn't heard any of the conversation she'd had with the first policeman upon initially opening the door to find him standing there in front of her. From the looks of things, the two of them had left wherever they'd been earlier that evening in a hurry. The bag contained only their necessities, toothbrushes, changes of underwear and their school work and the such.

We lent them a day or two of solemn contemplation. Mama'n laid out strict orders that they weren't to be messed with, or pestered by us hitting them with all kinds of prying, none-of-our biddnazz type of questions. We respected her demands. Neither of us wanted to have to sleep outside in the backyard, with Sabu', possible consequence for stepping up to go against her sternly placed word.

We eventually learned the full story of the harrowing ordeal the two of them together had suffered.

Their mother, a hard working Woman from Las Vegas had worked as an LVN the very brief time we'd known them. Always on the move, charging ahead, and forever absent, Daniel and Rolanda had generally tended to themselves during the lengthy hours of treading sometimes-double shifts she pulled in earnest, trying to keep the three of their heads above water.

Turns out—those were the least of her worries outright. She was newly married to a very young, homicidally jealous, Nigerian manic and student, named Bobotu' Okwnonde. His brother, Obbalenda, often shared their apartment any time Bobotu' saw fit.

This was an arrangement Miss Dorris, Rolanda's momma, hadn't taken so easily to at first. She had a young, teen-aged daughter's safety to consider. But she quickly gave in under Bobotu's assurances that everything would be just fine.

"*Everry Ting' will Wok—oowut', Juuust find, my spring flouuwwa'. Yoou will seeee!*" He'd guaranteed.

Miss Doris saw all right.

She'd seen in the form of coming home one morning after slaving through a double shift, only to be met by an enraged Bobotu'. He'd stalked around, upsetting things inside their apartment as he' seethed there seeming for hours, the increasing nature of his rage incensed by an uncontrollable, boiling fury, threatening at any minute appearing about to blow. He'd made Rolanda and Dan's life hell as they all waited for their mother to walk unknowingly through the door.

All six foot five of his African massiveness, with his eyes bleeding a hampering, murderous red, took off after her, immediately, as she'd almost made it out of the cab that had deposited her in front of the apartments following her late return home that day from work. He pulled her morosely from the cab's doorway, before she even had a chance to complete her transaction with the frightened driver. After flinging little Daniel off his back, as if he were merely a bothersome fly to be swatted, he started bashing her against the outline of the vehicle. Her head slammed unrestrained, into the sloping curvature of the taxi's rear door. The driver had no clue what he'd just driven into. The resultant shatter of imploding glass from his rear window mixed with their mother's spurting blood as it splattered about what had been his side view showering him before he could pull the car into gear and speed away plainly to safety.

Dorris's mad Mandinka then dragged her limp, already lifeless form into the inner overhanging shadows of their apartment building. Once there, lifting his own head, he peered back at his brother, Obbalenda, who smiled widely, and he let out a blood-curdling, aboriginal scream. Showcasing thirty-two overly white teeth, their size and form set into a mandible more reaching the volume of an overly enraged gorilla, he then reached down ceremoniously into the hidden depths of his pants and produced an eight inch butcher's blade, six inches of which, he then plunged completely into the top of her skull—both hands wielding its stock, attempting to end her life swiftly.

Rising from overtop of her, to join his brother's celebration, Bobotu' then returned to the throne of *his* home, where *she* and *her* children had held the status of being only would-be-guests—beholden only *to him.* There he sat with a proud, arrogant bearing, until such time as the cops finally arrived, lent minimal aide to Miss Dorris, and carted his whacked out azz downtown to be placed up under the slammer.

Obbalenda was nowhere to be found at the moment the smoke finally cleared just a couple blocks up from our house. I think he eventually was apprehended, but got off—claiming that he too had been intimated with fear of his crazy brother and that he'd had no prior knowledge of his formerly bloodthirsty intentions as well.

Miss Dorris wouldn't tell. She was barely able to remember the events of the *accident* at all. (That's what the two Nigerians referred to the incident as amongst themselves whenever Obbalenda visited Bobotu' for a couple years more in prison) It took her a full period of about nine months to minimally recover.

Obbalenda got off scot-free, for a while—in a way.

What had occurred was Obbalenda and Dorris had argued earlier two days before. She'd confronted him with topics along the lines of his asinine unwillingness to do domestic chores such as—cleaning up after himself, doing his own dishes when he made a mess, and among other things his putrid disregard for his own, personal hygiene and his laundry as he loafed lazily about each day lying around in their tiny apartment.

Obbalenda had found it increasingly tempting, and had been just two seconds from reaching out, to strangle Dorris himself during the heated diatribe that had spewed between them. He'd felt, and would eventually state that he took her disrespectful claims to be expressly aimed *at his manhood,* her taking unlawful advantage of him while his brother had been away at UTEP, the school they both attended.

Realizing that his brother's retched temper command a jealousy that walked a finely taut and teetering line, he'd instead only raised his voice in reply to her ranting. He chose as an alternative the opportunity of steeling himself while concocting a scheme better than anything else he could have considered to make her pay for having put him down so with such embarrassing defiance.

The *problem* with her, as he saw it, was his brother Bobotu's lion to tame anyway

—Not his own. He'd just make it all happen, by throwing the hunter the cunning subtlety

of a skillfully placed hint on the end of an arrow; and the hunted, foul-mouthed lioness would receive all that she had coming, he was certain. A deeper anguish than even he would be able to wickedly stoke by himself awaited her. She'd be made to pay for keeping with her formerly intensive, idiosyncratic mannerisms of harassment she'd so obtrusively spat at him two days before.

All he had to do was whisper frantically to his brother that he'd witnessed a man of his bride's awful choosing pulling his car away from the curbside in front whenever he wasn't at home. He even added to this a miserable claim that he'd supposedly *almost caught the sucker* scuttling through the opening of the back window of his brother's own bedroom, while Bobotu' had been away, studying at the university.

He gave him the overacted air of impression, "*My broth-a', I could not hold it back, and away from you—any longer.*"

The fuel with which he'd tended his worthless fire immediately fanned out to enrage his brother's ire further. Bobotu's reaction was like that of a finally unleashed tiger that had been penned up, and not fed for adjoining weeks, as the criminally insane cycle inside of him churned, stepped up diabolically as it was engineered through the vehement acts of his brother—A man whose own jealousy at his sibling's relationship with Dorris was the actual reasoning behind the whole show.

He'd played the negativity of his unanswered desires for her out upon an unsuspecting flock of lambs, which included her wide-eyed, mostly innocent children.

I was overly jubilant when I found out, many years later, that that dog had actually gotten his own day beneath the warming lights of a cold table on coroner's row. The formerly very distinct features of his body had been mainly deemed unidentifiable due to the marred trauma he had undergone, making identification and solving of the crime a point of moot acceptance.

The recollections of a mind belonging to a grown, more—manly Daniel had returned one day to the scene of his mother's attack and torture. He was accompanied by other, very-concerned members of the family, from out of town. When the family members were well on their ways back to Nevada, they left the lifeless form of one Nigerian accomplice limply waiting for Monday's outhaul in a dumpster at the back of the very same apartment where he'd continued to live in stupidity following the *accident.*

Time had finally caught up with him, canceling out his wicked forevers completely as his days were stomped *(VEGAS STYLE!)* restlessly from him for good.

Rolanda's body was a genuine piece of hard-earned, distinctively defined work. At fifteen, she had curves, nips, tucks and crannies in all the places young women like her, who graced covers of a hoard of sold-out, choice rags command in a crowded room full of pubescent wide-mouthed boys to flock around, fawn over and see.

It was nothing to catch myself quivering nightly in a hover over the spread before me on *her* page three. I poured over them to devour her inviting shots hungrily as the two of us conjured up purely carnal images well into the later hours of many evenings when we were alone my bedroom behind closed doors.

Mama'n had vacated her own room to give the poor soul a semblance of privacy when she and her brother had first materialized at our front door. This turned out to be heaven for me. It wasn't more than a week after she and Daniel had come to stay with us that on a quiet evening, after everyone in the house was plainly asleep, that I was startled awake to find her poking her head quietly into my room.

"What you doing?" I whispered to her in a half-dazed sleepy stupor. I could see by a lofty moonlight to take in a full view of the naked outline of her body through the sheer nightie she wore, that it took only a second to remove.

"I can't sleep," she sent back. Shifting now, one fully stacked hip to another in a bothered huff of repressed frustration that seemed to play out all about her lustfully structured womanish frame.

"Got too much pent-up energy…Need some help getting' rid of it. You game?"

I just sat there for a split second. My mind not fully registering the gist of the meaning of the simple words she'd just said.

At first.

Immediately after tossing in her grenade, she wheeled about abruptly and returned to Maman's room. Secure in her confidence that I'd provide only one answer to her question, she had removed the nightie and waited for me properly, in the comfort of Maman's bed.

"Was I game? Pa-lease!"

I was more than game. It had teken me about two seconds to throw back the covers and bolt my ass right outta my own bed. Throwing little vigilance to taking the care to make certain to be as quiet as a mouse while trying not wake up the whole house, I was offering little opportunity for her to change her mind, given time. The expectant excitement of getting next to her that evening completely outweighed any caution, including condoms, that I might otherwise have given a fleeting concern.

Embarrassingly, it took me about as long to expend myself once I'd scooted between the covers with her and entered her sweetness completely bare.

I couldn't help it. I'd never yearned in desperate patience for something so bad in all my iife. I had built up very little skills of a stamina'd maintenance while only experiencing greatly with masturbation on such a grand scale up to that period.

Things got infinitely better. Being young and strapping, it was only a second's whistling of a cold Texas nights wind blow and I was *up and at it* again.

Overcoming her initial jeers and giggles at my original prematurity, she and I took our time the second time around. It didn't take the two of us long at all to amiably develop a unison of sweat-filled, mind-numbing rhythm.

Our conjoining tune lasted for the entire period, almost nightly, for the full six months she and Daniel stayed with us. Of course, we didn't hit each other up only in the comfort and sanctity of Maman's bed. We christened every area of the house and on the outsides whenever we were alone.

We felt, due to our sexual promiscuity, that we were plainly in Love. We never wanted to be out of the company of one another. We refused to accompany the rest of the family on outings and trips to the store and such, having better things to do once everyone else exited.

Of course, Mama'n wasn't stupid. She made this plainly felt one day as she returned to the house from an outing which had taken her grocery shopping. Rolanda and I were sitting on the couch watching TV as intertwined with one another as we could possibly be without shucking off our clothes completely. Exiting the kitchen, she reached into a bag she still held lightly before her, prior to sweeping through the front room area in route to the rear of the house, and she made a silent presentation of forcefully tossing an industrial sized box of latex condoms at me. Catching the object with quick reflexive action, I turned it over to see what it actually contained.

Seeing the item more now than I had at first, Rolanda hid her face in a couch pillow, giggling wildly, and feigning being overcome by embarrassment.

Who'd we think we were kidding?

Turning the item over, I saw it was a carton about as big as a container holding a specialty tea. It was a super-sized box of condoms. Mama'n had only tossed them in my lap and "*Harrumphed,*" continuing her motion toward putting away the rest of the items she'd brought in with her.

When the six months was nearing its end, Rolanda began to attend school less and less. Having more endearing things to do with her time, she'd leave the house with us every morning. But she'd split off and make her way toward other things not having anything close to do with school.

I'd often wondered, thinking about her time and time again before this, how she must have felt being the only fifteen year old, young woman, attending the eighth grade at Morehead Junior high among the rest of the class. She was far behind. But I'd never spoken to with her concerning this. I just left it alone and chalked it up to parental misgivings. We all knew what that could be like.

Before long, she not only stopped going to school, but she stopped showing back up at home at the end of each day. Our trysts in Maman's bed began to occur on fewer and fewer occasions. This soon materialized into just showing up on the weekends. At which time, she'd sleep all day and be gone as dusk began to gather. Back out into the lure of the streets where she'd come to discover a different life all together.

We moved once more.

Man…don't these landlords ever check with the landlords before?

If they did, we'd a' been assed out, sleeping in the streets. Maman's record for absconding without paying the rent was notorious. It wasn't even funny anymore.

This time, we landed in a really nice apartment complex just behind Coronado High school on the West Side. The compound was beautiful. There was a tennis court, recreation room, with pool tables and a swimming pool. We had three bedrooms, one for each of us.

But still no Rolanda.

By this time, their mother was fully as recovered as a person who'd been through the trauma she'd survived could be. Daniel rejoined her in their *new* apartment. But we lost touch with Rolanda. We'd heard she was hanging out in a project with an older guy, named, Harry, at his sister's house—off of Railroad.

I was grief-stricken for a time.

I really missed her.

But I never saw Rolanda again.

I missed her so much that I began to act out and do stupid things like getting in trouble in school. I even returned home from school one day, to find the little Mexican girl there, who Mama'n had hired as a maid. Yeah, things had gotten a lot better for us, just prior to moving up the hill, toward the high school. Mama'n had held a job for a time, doing transcription for a group of doctors at Sierra Medical Center. She just had that problem thang—with paying the rent when she was supposed ta'. For real! It was a sickness...

Returning home that day to find the maid there was a normal circumstance. What wasn't normal was not sharing my day with Rolanda. Being unable to toy with her and see her face and feel her warmth for another entire day was about to drive me crazy. The hardest part, after coming to care for her so profusely, was not know anything about where she was—whether she was okay. That ached and hurt me inside.

So for the first time ever, I got drunk.

Mama'n had always kept a full gallon of Manischewits on chill in the fridge. Besides, the approaching summer temperatures could have already fried an egg on concrete, literally that day in El Paso. This compounded the effects of the wine. And although there was rarely a shortage of that wine, we never had enough Kool-Aid or juice or sodas or sugar for the Kool-Aid and Mama'n wasn't playin' when she said, no A/C during the day—cost too much. Not only the outside temps, but inside the house too was sweltering.

It seemed Mama'n could never buy enough cold beverages to keep in stock three days after shopping. So, the only thing available to me as I stood before the cool breeze blowing at me from inside the fridge, was that oversized bulbous green bottle of wine. It was cold. It was sweet. And I had a real bad jones on.

It took me eight straight trips of turning that bottle up in increasing sips ta' get pissy snockerin' drunk. I got so bad, that I've been told I chased the little maid girl around the house, terrorizing her to a point she threw up her hands, murmured something about Madre' Mary and the DIOS and gathered her things and headed for the nearest bus stop as quickly as her scrambling feet could carry her. I didn't remember a thing.

She quit!

But that was all right. We were all getting tired of her boiled chicken anyway. It was the only thing she knew how to cook. And she only half-assed cleaned a good house. I think Mama'n had all but *Taken Her In*, as a project, as a favor to a friend at work.

But still, Mama'n was furious returning home from work to find me drunk, a full gallon of her wine…and her maid, gone—nowhere to be found, and facing the probability of having to once again do a full share of the housework she thought she had progressed past having to do.

It was way too much for her. She lost it.

Shades of the former, Pennsylvania Mama'n showed back up with a terrorizing complexity. She punched and bounced my sorry ass around that house like a grown man in battle with another as the fuel of angered rage ignited. I was too sloppy to even think about putting up much of a fight in reply. I do remember thinking she was truly crazy as she reached for one of my twenty pound barbells to toss at me.

We ended with her holding her head, as she scanned to take in the mess I'd made of the living room and with me snoring snugly in my room—sporting a new black eye that I couldn't even feel for a full day more when I finally woke up.

Mama'n bounced around for a minute, between men. We moved again from our quaint apartment, to shack up with a character known only as *Tha WolfMan.* Henry Clay Lewins, was his actual name. He was originally from St. Louis. He'd come to El Paso years and years before with the Army. And completely out of character, he was actually older than Mama'n, by a far cry. A veritable *Sugar Daddy* was what she'd hooked ole' Wolf into becoming. We stayed with him for an entire summer, more towards about six months. We moved schools and began to reestablish our centers of living in an entirely different neighborhood where we knew no one, and unexpectedly, amid a stream of rapidly changing settings once again, Toppa and I thrived.

Ole' Wolf was called that because he looked just like that.

A wolf.

Slight, slipper wearing and bow-legged, with a deep, slow, almost painful to listen to, Southern *Draaawaaal*, his was a peaceful countenance and he was affectionately known and respected by every G.I. in town. He ran the barbershop on base and made his living, although he could barely read and write, off of a miniscule wage accompanied by quarter and dollar tips he received every day. I had no clue how the Wolfman did it.

His lack of education and obvious illiteracy notwithstanding, he'd return home following the leg warying numbness of every shift and fill huge Sparklett's water jugs, bottle after bottle, with nickels dimes and quarters to amass his fortune—while he drank a case and a half of Budwiser he had, stacked six feet high in his kitchen, without fail daily.

Although his relationship with Mama'n would falter (it was inevitable. Weez, hadn't yet proven her ability to keep a man. Besides, I think that the break up was pretty much mutual) The time she required of him began to get in the way of his daily beer drinking. He just couldn't have that. That was all he did.

Get up in the morning, make us all breakfast (wonderful grits, thick slabs of ham and a mountain of fried eggs—We thought we had died and gone to heaven) drink beer, go to work, come home, drink beer, while sniffin' after Mama'n all over the house, whining and beggin' for some leg. Drink beer, go to sleep. Get up the next day, do it all over again.

The thing about ole' Wolf was that he could sit there and put down case after case of beer, and he'd never appear to get drunk. He'd just sit peacefully in his little chair and drink, eyes yellow, hair all wild and lambasted about his face, but he bothered nobody.

Wolfman, his drinking notwithstanding, was another shining example to me—of triumph over adversity. An adversity that so many young black men run from, instead of battening down and diving in to make their mark by embracing it as a challenge, as he had, in creating their own successes in a bustling American economy which many refuse to accept as their own.

Eventually, Wolf would extend out and away from the shop on base to open his own shop, just off of Dyer. Seeing how he could style and cut a head of G.I. hair better than most men three states surrounding, his clientele roved with him. And he prospered.

The last time I'd stopped in to see him, following Maman's accident many years later, he had greatly expanded his personal directions of wealth. By then, his holdings included the title as owner and landlord; he owned more than ten houses. With the fires of an entrepreneurial spirit fueled by need and depression burning brightly deep inside of him, he'd pooled the change of those water bottles to purchase and rent out houses, mostly dumps, but income-producing properties, still the same—thereby adding credibility to his formerly menial, Budweiser empire.

To think, people used to make fun of his slowness and meek, under-aggressive nature.

He wasn't pretty. With the sides of his hair fluttered back and with long, thick sideburns touching down to greet a nappy, wooly beard, he took on the features of a gray-haired, honey-colored wolf. And, even after all these years he was far from being book smart. He can still only read and cipher only enough to carry out his all-cash businesses. But—*Wolf* was tha-man…

He carried those jeers and taunts of underestimation he received, weekly, *ALL THE WAY TO THE BANK* with finesse.

And I Loved that old cat.

It was about this time Mama'n first met *The Dark Ranger*, Garvin Emanuelles. He was an Army air defense technician stationed at Fort Bliss there in El Paso. Garvin wasn't very much to look at for Toppa and I, at first. He was just another young guy getting laid. I think he was about twenty-four when Mama'n first became enamored with him (making her thirty-one). Tall, dark beyond lights out on a moonless night—dark, he was about six-four, solid, and thickly muscled.

Just like she liked em'. She began to bring him home, to spend the night—*NOISILY*-on a more frequent-almost permanent basis after about a month of pretending for him—to be a *good* girl.

Who was *she* trying to fool?

From the start, Garv, was doomed.

Once Mama'n had her talons firmly seated into him, He didn't stand a fleeting chance of ever finding happiness with her. It was impossible. She didn't really even *believe* that it existed.

We were accepting of the guy—at first. He had a *keewel'* new Celica and he always seemed to have money. Two plusses in our book.

I'd later learn, ages and ages away in my own adulthood, that the poor guy only appeared to be so free-flowing in cash, because he was so young, and he had no family or bills previous to taking us on to spend his pay on. For a boy fresh off a farm in Connecticut, Mama'n was an exciting, carnal derivative. One he couldn't wait to spend every cent of his earnings on in order to capture her and be able to call her his own.

Poor fool.

Although super quiet, to a point of almost appearing standoffish and reclusive, initially, he treated Mama'n the way so many others should have—but were either too selfish, too stupid, or too high to really bring off.

Things got real good for us—real fast.

I can only now begin to put together the positive complexities evident then, of finally having a man firmly ingrained in our household as a leader. All sorts of things changed instantaneously, when Garvin Emanuelles took over the place.

We moved again.

This time, our move was not the typical, former decamping leaning toward our usual nature, of running to escape paying the month's rent. Instead, we made a move more seemingly, toward something better.

A new house, in the Northeast section of the city, closer to Fort Bliss, on Decatur Street became home.

Garv and Mama'n appeared compatible. He was so quiet, seeming shrewdly to take his leads from her, while wisely manipulating the daily workings of our lives completely from behind the scenes.

They didn't even fight very much right away. Still, they kept Toppa and me up late nights, forcing us to fight through the heated grunts and piercing wails of their noisy Lovemaking. It was an encumbrance we were used to, having grown up with it, man-to-man over our youth. We really didn't mind at all too much as long as things continued to improve.

Things went pretty smoothly till Garvin, had to take a stint of temporary duty, first to Germany for a period of about six months, then following, to Korea, for an entire year away from us. While he was gone, the wild natural temptation of Maman's bad girl reared its ugly head to revisit and once more turn our World topsy-turvy, upside down on its head.

It was as if she'd been holding back the former, party animal grill within herself while he'd been there. And with him gone, it came bustling forward with an idiotic rage, all but crippled with a helpless explosion to chart the beginning of the end of her relationship with Mr. Emanuelles.

Years into my future, I would experience and witness the exact same thing in many of the Filipino women I'd encounter on the many trips I'd take myself, overseas with the Navy. These women, the sweetest, most down-to-earth and honest souls you could ever meet, would all but sell themselves to the highest bidder, nightly, inside the sparkling lights of the hundreds of night clubs and discos lining Magsaysay Street in Olongopo, a city in the Luzon province of the Philippines.

Their only goal, besides providing sailors and Marines, literally, *THE TIME OF THEIR LIVES* sexually, was to get married. They had an almost innate programming to snare a service member, convince him he couldn't live without them, all during the course of perhaps a week, in which she'd cook and clean and suck and fuck him like he'd never seen done in any imaginary fantasy he could have ever conjured up. And before you know it, she'd be hooked in to a fiancé visa, complete all the preparatory paperwork which would get her back to the states…and a follow on plan for getting the rest of the remaining members of her family, still in the islands to the states as well was actively thrown into motion over time.

You almost couldn't fault them. They were just like everyone else and seeking a better lifestyle. Searching for the best life had to offer them.

Big-Ups to them.

But what I didn't understand, at first…

Was what happened to these poor transplanted souls, at their own engineering (most of them) once they made it to America's opportunistic shores. Once here, they'd set up house with the sailor or Marine, as they'd previously advertised. They'd continue to be good to their betrothed, for a minute anyway.

It was once they'd been able to finally get here and become firmly ingrained in the way things worked, that the surface of a myriad of socio-fidelity problems would suddenly take foothold.

This would be far after the nuptials had taken place and maybe even after giving birth to the G.I.'s baby—Of course…Had to make certain they were legally entitled to whatever empires they'd be subjecting themselves-to *half* of—upon signing on the dotted line of the marriage certificate.

And then the *"far-ty"* would begin.

They almost couldn't help it. As couldn't Mama'n

For so long they'd only known one lifestyle. That of getting' ahead using the wiles of their body's as best they could. You couldn't expect them to simply be able to turn the lure of the streets, the allure of the *many*-dick, no matter the continent or surrounding, off inside of themselves. If you did, you had another thing coming.

All you have to do to witness this even today, is take a drive on a Friday night down National City Boulevard in San Diego—to the *Trophy Lounge*, located just outside the back gate of 32nd Street Naval station's dry-side. They had become so used to the variety of an entire fleet of men, back home on Magsaysay, that individual couplings with a single man over a lengthy period of time held them bored now, cooped up, feeling caged like chickens and unsatisfied.

This fact has always held me curious and I've even asked a fair amount of these women what things drove a great number of them to being such unfaithful wives and sometimes less than adequate mothers to their spouses and children.

Most would give an almost identical answer.

"O'-O' ("Yes," in their native language, Tagalog') Hun.... I know what yoo mean..." And she'd point at me. "Yoo know what I mean too, huh, hun...Can yoo live on ham-bur-ger a-loone? No, sum-tine not just the maaan need to have a leetle lobster too huh, hun?" Turning to lightly high five her girl, sitting beside her on a bamboo barstool, the particular girl in question went on about her business as she overacted her salacious sucking on a red lollipop, in an attempt, with increasing success, to get me to envision it as my dick.

Stepping closer to me and reaching down to grap my crotch, she tossed her head to one side and offered nonchalantly, "I'm a good mu-ther, hun....

It's just sum-times, I need steak tooo."

It was weird. This wasn't the Phillippines. This conversation took place in San Diego, in good ole U-S of A. They weren't bad people or hookers or even sluts. They didn't even make excuses. It's just the way for them that things ran.

Take it or leave it.

Don't get me wrong, there are other examples in which those relationships worked out like clockwork. Cases, I suspect where Love and not merely the perpetuation of falsehoods in the quest for a better life was involved. But those were few and far between, by comparison.

Maman's past had caused her the uncanny ability to play with fire—and win—more times than most.

Toppa and I had all but become immune. We had long before this begun to separate ourselves from the twisted occurrences, which took place in Maman's life. We'd developed our own, safety nets, per say. She began to once more run the streets and bar hop the shanty town establishments lining Dyer Street just outside the base at Fort Bliss.

It was also during this period of time when her luck would begin to take, with near-fatalistic irony, an almost drastic turn for the worst.

She had the ability to appear skilled at herding cats. All sorts of twisted, unruly maneuvers I've witnessed her come clean out of—smelling like a rose. But even with the best and at times the most terrible luck of any person, living or dead I have ever known, (call it blessings, Karma. Call it destiny. . . whatever) her nine-lives, inherited from her herd, were about to run a chilling dry spell.

She bought into her fate and explained as reasoning for both her good and bad fortunes, on having been born with a thin membrane, or a caul covering the front of her face as an infant. An anomaly which she professed brought her inter-phsychiatrical moods of discernible and clairvoyant powers.

Mama'n thought she was *Miss Laura.*

But I do have to give it to her.

There have been numerous times when she'd call me up from across country, and tell me she'd dreamed of fish and NETTIE'd turn up pregnant. Or she'd say she'd dreamt something was wrong with Toppa, who lived forty-nine states away. . . . And my phone would ring a half-hour later, with him pleading for bail money, because he'd gotten locked up following a scuffle with his wife, Monica—and the po-po's had carted his ass off to jail for pushing her around or for slamming her hand in the door and breaking it.

I've often wondered and wanted to ask why she never used any of that stuff (her powers) if she did have them, for the good of self. She only trudged along, appearing to step in life's shit droppings taking lumps squarely on the head as a daily occurrence.

Although I do believe she made attempts to helping others whose lives, believe it or not, were more unfortunate than her own. People like our adoptive sisters, Vette, and Nelle and Rolanda and her brother, Daniel.

Perhaps she did use the powers toward forwarding her own ambitions.

Once.

It was around the time a friend of hers, Cookie, and her three-hundred pound boyfriend, Bear, had had a falling out, and Mama'n had once again, with her own big-hearted misguided extension of goodliness allowed Cookie to stay with us to escape Bear's heavy handed blows. We didn't mind. We were used to some urchin or another being there to greet our homecoming following any given day's attendance at school.

Coming into the house to find Cookie there during her third week of squatting was nothing new. I was a freshman at the time, attending Irvin High School just down the street from our house. Garv, at the time, was still in Korea.

Things were wild.

I was ungodly tired. I remember I'd walked home, still half-in, half-out of my football uniform. I was too exhausted to take it off and leave it in my locker at the gym that day after practice.

She'd been sitting, watching TV when I entered the house. After shucking my gear and showering, I'd come into the front room, wearing only my robe, thinking I'd grab something from the kitchen real quick, take it back to my room and relax, where I'd begin to attack my homework.

Boy was I ever not ready for what happened next.

I guess I'd been moving around kind of stiffly. My toes, knees and other joints had all begun a painful rebellion following their workout that day previously at practice.

"You all right?" Cookie looked up, asking, *almost* in passing.

"Yeah...I'm all right. Just a little sore, from practice."

"Really?" She smiled at me. Cookie was a real cutie. But her smile held something else, altogether...wicked in store.

She was a petite *red-bone*, about in her mid twenties. Slender and a bona fide nice girl, with a very ample stack of always swaying titties, these were just a few of the benefits of having her stay with us. My eyes never seemed to miss that part of her as she passed by doing *whatever*.

"Yup. I'm cool."

Not even thinking where that yup would lead. I turned heading back into my room to eat the apple I'd retrieved and to start my homework.

"Well, you know..." she offered with a girly-girlish almost whisper, the softness in her voice changing subtly, "I've been known to give a mean massage. Knock them kinks right-out."

She'd caught me in mid-stride, patting the pillows of the couch lying beside her.

I'd turned back to face her. My apple caught up in mid-bite, still inside my mouth. Looking up at me from the couch, she then added, "Lay er' down right there. I'll hook you right up."

I'd all but forgotten that the only shred of clothing I had on was my housecoat. Perfect for a massage....Right?

Hiking her dress up in a sweet-smelling bunch about her pliable, baby-oiled knees, she straddled me softly while I lay on my stomach. She first poured then warmed the baby-oil she'd retrieved from the linen closet into her hands. Then, wistfully peeling me outta my robe, she began to knead and pull my tired, screaming muscles from one end of their soreness to the next. I felt I'd go to sleep right there, half-bucket-nekkid, on the couch, with Maman's friend straddling warmly atop of me.

Yeah....Right!

"How's that feel-*Baby*?" She bent down towards me, shocking me at first as she first whispered her question, but then followed it by licking lightly along the inner rim of my left ear.

I couldn't answer.

"All right." She then said, after working me over frontally for a full, fifteen minutes more.

"Turn over."

I just stared at her for a second. My mind blinded by purely carnal incantations of utter stupification. Furies of ingratiated hormones were all sweeping up at me, threatening at any minute to violently explode!

Looking at me incredulously, as if it should have been plainly evident to me, "So I can do the front, silly, she said."

Not thinking, at first, I turned over, without further questions.

Why'd I do that?

It didn't take a second for her to zero in, with a sweet, nonchalant flicker, on the engorging effects her hands had produced in me just moments before.

"Hmmmmph." She wandered matter-of-factly. Appearing not to be flabbergasted, or offended by my raging hard-on, which at the time, poked at a straight angle of attention directly up at her—She just spread a fair amount of oil in her hands, warmed them together furiously and began to spread them all over—covering my chest, my abs, and surprisingly, even my member in a slippery, glistening sheen of expectation.

She worked her way down the front of my torso. At first, with expertise, skipping over ole' *Appleseed* and his partners, appearing to ignore them, as she kneaded and tugged at the fronts of my thighs—all the way down to spending a year's worth of time on each individual toe—popping and bending them into pleasurable submission.

She then asked again, "How's that feel?"

I just moaned out compliance. Ready to succumb to anything she'd possibly pose right about that moment.

I thought she was done. Sensing a change in the aura between us, opening my eyes wide, I watched as she scuffled off of her perch atop me. Turning her back to me, I could only barely take in what she was doing just out of my view. But, she didn't leave.

Thank GOD!

Finished with whatever it was she'd been doing, she turned back around to me. Pushing me back down firmly from my half sitting, half lying position….She climbed back on top of me in a straddle.

She was in complete control of every nerve of my entire body.

I was at a complete loss for what she did next.

I was already most grateful for the simplicity of just the massage she'd already given me. And although a willing participant, I'd held no illusions of

Seated atop me, she reached between the heated crevices of the ruffled movements our two bodies made together, and grabbed me ever so lightly. I merely stared up at her, a vision of both shock and expectant awe playing taughtly to spread across my face.

I wasn't a complete doof. I knew what was about to take place. I was ready, not fightin' at all.

She guided him home to a heaven no longer covered securely inside the laced material of the panties she'd removed prior to turning back to me.

I gasped in an interrupted breath as the moist heat of her inner body rushed up to hit me in a whoosh, settling down in a pulse to engulf me fully.

Her own breathing increased to a husky whisper now as she looked down at me with a sweet smile covering the front of her own face.

Keeping to her previous form, she threw back her head and permitted the wet run of her tongue to repeatedly cover the outer ridges of her ruby lips lightly. She began to register in a satisfying whimper, her mounting pleasure, as she became further impaled upon me—Each increasing thrust forcing her closer to a powerful climax building inside of herself slowly.

"How," suddenly having to reach forward over my head to the steadying arm of the couch to remain upright....How...How's that feel? Ummm..." Was all she could get out right then.

And again...Of course....it was all I could do—Just to hold on.

There was no answer.

Maman's luck matched my own briefly.

When we were finished, Cookie looked down, peering at me more differently now than she ever had before. She shook her head rapidly from side to side, then went about the sordid chore of disengaging with that sweet, pleasurable terror that was just-spent passion, while popping her gum, she turned her head from one side to look at me deeply and only added, "Damn!..."

And returning to the persona of her former self, she asked, "Did your moms tell you, she won one of those radio show contests today?"

Me, being just a mere image of a man, only half heard what she'd said. I'd already tuned her almost completely out, no longer paying her any particular attention. Heck, I'd just gotten a *real* nut. I was chillin'—cool. And typically, like so many others who'd been on the receiving end of such subtle treatment from her, I'd already all but forgotten she was even in the room.

After coming from my second shower that afternoon, I again approached, with her looking up at me from her spot back on the couch in front of the TV. Smiling at me sweetly, she picked right back up, as if she was used to being ignored—after the fact.

"Yup, for real, I ain't shittin' ya'." I looked at her then with a smirk, thinking the lovin' had driven her mad and made her start talkin' crazy.

"She even won a motorcycle, some luggage and a trip to Acapulco."

Now I knew she'd lost it.

Maman seemed to be one of those people who was wholly incapable of managing her own life. Especially after Garv left for overseas service. Though the two of them had never appeared to get along all-that-great, in the first place, it was like Garv leaving had caused the little stability he'd instilled in her to come unglued irretrievably with his absence.

On a much smaller scale than we'd seen developed previously, she began to permit a more shady section of town to invade our formerly quaint home on Decatur Way. Instead of the abject junkies and smack peddlers, a more softened spectrum of functional drunks and weed smoking bums returned to begin to lurk around. It didn't really bother me. I remained aloof. Almost vindictively, I began to totally disregard people and things that entered and took place inside the walls of that home. For me, this had begun to materialize as a saving skill which held me distant from the ugliness of the things she permitted some of those surrounding her to pull her into.

So, when Cookie told me now that Mama'n had won some sort of contest, I just shrugged it off. Knowing, with Mama'n, just like with Cookie, I'd come to find out... Anything was possible.

Sure enough...

At about six thirty, later that evening, Mama'n came rolling up in our driveway, sitting atop a brand new Yamaha 400XS *Special*. She just sat there, gunning that throttle like she was a possessed mad-biker wench, till we'd all come outside to gawk at her. Queen *WEEZO'* and her mean, mean putt—puttin' machine.

I stood bowled over. I couldn't believe it.

She was all *dolled* up in full gear. Wildly colored helmet, leather jacket, her jeans covered sparsely by a pair of chocolate leather chaps which had dangling tassels at their sides. She even had on a pair of ultra dark specks—*Rayban's,* that the station had thrown in as part of her catch.

Good for Mama'n.

It was about time something good happened in her life. I could just see grand pappy, Ollie smilin' down at his little girl from heaven.

But this was to be a very short-lived thought in my own mind.

Mama'n had started messing with this smelly footed character we called only, B.J. The man had the worst smelling feet. The odor he could produce by just taking off his shoes was more offensive and stronger smelling than any other stench I'd ever experienced up to that point. So much so, that Toppa and I threatened to kick his ass out of the house, on numerous occasions if he ever took his shoes off again and tried to walk around inside the house thinking like that shit was some kind of normal. He knew.

We were serious...

We felt there was no reason the two of us should be forced to trudge through the cloud of funk his feet kicked up while trying to go about our own daily lives inside the comforts of our own home, just because he was seeing Mama'n on the sly while Garv was away.

Cookie went back to her abusive boyfriend, Bear. Her offerings to me had turned out to be very sweet, and also, as she had put it, "A one-time, sweet candy-deal type thang', *Baby.*"

I didn't hate.

Mama'n took some lessons and actually became pretty good riding her put-put machine. The running joke among my football homies, Mickey Rodrigo, Ben Azudo, and Mike-Mike Pauluto, was, that my mom's could take on an entire bar of Bandidos (a local motorcycle gang, notorious for their treachery) and win, drink a fifth of Scotch, and ride to the Carlsbad Cavern cliffs and back—all on a single tank of gas.

I wasn't studdin' them fools.

By this time, I'd long matured away from fighting over things my boys said about my mother. I Loved those guys. They were my true homies. "Besides," I'd tell them. "See there... She don't even drink Scotch. She's a Vodka and Manischewits Girl, to her heart."

And that's what just about killed her.

It was the day before Thanksgiving, 1981. I'd just turned sixteen, two months before. Mama'n had been home all day, preparing her turkey.

Sometimes, and I don't know how she did it. We'd have squat, abso-fuckin'-lootely nothing in our fridge, all year long, but every Thanksgiving, and every Christmas, she'd find a way to throw together *THA BOMB-Asse'd* feast and feed about twenty or thirty people who utilized our front door as a revolving swivel all day long feeding their faces.

And that year was to be no different.

Leaving *stank-foot* B.J. in charge of watching the turkey, she hopped on her scoot and high-tailed it up to make her rounds of the bars along Dyer to dole out merry *thanksgivings* while taking in a nip or four of getting' her drink on. Once there, she had her usual, Vodka and cranberry, *"Make it a double."* And, after socializin' a bit—the only way *WEEZ'* knows how, she got back on her bike and headed for home.

This time though, she'd never make it.

It was about ten o'clock at night when B.J. took the call. He had all but moved in with us. Garv was gone a long time and hadn't left anything resembling a wedding ring in his wake to remind her of her supposed commitment to him.

Giving Mama'n the freedom to play was a big mistake he hadn't calculated when he left us all behind to go on his overseas adventure.

B.J. shook me awake, lightly, and then stepped away from me with a quickness, before I was fully able to wake up. He was a slack, small little man, and he knew I didn't like him much, so he maintained his distance, even at such a horrendous time as that moment.

Inside, I knew he was genuinely a nice guy. So I didn't go out of my waym generally to give him too hard of a time.

All except for those feet...

"Your mother's in trouble," he half-whispered, half shouted at to me from across my room, pleading incessantly for me to get up. He moved closer to the open doorway than come near my bed.

"What?" I sent back, almost threateningly. "*What the heck was he doing waking me up at this hour of the night for? He'd never come into my room before like this.*"

I didn't like it. Didn't like it—or him, one bit.

"What... What—did you say?" I asked him. A mere bit of what he'd just offered beginning to register among the cob of sleeping webs crowding my sleepy head.

"Your mother...she's had some trouble, Blu. Now get up, boy! I ain't kiddin' ya'."

I began to slightly catch on then. And I began to shake the sleep from my mind to better think.

"Where's Toppa?" I asked him.

"He ain't home either," he sent back steeped with frustration

I looked over at my clock. Four—A.M.

"*Where the hell could he be?*"

After getting all of the particulars B.J. had, I called the number of an El Paso Police Detective who'd given his number when B.J. had taken the initial call.

I found out—Mama'n wasn't really in no trouble...She was almost dead!

She'd run the super machine into the back of a van that had stopped abruptly in her path, and was now in a coma, at Sierra Medical Center, the very hospital where she worked.

After speaking with the detective, I was dressed and out the door in a matter of minutes. At five-thirty in the morning, I began the trek of walking to Sierra Medical to see my Mama'n.

It took me four and a half-hours of walking. All the way down Dyer, up and around hillsides, Northeast El Paso, all the way to the northwestern side.

But I made it.

When I finally got there, I could no longer feel my feet and my legs felt as if, when I stopped, they would just fall off, right there where I stood. My inner thighs were chaffed and sore from walking.

Upon making my way into the hospital, I headed directly for the ICU. I knew my way around. It seemed we'd been there almost daily. Mama'n had worked there for a couple of years before.

Reaching the Nursing station outside ICU, a nurse recognized me and attempted immediately, with stern care to cut me off in stride, hauling up my steps.

At first, she held me at bay, an arm's reach away with her soothing words. And I broke down completely.

"I wanna' see my Mama'n! And I wanna' see her now!"

"Hold-on, Avery. Your mother's been in a terrible accident. And her condition is not such that we can allow her any visitors." The nurse said—all the while with me pushing my way toward the double doors, ignoring her—trying to get where I knew Mama'n would be lying. Waiting for me to show up

Realizing she was making no progress keeping me away from the doors, she turned me loose and headed off in search of help. I burst through the doors, mindful inside myself, that Mama'n wouldn't be the only person in the room, I slowed to a crawling pace, peering into the heavenly faces of each traumatized patient as I went about my business of searching for my mother.

When I found her, I was wholly unprepared for what I'd become faced with in the body of what awaited me lying in my mother's bed. She had tubes and monitors extending from her in every which direction. Blood still encrusted the rims of her broken fingernails, all ten of which had previously been self-manicured and stroked into a beauty of lengthy perfection but were all now broken off at jagged teeth clips at differing levels of each of her swollen fingers. The former talon'd length of each swiftly torn away following impact. Her hair, formerly naturally straight and marvelously flowing lay now, matted and encrusted as well with blood in heaping patches surrounding the extended puffiness of her face. She appeared swollen, from head to toe. She had splinting casts on a broken leg and one on a broken elbow.

She just laid there, a mere shell of her former, life-fulfilling self. A quiet, sleep-like unconsciousness making her appear surreal under the hawk of my watchful eye.

I called on the only thing I knew how to do under the circumstance of that current moment. Deeply, from a place inside of me that I never knew existed, I bowed my head and I began to half cry out, half whisper to GOD in prayer.

"GOD!" Don't take my Mama'n…" I begged him. "Lift her up, LORD. Get her up outta that bed and bring her back home. Pa-leaaassse! GOD, we need our Mama'n. Don't take her.

Have mercy LORD!…

And I turned about to find aunt Dee-Dee, another of Maman's friends and a registered Nurse who also worked at the hospital standing pensively, rubbing my back Lovingly there behind me. I felt totally helpless. There was nothing more I could do to help her.

I fell into her arms, exhausted from walking, crying and worrying. She was finally able to pull me away and after calming me more severely by further explaining the optimism of the seriousness of Maman's guarded condition, she convinced me that she would come over to the house each day and bring me back up to sit with her and I permitted her to give me a ride back home.

Ole' *WEEZO'* made a rapid resurgence. An astounding recovery to say the least. She stayed in her coma for about two weeks. She then just appeared to somehow, one day, snap out of it.

She came home, all a-fury of hustle and bustle, barking orders and creating ruckus.

We'd set up a donated hospital bed in the dining area of our tiny living room, one of those old, wind-away forever jobs that squeaked incessantly when you raised or lowered its head or tail. Toppa and I took agreed upon turns caring for her. It turned out, I did the most caring. I bathed and fed, and provided and emptied a bedpan for her when needed.

I still remember the first time I really had to give her a bath. The thing she said before I got started cracked me up to no end.

Looking down at me from high above the upper level of the bed, up on her pillowed perch, she said, "Now, Blu, one of us is gonna' have ta' close our eyes. Cause' you and I both know, you ain't sposed' ta' have to look at your Maman's, *Como Se ' Yama*. So, I'll just close mine and you can get on with your work."

She was a mess.

She might as well have had a glass bell, complete with a silver handle, the way she ran me ragged with the increase of her everyday demands. And I'll be honest. At times, during that period, I really hated her. She seemed to sometimes take pleasure and a sick advantage of the fact that I was always the one there, to wait on her, literally—hand and foot.

And Toppa, well, Toppa was just Toppa, never around very much when the getting' got bad and somebody had to step forward to the plate to take charge. I think even then, he felt it way too heart-wrenching to be able to steel himself against the anguish of having to see Mama'n in such a condition.

Who was I to complain?

The LORD had answered my prayers. He hadn't taken my Mama'n from me and he'd given her back with every ounce of her former ill-endearing feistiness.

This wouldn't be the last time he'd have to do that either.

Well, you know the deal. Rent came due... Twice!

We moved first, just down the block to another house on the same street but on the corner. We stayed there a piece, and encountered people like John Moore, another of Maman's conquests, and Leucille and Kevin. She and Mama'n had met while they were both sleeping with the same hustler, a punk named Roscoe, who'd played the two of them with impunity, till he'd finally gotten caught. Kevin was our six foot four, one hundred thirty-pound, *doorman*. Homeless when she'd first met him, he was about twenty years old and painstakingly loyal to Mama'n for her having given him a floor to curl up on at the end of each grueling day.

And he did what his title betold. He watched the door. Mama'n, quick to get back to hustling herself, even from a hospital, roll-away bed continued to deal during her recovery. I often wandered what good Kevin would do, should anyone make a bums rush on our door? Tall and lanky beyond stature, he was weak for a grown man. I used to throw him around whenever the two of us wrestled playfully. Sometimes I'd pin him in these ungod-awful holds and keep him there, till his cries for Mama'n would bring her out of her room, threatening me as all she had to do was look at me, to make me let him up again. His ego and machismo stained for about a week wherein he wouldn't even look at me without contempt until he'd finally get over it. Kev was like a weakling, big brother.

We all somehow formed for a time a completely hapless family. Somehow, eventually, Leucille and Kev got together and decided they liked each other's company way too much not to have to steal away from time to time to pester each other and bump uglies. They even eventually got married. I had a blast taking the drive with them, down to Huntsville, Alabama, so she could introduce him to her parents.

She had like eight sisters. All living on the outskirts of town in the comfort of a huge house their daddy had built on his farm.

Needless to say, it was a great trip.... For me, at least.

Mama'n once again cleaned out her closet and began to be a good girl. She kicked out all the smelly feet and hundred pound door squatters. She tempered her drug use to an acceptable purchase of *only for self-use* weed.

Ole' Garv was on his way back. He'd been gone for what seemed like an eternity.

And another anomaly returned to us, finally that year as well.

Miss Honey made her first summer trip to visit with us. It was the first time any of us had seen her since I was almost thirteen. She'd been seven the last time we'd seen her in P.A. She was now almost ten. Mama'n had somehow convinced Mr. George to let her fly down to Texas. I think he'd mistakenly felt she was somehow more stable, with ole' Garv around. She'd somehow given him this impression when we'd all packed into Garv's car and trekk'd across country and we'd seen him at grand pappy's funeral.

Both Toppa and I were ecstatic.

But the one it affected most—was Garvin.

He immediately fell in love with the little urchin, the second she stepped off the plane. And she liked him a lot, initially as well. He doted on her.

Spoiling her and treating her with genuine, fatherly care as if she were his own daughter.

I think that deep down inside, he broke down the worst, out of all of us, when we finally had to take her back to the airport to get back on the flight heading for Pennsylvania at summer's end.

Following that, we moved deeper inland into an even nicer house on Nike Lane. We were still in the Northeast.

We had just moved in that day. I was still busy unpacking boxes inside my room and had all but gotten everything put away where it belonged. It was getting dark. Toppa was out running the streets. He'd barely helped move his own stuff in, threw it all in a heaping pile in the center of his room and had taken off without a word. Garv had CQ (Command Quarters, meaning he was away for a twenty-four hour period—on duty) and Mama'n was three fifths into her fourth Vodka double, all but comatose in a snoring stupor position curled up in one of our large living room chairs.

I wasn't about to speculate out to take in the spoils of our new neighborhood. I was too tired from moving. I was headed straight for bed after ensuring all of my things were situated just right inside of my room.

I never made it to bed that evening. I became alerted to an assembly of male voices which suddenly seemed to be coming from what sounded like harmonies coming from just outside my window. It sounded like a lot of them too.

I wondered…Reaching up to pull back the curtain I'd just recently hung, I looked off in the close distance, down towards the corner. There I could barely make out the shadowy faces of what I could tell was a group of brothas gathered there.

Then, I could make out…Somebody…They…were actually—singing…

Those fools were old-time crooning. Right there outside of my house. I Loved it! I had never really seen anything like it in real life. I'd heard of the brotha's in the forties, fifties, and sixties hanging out on street corners, fine-tuning their craft with hopes of one day being discovered. But I hadn't actually witnessed the real thing in action. I was enamored and I quickly became consumed.

Getting dressed in a hurry, I slipped on my house shoes, and after making certain my pants hung just right, almost seeming to fall about my knees, I set out for that corner too—to join in.

When I got to them, they each introduced themselves invitingly. There was none of that, "Who-You? What you doin' on our block"—type hoodoin'. These brothas were a real friendly lot. Following introductions, they accepted me into their fold at first sight, without questions or threats.

There was Lonny and Johnny Williams. Both about six-two, and powerfully built man-boys. Both of them nice guys and extremely, gentle giants. Their sister Tanya Williams. You can only imagine how she was built if her brothers were of such mammoth size. Tanya was a female version and a year older than the twin brothers, about six feet tall and a Mack truck from the top of her head to her heaping, overflowing chest, down.

Gerwin Williams, another new homey in the group had a thing for Tanya. Truby and Auzelia Cale, were also intricate members along with their brothers, Fabe (FABEOUS) and Right (ALL RIGHT) Marley, all Jamaicans. Truby was way sexy. Tall, dark and pretty—Thick, and exotic—Stacked to the Tee's. There were also siblings, Dave and Pamela Burstow.

I first met the homeys, standing around, out there—singing on that corner, before I'd ever met any of the honeys. In fact, turns out, none of them actually even lived on my street. They'd all just been leaving the house next door to mine, over at the Pall's.

"The hardest thing to do is watch the one you love, love someone else"

Chapter Six
'STRAWBERRY'

The sisters, Lucinda and Kammy Pall, were an antithetical study in confused contention. It was they, through their actions, whom first taught me the lesson (although at the time I had no way of knowing it) that—you find the best jewel (even in a woman) when you aren't actually searching for one at all.

Kammy—small and slight.... Petite, quiet towards sneakiness, more approaching a calculating—slyness, was at the time the self-appointed star. She was more cunning than she was beautiful, and more lacking of intelligence than she was cunning. If I'd a known better, again, I would have run for the hills, the very second I'd met either one of them.

Lucinda, two years older, taller, obese—but plainly tolerant of her weight, which she wore well, offered an extreme contrast to her little sister, Kammy, whom she affectionately referred to as "Bey". Although very possibly even more beautiful than Kammy, Lucinda's style was to permit her inner peace to be overtended and surrounded by the immensity of her physical girth, which, although she peered at it with a helpless acceptance, it didn't extend her the air of self-confidence in her everyday dealings.

Extremely unsure of herself, and yet still outspoken, in a slapstick, jovial, *I can laugh it all away* matter of psyche, she depended on her little sister, gravely, for her leads in almost every endeavor. Rarely, if ever, could she be counted on to develop an individual, creative thought or capturing idea on her own. With Kam in the lead, it was a comical set up of a case of the blind leading the blind. And they both tended to head, no matter the situation, increasingly toward the encrusted edge of the nearest, most deadly sloping cliff.

I came to find out that very first night of living on Nike Lane that the Pall sisters were both promiscuous little erotic freaks. The two of them together as seductive teens were already skilled in the guile of feminine sexuality and ways. As well, I was also to find out that they were more than willing to play with the fire of unprotected sex amid sensual encounters the two of them joined in on with an earth-shattering frequency, as if it were mere child's play.

You had to think... With reps like that, what guy in his right mind would ever seriously think about marrying one of them?

Well, let's see...

There was Fabeous.

And then, there was me.

After meeting the fella's outside on the street corner, I'd invited them all inside our house, just to warm them up, hang out a little and take stolen nips at Maman's Vodka for starters. We hung out in my room for about an hour before we all began to conjure up better ways to be spending our time together on that particular summer weekend.

I think it was me who first suggested, "Hey, don't you homies know any hunnies we can call to come over and kick it with us?"

"Yeah...*Scraight!"* Gerwin answered, but then he just stood there, rubbing his hands together, back and forth, as he began to peer back at me strangely.

I had no clue what had just happened between us. It was *Right* and Dave who stepped forward to finally let me off the hook.

"Man, homie! You really don't know—*Do You*?"

"Know what?" I turned then to Dave to fill me in further.

By this time the whole gang was either snickering into cupped palms or laughing out loud so profusely that they bent over at the hips to keep from falling down in their pleasure at my darkened ignorance.

"Damn, dogg... You got the most down hunnys living in yo' lap right next door."

I was like—*What!*

"Yup." All the brotha's began to gather together with a faked glee club unison and they all bore sharp whitened teeth at me as they began to slowly arch their brows while shaking their heads up and down, gesturing with hitchhiker thumbs, pointing in the direction of the pleasure dome that existed not twenty feet away next door.

Fabe pointed to Dave. Dave pointed to Lonny. Lonnie pointed to *Right*.

Right set me straight. With his thick Jamaican drawl, he told me, "Well, mista' new guy on dee' block, you just happen to ave' just next ta' yo' door," He pointed once more toward the North wall of my room, the one in the direction of the Pall house. "Out dee' front, back, mittle' Wha'Evah', dee mose' willing, sex tangs in hour' en-tire school..."

Just then, he began jumping up and down, patting his brother, Fabe on the back as he became unable to control himself, overcome in the telling of the glee I should have felt for having the fortune of where I had moved.

Johhny stepped up with gargantuan ease and sought to shush us all and calm us down. "J"...was always the caretaker of our bunch. He didn't want Mama'n to be woken up to swoop in on us. There was definitely something brewing between us all. We could all feel it. And he didn't want her to get up and kick us all out.

"Well?" I threw back at them with the inevitability of a silently thrown challenge.

It was my turn to bait them.

My *"Well"* had said to every one of them, "Put yo' money where yo' mouth is, fools. Pick up the tellie and call them ho's."

They all stood around a second more before *Right* stepped forward with his aggressive stance and said, "You ain't said nutting' butta' ting'. Where is dee phone? I'll call dem'."

...And he did.

It wasn't long before we not only had Lucinda and Kammy, but Pamela, Truby, *and* Tanya, all close to bucket-nekkid, crammed up in my tiny room as the guys cheated their ways to peeks at nipples and hairs peaking out of bush panty lines over a game of strip poker while again, sippin' away at Maman's gallon jug of Vodka which we'd mixed with Kool-Aid we just happened to have enough of that day in the house.

It drives me crazy even today to think I met my first wife as she lay around, half-nekkid in front of a bunch of dudes, all half-drunk and chomping at the bit to take *another* turn at getting next to her.

But it's the truth. I did.

Immediately, the ruby red hue of her inviting lips led me to start calling her strawberry. From the very second I pulled her away from the rest of the fella's and took her into Maman's bed to have my *own* shot at calming that untamed beast between her thighs which appeared, from her rep, to drive her so incessantly insane, I thought myself at first successful?

How many of you know that I wasn't reaching for success at all?

Who was I trying to kid? I'd sweat and I'd sweat over top of that girl a thousand times of heated, sexual engagements and she never once had orgasm one. At least not until after the two of us were already married and we finally began to settle down and take time to learn and be taught all that we could about one another.

Thinking back, I've often wondered... Why was she having all of that sex back in high school if she wasn't able to experience the full joy of sexual completion an orgasm could bring?

But why'd I want her to do that? My teaching her to have the expectation of the build up and release of her own orgasm came to be the eventual downfall of our very short-lived marriage.

After asking her father for her hand, I quickly took off to return to Great Lakes to continue my Electronics Class "A" school with the Navy. I finished the school in February of 1984. She and I were married that same month and I flew her out to San Diego so the two of us could begin to set up (more-play at setting up) house.

We got a quaint little, furnished-studio apartment in North Park. At three-hundred fifty dollars a month, on a Third Class Petty Officer's pay, it was all I could afford, and keep up with my little car payment while ensuring we had the whopping seventy-five dollars worth of food we spent to keep us going every two weeks. Because money was so tight, and because I was transitioning from one school straight into another one, this one a Class "C" in which I would learn the total workings of the Navy's Close-In-Weapon system, we didn't do very much together, except make Love.

Stupidly, we even took our chances on trying to have a baby. In fact, we made Love so much, without protection or successes, that when I finally got over Kamm and had met "NETTIE", I told her that I wasn't sure I could even have kids due to the fact Kammy was never able to become pregnant.

I look back and believe that GOD knew what was best for me then. He knew whatever she and I produced as a blessing during our marriage would only be brought to suffer beneath the outright selfishness and vindictiveness of our natures which had no business even being together as man and wife at such early ages in our lives.

My involvement with Kamm came to a screeching halt about eight months after we were actually married. I had completed the final phase of my military schooling and had reported for duty aboard the guided missile cruiser, USS ENGLAND (CG-22).

From the second I reported to her, she was, as they say, *Haze Gray and Underway* seemingly forever. I'd leave on a Monday and not return for some times weeks. There were *Readiexes, Comptuexes, RefresherTrainings,* and drills, drills and more drills. Everything a learning sailor needed most if he were going to accept preparation needed to counter the mighty Russian war machine at sea during those Cold-War movements of the early 1980's.

I'm not sure if our union would have survived even if I'd been a banker or a garbage man. All of my Navy training could only be accomplished while the ship was out to sea. And Kamm was the kind of girl who couldn't keep her hands to herself when left alone inside the tempting venue of an empty candy store.

A candy store.... That's exactly what San Diego California became for her. As I've said before, the poor girl had *FREAKISMS* all locked up inside of her and she had a desperation of need for seeing to them—that they were let out, loosed to an end—with me nowhere around to take my proper place in providing her the key.

The ship had been underway for quite some time on one particular occasion. I remember I had held up a partner and friend of mine, D-D Plout, as he was preparing to depart once we'd pulled in. D-D was a disbursing clerk. He managed the pay of more than four-hundred men, without a hitch daily and with ease. He knew all the pay manual rules and directives and could spout them out, verbatim, upon demand, whether it was the lowest ranking Seaman or the ship's Captain standing before him in front of the half-cutoff service door of his office.

Catching up to him, I ventured, "Say, D! Wait up a minute man."

Throwing back a discerning look of impatience, he slowed his roll just as he was about to round the corner which led to an athwart ships passageway just behind the quarterdeck leading to the freedom of the brow. He raised his arm high in the air and shook his watch at me. Meaning I'd better talk and talk fast while not impeding the flow of his intensions for liberty.

"D? What do I have to give my wife if we ain't gonna' be married no more?"

He looked at me strangely for a whole lot of seconds more before replying. I could tell my words had sort of stunned him stopping him abruptly and caused him to remain cemented rooted in his tracks.

He then set his laundry bag down lightly on the non-skid of the deck and beckoned me coolly to meet with him closer near a lifeline outta' the way of all the other exiting traffic.

D-D Plout, was my maanss...He sat me down that very second and began my eventual schooling with the words...

"Blu? Now, tell me this before I hip you to anything. Are you and your wife really calling it quits? I mean," he shook both his hands exasperatedly—The tips of each of his fingers making distinct snapping sounds as they met quickly with one another in rapid succession.

I was initially taken aback by his reaction thinking he wasn't really taking the question I'd asked him seriously.

He stepped closer more. "Naw, little bro' don't think I'm throwin' you da' foo-foo. I feel you. I really do." He stepped back and turned a complete circle before settling back down in front of me.

"You just don't know how bad I've been wanting to peep you in on a lil' *sumpin'*-sumpin' I've been made privy of—concerning zactly' this very situation—you see." It was my turn to peer at *him* blindly for a long second. I had no clue what this fool was getting at, standing before me talking so excitedly in tones of jive ebonics, a term that hadn't even been invented as yet.

He went on, "I just wanna' know fo-sho', you hip...If you really made up your mind ta' finally kick that ho'in' foot-draggin' skeezer to the curv', *Knoa-I'm-Sayin'*?"

He had me off guard. What was this idiot thinking, referring to my Kamm in that manner of talk? Stupidly, I was finding myself beginning to get mad.

But, remaining on task, I quickly shook off what I should have been rightfully feeling had she been any kind of righteous wife to me in the first place. I forced myself to see through it.

I looked in to him hard and asked, "Wha's-up, fool—what you know?"

Almost dancing with glee at finally getting his chance to unload on me all that he'd apparently known for quite some time, D-D held no punches in drawing me in to see the picture of all he was about to paint for me. He brought me in, lifted me up and slammed me back down forcefully—just like this.

"Pa'tner', yo' stank-ho, cheatin'-azzed wife been creepin' on you fer goin' on six monfs'. I mean..." He could barely bring himself to contain the elation he felt at what he thought was him helping me straighten out my life's woes.

"Get this, me and Deebo an-em' was down at the barge one night runnin' the smoovies (dice) on some busta's from over on the USS Denver."

Our ship was going through a maintenance availability period at the time and all of those sailors who lived aboard or who were in a duty status slept on a floating barge that was tied up three piers down from where our ship was berthed.

"Dis one fool pipes up and aksss'.if we know a brotha', Fire Controlmen, a Second Class on our ship? We all know he's talking bout' chew' cause you the only brotha' Fire Controlman onboard...And Second Class ta' boot—whew! I wan-ta' slam him right there, cause' I knew what he was gone be gettin' at next."

D-D had to take a second to calm himself down. Walking over to the edge of the lifeline, it was almost as if he'd been referring to a tryst he'd caught his own wife in instead of us standing there talking about mine. He stared off out into San Diego harbor a full moment more before continuing.

"This fool goes on tellin' us all how he been pumpin' yo' wife, Kammy fo' more'n six monfs'. And how he be sportin' yo' wheels and takin' money from tha' crib and partying over there an' what-not while we been at sea all those times. I swear fo' GAWD, Blu, I was gonna blast da'mu-afucca', but Darryl and Ronnie an em' held me back, word is bond..."

I couldn't move. There couldn't have been a more raging fire sweeping through that passageway hotter than the insides of my nature as I took in all he'd just spoken to me. Suddenly I had no breath. My usually dry temperament moistened quickly to become instantly clammy. My mind raced forward with a thousand ways of killing both Kamm and this nicca' before that day's sun had met its eventual end.

D-D could see that his words had had a mind numbing effect on me. He reached out to place a steady mentoring hand lightly upon my left shoulder. I swooped away from him deftly, letting his hand fall slightly back by his side.

"Wha's is' name, D?"

He thought better at first of extending himself further to those lengths of filling me in on the vital statistics of what he felt was quite possibly a dead man should he pinpoint the particulars for me.

I glowered down on him. """Set it out, man! What's this fool's name?

After turning away, himself caught up now with a quickly developing indecision, D-D came back around and said, "Fucc-it! Ain't no skin off my azz'. His name's Billups, homey, Marvin Billups. He go by *Pimp-Daddy* and he a Seaman cook over on da' Denva'."

I then picked up my gear and I walked out onto the quarterdeck, presented my military I.D., saluted the Officer of the Deck, requesting permission to go ashore—and I headed off the brow—the USS DENVER, over on pier four, was my next stop.

When finally up her brow, I went through the same ritual'd routine, but this time requesting permission to come aboard. After being permitted to step aboard, I told the Officer there that I had to see a Seaman Billups. He dispatched his messenger to go off and find the fool to meet with me.

After a full twenty minutes, the messenger returned. I thought he'd gotten lost. Messengers were known for taking a half hour in which they *SKATED* (goofed off) to deliver a two-minute message.

"I'm sorry, Seaman Billups has already departed the ship," the Petty Officer of the Watch finally informed me.

I didn't know how to feel about receiving that info right then. I just stood, glued there, unable to put my hands squarely on what it was that was going to be my next step.

"Tis' there sumpin' else or another body I could call for you," the unknowing Seaman inquired of me.

"Naw. Naw, Tha'...That's O.K." I shook my head affirming positively. "I'm sure to catch up with him sooner or later." And I received permission and exited the brow once more. My mind raced exigently as I went back down the brow in search of my soon to be ex-wife, Kammy.

It hadn't come as a total surprise to me that Kammy would extend herself and the sanctity of our relationship to such despicable lengths. I wasn't a total fool when it came to her concupiscence. Heck, time and time again, while back in high school, there had been many occasions where she, Lucinda, and either of the Williams twins, Lonny or Johnny and I, would all gather into their mother, Mrs. Pall's Thunderbird and head for the lustful peace and tranquility just off a deserted patch of El Paso's Trans Mountain Road—where we'd pull the car to a stop and all save the first two up would exit the vehicle while the remaining participants inside would quickly shuck their clothes to begin the tussle of trying to fucc' each other's brains out, while the others froze their butts off, waiting their turns outside.

Hindsight kicked in for me years and years later as I was retelling the story of those encounters to Mama'n, while holding one of those heart-to-hearts we still have now and again as adults. Her reaction was, in that nonchalant way she had of not placing too much care in any one subject, just minimal shock. She'd always thought of Kamm as the sweet, wholesome, shy little lady, as this is how her cunning fascia portrayed itself outwardly when caught out in the open toward the public eye. She had no grasp upon the real persona of the ungrateful, selfishness and egotistical self-importance she fostered wrapped around a feigned materialistic loveliness which lurked on her front as it became shiningly apparent, blemished and sullen later as the truth of her treachery amid her devious ways began to materialize so plainly at her back.

In the only way she knew how to put it, "You were a stupid shit for ever marrying her," were her Loving words of counsel after I'd relayed the antics of the group's mountainous encounters to her. "You knew she was a ho' way back then, in high school? And you still thought you could swamp her down, settle her n' start a family?" Mama'n then threw her head back and laughed heartily at the magnanimous blunders of my marital stupidity.

"You sure got some nature about you kiddo—Some nature for sure. I don't know...And you say I got nine lives. Some of the shit you git' yo'self into and manage to get out of…I don't know how you do it; must've come from being *raised by wolves* in your youth."

She was right; I could do nothing more before her except begrudgingly relent, as usual.

I should have never proposed to Kamm. Shoulda' just kept right on hitt'n it, along with *Right, Fabe, Lonny and Johnny, Gerwin and Dave*, cause' I knew for a fact, they all hit, while I'd stood out in the sweeping chill of the Trans Mountain winds, freezing and waiting my turn.

But the fact that she was sharing out the goods to so many others, at the time, meant very little to me. I don't know what I was thinking. There it is again…*Thought I was a man—playing horribly at a man's game, perpetually losing*—like my Mama'n. Losses merely annoyances I had to make adjustments for as I went about my way of seeking out the real meaning of life at seventeen.

She was just like the Pilipino girls brought back to the states after whippin' that leg on some unsuspecting sailor. So engrossed in the smorgasbord of succin' and fuccin' an entire fleet round'-the-clock, that they actually went into dickmatic' withdrawals when forced to face their anxious realities of fact that the variety of ham they were used to was never again going to materialize into the steak and lobster of their pasts while they remained in relationships with men they had used solely for the purpose of seeking a better way of Love and life—American style—thus the premature reasoning behind so many of those relationships failing so miserably.

On one occasion, I had just returned to our little apartment from a lengthy at sea period. Kamm never came down to the piers to pick me up when I came back to port. Her excuse was: the ship usually berths at 32nd Street, either during the early morning or afternoon hours, and by that time she was already in school for the day and was unable to break away to come and pick me up.

I had engineered a way for her to get out of the house as well as learn a trade she and I might put to *work* toward beginning to build a future together. We had enrolled her in one of those rip-off nursing academy schools which used to be located just up El Cajon Boulevard, a stones throw away from our studio. You know the type you always see on those motivational commercials seeking to capture the minds and dreams of a horde of lackluster soap opera lovers during their mid-day afternoons where they say, "*Thinking about a career in the medical field? Let the Larcenous School of Laboratories show you how to make all your dreams come true in just twenty-three short months.*"

When what they really were all about was luring their students in, saddling them beneath the greed-infested gallows of perhaps ten thousand dollar student loans, the majority of which was payable, by contract—to the admin department at the school—the student actually getting to keep about a thousand, for books and necessities, the other nine thousand didn't cover, and they shipped them out into the work force following the twenty-three months of minimal instruction with a nurse's aide certificate which might or might not have been accepted by reputable organizations—to empty bed pans at old folks' homes and pinch and abuse non-compliant residents of assisted care facilities.

But that supposedly, had been hers and *our* dream for her, to be a nurse. Again, I was duped. The girl probably still ain't got the brains GOD gave a goose. She never even finished.

So I bummed rides home after pulling in from sea from all my homies.

After D-D schooled me in on *THAREALDEAL*, my next perplexity, after recalling myself away from my own determined efforts of ruining my life further by killing Marvin Billups, if necessary, right on the USS DENVER's quarterdeck, *was how the hell I was gonna' get home?* My old friend, Rastess Feldmen, came to my aide, just as he had on countless other occasions during the time the two of us had bunked next to each other down in ENGLAND's *Lower* Fox berthing in the division.

To us, Rastess was a sapient old cuss. Approaching thirty, he was by far ganglier and leaps and bounds more knowledgeable than the rest of us nineteen, and twenty year old kids that swarmed around him seeking wisdom in the division.

I was by this time the Close-In-Weapon System work center supervisor aboard the ship. He and I were of the same pay grade and rank, yet, although I was younger, I had been presented the lead by our superiors. Rastess and I got along fabulously. The relationship between us, like with he and just about everyone else, transcended the staunch regiment of rank and regulation. I never directed Rastess to do anything.

He was always there at morning muster to check in. But who knew exactly what it was he did with rest of his time during the follow-on minutes of every day's work?

Rastess was *my maanns'*...A gun *wizard* to be exact. Equaling my abilities to troubleshoot, diagnose and repair the system's extensive electronic search and track radars and computing modules, there was nothing that he couldn't do with the hydraulic gun system to make it purr like a quieted kitten each time we called on it during live-fire exercises.

From Port Arthur, Texas, a boot wearin', hat toting cowboy to a fault, Rastess had more street in him than most brotha's I had come in contact with up to that point. He took his Jack Daniels and his women exactly the same—straight up.

He was a *real man.*

He pulled no punches when it came to dealing with others on a straight and narrow level and he commanded and gave respect, no matter your rank—or he'd put your lights out, for good, if it came to that in the end.

Over the course of his travels up to the point where he attempted to become my unwilling mentor, he'd already been an engineer, working for a major government contracting corporation, and a bouncer at the famed *Gilley's* bar in Dallas, where he'd once shot a man for taking out his frustrations and anger on a little lady who had formerly been his girlfriend. Guess the pard had issues getting' over the fact she was no longer totin' his spurs, and Rastess cancelled Christmas for his azz' in a matter of seconds, leaving the dying embers of his ruined frame to rot along the filth riddled edges of a nasty trash dumpster for pick up.

He was a skilled craftsman of fine hand-made knives. These had polished deer antlers and glossy hoofs for handles, the kind you see refined and razor sharp inside the lustrous pages of a *BUCK* company outdoorsmen catalogue.

Rastess always had a weapon on him. You could count on his Mark X Desert Eagle making every trip with him. It didn't matter whether to and from work or down to the corner store for a frequent re-supply of *JACK*, he was always gainfully strapped hard. If he found himself unable to place hands on it in times of dire need, there was always one or two of the razed edges of one of his knives hidden in a manufactured crevice of one or two of the pockets only he knew the origin of about his person.

He was a quiet man. He never wasted breath giving any shit and he took none either.

I never pressured him and didn't even know most of the time whether he was even still on the ship at day's end. Only when we'd have a gun jam that one of the junior techs was unable to clear or correct would I utter the four words which kept me both in and outta' trouble for a couple of eventful years.

"Where's Rastess? Find him"

He'd materialize. At times, like a white ghost, appearing outta' nowhere—I'd look up suddenly to find him standing contemplatively behind me, as if he'd been stationed there to watch over me forever.

Pushing his always present tooth pick to the holding side of his mouth, he'd greet me with a clever, smirking smile and offer, "Whass-up, son? Got yer-sef' a problem?"

Twenty minutes later, after hulking up his sleeves and jumping in (if it took him that long) the gun would be fixed and Rastess would saunter on back to whatever motor generator room that day's card or dice game event was taking place in (they were usually his games and he took a cut of every draw or toss) where the juniors, after scouring the ship a quick twenty minutes, had pulled him out of.

Rastess and I for a time were thick as two ambitious thieves could be. He ran various payday scams or *slush-funds* aboard the ship as well. He always had money due to the many capers and salacious vices he had a hand in most times. He was always available for the young, fiscally irresponsible shipmate. A ten would cost you twenty and a hundred, two—on payday. And... You betta' have his money, on time or Rastess would dispatch an unwavering stable of ready henchmen to go get yo' azz', even at your house, in front of wives, mother-in-laws, neighbors. He didn't care. And they'd confiscate a T.V. or your great-grand mother's preciously handed down china in payment—Always leaving you with more bumps, scrapes and bruises than you had when they first showed up at your door.

Rastess was nothing the discernable man needed be playin' too much around with.

At the time, I was loft into the poignant turmoils of having to battle everyday with Kamm. And I wasn't too readily discriminate about the company I tended to keep as a result. My problems with her caused me to disregard my own registration of caring expansively about myself.

I accompanied him on numerous trips across the border into Tijuana, Mexico. Once there, he would purchase, for pennies on the dollar, infant Rainbow Lorikeets, Cockatoos, and colorful Parrots which he would dope up on mescaline and conceal, packed together like baby sardines in little pockets he had constructed in the armpits of his Texas Longhorn, trench coat duster. Once the drugging effect took, he and I would walk back across the border, birds in tow. The doped animals would merely sleep soundly during the trip and upon returning to San Diego, we'd get drunk while waiting for the narcotics to wear off.

He had prepared these huge, wrought iron cages he maintained in a room in his house in the La Mesa community for when they woke up. These stood six feet tall and were so heavy and wide around that it would take two of us to move them about. He had four of these aviary prisons lined up inside the vacuous interior of one of his guest bedrooms.

He'd station the birds inside, keeping better care of them than a mother of a gaggle of newborns and he'd raise them to a strapping health, until such time as he'd parlay them off to many underhanded pet shops throughout the county, oftentimes at exorbitant prices or for engineered bartered exchanges for other, more ill-reputed gains for them.

It was on a particular day when our ship was undergoing a maintenance availability period and we were in-port for more than a usually lengthy amount of time, that I got to take in a more sinister side of the pard I knew only as Rastess Feldman. He had invited me to come out to his house to gawk at a Pistola Rotazione, the Bodeo M1889, Italian pistol he'd *taken* off a customer—in trade.

Once there (I had ridden with him) we were met by his brother-in-law, whom Rastess referred to only as *Sonny—Buttfucc'* and whom he had also filled me in—was, "As useless as tits on a bore-hog, foreva' suckin' off his daddy's money tit without ever havin' a job ta' provide support on his own."

To me, it seemed *Sonny* was doing O.K. Turns out; it was his late model Porsche parked in Rastess' driveway we'd both had to squeeze by in order to make it up to the front door of the house upon our arrival.

Sonny didn't utter much in our direction as we'd entered the house. He was solemnly stationed at the dining table, head down and gulping a passel of Rastess' best black beans and rice as we passed by.

Rastess' wife, the striking epitome of a *fine* version of what most of the fella's referred to as G.R.I.T.S. (Girls Raised in the South) was there as well. She was a pampered—daddy's little rich girl—and was deeply engrossed in an excited telephone conversation with her mother back in Port Arthur, as we'd made our approach known.

"Mamma, that sounds like a wunnn-der-fuul idear! Of course, Rastess n' me would Love ta' fly down n' meet you'n daddy in Vegas this weekend." She looked up at us, overlooking me and smiling brightly with an accompanying wink, at Rastess; as she went on to solidify plans for *his* life later on that week. "We'll get all the fliii.ght plans n' call y'awl back with tha' par-ticulaaa's."

Rastess bout' had a fit. I thought the pard was gonna blow a brain valve, as we stood there listening to his woman seal the deal in the latter parts of her conversation with her mother.

Rastess' disdain for her plans began to register on her and she turned away, rapidly dismissing us with a realistic condescension, to whisper into the phone further. He looked over at me with a glance of incredulous disbelief residing plainly on the crevices of the well-cared for lines of leather which now contorted his tawdry-stricken face.

I knew a bit about their relationship. Guys at times talk too.

He was none too happy about the fact that she continually ran back to reach into the deep pockets of her daddy for a sustenance he felt he was doing more than an adequate job of providing her.

The woman boasted a full assortment of rare and precious furs. Every designer, from Louis Vouitton to Dooney & Bourke, Liz Claibourne, and Gucci had personalized shelves lining the expanse interior of another guest room Rastess had converted, expressly for her to closet all of her delicate gear. He had built safes into walls which warehoused the bountiful collection of expensive stones inlaid in customized, one-of-a-kind settings he had presented her over the three or four short years the two of them had been together.

Don't get me wrong, ole' girl was a bona fide knock out. Every lusting curve about her was picked, plucked, manicured or siliconed proper. The golden blond locks of her Dolly Parton style hair was always *whipped* to a "T" and she never sported a ride which cost less that a hundred-thousand dollars, a yearly gift that daddy had one of his minions drive all the way down from one of his high-end lots back in Texas and swap out with whatever one she had been driving

Rastess drove a cherried-out, '72 CHEVY Impala.

His ride was clean beyond clean, with an engine he'd built himself, the chrome of which you could cook on and feel as comfortable about eatin' eggs off of as you would a piece of flatware pulled from your grand mother's kitchen cabinet.

The interior was a collaboration of some of the most skilled craftsmanship his *connect* down in Tijuana could come up with. Pelted in-laid Texas Longhorns splashed about the dash and covered the seats in finely selected colors of softened, Corinthian leathers. He had dazzling chromed-out rims before most of the brotha's on a hundred sets even knew they were supposed to sport such items as icons of misguided ghetto fashion.

Some say the former president, Bill Clinton was a bad…bad "Black"-White man. Those who say that had never run into Rastess Eclipse Feldman.

I began to feel for the brotha', right about then. And I suddenly began to wonder about the loop ends of my own problems that were just starting to increase and creep up, more and more, with Kamm.

Did I really have it so bad? Damn! These folks had all the money in the world.…And even that still was unable to solidify a unionized compatibility between them.

The ire of Rastess' wrath seeped on even higher. Especially after he took in his wife's whining, "Maaamma? Rastess don't ever seem ta' wanna' go no where any mo-oor'…Keeps blamin' it on fi—nances' or sumpthin'. I de-claarrre! Sometimes I just feel like I'm one of those well-faare' wives! Livin' in tha' ghe-tto, unable to afford ta' do nuffin.'"

She caught herself. Looking up at me, she suddenly turned a crimson red, of enlightened embarrassment, as if her words had quite possibly stung me and lurched forward to smack the cause of injured feelings.

But I didn't care. She was just another whinin' wife to me. Her troubles, nor her words, had any effect over me.

Just then, I think the ole' boy lost it.

"Whaaat!"

He sprang up from the couch he and I had been sitting on. The sudden volatility of his actions had startled *Sonny Butt—fucc'*, and had almost caused him to choke on the last bit of vittles he'd been loudly scraping up and slurpin down, increasing Rastess' consternation as he next stormed across the room. I thought he'd knock her outta' the chair she'd been so daintily curled up in.

Instead, he repeatedly turned back to shake twisted, enraged glances at me. I think it was my presence which saved that little girl a horrendous azz-whippin' that day, as he knew I'd never sit idly by to watch him enter into the utter stupidity of actions that would change all our lives forever in the worst of ways.

He went instead for her purse. I settled back a seconds more of comfort—relieved, thinking *how much damage could he exact with that?*

He then dumped the entire contents of her handbag completely out on the floor before me. A potpourri of lipsticks and candies, and a full assortment of other things, still packaged tampons, her wallet and mini papers scattered in a huddled mess about the carpet.

He went for the wallet first. Snapping it open brutally, he let a falling flow of credit cards, Visa's, Mastercard's, American Express, Zales, Nordstrom's cascade out and away from him as the little plastic slips covering them all swept down to a length just below his knees as he held the bill fold high over top his head.

"Put that gawddam' phone up and quit bad-mouffing' me to yo' mother, you *biiitch!"* He hurled at her. Then, he blushed over at me and countered, "Blue? I mean it son; does this shit look like that *bitch's* on well-faaare?" He shook the culprit string of items at me. I didn't offer him a reply.

"We...eell? Does it!"

I figured I'd best say something in compliance with him, trying desperately to figure out what had just occurred, while searching for a way to get him to calm down and let that shit squash from blowing up even further.

"Naww, Ras', it's not welfare, O.K.? Say, where's that piece you said you were gonna' show me anyway?"

The situation began to develop even scarier when his woman plainly disregarded his demand for her to rapidly end the conversation she'd been having with her mother, talking about him. Just then, Rastess stormed over to where she was sitting and he reached down and slapped the phone completely out of her grasp. He'd struck her so fiercely, that that thing went hurling across the room, cord and all, and it landed atop the glass of the dining room table with an ear deafening clatter, almost landing in *Sonny—Butfucc's* stew.

It was then that the tiny hairs began to stand up at the nape of my neck, matching now the panting race of my quickening heart beat as I watched him bend to rip the entire line completely from the mangled junction in the wall.

Wa-n't' nobody making any more calls in or out on that line that day.

Just then, I peeked movement in my peripheral sights as *Sonny—Buttfucc'* seeking to add his own two-cents into the convoluted mass took two parrying steps of undecided venture towards Rastess.

"Now, just hole' on dere' a mole's minute Rastess!" Was all he was able to get out.

Rastess shot him a beleaguering glare of instantaneous blue-steeled defiance. Even I knew the telling meaning of this as he wheeled about to turn on him, offering him only, "You just sit yo' worthless cock back down and shut up—BOY! Fore' I dust yo' junky azz' off!"

Sonny huffed and puffed for a very slight minute more. But he did as he was told. He shut his mouth and sat his azz' down without murmuring another word.

He wasn't ready for the torrent of rotting anger and rage that Rastess had stored up just waiting to pelt out towards him. Guy was a wimp. Didn't even think about the same passionate leagues of ruthless natures Rastess easily sauntered through on a daily basis.

Ask me...*Sonny* was purely a wise man, sittin' down and the likes like he had.

Rastess' woman, on the other hand, wasn't quite as bright as her previously unvoiced brother. She clamored on, the now raining pitch of her voice reaching an excruciatingly high pitched fervor of squeak.

"You filthy Summ-an-a'-bitiiitch!" She screamed as she swung her head around, glancing wildly in an attempt to locate something—anything at all, that she could place her hands on to hurl at him.

"I'm outta' here, Rastess!" She bellowed at him. "Tain't no call at all fore' you ta' be slapping me n' puttin' yo' hands on me like that." The sweetness of her sweating palm rubbed lightly about the vicious hand print taking outline along the powdered side of her formerly pretty face.

Rastess kicked it up a notch.

Now towering over her frightened form, "Weeell…Git' yo' shit and *bounce* you simple *bitiitch!* I don't need you holdin' me down round these parts no mor'n I need a pair of tits don't move."

The poor woman near climbed up the back of the recliner she'd been in, almost appearing to scale the supporting wall behind her as she tried to extricate herself out of Rastess' field of fire. She scampered away frantically to exit the living room and disappeared toward the back of the house with a whimper.

The whole ordeal loomed at first startling to me as well. I mean, I'd been over their crib on plenty of occasions. And I had even borne witness to the little Love spats the two of their colliding tempers produced from time to time; but never anything as impulsively outrageous or inconceivably capricious as this.

Then, it struck me as being laughable, almost gut-wrenchingly funny. My maanns' had broken that ho' down like a newly purchased, store-bought puppy. Rastess wasn't a boisterous soul at all. Not flamboyant or flashy about his business dealings. So much so, that people merely mistook him for the simple Southern farm boy his countenance belied him to be.

Those who never crossed him were unaware of the gamey animal lurking inside his peaceable calmness. Those who irritated him received very little in the way of a passing liberty toward a quickly vanishing mercy when given just a single chance of approaching him on the correct side of his truly adversative nature.

His wife had somehow foolishly ran into their bedroom and closed and locked the door behind her. Unlike *Sonny—Buttfucc'*, who'd lit out at first chance, slamming his Porsche excitedly into gear, screeching the rubber of his Pirellis all the way down the block as he'd abandoned his sister to the whims of what was proving to be an entirely crazed man, she'd remained behind—not moving fast enough for Rastess, whose mind had already been made up. Was no turning back now.

"*That biitch...one way or 'nother...was gone.*"

Without slowing stride, he kicked in the bedroom door and just stood there, gasping at first with a silenced, haunted repartee. He again looked back at me and threw me the wickedness of a blazing red smile.

Something right then told me to get my own azz' up and begin to hitch down *Sonny,* to see if I could catch a ride with his scary azz' back down to the base aboard ship. Rastess not only concealed all types and manner of weapons on him at any given time, all you had to do was just look around the pad to find all kinds of differing manufacturer's fire arms thrown about idly—Glocks and Taurus', Winchesters and Remingtons, just laying out in the open—fully loaded.

I wasn't about to plan to take on the likelihood of being around to catch a stray bullet.

Rastess heaved into the room and seeing his wife on the phone there, became so enraged that he jumped at her and while clutching her firmly by the hundred dollar do' of her formerly pristine hair, he dragged her screaming, kickin' azz' back out into the front of the house.

"You musta' thought I was kiddin' wit' yo' stoopid' azz', you *biaaiitch!*"

He dragged her even more toward the opening of the front door.

That's when I finally did get up. Although this was their family business, there was no way that I could merely sit back and laze around to watch his abuse of her any further. It wasn't in me.

"*RASTESS!*

I yelled at him in that commanding tone of speech I'd perfected so easily when dealing with an obstinate subordinate back on the ship during work day.

I treaded ever lightly, reaching out a hand to steady him, hoping he would see the seriousness of the situation and reconsider the finality of his next menacing steps.

"Back tha' fucc off, Blu! He countered me. "This here ain't none o' yer parts." He refocused his endangering ferocity back on the trembling figure of his petite but mouthy, and terrified wife.

"Rastess, I ain't letting this go down like this any further. Turn her loose!" I ordered him, preparing for the sting of the battle brewing between the two of us that was sure to flow if he continued to resent my labors.

With her still firmly entangled in his grasp, he just stared at me hard. The shifting polarization of Buster metamorphosing, about to slug Toppa and lay him out at grand pappy's wake flooded back to warn me to be prepared for anything that came that very moment.

Then, he appeared to simmer down just the slightest bit. Releasing her gruffly, he almost slammed her to the posh tile lining the parlor floor leading to the front their door.

She scampered over more nearer to me. As if I had become the defining image of *her* fleeting savior. Don't know what she did that for...I sure wasn't there to fight *her* battles. I had no loyalty to her.

I only really didn't want to watch *my maanns* go out like that. I held more respect for him than to permit an outraged moment concocted by the brainless acts of a foolish woman to cause him to be brought down so futilely—and perhaps drag me down right along with him.

I had lost track on Rastess as he'd swept by me heading again for the bedroom. Endearing pleas of self-preservational flows bearing a flighty wisdom screamed at me inside to make my own exit then as well. But I held firm.

He reappeared suddenly. This time, he had what looked like one of those antique, pot-bellied gas cans in his hand, and he fixed his gape upon me—lending me just the slightest deviation of a loosely offered wink.

Then, he started again... While appearing to begin to outline the exterior edges of the room with the liquid contents the jug held.

" So...son, since she thinks you wanna' act as her guardian n' all, tell-at' *biittch* that she got just ten minutes ta' gather all she can carry and scoot on outta' here, for good." He smiled widely with the crazed glow of a sho'nuff' madman, "Cause' that's just bout' when I plan ta'set this mutha-a-fucca' ablaze."

My mind about collapsed on me. What was this fool talking about? He was actually planning on burning the house down.

That was enough for me...And his wife too. She didn't even rest to think about all the lavishness of her former belongings. She just peeled herself up off that cold floor, scampered over to the mess that was a mere remnant of the things previously held inside her purse, still lying about the floor—and she snatched up her keys—and was gone, almost flying out the door without ever turning to look back.

I meant not to be too far behind her.

I had had enough!

Shooting a dismay—filled glance over at Rastess, I prepared to bid him adieu, with a promise to alert the local fire department should I run into any of them on my way (about to walk if I had to) back to the ship.

He just stood there as I began to gather my bag and head for the sanctity of his still opened front door. Then...

He exhaled a loud burst of exasperated air and bellowed the heartiest laugh I think I'll ever witness in such a situation. It caused me to be held up once more, deeply enrooted, staring back at him with amazement my only emotion in front of him now.

He then lifted the gas can heftily and took a long pull from its contents, while looking back at me.

I turned my head, further confused at his movements.

He laughed on before pelting out a fiery breath and said, "*MOONSHINE*, son. Wanna' belt?"

The two of us crazy cats settled in even further and we drank plenty plugs on that gas can before getting snockering drunk.

I never did get to see that pistol. By that time, following all the eagerness of the events that had taken place, I wasn't any longer caring.

It had been Rastess who had dropped me off that day that Kamm was too busy to pick me up upon our return from sea. When the two of us had pulled up in front of my apartment, we were surprised to see my little car sitting idly in its parking spot out in front of the complex.

"There's yo' wheels right there," he set out for me as we'd rolled up to a stop.

"Damn...I wonder what's up?" I sent him back

Looking over at me with all seriousness, he began to languidly reach under his seat.

"Want me ta' juss' hang aroun' a spell—ta' get yo' back case this turns out ta' need some adjustin"?

I knew exactly what he was getting at. As I spied the glistening sheen of the baretta he'd just retrieved from its hiding place along the inner outline of his *IROC's* falsetto floor.

"Naaw, man. I can handle whatever comes up. See you in the morning."

But he wasn't letting it alone.

He exited the vehicle and walked around to begin to deftly inspect the outside of my car.

When I'd reached his position, he motioned for me to pass him my keys. I did. He unlocked the door and reached in to settle the key firmly into the ignition. I pushed past him and slid expectantly into the driver's seat, my senses already amplified by the peaking glare of his usually austere intuition.

I looked at him expecting him to jump back in his ride and peel off for whatever troubles awaited his existent deeds.

He just shrugged thoughtfully and shot back at me, "Juss' hangin' aroun' a second more ta' make sure everything's hunky dory."

I didn't care. I busied myself trying to pull my focus back to beginning to start the car. It started right up. An inkling of relief-filled glee shot through my already weary brain. Rastess began to head for his own car preparing to take off.

I began to push him from my mind as indications of the things D-D had relayed to me came sweltering back to bombard the interior caverns of my head all at once. I had to do something about Kamm. And I had to do it now.

Pulling away from the curb slightly, (I hadn't even taken the time to go up into the apartment just yet.) I began to be tossed, lurching crookedly from side to side, and my car began to belt out screeching noises as it became evident to me that someone (probably not Kammy) had ridden the padding of my brakes totally down to tunnel through and ruin the rotors completely.

I looked up to find Rastess again standing outside my door. I rolled down the window to talk to him.

He met me with, "Brakes shot out ta' fucc', huh?"

I just shook my head at him filled with disgust in reply.

"Yup...Can smell that asbestos burnin' and you ain't even travelled nary a mile."

"Thanks for stating the observably obvious, azz-hole," I shook my head again, throwing back at him.

"We...ll, need a ride somewhere's else, pard?"

With my own wheels so obviously outta' whack my plans had abruptly changed.

"Naaw. Think I'll just head upstairs and unpack.

And then, Rastess was gone.

I hadn't reached the first rung of the stairs before noticing my seventy-three year old Jewish landlord, Mr. Nelson, peeking out at me from behind a curtain at his opened window.

"Wait there just a minute more young fella," he implored, catching me immediately off guard. "You and I have distinct matters of fiscal business to discuss."

I leaned against the slim wood column put there beneath the staircase for the most part just for looks. I was exhausted. Each at sea period, for me, at nineteen was as exhilarating as an exciting prize fight. And I expended lots of energy seeing to the perfection of skill my nautical responsibilities demanded whenever the ENGLAND would pull away from her eventual berth. It took a lot outta' me.

So much so, that I barely held the reserve of any energy then to put up with Mr. Nelson's eclectic antics now as I stood there watching him frantically wrap himself in his smelly old robe and dance about inquisitively, searching for slippers I was certain as each day passed were getting harder and harder for him to find.

He finally found them and came out.

Shaking a grand fatherly finger at me, he withered, while cocking his head to a side to look down on me in that affirming notion most white men of his age held when they'd caught themselves a young American of African descent whom they felt might be up to no good.

"Prey-tell, young man... What exactly are your plans for offering your's truly a prompt response to the eviction notice I so cautiously delivered to your door stoop not more n' a twilight's haze ago?"

He had me there.

EVICTION NOTICE!

"Mr. Nelson, I swear..." Turning now away from him, intending to ignore him, thinking this another start to one of his miraculous stories he'd constantly held me up with time and time again previously. I at first disregarded his threatening nature of the messaging question and began to make my way up the stairs to my studio.

This was too much. I could barely see straight for all the litigious things life had jumping out at me so contentiously. I just didn't have time for Mr. Nelson's larking about right then.

Damn! After all…I was only nineteen.

"I ain't kidding around here this time, young Mr. Penn," he accosted me further, stepping up on the first rung of the stairway to match me height for height as he pulled himself taller to engage the step of manhood he felt I needed while employing his deepest confidence in bringing me to see he was in for the whole fight of the full situation I had had no clue that I'd climbed aboard.

"Whaa…Whaaa-t are you talking about? Eviction notice, Mr. "N"? I asked him.

Beefing up his zeal, he moved even closer to me. I could smell the salve of liniment wafting aimlessly in a strong waving cloud of haze as it hit me from his breath. "Now don't you try to play coy with me Junior! You know zactly' to which I am referring when I say eviction notice."

This was fast becoming too *fucc-in'* much for me to calmly stand by n' swallow peaceably; my mind raced suddenly, bombarding me with the need to begin to fast talk him once I finally realized that the course reality of his words actually held a validity of sense, meaning to cut my tenancy there off succinctly and for good at the knees with hollow accusations I could barely keep up with him now to swallow.

"I…I swear fore' *GOD!* Mr. N, I don't have the least bit of inkling what you're talking about. I have been at sea for the last three weeks, day in and day out. We just pulled in this morning. Swear! and I just got home this very second to find my car all *fuc'…messed* up," catching myself, almost forgetting the person I was addressing as he instantly cringed at the harsh slippage of my generally respectful words the sudden surprise of my nature had brought outta' me. But he brushed it aside, offering me a brief pass to take a step back then and peer at me longly, caught up in a deep sudden look of indecision, wondering if quite possibly there was any ring of truth to what I'd just offered him, I reached desperately for the break of the fissure in his own determination to see us gone, I slipped in lithely to break the back of his former sensationally applied contention with, "Sir? I'm quite certain, if you will permit me, that I can produce a written statement from my C.O. verifying that what I say to you now to be the Gaaawd;'s-honest truth. The first I'm setting foot on these premises, over the course of the past three following weeks has been now—as I return from sea to find myself hit up with this quite unbearable news."

A sweeping flow of a better command upon the English language had suddenly kicked in for me to aide me, as I began to draw on it to envelope myself in the stark seriousness of the situation's significant meaning. Not only had it just been established that I had a cheating slut for a wife, my only form of self-propelled transportation, back and forth to and from work sat apparently ruined, not more 'n twenty feet away from us on the street, but I was teetering quite closely on the edge of becoming a vagrant, kicked out on that same street! About to lose the first personally held apartment I'd ever had—all for nothing more than not being there while off in an attempt to support the very same, while working at sea completely.

Looking down at him now with weary debate brewing ever so slightly between us—I was really tired and not quite certain how much more of any newly borne development I could take—I continued, bearing him a soul-searching inquisition with, "Whasss really goin' on, Mr. N? Tell me... What is it that I was supposed to have done to make you race out her after me, your robe all on inside out and your slippers both on the wrong feet?"

He released his siege upon the step where he'd meant to stand firmly blocking me as he began to rub the gray stubble of his suddenly distorted face to pull in the uncertainty that I really had no idea what he'd been talking about when he had mentioned evicting me.

"You mean...?" He looked off up the stairs, as if stooping to recall the last minutes where he had previously thought me some accomplishing caste of a twisted nature of the caper he was before overly certain he'd caught me up in red-handedly.

"You weren't at the store last week when I stopped up to talk to yoouur', " He cringed up his face now, as if just the mention of the word, *"wife"* when referring to Kamm, had somehow caused the thick choking bile of his nature to kick up suddenly now shocking the tender insides of his widely thrown open mouth, as he sought to spew the word away violently *anywhere*, just to get rid of it forever.

"The store... Whatta' you mean?"

He took a second. And with his hand still firmly placed at fiercely rubbing his chin, he began to fill me in on all the ruddy excitement of things he'd witnessed taking place—in my *fuccin'* apartment, over the full course of the last three weeks that I'd been gone.

Turns out Kamm, and some of her *foot-draggin'* friends had had a party. When their music had topped the peak of what he felt he could no longer stand, he'd reached again for his robe and slippers and carted them up the full twenty-three stairs it would take him to plant himself firmly in front of our door to vehemently implore them to consider how late it was and to simply have some respect for the other tenants in considering just to turn it down. He'd initially asked to speak to me, being the old-school gentlemen he truly felt he was, believing that all business dealings were meant to be plainly discussed, between men, as had been conducted between the two of us since the commencement of our stay there.

Kamm, with her ease of slipping a forked tongue urgency of twisted truth in almost everything she said had lied to him plainly. She'd told him that I wasn't there. And that she expected me back any minute, from the store, where she had dispatched me for one useless item or another, and that she'd be sure to dispatch me further, to go searching for

him, to comply with his copious requests for an answer to a transgression I hadn't even known existed before that very second.

He informed me that he'd been all right with that at first, for a brief fleeting moment. At first calming himself to register the realization that the two of us had probably been just blowing off steam, perhaps celebrating some great accomplishment in my career upon just returning back home (He was one to truly understand the full complexity and nature of my job, having been a Naval veteran of harrowing sea battles himself in the big *Dubya-Dubuyou-Two*). But he placed his hand solemnly on my shoulder now. No more a landlord seeking aimlessly to get rid of a slothful tenant whom he felt had soiled the great integrity of his formerly perfected surroundings.

He was now speaking to me, with the care and heart-felt concern of a wizened, grandfatherly old man as he said, "Son, there comes a time in every man's life when he has to force himself to face some really tough decisions." I settled in beneath the comfort of his rusty old hands. There hadn't been many moments for me in my past like this. So whenever they did occur, I welcomed them, and I valued them so vehemently, that I went to great lengths to invariably record them, word for word in my head, just so I could play them back later, alone, at night lying languidly alone in my rack on the ship or in my bed of the studio to wring them incessantly for their bone-jarring simplicities of a sage course of knowledge and good judgment I put to use later in keeping my teetering personal ship afloat.

He looked down at me now sorrowfully. Seeking to keep the conversation enthralled, I'd relented my position upon the step where I'd only sought previously to continue the gait of making my way up to the apartment.

I cocked my head slightly at an angle looking at him now more closely. He was about to tell me something that had him shaken. A thing he felt no hard working young man should ever have to be faced with upon returning back to his spouse at home.

"Son…I…

I didn't only have to go up there once. I…,"

He then lowered his head in a quickly caste glance seeking a solemn grace as he fought forward with what he was trying to get off his chest to encounter me with. He rapidly cleared his throat and renewed his baby-blue gaze upon me.

"I actually went back up there another occasion. About three hours more of calling and banging on the door, trying to get in touch with you before bearing to bring myself to a decision of calling the authorities to aide me in getting at what I'd originally thought was *you* up there partying away in the wee hours of the night, disregarding the sanctity of our fairly quaint little garden of living here."

He shuffled about a bit more. Seeking to kick away the immensity of what he had to bring himself to lay out for me further. "But I never called them. Figured I catch you coming or going, just like this, and I'd speak to you about it, read you the riot act or something. Heck you two've been such good tenants. I really didn't want to let you have the place, better thoughts and all in the beginning. You two being so young. I felt for certain I'd be faced with tossing you out on your keesters, just like this in the end for sure.

But you turned me into a pestering old fool, always paying the rent on time-before it was due.

And you...! Always so doggoned respectful and hard working. Makes it so *damned* hard what I got to tell you right now."

"What is it, Mr. N?" I stepped up to stand firmly before him, the brunt of what I was about to face I felt sure was to be a gut-wrenching kick in the nuts. "Jusss let it all flow. Tell me plainly sir; do me the solid of cuttin' me quickly."

I took note of how truly hard it was for him to swallow what he had for me. A glazed over moistness of broken solitude had crept in to flood the corners of his sternly held eyes, shaking his world, turning it upside down. It was me who felt badly for him instead of the reverse.

He continued then with," Well, when I finally did creep back up them stairs, the music was so loud, guess no one inside heard me knocking. I stood outside your door a full ten-ta' twenty minutes more, trying to get you—or anybody to answer me at least. But no one came. So I began to get worried, you know. Didn't know what other thing there was I could do.

So I took my pass key and I let myself in." He swallowed hard once more. Imploring himself to move forward with perhaps an explanation harder for him than living through the harrowing barrage of German battleships unleashing life-threatening depth charges on his submarine with teeth-jarring accuracy so many frightening years before.

"Son... What I saw there... Was a whole lotta' nekkid' bodies, all just lying around, spread every which way and again. They'd all been asleep. Some of that Marijuana... You know the cigarettes rolled, was lying about all spilled over the coffee table. The one they had the booze bottles strewn all about covering over it. And there was your little wife, a participant." He shook his head slowly, even now standing there fraught with disbelief.

"Cept' she was sound asleep... But she was wrapped tightly in another man's arms."

"Blue..." He right then began to lose his compensity for being able to hold it all together and continue putting together his words wishing there was some way he could find in all of this to comfort me.

But he knew there were none.

I began to instantly feel sick. Standing there an enraging second more, I suddenly broke off away from him and swept past him at a trot. I quickly deserted the stairway heading for the pastured sideway of the apartments. Once there, I bent slightly at the knees, and I vomited so violently, that I peed myself, soiling my jeans throughout.

When I'd finished emptying the contents of my gut into the sweet, manicured string of his preciously plucked over lilies, I reached up to accept the crisply folded handkerchief he stood over me holding as he reached out with his other hand, just like grand pappy used to, when I was a little kid, and he touched me lightly upon my back to soothe me.

I pulled myself up tall to straighten. "I'm sorry, Blue. I didn't wanna' be the one for sure to have to tell you. What could I do? I haven't gotten a moment's wink of sleep since discovering this."

I consoled him, "I know...I know, Mr. N. T'ain't yer' fault, " Shaking my head trying to convince him and myself." Ain't your fault at all."

He looked at me then with a newly covering conviction. "So, what are you going to do about the eviction?"

I didn't know. Not right then anyhow.

"Can't you rescind it? I'll get the confirmation of my whereabouts these last three weeks from my Captain?"

He considered what I'd said for a long second. Then shaking his head again, replying negatively, at first. He said, "No...Not with *her* living here stinking up the place with such utter and despicable depravity."

I felt where he was coming at me from. He and I were thinking exactly the same. Our minds sweeping in together to cusp along the same identically recalcitrant line.

"What if she ain't here no more?" I countered.

He stood back to take this into thought again as well.

"Maybe. But you have to see to this matter now, son! You can't let it go on any further, for your own good. You got to place distance between you and that little trollup—once and for all. Or she's gonna catch you up in something you won't be able to get yourself out of."

I felt that too.

I could feel Mr. Nelson's genuine concern for me. He may have been a cooty old hoot. But this was one of those cases where I was to be sure not to discard the message outright just because the messenger was a little soiled.

I knew right away all he'd said was straight from the heart. It was just I had no idea what it was I was going to do next standing there before him. Something inside of me ticked away with a tugging urgency to pull forward and do exactly what he had said, "Place distance between myself and Kamm, for good."

"Well?" He looked down at me scornfully. "What is it you're gonna' do?"

"Don't really know right now. My head's all full of a million jumbled thoughts and what not."

"Well, Get it unscrambled boy. You've got too much going for you right now to be saddling yourself down with all the nonsense of this business." He turned around then to kick out of his slippers, transferring them finally to the right feet.

"Something else," he wheeled slightly to throw over his right shoulder and continue on.

I looked up quickly. He'd surprised me thinking he'd already be off to boil some turnips or something back to his own life inside the clutter of his tiny apartment.

"You straighten all this out. Come on back. We'll talk again about the matter of that eviction notice. But when you're doin' it," he removed his glasses and peered stronger into me. "Givin' that trollup tha' boot for certain, don't forget to ask her about the whereabouts of your Federal income tax refund."

It was my turn to look at him with a compelling concern. *INCOME TAX? What kind of tangent was he off on now?*

"Income Tax?"

"Yes, Income tax," he retorted.

"Seems to me the mailman placed yours in my box about, Oh.... A week and a half ago, by mistake. Instead of placing it back into the box, I merely placed it in the capable hands of your.... Well, you know...I gave it to her to safeguard for you until you returned home. That's all."

Mr. "N" was a trip.

I never cared to know too much about what he was saying to me previously before this whenever he'd try to engage me in conversation preparing to break into one of his lengthy stories detailing some minute happening locked away in a time warp stemming back before my thought patterns even existed. But now, I was beginning to feel as if I'd almost overlooked a veritable gold mine of sagely placed knowledge lurking right under my nose. I was typical of most people.

They usually don't really care to take the time to learn how much you know, until they're sure at first, how much you care.

It had been exactly that way with me and Mr. "N". I had looked at him as merely another eclectic old man. One of a dozen who walked, wrapped up in the starched saunter of *Brooks Brothers* suits, stuffy, high collared, English style shirts, and overly hot, winter hats, on a daily bases, in the sweltering heat of a California summer, walking up and down our street repeatedly, as if they were searching for a youth life lost a hundred years ago.

I hadn't given him the courtesy of thinking what he had to say might actually do me a young life's warehouse full of good.

But I knew now. I made a mental *note-to-self. "Begin to take the time to spend more quality moments with Mr. Nelson. Pick his brains of all the available knowledge dusting there before it's gone."*

Looking over just then, I spied Mr. "N's" bicycle standing beneath the weight of perhaps the eight thick, metal chains he had it captured under at the base of one of the unit's fake columns, just beneath his window. This gave me an idea.

Like I still say, where there's a will and a determination, there's the possibility of flinging open wide, previously closed doors.

"Uhhh....Mr. "N"? Can I borrow your bike?"

He looked at me with his answer plainly written all over the front ridges of his sternly held face. He was about to tell me NO! That bike was his baby. He used it each and everyday to exercise the life still left in him as he rode back and forth, up and down our street, checking on the various co-op and studio units he owned. I could see him sizing up the possibilities of having this routine ruined should I allow something sinister to befall his precious bike while it was in my care.

"Don't worry, Mr. "N". I'll take good care of her. You want me to leave you a deposit? Somewhat of a rental fee or something—ta' make you feel better about trusting me with it?"

He just turned around while fishing a string of about a gazillion keys from inside his robe pocket. Picking through them with a practiced efficiency, he produced the correct ones and began to head for the bicycle stationed beneath the stairwell and he started unlocking the locks of the chains holding it down.

When away on Mr. "N's" bike, I headed, deeply in thought up Collier Street to turn right on 35th, meaning to make it finally across University to El Cajon Boulevard. I was in route to Kammy's school. Things I had to say and do to her weren't waiting still until three o' clock when she and whatever fool she was messing with pulled up outside our house that day, shocked to find me there at home.

I pedaled the full six mile distance non-stop, and I'm almost sure, *it felt like*, at record speeds.

Once securing Mr. "N's" baby beneath a stairwell. I headed for the offices of the rip-off school's administration. Once there, I identified myself and requested to see my wife on an urgent family matter which just couldn't be put off till that day's classes had drawn to an end. The obese woman at the front desk rolled over thirteen, grease infected chins at me, "Be that as it may, sir, I'm sorry, but we are precluded from interrupting classes for any reason until an established break time has been visited."

I wanted to reach across the particle of the fake wood counter to grab her and just shake continuously till' she put down the doughnut and began to make some sense.

I turned my back on her and left out of the office complex. I stole out with plans for beginning a trespassing scour of the insides of each of the individual offices of the entire school until what would prove to be my life-changing conquest produced what I'd come there to find.

After about the tenth office I had peeked into, attempting to ask whomever's attention my presence there had drawn along the way, whether or not they knew the whereabouts of Kamm Penn, I finally noticed her, at the back of a class, *of course,* sitting beneath a desk, the kind we all had back in junior high school, popping her gum loudly while the frustrated teacher went about her day's rigor at the front of the room of trying to actually teach the basics of bed-pan 101 to those other students who actually cared. She was stationed directly beside one of her staunch accomplices and road-dogg runnin' partners, Stephanie.

Stephanie wasn't a pretty girl per say. But she had an assortment of ghetto-hewn curves, situated in exactly all the right places. She and Kamm made an inviting match. Kamm, strikingly beautiful, with her manicured features, hair I hadn't been able to pay the hundred dollar fee for to have done on a regular weekly basis. Nails sculpted to include individual artistic designs on each one. Bootleg designer clothes to match every hat, purse, scarf and blouse to swathe over her own curveless frame.

Where had she gotten so much of this junk? Ole' girl appeared everyday to be overly well-kept, just, we all knew now, that it wasn't by me. I was an honest man. A wage earner, not skittish about providing the things my scale of wages earned. But as I stood back to watch the two of them now, with them not registering at first my presence there, I hurt so badly right then thinking how much I truly Loved this girl so very much.

And she shit on me…

Stephanie had entered our lives along about the first couple of weeks Kamm had begun to attend the school. She was a welfare mom, living in the projects, off of Euclid and Felton, with her mom, who had lived in the same apartment complex, as she'd grown up, a sixteen year old, unwed mother herself, with her mom. Not cute or pretty in any kind of way as I'd stated before. She was almost homely, but had gotten her way with a full slew of young, unsuspecting guys, all living exactly identical lifestyles as she, with the availability of her body instead of with her outward appearances or with her mind.

This wasn't the first time that my own encounters with her would come to bring me to fall into doing things—and regretting them—when it came to this woman, Stephanie being involved.

I had just returned from another exercise at-sea and I had just settled into the apartment, beginning to unpack my things. (Kammy hadn't been there to pick me up again—Too busy, I guess, setting out the outfit she'd planned on wearing to cover that evening's events).

When I'd arrived home, after completing my unpacking, and following a lengthy hot shower trying to knock off the chill and sting of the shipboard showers I'd been forced to encounter while out, in which one moment you were freezing to death beneath the pelt of ice-chip temperature waters the engineers in the pit were offering you, or you cowered beneath the skin melting mist of *pure-D-steam* as the water came out scalding you in sensitive places for what seemed an eternity as you held your ground waiting it out beneath the barrage and glare of thirteen other guys shooting insults at you to hurry so they could take their turns at freezing or burning just like you.

I was out of the shower and almost dressed when the phone rang.

"Hello?"

"Yeeeaaah...Dis' here Tony. Dis Blu?"

"It's me," I answered, trying desperately to roll through the library working crazily inside my head to place the name with the face with an experience, recollection, or meeting with the voice on the other end to offer me recognition.

My search came up empty.

"Where I know you from, playa', "I sent back across the line.

"You don't!" Was all he appeared willing to offer me.

"But you will."

Now the miniscule hairs on the back of my neck began to stand obediently on end.

"What can I do for you?"

"You know Steph?"

Again, the studded racing of my mind's rolodex sent me querying. The only Stephanie I knew was Kamm's friend Steph, and I didn't really know her all that well to call.

"You mean, Kamm's Steph?" I countered back.

"Naaaww, Nigga', I mean Steph, my Steph. My bitch, Stephanie, fool, and right now, she out wit' some otha' *soldjiia'*, kickin' it, givin'-way my shit—about to bounce." He ended this tirade with, "What-chew know bout' dat', par'dna'."

"I ain't got no feelin's on it playa," I shrugged while attempting, without help to picture the fool I was speaking to on the other end of the line any more.

There was a long silence. I could almost feel this man's anguish as he waited a full second more before shooting back.

"You ought to have feelings on it money. Cause' it concerns you."

"What you mean?" I was beginning to feel him open up. Steadying myself for what I was sure was coming next—doom, heartbreak, poverty, guilt...

"Set it out playa' what you callin' me fo'?"

"Don't you see? I know where dem' ho's at right now! Juss' callin' you ta' see if you wanna mann-up wit' a nigga' and go handle this shit, proppa'?"

It was my turn to return him silence. This had been the first time Kamm had presented me an inkling of what our minimal futures together were to hold. Sure, I hadn't forgotten all of hers and my own promiscuities back in high school. I had just felt more of a commitment than she, I guess, to our non-developing relationship as husband and wife now, and had put all of that behind me, trying to make a life for both of us, choosing to overlook such things instead.

"What you have in mine? You talkin' *NINA*?"

"I don't know fool, I'm talkin' anything you want it ta' be. Peep dis'. I'm down wit' brang-in' whatever's necessary to da' table soldiia'. But you and me got to handle this shit and we got ta' handle it right now, fore' I'm ready ta' jump off a bridge or sumshit', thinking how dis' ho done been playin me *Yo*—for a-sucka'... WORD?"

"...Bet?"

I wasn't really certain whether I actually did feel his sense of world-ending urgency, his anguish, and his anger. Something about his answer to my reference about gunplay told me this guy wasn't all together too sure or serious about his own intentions. He was just another soul crossed up and caught within the battle just like me. I'd never met him. Didn't know if I could trust him?

Who knew? Sure would have liked to have taken the time to place a call to Rastess right about then. But I couldn't.

Had to conduct myself as my own man—Step up to the plate and handle my own business the only way I knew how—straight forward, diving in, then settling back to see what lay in wait there before me, making the best of sometimes horrendous situations as they came about.

Home-Run-or-Strike-Out—Strength and Honor Baby! No gray areas accepted.

"Meet me up here at Scorios, on the corner of El Cajon and 33rd. We'll jump off from there."

I left my gun at home. Kamm hadn't driven me yet to a point of emaciated wisdom where I could kill a man outright over her spoiled goods satisfying wanton needs of other men. Once I left the apartment, I had a foreboding feeling cautioning me to leave myself an opening, however slight when dealing with Kamm, this Stephanie, the guy on the other end of the phone, and whatever else I was soon to become faced with as I ventured out to meet with him in front of a convenience store just a minute down the road.

But as usual, I didn't listen.

Tony was a huge brotha', about six feet six inches tall, two-fitty' to gage the least. And black as midnight. . . I at first thought something was wrong with his features when I pulled up, exited my car, and walked over to meet him. I had never seen someone so black, even in the sun of my former Texas youth. But the brotha' wa'n't wearing a pitch dark ski mask. Didn't have scarring which gave him the appearance of something held out of place. It was his complexion that blotted out the moon that night for me. While it was Kamm, that had stomped out a flickering light, in my heart as it had burned brightly there, believing in her wholeheartedly completely before.

He and I set out for East Deggo', just behind FAM-BAM, the Korean owned, *BLING-BLING* warehouse where they sold the ghetto-bandits their too-big jeans, their faddish, rapper shirts, they had nail and hair weave booths, car stereo and hair-care shops among others where they peddled every kind of ware, including black art and a full assortment of the cheapest quality gold and platinum trinkets—and right in the middle of the hood. But they never once offered any of the brotha's and sista's there—any jobs. All the assistants behind every counter of perhaps more than a hundred shops—were Korean.

It perplexed me. So much so, that I refuse to ever shop there. I understand that as proprietors of a legally licensed, thriving business, that it is their right. To choose who and what kind of employees they are willing to permit to toil in their shops. Just, still the same, it's also mine not to patronize them.

But that wasn't what made me mad the most. Do you think Mr. La Jolla or Mr. Rancho Bernardo, Mr. San Diego Estates would purchase every stitch of goods he bought from only American people of African descent should all the stores in his particular neighborhoods be manned solely by that culture of peoples?

Heeell no! He wouldn't.

He'd find a way to mass together a posse of his most influential cronies and perhaps a band of his sheet-hooded, rope-totin' henchmen and he would engineer a way to buy, burn or gerrymander Bubba's azz' right up outta *his hood.* To set up his own Zigfield malls, complete with Zale's,

Ralph's, Nordstrom's and Ward's conglomerate stores, where he could feel happier about himself in buying from and thereby supporting his own people, his own culture, his own family.

But not those of us living within the communities of our own sacred hearts. For us, it had become a modern day, Willie Lynch success story. Where we were more akin to caring about looking better than, having better rims on our whips than, showcasing better weaves and braids in our heads than, the next brotha' falling down or the next sista' stumbling backwards toward us, over more sustaining values of stunning particulars such as home and business ownership, continuing education at the collegiate levels, and maintenance of our own relationships within our own families. Ones now in which statistically, three of every four homes was run solely by a weary American mother of African descent who at times forged beneath the sweltering necessity of perhaps two jobs, cause' her kid's sperm donor was no longer around and he wasn't about to take any food outta the mouf's of the twenty-eight other kid's he had spread out among *her supposed* friends in the same hood to stop for just a second and think.

Think about getting a job. Any job, nicca' in the morning and handing over that paycheck, every week to support yo' kids. And think about getting a job. Another job, nicca', in the evening, so you could help put mom's back in school ta' at the least get her G.E.D.—that you stole from her when you knocked her up at fifteen (and you were twenty-two) so she won't continually be forced to faced the fact that she'd forgotten about her own dreams and potential but had also overlooked, beneath a barrage of things she had no training for dealing with the fact that all the potential and promise of her little Ray-Ray or precious Die-eesha was fast becoming swallowed up too in the streets.

Their only role models, Pookey n' them... The same gang of cut throats and societal drop-outs that had just robbed the sun-times liqcka' sto' on their own block with stocking caps and ski masks clung tightly over their heads and had the guts and the gall to congregate directly there outside of the very same establishment the next day, getting' high thinking the inevitability of their actions to be beyond them. Or they were the ones tha' five-O had just picked up for jackin' some old white dude foolish enough to stop and *AKSSSS fo'* directions on a moonless night after finding himself lost in *their* hood as he tried ta find *POOKEY's* mom's house in an attempt to make his own little brother's life better, by offering him a full-four year, free ride scholarship to Stanford.

The old man would never make it. He'd bleed out on a cold gurney in the rear of a slowly respondent ambulance just outside a cluster of people gathering about to see what was going on two dwellings down from the front of Pookey's house. There sat his moms and his brother—Waiting for their very special visitor who would never come.

Pookey's little man would eventually take his rightful place in the gang as well. After Stanford had pulled its offer, fed up and frustrated with the remuneration of its efforts of trying to bring life to the hood while receiving only beef and danger for its messengers as they struck out, time after time again trying to penetrate the bitter stupidity of the hood. And he'd very soon be spoken of in only memorial terms as his own short-lived dreams became snuffed out with reality, like his brother before him, and his moms would then have to visit her boys—every Sunday, down at Simpson's Cemetery—on Imperial.

REVENGE-BEING AN ENTRE' BETTER SERVED COLD, I had attempted to steady my unsteady resolve prior to meeting with the Tony character and prior to me making perhaps the complexity of an asinine decision I couldn't get myself out of once my steps marked forward to cross a line from which there'd be no telling return. Good is the enemy of better. Better the enemy of best. And Best is not what I was using in the form of judgment in seeking to align myself with him now as we stood in the twilight of a summer day's dusk, planning, without a plan to charge headway into the iniquitous den of Kamm's and her friend Stephanie's back-stabbing desires.

We pulled up in front of the complex.

Oh! Whatta'ya know? There she sat, Kamm, my wife, in the back seat of a car, with another nicca', the two of them just sitting there talking, oblivious to my presence at first when we had just rolled up.

I quietly exited my own car which I'd followed in behind Tony's supped-up CHEVY *CHEVELLE* all the way from North Park to the hood. Sweeping up on them, I presented myself suddenly before the window on the driver's side where dude was sitting.

"Whaasss-up, homey? I offered him briefly. Keeping him in my sights, I glanced over at Kamm and instructed her to get up out the car. She looked up at me, awestricken; initially unable to make out the features of whose face it was who had been addressing her. Then, finally, I think I hit her heart.

"Blu…I…." That's all she had to say to offer me. No other words escaped her mouth that evening toward me.

"Ain't have ta' go down like that, playa," dude sitting beside her in the car tried to offer up.

But I wan't haaaavin…it! I hadn't come there to talk at him. I'd come to retrieve my wife. I felt it the correct and manly thing under the circumstances to do.

When I sensed a sudden movement from him inside the car, I reached quickly into the rear window before me, and I all but pulled-half drug him through that tiny little slot, punching and kicking him, as he attempted, with very little success to untangle himself and become extricated from within the clutches of a young mad man, a half-opened door and a tiny window area he was half sticking into and half-hanging out of all the same.

Kamm began to scream. I was beatin' ole boy so bad, that even my own subconscious mind began to pummel me to implore me to have mercy on him and let him up. Just then, I felt a sullen crack and a dull, ear-splitting thud. And the slow seeping stream of thick, scarlet blood began to saunter down the side of my face as my vision became interrupted by a wash of my own blood filling into both my eyes.

My legs suddenly threatened to slip out from underneath me. Then they did. The lights went out on my Love for Kamm for good.

Things began to peer around me with the slowest motion of solemn clearing memory. I recall seeing flashing lights of all twisting colors as they blared at me psychedelically from every angle. At first I was bone-chillingly cold, then excruciatingly hot, and then a subtle peace of feeling nothingness at all at once swept over me.

My eyes were still open. I could see a flux of movement bouncing all around me. But, I couldn't move. It was literally as if I was watching myself from outside of myself. And somehow, the self lying on the ground knew that this was quite possibly—the end.

The self floating around to watch as an assembly of policemen questioned looky-lieu neighbors and scene gatherers, with no luck at all, had other ideas.

I'd been struck on the head from behind by the butt end of a .357 revolver.

Knowing that, I appeared to have cashed in another of Maman's nine lives she'd unwittingly passed down to me.

How many did I have left?

Why hadn't he just shot me and got it over with once and for all?

I was transported to Balboa Naval Medical Center; where I underwent observation for three days following a serious concussion and a mounting list of other knitnoid scrapes and bruises I would eventually survive to get back out there again to cause trouble more.

I was visited by my ship's Chaplain. My Chief and my work center supervisor, Robert (Bob Painter) came down to make certain I was gonna make it through as well.

Kamm never showed her face. My uncles, Larry and Kelvin poked in from time to time to keep pace with a medley of doctors and nurses who fawned over me as well.

The police were the peskiest of all my visitors. They hounded me and mentally prodded to no end, as if they truly cared, trying to gather and piece together details of what had taken place that night in the project parking area three nights before. I told them nothing.

Instead, I healed...and I thought.

What had ever happened to the six foot six midnight mass,—Tony? That brotha' had sure done a piss poor job of watching my "*six*". He was supposed to have been watchin' my back, and me his, throughout; during our efforts of going there to reclaim what we felt was rightfully ours-the Love and tenderness and care—of our women.

How many of you know that we went there and we reclaimed shit...Nothing—Jack, Zilch, Nada'?

Apparently, upon seeing Marvin Billups (AKA Pimp-Daddy) as he'd heard all the commotion and was come at a stride towards us once exiting the inside of Stephanie's apartment, with a gun in his hand, Tony had broke and lit out on his own run, toward the safety of the awaiting *CHEVELLE*.

I should have expected as much. Not many men already of my past had stuck around to stand up for me. He'd left me to fend for myself alone.

After healing up and getting back to my life, Kamm began to spend her days and evenings with him for the most part. She and I had gotten back together only briefly. It was a time of what I'd felt was reconciliation between us, when I began to get the feeling she was back up to old tricks when I had queried my maanns, D-D Plout, about what I was expected to provide for her during the time of our eventual split.

The two of us had ridden home, down the full length of El Cajon Boulevard, on the back of Mr. Nelson's bike. While in route to our house, I had her as a captured audience, for once to question her about things that were nagging away at me internally.

I asked her straight out if she had gone back to messing with this Pimp Daddy idiot and his friend, whom I had mistakenly, beat up—Chuck Dogg?

Of course, she lied... Stating no, she had not.

I half-baked asked if my income tax check had come in the mail. She half-stated, half-whispered, that it had. I asked her what had happened to it. She stated she had simply signed my name to the back of it and then deposited and turned back around and withdrew the full amount from our account to spend. I didn't even want to know on what or on whom she had spent it all on.

I asked her how much the check had been for. She told me it had been for exactly $666.00 and she stated she had already spent up a good portion of the entire amount. The wafting waves of all-consuming chills that swept over me right then almost materialized to shake the both of us wit ease from the frame of Mr. Nelson's bike.

DAMN! The number of the beast...

I began to feel that there were other forces defiantly at work within the focus of our soon to be ended relationship that were at play without me fully knowing.

That info held me shook. I didn't pose any more questions for her or say anything else to her.

Till we got home.

After returning Mr. "N's" bicycle and thanking him for its service, I wheeled about, after catching the meaning of the look he'd lain upon me before pulling away from his door. That look said, "End it—End it now. Take care of this messy business and be done with her once and for all—for your own good."

He no longer had to tell me. I was feeling the force of negativity's flavor as it resided in my own house just a flight of stairs and a doorway away from me more.

When I had entered the apartment, Kamm all of a sudden had wanted the two of us to begin to *play house*. She suggested drawing a bath for us. After which, she alluded to having plans for sexin' me up real tight and proper, and perhaps, going out to dinner—on her (right…) later on.

I made a subtle rejection of her illegitimate sexual advances. I told her that I was exhausted. But that dinner out sounded like a really cool idea. I told her to go ahead and take a bath if she liked. I would call a cab and have it come pick us up because I knew the perfect little restaurant that she was just gonna' Love.

I had the cab waiting outside the apartments when she'd finally finished re-applying her face and tinseling up her hair. Our car, without explanation from her as yet, was plainly out of commission.

I had already greeted the cabbie when he'd first rolled up, with the staunch presence of Mr. "N" watching me, like an expectant father, from the window inside. I had given him a hundred dollar bill and filled him in on our eventual destination. Then I'd rushed back up the stairs to see if Kamm was finally ready to take off.

Our travel guide hauled to a stop depositing us only about two miles from our house. It took a full minute's unwariness for Kamm to realize that my cabbie hadn't registered us outside of a waiting restaurant to take in dinner at all.

We had both already exited the vehicle and we were now standing in front of a cream-colored office complex on Park Boulevard. The sign swinging languidly from the building's rafters read: "*ABAMCO DIVORCE SERVICES," Jose' De' La Vega de Guerra—Proprietor.*

Immediately upon taking this in, Kammy began to back away from the door leading into the establishment. She looked at me with an immense hurt shrouding to suddenly sweep to cover her pretty face.

"Blu…

I don't want a divorce," she near pleaded.

At first I didn't look back at her. This was quite possibly; even after all she had already put me through, the hardest thing I had had to do thus far as a man.

"We're getting a divorce Kamm, and we're getting' one now...TODAY!" I shot back to her devoid of any heart-felt feelings.

She began to cry. Those crocodile tears she'd been able to turn on—just for me in our past. But they no longer held any effect over me.

"Whhhyyy....?" She offered back weakly.

I then looked at her as if she was crazy and had just told me she adored the shit colored stains of the scarring my obtuse amounts of injuries suffered while dealing with her had produced for me.

"Look! I ain't playin' with your azz any mo' longer. And I don't have time to stand here now, after everything you've done to me—against me—as some kind of wife, to explain a fuccin' thing to you. If you don't carry yo' azz up them steps and sign those fucc'n papers, I'm gonna place a call to the Internal Revenue Service and tell em' that I never received a check for last year's income tax. And they're gonna place a trace on the check they originally generated and they'll find out you forged my name and cashed the check—and you're on your way to prison for at least ten years baby gurl'—for a felony!"

Thinking her options slimming to a point of being non-existent, she turned and went right up the stairs, where we met Jose' and I did all the talking. After about an hour more, where I took a brief respite to run back down and make certain that my ace-boon cabbie was still out there in front, satisfied and plainly waiting, we came out from under the swinging company awning and she made preparations to get back into the cab to go wherever. She just knew that the two of us were to be heading back to *our* home.

But I had another thing for her.

Brushing her aside lightly, I informed her, that from that point on, she was literally on her own. If she wanted a ride outta' there, she'd have to contract for that—Call up ole' Pimp Daddy and do that—on her own. This was my cab. She'd have to find another form of transportation to take her on the *A-train* down life's uncertain, rocky roads.

I didn't see or hear from Kamm again for a full couple of months. I thought at first that she would drop by the apartment to gather her things responsibly right after I had left her standing out before that office in the cold. But she made no moves to contact me at all. I took all of her possessions and emptied them without emotion into the trash dumpster at the side of the complex.

It wasn't till one sunny Saturday, when I'd been deeply involved with rockin' Carolyn's world, right out front in my studio, with her legs spread wide in both my hands, on the couch, that I began to take note of approaching steps as they made their way up toward the door leading into my house.

I hadn't heard their start at first. It was only when I began to register that they weren't heading in the direction of my neighbor's door that I began to listen for them more intently. Suddenly, and all-mind-blowing to me, the front door shot open, only the security of the chain I had deftly drawn into place before attaching myself to Carolyn held us both at bay from finding ourselves caught up then in the embarrassment our lustfully applied haste would have found us in.

Kammy poked what bit of her head she could fit between the door and the chain inside to begin to call out.

"Blue...? Bluuu...? Blu, I'm here to get all my stuff. Blu...."

After pulling out of Carolyn, I reached down to the floor to sweep up my shorts and I began to struggle into them thinking with a sigh, *damn! Am I ever going to be rid of this gurl forever?*

Carolyn ran off toward the bathroom. I sat a second more. I watched the smooth nekkid silkiness of her backside as it swayed away from me at a banter to disappear behind the closing sanctuary of the bathroom door.

Drawing in a full, clearing breath, I got up, minus any kind of shirt, and I released the chain to finally usher Kammy in.

Looking at her disdainfully, "What you want?" I snapped at her.

Visibly flustered a bit, she just looked at me with those bright eyes and smiled briefly. I could feel the beginnings of my heart starting to melt inside as I stood there fully, once again captured inside the crux of her beauty. I had to shake that shit off!

"I came to get the rest of my stuff," she answered.

"You ain't got no stuff here."

"What you mean? I ain't got no..." She began to try and step past me enroute to our inner storage closet door.

I stepped out of her way to permit her passage. Once there she saw that every stitch of all the shit she had brought with her from that little house next door to Maman's in Texas was gone. No longer there for her to neglectfully come and go as she pleased, forgoing it all for this time months before coming around to wanting to pay attention to it again completely.

She stood there in front of me a look registering hurt, anguish, tenderness hidden and surprise changing chameleon colors of doubt, distrust, frustration and hate across the sloping wave of uncertainty on her face.

"I tole' you. Your shit's no longer here. I threw it all out."

She still just stood there with her hands firmly placed on hips she barely had. It appeared she was trying to come to some sort of decision of just what it was she was going to do now without all her stuff.

"Blu...? I can't believe..."

Just then, Carolyn decided that it was time for her to make a return entrance to let it be known that she was still somehow in the mix.

With nothing but a cool, white cotton towel draped about the curvaceous temptations of her previously lust-filled body, she stepped boldly from inside the bathroom and she sided over to stand next to me at first in silence.

The man inside me couldn't help, even in that situation, but to feel the familiar sensations of arousal striking up once more briefly, knowing the nastiness of things she and I had been doing just before Kamm had placed the key I had forgotten to take back from her in the door to interrupt us.

Kamm and I began to argue over the whereabouts and costs of all her discarded belongings I no longer cared about. I could feel the fervor of hotly burning anger as it radiated out in the open coming from Carolyn. More and more she began to become edgy, shifting ever so slightly, foot to foot, appearing like a cornered cat, preparing to pounce at my side. She suddenly shot out to step forward to draw closer to Kamm. She stood facing her now between us. I was taken in by just how much she towered over the shaking form of my former Love.

I had no idea she was about to stoop to the lengths of what she was to offer next.

Letting go of the tops of the towel she had been holding closed at the apex of her ample breasts, she flung it off to one side and inched even closer to press those supple mounds of softened flesh completely into Kamm's quickly contorting face.

She attacked her verbally with, "Take a good look at what you couldn't give him, *bitch!* And... What I was givin' im' right now and I'm gonna give back to him, again and again and again juss-soon as you step back through that door n' leave.

She wasn't done.

And as if she'd come to a decision to take matters into her own hands, she leaned in closer and slapped the piss outta' Kamm with a resounding *WHACK*, shocking both of us completely.

I wasn't quite sure internally right then how I felt about that. I let it stand without a word.

Reeling back to take in the full brunt of the forceful blow, Kamm began to counter back preparing her own volley to further incite the afternoon's glow. It was then that I stepped between them soundly, trying desperately to pull the two of them apart.

It was then that I first noticed Marvin Billups making his own hurried preparations for taking the flight of steps leading up into my still opened doorway, two at a time, with haste. Unlocking myself from between the careening women, I met him just as he'd reached the final rung of the top step. Drawing back a perfectly placed foot; I kicked him with a sweeping force, the blunt bottom of my vengeful drive settling in the solar plexus region of his heaving chest to knock him backward. He went toppling end-over-end and came to lay motionless for a millisecond at the foot of the landing below.

At that moment, I had no worries of possibly causing his death. Demeaning shades of Buster felling Dusty escaped the conscious flow of volleys of chained, cell infested pictures of the wicked abuses and previously unthinkable molestations I'd have to fight off should I crush his wind-pipe completely as I had planned for him upon reaching his stirring form at the bottom of the steps below.

Mr. "N" reached him before I did.

Thank GOD!

When I did stand tall reaching the two of them, ole' Pimp Daddy was dithering in a wavering stupor, trying desperately to shake the webs of a star-stricken confusion from inside his head. Mr. "N" warded me off of him at the first.

"Now, Blu, stand down, boy. Stand down!—I mean it," he warned.

I lunged forward at them again slightly.

"But, Mr. "N"! That's the fool's been messing round' with my wife. Turn im' loose so I can give im' what he's come after."

The old warrior stood before me now, with fire in his eyes as he contemptuously looked up away from me to hear all the raucous throwing about taking place in my apartment above where I was certain Kamm was having her azz handed to her as well.

"So what...Eee's tha' one's been dancin' around with that little trollup." He stood his ground convincingly. With a grave set to his jaw line he went on.

"What's that matter to you? Look at you...Ought to be ashamed of yourself! Got that beautiful young lady up there (Mr. "N" adored Carolyn) fightin' all about, mixed up in your mess. Don't you know that if you don't show the person you love, that you really love them, somebody else will come along to show them for you. And that's what you ought to be focused on—what you're getting' new. You don't need that trollup in your life. All's she's ever done, instead of complimenting you since I known you in life...is complicate it for you.

Blu...Son, you got to learn to make betta' choices for yourself and find," (pointing off—up toward Carolyn above) "strength to stop believing in every Bettye who steps forward to say they Love you, cuz' you son, are just batty enough to might do somethin' else crazy like believe em'." He brought his rushed education to an end by offering me, "You just can't continue to give and give and give to them, if they won't accept it, Blu. Now let this piece of ruddy business be and let this here foolish malcontent back up to his own devices."

Marvin had pulled out of Mr. "N's" clutches and did the best he could at making an attempt to settled back down at a beaten stoop atop weary legs in a heap at the old codger's feet. He had all but gratefully given in to permitting the old man's waving protection to flag over him. He lay back now in the full fluff of the manicured grass and attempted to regain his efforts of bearing.

The wise old man shook a crooked finger at me. "Sounds more like she's—is' problem now...rather than yours. N'...I ain't about to stand before you now and watch you throw all your life away seeking a vengeance ya' will never be able to make reason with for why ya really need it.

Scolding me further, with a confident anxiety, "If you'll just settle down n' try to put all this jumble beside of you and put yo'self back together, Blu.

You'll probably be able to pull yo'head on up and out and be able to begin to focus on the more positive aspects of your life."

He was right. I knew.

I stood down the heaving shades of the ferocity of my previous anger. I attempted to replace it—with mounting concern...

...For who?

Carolyn or Kamm...

It wasn't long after that that they both materialized. Kamm first, as she sought to get out from under the thunderous blows Carolyn had been raining down on her unmercifully all the while Mr "N" and I had been masking together a fleeting calm outside.

She flung herself out the door—Took each step, seemingly four at a time, scooped Pimp Daddy's azz up from the green. Their two beaten forms limped brokenly on wavering supports back toward the lavishly upholstered insides of the awaiting *PIMP-MOBILE.* They lingered very little now in their determinated efforts to seek an escaping flight away from us for what would prove to be their very last time.

My moment in time with her was over, for good. The county courts in San Diego mailed the final dissolution papers to her parent's home, beside Maman's house, back in Texas.

On February 24th, 1987, for the very first time, I became a divorced man.

...For a minute.

I never saw either one of them ever again.

Chapter Seven
"NETTIE"
GOOD LORD; WHAT IS WE GON'DO

There are five simple tests toward happiness: Free your heart from hating any and all things; Free your mind from inconsequential worries; Live your life as simply as you can (never striving or stressing to have what you cannot or be what you're not meant to be) Give more of yourself on every occasion; And expect less in return as payment.

Happiness and joy for me had become a bit more relevant, yet still somewhat relative. I hadn't held much of an example of it from birth, leading up into my early twenties. But I refuse to stand around idly, skulking at that. Never one to harp too convincingly on the negativities of things that didn't go right for me, I just 'Kept-On-Keeping On', believing that the glass was *always half-full,* marching forward with *POSITIVE PERPETUAL MOTION* toward a future I originally had no idea I was setting myself up for. I was intent on making something, anything at all worthwhile, of myself. A great thinking man, Albert Einstein, said it best for how I have thus far determined to mold me.

He said, "Seek not to become a person of success…Seek instead, to become a person of value."

I met "NETTIE" June 10th, 1986. We were married, February 24th, 1987.

The First time…

It was the very same day my divorce from Kammy had become officially recorded and final.

I had lied to her originally—in a way. I'd never found cause to mention my still existent relationship with my former Texas neighbor when I'd met and began placing serious thoughts of forever in the impressionable aisles of confusion leaning toward negative vibes which danced wildly inside her head. Especially the fact that I was still a married man all the while I was building up her hopes for eventually causing the two of us to come together on an eternal basis, as man and wife. It was only just before she and I stepped across the threshold of a quaint little wedding chapel on Pennsylvania Street, located in San Diego's Hillcrest district, a lovely continuum of developing, upscale storefront structures chocked full of newly out-of-the-closet gay men, that I finally moxied up enough courage to let her in on what I felt no longer really mattered when launched beside my Love which burned completely incessant for her.

I had taken the requisite steps to correct the situation and had only been waiting on time to make it all complete. So, in my mind, there had been no reason to consult or concern her with the soiled details of the what's and how's of Love's previous business.

It was a simple ceremony. One after which we snagged a pint-sized bottle of *Jack Daniels* from a local store and we merely—went to the movies to sip and mix it inside our overpriced cokes as we talked so much in the excitement of finally starting out our lives together, that we thought we'd get the bums-rush out the door, so many other patrons complained heavily about our jabbering so loudly during the entertainment that the theater's manager actually took to stationing himself nearby to shush and calm our tirades throughout the showing.

But, we didn't care.

It was the beginnings of us beating an assortment of about a gazillion odds together. What was there to care for—from him or anyone else menacingly purporting to obstruct the paths we looked so eagerly toward? He didn't know it and thank GOD he was never unfortunate enough to have been worthy of being made aware. But, that very second, nothing at all would have been permitted the lazy eye of failure to come close to threatening our success bearing progress?

Boy! Did we not ever know? There was a bunch. Even after all that the two of us had already been through in our own separate lives, we were strikingly ill-prepared for what awaited us next on the doorstop of entrapment encircling life's fickle door.

For us, it was hardly to be easy. It's like I've said to her time and time again over so many years, GOD gave us one another as a gift. Our union was like a Loving promise from him at its start. Yet, he never included to-date that anything between the two of us would ever be easily accomplished or trouble-free.

I was still on the USS ENGLAND (CG-22). I was by now a Second Class Petty Officer, an E-5, and I made just about enough wages, in pay and benefits to keep our heads firmly above water. I was due to reenlist once the ship made one of its final voyages, to the Long Beach Naval Shipyard, where once there, we (with the help of about a thousand government contractors) would tear her apart, from stem to stern and install the latest weaponry and most state-of-the-art sensing electronics the world had ever seen up to that point, an accumulation of separate systems known plainly as the New Threat Upgrade.

It would take a full thirteen months to accomplish such a daunting task. During that time, I would begin to commute, back and forth between our tiny, two-bedroom apartment in Oceanside California, and the sometimes two hour distance it took me to get to work everyday depending on the flow of traffic. Some days it took me four hours, one way, of being clogged within the metal parking structure of the 405 or 5 freeways just to get home.

Fridays were the worst and the best…I bought another car. We still had my little blue Honda Accord. But I knew "NETTIE" and Britty had to have a way of getting around the tiny Marine infested town as well. So I purchased what was for me, up to that period of time, a dream car.

It was a 1976 *FORD* Gran Torino. Its engine was a 351 Windsor and that thing purred like a kitten, even when doing a hundred and five (which me and two other guys, one with a '69 *CAMARO* and another a '72 Cadillac Seville we'd all lent a hand at rebuilding the engine in to perfection) on I-5 on Fridays as we floated on whispering wings striking out from Long Beach heading home.

I quickly developed an unhealthy Love for that car. It even had a *CHOLO'd* out, little chain link steering wheel and I'd outlined the square of its license plates in a faux, chain link silver as well. It was painted *ala'*

STARSKY and HUTCH, white flames of death overtop a flushed glowing red to capture eyes and alluring stares while speeding almost abruptly down many a highway thoroughfare with an insolent disdain for the boundaries society had set for me. I'd caught a killer deal off a guy in my division, whom had previously caught a like-size deal from another guy in that same division a year and a half before. I paid $1500.00 for that rig and I drove that car nearly to its and my early grave.

We'd contracted for "NETTIE" to begin classes daily in San Diego, at a local business school formerly located on downtown's fifth avenue. There, her goal was to learn the trade of becoming a bank teller. We had a young, stay-at-home neighbor lady from South America, named Candy that we trusted to watch the sweet little Britty while her mommy and daddoo went off to work and school in support of keeping our fledgling little home life functioning.

Things went well for a minute or two. "NETTIE" and I went about the tiring chore of really getting to know each other. Our courtship had been brief. One which had us meeting in one night, betrothing undying Love for one another just three days more into that same week, followed by one, two week trip I'd made back to Portland during my Christmas leave...And *BAMmmm!* There we were, settin' up house, trying to make our way in life together, as a family—seeking success neither one of us had been given a historical model or pattern role to follow in our own lives toward . But we were game. We struck out, time and time again. But we stayed and we attempted to hold on, in search of that ever promising "home-run"—just like we'd seen Mike and Carol Brady of "The Brady Bunch" pull off so effortlessly each day after school while we'd watched episode after episode, as kids, unknowingly taking mental notes.

The Century School of Business presented us a bitter sweet ally. Its administrators demanded we take out a seven-thousand dollar student loan, guaranteed by the government in order for her to attend. All so she could drive the thirty-five mile distance, from Oceanside to San Diego every morning and learn the particulars of no-brain bank telling complete with fake machines and cheap, play monies. It provided "NETTIE" with an outlet away from remaining cooped up inside the confines of the apartment and it gave her a daily respite from the sweet rambunctious nature of our darling little Brittney.

It was all good!

You'd think...

It was there that "NETTIE" made her first friends in Southern California. There was Maria Slackey, your typical welfare legacy and single mother who continually perplexed me with her ability to make a great life for herself and her then toddler son, Rendell, all without ever having the responsibility, anguish and pangs of ever holding down a righteous job. I don't know what it was about Maria, but from the start, I just didn't like her.

I realize now what I could never fully recognize back then. Maria was simply another soul, an American of African descent MOTHER, on her own—No Man, trying to right things life had twisted up for her decidedly in her youth. And, believe me...Maria Slackey, even then, was doing a damn fine job.

Although I never let on back then, I was enamored of her. I think a little bit jealous too as well. The girl had tha' bomb townhouse apartment in a rent district none of any of our other friends at the time could even hope to touch. She had cable television with every channel, every amenity Ma Bell could offer on her phone, call waiting, call transfer, and call ring back...call-call! She could produce an assortment of credit cards upon demand. *Who paid for all that stuff?* There was Mervyn's, Ward's, and several Visa's. She went about life having nothing, yet appearing outwardly to have it all, and we worked everyday, seven to four (and me sometimes twenty-four hours a day when at sea) and we were struggling.

Not only did Maria have what it took to find a way for her and Rendell to live almost lavishly without ever lifting a single manicured nail in the effort, she had the sweetest outgoing countenance going for herself to match her plainly blessed progress. That woman would give a friend the shirt off her back, for real, if she thought they needed it.

Still, initially, I had no use for her. I became so caught up in my own conservative views of being unable to look at the struggles of life's other participants without the jaundiced eye of contempt and suspicion that I immediately tagged her a loser, although everything she did, every move she made spelled out a painstakingly earsplitting success.

I treated Maria poorly on every occasion in which I had the chance.

And she just smiled in that sweet little way she had of passing life's idiots by and she went on, ignoring my ignorance as she went even further to raise her children, by herself the best way she knew how.

There was Carnella Jones, an identical template of Maria. A bit wilder and younger, yet still a bastion of Motherly strength and fortitude, lending to the example of forceful might and level-headed guidance tens of millions of American Mothers of African Descent impart to babies with absent fathers on a still increasingly daily basis. Carnella was flighty, a petite, desceptively demure figure. I swore on a stack of bibles, upon first meeting her, that she could never be trusted with anything more than a pack of cigarettes and a cheap stick of bubble gum.

Again, just like with Maria, I was wrong. Foolishly, I'd based my own value and worth of these young women on the fact that they held down no jobs. Yet, they were out there, making it outright, and making it good, without men. For me, this was wholly uncanny. Backwards and to a point of being unacceptable in that day's discernable society. Carnella's actions ignored my own as well, just like Maria's. And for some ungodly reason, I refused to treat her with respect as well.

I think back now and I can only attribute my disrespectful treatment of these two indelible ladies to my own internalized frustrations with my own woman, "NETTIE". They were each there for her during a time in which she was at her stark worst.

I recall receiving a phone call from her after just returning home following the lengthy drive from the ship at Long Beach. I had already re-upped for an additional six year hitch and that brought with it the overwhelming immensity of a thirty thousand dollar reenlistment bonus.

Immediately it seemed, I'd just stepped foot inside the apartment to find it empty, no "NETTIE", no Britty—only the phone ringing incessantly greeted me once inside. I picked it up on its sixth ring.

"Hello?"

"Blu, this is Benita. Have you seen Mac or Maria today?"

"Nope...I haven't seen either one of em'. I just got in from work and nobody's here. Why? Was Mac supposed to come down to see "NETTIE" today?"

Benita was the wife of Marie's brother, MacArthur. The two of them lived up the 5 freeway going North in Garden Grove with their toddler children, Shay and Manford, about an hours drive from us in Oceanside. The tiny hairs at the back of my neck began to involuntarily stand on end and I felt that slight rumbling of nervous energy I always get whenever I encountered a sixth sense of awareness peek up to tell me—Something was definitely wrong. . I felt the jist of her conversation strike me as being just a little bit odd.

"What's wrong, Neet... You O.K.?"

"Yeah..." She exasperated heavily, suddenly swooped up in fretting thought.

"Man-Man's got a high fever and Mac has the car. I think I need to run him to the hospital before it's too late."

"I haven't seen either one of them. I'll call around to some of her friends in San Diego to see if the two of them have bounced around there. Tell you what. You do the same up your way and if we have no luck here soon, I'll come take you and the little bit to the emergency room myself. Give me about ten minutes and then call me back."

I tried every number I knew where they might be. No luck. My own mounting frustration was only increased when Benita never called back and she wasn't answering at their house as well. But all that was nothing compared with what I was offered next when the phone did finally ring again.

"Hello?"

"Baaabbby..."

It was her and I sensed instantly from the draw and tone of her voice that something was crucially wrong.

"What's up, boo?" I offered her softly at first.

"I need you to come up here and pick us up."

"What do you mean come up there and pick you guys up? How'd you get up there?" I had noticed our little Honda sitting in its designated spot outside in the carport when I'd first driven up. That was part of the beginnings of things striking me as odd upon entering the apartment to find noone home inside. I was totally unprepared, mentally for what I was about to face at the other end of that eventful conversation.

"Mac brought us up."

"Why can't he bring you guys back down? I'm tired, Babe. I just got in from the drive from Long Beach."

"Uhhmm...Um—his car. I think something's wrong with the brakes. He's got to go to work or something or he can't drive it."

I stood frustrated. "Which is it, "NETTIE"? He carted you two all the way up there, forgot he's got to go to work, and now he's just finding out his brakes'r bad ta'boot?"

"Blu.uuu? Damnit Blu! I don't know. Just come and get us, Paleeease!"

My heart sank. There was that sick feeling lodged in the pit of my stomach again. I knew, for some reason or other that she had just lied to me.

"Did Benita get in contact with you guys? She's been calling all over town trying to locate Mac. The baby's real sick and I think she took him to the emergency room. Is he there? Can I talk to him?"

Uhhh...No! He's o'-out-side, looking at the car or something."

I was just about *or...sumpthin'd out.*

I'd been so elated to be finally pulling into the driveway of our happy little apartment complex after such a grueling weekday afternoon drive from Long Beach to Oceanside. I still recall, I was in such dire Love with that girl, so overly smitten with the luxuries of newly wedded bliss, that anytime during my day when I had even the slightest thought of "NETTIE" and Brit, I got the anxious flutters of about a billion butterflies, all swarming and dancing around warmly inside of me, and I just couldn't wait till fifteen-hundred when it was time to be heading back home to them at day's end. The flighty comforts these feelings gave me tripled as I pulled up, parked the car, and took my usual shortcut through the complex's pool site which was located just beneath our apartment's balcony and sliding glass windows. Once there, and safely inside, I'd swoop them both up in hugs, hugs, more hugs and kisses as the two of them would register genuine surprise steeped with wide-eyed Lovliness as they both lent final meaning to my life, greeting me, and welcoming me back home with tender care and Love to assure—That we was gon' make it. Everything was eventually gon' be, for me, and for them too, finally all right.

But something had gone horrifically wrong that day. Someone had thrown back the depleated edges of an iniquitously oblique curtain on me. Behind it lay the all-but defeated sanctity and pureness and wealth of my very brief, formerly happy marriage. In doing so, they revealed a sorrow-filled truth to me. One I'd hoped and struggled against daily, on tenterhooks praying to have strength and courage enough to maintain it securely tucked away and hidden. But I was weak, fully unprepared. The legitimacy of what I was facing was flung towards me shadowing blindly in an irrepressible darkness which read: "You, my friend—have attached yourself knowingly, by your own hand—TO A MONSTER!"

The demon which plagued me billowed with a sweeping ferocity threatening to take my young family out with a ruthlessness I'd never personally contended with before. It was not only far from being mortal or phantom, thereby sentencing me to defeat, helpless, unable to fight against it completely. It had no mind, could not think or act and react on its own. But it held flesh, air, blood and the ability to breathe and take form in captivity all the same. It was akin to an eternally present ghost, one which harassed you ceaselessly, heaving at and hauling on you with a life-bending infinity which took clutch upon a body, and knocked it from atop everything good it had ever held out hope for or known. It assaulted as rapidly and as fully as a thing such as this could attack. It bore death and held poverty and debilitating anguish passionately in its grasp. We were goners' man... The finality of its presence was upon us. All before we'd even been given a fighting chance at making a healthy start.

It was nothing of my own doing—in a sense. Or was it?

It was both physical and neurological, yet not emotional. It had a name, sometimes a face—and even had a lengthy history—One of breaking down existences with looming ease or of wreaking havoc on lives, the rolling extent of its depravities throughout countless years briefly recoverable yet effusively unrecordable.

The horror which engrossed my Lovely young family and ripped through us threatening to tear us apart without ever having struck a commencing blow, reared its revolting head with alacrity. With an ominent malevolence and seemed pre-planned forethought, it took only about a minute's worth of seconds before this beast had almost escaped with the life's blood of all that had made our wonderful relationship whole.

CRACK-COCAINE had all but whipped up on me and put me out of the race once and for all—again.

. . . And all before the first tolling anniversary of six months of marriage had been attended.

"NETTIE'S" call had brought with it the insecurity of a soaring desperation as it crept amid momentary silences and lengthy, extended pauses to clutter and fog up the connections of our former early personal existences. I sensed the daunting edge of uncertainty accompanied by a telling, fitful longing which belied an ambiguous hesitation as it snuck stealthily up to linger along the now fringed edges of the formerly sweetened familiarity at the back of her voice. She was choosing her words carefully ensuring an almost ultra clarity in each syllable. No longer free-flowing in her banter as she'd expectantly been with me on normal occasion, she picked through them as one would while sorting a newly shucked passel of green peas after just harvesting them for a special dinner.

She'd been visiting with Mac allright. But, for some unspoken reason, she didn't want to be there any longer. I got the feeling from her tone that she didn't quite feel up to being with herself for any length of time while there as well.

"I'll be there in about forty minutes. "NETTIE", where's my baby? Is everything all right?"

"Yes, of course! She's fine. Her and Shay are rolling around playing right in front of me now on the floor."

Pensively, I told her that I Loved her and hung up.

I got to Garden Grove in about thirty five minutes. Me and the Starsky and Hutch mobile never played around when it came to chewing up the unworthy lines of multiple lanes along the shortening freeway. Specially when sparked by the urgency of need.

Destiny held that I was in for something ugly. Some kind of incongruity I'd never had to face before. The sick, kicking feeling of pending doom lay waiting, even if only inside the sweating den of the inspirations of my own mind.

I was sure of it.

Something was wrong! I'd find out and I'd convene with it once arriving there. And like anything else, up until the moment when I finally stepped foot across the threshold of Benita and MacArthur's apartment door, I tried aimlessly along the quickly paced route to prepare myself, one way or another for lending my own passions for ruthlessness toward engaging what that destiny intended. I'd see it through on its terms—And, I'd meet it like anything else—head on!

The first thing that struck me once arriving at the complex in Garden Grove, was the fact that Big Mac's yellow Thunderbird was no longer in its parking spot beneath the tin awning at the side of the apartments. I moved forward cautiously.

I was met by an opened door. Once walking inside, I was taken aback to have to sort through the sparcity of light sifting up there to greet me. The entire den was almost pitch-black. It took me almost two full minutes in an attempt to force my pupils to finely adjust in order to be able to see. My mind conjured up harsh similes of the poorly lit burrow of a clairvoyant's lair, a place where secrecy, chicanery and money-grubbing tricks played out to scathe the unwary.

I picked out the tiny free-form frame of my Britty. She lay, appearing to sleep in the middle of the living room floor. I at first sent up silent prayers of *THANKSGIVING* to a faithful GOD above. I could also tell that her diaper hadn't been changed in a long while. Then, almost instantly, I became furious. But I shooed such thoughts away quickly, keeping them all bottled up and away smartly inside. I was not completely sure of the next surprise and wanting to sagely conserve the cruxt of both my mental and physical energies for whatever it was that I would be forced to face next.

I stepped over her lightly while moving more deeply into the interior in search of a light switch. Flipping it on once there, I turned to find "NETTIE" curled up in a fetal-like position appearing to be sitting like a demure oriental urchin rocked back on her haunches. Her knees were tightly pulled up close to her chest and she sat while rocking back and forth in a tranced rhythm, ever-so-slightly humming to herself while sucking her thumb.

She wore a pink gaucho jump suit made of cheap, swap-meet cotton. The lengthy roots of her hair smattered about her face to lend the crazed image of a desperate, maniacal animal. When I walked in to stand in front of her, she angled her head just a bit and caught me with a sauntering gaze. The pupils of her bloodshot eyes widened the size of sable dimes as they struggled to register upon me.

I could smell her. Unusual for her, the effluvial aroma of her body's odors mixed with the absorbent materials of the baby's unchecked diaper. A fowl smack of unwashed sweat and feces tuned my stomach to flips as it plunged effortlessly about the stuffy interior of the tiny apartment. I could also smell the odor of another, perhaps her brother, who wasn't present now. I swooned briefly. It all hit me at once with an abrupt debunkment.

I sucked in a breath, trying to mask my obvious disappointment, or at least play down my individually outraged sense of utter disgust. Still, I implored myself to push forward. I had to almost physically prod myself to harden my insides against the things I was stepping into, experiencing and seeing.

I stooped down to rest on a knee beside her. I hoped to match her level with some minimal chance of trying to reach her—to get through to her any way possible. I wasn't finding any fortune there. She was locked in, off in that far-away place I'd feared she might have sought out for her own preservation. I'd found her in this protective state, one she'd already lost herself to, long before I'd even arrived there.

Was I in fact alone, even with her there?

Too late again.

I could barely stand to look at her. It hurt me so much to see her like this and know, without a doubt, how, if she kept on like this, she'd eventually end up.

....How we'd all end up...As a family?

Even with it all, at this, I wasn't all that too alarmed. I had seen her in these states before. Twice previously, I'd been startled awake in the middle of the night to reach over and not find the warmth of her body lying comfortably next to me. Upon rising with thoughts of seeking what had become of her, I'd looked over to the cornered edge of our bedroom to find her in this exact same inquisitive position. She'd be just sucking her thumb then too, rocking back and forth, her eyes locked into a seemed terror of paralyzed fright.

Upon first witnessing it, this thing scared me to no end. I had never seen anything like it before other than in the movies, for sure, not from a living, breathing human—My wife! She appeared lost, non lucent, as if away and as if she was locked tight in visiting some strange distant land of her mind's own making. And no matter how hard I tried, I was never permitted a speckle of entry to be brought along to make the journey with her into that place. The reality of the surrealistic natures of the adventures she encountered while gone on these trips was held closely only to herself.

It would take almost another year before the two of us (during counseling) were able to begin to develop methods of approaching the idea of stepping out to break down the reasoning behind and seek resolutions we could both work with, toward combating these fitful, unexplainable episodes.

Looking at her now, I just stood there…helplessly wondering. She hummed incessantly. A medley of twisted concertos seemingly pulled her away from me. There sat my "NETTIE". No longer the care-free inviting beauty that I had so many short months before fallen instantly head-over-heels in Love with, But now…A mere shadowed shell of her former self. One in which the vigor and stamina of life had seemed to've gone out of forever. I was scared—and like so many other times during my life—I felt the chilled, depleting wave of utter loneliness sweep in to take hold of my weary heart. That which I'd felt I wanted most (Her, and our Lovely little family) had all but abandoned me too.

In her state, she was incapable of Loving me like the dream angel had shown me, promised me, she would, if I sauntered down the guard of protective walls I'd maintained throughout the years and just let her. For her, there now appeared to be only one, true Love—The pipe!

It seemed that moment of her lengthy almost autistic fit would go on forever. For a time, I began to gather what I could make out belonged to her as things lay scattered about the interior of the still, dimly lit room. Her purse, her shoes, cigarettes, lighter, Britty's diaper bag and a steamy, putrid plastic bag of soiled jumpers found their ways into my keeping. I just let her be.

I then bent low to scoop the tiny little girl up into the determined protection of her new daddoo's arms. I held her cherubic face up to the light, ensured the rhythmic breathing patterns of her tiny little chest, kissed her Lovingly on the top of her head and I placed her gently on the empty sofa.

I then began a guardian sweep of the entire apartment with the goal of making certain we were still the only souls there. I found no others. I turned my attention back to what would be the most complicated task of *my responsibilities* that day—attempting to care for "NETTIE".

I was responsible for her. Whatever happened to her, good or bad, was on my head. She was Marie Antoinette Penn, *my wife!* That heart, that body, that name belonged to me. I was accountable inside, for all that happened to her in every day of life that she sported it.

Can somebody out there spell ENABLER WRAPPED DEEPLY WITHIN THE HELPLESS WEB OF CO-DEPENDENCY?

While trying not to give any resemblance of approaching her with any intimidating manner of movement I tried to talk to her. But, for a long time, she'd utter nothing and wouldn't really acknowledge that she recognized me or even cared that I was even there.

Just like back in Portland when I'd been visiting during the Christmas break, she sweated so profusely that the entire front of her blouse was covered in wet, clumpy stains of salty funk. I stood watching as droplets of perspiration beaded down unchecked spires at the sides of her almond shaped eyes. I did notice that she appeared to shiver as she rocked. I made my first move towards her then. She cowered back ever so slightly as I gently pulled forward to layer the soft cover of an afghan I'd found in a closet over her shoulders. I tried the best way I could to comfort her.

Just as easily as she'd appeared to be engaged in whatever voyage her mind had sent her off on, she made an abrupt return choosing to come back to me.

Looking up at me with the bugged-out awareness and blazing heat of enthusiasm reticent in the tweaking motions of the crack-addict, she shuffled about and drew down to a defining sitting position. The sorry slump of her shoulders with her head hanging down, almost between her thighs told me she was beaten, dogged and ultimately tired. She needed sleep.

I didn't care what she looked like. For her, I'd be her enabler, her co-dependent boo—If she'd let me…

With Love, I just wanted to whisk her away from there to safety and bring her lightly back to Oceanside to take care of her forever, in our own home.

She had different thoughts. Finally looking up to me, she grimaced that self-disgusting scowl wherein she looks at everything outside of the world crack-cocaine held her trapped in—as scathing and judgmental—offering nothing that would longer count her, a MOTHER, WIFE, PRODUCTIVE PERSON…as worthwhile. She appeared finally defeated by the enormity of the strength the drug fanned over all that was existence for her.

She motioned limply toward the baby, saying simply, "Take her."

I stood dumbfounded for a brief second. My mind searched wildly through its vastly equipped library, which was now producing a simple nothingness, trying to make sense out of the two words she'd just spat at me.

What had she meant, *take her*?

Take who?

A registered simplicity of relieving sense at having her at least appear to be back with me for an un-trusted moment, and talking to me, felt hell-a good. I Loved my "NETTIE" so fiercely that I hung helplessly onto every incredulous morsel of emotion, the slightest wince of a sweetly upturned mouth line for just a second's realization as I caught it struggling toward a sweet smile, the softening edge of a sentence I was already adept at finishing on occasion, before she even finished getting it out. I mean, I breathed, ate, slept and thought Miss Marie, constantly.

Perhaps that was the problem.

But I ain't never learned nothin'...Cause' not much has changed even today...

"Take who?" I countered, surreptitiously panning another sweep about the room looking for something or someone else I might have missed. Now she had me acting the part of the paranoid dope-fiend.

Empty...

The three of us were the only terrorized souls trapped there.

I continued on, helplessly, watching as my life's intentions, my dreams, my hopes slipped aimlessly, falling further apart by the millisecond.

I bent low to take hold of both her clammy, still struggling hands. I wanted to just wrap her up in a hug and protect her. I wanted to yell and scream at her for having once again jeopardized our lives and our Love so irresponsibly. I wanted to hit her for neglecting Britty. I wanted to somehow—just get through to her.

Silently, inside—I prayed...

And I stayed put.

Then, lightly, cocking my head slightly to angle at one side, I tried to bring her more fully around. "Take who, Baaaby?"

She looked up at me. Then, back down, gesturing toward the little button now sleeping soundly in front of her.

"Brit...Take her."

"Take her where, "NETTIE?" I could feel the ire of my already tested patience breaking forward threatening to betray what I knew would support me most in this role. It was deafening hard. But I had to remain calm.

"Far-away. Just take her away from me—I ain't no good for her."

I could feel the anguish of the exploding themes of nothingness and the abstract horrors the ends of disconnecting, twisted abuses had scratched her life into becoming that second as she gave in permitting them to sweep over her. Inside, the girl allowed herself zero hope. Emptiness sat guarding the untapped regions along the interior of her bewildered mind as she said this. Torment wasn't the correct word for what my aching heart witnessed my woman go through that sweeping moment when she had chosen to thrust her own baby's welfare into the arms of what she felt was a responsible stranger. She didn't really know me. And, obviously, I knew nothing at all about her. We'd just me, a short eight months before. It was more a pain greater than anything I had ever seen before than just simple torment.

"Just get her! Before I ruin her or hurt her too…" She gestured forcefully, thumbing in toward herself for the first time with conviction. "Like this. Take her away from me now! I know you Love her. Take her and make a life for my baby, *Pa-lease!* Be good to her. And…" She almond-eyed up at me, swallowing harshly. The swelling brinks of great rivers filled with unhide-able tears flung quickly as she turned her head away abruptly with an attempt of trying once more to retreat inside herself—to hide.

"Just…Just—leave me here to die."

My heart wrenched with each awkwardly scoffed syllable of her confusing words as I bent low first to scoop the baby up and place her gently on her Uncle's filthy sofa. *How could I ever do such a terrible terrible thing*? Take little Brit and leave Marie there to rot and decay in her stench without a semblance of hope? That baby was her life. I knew if anything at all would lend her a reason to eventually take the steps needed for her to finally kick that scathing habit, that little girl, lying peacefully on that couch, would have a large hand in making it all seem possible and somehow worthwhile for her. At that moment, I then made a determination that I would live with forever-to tha' grave.

I know…I was stupid, I was alone…I didn't care. Didn't matter how long it would take. I was Blu Penn. For me, after all I'd been through, if I never learned nuffin' I'd bought into the fact—That for everyone, as long as GOD was real, there always loomed hope—No matter what.

No way... Wan't goin' down like that...

I quickly began to lose the sizzling battle between my yearning Love and desire for her and the force of rage I'd previously staved off and had been able to hold timidly at bay, as I found myself caught up in being infuriated, mad at her beyond mad, for bringing us all to the never ending edge of this fateful cliff. I was so infinitely angry with her that if possible I could have swept that baby up and jetted outta' there without turning to look back, no longer caring about what eventually happened to her with the resolve to never return.

But, I couldn't.

I Loved her. For the both of us, that possibility would never be made a reality.

She was my wife. And, because that meant more than air and life itself to me, I could not permit her to let all of us down. More importantly, there was no way I could permit her to let herself down; There was nothing inside of me that would let her remain there indefinitely to give in to succumbing eventually to the enemy's beast.

The MONSTER had all but licked us, but I was reaching up once more, never giving up hope enough for the both of us, imploring her with a dogged ferocity, to dig down, just one time more and reach for something she never even knew she truly wanted.

I prodded her forward to reach for *FREEDOM*. Her release from the nastiness of this thing which held her so elusively gripped within the spiteful clutches of its terminating blackness as it breeded self condemnation.

I could not let her...Sentence us—to fail.

I spoke harshly at her. "I'm taking my baby fo' sho'! Taking her little butt out to that car and I'm strapping her into her car seat...

And when I get back, I'm gonna get yo' azz up outta' here too, whether I got to drag you, pull you, push you, or beat you. You're about to get tha' fuccup'...and we're going home!"

She looked up at me suddenly. The gaze of her impression shifted ever so slightly away from its previously clouded unknowing fear. It showed a brief respite away from her former terror. I think I sensed a sparse relief in her eyes. It said, for only the tiniest flicker of a split-second, *"HE STILL WANTS ME..."*

It also held something else. A warning which effusively challenged me in meaning.

She knew I'd never be able to bring myself to hit her. *Bet'Not*.

It said, "Just you try some shit like that... And you and I both'll die here on this carpet—fo' sho'."

I about faced, away from her, with *MY* baby now soundly asleep in my arms.

I tried to conceal how much her subtle reaction to my words (each one I surreptitiously meant) instantly filled and comforted me.

It told me that there was enough of *MY "NETTIE"* still left behind on this side of reality, not lost inside the former never-never land to shift upward in meaning to see to it that no shit like that was about to jump off up in those parts right then and there without the horror-filled immensity of the dreadfully endangering culpability of one of us pleading *NOTGUILTY* to a horrendous murder-suicide.

The ride home from Garden Grove to Oceanside was filled with lengthy periods of impregnated stillness uncomfortably wrapped in an eerie, uncertain silence. Occasional, but brief outbursts betrayed my simmering anger at her as I was incapable of keeping them from escaping to truck my mouth forward, spitting confounded emotions which lined the all-but-ruined rims of my worried heart out at her. With judgmental contempt, I told her about herself, over and over again. I foolishly set out for her, exactly how things were going to be for the three of us from that moment on.

I had nothing else, no therapeutic remedies to use, no experience. I knew nothing else to do. My life up to that point, as an adult, had wrapped itself securely in the glory and stability of structure a military regiment provided. I only knew the motion of moving forward. Retreating for me meant death and the hideous embarrassment of defeat. There would be no retreating. In this, every question had a proper response, every problem an achievable resultant answer.

All of this materialized in me being a pretty controlling character. One who espoused the infinitive of adhering to only one notion—That again, of—POSITIVE PERPETUAL MOTION.

And without appearing to step back to take a clearing breath to guide me, I charged forward.

The first thing I did upon reaching Oceanside was deposit "NETTIE" back to the safety of our apartment. Instantly, she plopped herself down atop the clean comfort of our bed and was asleep before I had exited the apartment with Brit still snoozing in my arms. Together, she and I, a Daughter and her *DADOO*, headed for our next move. And…it was quite possibly the smartest tactic I could have ever taken to snatch us back from a very real brink of death.

Britty and I made the thirty-five mile trip into San Diego. I knew, only there—existed the remedy necessary for all of us to eventually start off on a lifetime of eventual joys together. Without taking that trip with that little girl beside for strength, the three of us were through, destined to forever usher loneliness in as our only take.

Once there, I went to the 32nd Street Naval Station where my ship, USS ENGLAND was berthed. After paying my respects to the Officer of the Deck, I set off in search of the one man aboard whom I knew would be my only saving grace in this situation.

I sought out the ship's Chaplain.

I had no idea how I would approach him, or even how I would begin the process of telling him the stark raving immensity of all my problems.

I didn't care. My family was in trouble.

Only GOD could help!

And I was in search of his trusted agent.

It was only a fleeting second of encountering embarrassment that I even slowed at having to lay down to a stranger the details of what had been taking place inside my home. The military establishment of the day judged harshly on any gray matter remotely approaching to relate to illicit drug use. Didn't matter if it was yo' Momma, yo' Brother, a live-in Cousin, the President or the Pope. If you did drugs, illegally, sans a bona fide prescription, your name and your reputation was mud—they made certain of it.

But I say, "*I was a million miles further away from caring*" about what repercussions might be brought to face me upon letting my needful skeletons shine free into the light because I had larger worries to contend with. Things more important even—than my career—and at that moment in time, that was a mentally engulfing mouthful were falling heavily around me.

Already, through the inevitabilities of being brought to forcefully face the reality of the things "NETTIE's" addiction brought with it, I found myself growing exponentially.

The Chaplain, a sullen, slight man, held a position aboard the ship of quiet, demure obscurity. Generally holding services only during underway Sundays when the ship was at sea, over the course of a normal weekday import, his congregation consisted of himself, an almost handful of genuinely faithful, and the overtly homosexual Religious Petty Officer and his Yeoman First Class Lover, both whom he was more professionally bound to accept that he was spiritually. Other than this, he was incontrovertibly bored out of his mind with the modest demands his job—of not really having a job—presented him. His services were rarely called upon, other than an uneventful benediction during a templated retirement ceremony or mundane burial at sea.

For him, and for me...GOD is so good—ALL the time...And all the time GOD is good!

Our individual troubles, his of bored professional plight and mine, of marital dis-constitution, were right up each other's alleys. With a perfecting glaze of necessity, he and I hit it off from the start, almost as if the two of us had been steered toward one another, unknowingly, for exacting and identical reasons. Little did he or I know...

GOD was tryin' ta tell us sumpthin'.

In a matter of twenty very indecisive minutes, with the solemn skills of a seasoned counselor who'd begun to doubt even himself while steeped inside his own idleness, Chaps pounced upon me and my problems with an almost frightening alacrity. Calming me down enough to offer me a chance to rapidly tell and retell the events of my day in full, he had appointments made, audiences requested with the ship's Commanding Officer, and leave papers drawn up, all before I could think to spell NAVY.

Captain West, the vessel's commander, sat in shocked awe at all I told him once being shuffled into the stale airway of the passage leading op to his quarters. He just kept repeating, over and over again, "Petty Officer Penn? Are you O.K.? This is just so hard to take in! So hard to believe..." He peered deeply into my face seemingly for forever.

"Son...Are you sure you're all right?"

Then he shook his head profusely, in the negative, from side to side.

Taking in the pleased figure of the Chaps, he counted briefly inside his head for ten steadying second before moving on. "Chaps, anything. . .Anything at all we can do for Petty Officer Penn and his family?"

Right on cue, and taking his lead from *THE OLD MAN,* the Chaplain began to shake his head in the affirmative as he laid out for the C.O. all that he had already set in motion toward getting me the assistance I needed.

"Yes, Captain. . .Petty Officer Penn is extremely clear on everything he has to do. I have provided him with the name and num. . ."

"Very well, Chaps. . .Good." The Captain had already cut him off and shut me out in the comfort of feeling problem identified, problem attacked, problem destroyed. Problem no longer existent. . .Move on to the next engagement. . .Find, fix, and finish while maintaining the daily discipline of an up till that point a completely neglected calendar's schedule.

I didn't mind. Heck, just getting a chance at having a positive audience with the ship's most senior executive was more than most young sailors received over the lifetime of an entire career. I had my shot. I told my story plainly. I didn't need the C.O. walking with me every step of the way to get to where I needed to go.

Besides, I had GOD's trusted agent in the form of my very own Chaps in my pocket and on my side, almost at my beckon's—call.

First, Chaps hooked us up with a non-availability coordinator at the then Balboa Naval Hospital located in North Park. Once there, I was more than surprised to find the absence of a *drug* issue stigmatism I had formerly feared would be present as it tended to surround the indelible immensity of such personally engineered problems. We were met only with compassionate determination to help as door after door was flung effortlessly open assuring our paths.

We were Champus'd out to SHARP-REES-STAELY's in-patient drug treatment center. The military was unable to provide drug treatment care for her directly at the hospital, due to the fact they were filled to the gills with their own Addiction Rehabilitation Center processes as they lent encompassing assistance to the scores of SAILORS and MARINES it was trying, at the time, to rehabilitate and keep following the brash commencement of its own zero-tolerance substance abuse programs.

Instead, the United States government and the Navy footed the entire bill, a sum of more than nine-thousand dollars to support my family in the way of providing financial assistance for "NETTIE" to take part in SHARP's thirty-three day program.

Britty and I saw her off to begin the five days of primary detoxification where she would be permitted minimal contact with those she knew best and counted on most. No drug dealer on multiple corners, no coercive accomplices, no freedom of cars to ferry her to and from her drug of choice. No regimented husband…No child to care for. She would be all but caged inside the four walls of a simple room bearing a single protected light at the ceiling with only a sheeted bed with a pillow upon it, a toilet when she needed it and that was about it. A generic pair of light pajamas furnished by *The Program*, cotton, granny panties and a bra were the only items of clothing she would be permitted during the full length of her stay.

No telephone, no television, radio or other contact with the outside world, not even family, was permitted for the entire nightmarish haunt of her detox and follow-on thirty-three day period of self-inflicted incarceration.

Following the initial five day detox and subsequent thirty-three day program where she first encountered the stability of *Twelve Steps* leading toward recovery, she came home an apparently new person. It was a period of renewed hope and determination for all of us. Freshly released, and with a new after-care counselor, she began working at a different bank as a teller and she went about the chores of regaining her life while encased inside the protection of daily *Narcotics Anonymous* meetings among people just like her who were grasping with desperation at just one more chance at normalcy.

She didn't use…For a while.

It was about this time when we were pleasantly surprised to discover that GOD was once again working his magic within the turmoil that was our lives.

Turns out, *SHE WAS PREGNANT!*

I tried to lend her what support I knew how. But it wasn't much. I was just as stupid, even more-so-than she, when it came to trying to understand the kinds of things, emotionally, mentally, and neurally she was still waging a horrendous personal war with.

I had been unable to attend the vitally important week of family counseling SHARP offered at the tail-end of her treatment. I'd used up all my leave to be at home with our baby while she'd been gone. Had I been smarter, I would have turned over heaven and earth to be there with her to take part in that. I held no personal value of the entire addiction treatment facility nor in its life-changing therapy. I merely felt I had been doing the right thing in my initial efforts causing her to be able to attend there.

I would know, almost after it was too late to save us, that inside the antiseptic halls of SHARP REES STAELY, there was a place I know now with final enlightenment exists where I would have been sure to learn the idiosyncrasies of issues such as Enabling, Co-Dependency, Self-Preservation and forgiveness. But I didn't.

Instead, I ferried her to her appointments with her new counselor, a genuine social genius name Issaic Maclemore, and with my stubborn tenacity at refusing to accept and embrace addiction as a bona fide disease, I did all I could, unwittingly to sabotage the very concept of her eventual recovery.

She met a full assortment of new friends and acquaintances who she tried to use to replace those who had led her down such a twisted road toward destruction. Issaic tried his best to help us both. I take my hat off to that man. His unshakeable determination to remain patient with me and his counseling mastery held up against the unabashed ignorance I threw at him weekly. This was coupled by a growing uneasiness stretching forward inside of Marie, to return to visit him, with me, as scheduled. I didn't blame her. I was glad when we finally stopped attending together.

She continued her sessions during the entire third trimester of her pregnancy. And, she remained clean and sober until its end.

Our youngest daughter was born at the TRI-CITY Medical center, a block from our apartment in Oceanside. We named her AshLe' Antoinette. Her birth was the most beautiful expression of Love I had experienced up to that time. I watched as she took her first breathe, her tiny mouth agape widely seeking expectantly as she took her first chance at reaching toward life.

I had never seen anything like it. I cried like a sobbing puppy as the O.B. nurse cleaned the gray matter from her, stuffed her tiny head beneath the warming cloth of a knit skullcap and wrapped her tiny body in the comfort of a hospital blanky—and handed her to me.

Like every other facet of our relationship to that point, there had been nothing easy about the entire ordeal of the pregnancy itself. "NETTIE" had a very low threshold for any kind of discomfort and resultant pain. Who could blame her?

For me, it was my first. Everything and anything dealing with the baby was new to me. I relished in every laborious stage of it. Easy enough to state if you're not the one huffing in excruciating pain as your body is split open involuntarily by a determined fetus not taking no for an answer.

We went through filling periods of wild sexual encounters. Then there were months and months of dry, *you-betta-not-touch mee's*… There was a period towards the end, when we fought so incessantly that, Marie had had enough of me, the pregnancy, of being homesick for her Mother, Brothers and Sisters back in Oregon, not to mention the internal anguish of remaining stoic in her determination not to digress back into the denigrated hell-pits of using. It was all too much for her to take on and weave within with any kind of sustainable success.

She decided at about the seventh month of her pregnancy, during one particularly brutal confrontation, that she was leaving me. I was about at my wits end and for the most part didn't put up too much of a fight to cause her to stay. I packed her up in the Torino and deposited her pregnant form of constant frustration in front of Oceanside's GREYHOUND station. Once there, I helped her and Britty out and saw she and her one lone piece of luggage aboard the waiting cruiseliner.

When the bus began to make its eventual exit, the immensity of the loss of my family for good kicked in and I just about lost my fucc'n mind right there in the GREYHOUND parking lot.

Well…

For me, that just wouldn't do. I Loved her and could never see myself ever getting to sleep at night—EVER! Without her by my side.

It was harder than ever for me to just be able to let well enough alone and simply forget about her and *my* baby—just let her go.

After taking stock in my own digressive stupidity, I revved up that *STARSKY & HUTCH*—mobile, and I lit out after that damn bus with an almost maniacal abandon.

It didn't take long for the polished interior of the 351 *WINDSOR* residing beneath the hood to deposit me within a stones throw of the lumbering ga-zillion ton bus. I'd driven with uncontrollable madness to get there. I'm quite unsure how many lives I endangered in doing so—Not to mention the blatant disregard for my own…

Once catching up to the bus, I weaved in and out of its path with daredevil stupidity. Pulling in front of it, blasting my horn incessantly while attempting to slow to a crawling pace before it, I begged and pleaded out my window for the driver to stop and return my everything I felt I had to live for that he would rip from me completely should I permit him to peacefully travel on.

He kept right on trucking up Interstate—15.

Inside the bus, my blatant acts of disregard for the expectant safety and welfare of the inhabitants residing there began to cause an uproar of excited pandemonium to break out all at once. Finally, my antics had began to develop so dangerously that the driver began to have enough…He queried his passengers if any of them knew this fucc'n nut who was trying to cause him to stop. "NETTIE" informed him that it was her nut trying to cause him to make her get off the bus.

Wisely, the man drove on. He didn't slow the bus until he'd reached the haven of a Border Patrol outpost leading into the outskirts of the city of Temecula. Once there, he stopped the craft immediately. I pulled up directly behind him. He didn't make any moves toward me. He only locked the bus door and disappeared inside the outpost's main structure. It wasn't long before he'd returned with two burly Border Patrol agents shadowing his shaken form in tow.

The agents headed directly for me. They accosted and further informed me that I would be detained for an indefinite (Federally mandated) period of time if I continued my attempt to interfere with what was deemed any portion of *National* transportation efforts.

I looked back with desperate helplessness into the blacked out smoke of the bus' mirrored interior. I hoped beyond hope that *My* "NETTIE" would see the effusive aimlessness of her willingness to leave me.

She remained inside the vehicle and I watched with the two agents standing menacingly side by side me as the rambling vehicle stole my whole world with nothing more that I could do…but cry.

I returned to our tiny apartment back in Oceanside. I went to bed at five in the afternoon. I didn't hear from "NETTIE" for another ten days.

What was I to do? I didn't have a clue. But, in keeping with my former ignorance in adhering to the concept of never falling prey to anything less than a *HOME-RUN or STRIKE-OUT*, I moved on.

I gathered all of her belongings while preparing the rest of the interior of the apartment for what I touted as the world's greatest garage sale... And I sold every item she and I had possessed, at what was despicably equivalent to virtually pennies on the dollar—just to get rid of it and begin to be able to place she and our children forever out of my mind's ranting eye for good.

I gave up the apartment and returned back aboard ship to lay staring up at the brightly lit rack light which peered down mocking my failure each time I opened my eyes.

She remained in Oregon until right before our baby was due.

It was a period of more stark-raving loneliness for me than I had ever experienced up to that point in life thus far. It was nothing like what I'd been through previously with Kammy before. With her, I'd only lost a woman pretending to be my wife. With "NETTIE", I'd lost an infinite amount more.

I'd lost my soul mate, my help meet, my life.

I began to throw myself back into my work. The USS England had returned to San Diego from its extended overhaul period to which I'd been making the two and a half hour trip, Oceanside to Long Beach, on a daily basis over a period of a tenuous thirteen months. I began to study for the First Class (E-6) exam. I took the test and had studied so profusely leading up to it that I finished the entire test in an hour and pushed away from the testing table knowing confidently that I had mastered the material well enough to promote in the first cycle. It was a terrible trap I had permitted myself to operate inside and fall stupendously into.

My home life had continuously fallen apart while the particulars of my professional progression screamed forward to sparkle with an unchecked flourish.

"NETTIE's" stay in Portland lasted just until right before the baby was due. About a week and half prior to the big event, she called to inform me that she would be arriving on a flight later some unsuspecting evening. It was my job, of course (once again) to be there for her, to pick her up, as well piece as to piece all the parts together—on her whim, that it would take to once again bring us back to a tentative stage of being a family. It seemed, even after only knowing her such a short time, that I had supplanted any inner-personal feelings of self with all thought and feeling for what it would take to again place things like a roof over our heads and food in our bellies, while trying to somehow gain an angle on the complexities the new experiences being married to her shot at me from every direction.

Turns out, it was Maria Slackey, "NETTIE's" old bank telling school friend, the one I'd gone out of my way to speak so harshly of and disrespect so often, who stepped forward to save the day for us. That girl opened up her home to me and my evil pregnant wife without thinking twice about it.

When I say evil, I mean devilish. Pregnant, "NETTIE" was akin to a dead wringer for Doctor Jekyll's Mr. Hyde. Mood swings for her occurred at the drop of a hat. Boisterous outbursts of fury, during which you could easily find yourself reeling from a backhanded slap viciously applied for an infraction as minimal as disagreeing on what television show to watch were common.

This period of time was so confusing and uncanny for me, I didn't know if I'd get through it. I began to take on the realization of feelings that somehow I'd suddenly found myself trapped back in the dung and stench of that projects bathroom, with shit piling up macabre...And whom I'd thought I'd safely extricated myself from forever up to that point.

Yet here she was again. She was just like Mama'n!

From her unwillingness to commit to a dedicated effort to clean up our home when needed, to her refusal to make Love to me for often months at a time, topped by her penchant for just being a stumble-bum when it came to picking up after herself on a. general hygiene basis. I could handle it, for the most part. But, the worst for me, when she wasn't even pregnant, was having to be faced with her soiled sanitary napkins, all rolled up neatly in strips of toilet paper as she'd deposit them at the base of our toilet, for only GOD knows what reasonable safe-keeping could she have been thinking of; when the bathroom trash can was within five feet of the very same commode's reach. That's what went a long way toward driving me fucc'n nuts.

But, I'd just pick them up and pitch them away with only the briefest hint of suggestion or pleading word to her. What was I going to say to her that I knew wouldn't cause her to light out after the first GREYHOUND station a cabbie would bring her to and deposit her and now *My* two babies on the first coach steering North? But, *Maaan*...Her filthy habits were literally beginning to grain on my teetering consternation of beginning to form the opinion that, baby or no baby, Britty or no Britt, I was fast approaching the reality that I just didn't like her very much anymore.

I dug down deep while determining with what I felt was an unshakeable resolve to duck through the storms of her unexplainable demeanors and win the contest of wills eventually by waiting the immensity of her *Jones's* out and simply holding on.

We moved out of Maria Slackey's place after about three weeks of solid imposition. The poor, sweet girl never once let on, but I was certain, by the time we had packed our meager shit and prepared to depart, she too had stretched the previous warmth of her overwhelming hospitality to a point of being unable continue to peer at us as friends. In this, she'd by far exceeded the greater boundaries of what any normal human could have been expected to be called upon to reproduce through and through.

"NETTIE" was very close to giving birth to our Ash Le' and we moved this time closer to San Diego. My ship was out of the yards and I was fast on my way to reporting to a new assignment. One in which I hoped I would finally be able to settle into and engineer a steadiness about life where we'd be afforded a breathable calm in the former roller coaster uncertainty of our previously detrimental surroundings. Reporting in, I'd already be promoted to First Class Petty Officer and be successfully departing a shipboard billet where I'd been presented the opportunity of becoming a senior, Leading Petty Officer within the very same division which had nurtured and seen me through almost every stage of productive development of my still fledgling Naval career.

We moved to North Park, a portion of San Diego more known for its community of actively living retirees. We'd chosen that particular area more so for its extremely affordable lifestyle than for anything else. Our apartment had two bedrooms. The building was fairly new and well groomed inside and out. It would be there that "NETTIE" and I would once more attempt the tough chore of getting to a minimal stage of solitude in our marriage, where at least we'd learn to get to know one another a little bit better. Only in this way would we stand a chance at survival and perhaps not want so much to kill each other so often during the many heated confrontations it felt like we were having for a better part of a daily basis.

Because of our extensively disproportionate amount of distending turmoil (the drug abuse she utilized so as not to have to be forced to deal with what she felt were both heaping personal and inter-relational shortcomings, as well other baggage we'd both deposited before the threshold of *the broom* before jumping) within items way too monstrous and overwhelming for her (in her own minds eye) for her to place faith in trying to gain working skills toward practically overcoming, she seemed adept enough only at hiding behind the trivial pursuits of running away from our self-inflicted predicaments with very little in the way of success.

Instead of growing together and becoming more naturally bonded as we should have, we wasted almost a full year's worth of valuable time dealing with the kinds of *peering from behind, no-hope-of-ever-catching-up* issues the two of us should have never had to face plagued us incessantly. Had either of us entered into the union fresh from functional pasts steeped with wholesome narrations of upbringings bearing the fruits of positive possibilities, we just might have stood a more winnable chance from our start.

We'd instead chosen to step out on the limb of taking the risk of being plausibly unwilling partners subjected to each other's fucc'd-up whims of how we each thought the worries in our life should be haphazardly played out.

We continued on together, albeit not ever truly developing a soul-filled determination that we actually Loved one another. Hell, we barely even knew one another, let alone like each other.

I transferred to Naval Station 32nd Street's Fleet Training Center a few months later. I attended Instructor training and followed that with beginning to teach the Close-In-Weapon System, the very same radar guided, computer controlled shipboard anti-aircraft system I had all but easily mastered with minimal difficulty while in the fleet.

We moved again. The manager at our old place started getting shitty about wanting to fix things and in a matter of about six months, the place very rapidly began to fall apart all around us.

With our new baby in tow, this time, we traveled just down the street, into *CRACK-VILLE,* off of El Cajon Boulevard, to 51st Street. Our apartment again had two bedrooms and the building was brand-spanking new. It was huge!—About eleven-hundred square feet, almost a mansion, in both our eyes, compared to where we'd just come from.

Instantly, upon feasting our stupidities upon the spacious interior of the dwelling, we'd both been bowled over and fell immediately head over heels in Love, with it—Internally, we were both still ignorantly uncertain about how we still felt about each other.

We felt, during the initial stages of negotiation with the building's owner, that *we* were in some way *gettin' over* on him. After all, he was a former Naval Officer who'd started his own construction company and had placed his heart and soul into the construction of what was (we discovered) his first building. Based upon his confidences of my being active duty military, he'd even gone as far as to permit us to sign a year long lease without the sanity of requiring a credit check.

WHO WOULDATHUNKIT?

In the end, turns out, it was him who'd easily gotten' over on us.

Situated just off the rear of another, more dilapidated single family dwelling, the back portion of the apartment poured out into the sinister narrowness of a purely stench-filled, wickedly vice encrusted alleyway. It was there that I first learned that it would do me prudent to tote my pistol with me when doing something as menially mundane as taking out the trash alone there after dark. All manner of ill-repute, underhanded gang, drug and prostitution transactions, amid other forms of ill-reputed skullduggery was surreptitiously cultivated and engineered back there nightly without end.

We lived on 51st and El Cajon a couple of obscure, very healthy months before our bubble burst once more and the inconsistencies of the world viciously returned to take shape, cruelly, to creep back up and knock us on our asses once again.

Toward the latter period of our stay there, I found myself fast approaching a development point of professional mastery. I effortlessly threw myself at my work with a vengeance. Complex strategies of imploring, motivating and at times belittling my students in their journeys toward learning the material I presented them very quickly began to materialize as internal educational genius in the eyes of my co-workers and superiors alike.

I enjoyed the hell out of being thrust into the spotlight while instructing at the podium. So much so, that I began to be awarded instructional accolades (which generally amounted to taking on more work) and, to "NETTIE's dismay, I would effortlessly pull double shifts while even volunteering to take on the newly established night instruction classes; developed to assist those students exhibiting difficulty grasping the lengthy volumes of technical material we entrusted them with.

It was a grip. Although working so many hours, I tried with mad difficulty to establish a finely-tuned balance between engrossing myself so deeply in developing the skills necessary to rapidly hone my delicate instructional intricacies to a point of affording me the awarded distinction of becoming one of the Navy's strongest, West-Coast, Close-In-Weapon System instructors, and finding a way to successfully manage an equalizing effort of maintaining what was a feeble grasp on the most often negative undertakings playing out daily in my life with "NETTIE" at home.

You know a brotha' was crazy unsuccessful!

This would all come to a life-changing head one late Friday evening after I'd exercised an early, unauthorized dismissal of my entire class, well before that day's scheduled departure. This, I felt was a reward for all of them having amassed passing scores on a particularly tumultuous, hundred question exam I'd blasted on them without warning earlier during the evening's caseload. Our normally scheduled release time on a Friday night was twenty-three hundred (Eleven, P.M) for most land lubbers.

Following a very minimal, daily field—day, I dismissed all twenty students promptly at twenty hundred (Eight, P.M.). Gathering my things, I hi-tailed it out to the ride and headed for *CRACK-ALLEY* just off of El Cajon Boulevard, towards home.

Taking the landing stairway two-by-two, my inner senses soared within being wrapped up in a jovial excitement at getting off early enough to spend some quality time with "NETTIE" and the girls before evening's end. Due to my misguided compunction of offering the best parts of myself to my work, it wasn't very often that she and I got the chance to simply relax with one another and just live what was left of our lives in quiet enjoyment—OF JUST US. Times like that for us were purely visions of illusive grandeur, and up to that point, wholly, non-existent.

Slipping my key quietly into the lock, with my mounting expectation increasing leaps and bounds with very step (I still get those butterflies of excitement in my stomach any time I'm about to return home to them—

That's how much I enjoy being me with them) I let myself into the apartment meaning to exude as much *rico-suave'* sensuality toward my baby as possible.

But, once inside, I was met by an empty interior. No Nanna's...No Stankawank...and worse yet...no "NETTIE".

Instantly, my first inclination was to play it all off. You know, not waste too much time pining or putting too much thought into falling prey to bearing fantastic visions only multiplying in negativities. The trio troupe of my most precious girls could have been anywhere.

At the movies, out visiting friends, or down the block having a wine at the neighbor's house while watching the excitable antics of the ongoing bid-whist game or something.

I wish now they had been. Anywhere...Except exactly where I found them.

Moving more deeply into the apartment, I passed the girls' room. I took note of both their tiny forms (Britt was four, Ash, almost two) asleep snugly in their own beds, just like everything good about life's precious wonders would have had the two of them be while their Daddy was off working hard to bring all of the great things in life to reality for them.

Relief swept over me with an instantly gratuitous emotion. Two third-parts of my entire world were verifiably exactly where I would have placed them, had it been my choice—and they were engulfed in doing exactly what I would have had them doing at that gentle hour of day's end. Both those knuckleheads were knocked out cold, altogether oblivious to any of living's incongruous idiosyncrasies.

But, where was "NETTIE"?

I knew she hadn't left our precious babies alone there inside that apartment without help to fend for themselves.

My previous fervor of inner apprehension at arriving home to an unusually quiet, empty house returned. Instantly, my insides balled into a twisted force of unexplainable consternation.

I felt it first, before it hit me and I knew, without a doubt...

Something there in my own home...Just wasn't right...

Hoping for at least—*Half Full*, I prodded myself to concentrate on the millions of other more pleasantly thinkable possibilities which could have explained the horrific inevitability of the next perversion facing me.

I found "NETTIE" in our bathroom. We only had one. It was crazy tiny. Because of this, we generally permitted each other undisturbed solace whenever one or the other was in there taking care of *bidnazz'*.

Calling out to her, hoping beyond hope that she was all right—I mean I'd been home for a short while—without even the slightest indication that a body had even been alive in there. I edged nearer to the door to try my best at briefly trying to connect with her more closely.

"Nett? You…A'iigghht?"

"Mmm…hmmm." Was her only terse reply.

I left her alone—approaching a whispered period of perhaps another solicitously uninterrupted hour.

With my baby girls soundly sleeping, and my woman, in my mind's eye, perhaps languishing inside the tranquil, relaxing comfort of a hot bath setting, I had nothing to do with myself.

I decided to spread the tubular prints of my work schematics fully out on our kitchen table, pour myself a snift of my then favorite, E&J Brandy, and settle in to getting a jump on the new area I would be instructing come the next Monday morning.

I found myself alone and doing this for about another hour more. After my third drink, and still no "NETTIE", the apprehension of my prior intuitive emotion felicitously returned. Rising up with thoughts of this time placing eyes on my beautiful wife (she was always so completely soft, head-to-toe, and forever smelled so good, just following a bath) I reached out for the bathroom door while calling to her for recognition once again.

Surprisingly, the door wasn't even locked, as usual. It was no thing for me not to bother her while she bathed. I was a patient man. Besides, when she took the time to meticulously groom and care for herself, I generally was the rewarded recipient of the eventual outcome her efforts produced. I was a sucker for those times.

But this wasn't going to be one of those moments for me…. Was it?.

As the door drew open, away from me further, instantly I was hit by the searing stench of what smelled like a school yard full of children burning stacks of sticks containing putrid piles of what smelled like suffocating chalk. Edging more fully into the tiny room's interior, I searched my mind's internal library seeking feverishly for an answer to the question immediately plaguing me. My inability to place it immediately came around full circle to slap me in the face with a common-sense-blocking, surreal motion.

WHAT WAS THAT SMELL?

As I tip-toed a slow walking groove into the room, everything inside me screamed with a gripping, bone-jarring intensity as clearing recognition took grip of me.

STOP!—Don't look inside. "*Turn your* azz' *around, Blu! high-tail it outta' there... You don't wanna' see and know what's inside.*

RUN!"

"NETTIE" pulled a slow, scowl-filled gaze up to greet me.

The hurt...

-Hers...And...Mine!

The epitome of defeated anguish that leapt out at me from within the globular postules locked inside the scattery movements her pupils made instantly felled me. The pain of the deeply sorrowful expression she held me in was a combination of culpable apology mixed with a wildness unleashed, an imminent, terror-filled ferocity dancing hauntingly overcoming her. I could see her frustration at finding it increasingly difficult to focus. Repeated, unrewarded attempts at embracing the uncontrollable rage ricocheting unchecked inside her, told the telling truth of the debilitating events of her evening.

The pictures captured in my mind of her that minute were incapable of being frosted over in whatever lie she could offer.

She was high!...Pipe still locked firmly a-hand.

I found myself fully incredulous. Didn't know what or how to do what I would be called on to do in my life—*without her*, from that moment on.

I moved in, meaning only to engage her closer. But, instead of going about it with a more pensive motion of plainly explainable peace, which might have gotten me further—before the fight, I moved in, unconsciously reaching for the fluted tube she clutched possessively, wrapped securely inside the white perfection of a scented face cloth in her right hand.

She beat me to it.

Slamming the fingers of that now balled up fist shut with vice-like precision, she firmly ensured there wasn't much I could do off-hand to outsmart her towards coaxing it away from her.

I tried talking her out..."NETTIE".... *WHY!*"

She didn't answer at first. Only began the simplistic motion of that rhythmic rocking I'd borne witness to more times already than I cared to count.

I kept imploring her, while conjuring up every effort, telling myself talking to her softly would work...Just remain calm—All the while keeping my eye firmly on the reason for every one of our marital problems—that *fucc'n* pipe.

That, to me, was the enemy. Not my baby...Not my job. My friends, her friends, our relatives, even our still soundly sleeping babies, my own internal demons, all paled that second by realistic comparison.

All she had on was a thin chiffon of a barely there, baby-doll nightie. Salt water taffy green, no bra, no frilly wisp of matching panties to cap these off, she was wide open for me to gaze at her private delicacies with full view.

I watched her more intently waiting for that specific opportunity to make my previously internally held, intended move. Seeing my mark, I focused in on and lunged for the pipe. I meant to rid our lives of at least that one sordid symbol of death and dying destruction...Right then and right now!

She twisted away from me with the smooth stealth of an embattled mother cheetah protecting her birth. But I wasn't to be deterred. With maniacal, animalistic cantor, she

had other visions of possible outcomes speckling confusedly inside her head.

This...*SHE!* Was my entire *FAMILY.* No way I could simply back off, pull out or walk away and let things meander unchecked now looking at her there as she stood.

I wasn't about being dissuaded. My Love for her...and my need to have her there—healthy—by my side, raising our children together, struggling through life as one, shattered any sensible strides of wisdom or saving reason I might have had, had I been somewhere else, in a different situation, staring at possibilities bearing more productivity of promise.

Instead, I was a twenty—four year old co-dependent, lost inside the vicious cycle drugs, deceit and unfettered Love presented me seemedly on a daily basis.

I was a mess.

I struggled with her till she finally tired and gave in, finally relinquishing her trip upon a claim towards death that I was just too stubborn to let her go to trail down just yet. The wicked vial goblet lay now in deceiving obscurity beneath the softened fabric of a tiny terry cloth towel.

Sensing the sweet node of victory within reach, I effortlessly flung the cloth aside. I stood there a millisecond more meaning to try and piece together with some crazed sense the chaos my life had so abruptly mushroomed into. Taking the time to finally peer down at the nemesis of my marital existence, the black encrusted surface of the tube screamed nerve ending caution back up at me. Instantly, shock messages screamed with deafening clarity as an indescribable pain clawed its way from the extension of my outturned wrist and palm, and slammed into my brain with excruciating finality. *That damn thing was still skin curdling hot!*

My reflexes caused me to instantly contract the muscles of my right hand. In doing so, I caused the subtle structure of the glass to burst with a loud shotgun pop. That thing appeared to explode effortlessly inside the frustrated clutches of my now ruined, clenching grasp.

She and I took a brief double take. The sudden silence which swept up into that room was deafening in its opaque clarity.

DAMN! What else could go wrong?

The two of us stood in silence momentarily, as if preparing ourselves for the horror of what part of this macabre show we were supposed to enter next. The previous nerve shattering contention of pain was immediately replaced by a new quality of terror. Looking down, I took in the now mangled interior of what used to be my inner hand. Suddenly, streaming floods of warm, reddening blood began to slide a slow definitive trickle of increasing droplets away from me. Precious pools of life began to collect in tiny lakes about the floor surrounding my feet.

I remember mentally willing it all to go away. The crack, the pipe, "NETTIE", NAVY nights teaching undisciplined students. I prayed...implored, begged, willed with all my might...For my blood to stop seeping from my body.

It didn't work.

I reached up and took hold of the nearest towel hanging loosely from a half twisted towel rack swinging at one wall. I wrapped my hand quickly, never knowing what to expect to come my way next. I was right to make such haste in my triage and treatment, cause', with an apparent dis-connect of concern for my developing condition, "NETTIE" stepped forward brashly with intentions of reclaiming *her* pipe.

...And she meant to put up a mean, *know-she-was-there* fight.

She developed that look. You know the type I'm talkin' bout'. That stare Buster used to glaze over in, just before he sent a searing blow to your adams apple and secured your wind for the duration of the bout. That gaze the fully-grown pit gave, right after he'd finished feeding on the two pounds of raw hamburger, completely mixed with the habanera peppers, jalapeno juice and gun powder we used to feed him, and he took off after the weakest of the eight week-old, Husky puppies which also inhabited our backyard, meaning, with every malicious intent, to make a rapid kill of its tiny form, and eat him, just to get the taste we had engineered for him completely outta' his mouth any way he could.

For us, the battle was on...

She struggled with me intensely, bringing a fist full of pounding flurries as her Love-filled offering.

We did everything we could to tear up every inch of that little bathroom with our efforts. Tore down the shower curtain. Then came the flying metal of the rod which previously held it up. Somehow, the medicine cabinet mirror exploded. And, I don't know how, but at one juncture, the rectangular porcelain of the top of the toilet tank bounced, ringing off a wall or another, to land in three or four pieces covering the floor before it was all said and done.

I remember thinking, *This B'...done really lost her mickey-fickey mind.*

After all the time and effort she'd spent picking out just the right bathroom accessory to match the perfect rug, curtain, toilet-back combination. After the many moments of internalized anguish I'd voluntary suffered, watching the kids, while she'd spent, like hours, shopping for everything, spending money we didn't have (Haven't I heard this story somewhere's else before). And she could now, just throw it all away, tryin' ta' kill me for tryin' to *help her* out without remorse.

Smell-good trinkets and preciously held novelties, items previously touched upon the penalty of instantly incurring Mommy's wrath, flew from their grandly particular places in every which direction as we jammed from wall to wall, each of us attempting to find a foothold amidst the piling shit beginning to stack up around us.

Believe it or not, (Right now it seems so fucc'n incredulous) we fought for control and eventual possession of that ubiquitously searing cylinder—THAT CRACK-PIPE!

Encased in the battle, I hated her so much very much that second.

For putting me through that shit.

But, still...I Loved her even more.

So much...

Still, I was not entirely naïve. I realized the odds were mountainously stacked against me from the start. And perhaps not so wisely, I still felt, inside me: That the person winning that fight, and coming away with that pipe held the upper hand in deciding the course and pathway that our lives were to take in shaping the follow-on movements and moments of our entire family's future.

Plus, I didn't want her to continue to kill herself. All sorts of terrifying thoughts of horrific possibilities of things that could have happened to her along the route of her quest for attempting to support the animalistic nature her habit had forced her to become plagued my mind from that very second of discovery, up until the time when she finally kicked the habit and the lifestyle almost three years later.

I knew here and now was where I had to make my stand; had to simply roll into the fight with her, no matter the cost, to save her—and us. This was the co-dependent, under-educated side of me talking. I could care less. I intended with every last ounce of courage and conviction inside of me—to ride to hell and back with her, just to chase away for good, all her demons.

We met in the living room. By this time, *and I say this with full humility,* I was in full physical control of her every movement. Fight had all but been swept out of her throughout the ferocity of the struggle we had gone through as our efforts carried the two of us together, from the bathroom, to the front room, into the kitchen, and leading, *unknowingly to her,* toward the front door.

The entire time of struggling with her, the finality of subsequent planning and follow—on thoughts of making my next move began formulating enlightened decisions and ultimately necessary determinations inside my own now ranting brain. Thoughts on my own, of how life would be for the girls and I—without her, began to firmly formulate for me in becoming more clear.

Had ta' do it. Loved her crazy n' all. But everything proppin' up my role as Father and as Man implored that I had ta' get rid of her azz... For as long as she continued to place her drug, her, pusher, her *jones* before me n' dem' babies, she would never again be mine or be a part of our little girl's lives.

I just prayed that it wouldn't have to extend to being for too long. As she stood there, firmly in my grasp in front of me, I steeled myself against the pain and sorrow of being without her. I missed her already and I hadn't even put her azz out yet.

Wan't nuttin' more that I could do for her, cept' pray.

I drug her now almost completely limp form toward the open doorway of our apartment. I shrieked at her, *"THIS WAS THE LAST FUCCIN' STRAW. SHE WAS OUTTA' THERE. I WAN'T PUTTIN" UP WITH HER MESS NO MO'."*

These words seemed to instantly bring the sad truth of fighting fright back into her.

Wasn't no way I was puttin' her OUTTA HER OWN HOUSE!

The ensuing battle this brought on was even more vicious and physically draining than the one we'd just gone through battling over the pipe.

I'd wrap my arms around her in a big bear hug and cart her five steps through the front room, almost reaching the door. Thinking my job there almost done, I'd put her down seeking a slim respite. She'd find a way to scramble back into the interior of the room. She'd attach herself to a piece of furniture, a corner of a glass-topped, faux brass coffee table, the pile of fluffy pillows sewn to and attached at the armrest on the far side of the couch. I was past a point of caring. Meaning to drag *all-lat'* shite outta' that house if need be, I upset the table, smoked the glass top of the coffee table with the perfect placement of a single kick, and nearly ripped the pillows from the couch.

SHE WAS LEAVING AIIIGHT! It was just up to the both of us to determine how.

Then, I had an idea.

Why'd I do that?

I'd leave her be a second.

And then, go get my gun.

This one decision was fraught with all sorts of possible stupidities of failing to properly take time to exercise forethought on my part, that I wonder now how either of us made it out alive.

It was a Taurus 38 special snub nose. Black and weighty, I'd only fired it once while up interstate eight at Kitchen Creek Road where the county used to permit gun owners to bring registered weapons out in the boonies to conduct target practice.

I'd played with and cleaned it a lot. Had taken it with me, to take out the trash back in the darkness of the vice-infested alleyway, and had even packed it on one occasion when I'd followed her, when she had the babies in the car, as she drove around, dealer spot-to dealer-spot seeking to cop.

"You wanna' die?" I roared at her while brandishing the gun in my most menacing, *BITCHIKILLU* stance. Waving it about, like a stupicidal maniac in front of her face, I watched her intensely hoping for a particular reaction.

At first, I was happy to see the beginnings of the response I sought begin to take form. Her eyes widened suddenly. Her formerly consternated façade of determination in fighting me slipped pensively away at an instant. Instead, only the twisted cover of sheer disbelief *that this fool in front of her actually had a gun, and was waving it around like a madman* registered upon her with a sobering cerebral lucidity.

"You drove me to this! You wanna' kill yourself, out here smokin' that shit. No concern for our babies—no care for me—no self-respecting thought even about yo'self...How bout' I just plug your azz right now...Get it all over for you, punch yo' ticket...Put you out yo' misery here and now, once and for all?

That what you want?"

I stood a brief second more, not sure of what she'd throw back at me. She appeared at first wholly unable to gather her thoughts.

When she had, what she offered back was nothing close to what I'd initially prayed for or had even touched upon as an inevitably expected outcome.

Instead of seeing logic, and the fact that the two of us were through, and just melding away into the no-longer-sought-after friction of our pasts, she twisted around out of my grasp with seemed ease. She then reached down to take hold of the hand still holding the gun. It was now my turn to be caught unaware and off guard. With a softened determination, she drew the hand up.

...And, plainly placed the muzzle of the barrel at the softness of her left temple.

"Go head', Blu...Kill me!"

I was shocked to incomprehension by her actions.

She knew, just looking at me, that she had me. She followed this up with, "I ain't got nothing to live for no way.' Shaking her head negatively from side to side with mounting dejection, "I done fucc'd up your life.' Waving back deeper into the apartment toward our still sleeping girls. "Fucc'd up their lives too. Ain't got no reason to go on livin."

It was then that she concluded the process of tearing my heart out and breaking it completely.

Looking me dead in the eyes, holding me firmly, she said, "If you really Love me, bring all this pain to an end for me, right here, once and for all. Shoot me baby!"

I stood speechless. Locked deeply within the indecision of a moment I hadn't counted on. I didn't know what to do.

She'd outsmarted me. Had called my bluff something fierce, completely. Suddenly that gun in my hand became about as hot as that fucc'n crack pipe had been at it's burning height. It was all I could do to get that thing off her head, outta my hands and put away safely before something unreturnable actually happened.

But I didn't. I just stood there. I had no clue what it was I was gonna' do next. My loss for thought or words consumed me. All I could come up with is, "You a crazy *biotch'*..."NETTIE"

I then began to shove her more forcefully toward the door than I had been previously. She felt this fact; that the meaning in my movements had somehow changed.

It had.

I had to get her away from me and my girls...But fast...Before something really jumped off and happened—and our babies had no parents, or one locked up and another in the ground.

Meanwhile, through all this, I was still bleeding all over the place and had no idea just how much blood I'd lost during the seemingly slow motion of events which had taken place over what was actually a time span of about four hours.

Upon finally coaxing and pushing her outta' the house, I shoved her down the stairs ferociously and told her not to ever darken our doorstep again, for no reason. Suddenly coherent and seeming fully aware of what my mindset had finally permitted her to bring me to do, she pleaded with me not to do it. She looked up at me with those sorrow-filled, almond shaped eyes, and all but begged me to open my heart, to forgive her one more time. Welcome her back into my arms again, just Love her—one last time.

I couldn't!

Instead, I cursed her with every negative connotation I could saunter up and I called her outta' her name with aa vehemence reserved only for your very worst enemy…and I ran after her, threatening to kill her with that gun.

I even squeezed off a shot for authenticity's sake.

Wan't no big deal, I thought. We lived in the ghetto. We were forever cringing in our sleep to the sounds of wayward gunshots reaching out at us from afar.

She lighted out, heading up the steep hill just to the left of our apartment. Without turning about to look back, she went up over the crest of the hill…and disappeared.

My heart raced incessantly inside the wheezing cavity of my sweltering chest. I then went back up the landing of steps leading into *my* house. I looked out over the balcony of the third floor unit, through the sliding glass window, and I prayed.

"GOD, watch over my baby. Keep her safe. Help her to get clean. Bring her back to us soon…for good!

Then, I sat down in front of that window. I crossed my legs in front of me, let my head fall aimlessly into the wells of my palms…And I cried.

Seems like I sat there, in that predicament, for a long time. It wasn't until almost an hour later that the ringing of the phone shook me loose from the broken-hearted torment and inevitability of hell I thought I'd entered into to become lost to forever.

I got up; stumbled over fuzzy feelings shooting up and down the insides of both my legs and I answered the phone on the sixth ring.

"H-ulll-o?"

"Yes... This is Sergeant Stoddaert of the San Diego Police Department. Is this Mr. Penn?"

Initially, I was shocked to silence. My mind had yet to connect the dots of the evening's previous, unbelievable events and the purpose now for the sergeant's call.

He continued, almost forcefully. "Mr. Penn, the reason for my call is to ascertain the status of the welfare of your two young daughters. Are the two of them in good health and would it be possible for me to make a distinct verification of said health within the next couple of moments?"

I was mentally clouded, at first. It took me more than an escaping couple of moments more to finally bring myself to piece together all the intricacy of the various nouns, verbs, who's and what's of what he'd just spoken to me.

"Uhhh...My-...my girls?

Of course... Yes, they're all right. They're both sleeping soundly, in their bed, in their room."

He switched it up on me suddenly with, "Mr. Penn, do you own a fire arm?"

"Yes, of course. Yes, I do."

"Mr. Penn, I'm going to ask that you unload said weapon. Place it in a purely conspicuous location where it can be seen upon first entry to your domicile. Take off any shirt, shoes and belt containing any shiny material, anything, a buckle, per say, which might give off a reflective glare to make anyone the slightest bit antsy, and come outside and have a talk with us."

Again, I stood dumbfounded. I meandered, caught off guard suddenly, swept up in a quagmire of flooding, confounded visions and depictions of me getting locked up, railroaded along the trail of a litany of trumped up charges which would effectually label me among so many others who'd come before me who'd traveled down life's bamboozling pathway, all the while skipping wistfully along to the surreptitious melody of *the black man's jig*.

Or worse yet... Me lying fallen, choking unassisted, while lying in a spreading pool of my own blood, the covered-over victim of an edgy rookie's hot trigger finger.

I'd seen it before. I was in no hurry to make the byline of some liberal media scuff who'd attempt his worst to piece together the sordid details of *my* twisted story, no matter how altogether remote from an attendance to the assurance of facts his report would be.

I re-engaged the voice of calming control and assurance that faced me on the other end of the line. "Mr...Uhhh, Sergeant, *SIR!* I believe I'm within my every right to have a weapon within the confines of my own home. It's registered...And, no, I will not do as you say and take off my clothing and unload that weapon to come out and have a *talk* with you as you suggest.

I very quickly found out that the ole' Sarge, wasn't one to be easily dissuaded and put off.

He countered ultra quickly; as if his intended response was one he'd held waiting, just for me, months prior to ever even receiving the call.

"Mr. Penn, my only concern here in this matter is verification of the health, welfare and safety of your two young daughters." He followed this sternly with, "If you would sir, I would both implore and caution you to take a slight glance out the window of your balcony door and tell me what it is you see unfolding there."

I half-scooched, half peeked my way to gaining a definitive glimpse out the window as he had suggested.

What I saw there held me locked inside an exploding apparition of pending doom which played itself out before me with my own clearing focus of a self-telling sense of certain, life-ending horror.

A S.W.A.T. VAN!

Taking this in, I returned my attention to my deadly serious caller. "Uhhhm...Sir, I...I'll—I'll be right out."

He left me, before disconnecting on the other side of the line with, "ummm, one more thing, Mr. Penn. Do all of us an extremely vital favor. Keep your hands in plain sight, extended high above your head where everyone can see them; and we'll all make it out of this without a mistake or a busted bubble of any kind, and I can go home tonight without having to be caught up in too much more paperwork than this thing's already going to cost me.

Following a checked-over assurance that I'd made every preparation necessary—to a "T"—that he'd formerly required of me, I edged open the apartment door and stepped an apprehensive toe out to greet the miniscule minutes of my life's next few hours, all the while offering up prayers of desperation to a GOD I begged to listen, as I infinitely sought blanketed forgiveness for any and all iniquities I might have ever previously attempted to cover.

I stepped out on faith. What more was there for me to do?

I trusted GOD.

And, for some strange reason that I couldn't quite put my finger on, I trusted Sergeant Stoddaert too.

I was greeted by the surreal comprehension of the pound and sweep of swirling law enforcement helicopter blades as two of the burly beasts crisscrossed the night skies noisily keeping a burning light shining steadily on me to blind me. They tracked my every movement. As I approached the top of the landing stairs, I took note of the fact that there were uniformed men, encamped in secure positions all about me. *They must have cordoned off the entire street.*

At the base of the landing, I took in the gnarling, wolfish grins of two highly trained, extremely healthy German Sheppard K-9 officers. I hoped those suckers had heeded their training well. I was intent on giving them no reason to put said training to use. I chose each of my steps with utter attention to the utmost care. Had I not, I just knew, *that for me, this was to be a painful end.*

I resumed my attention to maintaining the internal chant of my silent prayer. "LORD, don't let em' shoot me. Help me FATHER. Stand with me, walk with me down these stairs...Don't let em' shoot me!"

At first, I began to stupidly think, that the always-present interceder had forsaken me. That he wasn't listening now that I'd decided it was time to call on him here in the dire moment of my sorry-azz'd need.

Upon meeting the last wooden wrung at the bottom of the stairway landing, two bodies of quickening force collided with me simultaneously in an instant. Suddenly, the former calm of the surrounding nightline exploded into a fettered fury of twisting, struggling bodies of coagulating mass mixed in with the raucous chatter of helicopter loudspeakers as they repeatedly warned the developing hordes of boisterous looky-loos crowding around—to remain back. This chimed in with radio calls transmitted with secretive, numero-phonetic cadence.

...And me, lying upended, securely hand-cuffed and nearly hog-tied in a position of subservient defeat, the cold-damp surface of the apartment soil, my calming ground.

A frightening chill of unshakeable uncertainty waved over me. Replaying the evening's events in rapidly isolated frames of twisted motions, over and over again inside my head, with an almost too solemn sense of overshadowing calm, I searched within myself for clarity.

WHAT HAD I DONE TO DESERVE SUCH TREATMENT?

I knew.

Should've never fired that damned gun.

Resigning myself to taking on the resultant responsibilities of that singular stupidity, I just hunkered down. I waited the play of the outcome—that that one act of unthought-out hostility would eventually produce.

It began to drizzle.

Somehow, this tended to increase the feeling of finality and peace inside of me. I'd always Loved the rain. Lying prone there on that pavement, I welcomed the covering drops beginning to seep around and creep inside of me.

While enjoying the eventual downpour of a sweet, calming sprinkle, I began to play over, in my mind, everything I stood to lose by just being there in that body, on that ground, caught up under those circumstances that night.

It was a given that I would lose my wife. What would become of our two, very precious children...? My job—my career—my students?

My dreams, my goals and my wishes...All of this shot before me with a fading immensity.

With the sound of choppers and the beat of what seemed like a million feet swirling about me in excited, counter motions, I held everything not meaning anything securely blocked out. In this way, I afforded myself the slightest chance of beginning to be able to forcefully regain the slightest amount of discerning control over things taking place so rapidly around me. Sergeant Stoddaert was a stark-raving professional.

This lent hope to an otherwise hopeless set of circumstances playing out before me.

He knelt down on the cold, wet concrete...And, he began to just talk to me.

"Mr. Penn, I'm going to ask that you attempt to exercise calm and please try to understand that the handcuffs are for both your protection as well as for the protection of my men as we attempt to diffuse the uncertainties of the situation here."

O.K. Who was I to offer him any annoyance? I lay, trussed up like a Thanksgiving turkey. My every control and effort in life taken from me as freedom, for me, began to be rolled up and *put*-away as it began to appear more and more increasingly bleak by the second.

When he felt he had completely secured *the situation*, and after receiving radio and voice calls of, "CLEAR" from his many outposts of bivouace'd storm troopers stationed seemingly from as far away as three blocks cordoned away from my own, he sided back over to me and had his men bring me first up to a crouching position at the knees, then to a full height of being brought with finality to stand before him. I peered at him full of defeated improbability and certain respect.

The impressive figure hulking down at me from an intimidating distance of mere inches was gravely stoic in his build. His absolute sense of command of the immediate surroundings was unquestionable and absolute. His overall stature was imposing at best. A good six-foot four and a solid two-fifty of steeled musculo—physique, he belied this with a gentle, understanding nature which offered instead a cooling—moderate countenance causing me to almost be able to relax to a point of being able to believe that circumstances actually stood a chance of not being as severe as I had at first calculated.

He engaged me completely seeking information. After gathering confirmation that I was who I said I was and that I did in fact belong where he'd first encountered me. The invasive questioning of trying to piece the evening's events together, from a backwards stance began.

"So, you're telling me, you came home and found your wife, uhhh...Marie,—using the illicit substance, cocaine, in the confines of your apartment bathroom?"

I knodded in uneasy compliance.

"...And, how long had you been in the dwelling, prior to discovering that she was in fact occupying the premises and partaking of the alleged substance?"

"I...I don't know, an hour, maybe two."

I could sense from his quick shift of demeanor that he wasn't warming to the increasing vagueness of my short, unthought-out answers. I immediately shifted tactics and began to spill all I had inside me of the events that had transpired. When I was done, he countered me expertly.

"You expect me to stand here and foolishly take all of this in and believe you come home to all of that and you didn't once, with the slightest bit of hankering want to tear into her and give her the business, a slap or two—once or twice—for dragging you and your little girls through all of this, time and time again? That's not what she's telling us.

She says you tried to strangle her and that you shot at her with that burner."

He darted a gesture over to one of the junior patrolmen who stood with my pistol wrapped securely inside the thick plastic of an evidence bag.

His words caught me suddenly off guard. I began to feel baited. This caused me to want to slip into a more verbally confrontational mode. No longer a *Chocolate Chicken*, but a living breathing, viable adversary in the right, wrongly accused. But I held off, I didn't permit his efforts to cause me to sink deeper into what I felt was plainly a world better suited and waiting for the *BUSTER's* of this world than for myself. He was attempting to splay out rope enough for me to unwittingly hang myself within the definitions of my own terms.

"S...sss-at' what you're trying to bring me to believe, Mr. Penn, that your only part in all this was to come home to be faced with all that you found and you have zero culpability in the resultant facts or actions which have brought us all to where we're at right now in this very momentr"

Fully on-guard at this point, I just stared up at him and nodded a solemn concurrence to all that *he* had displayed.

He squared off with me again completely. The full tip of his pointed nose, not more than an invasive inch from my own, he scowled at me from beneath sharply clenched, extremely *white* teeth.

"Well, smart guy, we'll just see about that. Cause' I got a little secret for ya'. At this very moment, a female patrol officer is in route to the scene to investigate the person of your wife's body. She will be searching for bruises, contusions and abrasions." He turned away right then, appearing to swirl about in an aggravated semi-circle of frustrated, pent-up energy before me.

Returning, quickly in front of me, he spewed out, "Ohhhh...Just let the report be that she finds a sole, solitary scratch, a lonely knick, or a single bruise ten days old.... Your ass is mine, Mister Man! You're goin' down for the long haul."

I knew he wasn't kidding. Things the way they were in California, and all over the country, regarding the atrocities and horrors of Domestic Violence, there was no way I could expect anything less, should the results of the officer's inspection prove contrary to all of what I *was not* saying.

I did trust this trooper. And I knew I owed him more that very moment than I had already given. But I was extremely wary of giving up too much and perhaps endangering my own, and the girls' circumstances any further. Besides, I felt I could see through him. Even with all of his antics and efforts of appearing to break me down...Make me confess...I sensed he was somehow, with me. In a way, he was coming round' to pulling for me and on *my* side in it all.

I was far from being wrong in this.

The female patrolmen arrived and escorted "NETT" back up the landing stairs to re-enter the inside of our apartment.

The Sarge kept it up at me. "Guess you don't wanna' tell me where all the blood inside that little room up there and all over the front of your wife's night dress came from either, Do ya?"

I only lowered my head, still silent. At the same time, I unconsciously began to flex and reflex the tender area of my right hand where the heated pipe had popped and imploded inside my clutches. He caught wind of my movements and caused me to bring the hand up into the light out into the open.

Peering down at it more closely, while a junior patrolman shined a blaring flashlight for him to better see, another produced a Polaroid camera and began snapping pics of my hand and its coagulating bloody matter. "That's quite a little battle scar you've got yourself there, boy-o'. How'd you get it?"

I felt trapped all of a sudden.

I had to give in as I answered, "Got it when she came after me for the pipe."

"How.?" Was all he sent back.

"...Reached for the pipe. It was lying on the floor behind her, under the toilet. She lunged at me. Tried to take the wash cloth from me..."

"Wash cloth? What wash cloth?" He countered.

"She had it wrapped inside a damp, white cloth."

"O.K. Go on."

"She tried to wrestle it away from me. I didn't want her to have it. The thing was so hot and it just-like popped inside my hand and cut me on my palm."

I then lowered my head once more and stood there sorrowfully, shaking my head from side to side. Boy! What I wouldn't have given right then to be somewhere else or to hold the power to replay the night's events to be able to cause them to play out in an eventual different outcome?

"Ssss-at when you slapped her?"

I brought my gaze back up to hold him squarely, for effect. "Never slapped her, not once," was all I sent back.

He left me in the company of a gathering of *his* boys just then and walked over to take in the report from the female officer.

Just then, a uniformed Watch Commander arrived. He shucked about, questioning everyone in his path as he passed by me seeking Sergeant Stoddaert.

The two of them huddled together briefly to quickly compare notes. I watched the other newby intently. I could sense that he was the controlling, pushy, persuasive type. I wanted to ensure that he didn't sway the Sarge in the wrong direction in his eventual decision of how he intended for me to appear in this case.

They broke their huddle with a force of disagreeing contention lingering between them.

"You are well aware of your responsibilities in this instance Sergeant."

"I am at that," Sergeant Stoddaert spat back over a shoulder without turning back to look at the man he addressed with a thickly mounting contempt.

The Commander continued on, "If the perp goes back in there tonight and kills this poor woman, there'll be hell to pay. It'll be on your head and your head completely—*ALONE*! You understand me?

"I understand you, SIR!" He still addressed the man without turning to face him. I could tell that this was perhaps not the first of such occasions the two of them had butted heads on an issue. "I just am not taking this man to jail for something he did not engineer or do."

The Commander forced himself to be looked at then by striding up into the SARGe's face just then. "You know the newly established code in these matters. We don't make the call. We take the call. A perp's got to go."

PERP! Who was this bum calling a perp? I was with Sergeant Stoddaert. This guy *was* an asshole. He had to go, not me. All I'd done was try to failingly preserve what was left of my fledgling family. I hadn't hurt "NETTIE" in any way. Through her actions and through her inability to seek and accept help to overcome her addiction, she'd inflicted a life's barrel—full of hurt and harm on herself and on me and our girls than I had ever brought about during the heated period of our former struggle.

Turns out, Sergeant Stoddaert and I had been wandering along similarly held lines of thought. He turned to look at me briefly, and then allowed his gaze to slowly peer up the landing at Marie. She stood languishing in the aire of what she'd hoped was that of the victimized necessity bearing compassion under the protection of the hovering patrol woman.

He gestured up to the woman, beckoning for the two of them to come down. I watched him intently. Cocking his head slightly to look at me once again, it was almost as if I could read the internal workings darting about excitedly inside the animation of the man's mind.

He was sizing me up once and for all—Trying to throw all that I had told him and presented to him up against the wall of his judgement's ire to see if anything about me or about it didn't stick. And after whispering a covered order to the patrol woman, he sided behind me and he began to unlock the cuffs I'd been standing in, barefooted, and bare-chested for more than two and a half hours of peaceful but chilling rain.

"Mr. Penn, you have a nice evening. Take good care of those two little girls. Your wife is going to jail—for being under the influence of a controlled substance in public."

And that was that!

You'd think so?

To her ultimate shock and dismay, "NETTIE" was subsequently handcuffed and placed in the back of a squad car that had been earmarked expressly for me. In her mind's eye, I could tell, from the smug smurks and self-assurant glances of "*I got yo' stupid ass, Blu!* That she'd been jeering down at me from the landing while the Sarge had been battling, mostly within himself, over which way to turn, that car she now sat in had all but but had my name written all over it, not hers.

GOD IS GOOD…

ALLTHETIME.

Needless to say, Stupid me showed up on the stoop of San Diego's Las Colinas Women's Detention Center, bright and early, with an arrangement of bail money to get her out. I'd called ahead to my job and filled my Chief in on what had transpired the evening before. He'd had no problem incredulously affording me time to try and bring some semblance of right back into the wronged crevices of what had become my world.

"NET" didn't have much she wanted to discuss with me after I had pulled our car away from the curb departing Las Colinas.

That was all right by me.

I told her I didn't want her coming back to the house if she still refused to get help for her addiction. Still she offered me very little and instead instructed me to drop her off over at her friend, Maria Slackey's place. She informed me further that that would be where she could be reached and would be staying until such time as I heard from her further.

Boy, did I hear from her further.

Her next move was to go to the local Tricare clinic and attempt to gain a doctor's approval for the amount of time she had missed that day at work. My next move was to seek a restraining order against her to prevent her, legally, from further affecting our kids.

She received her pass of approval, with a reason behind her absence being listed as "*Physically Abused by Spouse*". I received a temporary injunction against her. We were both afforded a court date to air our gripes before a judge just three weeks into the future.

All sorts of sweeping changes took place in all of our lives over that very short period of waiting. She was still staying with Maria. I had enlisted the aid of Uncle Larry and Auntie Mattie in taking care of the girls while I continued to teach at the gun school at 32nd Street. Things shaped up briefly to a bearable planning of just bare existence.

Just prior to our court date, at a time during which I was actually contemplating softening my stance on not permitting "NETTIE" to spend more quality time with the girls, I was hauled into my Executive Oficer's office and informed that I was being accused of battering my wife, pursuant to a report taken by the Naval TRICARE outpatient clinic connected to Balboa Hospital. According to the Exec, my only recourse, other than expulsion from the Naval Service weighted beneath charges of unsuitable conduct, was for me to enroll myself, on a weekly basis, into a voluntary anger management program run by the Navy's Family Advocacy Program.

I found myself caught up once again. Trapped like a rat in a trap of my own making.

Life for me and the girls began to take on a newer light of prodding self-protection. Needless to say, my former softening stance on "NETTIE" spending more time with the girls went out the window. Every Thursday evening for an entire year, from 7 to 8 P.M., I found myself thrust before a circle of like *batterers* in a classroom up at Balboa Naval Hospital, an accused scoundrel of spouse abuse, no matter the fact that no proof had ever been presented against me to corroborate the allegations.

The place was run by NAZI-like, male-hating she-femmes, complete with overly applied, caked-on mascara, choking concoctions of the most hideous perfumes and the ever present shine of storm-trooper boots. The immensity of their strong-arm tactics in attempting to belittle and disrespect every participant there was held up only under the enormity of power their return reports back to each member's parent command wielded in the Navy arriving at a decision to permit that member to continue on in what for some were already quite lengthy careers.

I endured this treatment for about three months before finally blowing. The reports reaching back to my command held me as combative and uncooperative. I was nearing the trouble of being forced out of the Navy without recourse. My overall participation grade was deemed as poor. It was only after presenting my Exec with a clandestinely recorded meeting with my supposed counselor, during which time she berated me vehemently using an assorted variety of spiteful expletives, all because I maintained my initial stance of having been innocent of all I'd been accused of, and I continue to refuse to acquiesce to a point of admitting and taking responsibility for the testosterone-filled iniquity of having battered my wife, that I found myself relieved of the mandate for attending further sessions and presented a clean slate of service, free to resume my prior stride toward eventual accomplishments. .

AND…ALLTHETIME…GOD IS GOOD!

Our court date came and went prior to me beginning and ending the classes. When we had arrived at the court house on Fifth Street downtown, "NETTIE" presented herself sharply. She sashayed in, decked out in the hip-hugging swagger of a finely tailored, blue, business suit. Her hair was whipped up to a flowering, sweet—"T" and her nails were manicured and cultured to an explicit perfection.

DAMN! She looked good. She appeared healthy. I took solace in that small fact, for her sake. The usual caste of yellow in the dens of her formerly drug infested eyes was gone. This was replaced instead with the piercing clarity of an overall outward sobriety encased by a lucid determination. One which would have me further put down and thrown off course in my quest at maintaining my stifeling hold upon *our* children I was sure. One whereby, she felt she could dress up her internal wounds while showcasing her supposed outward ones as well and regain all she had lost so pervasively during that one rainy night more than almost a month gone by.

Looking at her as the two of us met at the front of the court house entrance prior to going in, the hair on the back of my neck stood involuntarily on end. I was a bit apprehensive about the day's outcome. She was prepared for a battle. My fight there, with her, held out to appear as if it would be more arduous than I had at first envisioned.

She presented herself so plainly and with clear thought of articulate manner when somber and high thinking. I looked at her once more before following her in. She was succinctly prepared for a lengthy fight.

…Or so I had thought.

We were ushered in before the judge on a docket of perhaps a hundred cases the poor man was to entertain that busy day. He took one look at "NETT" another quick glance at me, all trussed up in my best summer, dress-whites, complete with colorful medals and upon hearing mention of children involved in our case, quickly slammed his book shut and banished the two of us off and out of his courtroom with a hasty judgmnent toward what was called "Conciliation Counseling".

We soon found ourselves outlaying our differences in ideas and philosophies of childrearing before the staunch personality of an extremely bored Conciliation Counselor lady.

Her very first question to me told of the completely uphill mêlée I was in store for in attempting to safeguard the wellbeing of my children.

"So, tell me, Mr. Penn. What kind of visitation schedule did you have in mind for maintaining contact with your children? Let's see..." She shuffled a heap of unkempt papers about in her lap half-heartedly. "You have.... A two year old girl and...?" She looked up at me with question, somehow enlisting my help.

"...And a four year old daughter, Ma'am."

"Yes...Of course," she smiled with fake vagueness. "There, now we have it straight. What did you have in mind for reasonable visitation?"

I sat stoically, in shock.

"Excuse me, Ma'am? I'm not understanding. What do you mean...? What do I have in mind for visitation?"

She turned sourly towards me in that skulk of shaded memory I recalled the NAZI-bitch, Family Advocacy counselor use on me. "Yes, it is of course the state of Californioa's intention, for the most part, that under most circrumstances, all minor children remain in the physical custody of their birth mother, barring any extreme realities."

My heart beat so fast in my chest, I felt like I was going to scream! "What are you talking about lady?" I'd quickly discarded any formerly held courtesies.

Smiling serpent like at me and shaking her head in the affirmative, "I'm certain you understand the theorized reasonings behind such a policy, Mr. Penn."

That was it. She had all but exhausted my last nerve, in record time.

"NETT" sat smug-faced, the epitome of the Cheshire cat with the house-pet gerbil's tail still dangling culpably at the corner of her tightly held mouth.

It was time for me to exhibit my own sense of strengths in what appeared an already hopelessly lost battle.

"Errrr...Missus uhhm...J-Jenoa, is it? What do your sanctions and directives say about awarding physical custody to a female parent or birth mother who has been clinically diagnosed as being drug-dependent?"

There it was. I'd placed every card I had in the deck out there plainly on the table for GOD and everybody caring to witfully see.

Feigning an apparent shock coupled with distasteful contempt, the former cool demeanor of the staunchy public servant took on a materializing shift of heading an entirely differing direction.

"Drugs! Ummm…" I could sense a squirm working its way up. "To what could you possibly be referring, Mr. Penn?"

That's when I hit her with the immensity of the copious amounts of documentation in the form of police reports, drug rehab records and mandates of psycho-therapeautic counseling I had bundled up to enter onto the field of battle should it prove necessary.

The lady, Missus Jenoa, sat awestricken at first at the defining nature of the detail in which I had come there prepared to counter the stupidly waged senselessness of her formerly pretentious statements. She began to fan herself liberally. *Dare ya' go, Miss Biddy. Fan ya'self wit' dat fo' facts a while… won't cha'.*

An extended storm of silence wafted through us to hang thickly inside the room.

By now, even "NETT" was fidgeting; her prior façade of self-confidence and impervious togetherness blown to smithereens at the force and structure of my very first blow across her bow.

Turning toward her, the lady all but redirected her efforts as she began to pounce in a new direction with the full vigor she had fully intended on using to stop me firmly in my tracks just moments before. "Well… Ummmm. Mrs. Penn? Is there a viable explanation for what Mr. Penn is telling the court?"

I continued to press forward, cutting off her cross-examination without even a feign at a concealed disrespect. I fully realized that my only hope of being crowned the victor in this court of idiots was to maintain the pressure of the upper hand I could already sense I was commandeering.

"I hereby request the court mandate that Mrs. Penn submit to a hair follicle drug test for illegal substances prior to entering a judgement one way or the other in these preceedings. No matter the expense, I am prepared today to remit the cost of said testing."

"NETT" was really nervous and restlessly squirming about in her seat by this time.

Standing straight suddenly, appearing to try to pull her eye's view in on the nearest door leading outta' there, "I ain't taking no drug tests for nobody! Not today. Not tomorrow...Not no damned day!"

I smiled inwardly. I knew then, that I had her. Sad as it may seem that I had been lead to such depths of, call it informed divergence or wisened treachery, I fully understood the vast nature of what it was we were entered into there that day. I was engaged in a conflict which could very well mean the total anihialation of my young family. My every right, as a Father, stripped away, senselessly—all on the whim and torture of these two crazy bitches' words.

There was no way I was going to come in there anything but completely, if not overly prepared. I could never permit her to use the tongue in cheek smile on the outside to belie all the drudge of soiled debris maintained in a twisted nesting accumulation on the inside while standing by to aimlessly watch as she attempted to use such trivialities in threatening the continued welfare of our two young daughters.

NOWAYINHELL!

After attempting to clear a frog from her throat for what seemed about the millionth time, Missus Jenoa enunciated very plainly, "Well, Mrs. Penn;" Her expreesion appeared pain-stricken and outright annoyed. I could tell it was killing her to have to continue forward with the recommendation she felt bound by the law to have to put before the judge and the court in this case....Just *Killin'-er...*"In lieu of the developments of circumstance surrounding the information presented to the court and pursuant to your refusal to submit to and grant the court a random sampling of, be it hair or urine, for subsequent drug screening, I can only recommend that Mr. Penn be awarded sole custody of the Penn children for a period not to exceed three years, or until such time as you are willing to tender proof otherwise detailing your willingness to undergo testing as ordered by this court."

And that was that...

We never returned to see the judge. We weren't required to. I received the appropriate stamps of judgement on my paperwork and I departed to reclaim the girls from Uncle Larry's. "NETT" went back to wherever it was that she had been staying.

This lasted a month or two. Then, the two of us began to talk once more. At my suggestion, she had re-enrolled herself in SHARP REES STAELY's outpatient substance abuse program. She was rooming out in Spring Valley, California, with a middle-aged recluse drunk, named Susan; she had met in *THE PROGRAM.*

It wasn't very long after this that we began to once again begin to spend more and more time with one another. We were hopeless. In what we tried to snift out in our union as man and wife, we were unable to completely stamp out altogether. For the both of us, it was plain. The one was ultimately hapless without the other. There was just no keeping the two of us apart for good.

Due to this fact, it wasn't long before she and I had decided; restraining order be-

damned... We *needed* to pull our shit back together and make things right once again for our family.

She moved back in. We moved outta' *CRACKVILLE* central and leased a quaint, townhouse apartment more East of the main city of San Diego, out in the suburban surroundings of the city of El Cajon.

I continued to teach at the Navy's West Coast gun school. "NETT" sought out and got a new job, working, believe—it—or—not, at SHARP REES—STEALY, for two super Orthopedic surgeons, in their clinic, as an administrative assistant.

She wasn't using. I was trying my best to be good to her and to our two little girls, while continuing to work what amounted to crazy hours while doing everything in my power to move forward within the ranks, the only way I knew how, with *that* positive, perpetual motion.

It was all good....For a while.

...Till E & J took over one evening and got in the way.

It was late on a Friday evening. "NETT" and I found ourselves just broke enough to afford a bottle of our then, old time staple, E & J Brandy. We drank it cause' it was palatable, it was handily available down at the local rot-gut store, and...it and the coke we mixed it with were cheap.

This particular evening, I remember, instead of ending our drinking festivities locked in the blissful state of heated Love-making, we brought the finality of our merriment to a spiteful close fright with an altruistic verbal confrontation over something so simple so as not to even be able to remember the actual topic right now. It could have been over anything. Her drug addiction, her unwillingness to spend time snuggled up with me locked in tongue-twisting splendor (I Love to kiss—in that wet, slobbery lip-smacking way that you envision encountering for hours on end with that one, special, best-smelling, most beautiful girl in the world. She couldn't stand it) or even something as trivial *now* as her inability, at the ripe age of twenty-two to be able to bring herself to completely break the habit of comfortably sucking her thumb (which she still does to this day and I've found a way to peer at it differently, now ultra-hypnotic and Loving instead of vindictive and accusatory)...My continual, brow-beating, controlling impatience with her...

-Could've been any reason.

All I know or remember is; we ended the evening professing our undying hatred for one another. We even assured one another that, "C*ome morning...This here shit was O-V-A'...Over!*

She stormed upstairs. I stayed downstairs to finish off the last of perhaps my twelfth drink of that evening.

The very next thing I knew, Marie was shaking me awake. She did so, completely covered in the sweat and fervor of a plainly evident, idyllic rage. She screamed and cursed at me like I was the personification of her most dire adversary instead of her sorrowful, companion; already remorseful of the hurtful words of evil I knew I had spewn at her just hours before during the previous evening.

Peering up at her, I began to take in my surroundings to focus in on the fact that I was not lying in the comfort of the bed she and I shared together, yet, instead, as the full depiction of my immediate surroundings came into full view, I noticed, that I was actually lying in our girls' bed. The forms of the spots where their warm little figures had lain just moments before, still outlined in tiny, baby-like forms among the covers from which their now irate Mother—my wife had just forcefully snatched their two little bodies away from me, her eyes bleeding murderous clamor of impending vigor as she stared down mouthing a venomous diatribe at *me*, their culpable father.

"Why you molest my baby!

I just laid there. Trying to gain a grip on my composure, while attempting inside the coagulated cob webs loudly clouding the aching crevices of my pounding head to make some sense out of the unbelievably inconceivable and wholly controversial complexities of the things she was trying to spit my way.

She's CRAZY! Was the gist of the majority of feelings I was experiencing right then. I knew it... Guess I had always known; from the very first minutes I had at first held her in my arms, and she cried like a baby—for no apparent explanation or reason.

"What you talkin' bout, "NETT"?

She bounced a step back, but didn't remain in that position very long.

"You know what the *fuc'* I'm talkin' bout'—*YOU-SORRY-MUTHAFUCCA'."* She stood there before me, her mind and her movements all trussed full of motherly wrath.

"You molested my baby!"

"I did... Whh... What?"

"You know what you did, you sorry assed-punk. You think you're so high-and-fuccn' mighty all the fuccn' time. Bet you won't be held so high once your precious *NAVY* finds out what you did."

Suddenly, the immensity of the realities of her accusations began to sink home. I began to focus further in on the things she had just said to me. I became instantly aware and overly, at-an-instant... *SCARED!*

At first, I did all I could to calm her. I knew, no matter what, that I was in deep, deep trouble. The things I'd said to her the previous evening were mere clouds of devilish mouthing to me by this point. But, obviously, to her, these things were living, breathing embodiments, still fresh in her mind, and I was going to be made to pay for them, in whatever way *she* saw fit now, even if it meant total abandonous ruin brought about by false accusations of the worst order.

Next I knew, "NETT" was on the phone. A full slew of her fifteen brothers and sisters, and her Momma had been duly informed of my alleged pedophilic atrocities. I attempted to plead with her while she was still on the phone for her to simply get off the phone and talk with me.

She refused... Wan't listening... Had no words for a brutha'...

Instead, she shored up plans for her oldest sister, Pamela, to fly down to San Diego on the soonest bird heading our way, with hasty intentions of fully wrapping up our disheveled little household—for keeps. No sooner had their brother, Bruce, and I finished loading the U-HAUL mini-trailer we had gotten hitched to the rear of "NETT'S" new HYUNDAI, than the two of them drove off toward the Oregon crest line. I remember him and I standing about, looking at each other foolishly, no words to be said between us as she, her sister, and *my* two babies drove off.

With fretful tears banked in un-surety welling in both our eyes, we just stood there and watched them all disappear from my life in a cloud of exhaust for what was certain to feel like my forever eternity.

I returned to work the following Monday morning. Trying my best, due to the events that had taken place over my very recent weekend, I found it increasingly hard to concentrate on any one task. I hazed through each of the day's classes I was scheduled to teach like a zombie. It was the beginning of a period of waiting for the other shoe to drop as I forged uncertainly through the rigors of life's events while behind each heavy step loomed the possibility of pending accusation and certain publicized scorn.

Time and time again, I tried to call "NETT" at her mom's place in Oregon. My every attempt was met with the blocking irony on an incensed brother or the mouthy fervor of an irate, stalling sister, as my name in that household had been made to equal nothing elevated higher than a nasty derivative of a despicable mud.

When I did chance to call and actually was enabled to speak with her, our terse conversations always began and ended in an identical way.

"Why you do that to our baby? How could you have done that to my little girl?"

I forever met such questions from her with identical answers. "NETT, what do you truly believe I could have done to hurt our precious baby? I Love that girl like she's my own blood. I would never do anything to her and I'd be the first to kill another for even thinking about harming her."

"I saw you lying in that bed with my baby,—with no clothes on."

"NETT, sure, I might have been llying in that bed with the girls, but I had my boxers on. I didn't do anything to harm our daughters. You've got to believe that baby. You know…I wouldn't…ever…"

"I don't know what you're capable of, Blu. I don't really know you at all."

"You know me, "NETT"."

And that was the general nature of our conversation spanning a matter of months.

That was, until the nature of my calls with her began to take on a more different, demanding turn. She began to make more increasing demands along the lines of monetary claims on me. In a manner unbecoming of the sweet, troubled girl I had seemingly mistakenly married, she began more and more to ask for and insist that I begin to send her even more money than I'd already been sending.

I was already wavering beneath the financial weight of more than I felt I could spare or afford comfortably supporting her and the kids in Oregon while continuing to maintain a hollow existence, including our apartment, other extensive amounts of bills and our car payments.

Toward this, I just flat out told her no. I had given all I was going to give at that time. This always tended to bring a rapid end to any conversations approaching reconciliation the two of us might have entertained.

It came boiling to a head one fateful afternoon as I was busy with a group of students during practical labs, when an instructional patron of mine summoned me over to pick up an available phone line in the lab's interior.

"Who is it?" I remember saying.

"I dunno', said it's your wife."

"Do me a favor, shipmate...Pick up that other end there and listen in for me." He was a bit incredulous, at first, but did as I'd asked with very little cajoling.

My situation with my wife had become a well-known thorn in most of my co-worker's sides. For a large while, it was all I could talk about when engaged in any conversation for more than two minutes at any given time. So, it wasn't too outlandishly unthinkable that I would drag him into this conversation with her now. He merely rolled his eyes at me and went to station himself at the open extension at the other side of the room.

"Hello..."

"Hey. What you doin'?"

"I'm in the middle of teaching a lab, "NETT", what's up?

"We need to talk."

"O.K. What about? There's some Naval Investigative agents scheduled to fly down to Portland to interview me on Friday."

My mind quickly ran over an internally located calendar. Today was Wednesday. Two days more and my whole world would quite possibly blow up into a wickedly twisted scheme of bile raising never-nothingness.

"All right. What is it you think I can do to effect the outcome of that. I've already stated my position. I asked that you take our daughter to be examined by a medical professional. Have you done that?"

"No, I don't see any reason as to why I should have to. I know what I saw, Blu."

I was about to lose my good graces with her in that very conversation, just as I had a million other conversations before, but I remained excruciatingly calm.

"Why wouldn't you? If you believe so vehemently that I'm some sort of monster pedophile, why would it be so damned hard for you to take her to a doctor, get her checked out, head to toe, to determine, once and for all the extent of, or whether at all she has even really been subjected to the molestation in the manner you are now accusing me of?"

"Look, Blu...I don't want to ruin you. All I want is five-hundred dollars more a month and I will tell those agents nothing happened and that I was confused about it all from the start. Blame it on drug use or sumpin'...you know the drill."

My heart couldn't have broken more completely that very moment had she told me she'd never held any Love for me at all or that my babies were never none o' mine and that they belonged instead to the local preacher she'd been spending time with during a supposed, weekend, spiritual, bible retreat.

"What are you talking about, "NETT"?"

"You know what the hell I'm talkin' about, Blu."

"You know, I'm really starting to believe you're fuccn' crazy! This conversation is over, baby. I Love you, good-bye."

...And I hung up.

Turns out, putting my co-worker on the other end of that line was perhaps the smartest thing I had ever done since meeting her so many months before.

When it all did come down, and when the shoe I'd been fitfully pining away in fear of daily finally did drop, it turned out that I was the number one candidate at my station in line to be awarded the coveted position as the command's Senior Sailor of the Year.

This was a monumental career milestone in the pathway of any young sailor's procession leading to the highest peaks of professional achievement and an increasing endorsement toward a coveted excellence. Once awarded such a distinction of sustained superior performance, eventual promotion into the ranks of the Chief Petty Officer was never far off on the horizon.

It was an achievement I'd strived everyday for, for more than a year of late nights and extra professional duties and chores to amass.

...And I think she knew it. No! I knew that she knew how much the fruition of my efforts in this arena meant not only to me, but for our family as well.

Days rolled into weeks. Weeks turned into months, and still, following a lengthy interview process, in which I felt I'd faired exceedingly well, there was still no public announcement by the command declaring that year's selection. Nothing more than whispers each time I found myself approaching the topic while in the company of counterparts. Hidden snickers and daunting, procrastinating put-off statements from superiors I engaged on the subject as well.

This went on with undue course until I'd finally come to a point of no longer being able to stand the pathetic endurance and patience required of me in awaiting the outcome. Taking *the bull by the horns,* I charged, headlong into the command's administrative offices which housed the Executive Officer. On an afternoon, just after releasing my students for the day, I barged into the outer offices of Commander Consuela Green.

I relayed to her assistant to please extend to the Exec—, "that Petty Officer Penn, would respectfully request to be placed on her afternoon calendar. And that it didn't matter the amount of time I would be forced to wait in order to accommodate her already busy scheduled of that day's events. I would wait...No matter how long it required.

Unexpectedly, I found myself being ushered in to see her immediately. After making the proper respects of military courtesy, I thought I would begin with telling her a simple story. One in which I would detail the cumbersome frustrations and failings encased in what had developed thus far in what had become my fateful marriage.

Turns out, I didn't get very far in telling her much of anything...

At first...

Peering into me deeply with seemed, all-knowing Maternal intellect, the Commander chose her words carefully while sizing me up clearly with an angled glare.

"Petty Officer, Penn, I don't think I have to tell you this; but, you've got a very serious problem."

I returned her glare, wanting to blurt out, "*Are you kidding me*?

I knew better than most the power and gleen of the darkened horizon which lay before me. With the stressors of vociferous rumors and half-truth, whispered accusations I was bearing up under, there were times during this period of ordeal, that the sudden, threatening weight of just attempting to maintain a normal, military appearance loomed all-too oppressive. Being able to aptly present the students I was instructing a just account of the daily curriculum that normally I was adept enough at to recite backwards in my sleep became nearly impossible.

She was singing to a choir that just wasn't caring much about being heard.

Pushing back a willingness to lash out toward her with words, I found myself instead gathering together my best attempt at reaching out to grasp at a fading humility. I knew under such circumstances; that, was the only fleeting possibility which would suit me best. I offered only a sullen, "Yes, Ma'am. I do have some problems I think I need your help with."

Casual to her usual course, she pulled no punches as she moved forward into a more favorable striking distance.

Approaching me austerely, she exited her former position from within the enveloping comfort of the high-backed, red, leather chair she'd been working in, and she sauntered slowly towards me. She finally settled into a relaxed posture along the front edge of her heavy oak desk in front of me...

And...She just sat there for a pregnant moment, one which overflowed between us with a propensity for unspoken anxiety. She stared a wondering sternness into me, piercing my soul, my knowledge, my manhood, my character...seemingly forever.

Starting with, "I'd be willing to bet that you thought you were climbing all of those stairs leading to my offices to engage me about the status of my decision to announce this year's recipient of the command's Sailor of the

Year program, isn't that so, Petty Officer Penn?"

I nodded, obediently. "Yes... Yes, Ma'am. That was one of my reasons for approaching you in such a manner, Ma'am. Please pardon the..."

She cut me off with, "It's not going to work, mister." She sealed the thin air surrounding my next volley of words, pinning them deeply inside my chest to be left unspoken.

I stood still, tazed into shock. Her gruff, almost abrasive nature was totally out of character for the kind, loveable Exec not one person at the command did not Love as much as they did their own Mother.

"I'm sorry, Ma'am, I don't understa..." I attempted to wage forward once more.

She held me firmly in my tracks with, "Oh, I think you understand perfectly, Mister."

There again was that jaundiced eye of the unbeliever she now held me in so accusatorially. Returning back around to the disheveled, business side of the great oak, the respected Commander began to shuffle through the leaves of a particular stack of paperwork she'd set out before her in what for her had amassed to being an overly organized conglomeration of untidiness.

I studied her intently. Attempting to gauge every nuance of heart beat, reaction and run of her excited senses, I couldn't help keying in on the fact that the air venting almost vehemently from each of her nostrils caused each of the overly sized caverns to rifle the edges of the papers she now clutched begrudgingly before her.

Something was indelibly wrong here.

I peered up at her. "Ma'am, I don't..."

She blew out one last exasperated breath and then hit me full-force with all that she had in store for me.

"You see, Petty Officer, Penn, things appear to play out thus; It comes to my attention that every Chief Petty Officer at this command has voted to award you the distinction of running with the honors of being anointed this year's Sailor of the Year.

...But my hands are tied."

I stood stupefied. Seems every word and response I could have given her right then lay stuck, forcefully distended inside of me, unable to be pulled forward as a formed reply.

Lowering my head to make preparation for sliding through to the next set of obviously awaiting let downs she held in store for me, it was all I could do to maintain the composure I'd so strongly prided myself on maintaining under even the most harrowing circumstances in the past, she gave it all to me full-brunt, without even the slightest propensity for hesitation.

"You are being accused of child-molestation!"

Her words all but threatened to floor me where I stood.

I mean, what response was warranted at such a stifling, fucc'd-up juncture in a grown, responsible man's life?

In a flash, though I had known that the possibility of that moment becoming a reality for me was excruciatingly near at hand, I almost wavered beneath the utter immensity of it as it faced me suddenly then, surreptitiously canceling out every great deed, every carefree whisper, every warm, rainy day I'd ever experienced in mylife up to that point.

Her strict words of allegation sucked the breathing air right outta' me. I became helpless, unable to prevent the sullen rivulet of at first, a single tear from slithering its darkened betrayal down the side of my quickly contorting face, and over all powerless to stem back the ensuing tide of more of the same as they soon seemed to flow unchecked—forming the first of many lonesome cries that have swooned to swell up inside my eyes—all because of this despicably conniving and deceitful person I so lovingly referred to as "NETTIE".

Looking up to her, and abjectly burdened with the pressing materialization of immediate physical and emotional pain, "Ma'am....I...."

"Have a seat, Petty Officer, Penn." Then she recanted, Better yet! You just stand there," she spat. "Yes...Just you stand there—*AT ATTENTION!*" She directed, scolding me crossly with glaring eyes.

It was only following an hour or so of comprehensive explanation, during which time I extolled for her the full propensity of all the things I'd been striving through with "NETTIE", that I began to feel with a glimmer of unbelievable hope that there was a slight chance of her placing a smidgeon of trust and faith in the fact that I might just be telling the truth. In these explanations I implored her to enter in the possibility of thought; that I might just be innocent of all the things the Naval Investigation preliminary report had outlined previously in their sloppily thrown-together case, one in which they'd spent only a single day's execution entailing simplistic phone calls and amassing amateurish conclusions and stamping the monicker, *Investigation* on them in their so-called gathering of *tha-fact*s.

I knew that my only chance was in getting her to rightfully see me for who I really was, to impound her with the truth, regardless of how graphic, while irrefutably showcasing my own facts, that I was more than a heartless beast capable of' committing the most heinous of the worst of atrocities.

It became so bad, for her, towards the end, as I detailed the countless times I had tailed my wife, along with the two blameless, unsuspecting lives of our two young

daughters, strapped securely into toddler car seats in the back of her Hyundai, as she tweaked on in an unremitting adventure—on-the-prowl, weaving through the streets of San Diego, in her debilitating witch-hunt for crack cocaine, that she too began to droop beneath the pressure of such a damning reality of circumstances as I'd lain them out plainly before her. I began to sense her developing a need for a nearby box of tissue all her own. While I continued pouring out my soul, the continuation of my every word began to cause her (she a Mother and a Grandmother as well) to gasp in disbelieving horror at the craziness I'd agonizingly re-lived for her that afternoon in her office.

Finally, at a point where she felt she just couldn't take any more; (I believe, I was just about to approach the gut-wrenching, re-detailing of an entirely new medley of more additionally carnal infidelities) that she stopped me abruptly, herself unable to withstand the immensity of the mayhem I'd thus far been able to stand up under—all in the guise of Loving and wanting to be Loved at the cruel, witless hand of my beloved "NETTIE".

Shaking her head slowly from side to side, she became aware embarrassingly of inadvertently catching herself dabbing lightly at the corners of each of her eyes. She left her chair abruptly and quickly stood glaring out her fifth floor window with her back to me. She stood there for a long pause before whirling around to face me once more. Still incredulous, I could almost feel the machinations swirling about inside the emotionally strapped entanglements of her mind.—There's no way I could have simply made it all up...

The story lines ran too well together. The ends matched the beginnings a bit too concisely for me to be standing in front of her now, at attention, and lying.

Peering even more deeply into me then, she sat back down directly with an almost frozen, exasperated clump. She blew out a frustrated sigh, yet said nothing.

Hers was an eerie, but all telling silence. Her inability to draw forth words any longer reached out to chill the sensitive reaches of my bending spine. And at the same time, that moment became caught up in the vacuum of screaming at me all too loudly.

She just sat there looking at me in silence. I forced myself to catch her stare squarely, refusing to drop my own gaze as I remember focusing in on the rhythmic heartbeat of the widened crevices aligning themselves with great stress at each of her beating nostrils. In and out, in and out they moved, hawking at me steadily, wondering, delving, searching in a steady tone of her own inwardly held conjecture amid speculation that if she chose wrong in this case, if she made the incorrect decision, even her world could end up topsy-turvy, turned on its own upsetting axis of spinning side ways.

Seemingly without end, she tapped a lengthy, manicured nail noisily about the edge of the plastic corner of her desk calendar. She seemed so torn. Caught up against the grain of her position. Between making a quick, done-by-noontime case of this thing and merely dismissing me off into the easily pre-judged shame of immediate discharge and follow-on federal indictment, a decision which would surely force me to walk an inevitable, never-ending plank of having to incessantly attempt to clear myself before a world-wide court of opinionated, yet closely, judge-worthy ears—to always be searching for that thing she held the reins to now that very moment—my future…to seek out a never-reachable forever.

Or…To take the equally frightful step of placing her everything, her faith, her job, her visions held internally for her own members of her family…Her worries, her cares and her concerns unevenly on the alter of the mere words of a young sailor she barely even knew.

"What am I going to do with you?" Her words hit me about as softly as a ton of bricks squishing an upwardly turned, helpless beetle.

It was then that I felt I had her…Mistakenly; I began to permit myself a moment's respite in which I felt I could finally begin to relax.

Suddenly, and just as promptly as she had before, she bolted upright from her chair, was onto her feet, and at me preparing with a stealing resolve to swoop into engagement mode again. I sensed her actions to be nothing more though for me than just another series of tests. Her return to another round of what seemed a torturous encirclement of excited, pain-stricken, internalized grief as it surmounted even for her and not just I amidst a streaming flux of both anger filled accusations and undirected frustrations inside of her own self all had their reasonings. Turning about to face me suddenly, her face completely contorted she tried to flush the straining truths or untruths from me with blow after blow of an unending, knee-shaking onslaught of both leading and misleading questions.

Once again, we went back over every excruciating detail of all I had already infinitely imparted to her. Times, places, people, faces, facts; "Who was there? Who wasn't? What day did this occur? Whose home did you say you were at? Do you recall the exact address? Give me their contact number!"

"What extension of proof can you provide? Can you corroborate, to the minutest factor, every single extent of each far-reaching aspect of what you've just relayed to me? Who else at the command would be willing to verify your repudiation of each and every one of these supposed facts?" She shook the paperwork she held balled in her fists at me.

She all but stood over me now, threatening. An all intrusive Den-Mother, brandishing the stack of menacing, manila folders containing the dossiers as if to remind me of the sanctity of her word within the far-reaching community of her world and of the earth-shattering significance of what her allegiance in my situation could fetter out to mean. We both realized that it was she, and not the documents encased inside those dossiers, that held what was to be left of the follow-on continuation of peace for me within life that very second.

I could sense and feel her sway. Now that she'd had her own staunched sense of propriety shaken, through just a tiny gape into the still greatly untold horrors of my lengthy tale, she'd been able to envision just the slightest forming of a shimmering fissure as it began to shatter and dot the infringing edges of the summarization contained inside the previously irreprehensible report which the Naval Investigative Service had gathered or rather concocted, at "NETTIE's beckon, against me.

With a heightened clarity fueling her efforts, the previous fervor of her ball-busting energies began to turn away from me and instead instantly began to claw with jaw-clenching aspiration toward a direction more aptly deserving. One which would go a long way toward finally affording me that which I needed most that moment—REDEMPTION!

As I was shooed from her office with the dismissive backhand of a happily received swoosh, she was just settling in, with salivating grandeur, as the Western Region head of the then, Naval Investigative Service closed his own office door with quieting exasperation before settling in to take her call.

For her, the wizened enlightenment of the facts and truths I'd presented and had gone to great lengths to corroborate in countering the hastily constructed accusations had become a light force.

For me, to have it all become coaxed to a forward-thinking resolution of life-saving legitimacy; after explaining every detail to her, leaving nothing out, showcasing minute particulars about my battles with "NETTIE" and our young Love, complete with sordid, blunt and morose details which would have brought even the devil himself to cringe; after, re-hashing the many phone conversations I'd received at work demanding more money amid shocking threats steeped in blackmail, and providing a rather extensive list of others at the command who'd willfully taken part in each of those conversations, on remote extensions as silent listeners, and after being quickly dismissed from her presence with a joyous internal and re-constituted, defining grace—I was finally again able to breathe.

Her ultimate reaction and emotions to all that I'd lain out for her in my defense were ungageable. I couldn't tell if, in her, a powerful ally had developed, or, if still, somewhere at the back region of her mind, she looked upon me contemptuously, stamping me as much a verminus pedophile, one far from deserving of rights, her time and her efforts, as I had been unctuously accused.

I never heard from Commander Greene again. The only words she offered me on any occasion were in passing. I'd see her coming my way, I'd step to the side to offer her a respectful lee-way, she'd nod, speak just three words, " Petty Officer, Penn,"...nod her head amiably, I'd reply,

"Ma'am."...nod my head as well, and that would be the end of it.

Through it all, I maintained a safe grasp in my previously strong-willed belief in the system. A coordination of societal rules, strengths, injustices and adjudicated acquittals developed even more staunchly inside of me as I stepped out of the foyer of her outer office, a new person.

I was strong and young.

I was free; I was exonerated completely following the completion of her phone call.

I was still a Daddy, still an honor-bound Veteran, still a Man!

...And get this, by distinct order of the station Commanding Officer, at a special conference, called expressly for that purpose, that following Friday, I became the Fleet Training Center, San Diego, California, Sailor of the Year!.

It wasn't until I was eventually brought onto stage that fateful afternoon, and awarded the distinction and accolade as Sailor of the Year, that I knew GOD had delivered me of "NETTIE's" evil wickedry.

Finally, I felt as if, once again, I had been saved from the life-long effects of the sting of her venomous traps.

And...For me, that was when my life as a professional sailor in Uncle Sam's Navy truly began.

"NETT" and I had split...*for good, this time*. Not able to find enough family or friends who would blindly put up with her selfish, maniacal ethics either, she had long since returned to San Diego from Oregon. All I knew, she was rooming place-to-place, moving about with nomadic squalor, from friend to friend.

By decree of the courts, custody of the girls was returned to me. The three of us eeked out a pseudo existence of not really happiness, with the two of them spending most of their time, either at the baby sitter's, while I continued to teach at the gun school at the Naval Base on Thirty-Second Street, or over at Uncle Larry's.

The whole sordid time period seemed twisted, encased in the macabre,...totally out of place and comfort for me. Seemingly somehow, as if I'd again been on the outside—looking—in on the horrific tale of some other poor bum's fucc'd-up life.

What right-minded woman would affect those kinds of variables so negatively in her own life which would play out in the culmination of her losing custody of her own children? What right-minded person would trample on such a feisty, fulfilling Love that I felt for her?—All over a sweetly soured mixture of crack, cocaine, vindictive emotions and lies?

Lies and crack-cocaine... Was she crazy? Was I?

Because, deeply rooted, down inside...

I wanted her back.

Britt and Ash were three and one years old. The three of us went through a mountain of stove-top macaroni and cheese boxes, not to mention about a million diapers, freeze-pops, Frosted Flakes and animal crackers. We did our best to get along in a world that had rendered us Mommy-less.

Last I'd heard, at the time, "NETTIE" had flown back to Oregon (the girl was a veritable free-bird, taking various trips between California and Oregon, as if the distance was merely that of the area between here and the corner store). She rarely ever called or even came by to see the girls before leaving. The gripping throes of her addiction had only strengthened after losing custody of her girls; and she began a downward slide toward nothingness, peaking assuredly toward an eventual, certain death.

Her emaciated physical condition, complete with sunken, sullen eyes atop an almost skeletal frame had even me, the one person in the world she'd attempted most ardently to bring to undeserved ruin concerned and fearful for her fate whenever I had had occasion to run into her.

There was nothing more I felt I could do.

So...I let her go.

...And I filed for divorce.

The dissolution of our marriage was final May 15th, 1989. I remember receiving the papers in the mail. She still claims to this day, that we were never divorced, due to the fact I'd asked the courts to forward her paperwork to her mother, Miss Carrie's house, in Oregon; because I knew that locating her when the time came for final signatures and recording would prove to be a next to impossible caper.

So the girls and I moved on... Without her...

I had never really known or experienced depression like I felt right then at the moment I stood, after returning from the mail box, with papers of finality in hand. Not even when I'd first been brought into the light of Kam, my first wife's infidelities, did I remember such an overwhelming feeling of loss, deeply rooted anguish and lack of strength at the daily absence of the woman I'd previously felt certain would be there with me throughout eternity; be there for me, supporting my every dream for our family…to grow up, grow old and be together, forever.

Following a good drunk, one in which I'd deposited myself at Uncle Larry's house in Murphy Canyon, turned over care of my girls to Auntie Mattie, I went about the task of attempting to console myself at the loss of *my* "NETTIE".

Following this brief period of self-serving respite, I once again became immersed in my job. I toyed with the idea of putting together a submission of my record for consideration as a candidate for appointment as a commissioned officer, but I faltered and didn't do it. I continued teaching and operating with excellence, while devoting myself ruggedly to the care and comforts of my two darling girls.

Chapter Eight
TAI-LAND

You know, even this didn't last long. As a wise woman once said, "Man cannot live by hamburger alone. I was strictly tuned in to coming up with things the girls and I could do together. The three of us were constantly at the park, a parade, the zoo, or on station as an established staple group at numerous birthday parties.

Before long, I found a way to mix most of these pleasurable things to include all of us, no matter the venue. San Diego's Mission Beach, during summer was extremely helpful. It was there, on a breezy and lazy day, that I found myself *caught-up* in my next big romantic deluge.

I had just placed Ash on a swing when, from behind me, I heard the banter of a pair of clearly female voices, as they hmmmph'd, mmmmmph'd and haawwed their ways into my existence without first being asked.

I wasn't a vain man. Yet, at the same time, being newly divorced and overly stressed by the immensities of my many responsibilities, I'd taken up the practice of most times not eating properly. Although chunky by trade and legacy, because of this, I had very rapidly and easily slimmed down to a fightable hundred and sixty pounds, all of it rip-rocked hard, due to the fact I was still ever faithful, at the time, no matter my troubles, to my daily work out with weights at the Thirty-Second Street gym.

"Mmmmph' *Huuuunnny!* All of that man out here by his lonesome...He betta' be careful gurl' I'm thinkin' bout reachin' ova and sss-anatchin' me a piece right here, chile!"

I knew, but could hardly believe they were talking about me. Things like that had never happened to me before in the past. I looked up and back over my shoulder, stealing a glance. Catching their eyes, they both giggled lasciviously, while shooting me the pearly whiteness of two sets of perfectly groomed teeth.

They waved at me coquettishly, feigning an abrupt, *we'll eat you alive* shyness between them at having purposefully permitted themselves to have gotten caught.

Their names were Tai and Trinity, cousins, and apparently partners in the accomplishment of more wicked things than even I could have imagined at that time. The three of us talked for a brief moment. I couldn't believe my nervousness at being so tightly drawn to the two of them.

Tai was the more beautiful of the two. Tall and slim, with almost blue-hazel eyes, I remember trying desperately to ascertain whether they were really hers (They were) or the colored contacts so many people had just discovered and were wearing as if blue was best and brown was somehow out of style. She had a heaping mound of ample, protruding breast line, trying incessantly to make its way nipple free through the tiny lace of what could've passed for a negligee top she was wearing. Her hair was swept up and curved about the soft nape of a long, succulent neck, braided expertly, as was the style, and rave of that day's bursting African culture. She had no other body to speak of. Very slender, not many curves, you could tell that she was very young and had as yet to fill fully out.

I found out Trinity was the older of the two. She was a heart-stopping nineteen, and she sported a little girl of about two on the hips of a young woman who'd already experienced the anguish and pain of becoming a Mommy. I approached Tai first.

Heck, Trinity was a rave to look at. She actually did have the matching bustier of her young cousin, plus she was bootied-down with all sorts of deliciously inviting curves backed up by a full spread of wonderfully soft-looking, widening hips. But Tai was a definite knock-out by comparison. Plus, it's probably verbose for me to say this, but...she didn't appear, at the time, to have any kids.

She was the talkative, fully-animated one of the duo as well. *Miss Mouth*...Hemmin' and hawkin' at a grown man, like she didn't know if she kept it up like dat' there, messin' with me, she was about to get herself *fucc'd.*

I calmed down enough to reprove my former practice of being able to at

!east fake being an on-the-spot suave-y' and I was able to get both their numbers. I had almost blown it. My original intentions had been to gain access to both of these young, supple hotties and merely toy with them over the course of the approaching days of summer, then discard them, like spent trash, without even the simplicity of a returned phone call, after having gotten' *tha-panties* and forever-after appearing to be on the run. I wasn't even thinking about playing either one of them—for keeps. That, I'd promised myself and an entire slew of tired-of-listening-to my-shit family members, was no longer my style or part of my forte.

I'd almost blown it, I said, because I'd insisted on Tai showing me her I.D. before I really started jawing at her. On mere looks alone, I more trusted my efforts with Trinity, the obviously more mature of the two. Even if she was a bit underage (I was twenty-four) she had the walk, mature talk and responsibility of parenthood going for her. But Tai, all she had...was this peevish look of pure-D-sex about her. It was written all over her. Tha' girl reeked of trouble and with that came jurisprudent havoc in her every scheme, and that spelled trouble, because it invariably showcased her inexperience, which truthfully belied the fragility of her evident youth.

She was but eighteen, fresh outta' high school and she had no clue what kind of murky circumstances came with getting herself involved with a man like me.

I wasn't a bad person, by far. I'd just taken part in and been through far too much for a young man of my experience. I was the kind that Loved fiercely...wore my heart and my propensity for courage on my sleeve. And, once seeking and finding something I wanted, I would very rarely back off or leave sleeping dogs lie, as they say, until I was able to exact precisely that for which I wanted, without failure.

And from the minute I first heard her wayward catcall and had turned around to take in the pure sexiness of her pubescent features, I wanted her.

And, needless to say, I got her...

Our's was a fiery relationship, steeped in disputation. Tai came from a long line of strong-willed, single women who'd settled in San Diego almost a century before. Her Mother, Miss Glorietta, who owned her own home in National City (a seedy, low-rent suburb of San Diego, right outside of the Naval base) held down a secure position as a shipyard longshoreman at the

National Steel and Shipbuilding Company (NASSCO) adjacent to gate nine of the Thirty-Second Street Naval Station lining the harbor shores.

Her Father was, of course, non-existent. Sparse mention was made of him, as a no-good, drug-addicted drifter who very rarely paid the hedgling family any mind. And, her Mother had about six sisters. All of them grown and living on their own, some of them too, living off the spoils they were able to wrangle out of unsuspecting sailors.

I saw the scene exactly for what it was. Here you had a strong-willed beauty, who'd been trained by a host of the best, when it came to wrangling what they wanted out of men, outta' sailors explicitly…

She'd been a studious pupil and had definitely learned her lessons well. Spanning a period of about a month, it had taken all of about three trips to the local motel with her for me, before I was, like I said before, *CAUGHT-UP* in giving in and providing her every whim and need, simply upon demand.

Man…I mean, the girl was wild! And I was living it up and eating it all in with abandon. She Loved my girls and was good to them whenever the four of us were together. The whole thing; once again (her penchant for using me and bleeding me dry financially notwithstanding) felt excruciatingly splendid.

It felt…*ALMOST*…Right.

Until she became pregnant!

After receiving this news, I fought with myself persistently. What should I do?

Do I marry her?

Pay for an abortion?

Move her in with me to finally become *her* man, as well as take up my right-filled position as *her* baby's Father?

I was stupefied by all of the complexities of daunting variables that came hurling at me more than a million miles a minute, seemingly all-at-the same time. I wanted to do the right thing. I didn't really know if I truly was *In Love* with her. Heck, I don't even really believe that I Loved her at all.

I was *In Love* with getting' at the newness of all that *strange* after having just come off such a horrendous set of circumstances with "NETTIE" just prior to having met her. I was in Love with the heaping pile of goodies she offered. To tell the truth, it wasn't until years later, that I actually took the time to take a step back and actually look at her and peer into the meanings and propensities of her very immature actions that I finally began to realize who exactly she really was, as a person.

WHATTAYATHINK?

Of course, I took steps toward doing the right thing by her, making the appropriate moves for both she and for the baby.

We made plans to get married. We paid overly-copious amounts for very low quality furnishings, for the apartment the two of us would move into together. I would give up my current living situation with my girls, all because she didn't like the size and shape of the complex pool, or something or other just as mundane and inconsequential as that. We placed about a gazillion bucks worth of maternity items on lay-away at the local K-Mart.

We bought swing-sets, frilly, softened shams and baby comforters, bottles, bottle washers, breast milk squeezie machines, brasier, nipple leakage pads and the whole kit-and-caboodle. That baby was about to come into the world playing it right. . . with nothing wanting for its health and happiness forever after.

I was as frustrated as any man could be with a pregnant girlfriend. I remember continually looking at myself each morning in the mirror as I shaved. The shadow of the figure leering back at me peeked a cruel and condescending mantra at me continually from across the tiny sink.

"Ya' happy fool.?. Ya' happy? This, is what YOU want for your life? What about the girls? Ya' happy...fool?

The unmistakable answer kept ringing back at me loudly with clanging abandon.

No, I wasn't happy. I was far from being anything nearly approaching true happiness. I was trapped. That's was what I felt. I was caged like an unintelligent animal, life and its inexplicable occurrences, my confine.

Subliminally, I know now, that I began with a deeply rooted earnest, to search for a face-saving way—of getting out.

My out presented itself, almost eight months into her pregnancy. I had put up with about all I think I could have taken, watching her Mother and her aunties' toy with and manipulatively amuse themselves, literally, all at the expense of one or another, young, hapless sailor. Time and time again I'd made it known among them that I wasn't to be counted in amidst the lot with all of the rest. I wouldn't permit myself to be lumped in with the sortless souls of suckers they were at times playing off of one another, just for the simple fact of attending to the gains and spoils of *their* soul-less, sullen pleasures.

Out of about ten women, to count them, all sisters, daughters, aunties, cousins, somehow of the same plighted family, there appeared one who had taken me deadly serious…And Tai was not to be listed as that one.

It was Trinity…

She was always the third wheel with Tai and I. Always hanging out at my place, sleeping over with her boyfriend, Dre', the three or four of us attached at the hip, attending concerts and fairs, going to the movies, or scheduling cook outs together down at the beach in Mission bay.

We fried a turkey once at the beach. We did this atop the crusty surface of my charcoal grill, for Christmas that year. At the time, we all thought that was the neatest thing since glow-in-the-dark condoms.

Good ole' cousin Trinity had accompanied Tai and me on an outing to K-Mart one raging, sweltering summer afternoon. Once there, the three of us exited my tiny little blue Honda, and went into the store so I could finish paying off the items she and I had picked out and placed on lay-away there some months before. Inside the store, things took on an entirely different reasoning away from what we had originally intended prior to even setting out to arrive there, or so I had thought.

I set off in the direction of the customer service counter. She and Tai immediately headed in another direction, I think, towards the women's lingerie section.

At first, I thought nothing of it. Trinity was a talker. Always wolfing about the wonderous sexiness and crazed debaucheries she and the very fortunate boyfriend, Dre' were always finding themselves twisted into. She had mentioned that she was sorta' looking to buy something special the two of them could slip out of during the approach of whatever nastiness she had planned for him that particular evening.

As usual, I paid her scant attention as the two of them headed off into their own direction and I found myself behind a grotesquely obese lady in the customer service line, intending only to retrieve our lain-away items and get tha'hell outta' there.

Darkened moments of capricious laughter and impulsive neglect greeted my mind's terrible ire as I stood behind that lady in that line. Bile and acrid stench of the decay of a relationship that had never quite held a chance from its inception haunted me increasingly as both my conscience and my intellect bombarded me, labeling me *tha' fool, the sucker, the mark*, as Carolyn's brother, Stoop, had once referred to me as, thinking I wasn't listening in passing.

Doing my best to languidly press the immensity of such thoughts behind, I stepped to the front of the counter at my turn, gave the lady my credit card, and without even caring to watch the amounts she was seemedly joyously ringing up, I retrieved all of our items. This took me the full energy of making three complete trips, back and forth, out to the car, and I then turned about, meaning to re-enter the store to go in search of the two, diabolical cousins.

Then, it hit me. This thing stopped me abruptly in my tracks. I never took another step toward seeking the young women out. There was no way anything could have brought me at that moment to re-enter the cool breezeways of that gigantic store that very moment. Something along the trails of my inner stomach sent waves of shocking foreboding to me, suddenly and all at once.

Something wasn't right.

I was at a loss for pin-pointing exactly what it was. But, I knew, deep down (...and I still get these feelings—to this day, whenever something about my earth's center is approaching or appearing to be deftly out of whack and wrong) something was morosely off its kilter. And, I knew it hadn't happened yet, because mine was a fate that was brutally honest and unmercifully terrorizing at times when it came to the tellings of immense let-downs, disappointments and vaunted truths.

I settled behind the wheel of my car, seeking some way of putting off the swooning discomfort of the mid-summer's heat. I played the radio for a while. I dozed. And when I woke up, all I recall was looking up to witness the voluptuous form of a streaking Trinity as she made her way out the store, and headed a bee-line for the spot where I sat parked in the little blue car which was almost completely filled with all our new baby-junk.

It was almost as if I knew what she'd tell me once making it completely over to me. My conscious nerve of steel resolve started messing with me. Almost as if preparing me for what was about to be played out next.

My mind shunted a haunting, "*Awe... Here... We—go!*"

I continued to study her every step, taking in the increased swell of evident frustration and apparent anger of what was generally, for her, an easily appeasable temperament covering her face.

Plus, I have to admit, after being around the swelling physique of her cousin for the previous eight months, an opportunity to simply kick back and take in the seductive swagger of the bumps and grinds of her every excited step, wasn't too hard a thing for me to do either. I waited for her to draw fully upon my position.

Once there, I greeted her with, "What's up,-T…?" Ignoring the greeting, she instead yanked at the handle of the back door of the ride, only to find it locked. This, I sensed, only infuriated her miserable condition even more.

"Open the got-damned door, Blu…"

There was that proverbial Barker family respect and adoration I'd so grittingly come to Love. The crude ruthlessness of her unprovoked outburst held me a brief second in shock. Trinity had been the one hole card among the entire slew of debilitating, using, self-centered party of Barker females whom I'd previously held out the most hope for.

Generally soft-spoken and sweet, her enjoyable countenance had always been a contrasting pleasure to those of her raspy voiced Momma, her swindling aunties, or her cut-throat cousins. As long as the two of us had known each other, she'd always been a pleasure be around. Her smile and her physical nature at best was an easy combination to endure. Always playful, her's was an innocent streak of gut-wrenching laughter that could always be counted on to take even the most biting sting out of the most serious of situations.

A pinging service of a relentless deja-vu' quickly overcame me. Taking the feelings seriously, I steeled myself, knowingly waiting for *tha'-other-shoe-ta' drop.*

"Come on Blu, open the door, man…"

"Hole-on, girl. Dayummm…"

I reached back and politely pushed a portion of the massing pile of what I still considered, junk outta' her way, and I released the latch on the top of the door so she would be able to make her way in.

"What tha' hell's eatin' you, Miss—T?"

She stared off up and out the window, as if seeking to find the answer to my question in the brightly lit canopy of the blue-covered heavens. I chose to leave her alone a moment. Let her gather her thoughts in peace. Who knew what had happened in that store to cause her to return to the car so obviously upset?

It felt like a long, pulsating stretch of silent moments before she finally set up and perched herself between the seats behind me to finally begin to talk to me. It was then that she did something she had never ever done before.

She touched me.

Running the smooth softness of her slender palm up the back of my neck, she cocked her head sweetly to an angle at one side and she began.

"You know, Blu, you're a great guy."

A bit confused and extremely dazed as I sat there willing the beginnings of a familiar stirring beginning to rile up in my lower pelvic area to *STOP IT!...AND BEHAVE YOURSELF-FOOL!*

She went on.

"...It's that damned gurl-frien' o' yours..."

I remained stoically turned around, facing the front of the ride. The fully uncomfortable rhythmic medley of the sweetness of her breath on the back and sides of my neck as she talked was beginning to do strange things to me up there in the forward compartment.

I stayed silent.

"I never seen a more selfish, self-centered woman, in all my days, Blu. I mean, you've given that gurl' everything. Taken her places and provided her opportunities to do things she never woulda' had she hooked up wif' one o' them scrubby Nicca's she so fond of talkin' about."

She shook her head pensively for a second. With me watching her intently, using the opaque presentation playing out before me in the car's rear-view mirror.

She'd stopped talking for a brief moment. I looked down to take in the dial of my watch. Man! Had we really been there, in that K-Mart parking lot for going on—three dogg-gone hours?

"See, that's part of what I'm talkin' bout', Blu. That gurl' knows you sittin' out here wif' all this shit you done went and bought fo' dat' baby, and she's in there, wif' er' ole' dumb, stupid, pregnant azz—tryin' on lingerie she can't even fit."

She had me dumbfounded, extremely confused. I sat wondering suddenly, *was I just not getting the full brunt of the immensity of the thing that she really wanted to be talking to me about? Cause' somehow, I could sense and I knew that she really wanted to say something else. Why would Tai's stupefying propensity for taking all of our time for day-dreaming about the day when she would once again feel desirable and sexy with her figure restored, following the birth of our baby, cause so much strife and grief for her cousin, who was supposed to've been her road dog and ace-boom-coon?*

Perhaps I was the one who was stupid and blind, the one, even at twenty-four, who was most immature and pliable among the three of us.

She edged even closer to me. All former thoughts of sexual excitement I had so wickedly conjured up within myself toward this young woman's supposed advances faded quickly, like traveling wisps of lightly pursed puffs of transparent smoke.

She hit me with an inviting burst of her very familiar laughter just then. Except, now, I'd felt I was able to catch a small bit of the more incredulous irony in what for her, was rapidly developing to be a stricken bout with soul-torn mirth, rather than the fulfilling splendor of pleasurable release her hilarity had usually held out for her.

She was suddenly up-in-my-face...Man!

She screamed at me. Both hands held tightly about the sides of her pretty head, as if she knew for sure, if she didn't get this off her chest right now, if she let go, for any reason, her cranium would surely implode or burst open and explode with the stress of all she had on her mind right then for the tellin'.

"Blu...Wake up, damnit!" She implored me, almost seeming to beg me to see clearly a point she had yet to make.

She'd caught my attention though. It was then, that I'd been the first among the two of us, to spot Tai's bloated figure peek itself around the corner of the outside comforts of the air-conditioned store. Her tiny frame drew itself up to peer around, with her hand atop her head, shading her eyes from the sun, looking for us, as she tried to remember where we'd parked the car hours before.

The sheer emotion and immensity of the thing Trinity was trying to bear her soul about to me was on its way, I knew, to being stifled, caught up inside her chest and memory forever, if I didn't help her get it out that second. I tried to coax her along with her telling.

Turning my upper torso around to face her more squarely, I engaged her in all seriousness of nature.

"—T, what you tryin' ta' tell me? Is it Tai, tha' baby...Something wrong? Spit it out gurl' cause there she comes."

Pain-stricken and suddenly more panicked than I'd ever witnessed this extremely calm and confident young woman be, she all but blurted out her every feeling concerning Tai's and my relationship—in a nutshell.

"Tai's my gurl' n' all, Blu. We cousins till tha' day we die. But you too good a man to not know this—all the stuff you done did to bring that gurl's life up and outta' where she was shore n' nuff headed before she met you. She's crazy ta' do tha' things ta' you she does. I hate the way Momma n' em' treat and ruin all you good swabbies." She was then back to shaking her head with that same contemplative nature she had enacted before.

"See, that's why I never called myself tryin' ta' date none of you. Didn't want ta' even have all y'all round' wif' all of that. Want a real relationship, wif' juss one Nicca'; even if it gotta' be wif' a thug in da' hood. Not one where all's I'm in it for is tha' money. Hell, most of y'all ain't even got much money anywayz ta' speak of, just a steady paycheck of itty bitty amounts is all y'all got."

We could both see Tai's recognition of the car about three rows of empty, parked vehicles in front of us. I peered at—T through the mirror, silently willing her to go ahead and continue the crux and get to the point of what it was she was so painfully trying to offer up previously.

Drawing her hand up over her mouth, as if frightened that the enormity of her words could've been heard by Tai's approaching form, perhaps a hundred feet away, she let it all flow out rather quickly then.

"Why you make me do this, Blu? Damnit, dude...That baby's not yours. Neva' was...and now, I'm certain, never will be. She been treatin' you so bad, baby. I just couldn't stand by watchin' it, or you, no more. Using you up like a broke-dick mark...Playin' you for a sucka' man...I know it.

Aks'er' ta' see what's in tha' bag when she come ova' here. How much you bet it's some crazy-azz maternity lingerie and a cheesy-azzed pick and a razor she done bought wit' yo' money, for tha' Nicca', Tyree."

"She make me sick…"

I could make out the distinct tumble of a slowly flooding swell of Love-filled tears begin to stream from their dutiful wells in her eyes through my view of her sulking figure in the back. I sat gazing at her, for what seemed a long while, with heart-felt compassion, I looked at this grown woman sitting in my back seat through the rear-view mirror—for perhaps, the first time.

As Tai made her way to the car, I stole a glance back at Trinity. I'd jumped up from my seat and scanted around to the passenger side of the vehicle (force of gentlemanly habit) and took her bags, while I got the door for her as she shuffled and slid the girth'd immensity of her still pregnant but tiny waist line glibly into the car.

She held her head in her lap, away from my view. Apparently she was attempting to reconcile herself after having so strongly and openly betrayed her cousin. Or maybe she was just trying to re-gain control of herself. I guessed, before presenting herself once again before her soon-to-be-ever-so slighted victim.

My only thoughts during the short ride home were ones of hurt, pain, grief, and outrage…I fumed all over, re-hashing and re-taking in everything she had spoken of to me when it had only been the two of us in the car together.

But, I gave away nothing. I kept a typhoon of un-satiated emotion and just-deserving, passionate fury pent up like a jilted viper inside of me.

Tyree…?

I knew that Nicca'. He was a small fry hustla', complete with early model Cadillac, jacked up on switches, a blue bandanna, accompanied by a gun, a rep, some said in the streets he'd stolen, from his brother, who was doing a bid in San Quentin, for a break in, robbery, and murder of a rival gang crib he'd had nothing to do with. It had been Tyree's masterminding of a simplistic plan that had taken almost a full set of Pyroo men, women and children out that night up in Skyline. Himself too scared to come outta' hiding, he punked hard and settled in to the realization that his brother (at 27, who had all but cleaned up his act and had gotten a job, while taking steps which would be the beginning of his distancing himself from the activities of his former gang) would face the rap, staunchly, with a closed mouth and an even harder resolve than he knew himself internally capable of producing.—Plus, he was reputed to have a verifiable harem of women, and toddler babies in barely kept up stables all over town that all seemed to shamefully support his lies and half-truths he doled out to them in compliance with bringing the entire charade he chose for a life to a chilling, bone-bending falsetto.

Who was I?

What did I have?

...Only a promise to try and do my best for both her and what I thought had been, our baby. A willingness to work, instead of fight—to-the-death, for no extreme, a commitment, to ensure that our growing soon-to-be-family had every lavish amenity the world could invariably offer and afford. I had a budding, albeit misplaced, sure-enough growing Love and hard-earned respect of, and for, *her*.

I had a thing I held firmly in hand, for all of us.

I had...A future.

But, she didn't want none o' dat'.

I drove home (wishing I was, at that moment, alone) in silence. So self-centered and ill-conceived of personal meanderings she was, that she barely noticed the fact I hadn't uttered one word to her during the lengthened stretch of travel back to her house, which fastly become, for the two of us, our final—*TOGETHER* trip.

It was hard for me to get over the immense anger I had for myself.

I was madder at me than I was truly—at her.

I felt more stupid than I had for a long while...

Cause' I'd from the start—picked tha' wrong cousin.

I had a grip of shit at her Mom's house. But, all's I did, upon returning there from that fate-filled outing, was make excuses; that I had to go pick up the girls from some party or outing the two of them had been on, without me (Go Figure)...

And, I left all of that shit behind, and I did go get my babies, from Uncle Larry's

.... And the three of us went home together—still an almost united, nuclear family...

I didn't call or go around Tai, her Mother, or any member of her family for a good while. It was clear into July before any one of them again heard the feinted zeal of my inviting voice of friendship again. All she kept wanting to know, was, "Why'd you dog me...? Why you leave me here to fend for me and my baby—all by ourself?"

I offered her no answer. See, still, I didn't want to do anything to hurt her. I wished her no harm, no ill-respect. All I wanted for that poor urchin (who, number one; was too young to be pregnant and alone, at eighteen, out here in the world doing things she'd barely be able to contend with, even when she was more mature, and thereby, a more fully-grown woman) was the best.

But, I was no longer the one who was capable of giving it to her. I left her feeling zero responsibility, Nothing in the way of husbandly emotion, or ultimate culpability for whatever happened to her and *her* baby after that...forever.

GOD is good...All the time

And—All the time...GOD is good.

Chapter Nine
WAR

It's amazing *all the time* how GOD works. I can and always do say, that there's never been a prayer HE hasn't answered for me and believe it or not; ninety-nine out of a hundred times, HE has always granted my ever wish and especially my every wanting need. HE has steered and directed my life in such a way, as if his vision and plan for my soul is so incorruptibly sound and overwhelmingly complete, that I place total faith and belief in his at times, whispering direction.

The week following my departure away from Tai was life changing, not only for her and her entire family, but as well, for me and mine. Frustrated and a bit aloof at work, with so many rapid changes taking place over the course of a mere weekend, I found it increasingly hard to focus or concentrate as I should have.

It was May 21st, 1990. I was at the gun school and in between podium hours (the time when you were actually on platform, instructing classes) and languishing, attempting with minimal clarity to construct an assembly of more positive thoughts other than those shaping and all-but-plaguing the events of my immediate past. I was all but snoozing at my desk in our gigantic, open-bay office, when a particularly jovial Senior Chief Petty Officer, Baca, strode in and announced in a deep, bellowing voice, "Attention in the carroll…Attention in the carroll, I just got off the phone with the detailer. He's searching for a First Class Petty Officer to go to sea up near the bay area. Now…I don't have all of the particulars, but that person selected, would be slated to fill a billet aboard ship, where he'd be the leading Fire Control technician aboard."

When most people hear the term *Fire Control Technician*, they generally conjure up images of groups or individuals whose task it was to control and put out raging blazes. Not so when categorized in the terms of United States Navy speak. A Fire Controlman or Fire Control Technician in the United States Navy is a sailor, generally of more than above-average intellect and state-of-the-art acumen, with a general I.Q. just below that of today's practicing Nuclear Power Technicians, and some I've known, were smarter (A particular shipmate comes to mind, John Hogemeir, who was quite possibly the most extremely intelligent guy I've ever known). The available thought levels and visceral power encased inside the minds and brains of these nautical mental-warriors sometimes proved to be even diabolically frightening.

Fighting fires could not be farther away from the at times cryptic, TOP-SECRET job descriptions attached to assignments I've held during more than twenty-two years as a qualified Fire Controlmen in my selfless dedication to the country's Naval service. Instead of squelching and extinguishing blazes, in a way, I guess you could say, if done correctly, the job of even today's Naval Fire Controlman, is to initiate havoc, start fires, and rain death upon an unassuming enemy, as we held the capacity, contained the hardware, and were prima-donnas in our goals of presenting the enemy our capabilities of striking both offensively and defensively in postures whereby the results of our efforts were stridently evident, straight outta' the heavens, anywhere in the world, almost silently, at first, from afar.

If you recall the opening moments of the attack on Baghdad in January, 2003; a veritable high-tech fusion of all-out terror, one developed and successfully promoted by a Naval intellectual, of the day, Harlan Ullman, and which our President, the honorable G.W. Bush labeled as '*SHOCK & AWE*', the overly impressive depictions of streaming misery brought by as many as 800 cruise missiles as they bore down on the city, were the perfected results of quite possibly twenty-four to forty-eight hours of meticulous peeking, checking, re-verification of both coordinates and settings, accompanied by the diligent tweaking of a multitude of Fire Control radars, computers, guns and launching systems, all operated, guided, directed and maintained, without the luxury of a restful night's sleep before the *pulling of the pickle*, by the Navy's Fire Controlmen aboard ships—some as far away as a hundred miles from the susceptible recipients which were to be their intended targets.

I was a Fire Controlman.

It all stemmed from that single wager, made by my Mother's second husband, Garvin, and I, when I was sixteen, almost seventeen, twenty-two years before as I was just out of high school.

I played the Senior Chief's proposition over inside my head. *It wasn't such a bad idea at all-at first thought. After all, even though I'd been exonerated of the charges brought by "NETTIE" previously, and had been made the command's Sailor of the Year, a gross stigma of rotting scandal still loomed over me, like a plague of pending doom at every crevice of my teaching existence while still at the gun school.*

In the eyes of my subordinates and of my superiors, in passing, I was a topic which generally went: *"There goes the kid who had those horrendous charges against him and beat the rap.*

Did you even know he was the command's Sailor of the Year?"

Through the Senior Chief's words, I'd envisioned a possible, face-saving avenue in which I'd perhaps be able to re-claim and re-build my since—ruptured professional and personal dignity, as well as afford myself an opportunity of reaching for somewhat of a fresh and new start for both me and my tiny family.

After two seconds thought, I jumped at the chance to terminate my assignment of shore duty and go back to sea. All of this came to play during a time in which the imminence of hostilities brewing among the factions of the United States, Al Qaeda, The Taliban, Afghanistan and Iraq was all but established and fast approaching a point of boiling over.

War, of course, is always a double-edged horror. In its wake of dead men, women and children, its steadying flood of flag-draped caskets flown home, always in the still of night and into secret locations, lay for some, the reality of eventual prosperity.

...And I could see it coming from afar.

War, for me meant the same as it does for any man. The possibilities of death and of dying always loomed near. Yet still, for some reason, we were ingrained with the practice and training of being able to pursue combative goals while garnering the fortunes of talent to stupendously push such thoughts of demise out of sight and behind us.

Everything we did, as Fire Controlmen, appeared to have the vaulted touch of gold and we did our best to ensure that the particular tragedy of loss, grief, anguish and mayhem befell instead our enemies who leered at us, in fear, between the cross-hairs of our sights instead of upon ourselves.

Once aboard ship, and at war, I would finally be able to showcase those talents and bring the full brunt of my training to bear. Success in battle brought with it recognition. Recognition following battle fostered praise and accolades.

Praise, accompanied with that heightened level of accolade, brought promotion.

Without a second's breath of hesitation, I was on my way.

I strode over to the area inside the carroll inhabited by the boisterous, town-crying Senior Chief. After respectfully gaining his attention, and after waiting for his recognition of my presence and eventual invitation for me to pull up a chair and take a seat, I waited, for him to start the conversation.

"What's on yer' mind, sailor?"

Prancing butterflies of nervous chatter danced ferociously inside the unsure annals of queasiness inside the caverns of my stomach's lair. I wasn't quite certain what it was I was getting myself into. I was equally as unsure of whether I was in fact the man to answer such a call. Everything about the decision I'd already made, to step forward and heed the harkening of war, screamed at me—that I was in some way making a heaping and quite costly, indecisive mistake.

...But I pushed forward.

"Ugghh, Senior...I, ughhh, wanted to talk with you regarding the detailer's request for a volunteer to go to sea up in the bay area."

All the while I'd been there, standing before him, waiting for his recognition, he'd continued to busy himself, shuffling through papers, viewing reports, and filling, drinking, then re-filling his coffee cup, barely paying the fact that I was even there at all little attention. When the reasoning of my presence before him finally began to sink in and take effect, he hauled all of these antics to an abrupt and sudden halt, turned his massive, high-backed leather chair, swiveling about on its axis to face me.

And...He sat there, stoic and bear-like, staring at me with both barrels of his dark, piercing eyes boring into me intently.

Breaking the nervous silence, he countered with, "Well, what's it gonna' be?" He swiveled back around toward the completely disheveled area of his desk and quickly rifled through a shuffle of papers, coming up with the one he was so absorbedly searching for.

Making plans to speak.

He cut me off rudely. "Says here...The ship's the USS KISKA (AE-35) an ammo-gas hog—outta' Concord, California."

I swallowed morosely. A gas hog meant never-ending sea time. Ammo-ship, meant constant stationing and re-stationing, sailing hundreds, perhaps thousands of miles each steamy night, back and forth between the front and rear lines of combat zones lining both the North and Southern Arabian Gulfs.

"What about your girls? You got someone to care for them while you're gone?" He pulled his chair up closely toward me. He brought himself up to a position so close before me that I could smell the dank, staunchiness of his heated, coffee-encrusted breath as it assaulted my senses. I could see the peeking whiskers of areas he'd missed shaving that morning in the dark of the morning's fog at home.

And he exacerbated this with, "Cause' brother, I'm here to tell ya', once this shit jumps off, and you're out there in it...Ain't no turning back to heed the call of slippy diapers and what not...Once you're gone, you're goose is cooked.—You're ass-holes and elbows up to your neck, twenty-four-seven, in tha' shit. No turnin' back.

"My girls.?"

He was right.

What was I going to do about the girls?

Prior to deploying, all service personnel who are single parents, are required to indicate via a custodial care form, who they have delegated to provide care for their children in the event of their absence due to all-out war, which for us brought the utter reality of arduous and lengthy, extended deployments. Given the shade of World events at that time, there was a stark possibility of life-threatening hostilities in the military every where you turned.

He had me peeked, penned-up and closeted for a brief amount of minutes.

I stood there stupidly with my hands dangling uselessly by my sides.

As if dismissing my actions for shear hollow bravado, he shrugged a whimsical *hmmmph*…Screaming a quiet murmur my direction; as if to say, "*That's about what I thought—Family Boy!*" And he swiveled the girth of his fattening form back around and once more began to ignore me while reentering his former attendance toward attacking the remainder of what looked like a year's worth of work atop his desk.

I thought for a second, about to relinquish my former efforts and merely sidle back to my desk, defeated. But something inside wouldn't let me be.

"Uuuugh, excuse me, Senior."

Whirling back around, he displayed an *ALLRIGHTI'MPISSED NOW* annoyance at turning to still find me interrupting his untidy solace.

"You still here?" He echoed the thoughts spreading to widen and become his overall facial expression. "What is it I can do for you, Petty Officer Penn? No! You're not the one the detailer's looking for, all right!"

Capping this off, he stung at me further with, "If you must stand there stupidly, wanting to hear the words straight off my lips for yourself."

I was dumbfounded. What did he mean? I wasn't the one. After all, there wasn't a soul there in that carroll who knew the in's and out's of our particular weapon system with more in—depth detail than me. I could smell the burning stench of challenge creep its ugly head up to poke at the simmering embers of both ego and indecisiveness which held me there firmly in front of that man's desk.

He beat me to the punch of moving forward with, "Besides, you're the command's Sailor of the Year. No way the *ole'* man's gonna' send you off to war and not have a representative at the Admiral's luncheon table this time again next year."

Then I began to feel I had him. The sheer pettiness of the explanation used in his argument hinted to me the fact that his justification for refusing me a request to be counted in among those vying for the assignment loomed baseless. I even later found out, that I was the only member of about forty of my eligible contemporaries who'd even approached the Senior Chief about possibly taking him up on his proposition.

This peeved me to no end. I attributed the Senior Chief's ignorance and unwillingness to deal with me to an uninviting circumstance that I had frequently run across during the full spectrum of my stint in the Navy, a period extending twenty-two challenging years. It wasn't so much that he was being discriminatory against me, because I truly don't believe that was it.

What he was doing, instead, was underestimating me.

From the first second I'd stepped foot across the threshold at the Naval Training Center at San Diego, in March of 1983, I'd always felt my efforts to excel and be counted among the excellent to have been ignored, discounted, or made out to become invisible to those whom were the powers-that be at the time, and yes...and no...it was, I believe and I do not believe, all because of the color of my skin.

Naval society, up to that point, did not have a face-saving, firm grasp upon embracing the allure, and gigantic minds of intellectual, young American men of African descent, such as me, who'd come before them seeking the spoils of perhaps a better life. Yes, federal law had mandated inclusion for us, yet, acquiescence within the ranks was far slower in reaching accord with regulations on the inside of the lifelines which held a ship's crew in good health.

I believe it was more because of history and the ill-account of actions on the part of wicked deeds still held high by a great majority of American culture, that the American man of African descent was, in 1983, still watched more closely than his white counterparts, was still distrusted along the scale of advanced programs we were permitted entry to, and still pigeon-holed into menial labor jobs inside the force, simply because we'd been born with different colored skin, had received sub-standard educational opportunities in the haunts of big cities falling down around us, and held a past and a history of being held back and away from achievement for a period longer than four-hundred years.

But...

Because of all of that, we, as Americans of African descent had and still have an even loftier responsibility to this great nation, which was built, by those of our ancestors forced to come here, and whom had an exacting hand in its overall development from its inception.

Not because of Jim Crow, Not because of lynching, Not because a sweet little boy, just fourteen, was stomped and bludgeoned to death down in a place called Money, Mississippi, allegedly for whistling a cat-call at one of the perpetrators wives, Not because of unwed pregnancies, not because of illicit, illegal drug sales and abuse, not because of alcoholism or because of black-on-black crime, not because of the absence of millions of American Fathers of African descent in the home, not because of an unwillingness to reach out to grasp the sparse opportunities of achieving higher educational status which are still increasingly being opened up to us, not because of filfth-ladened, glass ceilings which held lessened chances for improved promotion, not because of sub-standard existences inside piss-filled hall ways of dusky, high-rise project apartments, not because of menthol cigarettes, not because of increased rates of cancer, not because of more-increasing rates of the contraction of AIDS among American youth between the ages of 14 and 24, and not because a documented one-fourth of the youth among all American men of African descent lay wasting away idly behind walls constructed by a system fearful of what they could possibly offer society, if rehabilitated correctly, is the stigma of under-achievement, accepted denigration along the fractured sidelines of the experience of our American society and of our American culture a wicked lie so many within that society ignorantly embrace as legacy.

...And this can be applied to both sides of the Black-White scales of American culture who still think along these lines.

Not because of the failures of a generation's generation past are we doomed to continue in the daunting cycle which threatens each day, with the telling and re-telling of news reports showcasing *our own* self hatred, and *our own* refusals to buy into, with faithful aplomb and vigilance, the omnipotent reality of available successes which still lie in wait for those of us who see freely, and are willing to step out and away from failure towards achievement, instead, to reach out and grasp the truths self-evident within the possibilities of embracing what is still a healthy American dream.

Chocolate chickens rely upon and steel themselves within the negativities of their's and their ancestor's pasts. They remain confined inside coffins of deceit and lasciviousness, thereby continuing the decaying structure of non-productive familial legacies. For those permitting the structure of their beliefs and actions to fall within this category of negativity, under-achievement, and spoil, empty cries syrup'd in baseless excuses are the only dividends which they persistently count on to compound exponentially toward a nothingness which feeds upon their individual strife continually.

Such baseless truths of nothingness is the root upon which a greater majority of America's society of citizens of African descent continue to cash welfare checks they haven't lifted a hand to work for, call for increasing numbers of newly proffered social programs pitching them rotting fish; instead of calling for and supporting the teaching of appropriate skills by which they could earn and save, and perhaps purchase a boat, some line and a jumbo pack of hooks to catch their own fortunes at the end of a day in which they've labored personally to reach for their own successful achievements.

That's a legacy worth passing down to your children.

The time is long past for excuses and blame, upon the *white man* and the system, for the plight of the Chocolate Chicken whose faceless pity numbers well into the millions among the culture within American society. A call for unity among the diverse customs making up America, and for finding a way, from the stoops of every house, from inside the busted elevators of every apartment tenement, from the vast graced-lands of every farm, for American people to begin to consider themselves first, AMERICAN, then Latino, of African descent, Indian, Chinese, Irish, Italian, Polish, German, etc.

The time for dissension among Americans toward Americans has played out its unsupportive welcome. Time to wrap up that sentiment and send it packing, like a foul-breathed cousin, who arrives every summer, unannounced yet forever present, and who refuses to pull his weight around the farm, and still shows up early at every meal setting, choosing first the choicest cuts of beef for himself.

The time for Americans of African descent to step forward from the halls of universities and colleges such as Spellman, Morehouse, and Howard, with plans for positive schemes encased in entrepreneurial networking collages spilling forward from the veins of their freshly sharpened minds to support and uplift one another, so that every American can begin to build both a broadening spiritual existence first, which is easily supported by a healthy financial contentment, next.

The time for greater America to begin to witness and see their own part in all of this clearly, for what it is as well, is of equally paramount importance. Should they continue to peer at the American of African descent with condescending denial, thereby fostering a continuation of the rejections of their own fore-father's generations after generations before, they succumb themselves, and the continued positive prosperity of the nation, to a medley of continued hit-and-miss accomplishments steeped in almost-thought-after achievements each individual culture holds the possibility of offering, when the spirit of truly invitational freedom sets in by the root and provides an avenue of goodwill and faith among the country's inhabitants—to live their lives together, whereby every citizen pulls their own weight, gives back their fair share, and once again begins to look out for the deserved welfare of others with a genuinely heartfelt sense of concern and care shrieking through them.

Never of a character to simply accept the failures of a former period within society, the Senior Chief's words only sparked a more endearing desire, instead of resentment and a sense of lacking self-worth in me. His refusal to reconsider my requests placed the two of us on a path toward contention when it came to the matter of the detailer's call for support aboard ship. Instead of outright bucking the system, I went back to my desk and fell into a deeply stouted mini-second of thought.

I played over all of the variables: my girls first, other plans I had made within the grind of the very near future, prior to that day, and also, I angled over how I was going to handle the invariable refusals of the Senior Chief, who could very well begin to make my existence at the gun school a living nightmare should he feel I've over stepped my bounds to cross him, even though he had so plainly registered his demanding declination of my request for consideration from the start.

The answer came easy to me. I owed the Senior nothing. In the way of proper military respect and courtesy toward him, my every action could be held up to stand nothing short of impeccable. My work habits, while on platform, were a proven selection of superior grades each time I had received critique from the Department of the Director of Training.

I was *Up-to-and-touching* as far as my military responsibilities as well. So, taking all of this in, I could ascertain only that the man's reasoning for denying my consideration for the bay area billet to be circumspect yet still, bordering along the lines of proving illogical.

So I did the next best thing.

Tossing all former thoughts of caution to the wind, and telling myself that it didn't matter if he made my life a living hell for the eternity I had left there, I went over his head.

Steeling away to a corner of the carroll which was at the time still uninhabited, I placed a call to the detailer on my own. Once connected, I informed him of my desire to accept the billet assignment aboard the KISKA. I relayed my command's reluctance to release me to make the transfer become a reality.

He instructed me to say nothing more to the command concerning the transfer.

"Are you certain you want this billet, Petty Officer, Penn?"

"Yes… Yes, Master Chief, I'm one-hundred percent certain."

"You're fully aware of what kind of arduous sea time you're looking at then? All right…You've got it, sailor…And don't worry about your command. This is a CNO (Chief of Naval Operations) priority fill-billet. Sailor of the Year be-damned—I can over-ride your command."

"Thank you, Master Chief."

"You'll receive confirmation of the orders via fax in…Ohhh…' I could almost see him lifting an arm up to take in the dial of his watch, 'About, fifteen minutes…"

"Roger that."

And, for me, life had changed at an instant once again.

Senior Chief Baca, hit the storm drain upon seeing orders for me to report to the Kiska come floating across his desk about an hour later.

Stopping by my own desk very briefly, with the papers in hand, he glared a glowing red of tenacious displeasure at me and he tossed them at me with an almost challenging, disrespectful vigor, without offering a single word. He then strode away, calling back over his shoulder to my carroll leader, another Chief Petty Officer, Joe Saldado in passing, "tell dirt-bag there, that he's gotta be bagged and tagged, ready for shipping out, no later than 16 July, with a port-O'call for Concord, no later than the seventeenth.

The seventeenth? That gave me zero time to prepare and ship what little amount of household goods I did have. Not to mention the ultra necessity of preparing two babies, four and two, for the rigors of a lengthy road trip across state.

I took the time then to get out of the building and went for a walk around the perimeter. In doing this, I was able to think clearly while pasting Senior's last vindictive shot across my bow (Not providing me an appropriate amount of travel, proceed time, and leave to correctly get my affairs in order before being required to report for duty) securely away in the garbage compartment of a mind merely dripping with positive thoughts of perpetual motion, instead of standing up to harp senselessly on the in-sensibilities of those more negative trivialities he was so aimlessly attempting to force upon me.

I placed another call to my detailer. This time around, I placed a demand upon him, instead of the other way around.

"Master Chief? I will require a full, thirty day leave period prior to deploying.... And how much travel and proceed are generally offered for going a distance of about eight hundred miles on the norm?"

"Leave and proceed granted, Petty Officer Penn. Travel is eighteen days, plus leave. I'll pen the changes in the ord-mod (modification of orders) immediately. Prepare to receive the changes within the hour. Welcome to the fight, shipmate, good-bye."

I hung up with a warm satisfactory feeling of having mastered the spiteful Senior Chief at his own game spreading over me. He would have taken a different road, had he realized that what he'd actually done that day was teach me a very valuable lesson; one which I would take on board and learn infinitely well to my telling advantage.

He taught me the vital importance of learning every facet of the in's and all of the particulars of the out's in a system bound profusely by regulations and rules; so that my increased level of successes—at bending the same—to an unverifiable point of almost breaking them, in support of my mission, was assured—no matter the obstacles.

Thank you, Senior Chief Baca...

I detached from the Fleet Training Center, Thirty-Second Street command on the date of the sixteenth of July, 1990. On the seventeenth, I'd already driven, with my girls in tow, the entire distance between the sunny shores of San Diego and the sweeping hills of a dusty, Concord, California.

Upon pulling up to the outskirts of Concord, I checked in to an available room at the local Holiday Inn for rest. I'd driven a full eight hours, almost non-stop. Me and the girls were plain beat from the rigors of the drive and as evening approached, our only goal, was to plop ourselves down on the twin beds the room provided, and sleep for-forever, if possible.

How many of you out there know that this was wholly an unrealistic endeavor? With two young babies all aglow in the lighted excitement of the trip, the looming uncertainties of the upcoming war pending, and still not knowing what I was going to do with my girls, come time for shipping out to deployment, it was a fighting displeasure of never gaining the comforts of fully falling asleep that I was faced with during our stay there as well.

About eight o' clock, P.M., I called out to order pizza for the three of us to pick at. With their little tummies full, my two sweet bunions finally drifted off for a few hours of comforting slumber. With one eye open, I tried to match their efforts but met little success trying.

When it felt as if I would finally meet my fatigue successfully, with sleep, something jarred me fully awake, causing me to bolt upright while feeling my way around the still fully unfamiliar bed.

There by my side to accompany me again, was that fear…

The very thing I'd felt I'd been able to overcome in my youthful days back in P.A.

I searched incessantly for a reason for its reappearance now in my life. I couldn't pinpoint its waking accomplice. Everything seemed so jumbled and thrown together at the time. An ark full of wavering possibilities matched by an entire stream of untamable variables all stood out looming over me threateningly without end.

It was times such as these when I found myself carefully giving in to whatever the dark held out of sight in store for me. I forced myself to remain calm. It was the only way, I was certain; that I'd be able to gain a grasp on whatever it was that had shaken me so devilishly. After peeking over at the two little cherubic forms sleeping soundly in the other bed beside me, I got up with something untouchable plaguing my mind. It was a hidden malady that I had the most trouble putting a finger on.

Just then, re-grouping and finally being able to lightly pull myself together, it came to me clearly hitting me like a ton of bricks.

…I had to find "NETTIE".

Looking at my watch, I saw that only two hours had passed since we'd first begun eating our pizza. This being the fact, for some reason, somehow, my body felt quietly rested. The single hour of power napping, along with my newly discovered realization of what I had to do reinvigorated me and sent me off on another live changing journey, this time, eight more hours away, up to the lush green hills of the state of Oregon.

I'd placed a call to Miss Carrie, "NETTIE's" mother.

Miss Carrie, for the entire time I'd known her, had always had one of those numbers you were totally incapable of forgetting. I'm not quite certain if it was because she was always a bastion in the darkened plunder which senselessly accompanied every storm—to everybody, or if just because the digits of her telephone number were simply easily remembered.

I was certain I would wake her. She had forever been an early riser. Her daily routine had her up before the crack of dawn, out of the house in her tiny, newer model compact car, only to pull up, just seconds later, at a bus stop, just a few blocks away, where she waited with co-workers, friends and strangers, to take the bus downtown to her job at the phone company.

But I couldn't care at the moment about waking her. For me, the entire past year of my life had appeared one storm after another. Miss Carrie was for me, at that moment, the only mainstay providing the knowledge necessary to make things right that had been wrong for so long in my life up to that point.

After exchanging polite niceties of me asking how she was doing, and her providing her usual, softly put phrase, "*Ohhh, Tollerable fa' Ole'-Folks Chile... Tollerable fa' old folks*," she inquired after the kids. I told her where we were, what it was I was doing and that both of them were sleeping soundly at that moment across from me. I asked her about the whereabouts of her daughter, my former wife, "NETTIE".

In her giggly, sweet way of putting things delicately she almost cooed at me Lovingly, with a worried chuckle... I held my breath; the anxiety of an expectant doom at what she had to say crept up inside to sweep over me.

"Child, now you know Maria done gone down to Eugene and checked herself in to one of those rehab clinics."

"No ma'am, I didn't know...

"You must sure have some good insurance for her to be able to just go on down and walk in to one of those joints, I'll tell you. Naaaw, she been down there going on a month or two. You know... I'm praying she really gets it together this time and maybe the two of you can sit down, with clear heads, and talk this thing out and maybe just make one more try at putting your family back together again."

I bid her good-bye before dialing the number she had given me for the rehabilitation clinic in Eugene.

I found in calling, that telephone visiting hours at the clinic were held strictly between the times of 1P.M. and 7P.M., Monday through Sunday. I would have to wait until the following morning to call and talk to "NETTIE".

Upon hanging up, all sorts of rapid fire ideas, plans and blundering woes attacked at me simultaneously. But the one thing sticking most prevalently in my mind, was the fact that "NET" had already been through two stints at an equal number of different rehab facilities, and neither of them had been able to garner a lasting relief for her wanting addictions while there before. Was the third time to be the charm? I held out a still optimistic concern for her. One steeped in care for her eventual prayer-filled recovery, and one encapsulated with an eventual clarity of mind which would present her, if even just for the sake of our girls, a capacity for maintaining a firmly held grasp upon something which would provide her a sense of lasting, self-respecting hope.

You know, it's been said that an addict has to hit rock bottom before they're finally able to place knickers on their own sense of nerve-bending denial. In only this way, can they once again take baby strides towards building simple barriers between themselves, their lives and their substances of choice, in order to find a way of once more becoming a viable cog in the wheel of a society that keeps right on moving without them if they never are able to conquer this before wasting away and taking that final wayward leap toward an untimely, unexpected death.

For "NETTIE", all of the signs of her reaching forward, instead of continuing her downward slide backward beamed resonantly out to me through the words her Mother had just relayed during our brief conversation. *SHE had taken the steps, on her own, to check herself in to a facility that would help her.*

And this time, something inside of me knew...She would do it—for good...

All the other times she'd been through the re-hab process, had always been for someone, or for something else. Never for herself; but for her job, which was about to begin random drug-testing, for her family, because she could sense a fading grasp upon the continuation of our lives together beginning to slip endlessly away.

But...Never...simply because she wanted to do something good—solely *FOR HERSELF!*

At first light the next morning, I placed another call to Eugene. I reached a receptionist at the front desk of the clinic. I was able to convince her that I was "NETTIE's" estranged husband, just preparing to ship out to a war everyone on earth knew was in the infancy stages of mobilization—and was surely on its way, bearing down on me and countless others like the peaking light of a freight train heard off at a distance, still out of sight, hidden by the fog.

The receptionist had a heart and put my call through to "NETTIE".

The person who reached out and answered that call was far from being the woman I'd left so long ago back in San Diego. A breath of freshly renewed vision could be heard to cap off a very familiar hello on the other end of the line.

"Hello, "NETTIE, how are you?"

An instant recognition shot out at me through the circuit in her instantly excited reply.

"Hunny? Iz-at' you?" She squealed with sudden elation.

I could almost see, if not certainly feel the wide beam of a brightly lit smile as it spread out to cover her high cheek bones and liven the almond shaped areas around her eyes upon fully recognizing that it was in fact me on the phone.

"Heeeeyy! What's going on, babe...How are my babies doing?"

"Ummm—They're doing just f..."

She cut me off quickly with, "Hey, listen, where you at—Cause' they're having a family week counseling session up here and I'd really think it would do you,' She stopped, catching her slip for a moment, 'do us...some good.

Can you make it?"

I smiled inwardly as well. That was one of the things that I Loved most (and on the flip-side, drove me so crazy) when it came to "NETTIE".

She'd always had a proclivity for stating and assuming that which is not clearly obvious. As if, just by saying it, she could somehow make it all exact, without a truly viable substance, when time came to play it all out before herself at a confusing stage of the present. But she'd lay it out there boy-o...That was for sure.

The more frustrating part about when she tended to do this to me came in my own weak efforts of still feeling the importance of being able to provide for and please her.

I had the hardest time, even then, telling that woman...*NO!*

"NET", we just drove eight hours to get here—All I was trying to do was catch up with you—ta' see how things were going for you, and to let the girls talk with you for a moment. I'm sure I can't..."

"Oh...O.K. It's all right. Just thought you'd enjoy the chance at cussing me out, in a safe atmosphere, for all of the nasty things I've done to you through my fucc'd-up addictive nature. If you change your mind, the sessions begin tomorrow at eight A.M. sharp. And she gave me the address. Before ending our conversation, she hit me again below the belt with...

-"Hunny, I just want to say that I'm sorry—For everything...I know you're a good man and I know I still am undeserving of all of the goodness you've brought into my life. Please take care of my babies, and maybe I'll see you guys soon, after I get my own shit figured out. I Love you, Blu, a-bu-bye."

She'd hung up. Damn her!

She hadn't even waited, to give me a chance to rapidly bring myself to a point of being able to process so many of the heart-felt feelings she'd thrown at me so suddenly before hanging up.

She'd simply edged the door open slightly, peeked her pretty head around the corner to make certain I was still there, and had rolled in her heart-bending grenade. Then, she reached back out, before I could catch her, and she *slammed* the door back shut securely, trapping me inside a vault of indecision edged only with the creeping fringes of an utter loneliness.

Don't you know, later that evening, once the sun drew down and the girls and I had finished dinner (They once again had demanded pizza) the three of us packed our sparse belongings, and we lit out on an eight hour trek, with Oregon and an idea of re-uniting them with their Mommy, our ultimate goal.

The drive just killed me. It pulled the final plug on my increasingly weary sense of fatigue. I made the distance to Portland first, in just under eight hours.

When we'd pulled up in front of Miss Carrie's house, both the girls, once informed that we were at Grandma's house, broke out in their own sweet little chants of, "*Mommy... Mommy... Mommy!*"

I told them Daddy had to go to a place where Mommy was after dropping them off to stay at Grandma's for the day... But that Mommy would be coming back to Grandma's very soon and that the three of them would probably all live together again while Daddy was away on the ship, at sea.

This seemed to appease them for a short while. Or had it?

The first words out of Britty's four-year old mouth upon greeting her Grandma at the door were, "Daddy's gonna' go get Mommy so's we all can go home to Saaan Dee Eghoo, Grandma!" She looked back at me seeking reinforcement of her words. I smiled at her.

"Ain't you, Daddy?"

Guess the kid didn't place much stock in my smile. She had to hear it straight from the horse's mouth. Cause' I'm certain her tiny mind believed that there was no way

Daddy's were capable of telling lies in the vaunted presence of someone as special and precious as Grandma.

"Yepper-Scupper, baby, Daddy's gonna' leave you two here now, with Grandma and Grand-Pa, while he goes to see Mommy, O.K.?

Ash waddled off toward the kitchen where she'd already spotted one of her favorite Aunties preparing to open up the refrigerator. In route, I heard her baby-talk murmur as she seemed to be reassuring herself with a two-year old swagger, "Mommy, at da' hos-pi-tuull. Mommy, at the hos..."

Looking up to the kind, all-knowing face of Miss Carrie staring back at me, Lovingly, nothing more could have broken my heart more deeply that second, than the full realization of the toll "NETT's" and my troubles together had taken on our two, very young and impressionable children.

My wonderful Mother-in-Law, keenly sensing the stress of my frustration, shoo-shooed me out the door and I was back on the road—this time, my destination, Eugene Oregon.

Taking the I-5, back toward the South, I hopped onto the I-105 and arrived in Eugene about two hours after leaving Portland. After locating the clinic, I parked and made my way nervously through the front door into the reception area.

The receptionist paged someone who appeared up front briefly, then disappeared just as suddenly to run off and alert "NETTIE" that *HER HUSBAND* had finally arrived.

Upon seeing her walk toward me with that sexy-ass'd sashay I'd always been so crazy about, it was as If I was justly seeing her again, for the very first time. Her eyes had lost that yellow, jaundiced quiver I'd become so used to throughout the period I'd been with her during the experience of her addiction. That was instead replaced by the shining whites of clarity indicating sobriety. Her hair was a mess, albeit a pretty mess, and she'd put on some weight. Somebody in there had been feeding my baby well. She'd somehow, somewhere in there found the beginnings of having some hips.

She hugged me fiercely upon hauling up her steps in front of me. The passionate beginnings of tears matching each other began to roll silently down the sides of our faces as we were totally incapable of controlling the swelling ruptures of happily displayed outputs from either of our eyes.

We didn't say much to each other, at first.

Taking a quick step back to look me over more fully, she stepped forward once again and reached out a hand to punch me lightly in the arm, saying, "You told me that you weren't coming! But you're here now, and I'm so happy, hunny."

I answered her with an un-reassuring, "I'm happy too, baby…"

…And she whisked me off to begin the first of many co-dependency and reconciliatory forums the clinic had set up, more expressly for visiting family members, than for the patients.

I had the damned-est time staying awake through all of the sessions. I mean, Over the course of the previous seventy-two hours, I'd just spent more than sixteen of them, on the road, or Lovingly caring to this or that need of one or both of my girls.

Up to that point, I was still not one to fully place a heaping amount of trust in the satisfactory evidence of value such counseling and referral processes held for those who had full faith in them. But I went along for the ride, hoping only to become a ready citadel of support myself for this Lovely young woman, whom all I had to do was look at to tell, that I was still hopelessly, head-over-heels in Love with her.

Both inside and out of the forum classes, the two of us talked and communicated more closely than we ever had during the entire period of our former marriage. I think it was at that time, when we both began to feel, with a more mature recognition, that we actually liked being around one another when a healthy sense of productive thinking was the tune bearing laughter between us and which stood out so plainly in our every thought and word.

I became utterly confused internally. I'd made so many plans outside of the consideration for this woman that as I sat in the crowded forum rooms, silently contemplating the moves of my next step in life, yet, none of them appeared sound to me then, if they did not include her as part of the ultimate equation.

Following a full week's worth of sessions, the patients were then free to be discharged back into the bustle of a still-roving society, to once more try their hands at fending for themselves, hopefully, for most of them, this go-round' *drug-free*.

"NETTIE" had insisted on me dropping her off at a *recovery home* in Portland that her counselors had contracted with for her to stay at for a period quite possibly reaching out to extend into the next six months of her sober life.

"I'm doing this—For me," she continued to tell me.

"See...I figured out that I'm a shit Mom and a shit wife when I use. And I want to ride this trip to my sobriety forever, the right way—for once."

She wasn't getting any argument from me.

I was blown away into a solitary silence at the utter sincerity of her words.

She did get one thing outta' me though...

As we found ourselves walking through what could barely pass for downtown, Eugene, I hauled up abruptly and took her into my arms, and kissed her with, "Whattayasay, Kiddo? How's bout' you and me gettin' married?"

I didn't even have to ask her twice. Although she did have a grave amount of misgivings about re-entering a relationship so soon after successfully completing her stint of recovery, the girl had learned so much doing this thing for herself this time, that she amazed even me on a continual basis.

I explained to her that we could take it slowly. She could go ahead with her plans for maintaining a residency at the recovery home. Her Mother, through clandestine conversations held at the ends of each evening, when I'd called back to Portland from my hotel room in Eugene, to talk to the girls and *make my report*, had already agreed to keep the girls at her house, for however long as we needed, while I was off to meet my ship and "NETTIE" busied herself taking the necessary steps to becoming the best, sober Mommy and wife for all of us that she could possibly be.

But, and I told her so, I didn't want another day to pass in which she was not legally and soulfully my wife again.

We didn't even wait until we got back to Portland.

The date was July twenty-third, Nineteen ninety. Wearing jeans and sweat shirts, we sought out and found an anointed preacher, located far up in the Eugene hills...And he joined us in marriage, while his wife played the keyboard, and snapped Polaroid pictures as our witness.

And once again, the Penn family was a unit.

...And boy, were we ever so happy...

I spent a lot of time with "NETTIE" and her family, before finally deciding to leave our little car with her, and fly back to San Francisco. From there, I'd catch a cab down into Concord.

Following that period of reunification, I no longer held any misgivings about going off to war aboard a strange ship I'd never set foot on before. I trusted and held a strengthened faith in GOD.

After all, he'd stood by me and watched over me, often times carrying me forward when I felt I just couldn't muster up both the physical and mental strength to go on.

With my family secure, my girls safe, my woman on the right road, this time, toward what's proven to be fifteen years of recovery, I hadn't a care in the world.

GOD is good...

ALL THE TIME!

The Kiska (AE-35) turned out to be a veritable rust-bucket work-horse. She was more than twenty-five years old and had a single weapon system aboard. The MK15 Mod 1 Phalanx gattling—gun Close-In-Weapon System. It wasn't so much the gun which made the system reliable and worthy, but the anomaly of ancillary systems of radars and electronics which actually controlled and guided its twenty-millimeter bullets, streaking across open skies, as if walking themselves up invisible ladders at *blink-of-the-eye* speeds seeking out the blunders of low-flying enemy aircraft and sea-skimming missiles which tended to pose threatening postures to the ship when she crossed damning paths inside the lines of battle zones.

She carried enough ammunition, JP-5 fuel used to refuel choppers, and DFM (Diesel Fuel-Marine) to stock and supply an entire battle group, including two hungry aircraft carriers and their entire sorties of picket and support ships for weeks on end, without requiring replenishment for herself, which we also conducted, rather seamlessly, while out to sea.

I spent more time, at sea, on that ship, than I had during the entire span of my full career up to that point. She was docked or home-ported in a delta along an eerie ghost town, on the outskirts of the cities of Antioch, Pittsburgh and Concord, called Port Chicago.

Port Chicago held a sense of notoriety for those in the know who followed history. In 1944, two ammunition ships had blown their upper decks and every compartment below their waterlines—to smithereens, following a race of ammunition loading off of trains, upon which White Officers wagered on, while their crews of young, American men of African descent continually endangered themselves, forced by those same officers to take part in the antics resulting in tragedy for more than six hundred men, the remains of those onboard who not even the smallest slivers of pieces were ever found. The small city itself is still, to this day lined with stop signs and black-topped pave ways leading twisted direction to nowhere. There are no houses still left standing, no street lights, no stores and no life, outside of the crowding meanderings of a farm's amount of cows guarding the swaying sweeps of hills surrounding underground bunkers containing only GOD knows what kinds of lethal munitions.

But, we weren't there much. An ammunition ship's job was only conducted—at sea. And, from the time I checked aboard in July of the year, 2000, that's exactly what we did and exactly where we were at,—all the time…At sea.

It was aboard this ship, that I was finally promoted to the rank of E-7, thereby buffering me in to be counted among the prestigious ranks of being able to stand tall in calling myself a United States Navy, Chief Petty Officer. It was also while aboard there, that I'd proven the expertise of mastering my own responsibilities so voraciously, that the vessels Commanding Officer saw fit to strip duties away from his own officers aligning his wardroom, and stuck them heavily, on me.

At the time, in 1991, I was perhaps the only ship's Maintenance Officer and Welfare and Recreation Custodian that held the rank, as a Chief Petty Officer, and not that of a full-engaged, commissioned officer in the fleet. It was a promotion of my abilities, without actually having been risen to the official level of being made an officer.

Although extremely busy with my normal duties of holding down a billet as the Leading Chief Petty Officer for an entire Operations Department, and as Lead Fire Controlman until my boy, Big-Bad, Bob Painter, checked aboard, I Loved it.

It was also aboard the KISKA, that I finally got off my duff, fine-tuned my military record, and finally applied for an appointment seeking a commission as a Limited Duty Officer. This came to fruition as I'd finally reached my boiling point's end and had become fed up with my own Division Officer, a young lady of about twenty-five who had also come from the enlisted ranks prior to receiving her own appointment into the ship's wardroom.

Her name was Liza Medira. She was perhaps the most caring, gentle officer I'd ever witness cross a ship's brow requesting permission to come aboard. She was fast-talking, in Love with the ship's Electrical Officer, whom she lived with, on the sly, and who would use her, from time to time, as a veritable punching bag whenever he felt like it and it was just the two of tem alone together, at home—And... She was inept.

She carried around an ever-faithful clip board, everywhere she went onboard. Whatever was mentioned to her, at any given time, relating to any given subject, somehow wound up onto whatever tiny, sliver of open space still existed atop the paper of her clip board.... Needless to say, her filing system wasn't very supportive of a success-filled tour for Miss Liza Medira aboard the ship.

It wasn't long after taking over the duties of becoming her Operations Department Leading Chief Petty Officer, that I very soon made the career-saving self-determination, that Miss Medira would never be allowed the luxury or permitted the solace of failure as the Operations Department Division Officer—Not while on my watch.

If she failed, that meant I too, as her Chief, had failed her most—thereby instantly brandishing me—a failure as well,.

...And that was not about to happen.

So, in the way that only the Chief can engineer or correctly pull his Div-o aside and explain, she and I came to an understanding—One which, during my almost two years aboard, played out to prove highly beneficial to both of us.

Instead of attempting to immerse herself in the day's daily running of the Division, I *instructed* her, that she was to focus solely on gaining her Surface Warfare Officer Designation, and leave every facet of running the Division to me. She appeared a bit hesitant to relent and give in to what I was suggesting, at first. But, when she'd realized that I'd had a few of the more-cock-strong Boiler Tech brothas' *have a word* with her Electrical Officer boyfriend, down in a darkened area of *the pit* one day after watch, concerning the unhealthy nature of him putting his hands on her, in a violent way, she began to instantly begin to develop a solid trust in me.

Following this, things began to go more smoothly for Miss Medira, both at home, as well as aboard ship.

It was while we were stationed in Concord that "NETTIE" kept renewing her demand for another baby. I mean...I was all for practicing and all, but we'd just begun to become comfortable with the surplus of my Chief Petty Officer's salary, she was far from chasing the evil dragon of her cocaine addiction, the girls were adjusting well—things seemed great, and I thought we were happy.

But, she wasn't.

She hated being stuck in *sleepy little Concord.* She didn't work. Had very few friends whom were actually on her mental thought-level, and she generally had nothing positive and worthwhile, besides her immediate family and our tiny little apartment, to fawn over.

So, in April of 1992, my *BOOMER*, Avery Lee Penn Jr. was born.

I, of course, was on extended deployment at the time of his birth....(Nine months spent at sea, off the coast of Iraq in support of Desert Shield/Desert Storm)—Add in a lengthy stint of another six or seven months spent offloading the entire contents of the Naval Magazine located at Subic Bay (Republic of the Philippines)—cause' the government there had finally come to its wits end and was no longer sitting reticent while the great American machine pillaged, raped and robbed their country, so they were kicking our butts out) The KISKA had deployed at the start of the war. I distinctly recall, that the initiation of hostilities began on the 17th day of January, 1991. It was the day our big girl, Brittney, turned five years old. I didn't return home until well after more than nine months celebrated its final end.

I had requested and had received permission to fly home, from Hawaii, as the ship docked there, for a period of rest and relaxation, following cruise. All the while, immediately following the birth of my son, "NETTIE" and her sister Katie, who had flown to Concord, from Portland, to be by her side for the delivery, had only referred to him, as *the baby* during lengthy conversations filled with a happy longing for me to return home by the shortest route possible.

Twice, her OB/GYN had conducted the most up-to-date-ultrasounds on her, and had both times, declared us to be having a healthy—*BABY GIRL...*

So, when I spotted her preparing to make her way up the escalator, coming toward me, after I'd landed, still on cloud—9, anxious to meet my *new* daughter, whose name we'd both agreed would be Courtney, I was thrown into shock by what she presented me once reaching my station at the top. I first embraced her sweetly; planting the softest of soft kisses upon lips I'd yearned and waited for—for so very long.

She re-gathered herself while looking into my eyes strangely...At first. I couldn't quite put it—what it was that had her gazing back at me so eloquently, her stride all bubbly, with a searing stirring of cuckolding pride jumping off of her, shooting out towards me, screaming shrieks of highly-worn pride covering her stark-raving beauty in an instant.

Just as suddenly, she reached out in front of her and held out what looked like a sleeping little teddy-bear to me.

Without a word, I accepted it. Thinking she'd stopped and bought the thought-filled gift at a store in the airport mall or something. I almost dropped it, not being prepared for it to be so heavy once she'd thrust it into my arms and had already let go and prepared to step back.

Holding it, I looked down into my arms, then back up to her quickly saying, first, "Ohhh...You bought me a bear. Thank you, Baby."

Stuffed Teddy Bears had been her thing for a while. So my mind registered it ultra-special that she had taken the time to bring me now something that she'd held so personal and Loving for herself.

"No, silly…I didn't bring you a bear.

It's your son!"

Looking more closely, I reached into the get-up, peeled back the fluffy flaps surrounding the little bear's face, and low-and behold the fattest little, chocolate brown man I'd ever lain eyes on.

There lay my first and only son.

There was no more room in my heart for Love. No space on my tongue left for words. I was a babbling, crying *Bitch*—all the way through baggage claim and out to the car as well.

I couldn't drive. There was no way. The jaws of life couldn't have torn that boy from my arms for a very long while.

I think, not only was I happy and overjoyed to have *Boomer* there, finally, as my son. I think then, that every time I look at him…And even now, the total make-up of his every physical feature just jumps out at you as—*PERFECT.* He was the most cherubic, fat-fat little brown ball and I was having ever-increasing feelings of inadequacy holding him, staring down into the little dark orbs of his brightly lit eyes…Cause' it was truthfully hard for me to admit and believe, that I'd created him, that something so perfect had actually, in fact come from me.

But he had. And I was more than proud. Even more so, today.

Following his birth, things again became rocky for "NETTIE" and me. She began to make demands and chart threats, that something woefully wrong was going to jump off, *If I didn't get her outta' Concord, where she was going stir crazy, sitting at home pretending to care about the motley issues of so-called female friends*, most of them stay-at-home, bored, military wives like herself, *and if I didn't get her BACKTOSANDIEGO! By any means necessary…*

I explained to her that my tour on the KISKA was due to be up very shortly. I was in line for a split tour, which could have very well landed us—anywhere. I asked her to be patient. She agreed. Yet, with "NETTIE", the thing she agrees to today could very well draw up to becoming—the straw breaking over the camel's proverbial hump just one hour later—at the drop of a hat.

It didn't stick.

I told her that if I called my detailer and requested orders so out-of-the-blue, that he'd be sure to oblige my request, but that it certainly wouldn't be to any shore duty, or cushy job he'd been eyeing for himself, upon transfer, or was holding in wait for perhaps six long months for a career-long crony of his he knew to be gearing up to come along at the same time.

Nope…

My ass was headed right back to an arduous deployment ship, right back out to the long, lonely life of a sailor away-from-home at sea, on a vessel setting sail for the far east as soon as I stepped aboard.

She intoned ferociously, "I don't care. We'll handle it. Just get us back to San Diego."

And of course, I did.

We made the drive from Concord down to San Diego on a crisp, clear first day of November, 1993. We arrived at Uncle Larry's house in the wee hours of first light. And spent the next few frantic hours searching for a place suitable for a Chief and his family, in a decent neighborhood to live.

We settled on a brand new townhouse situated on the same street in the county's east corridor, El Cajon, as we'd lived in before, back when she and her sister, Pamela had packed up all our shit and left me standing, high-and-dry, amid illustrious schemes of child-abuse with the despicably false charges of molestation hanging wildly overhead threatening to bring about my ruin.

I didn't care. The street, Mollison, or the city, El Cajon, had never done me any harm. She had. And yet, she was still there, hanging around.

On the second of November, our household goods shipment arrived. Working way into the slowing hours of the night, she and I went about the task of ensuring that the movers had set up beds and broke as little as possible along their route.

Come the morning of the third of November, I, with little sleep, dawned my most sharply pressed, Twill, dress-whites, hauled my fully crammed sea bag over my shoulder to deposit it in the trunk of our car. And she and I made the twenty-five mile trip down to the base at Thirty-Second Street.

All the time during the drive it seemed we both kept coming up with reasons to be as nasty and deplorable as possible to one another. Not a caring word, Loving caress or heart-felt blurb was uttered between us.

Upon arriving at pier four where my new ship, USS LEAHY (CG-16) was berthed, "NETTIE" pulled the car up and swung around before the mighty gate between the pier, quay wall and the ship, and she just sat there, with the engine continuing to idle.

This pissed me off even further. She wasn't even going to pull up and park and send me off for GOD only knew how long, but for sure, at a minimum, of six long and lonely months (For me) with in the least, a proper good-bye.

I was again heartbroken. I got out of the car. She popped the trunk from inside. I retrieved my sea bag. I stood for a million minutes of thought riddled silence. I could see her reflection looking back at me, sharply encased with nothing more than a heartless, cold air of utter contempt.

I closed the hatch.

She spun out the tires of my car.

And drove off.

She and I didn't see each other again for more than six months.

I returned home in May of 2004.

While aboard the aircraft carrier, USS KITTY HAWK (CV-63) during my deployment, a crabby, little old man, waddled his way up to me one day in the ship's medical facility where I was receiving treatment for an injury (Most notably—a broken heart) I'd been medevacue'd over to the great bird farm to have catered to.

It took me a full period of confusion and disbelief before I was able to make out the importance of his visit. He was a sparse, little white man, all of about five-foot-two in height, but he carried himself with that Jimmy Carter assurance, aloof and all-wise, ever knowing...

He had three shining stars blaring in strict unison at his collar. His name, was P.J. Cody. He was the man overall in charge of the entire battle group of more than sixteen ships encompassing perhaps more than ten thousand souls of ready and willing combatants at his beckon-call.

...And, he was here, taking the time to travel down thirteen decks of ladders, to see me?

My immediate thought, after realizing the sheer magnitude of meeting *The Admiral* under such circumstances was: *Who'd died*?

I began piecing together an anomaly of possible solutions and answers to an entirely unanswerable question dancing about morosely, finding nothing more than stark-raving misery as it ricocheted loudly inside my head as he'd approached.

"You Chief Penn?" He waddled up next to me reaching warmly for my hand.

"Why... Yes, Yes, sir... Admiral. I'm Chief Penn."

I stole myself to silence, curious, but still all the while wishing this little old man with the sparse locks of hair he wore in a shamelessly useless comb-over would disappear and go away, falling back aimlessly into the horrors of the nightmares my life had become following first falling head over heels in Love with my "NETTIE".

His face broadened to explode as it broke out suddenly into the widest smile I'd seen on any member of the ship's crew since being flown there a few weeks before.

"Congratulations, sailor! I'm here to tell you that you've been selected to receive an appointment to a commission, Chief. How's that grab ya'?"

I stood stoned. The stunning proclivity of his announcement had sent clashing waves of ironic shades of both glee and sadness storming through me.

I had wanted that commission, almost more than any other professional milestone I could have achieved at that point in my career. But I knew as well, that the Navy wasn't putting up with providing commissions to personnel it deemed unworthy. And right about that time, with my home life in all but shambles with "NETTIE", I knew wholeheartedly, that my chances for admission to the vaulted ceiling of becoming a highly-paid, career manager among the profession was about at a rate of being counted slim to none.

With her by my side, and her penchant for immaturely acting up—I was more unworthy than the next guy they'd passed over to jump to my selection.

Chapter Ten
LOVE's-HATE

The day the Leahy made its return to home port in San Diego, "NETTIE" and the kids all greeted me on the pier with abundant happiness. It's always like that. The first few moments, minutes, days, if you're lucky, weeks, are filled with the quiet, stolen flashes of pure-D bliss at having returned safely home to a family that still held the same amount of fingers and toes as it had six months before prior to your leaving.

...And then, the stank-bite stench of *THAREALDEAL* creeps its ugly head to snap you back to reality, once the peel begins to toss back the actuality of the way your woman's been conducting herself and living during the entire period that you've been gone. At times, and for most sailors, it's all the same, the things you become faced with are items you wished that ho'd just as well kept to herself and never told you about at all—just to preserve, if even an unhealthy, untruthful saving of the union you both had together at your beginnings.

Other things were more plainly obvious. Evident items which didn't hold the luxury of being hidden away from your immediate view, like a boyfriend, Jodi, she's been maintaining on the side, just for selfish purposes of having her pussy surreptitiously waxed in your absence, or the fact that, because of her lascivious amounts of ripping and running, with her new gurl, Stephanie, she'd overlooked making payment on more than four-thousand dollars worth of bills, cause' she'd spent most of the money you'd been sending her on a faithful, monthly basis, on taking care instead of the needs of the latest *Daddy-Long-Dicker* she'd found herself caught up with.

And, just as my luck would have it, my "NETTIE" had seen fit to get herself caught up in both.

I was taken aback a brief moment when we returned from the Naval station the day I returned home, to find Stephanie at our house, waiting for "NETTIE" to return. I was hurt even more, when the two of them advised me ever-so-non-chalantly, that they'd made plans for that evening and were deeply enthroned in taking what was supposed to have been my time as soon as we'd bounced back up into the crib, in painting and dressing themselves up in complete whorish splendor to once again hit the skreets—in search of what?

It had only taken me only a moment to figure out the first part. She had ever-so-responsibly separated and stacked each of our unpaid bills expertly, each in their own piles of menacing neglect, along the outer edges of our dining table. I all but lost my breath, not to mention my salvation, as each letter, piece of paper, warning, and intimidation leapt out at me threateningly each time I passed by in route to our tiny kitchen.

The harsher and even more possibly deadlier blow came to me in reality, as a young man of about my age, size, height and professional stature appeared at my door one evening, as I was at home (baby sitting) while "NETTIE" and Stephanie were once again out and doing what dirt it was they did on their tirades.

Turns out the young man at my door was none other than "Dewayne "DOOKIE" Banks. He was a wild, loudly spoken Missouri boy, and he was Stephanie's husband. He bounced into my life with a whirlwind of boisterous veracity and full of contemptuous life. In the Navy, like myself, it turns out, he at the time actually knew and worked with Uncle Larry at COMOPTEVFORPAC, on North Island.

I didn't know what to make of him at first. He talked so loud and said so much, all seeming to run together, one sentence running undisturbed into the next, that it was really hard to keep up with his loosely changing flow. Up until that time, I'd never really been big on having very many male friends in my life. I still had trust issues plaguing me, reaching as far back as my own relationship with my brother, Toppa, in childhood, until even this day, so, from the very beginning, I was a little on edge at having him show up on my door step that night uninvited, and unannounced.

But, the one thing that stuck most in my mind when it came to "DOOKIE". The Nigga made sense. Although he appeared to be rambling, and not saying much—all the time, if you ever really took the time to sift through the things he was actually saying, he very rarely minced words, and for the most part, came straight to the point of being brutally honest in the tellings of strict truths he very eloquently put out there for whoever,—he didn't give a good-*got…dayum, to see.*

He greeted me, upon me opening the door, as if he'd known me and my family a lifetime instead of the very short period of appearing at the door just then and introducing himself, waiting for me to let him in.

"S.sss.up!" Glancing around with a chuckle lodged deeply in his voice, "Got yo' azz stuck up in ere' baby-sittin like a mua-fucca! Dayum…. Can't believe you let dem' scandalous hoes set you up like that bruh."

I stood there, shaken and shocked all at the same instant—a fever of incongruous fuming reaching up instantly to amount to a rapidly brewing mountain of finely boiled rage…inside of me.

Who the fucc' was this crack pot to come into my house and toss such grenades of utter division and extremity at how I was living my life at me?

Who the fuc…

Then, it hit me…

This brutha was stone-cold, dead to rights, spot-on…

"I had yo' azz pegged from the very first time Larry told me about you. Super—Star, Fire Controlman, precious nephew, with all the brains in the world, but not enough sense to know what's-fucc n' what,' He side stepped toward me mockingly suddenly, holding his sun glasses pimply in one hand, pinky up, the other hand gripping at his nuts, '…or, is it guts lacking here, brrr-u…tha?' Guts a brutha gets, instantly, that makes im' take charge when it's plainly obvious that his woman's creepin' out on him and dogging his whole family at the same time?"

At that, I didn't have anything to say.

While she was what?

"Why you let her do that to you, Homey? I tole' Steph, whenever she plans on steppin' out, get a muah-fucc'n' baby-sitter for Dina (their five—year old daughter) cause my azz is right behind her, out de' do', fo'-sho'."

…And then it began to dawn on me, after a full minute' of self decipheration, as I played back everything mentally, his fast throwing, slightly

Southern drawn articulations had thrown at me.

Why *had* I banished myself to a hermit's existence, at home, alone, after just returning from deployment to the Western Pacific, while she and her lust-filled cronies opened and closed more than the streets, spreading Love, cheer, and thighs—belonging to sumbody else, for only GOD knew who, along their ill-begotten ways?

After warming up to him and after being able to look at him now a whole lot differently, following our talk, he and I set up a plan to begin to do a little bit of creeping all our own the following day, which was a Saturday.

Of course, "NETTIE" and I had had an argument about the whole thing. She feigned misunderstanding of my reasons for wanting to step out in the exact way she herself had been doing for quite some time, I found out, the entire time I'd been gone.

It was while "DOOKIE" and I were inside one of our favorite haunts (The VFW on Forty-Third Street) that I first met a fine, young lady, named Anna.

During our initial conversation, she had noticed my wedding ring and had put me on the spot in asking about it. I came out cleanly and told her that I was married. "...Thinking bout' getting' out of it. Don't know..." Was how I put it at the time.

She asked me, "Got a picture of your wife? Cause' you look way too familiar to me for us to be meeting for the first time."

I told her I did and produced a wallet sized snap shot from my back pocket for her to take in.

Upon looking at it, her breath became caught up and she flung the back of her hand up to cover her mouth as she reached for her glass atop the counter of the bar to take a long swig of whatever poison was her pleasure at that moment in reaction to the images on the portrait I'd shown her.

Laughing almost sadly, she then said, "I know your wife."

Naaawww...Couldn't be. The world was just too big a place for that to be happening to me right there and then, not now...

Registering my confusion, she brought me up to date slightly with, "I work with her." Then she took another long pull on her glass and followed that up with, "Plus,' shaking her head now, from side to side with an incredulous disbelief mounting, "She's been sleeping with my ex-old-man, D.J. for the last six months. I'll bet you know her gurl too, Stephanie. She's bangin' a good friend of ours, his best friend, Jada, too. One big happy cluster fuck of friends." I could see her evident amount of disgust and contempt she felt for the unhappy four-some of ex-hubby, friend, and their two conquests as she sat on that bar stool and fed me a dangerous brew of trickery that my Lovely young wife had poured out upon me unknowingly, once again.

"DOOKIE" had been there the whole time, over one of my shoulders, glibly taking it all in as well.

When she'd finished the telling of how the two of them had gotten married and how her parents, as a wedding gift to them both, had bought them matching corvettes, his black, hers red, she intimated that she just couldn't put up with his maltreatment and whoring around any longer, so she had cut his ass loose—on the quick.

She even went so far as to leave the club, go outside to her own wedding present and return with a picture of a beautiful young lady, lying seductively atop the hood of a crisply washed and waxed, black corvette, the sweeping flow of her healthy breast threatening at any moment to flow out and off the picture to push at you seemingly if held at an angle-just the right way.

She handed it to me.

"Here, you can keep it. One of my kids brought it home one day after visiting with their father. I didn't know what I was gonna' do with it... Until now..."

She looked at me sweetly, her expression one now of far-off care and pity amidst a mixture of, was it... Satisfaction?

"Ain't GOD funny bout' how he handles his business so fast and man-like?"

I just stood there reeling. Looking down to the picture again, I could barely make out a second image I hadn't registered before, off to the side of the vehicle.

That must have been her ex.

The other... was "NETTIE".

I stood there in front of this woman, floored—in total, helpless shock. The sudden urge to scream a crying bellow of pain and pent-up anguish leapt from inside my once more tortured mind, threatening with each shortened breath, to pounce from my body without the self-saving possibility of a covering restraint.

My thoughts raged on, after leaving the club. "DOOKIE" and I had agreed, upon taking receipt of such information, that that was about all the fun both he and I both could stand for one evening.

On the way home, he and I went over the facts plainly.

"Well, my Brutha', ya' gotta look at it like this, I know what you're thinking...How could she do this to me? Ain't I right?"

He was dead-on. Hell! Of course he was right. After all of the endless amounts of shit I had withstood and had put up with already, for her azz.

"Yeah, Nicca', I know I'm right. But, like I said before, and you gone go and make me say it once-ta'-gain', you can't fault yo' woman—for doin' the same exact thing you tryin' ta' do, when you out here messin'-roun'-n' she ain't no-where's in sight, n' you runnin' da' skreets."

His words caught me off-guard momentarily.

"I wasn't out trying to do nothing with nobody," I shot back, my feelings still wavering and unsure about what it was I was saying."

He drove on, toward home, at first, in silence, giving his yet unspoken words time to marinate inside himself before responding.

Then, as if, recess was over—for good, he started into me with just the slightest bit of condescending humor. "You certain?"

He looked over at me out the side of his face, shifting the ever present cool-guy tooth-pick around in his mouth, from side to side.

"You mean to try and sit yo'-lyin' azz right there in my car n' tell me, that if that ho, what's er'name, hadn't burst yo' bubble with this, *Ohhh...Gotta-tell-it* news, and had invited yo' azz out to da' parking lot behind tha' club to suck yo' dick,—*You wouldn-a' gone?"*

"Hell-No! I wouldn't have."

He went to great lengths to bulge out his already bulbous eyes at me, while shaking his head slowly, from side to side and perking his seemingly overgrown lips to peer at me grossly from one side. And he just remained there looking at me incredulously... Yet, he stayed silent.

As we were about to creep up to my house and he was drawing his ride to a glide preparing to let me out, he peered at me deeply, after catching my hand in a vice-like grip, following our *dap* good-bye, and he held me in his grasp a moment longer than he needed.

"Just remember, Ba-ruth—aaa! Don't judge too harshly for that which you yourself are prone to mighta'-coulda'-shoulda' done..."

And he put his ride into gear and began to slip slowly away, at first. Then, as if thinking better of it, he threw his closely cropped head out the side of one window, let out his infamous "*A-PHI*" shriek, then yelled back loudly, holding the break with one foot, the other toying childishly with the gas as he did his best to build up to a tire-screeching crescendo without causing his drunk-azz to screech careening head first through the windshield, right before slamming into one of my neighbor's vehicles parked nearby (just like "DOOKIE"—at two-o'clock in the morning, just outside military housing) he sped off with a boisterous call over his laughing shoulder,...

"You a lyin' mua-fucca!"

And off he went. Home to his own cheating spouse, whom he didn't really seem to hold all too accountable.

Me? Being that I'm a reality based, *HOME-RUN or STRIKE OUT* kinda' man.

Just couldn't bring myself to aimlessly rationalize it all away as he had.

"NETTIE" swore up and down, Claimed she was ready to put it all on-a-stack o' Bibles, that I was crazy and that I'd gone out, gotten drunk, and was crazy as a bessy-bug, done made all that shit up when I confronted her the very next day.

...Until I broke her down finally by blasting on her in an all-too-righteously perfected prose and I showed her *her* picture atop another man's ride.

There wasn't anything more that she could lie about in this case. All of the pieces fit far too succinctly together for her to even attempt to wiggle her way out of this one.

I didn't want to *roll her under-the-*bus completely, because, stupidly, no matter the infraction, I still wanted to keep my wife. I had learned a very valuable lesson from my dealings with my former cheating wife, Kamm. In that union, I still feel that I was way too quick to toss her and the marriage out with the next day's garbage after realizing she'd become way too easily dickmatized by the guile of her SMOOV-TALKIN' *pimp* daddy.

Given the opportunity for growth and a chance at being able to buy into an increasing maturity, I am certain, like with "NETTIE", that no matter the cause or breach of matrimonial contract, Kamm and I would still be man and wife to this day.

So, instead of discounting the value of what she and I both felt remained in what was left of our relationship, I laid down a strict set of conditions for her, if the two of us were going to continue in our extremely dysfunctional marriage.

One, she had to fully renounce her dependency on whatever held her bound to the iniquities of things she held dear in her relationship with the nefarious Stephanie. I mean, she had to drop that shit like a hot rock, never see her, call her, never talk to that hoe again, for as long as she wished to remain married to me. That's right...I placed most of the blame for both their incorrigible efforts squarely on the head of her new-found, adulterous friend, DOOKIE's so-called wife, Stephanie.

Heck, we'd never had these infidelity issues before, prior to her hooking up with that tramp. All's we had to deal with back then, was crack cocaine and her staying gone perhaps three or four nights out of seven during a normal week.

Now that shit was manageable...Let me tell you.

Two, she had to get a job and begin to make a way of paying off all of the bills she'd permitted to lapse during my just completed deployment. She and Stephanie both had found that they were unable to hold down jobs which came with completely understandable supervision at the management level. They were hard pressed to locate a place where their bosses overlooked them draggin'-azz' into their offices, late, hung-over, disheveled, still plainly outfitted in their best, Sunday night party clothes and reeking of souring remnants of Long-Island Ice-T's, and Cosmos' their acerbic gasps gave way to with every breath—So both had gotten fired. And although they were no longer bringing in substantial incomes with which to make a contribution to their households and to fuel their squalid endeavors, they still continued spending, placing both "DOOKIE" and me in the veritable *POOR-HOUSE* for months and months to come as we both took our financial and marital lumps solemnly, without discussion in trying, the best ways we knew how—by hook or by crook, to engineer ways of catching up.

I think, at the time, embarrassingly, that I was perhaps the only Navy Chief Petty Officer, who held the chance of running into one of his subordinates on a nightly basis, as I ran up to their doorways, delivering pizzas, for Pizza Hut, each day after work.

I know I was one of the very few who had a credit rating below that of a homeless stumble-bum. With all of the delinquent and late bills we had, due to her fiscal negligence, it was all I could do to put at least the smallest dent in the overall propensity for failure I found myself facing.

Third, she had to devote herself to placing her relationships with all other men, outside of myself, forever on the back burner of her personal, yet unrealized fantasies, in order to save our besieged relationship. She had to say good-bye to all of those things she was valuing misguidedly, and which were successfully threatening to sink our struggling family.

And for a while, a very brief while, she did what she said she would, and we went about our way of bringing repair to the widely opened fissure that had crept in to wreck our progress.

Continually, in that situation, I asked myself, over and over again *What was wrong with that woman?* Still, to-this-day, I catch myself asking the same thing, under other, less unpredictable circumstances with her.

She had everything! Wanted for nothing...Not Love, or validation, never respect, or companionship, not freakisms or fantasies. Cause' when I wasn't on deployment, and when I was home...I mean, baby, I was there!

More than ready, willing and able to mean all of that and more for and to her, upon demand.

But, I realize fully now with the fortune of a truly more mature hind-sight, that that in fact was a greater part of our problem.

Because of the way I had chosen to support my family, as a wayward and often traveling sailor, I was not in fact there—to scratch where it itched, tickle where it pained or pick up where things had fallen. During the beginnings of our novel marriage I was just never home to be all of that when I needed to most.

And because of that...

The absence of solidity in our marriage took its toll in us paying a very heavy price in both time and lost progress from the start.

But there was no way that I was gonna' let her off easily. Because I did what I did to support and uplift our family lent her no excuse for the horrendous natures of her despicable actions.

By the fall of 1994, "NETTIE" had gotten her first job at Sharp-Rees-Stealy. She was a receptionist for a group of highly successful and very busy orthopedic surgeons. She did well in that job—Until she began to relax into it a bit too much and this brought with it, the inevitability of her letting her guard down. She fell prey to a vindictive, drug-supplying co-worker, named Beth, who got her hooked and strung out on a mixture of California's new crack, a mixture of CRACK and Crystal-Methe.

It was at this time that I was making preparations, once again, for leaving; this time I was off, for thirty days, to attend what was known as *Knife-and-Fork* school located in Pensacola, Florida.

It was there that I was supposed to be taught the refined nuances of etiquette and culture that it would take to turn me into the consummate, productive commissioned Naval officer.

After patiently waiting almost thirteen months following being selected, I received my commission on the date of April first, 1994. My ceremony was held in a dimly-lit foyer of what were then the offices of the Commander Amphibious Group Nine, in San Diego. It was there that my detailer had stashed me for some months subsequent to my successful deployment aboard the USS Leahy and another very brief follow-on stint in which I decommissioned the USS Gridley.

One of the cooler points about my commissioning ceremony, was the fact that Mama'n flew into town, from Texas, to be present for the festivities. She cried like a whaling banshee throughout the entire day and she hashed and re-hashed the story of how I'd forced her, so many years before to sit through a horrendous phone call in which I told an ARMY recruiter, back in El Paso, that I was declining his offer of a full-ride

scholarship to an ARMY preparatory school, which would have almost assuredly seen me gaining an eventual appointment to the U.S. Military Academy at West Point—All thrown away—to-the-winds...because I wanted to get married to Kamm.

"I just knew he was gonna' make it somehow...Cause' GOD is good," she'd look over to and say the same sentence, over and over, to anyone who would listen.

I had just discovered "NETTIE's" return to the former scorn of her affinity for drug use and hadn't had any time at all to take the steps I knew were necessary before departing, to combat it, once again, for the sake of our family.

So, with Mama'n still there for a couple of days more…I picked up my stuffed sea bag, kissed my babies good-bye with a silent prayer for mercy, and I left.

I set out in my little red Nissan heading east, toward Florida.

The entire time I was there, at the back of my mind, no matter the nuance and excitement of the new environment I was in, I was held captive in a pseudo-state of personal terror and frustration. I had no clue what was taking place more than one-thousand, nine-hundred miles away, back at home in California.

The only thing I could do, to make my way through all of the things bombarding and coming at me, seemingly, from every angle, was press them forcefully toward the back edges of my mind as I lent my full effort to offering excellence toward my military performance while enrolled at the school.

When the school was over, and me and all my classmates had said our fond farewells as each of us were scattered to different assignments all over the globe, I set out for home with the vengeance and determination of being in a position of not really knowing what I'd find once arriving there.

I made it back to San Diego (Believe it or not…) in exactly eighteen hours after I'd first pulled out from Pensacola. Not taking the time to stop for anything, I mean…I pee'd in empty two liter soda bottles along the route while eating a full assortment of cold cut sandwiches, cold, potatoes I'd cooked in a microwave prior to leaving and of course, washing it all down with the soda.

I was so motivated toward reaching my ultimate destination that I really hadn't taken into account exactly how fast I was actually moving until I'd flung by what seemed like my millionth underpass, and low and behold, guess what, or whom, was waiting for me there beneath it…

I was literally five miles outside of the California border, just inside the boundary lines of Arizona. I spotted the Arizona State Trooper, as I whizzed by topping out at a crazy hundred and ten. When one spotted the other, it was as if time had suddenly slowed down to a baring saunter.

All I remember, as if he and I were close enough to feel the heat of the mid-spring afternoon as it rolled off his tongue below opaque, mirrored glasses as he permitted the slightest edge of an infinitesimally upturned smile creasing ever so slightly at the glistening edges of corners of dry, cracked lips to escape, was a sudden blur of a set of swirling, brightly lit red, white and blue bulbs as they exploded in my rear view appearing out of nowhere when he began to charge his own car into action. He raised a single digit, his index finger, up to touch the front of his nose lightly (As if to gesture—"I got you!") and, after that, he seemed to be taking his sweet time pulling on his own, dime-store leather racing gloves. And...following that, he slammed his patrol car into gear, and lit out after me with a vengeance all his own.

There wasn't much that I could do. He'd had me dead-to-rights. I was wrong and I was trapped, caught like a rat.

So I brought the red monster Nissan to a crawling stroll and I pulled off to the side of the shoulder, and I sat there, waiting for him to finally catch up.

When he'd finally pulled up behind me, I was ready for him with driver's license, registration and proof of insurance. I pulled the old G.I. trick of fumbling with getting my license out and stumbling over the unmistakable coloring of my military I.D. seeking a rapid savior in this instance.

And, of course...It worked.

Instead of carting my azz off to tha' pokey, for doing a realistic hundred ten, he wrote me up for doing a healthy seventy miles per hour in a sixty-five. It cost me three-hundred sixty-five dollars, but was damn well worth it, seeing how I drove away from there a free man and was home in an instant after that.

I came home to a wife who was trying her best once again to assemble a grip upon the demon still bouncing around unchecked inside of her. But even by this time, I still didn't have the answer which was going to cure what ailed her. But I knew definitely, something had to change.

And...For the first time in our lengthy history of waging battle against her fallen sobriety, I finally made what I felt was the smartest move yet.

I did absolutely—NOTHING!

CHOCOLATE CHICKENS DON'T TASTE SO GOOD WHEN MIXED UNWILLINGLY IN VANILLA SOUP

We moved from the townhouse condo we'd been living in for almost a year into the inviolability and security of Murphy Canyon Military Housing—on the Officer's side. I checked aboard the aircraft carrier, USS Kitty Hawk to begin my first tour as a commissioned officer, and we lived.

But did we?

We stayed there for a period of about eight years.

In this, it was I who'd permitted myself, like Buster, to play the role of *CHOCOLATE CHICKEN.*

The entire time we lived there in government housing, I was forfeiting a large amount of Basic Allowance for Subsistence (to the tune of thousands of dollars per month) which the Navy provided me, as an Officer, to go towards paying a mortgage in the extremely high San Diego housing market. And I stupidly, never took advantage of it when I had the chance to purchase a home on the outside market, which could've quite frankly amassed enough equity today to have been well worth over a million dollars or more.

But, I was scared…

Already, I had shit credit. And there just didn't seem any solution away from that for me at the time. So I didn't even permit abject hallucinations of us owning our own home to even minutely creep into the center thought patterns of my mind to mock me further.

I couldn't see or invite such a vision to skulk its way into breaking the staunch negativity of the loser fiscal mentality I'd permitted us to become caught up and rolled into. What I pictured instead, would be a forever without even being able to think creatively enough to somehow find a way out leading toward success.

So, when issues bordering on actual prosperity came up, I pushed thoughts of my own successes, and those of my family's, as well, safely (Like a *CHOCOLATE CHICKEN*) outta' mind. And then, I was once again safe.

Big man…Alpha-Dog! I was in charge. I was going down credit-wise, asset-wise, fiscally, and because I was the boss, me and all of mine would go down with me.

And we went down—not really living at all. Just keepin'-on…

Caught up, like the undereducated, ill-motivated *chickens* that we, rather I, had allowed us to become. We merely existed instead of reaching out—forward, to genuinely strive for attempts towards reaping the rewards of both our daily hard work and to see and realize the indisputable nature of things we could all perceive everyone else amassing and gaining, yet we remained behind, and therefore out of view without progression.

It wasn't until approaching the fall of nineteen ninety eight, that things began to unfold and turn for the better, depending on how you look at it

Chapter Eleven
MAMA'N & GOD!

It was Thanksgiving Day. I was then a full year into a new assignment as the C4I (Command, Control, Communications, Computers & Intelligence) Department Head at the then Special Boat Unit Twelve located on San Diego's Coronado Island at the prestigious Naval Amphibious Base. It was only my second shot during the entirety of my then fifteen year career at having an honest-to-goodness chance at a real tour of shore duty; where I would go home every night to my Lovely wife and have every weekend free to spend with my brooding kids. By this time, all of us had settled into our set of circumstances and we'd very rapidly become a very broke, but still growing, mature family.

We had bundled the family up and were heading North from San Diego to Los Angeles to have Thanksgiving dinner with one of "NETTIE's" brothers and his family. We'd meant to take full advantage of the simplicity the rest, familial camaraderie and relaxation the fullness of the extended weekend would present to us.

How many of y'all know that there wasn't much rest or relaxation to be had on that particular day or during that particular trip?

The date was November 28, 1998.

My little sister, Miss Honey, (Melania) who was in Pennsylvania, was the first to call with the alarm that she'd been unable to locate tha' Weez (Mama'n) and that she'd been calling and calling her house in Chaparral, New Mexico all day without any positive response. She'd reached me on my cell and relayed that she had spoken to her the day before and that Mama'n was overly excited about making preparations for her own holiday meal, one in which she'd already invited a full assortment of about nineteen people to her house to join her in the festivities of her own Thanksgiving dinner.

I was right about at the Border Patrol checkpoint on the I-15 when I took her call.

She said she'd already spoken with Toppa. He hadn't heard from Mama'n either.

I asked if she'd queried all of the local jails and hospitals in both El Paso and Chaparral. She said that she had, with equally exhaustive results. It would not have been unusual to suggest that we might stumble upon Mama'n locked up in some sweltering hooch-cow or, although she was fit as a fiddle, and otherwise doing terrifically well at the time, to have lost her within the confines of some hospital somewhere attempting to convince some young, and handsome intern to prescribe her the benefits of some illicit drug in treating whatever ailment or malady she'd concocted up to garner attention that day.

I told "NETTIE" what was going on and asked Honey to call me back if she heard anything, and I drove on, still heading North towards the city of Angels.

We hadn't made two miles of progress from the point of taking her original call, when my cell chirped again.

Before taking the call, I remember experiencing that same sick feeling of foreboding apprehension that GOD has instilled in me to prepare me for charging headlong—into trouble. It was a gut-wrenching offering which at times has maintained both my sanity and safety when faced with sudden situations steeped in utter turmoil.

It was her again.

This time a more distraught and barely recognizable voice of my little sister jumped out to greet me from the other side of the phone.

"Honey?...Zzzzat' you?"

"Yeah, Blu...It's me..."

She took a long time to get a grip on the overwhelming senses of emotion I could almost feel from the other side of the phone as she attempted unsuccessfully to get herself together. It took her so long between the period of her very first and her next words that I thought at first that we'd blown our connection.

I braced myself, waiting. It was almost like that feeling a parent gets when they have young teens who aren't in the house on time on almost any particular weekend, and it's three in the morning, and the phone rings.

With the only thing you can do in between the silence while waiting anxiously for the resultant reality to hit, you pray. Cause' you just know. Something's just not right in your world—somewhere. And... This time, it's actually gonna' affect you...

When she'd come back on, she sadly muttered three, barely legible words which have gone a long way since in changing my life forever.

She said, "We found her..."

I pulled over once again onto the side of the road, just off the exit leading to the Pechanga Indian resort and Casino.

She relayed that she had found Mama'n at the William Beaumont Army Medical Center in El Paso.

She'd been flown there as a result of a horrendous car accident.

I was deeply out of breath suddenly, sitting there taking it all in. It was almost too much for me to simply sit there and take it all in.

Immediately, tears of not knowing amid the confusion of being unable to be there for Mama'an, to help her, covered me.

After hanging up with Honey, it was all I could do not to just sit there in a stupor and swoon. Thank GOD for "NETTIE" and the bunions being there with me and for me.

She knew (herself no stranger to loss when it came to family) after my having taken the time to explain exactly what I knew up to that point of what had happened, exactly how to proceed.

She'd lost both, her brother, Macarthur, and her oldest sister Pamela, one seemingly right after the other, Mac in 96' and Pam, that same year, 98'.

All I could bring myself to think, during the hours following that tumultuous time was, *Dayummm... Not again...*

Mama'n!...

I swapped seats with "NETTIE". I didn't know full well whether I'd be able to turn the truck around and begin to make the hour long trip back to San Diego without getting all of us killed. So she drove, and I began to take the necessary steps of finding out more information about the screaming moments of the prior twenty-four hours which made up possibly the last few ghastly moments in my Mother's life.

My second call went out to the personal battle cell of my Executive Officer, Commander Gary Lumpkin, back at the boat unit. Once getting him on the line, I played over the scenario of my Mother's situation and informed him that I was leaving for the great state of Texas that second, no questions asked. Initially, he attempted to have me drive into the unit to execute leave papers. I further informed him that I wouldn't be stopping back at the unit for any reasons, and that he could, from that very second, count me AWOL if that was his choosing, and I hung up.

My first call following the realization of the seriousness of the accident was to a child-hood friend in El Paso, Dave Walterstein. Dave was a doctor there who frequently made rounds at the ARMY hospital, among other places.

Then, as "NETTIE" all but flew us back to San-Dog in my 96' GMC Jimmy in record time, we arrived back in Murphy Canyon, packed what bags we felt we needed for the trip and, with foreboding visions of being brought to having to re-live the horrors and uncertainties of Maman's previous Thanksgiving nightmare so many years before as these things bounced and danced around wildly inside my head, we set out for El Paso, poste-haste.

As we were about eight hours into our trip, headed out the I-8 East, and already reaching for the I-10, my cell chirped again. I picked it up, wishing instead that I could simply fling the damned thing out the window and have all of this become some sort of twisted mess or dream I had the ability to eventually wake up from. But I knew it wasn't. So I took the call.

There are miracles of nature which simply occur as a matter of planned innate procession. Then, there are those traveling mercies. Things GOD has in his goody bag, just waiting and teeming with Love, and the infinity of a precise pride that he can provide them for you.

...And all you have to do, to get them...

Is just ask.

The call was from Dave.

He informed me that he had attended to my Mama'n, as soon as the Life-Flight helicopter had landed on the pad. He and another of my childhood friends I remember as being a gangly kid and veritable genius cum-laude of our motley crew of bandits, Joe Cid (Short for Cidarella—but that pronunciation generally landed us all in fights if anyone outside of our group toyed around with it) had taken her directly to surgery upon arriving at the busy med-center.

"Man. . .Blu', I'm telling you, your Mom shouldn't even've made it here from the accident scene dude!"

GOD!

Dude, we had er' on the operating table for almost six hours. I'm sorry to have to tell you like this, bro. . .Over the phone.

But I gotta' cut you as quick as I can.

It doesn't look good."

"Whattaya' mean, not good?"

"Blue, damn-it, man. . .I'm sayin' not good. For Christ's sake, your Ma had a hole in her heart the circumference of a quarter."

Standing ther taking all of this in, I felt my own heart might've stopped!

"Her ribs were all busted to hell, puncturing the lung cavity and the outer lining of the heart wall. Joe was able to halt the bleeding and fix all of that the best he could. We patched up her lung and got it working again, slightly. All of that may heal, given time.

But Blu?"

I was full on twisted up by now. It seemed every emotion I'd ever felt in life came rushing to flood at me in a mere twenty seconds, almost smothering me.

I all of a sudden couldn't breathe.

"Don't tell me there's more, Dave."

"There is, pard, hole' on."

"Hit me. . ."

"She's in a coma, Blu. GOD only knows when she's gonna' come out of it. Or if. . ."

"Don'tchew' say it, Dave. . .Don't you even fucc n' think it!"

"I know. I know man. . .But we, which means all of us, have to be realistic about the minimal prognosis of her chances for pulling outta' this.

When you getting' here anyway?"

I forced myself to calm down and think.

"Be there in about three and a half hours. We're driving."

"Good, if you and the family need a place while you're here, you can stay at Dad's old house off of Ressler." We prepared to cut the conversation short.

But then he hit me with, "Just one more thing, Blu; results of all the neuro-functionality scales we've conducted came back, first try, looking real bleak."

"What's that mean?"

"Ain't showing us very positive signs of her ability to have much of a life...If she does come out. But we can't conduct a consult to delve any further into that until we're able to coax the swelling on her brain down a spell."

This shook me to no end. "You telling me...?

Maman's gonna' be a vegetable—if she pulls through?"

"No, pard...I'm telling ya'—That that possibility does exist. Just want you to be fully loaded, if that's what we face here in the near future, O.K.?"

I fixed my lips to prepare them to tell him that he was wrong.

Dead wrong.

CAUSE' I KNEW...GOD!

Just then Joe snatched the phone away from him and began to present me a lighter, albeit identical picture of what the verbose, mundane-speeched Dave had been filling me in on seconds before.

"Nothings definite paisan. Don't listen to all that hutzpah. You know Dave. How'd your Ma always put it? Ain't wrapped too tight and all."

"Ugh-huh...I know. I wanna' thank both of you man, for being there for me and Mama'n."

"Of course—dog...What are paisans for?"

GOD!

Neither of my two dear friends was at the Medical Center when we finally broke the Franklin Mountains, coming in from the East side and headed directly for the great hospital up on the hill. We tip-toed our way around until we had a proper bearing on the expansive interior of the now modern buildings; the place suddenly appeared so foreign to me. But too, I was amazed at how quickly my memories of the now fully upgraded facility were brought back to me as we strode through the ice cold lengths of its sullen halls.

We found our way to a special intensive care ward. Sort of a SPEC ICU's—ICU, maintained for the very, very sick and weak, folks whose injuries and ailments could cause them to kick off and depart the earth at any given moment.

I had "NETTIE, the kids—and my bible with me. So, I came fully armed. This included an accompaniment of already developed prayers as they were constantly being sent up to the heavens, with a clarified, strength-filling intercession on Maman's behalf, by the entire congregation of North Park Apostolic Church located on 54th and University back in San Diego.

Upon seeing the form of what used to be my Mama'n lying docile, not even able to do her favorite thang', (run her mouth) hooked up to perhaps a hundred tubes, monitors, and other medical gadgets, a thermometer looking device sticking out, in plain site, directly from the top of her head, her swollen nodes and limbs causing her to become at the most unrecognizable, even to me, who had entered this world through her womb, I felt, I was about to pass out under a complete sheet of the sheer heart ache and stress seeing her like that hit me with.

I cried. But I only permitted myself the very briefest respite of languishing beside her bed steeped in tears.

I had other things to do and I was gonna' do them right there, right then and right now!

I hadn't only come there (Thinking to myself during the entire trip, while my sweet, supportive "NETTIE" did the majority of the driving in route) to comfort and see Mama'n through to a level of better health, but I'd traveled there, bible in hand, particularly, for one and only one reason.

I had a mission to complete and I immediately made preparations around her for going to work.

I stretched out my prayers. I wailed like no possible son could wail for the continued existence and presence of his mother. I prayed for grace. I prayed for intercession. I prayed for strength for Mama'n. I prayed that every good thing in my life GOD had in store for me, for my future, to be taken, ripped away, snatched from me, at that very second—and given to my Mother.

I stood over that bed and prayed and prayed and prayed—out loud and with a fully vociferous abandon. Not a doctor, not a nurse, not "NETTIE", not any of the staff members present sought to take steps of quieting me.

The air surrounding me and the bed where Mama'n lay became instantly clear and sweet with the magic and power of GOD's Love at listening.

It was uncanny, very eerie and bordering on the mystical.

Somehow like it had become Mama'n, JESUS, and me as the only characters nearby as the room—enveloped, with all other worldly cares and petty concerns cast aside into an abyss of another era—for us to deal with them, once faith, Love, and heart ache had brought us through this ordeal safely. The stress and pain of not knowing loomed heavily around us clogging the present. But, as well, faith assured us, me. . . her—that, for real, all we had to do was believe—and anything at all, was still possible.

We remained in Texas for a full two weeks.

Mama'n never recovered from the coma.

—While we were there, the realistic time clock of the leave the Commander had granted me approached a very rapid end and then finally ran out. I had to be gracious and understanding of his position, as well as for that of my own and make preparations for returning to San Diego.

A bit disappointed, I guess expecting GOD to arrive and show himself there infinitely, on my time, we had to leave Mama'n alone and desolate, trapped within the deserted atoll of her mind's own wilderness and go back to California.

During the two week period that we'd spent there, Toppa had dropped in from Colorado. Instead of solidifying our relationship and perhaps pooling our mental, emotional, physical, and financial resources in order to ensure Mama'n was taken care of squarely, we fought. It was as if we were fifteen and sixteen years old again. We argued about who would stay at Maman's trailer, his family or my family, who would make preparations for getting her a lawyer, which lawyer we would retain, whether he and his family would assist me and mine in attempting to clean up the mess that was the inside of Maman's trailer. Although he wanted his family to stay there during the ordeal, he flat out refused to permit his family, and boldly forbid them, to lend a hand in picking up the place. He and his wife actually sat outside in their car while "NETTIE", the kids and I made the place presentable for visitors, and for them, while they stayed there.

We took up my friends on their offer of putting us up while there.

He's never taken the time, as yet, to tell me or explain to me exactly what or why it was, during that time, that he was so mad at me. So, as well, I've been left to my own devices of developing reasons behind the literally seven full years since the initial anniversary of the accident; that he has still not spoken a word to me.

This has gone on to play out so, that when I call his home to wish him well on any particular occasion, (His birthday, Father's Day) all he gives me, is ignorance in the form of one of his kids stating plain nothingness on the other end of the phone line.

"Sorry, Uncle "B", Dad won't talk to ya."

And I'd feel even worse for his children, having been forced into such a dividing line between their own father and their family, without the common courtesy of providing even them a parental explanation.

Over the years, I've simply stopped calling.

Instead of matching his stupidy with my own anger, I've made the choice to believe, through his own helplessness to offer Mama'n assistance, that he chose instead to simply distance himself, from her, from me, and anything else which might crop up to bring a reminder—that he had nothing to offer to our Mother during that, her most ardent time of need.

Perhaps he thinks that by simply sticking his head in the sand and trying to ignore the fact that *we* needed him, it, and we would all miraculously—just go away.

At this time, that's all I can bring myself to say about that...

So, instead, I threw myself into making sure all of her bills were paid, lights were turned off, gas, water and sewage lines were placed in secure positions, and I, for all intents and purposes, after giving her pack-rat's-haven, full of boxes, old pictures of us when we were little, items she'd retrieved from her own Father's home upon his death so many years before, a once over to prepare her place for that time...once she'd made a full recovery, when she'd finally, once again...come home.

I wrapped up her little trailer and made my own preparations, after one final trip back up to Beaumont, to head back towards California.

Mama'n remained in a coma for a full four months. Time and time again, I received various phone calls, first from her immediate doctor, a new guy the Med-Center had assigned to her case, David Brill, an ARMY intern, then from other, more higher up personnel in the ARMY, all intending that their call was for update, informational purposes, but all ending with the same identical themes..."Your Mother's not getting any better, she's showing no signs of progress…It's time to—*PULLTHA" PLUG* and let her go on home—to JESUS."

You know…

I wa'nt having it!

Short of cursing these mangy mongrels out, I told them very succinctly, not to ever call my house again, unless they had good news about Maman's developing condition.

CAUSE' I KNEW GOD!

Mama'n lay in that SPEC-ICU unit for an additional three and a half months. I finally did get another call from Dr. Brill.

It was on a particular Saturday morning. I'd just returned from my daily trip to our tiny bathroom inside our master bedroom, where, daily, I'd climb into the tub, fully clothed, and I'd wail and plead and beg GOD to *OPEN DOORS AD HAVE MERCY ON MY MOTHER.*

I made the mistake of promising GOD, that no matter the condition that he gave her back to me, I would Love her and find ways and options to care for her te best way that I possibly could.

Just, don't, take her away!

…And he heard…

…And, he listened!

The very first words out of Dr. Brill's mouth were, "Man…I'm telling you, Blu, you've got some faith."

"I'm sorry, Doc, what was that?" I replied, not even beginning to understand his elated mumblings.

He all but carried on, "Your Mother…I mean, Misses Daniels, she's back—YOU DID IT!"

"Sorry, come again?"

"She awoke from her coma this morning. She just woke up. She's coherent. And she's asking for you. I don't know what kind of connection you've got guy, but I and all of the staff and administration here at the hospital are calling it nothing short of miraculous."

I almost dropped the phone as tears of pure-D thanksgiving that still swell up in my eyes this very moment whenever I think of GOD's mercy for my Mama'n overtook me suddenly.

"Yes, Blu, I'm saying she wants to speak with you. Hold on a minute, O.K.?"

He put the phone up to Maman's ear. I could hear the steady hiss and track of the trach-machine, still breathing for her, as she struggled as best she could, and in her own way of trying to make me feel better, she half-heartedly tugged at my heart with, "H…Hi…Hi, ba-bab, baby…Gue.Guess w…wha.what?"

I suffered through tears of endearment, forcefully attempting to fight back and push through a plethora of my own over joyous emotions.

"What Ma'…?"

I could feel her smile at the other end of that line.

"We…We all…—heard you…

I'm b…ba.bac…back!"

I had to give the phone to my "NETTIE". After experiencing that, I broke completely down as I fell weak and was a crying bitch of a mess.

She spoke with the Doc for a while and I tried my best to pull myself together, because, for some reason, I knew…

That the real, hard—work, for me, was just about to begin.

Through talking with the Doc further, I found out that it had become life-and-death imperative, for Mama'n, that we develop and option for getting her out of the SPEC-ICU as soon as possible. She was in trouble once again after having been in there for so long, she'd contracted a blood disease that, if not treated properly, in a more sterile environment, would sure as snot kill her in a very short matter of time.

I was flabbergasted.

What did he mean…Kill her? After all that she'd been through and survived?

This man had to be crazy. He must not have known what I knew.

CAUSE', I KNEW GOD!

The very first thing I did, after closing out my call with Doctor Brill, was head straight for that bedroom, and I got my azz right back into that bath-tub, full-clothed.

I wailed and wailed and wailed some more. This time, offering up the most heartfelt thanks, praise and thanksgiving that I could possibly offer up to GOD. I thanked GOD for a full hour or more. When I finally did unlock the door to let "NETIE" and my family in, I was sweating profusely, from head to toe. My clothes were soaking wet, as if I'd been in there showering with them on.

But, how many of y'all know, that it wasn't from any shower that I was pouring water out from every pore in my body?

It was instead, from work. The spiritual kind, where you truly believe and you throw every ounce of audacity, might, courage and effort in to ask *THEMANUPSTAIRS* for additional pleasures, when he's already opened up the flood gates of the heavens to provide you with perhaps the sweetest gift he could ever offer... And you've taken the selfish liberty of wondering to the well—a time again—asking for more.

The first thing I did when I returned to work that following Monday, was head directly for the personnel office at the amphibious base. Once there, I encountered a First Class Personnelman, and I told him my story and that I had a need to make my Mother a Military Dependent, and that I didn't have much time and had to do it fast.

He was a Filipino gentleman and he met my excited efforts with, "I'm s-a-r-iee, suuur, it bill take you a-ffroxi-mately six peeks to have you're a-fflication consiiiduurrred py the bureau. I hap da f-aper-work right here dat you bill need."

Poor guy. Cause' I all but exploded on him, pulling rank, making him the bearer of my troubles with the red tape of the overall process.

I all but forced him to place a call to the Defense Finance Center located in Cleveland, Ohio. I instructed him to relay that I wanted to be able to fax the dependency application and that I wanted it all to take place over a day's time.

We were handled by a guy named Alexander Page on the Cleveland end. Mr. Page informed me that I had to fill out a Dependency questionnaire and mail it to Cleveland for consideration, and that they'd get back to me in due time (meaning six to eight weeks) with a decision on Maman's status. He said, primarily all applications for dependency had to be physically handled to support due process, and that they did not accept conducting business of that sort at all via fax. I implored this man to make an exception. I relayed and went over and over the propensity for failure and the decreased timeline I was working with while my Mother's life swayed heavily in the balance.

He kept saying no.

I kept him on the phone an hour, working on him.

Finally, I guess he'd gotten tired of my very excitable antics and wanted just to simply get me outta' his ear for the rest of his day. He promised that he would do his best, once mailing out the questionnaire to me, and following my receiving it and filling it out correctly and in complete form, to personally see that my application was expedited (That could very well have meant three to six weeks before I received resolution).

I told him that that wouldn't be good enough!

During the *eleventh*-hour of me attempting to sway him, I reached down into the folder I'd been carting around, with all of Maman's legal and personal papers I'd lifted from the trailer back in New Mexico, and I spotted a thick pad of papers I suddenly remembered picking up while "NETTIE" and the gang and I had been back in EL Paso during our stay there. I remembered going to a personnel office very similar to the one I stood in that moment, at Fort Bliss, and I recalled asking the clerk there for the Dependency application. He'd produced it and handed it over immediately, without question.

GOD…

This further sparked my own internal insistence that what the Filipino Personnelman, and now Mr. Page, were telling me, was a bunch of lazy, albeit impervious, amount of bull-shit, and I pulled no punches in letting the both of them know, exactly that.

Now that he had no more excuses to cause me to permit him the time of *mailing* the documents out to me, Mr. Page gave in.

"All right, Lieutenant! Fax me the completed application." And he provided me his direct fax number.

"But, I'm not assuring you that this thing will be completed in any particular amount of time, only, that I'll do my best, O.K.?"

I said O.K. And then had the shaken Personnelman lead me in the direction of the nearest facsimile machine.

I transmitted the fully-filled-out; five page pad of documents to the number Mr. Page had given me. I went back to the Boat Unit, and waited for a full, twenty-four hour period, and then I phoned him to verify that all was in order; he'd received my fax and that there was nothing else needed to facilitate a rapid processing of my request.

I was certain that he was going to tell me that everything was in order and that he had taken receipt of my fax, and that he was now in full force of considering the application for approval.

But, he didn't.

Nothing could have been farther from my hopes in the answer he provided me.

I asked, "Sir, have you received my fax? Can you tell me how far along in the process of consideration are you?"

Strangely, he met me back with, "Now... I'm not going to tell you that I've received it—and, I'm not going to tell you that I haven't."

I was like, *WHAT!*

Immediately, I chalked it up to him trying to stall using a very simplistic form of bureaucratic double talk to stave off another challenge of his position by me.

I said, "Come again?"

He repeated himself, "I'm not going to tell you that I have, and I'm not going to tell you that I haven't received it, just transmit again, if you will."

I did just that.

But this time, I only waited a mere twenty minutes before calling him back.

"Mr. Page? This is Lieutenant Penn. I'm again attempting to verify that..."

He cut me off with, "Again, Lieutenant, I have to tell you—That, I cannot confirm that I have received them, and I will not confirm that I haven't."

I was about to come unglued. I felt helpless, standing there trying to bring closure to a situation with a man who was more than four-thousand miles away from me. Only the distance prevented and held me back from reaching out to choke him for the true idiot I felt he was at that moment.

He continued, "Please... Transmit again...

I told him I wanted him to remain on the line this time while I re-faxed the application to him. He hemmed and he hawed a bit, but he kept his butt on that phone while I sent to him.

When I had completed my fax, for the third time in a two day period, I approached him with, "Mr. Page? If you tell me now that you cannot confirm receipt of my documents, my next phone call will be to a four-star Admiral, seeking immediate resolution in this matter. By the way, sir... Will you please provide me with the name of your boss?"

All of a sudden, the man holding all of the purse strings, on his high horse back in Cleveland, became nervous, suddenly on the hot seat himself.

"Ummm, my ughhh...Boss?"

"Yes, sir, please provide me the name of your immediate superior, sir. I've been in this business for quite some time now sir and even I realize that we all have to report to and be accountable to someone."

He began to suddenly stutter. "N.nnn.Now...Lieutenant, we don't have to go there and take this matter to such extremes. I've got the paperwork in my hand as we aaah speak and just looking it over...ummmm...now, I can unequivocally assure you....

That she is—APPROVED!"

Hallelujah!

GOD!!!

This time around, it was he, Mr. Page, who faxed me the fully approved documentation which made my Mama'n an approved Military Dependent.

...And it had only taken two days of haggling instead of six to eight weeks of impatient waiting and wondering if red tape would be the deciding factor in whether she would die or be presented a chance to finally begin to receive the best care, from the best medicine and doctors in the world, without question.

GOD!

Right away, after securing her status as my bonafide dependent, I headed in the direction of the county welfare office, on Ruffin Road, in San Diego. Once there, I fought and cajoled and all but extorted a very unkind clerk, trying to make Mama'n a California resident.

The only way I would be able to afford the fifteen-hundred dollar per day cost of her care in what she needed most, an acute care facility, was to enlist the uncertainty of assistance from a state organization, like welfare.

As I was becoming more and more discouraged, and was already out the door, heading for only GOD knows where next for help, a middle-aged lady of African descent approached me from behind, asking, "Chile, is everything all right?

I almost broke down right there in front of that sweet lady, whose name

I just cannot remember in the telling and rehashing, for the millionth time, all about Maman's major predicament.

She comforted me with the patience and clear vision of a true angel.

"Don't you worry yourself none, baby... We're gonna' take care of all of this for you right now."

And, she did.

The second time I left that office, I did so, with a briefcase full of new papers to fill out and submit, as well as with a more lightened heart overflowing with a mounting debt of genuine thanksgiving.

Upon taking my follow on call that all was set as far as Maman's dependency status and as far as me securing a spot to place her once she was in California, (With her blood infection, a myriad of facilities wouldn't even consider her for admission, fearful for the care of their other patients because of the contagious nature of the disease), Dr. Brill quickly kicked into action on his end.

A mere day later, I met my Mama'n, as she was gourneyed from the newly landed interior of a Lear jet at John Wayne Airport in Orange County, California. The only passengers on the jet were Mama'n, and a lone medical technician who'd overseen her condition during the four hour trip.

"NETTIE", Boomer, and the girls and I all waited excitedly as we witnessed the small plane hit the tarmac safely. We ran over to the outer edge of the flight line where an ambulance waited to whisk her off to the Pacific Coast Acute Care facility located in Laguna Nigel, just off the winding coast of roadway skirting the Pacific Ocean.

I recall the wild, frightened look in her eyes as the ambulance crew assisting the technician brought her safely from the still taxiing craft. Moaning from time to time at the gruff demeanors of her saving handlers, she first looked to her right, then to her left, and it had to be exactly akin to the first moment we ever set eyes on each other following my birth.

She offered the slightest whimsical smile in my direction, and like Tommie Smith and John Carlos, of Nineteenth Olympiad fame, both attendees at that time at San Jose State College, who'd shocked the world by raising the *BLACK POWER* salute on the victory podium in 1968, at Mexico City, following their first and third place finishes in the 200 meter dash to represent both *Black* Power in protest against racism in America and *BLACK UNITY* in the same way, she struggled to raise a single, high-yellow arm to the sky in a fist, and keeping that smile, she only whispered as loudly as her softened trachea would permit her,

"I knew you would do it."

GOD!

And we whisked Mama'n away, off to Pacific Coast Acute Care—to begin her recovery.

She was perhaps the worst patient a patient could be. The accident had wracked and mangled her body something fierce. But, somehow, it had left her mind as sharp as a tack.... And her mouth very soon after caught up as well.

She gave those poor nurses and attendants hell minus any mercy. They merely put up with her complaining and cursing them out while offering her better care than even I had imagined was possible.

I was driving the seventy mile distance, one way, everyday, following my day's work at the boat unit. I'd sit with her, comb her hair, and argue with her about facts involving our family history, which, to this day, she swears on-a-stack-of bibles she is the only living aficionado about. And then, once she'd drifted off to sleep following her meds, I'd jump in my car and head back down the I-5 freeway towards San Diego and home.

This went on for a period of about seven months. That was until I explained to her how much driving all that way, a hundred and forty miles, round-trip each day, following work, was killing me.

That was the first time she began to pressure me (Y'all know Mama'n was a champion and very skilled at manipulation) to find a place closer to home that would take her, in San Diego. The acute care docs had been able to rapidly beat the blood disease and she had even had her gastric feeding tube removed, and was constantly driving the staff crazy with her gluttonous demands for two and three portions of particular foods, as if she had her own personal chef to artfully prepare each meal.

So, although very professional in their dealings with Mama'n, the staff at the center was none all too unhappy when I informed them that we'd be transferring her to another facility, Tempored Gardens, in San Diego, in about a week.

I'd tried my best to research the place prior to placing her there. But, all in all, it was the only facility that would accept her with her recent history of having had the now defunct blood infection. So, I was stuck…

I appealed to Mama'n; to try and stay at Pacific Coast a while longer. I told her that her moving to San Diego, just to take the strain of driving off of me was purely a bad decision.

"It's…gonna' be like going from Bel Air or Hollywood, straight from paradise, into the ghetto, if you wish to do this Mama'n," I informed her.

Still; don't know why I listened. She didn't give a rat's azz about the level of care she was running away from and getting herself into at the time. Only that she'd be closer so that I could come visit her more often.

She was content and hell-bent on sticking with her decision.

Until we got her there…

The place appeared well-kept, everything in its proper place, all clean and tidy, yet it held this perfunctory odor of old shit about it, no matter where it was you traveled inside. It wasn't exactly a pristine, acute care facility like Pacific Coast, but more an old folk's retirement home. I'd known we were in trouble the very minute after we'd deposited Mama'n in the freshly clean sheets of her new bed of her new room.

The *institution* director was a man named, Harry Stanislawski. A tall, thinning man with disheveled, albeit professional clothing, beady, shifting little eyes set beneath perhaps the worst comb-over of what little hair he did possess that I'd witnessed so far up into my own period of experiences.

And…He always seemed to be tripping, and stumbling over himself, each time we visited, lost in his eventual inability to reassure us that Mama'n was receiving the highest quality care possible while there.

This all boiled to a blistering head after about six more months of her suffering there.

It seemed the place was teeming with cutesy, little oriental nurse's aids and extremely attentive medical technicians, all whom would race into Maman's room projecting the image of providing an impression; that they'd been fawning over her for hours on end prior to me getting there. And they'd be certain that at least one of them would remain inside of her room, as unwanted sentinels, (attending to her like SHEWAS DA'QUEEN) during the entire time of my daily visits.

I began to take note and make sense on these occasions, just by tuning in to my Mother, and by catching subtle images and subliminal messages she cast off implying feelings of stark terror and shocking grief as these images fanned across her face, lighting up plainly in her eyes each time one of them came near her when I was there.

But, I said nothing.

Instead, I brought her a miniature tape recorder which I placed beneath the security of her now ruddy and stained pillow case. It appeared her linens hadn't been swapped out the entire time she'd been there.

...And, she was starting to stink—really bad.

I took to arriving at different times, altering the pattern of my visits and staying longer to personally bath her each evening.

Now, this, other than having to wipe her butt whenever she soiled herself, because an aide would suddenly be *unavailable and busy elsewhere,* was perhaps the major of all the adjustments I had to make, internally, during her stay at the already very suspect institution.

But, true to her pre-accident form, she handled it comically and rather well all the same.

Prior to my giving her the first of many baths I would give her there, she smiled gently, commenting that, "One of us has to close their eyes. And I think that'll be me, cause' you know you got ta' keep yours open; you got work ta' do—but you ain't got no business seeing yo' Momma's Como' Se' Yama'."

I gritted my teeth and laughed at her. And she got the best bath she'd had in six months. The more I cleaned her, the madder at the facility I'd become. Before starting her first wash down, I'd forced the waiting sentinel to leave the room—out of dignity for my Mama'n. This didn't go over too well with the administration at the establishment.

So much so, that the very next day, ole' Stanislaw encountered me on my way in and asked if he could have a moment of my time before going in to visit with Mama'n.

I told him, "Suuurre."

After entering his office, he asked me if I minded if he closed the door.

I said, "No problem..."

Once seated behind the pompous block of his opulently outfitted, cherry wood desk, he produced a crusty looking pipe, which he lit staunchly, taking his time, as if I wasn't even there, before coming back around to his request for requesting a meeting with me. Then he went on to tell me that he no longer could permit me to visit the facility while dressed in my battle dress uniform fatigues. Said the staff was intimidated by them and that he just didn't think my wearing them there was supporting good order about the place on a daily occasion.

I informed him that I visited the establishment each day directly from work. He remained adamant about *his* new condition that I change prior to coming in. I told him, in just these words, that I thought he was a *fucc'n* nut. And that I don't tell him what draws to pick out and wear each day and that I would be there tomorrow, in BDU's, to see my Mother.

What now! Fool...

I then stormed outta' his office and went in to visit with Mama'n.

But, when I got to her room, the door was closed. So, for a brief minute, I waited.

Then, lost in thought over the immense oddity of my former meeting with *THEMAN*, I thought I heard Mama'n cry out in pain.

Wasting not a second more, I burst into her room and witnessed two of the little aides struggling with her profusely. The three of them were all locked up in a tangled tussle of feminine wills, arms wailing and weaving throughout one another, shouts of the aides and the hoarse cries of my Mother ringing in my ears inciting me to a point of perhaps causing an equally meted out portion of immediate mayhem to both of them right there on the spot.

When I'd rallied them away from her, I found out that they'd been trying to grip the remote control to the tiny thirteen inch television I'd set up across from her bed, for her to be able to watch her stories during the day away from her. Mama'n, having lost all control of everything she ever held dear in life, not to mention her personal freedoms, wasn't having none of it.

Looking up to see me there, her eyes met mine, filled with instant relief that I'd finally made it there. Then, she rolled her head over at the aides like Linda Blair, in the movie "The Exorcist" and began to tell it all.

"Blu!" She pointed forcefully at the two ladies speaking gruffly. "That bitch there, just pinched me! And the other one was sitting on my arms while that one there was trying to steal my remote."

It was all I could do to maintain personal control over the seeping rage that shot up through me that very moment. One of the ladies made a bee-line for the door exiting rapidly. The other stuck around and tsk'd and slapped her lips, trying to lend the impression that Mama'n was delusional and didn't know what she was talking about.

Mama'n lifted an arm and implored me to take in the swelling welt of an already reddening bruise appearing just below the crevice of her right arm pit. Mama'n is high yellow. Any bump, scrape or bruise is bound to show up with an alarming instance anytime she is either injured or she injures herself without fail.

Taking that in, I swooped across the room and lost my *fucc'n* mind…

I grabbed that tiny little menace by the back of her hair and pushed her azz through the door leading her all the way in to the director's office, with a full hoarde of her co-workers all screaming at me loudly in tow.

"Call tha' Fo-lice," I heard one of them screech out.

Looking back, just as we were about to bust through ole' Stanislaw's door, I called back, Yeah…. Call them, so I can have all of you bitches arrested for assaulting my Mother."

We dumped into Stan's office all at once, me holding the solidity of the tiny tape recorder firmly in hand.

Once planted inside, the tiny, twenty pound bitch slinked her way back outside, fearfully—closing the door behind her abruptly.

Stanislaw rose from his desk almost forcefully upon looking up to see me back in his office.

"What's this," he blurted, seeking to maintain his position of authority over me, his pipe now smoldering a shit-smelling yellow plume as it reached up to graft to the insides of my olfactory nerves inside my nostrils.

"I'll tell you what it is you puss-bag Mother-Fucker," I countered, stepping two gigantic steps in his direction to suddenly have him caught up against the backdrop of his messy desk. "I just witnessed two of your *fucc'n* employees giving my Mother tha' once over in her room. They had her pinned down in her bed while they were abusing her."

He tried to mutter some sort of incredulous response. That's when the devil in me came out completely, with him bearing the brunt on the bitter end.

I reached up and took hold of him with ease, holding a clamping grip upon the front of his larynx as I twisted his scrawny little neck to an odd angle while I held him firmly in place and continued talking.

"You betta' get this shit straight and you betta' get it straight now! I've got your girls' abuse on tape."

The bulging whites of his eyes began to fade red as the straining corpuscles swung wildly down to peer at the deceitful little device I still held in my left hand. I was tempted to bop him with it a couple of times, up-side-his *fucc'n* head. But I didn't want to invite demise or deterioration of the situation any further and perhaps take the risk of ruining the contents of the tape or of actually being hauled off to jail without a strict recourse to follow up on.

So I held him there, feet dangling in place catching only thin air.

"My Mother had better never experience this again, ya' hear! Cause' if she does, it won't be one of you tiny nurse's aides I'll be dragging in here."

I let him down. Then, flung his azz backwards into the plush, overstuffed sanctuary of his leather chair.

I could smell the stark tremor of life-ending fear emanating from him unchecked.

I pushed one lengthy finger at the protruding cartilage lining up with the tip of his crooked nose, "I'm coming for YOU! Let this shit occur again... And I promise you—I will *KILL* you, right there where you sit!"

And me and the trusty tape recorder exited his office out into the foyer. Not a solitary soul could be seen on the entire floor as I made my way back toward Maman's room.

I half expected to feel the heated presence of a million law enforcement officers, as they beat their way in, storm-trooping into the front of the facility forcefully, to once again apply full come-uppance, by way of whatever new choke-hold they had perfected, in tackling and shackling another deserving brotha', who'd *once-ta 'gain',* forgot himself out in public, seeking to right a misguided injustice—by literally taking the law into his own hands.

But I was met with nothing.

Once back with Mama'n, I begged her to hold on. I changed the tiny cassette in the recorder and this time slid it woefully beneath the sheets down at the bottom of her bed. Even she hadn't seen me do it. Then, I promised her, that I was taking her outta' there—fo' sho', the first opportunity that I could prepare.

Inside, that little man of common sense poked his head out in leering at me, imploring me to tread lightly, with caution. But, did I listen? Of course not...

And I didn't know how I'd get her out. All I knew; was that I had to do something...FAST!

I kept going back everyday and even popped in on her, just up the I-15 from my job, across the Coronado Bay Bridge at the amphib base, from time to time, during many of my lunch hours. I was intent on lending the realization to the full accompaniment of staff there, that I had my eye on them—and that I was keeping more poignant tabs on the level of effort that was being expended toward the maintenance of her daily care.

I didn't have to go as far as snuffing no'body. But, what I did do, guiltily, was finally complete the homework I should've been up on from tha' git-go. I researched the facility in the county records and I found out who owned the building, who was making ends from the services supposedly provided there, and I placed a single phone call to a lawyer friend of mine who made time for me immediately, once I filled him in on what it was I intended for my next move.

He charged me a mere two-hundred-ninety five dollars to contact the conservative holding company that owned not only that one, but about a hundred other *care* facilities throughout the Southwest. Once gaining a sit-down with their representative, he played the cassette I'd more than happily dubbed and presented to him for exactly that purpose.

He tried, during most of our more personal conversations, to convince me to fully unleash he and his firm in a full-on lawsuit, seeking punitive damages, but I held out, more cautious and scared, than anything else.

At that time, I felt I already had enough on my plate and wasn't up for the perhaps years of battle it would take to bring down such a large conglomerate as he and I would be facing.

All I sought was decent care for my Mother.

His efforts were able to gain the immediate, uncontested dismissal of my man, Harry Stanislawski. The parent corporation extended itself in producing a finely constructed, written apology, and offered to provide Mama'n indefinite care in any of their facilities, nation-wide, free-of-charge.

Why didn't I take em' up on their offer?

Y'all know why…

It took me about two weeks of convincing and cajoling "NETTIE", but I begged her, to find it in her heart (She and Mama'n had always been the best of friends, thick as thieves, often-times banding together to gang up on me even during *our* times of marital distress) to offer her blessing for me to bring Mama'n home, to our house. That way, I would, through my now solid connects at the American Disabilities Union, and the wonderful Grandmotherly lady at welfare, be able to contract for in home health services to assist with her care on a daily basis and we would know for sure that she was being seen to correctly.

It wasn't until after I'd convinced her, that if we were to do this, I would petition the Military Housing authority for a larger house, (We'd previously taken our names off of the four-bedroom list when a three-bedroom model house had come available immediately following our initial application, three years before, when we'd finally made the decision to move out of *the economy* and seek the feinted savings of *free* government housing instead) that she finally gave in.

I went down to the Naval Station at Thirty Second Street the following morning to offer the application. Once presented the verification of dependency paperwork, detailing Maman's newly approved status, we were immediately approved. We moved immediately and the very next week, with my Lovely wife's blessings and promises of a commitment to help me in whatever way she could, we contracted an ambulance to ferry Mama'n home.

Peace and tranquility bounded abundantly in our home, for a full three days after her arrival. AshLe', who was eleven at the time, was livid at the fact that although we'd moved into a larger home, that she would be the one who'd have to give up her new bedroom for Grandma' who was coming to live with us for an indefinite basis. Britty, who was thirteen at the time, was her usual, non-committal self, never one to seek out the position of inviting conflict, and perhaps be tagged as *making waves*, she remained silent. Boomer, at seven, Loved the fact his Grandmother was going to move in with us—forever…He was the one of my children that Mama'n had, in the past, fawned over and doted on the most.

"NETTIE", was an entirely different story altogether.

Surprisingly, she appeared to instantly develop a deep resentment of Mama'n.

Looking back now, with a healthy hindsight, I clearly see why. Mama'n, although being a party to the overall generation of the plans for bringing her into our home, offered nothing, zero, zilch—in the way of a humbled graciousness at having been permitted an entry into our most personal of personal lives.

It seemed that she went out of her way to be rude to "NETTIE", and to the girls. It was almost as if, because of my Love for her, that she demanded further recognition from them, that she was now head *bitch of the dome* and that they had best see what was good for them, if they knew what was best—for the family.

"NETTIE" would help with her shower. She would curse her out in the process, if she wasn't doing something as exacting and right as she would have done it herself, had she had use of her hands and other limbs, which were still, up until that time, dead and opaquely limber. I would help her when she couldn't maintain control of her bowels and soiled herself often. Throughout this, I'd be made to listen to all sorts of bad-mouthing she had for both my sweet wife, and for my little girls as I tried aimlessly to referee and play eventual peacemaker, while trying to keep my soon to be certainly violent home together and in-check.

This all came to a head one fate-filled evening when "NETTIE" and I found ourselves doing what we'd done more frequently to pass the time most, when it came to discussing the seemingly never-ending saga of the perplexity-filled circumstances surrounding Maman's living situation.

...*ARGUING!*

She and I were just going at it. Her vehement insistence that, "*That woman has got to be outta' my damned house—as soon as possible!*" Had me all discombobulated and overfilled with the frustration of not knowing what was best for me to do next.

Oh...I knew what the necessary move was to know what was best. I just had no idea of how to bring it all off, short of laying down the law and kicking my still invalid Mother out onto the streets to fend for herself completely.

I mean...Come on...

This was my Mama'n. No matter her faults, this was the woman who had given me birth.

And...She, was my wife...

I was having nor entertaining none of that. I sought to ignore her. So, as the fight and the evening dragged on, I finally went into our bedroom, closed the door behind me, locked it securely from the inside, and settled down, playing her off on herself, meaning to go to sleep.

How many of y'all know she wan't having none o' dat?

She next came to the bedroom door, demanding entry and meaning to continue the struggle. Surprised at finding the door locked, she did the next best thing...I guess. Drawing back a scrawny little leg beneath her hundred pound frame, she kicked the door in completely, knocking it off its hinges with a rage-filled vengeance. I got out of bed and immediately had had enough.

It had come down to supporting my Mother, a veritable crazy woman who'd birthed me, or stand around idly while an identically crazy woman, *my wife*, whom I felt I'd already put up with about a horse load of shit from—enough to last ten brotha's a lifetime, act up in such a way that I was certain—it was time for *her* to go.

I called the police.

LORD! Why'd I have to go off and do that?

Tha' Man showed up on our doorstep, lights blaring, sirens wailing, for all the nosey neighbors to gawk at and see. Guess they were a bit taken aback when I ushered them calmly into our abode, filled them in on the particulars of what had just transgressed over the course of that evening and told them that I wanted her out. The two peace officers seemed almost disappointed that they wouldn't get a shot at roughing up a brotha' at all during that call that night.

One thing I have to give the two professionally catering officers once they were there inside our home, they gave me countless chances to change my mind and revert back to common sense and not insist that they force my "NETTIE" to leave or have them cart her sorry azz off to jail beneath the ire of being charged with a domestic violence rap.

But, stupid me...I refused to wisely relent.

Finally, after coming to a definite realization that there was no changing my intentions, they asked her politely, to place her hands behind her back, and they carried her off to Las Colinas, for the second time during a marriage, and I tried as best I could to meaninglessly console our children, after them having seen their Father acquiesce weakly and have their own Mother taken forcefully from *her* home and sent off to jail.

I was a sorry sucker following that.

My heart ached so badly. I felt caught up in the despicable quagmire of life's wicked gambles. I had no where and could think of no one to whom I could turn. I had messed up my own marbles with the stupendous iniquity of my decisions. I'd made my bed...Now I'd have to live in it.

"NETTIE" bailed out, with the help of one of her brothers the following morning. After phoning and explaining the full immensity of the situation to my Executive Officer, I'd taken the day off from work. She arrived at our house, a couple hours later, for one thing—or a group of one thing...To collect—Her children!

I was a beaten man. I didn't even offer her a fight. She and the bunions moved out that same week. They'd stayed with her friend, Leslie, for a short while and then they got their own tiny, two bedroom apartment, in El Cajon, a few weeks thereafter.

All's that left me, was a broken heart, chocked full of guilt...And Mama'n.

We went about attempting to mend the individual pieces of our lives, this time, by ourselves blindly, instead of having each other's support, to count on. It would be almost the full year of 2001 that we were all apart. "NETTIE", having developed over the years into the strongest of strong American of African descent, decent persons, mothers, and wives, strode right through the turmoil of our separation like *butter.*

Me, Mr. *Know-it-all*, consummate military officer, leader of my home, intelligent confidante, I was a hot mess.

She quickly got her tiny apartment together and waved through maintaining her job, and our children with the character and strength women of her ancestry have been known to possess and had thus internally prepared her for, for centuries. Sure, she too was waylaid and shaken off course by the horrendous events that took place culminating over almost a full year and a half of putting up with the stank-bite shit of having to deal with everyday life, compounded by the complexities and trappings of managing the situation of caring for my Mother—and putting up with my shit.

So, she was ready.

Throughout the many years I'd already known her, it always surprised me (I don't know why—Stupid ME) that whenever we would argue to a point of finally deciding to call it quits, she would conduct herself, her business affairs, and the rest of what life would deal her, with the utmost clearing vision, commitment, and delicacy of detail which held her at least *appearing* to be unfazed by whatever negative outcome events of the day held in store for her.

She was the proverbial cat. Always landing on her feet and showcasing, in her past, and now, in her present, the inane ability to expend just a wee-bit of each of the more than nine lives she'd been given.

Mama'n and I lived together, in "NETTIE's" and my home, in Navy Housing, on San Diego's Nereus Street, for a period of about ten months. Each day, for me, was a twisted hodgepodge of hopelessly maintaining norms—of up before dawn, preparing my uniforms, seeing to her immediate toiletry needs, prepping for the arrival of the In-Home-Healthcare Assistant, who would cook and feed her breakfast, wash her clothes, bathe or shower her, and tidy up the house before leaving, after having spent three to four hours caring for her in such a way, that, due to me being so handily beaten down and at wits end by every negative aspect of what it took to be her son and offer her support, that she and I quickly fell into this solemn routine absurdly—so much so, that I found myself beginning to simply accept the situation and began to push thoughts of making attempts to recapture the Love of my "NETTIE", and of my children firmly out of mind while the edges of my heart imploded increasingly, becoming more lost and darker, just a smidgen at a time, without my family, day after day after longer day.

Totally unlike my own character, I was rapidly developing complacent thoughts of giving in, by offering acceptance of the newly developing lifestyle and merely *going along with the flow*.

Inside, I was caught-up, trapped beneath a maniacal, killing sheath of personal turmoil, as I'm certain "NETTIE" felt too.

We'd come so far together, up to that point, almost bearing the solidified determination and comfort of emotions—That, after all that we'd persisted through, and had grown up with together... Nothing could've *put us under;*

if we just maintained the vision and clarity of rapidly advancing the health of a Love forecasted by faith—to last lifetimes of lifetimes, beating back the odds, striving towards the future, having each other's backs, without failure, *NO-MATTER-WHAT*; then this too, I knew, deep-down, subliminally; somehow, we'd find a way—to right the wrongs of hurt feelings and of perceived and truthful betrayals—to reshape and mend our family again toward rekindling the necessary strengths of support which would present ourselves, and our children again, the positive amenities of that future never actually promised.

But, the key was: How would I ever go about making it all become a reality?

At first, I had no infinite clue.

I felt lost.

Impiously caught-up in becoming the fool who had chosen Love for his Mother, over commitment and dedication of the very same—for his wife.

After about five long months of more of the same, I found myself, like I said, giving in. She and I barely spoke or communicated with one another on any occasion. One rarely caught sight of the other in public. We were such opposites on every scale, that we simply didn't hang or run with the same people or even delve comfortably inside the same circles.

I saw her very sparingly during this time. Twice on occasions when I'd answered the doorbell, in the early approaching hours of the evening, only to be shocked by the surprise of finding two of San Diego's finest standing before me, professing that they were there to ensure a peaceful transition of her reappearing, only for the case of permitting her entry to *our home*—to grab more of her left behind belongings, to take to her apartment which she was now firmly engrossed in making *her home.* And at Boomer's "Next Generation" basketball games held at a local gym, up Balboa Avenue.

But even there, she and I would rarely speak. Those outings, for me, were life-savers though. They were times when I would get to safely interact with my children briefly. Hug them and reassure them silently that—*Don't worry, baby...Daddy's working on it, coming up with a plan for all of us to be back together—a family, under the same roof, once again.*

But in reality, *Daddy* was just as confused and misguided as they were.

Daddy didn't have a clue how he was going to salve the hole HE'D created in Mommy's heart and cause her to Love and want him again, just like she had for years and years before—Before he betrayed her and called the cops on her and sent her to jail, for no reason—Like some puss-filled sissy, running from his troubles, relying on—THE MAN to run his household instead of stepping up—and handling the situation—LIKE A MAN!.

I knew that she'd begun dating again, or at least *seeing* other men soon after our separation. This drove me nearly to the edge of a rapidly decreasing sanity—more than once. I held and had fought down an immensity of hell-sown visions, of stalking her and creeping up on her, catching her up in one of these encounters—and killing her, and the unsuspecting guy as well; just for him having the audacity to even try to eat the sweet leftovers from a still smoldering plate which was still, in my mind's eye, rightfully mine.

I'd do her, merely for setting the plate out and for making the offering.

But this, prayer and the Love for my kids, and their Love for their Mother, got me through it.

Finally, at about the seventh month mark of our disjointed separation, something began to take form in developing in me. Some, untouchable, faceless thing, which, in a productive way, would and could no longer accept the situation for what it was and for how it really and truly still is, to this day.

Above all else,—ALL ELSE! I Loved my "NETTIE".

And…I was a better man, better husband—Friend, a better Father, than this…

Mama'n was making ardent strides, on the sly—Cause' she thought I didn't know—that she had regained the ability to walk for herself, feed herself, and generally provide a lot of the care she had everyone believing she still needed help with on a daily basis.

My time was still caught-up in ferrying *her* to hospital and doctor's appointments, putting *her* shoes on, cooking *her* meals in the evening, prepping and preparing *her* linens and bed things. My every waking moment had become lost in shuffling around (Like *Step-and Fetch it*), attending to *her* wants and *her* needs while pushing my own deeper and deeper down into the wood chips, denying myself an actual life.

…And, did she appreciate it?

Well…She sure didn't show it.

With Mama'n, I understood her thought patterns and philosophies when it came to children. They were twisted streams of unproductive idealisms that she herself had gained from her own Father, my Grand pappy, Ollie.

Somehow, inside of her own head, because she'd been so busted up and unable to care for herself following her accident, and because she hadn't taken steps or made preparations for a good life all her own, which would have better held her up and supported her ability to get through this in her dire time of need, I owed her—my life.

I owed her my home.

I owed her my own children...

I owed her my marriage!

For these same reasons, the realities of her own life, which were now making my life so miserable, identical explanations, for what made me so strong-headed, so will-bound, so successful, were all her doing as well—She can smile inside herself and take the credit—I don't mind. In the way she had neglected me, because she neglected me, In the way she taught me, utilizing mainly a style of authoritative, negative reinforcement, because she had taught me, In the way she'd abused me, beating me down in my youth, almost to the point of me being so confused about my own self-worth as a child, that I didn't know whether I was of any value to this world at all, Because she abused me, In the way she Loved me...no matter what *she* did to refute it aligning along a system bearing an almost backwards scale of warmth, tenderness amid a shocking scheme of constant guile, because she Loved me; I came to my own epiphany of realization—That...It was time to kick Mama'n, and all her worries and troubles and *fucc'd-up* ideologies—TO THE CURB!

It took me about a month's more of management of all the possible variables, coordination and re-verification of processes and regulations, but, before long, I had put in place the necessary steps that it would take to get *that* woman outta' my house, and onto the proper roads to re-starting her own life; and then, and only then, could I begin to make the follow on steps of identifying just what it would take—to reclaim the truth in the tenderness, Love and care that my own distraught family so richly deserved.

It was May of 2002 before I'd finally been able to simply break it all down to Mama'n and tell her finally and forcefully, that she had to go. No longer did I permit concerns for her feelings, concern for her welfare, concerns for her ideas to overshadow the immense longing I'd held for so long deeply inside of myself, for offering my family the happiness and sanctuary of a safely administered, peaceful, Loving home.

I put her on a Southwest flight on a Friday evening.

Immediately, after watching that plane take off, all measure of stress and unrealistic certainty, that I was no longer myself, but Audrey's boy, disappeared plainly.

...And it had only taken me thirty-seven years to realize that I truthfully had it in me to be my own man, conduct my own life, make and stick by my own decisions—weighed and made positively, without any help—from her.

Chapter Twelve
CHICKEN-SHIT

I next began to formulate and put in place the things that I would say to "NETTIE" in the hopes of touching her heart to get her back.

I began calling her more often. To her credit, even after all that I had put her through. . . *MYTURN!* Her only insistence, or condition, if you will, for a serene return to the norm in our lives, was her demand that Mama'n be shown the door, no matter how slight, or how perverse the showing needed to be— She was at a point in her own frustrations, where she could care less how it was I was able to bring it all about.

JUST GET ER' DONE!

And I had done just that—*FINALLY.*

But we didn't get back together to mend things right away. She had other demands, slight ones, as well.

She wanted the two of us to attend counseling. Marital/Couples counseling, with a credentialed Marriage and Family therapist. And I had to be the one to research and locate the right one. *Cause' it was* my *fault that we were all in this mess from the gitgo.*

This was a very tough point of relenting for me. Even though I had learned an immense amount about coming to rely upon and trust the results and completely clarifying edge evident in being able to successfully buy into, attend, and complete counseling, there was still the nagging edge of distrust for the entire field of counseling lingering in the back of my mind copiously.

But, there was no other choice. . . Was there?

If I was truly a man who said what he meant and meant what he said, I would do anything at all to right the grievous stack of wrongs I'd selfishly forced upon my family during the entire charade and ordeal of pretending more to care about my Mother, and her needs and her life, than I had concerning my own.

I located a man, named Jaime Issacson, a brotha'. I felt for certain, he would be able to peer into and see that I was right ninety-nine percent of the time, and that she was wrong the same percentage, and that he would be professional enough not to be skittish about taking *my side* in letting her know *her* faults. He was local, just off of Carrol Canyon Road, five minutes up the I-15 from our house, in a quaint little office, inside a shopping center which we could easily reach even during the most overbearing traffic days at the time.

Jaime, for us, was pretty cool…at first. We both sat down, explained all our issues to him, cried a lot; and seemingly left every session, at least for me, more mad and pissed off—at each other, than we'd been prior to pulling up into the parking lot to get there for our weekly appointment. The sessions were quite expensive, but we didn't have to worry. My insurance under the Navy paid for everything.

It didn't take me long, to fully become irritated with the style Jaime used in attempting to help us deal with our own shit encased in our own situations with the expertise of a quiet demeanor and an extremely professional style I was blindly unable to see at the time.

He constantly flipped our troubles around to compare them to something he had experienced, whether with his own wife, his children, or with friends he'd encountered in everyday life. And I didn't take too kindly to that—at all.

I believe that I'd expected and wanted him—to fix us, *and fix us now*! I was extremely impatient. And because of that, I feared that he would never be able to bring it all off and that held me apprehensive and scared inside. So I began to alienate him.

Challenging his sage suggestions and countering his recommendations at every turn, with an airy alacrity—Cause' I was a smart guy, as intelligent, if not more, than he, and I knew what was best for my family more so than he did—*He* was just a stranger, for all intents and purposes, a highly overpaid listening ear whom we were stupendously trusting to perform a miracle for which I had no idea just how long it could possibly take.

He didn't really KNOW us…

Still, "NETTIE" and the bunyions moved back in. We rented a U-Haul and carted all of her things back home to the house on Nereus Street. I was elated at having them back. But, for us, not a whole lot had changed involving the scarring pangs of hurt and guilt, of deceit and feelings of having been betrayed, on either side.

But still, we moved on.

After only a short stack of sessions, we stopped going to see Jaime. It became a point of deciding to just make it happen—together, on our own—just like we'd started so many years before, without help. One way or another make it happen through the hit and miss of dedicating ourselves to taking positive steps which would eventually play out to preserve the hopes of a family still greatly in need.

Once again, like a million times before, we Loved, we fought, we struggled…But we remained firm, stuck it out and actually, the dividends that simple determination has paid, has maintained our existence, as a family for quite some time, and has followed on toward producing a wonderful success.

We tried approaching and seeing another therapist, Clarita Johns, a nice, white lady, whose office was actually within walking distance, in a Tierra Santa office project a mere mile or so from our house. Clarita tried her best for me and for "NETTIE" as well. But, once again, things still didn't work out with her for us. I am shocked that one of these two, highly educated individuals had never come straight out and recommended for us, "Why don't the two of you just get a divorce at last and go your separate ways. Why are you still together?"

I think, given the shoe on the other foot, I might have tossed all professional caution to the wind and suggested just that.

But they hadn't.

…And she and I still maintained, barely able at times to continually stick it out.

Our counseling woes over, I began thinking out creating or coming up with a new endeavor to take our minds off of our personal, marital troubles. That was getting us out of Navy housing, and entertaining the idea of perhaps getting in on the highly lucrative, California housing market.

We'd been living in government, military housing for a period of more than eight, wasteful years. And during all of that time, I was aimlessly permitting more than about eighteen hundred dollars per month, that the Navy would have provided me as a portion of my pay, to live out in town, buy a house, or just rent and pay someone else's mortgage (As equally stupid, if you think about it) to go down the drain untouched.

So, we actually sat down, time and time and time again and began to dream of all the *what if* possibilities our visions of reaching out to better the lives of ourselves and our children held.

Number one, we had horrendous credit at the time. My idea of balancing our financial situation, had been to make minimum payments, sometimes not even that, cause' I'd heard somewhere that your creditors are prevented from suing you in court, if you just pay them something, a dollar, a dime...

Something other than just—no attention at all. But this still didn't preclude them from dinging the shit outta' a credit report on a very strictly adhered to, monthly basis.

And our report looked more than troubled.

Secondly, we were fooling ourselves if we thought we could ever come up with the minimal five, ten, or twenty percent most lenders required as a down payment prior to authorizing financing of any new home purchase.

What was a fella to do?

I knew that the immense reality of the American dream, home ownership was out there. But, just like driving fast new cars, and having extra money to spend—on whatever, it was all an assembly of our imaginations primarily for us, things to be looked at and envied as they passed by or were lived in and driven or expended by and on somebody else.

But this thing just wouldn't let me go. Somehow, someway, I became hell bent on breaking that negative cycle of sub-prime credit, throwing away those lifelong, wasteful spending habits, and of finding a way of perfecting the inclusion of *my* family along the same lines as so many other (generally white) members of society who'd had already taken and made great strides and realized the dream towards amassing the same in their own lives with a seemed experienced ease.

I refused to remain on the sidelines, watching everybody else enjoy themselves while they correctly played the game.

I wanted in.

Again, I've taken to heart—that the difference between being a boy and a man are the lessons that you learn. Those lessons don't take very long to teach you, once and for all, that—in this game of life, experience is priceless.

It's just a shame it takes your entire youth to realize this. If imitation is truly the most sincere form of flattery, I had my eyes set on putting away such stupidity of continuing to follow along with all my contemporaries as each one of us made our idiotic ways straight into the poor house.

When I was enlisted, I was forever just a proving step away from Captain's Mast (the Navy's Form of Non-Judicial Punishment) where you were *AWARDED* things like: forfeiture of half a months pay for two months, restriction to the ship for forty-five days and a reduction to the next inferior pay grade, for having broken some sort of time-honored rule steeped in Naval and societal tradition.

For the most part, I was a single man, uneducated to the ways of how I should have been living.

Instead of striving and seeking out a higher principle of learning, one which showed me and prepared me further for the ins and outs of intricacies of items such as price to earnings indexes, the valued commodity of investing in various, high—producing mutual funds, and the individual dividends of raising your family, including disciplining your children steadily, and correctly, with a vengeance, where you spent more time working at that than you did making weekly preparations for stepping out to the club,

I was merely living on the edge. On the edge of a disaster which is largely unrecoverable increasingly, with the un-tethered passing of each wasted moment in time.

Once commissioned as a Mustang Ensign, I attempted to turn the tables on time by adhering more abruptly to a thought out, personally held axiom of, *Learn All The Rules—Completely. So You Can Break Them All…Just The Same.*

It was through being able to use this that I sought to finally place a break in becoming a shadowy figure continually fraught with finding himself ensnarled, caught, and captured while swimming up stream against the grain. I broke with statistics. I took steps of refusing to become further included in facts such as: although the national unemployment rate in our country, specifically for Americans of African descent looms scarily more than a whopping ten percent and rather than placing faith in abstinence, education and experiences of fore-fathers, our simplistic results have us spending more and saving less at alarming rates leading to shallow futures of perpetual denigration.

In 1992, according to research corporations that track such details, Americans of African descent spent more than twenty-two billion dollars in this country on clothes alone.

And this was during a heavy financially ladened year in which the economy was not doing so well as a whole.

We spent more than three billion on electronic toys, computers, software and gadgets and more than eleven billion on furnishings for homes most of us had no real propensity for even thinking about owning.

We have continued to place value in the wealth of fancy cars, with spinning rims and to ply ourselves not-so-discretely with all sorts of booze, drugs, depressants, and stimulants to try and hide in the face of our shame that we are so obviously far behind in the struggle for reaching towards personal equalities solely because we don't create and provide chances for ourselves.

Although we make up more than twelve percent of the populace of this, our great nation, we are stupendously responsible for more than thirty percent of the country's consumption of alcoholic beverages. More than forty six billion dollars was spent inside the American cultures of those of African descent on cars, that the emblazoned auto makers have done, exactly what we have permitted them to do with us, and that is take and use the greed and fame of ourselves and of that of our home-grown celebrities to design and create *special edition* vehicles targeting sales mainly in the more poor, undereducated sectors.

Anybody know how much one of those finely crafted machines of vehicular performance appreciates the moment you drive it off the lot?

Here's hoping that you do.

Know how much a home can appreciate after just six months of ownership?

Sadly enough, the only reported statistic that we've been *SMART* about and have actually decreased the level of our spending in demonstratively, is in our decisions to purchase books.

WHAT!

That's correct. The communities of Americans of African descent actually shelled out fifty-three million dollars less during the year 2003, than they did in the previous year on books.

What does that say about our unbridled commitment to the health, excellence and welfare of the many children we are continuing to have (Out-of Wedlock) every year?

How could we ever expect to bring this thing up from behind?

How can we offer our children the hopes and dreams of demanding a self-expecting equality from society, when we don't present society any hopes that we truly care about ourselves? Have we forfeited our hopes and our dreams and our ability for striving for success simply to become complacent, drunken braggarts, hell bent upon *looking good on the outside*, while continuing to hasten our own extinction through the demise of wasteful thinking and while killing ourselves head to toe—on the inside?

More statistics founded inside studies conducted by the National Urban League have less than fifty percent of Americans of African descent whom can call themselves home owners. This is compared to more than seventy percent of our white brothers and sisters who can confidently express the reverse. To carry it forward, other documented studies showcase the fact that whites saved more than twenty percent more on a monthly basis for retirement.

Most Americans of African descent, at least the thirty percent with incomes extending over one hundred thousand dollars per year, chose to place such a decreased emphasis on retirement, that their numbers show less than five thousand dollars, on the whole in retirement accounts to support healthy futures.

Do we have futures of fortune?

Do we care about having futures at all?

How many of us have taken the time to learn about and teach our children the values of investing?

I'm here to tell you, that more than seventy-nine percent of all American whites invest their hard-earned monies in the stock market and they raise their children with the solid knowledge of how to follow in their footsteps by doing the same. We find ourselves behind in this too. Only sixty-one percent of Americans of African descent discover the value in doing this.

Americans of African decent in this country alone wield a healthy six hundred thirty billion dollar spending ability. I say it's high time that we pull our heads—out, of the sand...And begin to make the dreams and realities of a forward-thinking prosperity a viable risk of common sense we can all make deposits into, in seeking better futures of fortune for both ourselves, our families, and overall to offer our own increasing levels of support to the continued national health—of our great nation, for our country.

Heck, our ancestors had a great hand in the economic well-being and structuring of this country. Some would even report, *that we built* it. Why not make its rights and its wrongs work productively, as do our white counterparts, for ourselves?

Accepting defeated lifestyles, those encased in disappointment, and offering legacies of failures we are all doomed to continually pass down to our offspring; the very same offspring who will not be fully prepared, and who themselves will look at life with our identical despairing mentalities, is the true chain of assured death sprayed across our incomplete cultures using our failures as their example for not achieving.

Such is the daunted future that has remained true to the force of promising more than four centuries of the ever folding, *CHOCOLATE CHICKEN*.

As Fathers, Brothers, Uncles...and as elders, don't we owe more to our children?

How about—To ourselves...?

Isn't it *OUR* responsibility to teach them and re-enforce within them, as the great man, Malcom, once said, *"By any means necessary"* to create within their minds the propensity of profit in having the wherewithal to identify sound foundations steeped in more plausible legacy and offer to our children, whom we so often profess—to Love, a more firmly rooted likelihood at making more positive choices supporting productivity in their own lives?

Yet...*CHOCALATE CHICKENS* fail to adhere to a sense of common assimilation, time and time again, that says, "you cannot continue to live in Rome, and prosper, while refusing all the while, to ever learn to speak Latin.

Falling under the heading of supporting ignorance, becoming unusable to society and bearing nothing to offer, places us on the path to quickly becoming used to lives as *CHOCOLATE CHICKENS;* thereby perpetuating the sustainment of a hoax and purporting a sham, which sells the tale—that it's acceptable to do less than your called to and that it's O.K. if you only achieve at the very minimal scales of your overall ability.

A cop-out—For certain, if dumb enough to place credence in it at all.

Don't get me wrong, throughout my twenty-two year career in the Navy, I've been guilty, a time or twenty, of falling prey to the same perpetration of false-hoods, most engineered largely from inside myself.

To me, *Sum-body 'was always out ta' get me, underestimate me, not understand me*—all because I was *BLACK!*

But, I'm not...

Black, that is...

I cannot be characterized by a color. What I am—IS AN AMERICAN (FIRST...and foremost)—OF AFRICAN DESCENT!

I'd thought in 1996, while aboard the aircraft carrier, USS KITTY HAWK (CV-63), that *THA-MAN* had it out for me—fo' sho'. It was during a two year period in which I had been doggedly studying for the prized, shipboard qualification of becoming a Surface Warfare Officer (SWO). Once completed, every officer that completes this qualification is presented the coveted brass (they appeared golden) cross-cutlasses to wear above their pocket, just over his or her left breast. This signified to every naval patriot your willingness and determination to seek out, research, memorize, and perform up to a par of nothing short of excellence—under stressful situations and conditions, while continuing to learn.

Is *RACISM* today still alive and well within the Navy today?

I found, that it was just like in society, when having dealings with some—it was, and when dealing with others—it was not.

Like anything else, you had a fifty-fifty chance of winning and becoming successful, of losing and failing or being denied the chance to succeed, or just merely of gaining a push.

Up until that point, I'd found a way of operating beneath the at times wandering scale of these odds.

The most blatant circumstance in my own history remains that period aboard ship where I was charging forward with hopes of gaining the distinction of being presented a SWO pin. This was eventually craftily thwarted, I felt at the time, by the USS Kitty Hawk's most senior Officer, the Captain, Jared Pomaskewski.

The Captain was himself a product of Polish lineage, only two generations removed from experiencing the same pangs of the greater American prejudice firsthand, by name.

You see, the major angst of the racism disease is that it has in its repertoire the ability to become as smoothly played out and taught in modern times, as it has during the past, as it is finely capable of enduring strangely, in silence and of remaining skulkingly invisible, until the creeping, encrusted edges of iniquity and resultant backlash begin to raise their unattractive heads and reach forward to threaten any progress those refusing to take part in its generation have rightfully realized through their own extremely hewn senses of hard earned sweat and effort.

For those seeking regeneration of such a disease, and even for some who do not, yet whom permit its endangering feces to incubate unchecked around and inside of them, it becomes *like childbirth pains to a woman. Mostly forgotten following many years separating the past and present between occurrences.*

But it's still there, lying dormant.

I felt betrayed and let down, by Captain Pomaskewski. To coin naval phraseology, *I felt—Thrown to the wolves, or rolled under the bus* by a system I'd gone that extra step toward assimilating—to a point where I felt I could let down my guard and finally begin to place trust, might be a more closely descriptive expression of the faith I had formally place.

Today's military's scheme of racism holds the possibility of being even colder and more exacting than that of plantation owners and overseers of a hundred-forty years ago.

Surely…they could no longer track you down on horseback, threaten you with the hunt of coon and hound dogs in an intrepid battle of wits as you pointed hopefully toward Northern waters, or lay you open in bloody filets of strands of a cold, strapping steel-like, punitive whips.

What they could do, was foster insipid images of crafty ideas of presenting you life-changing sweets—things like increasing wages, steady jobs, schools for your kids in neighborhoods which are not steeped in mire and gang warfare amid a supply of illicit drugs pumped in through pipelines originally established by the same government—which repeatedly voiced an insistence that it was determined in its efforts of *waging a war* against its creation, while steadily pushing an entire race of people, through its use, who were supposing to be counted among its citizens, firmly over the edge toward collapse and extinction as the overflowing inner cities are rocked solidly, year after year, by a neglect and failure in what some would stamp as being American genocide.

But who's to blame? Whose fault is it that today that situations such as these still exist. These are the faults of our country. Live with them or be crushed.

I've learned that no one system is ever going to be perfect. Just like in society, I encountered an overwhelming study, sullen at its forefront by stark and demeaning contradictions while in the Navy. The Captain possessed the capability of offering you these niceties. Well earned trophies, if you were worthy, but as well easily *yanked away,* when dealing with some, such as he, when it appeared you were getting too close too fast to matching and completing the largely intriguing and sometimes, seemingly impossible assignments of tasks he created, aboard *his* ship—and if you didn't following *his* timeline toward entertaining the successes of becoming a sea going Officer of the Deck on the bridge of the ship upon which he was master, you were nothing more than dirt.

After years of dogged study, through devices all his own, without reason (Cause' he was Captain and he wasn't required to give any) Captain Pomaskewski put a screeching halt to the advancement of my Naval career by refusing to look at me as *just one of the guys* inside his wardroom of officers, upon whom he was supposed to've been able to place any amount of faith and trust in, in any of our abilities to carry out his orders completely, no matter the drill.

Evil teaches evil. It doesn't matter if it's played out upon a single person, an entire race or if engineered by an entire nation against the peoples of an unsuspecting World.

Through Captain Pomaskewski's endeavors I bore witness in today's modern Navy, to the skulking face of a thing called racism. And I didn't falter. I simply looked at it and took it for what it was, at face value. I drew an angle on it after making a complete identification and subsequently quickly redrew the lines of my goals, removing Navy from my sliding scale of many future endeavors.

I don't feel special or unique in this. I am and was just a small smidgen counted among the many that have experienced just the same under equaling circumstances.

Picture seventy men, all of them Americans of African descent, in 1944—on a brightly lit morning, along a shoreline in Port Chicago, California, aligned in a dutiful daisy chain, passing bombs back and forth to each other unloading trainload after trainload of ammunition, fondling death in support of the war effort. The Port, a sleepy, one traffic-lighted strip of rolling hills and foggy bottoms, was located just outside of San Francisco.

They were there, each and every one of them, not because they were *CHICKENS* but more truthfully, because they wanted inclusion among society and they had found a way of making it become a reality through their efforts of wanting only to serve.

-Yet, not necessarily in such a capacity.

For them, at the time, this was one of the only jobs the Navy would assign them to. In keeping with the nationalized passions of the population, nobody else would or wanted to take on such dangerous duties. So it became a chore befitting personnel previously identified, by law to have only been three-fifths human.

Who cared anyway, they were only…*NIGGERS'*?

To make matters more interesting, white officers stationed there, just along a delta bordering the city of Concorde, California, would wager paychecks on whose group of strong backs could hump the most ammo from the most trains the fastest. They did this, knowing full well the inevitability of volatile dangers inherent with the loads they were handling as they gambled atrociously with not only the lives of their men, but with those of hundreds of the tiny town's citizenry as well, with a whimsical disregard.

When one of the trains did finally manage to blow, two entire pier side vessels vanished in an instant, along with any traces of the men still aboard which had previously made up the accompaniments of their crews. The ensuing force of the blast blew out windows in office buildings as far away as (forty-five miles to be exact) downtown San Francisco.

Of the hundreds of American men of African descent who had formerly taken part in the Officer's blight-filled wagering during handling operations on the pier, only seventy of them survived. Most of these bore life-threatening injuries which they would eventually carry with them to their graves.

When the blast had settled, and a very brief, *inconclusive* naval inquiry was conducted, the United States government quickly determined that it was imperative to the war effort that the timely schedule of reinitiating the dangerous work along the delta be maintained.

The seventy young, American men of African descent flatly refused.

To resume their deadly assignments without proven assurances garnering more safe working conditions was, for them, a reoccurring nightmare simply waiting to happen. They held firm in their stances and would no longer permit themselves to be thrust unwary into a situation, even if for service, for a company which plainly showcased a blatant disregard for their lives and for their humanity.

The Navy Court-Marshaled each and every one of them, for mutiny. The occurrence had become a black eye for the Navy when rehashed and retold as it has for more than fifty years of non-written, non-newsworthy history. Downplayed within naval folklore, and known only in hushed circles as *The Mutiny at Port Chicago,* the occurrence will shamefully never become part of any middle school text book for open discussion and review.

All seventy have since been exonerated and have had their records expunged of all alleged wrong doings. Yet it took more than fifty years, after having had their lives ruined, over nothing more than by being forced to endure an already amassing hardship (Being of African descent) for close to half a century. They were permitted to seek out and live the American dream following their incarcerations and eventual release from naval service. It's just—for an extremely long time; They had to do it—That is, seek freedom, as felons.

This can only be matched by the still under-reported recollection of the crew of the destroyer escort ship USS Mason. The time was again, 1944. The vessel held a cast of American men of entirely African descent for an enlisted crew. Of course there was a well and full accompaniment of white officers who held the responsibilities of "*overseeing*" the operations that these brave men were charged with on a daily basis.

Most recently, the story of the Mason was touted as the 1st time Americans of African descent were permitted the privilege of holding roles inside the United States Navy of non steward or service oriented natures.

Surprisingly to most and knowingly to others, those aboard the Mason gained a silently held reputation and fame throughout the fleet for their dedication and bravery in making more than ten repeated trips across the Atlantic, escorting allied convoys. The men were so astute at their assignments, that their Captain, following a particularly harrowing mission, had submitted every man aboard for a Presidential citation. His write up had applauded countless confrontations with the enemy in which each crew member's performance had showcased heroism *above and beyond* the call of duty.

The Navy swept the Captain's recommendation to award the men a citation completely aside. It wasn't to be until, again, fifty years later, in 1994, that then President, William Jefferson Clinton righted the wrong and subsequently presented the remaining survivors a just due in commemoration of the sacrifices these men who were blatantly discriminated against had suffered.

The saga of the stories of the Mason, and of *The Mutiny at Port Chicago* was a far cry from the regal winds of the fervored celebrations and accolades-as they were up front reported, of millions of their white counterparts returning home to ticker tape parades, and cheers of joyous raucous following the war.

My last boss while at sea aboard the USS Constellation (CV-64) was a congenial man named Commander, Gary Meyers. Gary was a gentle, soft-spoken genius of a man who just happened to be a brave, respectable American of Irish descent.

We served together in the carrier's one and two Combat Systems Management positions during the heated uncertainty that was the beginning of the liberation of the country of Iraq during Operation Iraqi Freedom.

He and I would discuss race and its history as it was applied to America and her people from beginning to seemingly no end. While far from being a racist, he held the views that he owed America's citizens of African descent nothing, solely for the reason of the fact of him being white.

And, outright and blatantly, I openly agreed with him.

But, during this particular, friendly conversation, when he and I spoke about this, I attempted to impart to him and get him to try and understand my reasonings; for why it was that I felt he was entirely incapable of fully grasping the frustrations of how a hundred or more years of oppression weighs on a person presently, as they routinely continue to experience subtly changed expressions of the same things even today over the course of their daily lives.

He attempted to offer swift comparisons between the plight of the American of African descent to that of the immigrant Irish, his ancestors, who'd come through a quagmire of prejudice all their own during the torrential periods of the American twenties and thirties.

I posed for him seeking a respectful challenge, "Were they chained when they arrived; after being torn from their homes using cargo nets, whips, flintlock pistols and shackles? Did they have their wives and children ripped from them unceremoniously? Were they forced to mate for profit or submit to being raped, pillaged and tortured, most times to a point of being forced to abruptly succumb to being murdered?"

I almost felt sorry for him. I saw the pain registering inside him as he searched forlornly for the answers that he was fully unable to provide. I felt his shame. I experienced his embarrassment as the only explanation he could offer for a thing merely altered and given a new name, as he and I both knew, it still ran flourishing, even within today's Navy of professional opportunity and advancement—but still not equal, as it continues to prosper and exist.

I recall a reply to a question I posed for him during our conversation. I'd asked him why we never saw more than ten percent minority representation among both the officer and enlisted core aboard any ship of the United State's fleet. Those numbers become even more driveling if held up within the more specialized communities within the Navy, such as pilots, nuclear prototype, Special Forces and among the silent submarine service.

Helplessly, he had no option other than to take on the persona of every card-carrying dissident who has repeatedly beaten the derisive drum, bad-mouthing the positives of Affirmative Action within the country, on a grand scale, as we offered altering views to keep us busy during the mundane routines evident during lengthy and arduous deployments at sea day by day.

Fearing becoming personally suspect, he began to meet my questions, with questions. He also began to imply that he knew nothing of what I was talking about, even though he too had been in the service for more than twenty years, just like myself.

"What do you mean ten percent?" he asked me. "I'm not so sure those figures are accurate. Are you? Have you counted every ship in the entire navy?"

"I've counted all the ships I've been on and I've queried others about the demographic make ups of their own ships," I returned.

"But that's not entirely a scientific evaluation," he charged. "What's the demographic make up of the numbers of African American peoples within society? What's the number of African Americans in the entire Navy? Are you counting females?"

Oh, suddenly I was being made to become a statistician, bearing studies of numbers, complete with discernable derivatives, knowledgeable about things surrounding me that I had lived as truths, almost on a daily basis.

"I don't know that to be true—that there are only ten percent on every navy ship," he presented again.

Regretfully, I could tell that the stalemate, albeit reticent, over the course of our friendly conversation, was causing him no little amount of immediate frustration.

I hadn't meant to.

"I guess you'd be one of *those* who'd call for and accept reparations for African Americans—too, huh…?" he added simplistically.

He seemed to answer his own question.

"I just don't see why it is *I* have to pay, for something that took place more than a century and a half ago," he went on, shaking his head, busted up inside, with a wholly unearned familiarity of guilt.

"Who's gonna' pay it? Where's the money gonna' come from?" He continued to counter defensively.

"From out of your's and my pockets. That's where." And he then got up gruffly, having had enough and he made his way out of my office with a stubborned quickness. I heard from him next, in an e-mail he'd forwarded to me, concerning, amazingly enough the story which had just hit the wire about the destroyer escort, Mason.

When he'd first been sent a copy of the story, I could read between the lines. I knew that he couldn't wait to send it to me, as if somehow attempting to confirm a revival of his insistence that I was completely wrong in my initial indictment of the precious Navy *he and I* formerly had held so dearly close to our hearts.

"Great story on page 35....deals with facts more than perceptions. A story that should touch every sailor's heart....it did mine.

Vr

Gary"

Typically, the *Greater America* chided those falling prey completely, marking them as being ill-informed, or improperly equipped and depleted of details,—for mistakenly choosing, instead of science of fact, to *rely only upon perceptions*.

Although I'd never been taught about the Mason or been informed that a sleepy place known only as Port Chicago even held such an esteemed consignment of existence somewhere outside of the protected annals of our naval history, I had known, through other personal studies, about both events, prior to him having a chance to point them out as perhaps a banner of his attempts of trying to solidify his points.

Perceptions? Was four-hundred years of abuse a perception?

Was my Maternal Great-Grandfather, Wade Williams's grave of a coiled snakepit-where he'd been forced to enter, prior to being shot dead—only after having been chased and run down by a mob of white, American men whose only reasonings behind their angry actions were, because of his refusal to sell them his land in Virginia—a perception?

Where *are* those stories in our history books anyway? Why aren't they there? Is America so ashamed of its Masons and Port Chicagos that they have to stamp them completely from existence, while compounding the effort by dauntlessly denying me promotion through the ritualistic attainment of a caster pin, spray painted golden pewter?

My response to his email was tempered yet extremely direct.

"Gary,

I'm certain you know... That one of the greatest strengths of racism is its ability to imply the excused act of plying perception while artfully seeking the denial of facts. While it is an awesome story, showcasing a human strength of character under oppressive circumstances, a commendation awarded fifty years later could never possibly offer relief of the injustice the crew had to have experienced after having been treated sub-humanely by a government purporting to consider from its inception *that "ALL MEN WERE CREATED EQUAL"*. This, if you read it completely through, was evidenced by the remarks of one of the story's characters. In those, he offered up his inability to even discuss the atrocities he and his shipmates have been forced to endure, both as citizens and as sailors of the greatest navy of nations the earth's ever seen.

V/R

Blu"

The article had also indicated that a newly built ship, christened, The USS Mason was being commissioned.

Also; that more than thirty-one percent of her crew were scheduled to be Americans of African descent.

Hmmmm....

Wonder why it was that the Navy had felt the need to highlight such a fact?

Could it be that someone other than me and my boss, Commander Meyers, had finally caught them with their proverbial equality down and had spoken out?

I realized fully that Gary, and America, were not the faces of *the enemy.*

I hold no unmatchable grudges for a history I am aptly incapable of placing a dent in and therefore am virtually helpless to correct.

I also know, that deep down, most men are just that...men. And I know we all suffer our failures and shortcomings entirely the same. I know...That I know GOD, and have a genuine concern and commitment to the healthy right of existence—of all men. It is for this reason that, although I bear a resemblance to a history of racism that I could never, and do not internally, characterize myself as being racist.

My thoughts around the summer of 2002 were centered directly around the newly developing sequences of mind altering challenges of having to knuckle down to develop a way of coming up with about fifteen-thousand dollars that I would use as a five percent down payment on "NETTIE's" and my first home.

We'd fallen head over heels in Love with a home built just outside of Temecula, California and one weekend, while visiting one of "NETTIE's" brothers, who'd already wisely purchased one for himself, we entered the brightly lit comfort of the sales office preparing with hope, to make our dreams to come true.

She and I still believe that GOD rewarded us with our home as payment in full for us having *stuck-it-out,* although the real enemy, satan, had other devices in store with which to continually try to beat us down or rather to make attempts to trip us up, but, through our faith, we remained firm.

The agents there were nice, coquettishly appealing, sharply outfitted, white ladies, each in their early to mid twenties. My first question to them, upon entering the crisply air-conditioned space, was, "Hello, my name's Blu Penn, this here's my wife, "NETTIE"...Say, How'd I go about getting a job like yours?

Always on the prowl for professional opportunity...

...And, believe me, simply by asking, very near into my professional future, it paid off.

I recall "NETTIE" punching me lightly in the ribs as she quickly side stepped me and immediately got down to business seeking further knowledge about what exactly it was gonna' take for her to finally get her a house.

Before we knew it, we'd signed our names a gazillion times. We initialed each legal sized page in the lengthy purchase contract in the tiny little outlines which identified that you were initialing to verify that you had signed your initials confirming that you had signed. The quite loquacious sales agents offered us, "Our lender will be contacting you in the morning."

...And *BOY!* Did she ever?

The representative for *their* lender was a nice-enough lady named Lisa. She first congratulated us on the purchase of what she said was, *the finest quality home of the most attentive efforts at the production of increasing value.*

WHAT?

She went on then to begin to step through all the things, documents, verifications, title report requests, appraisal inspections, good-faith estimates, rate lock-ins and points and closing fee numeraries which would be necessary for us to make our dream come true for us for real.

"Let's see, you've purchased a five bedroom, two-story, three-thousand square-foot unit, with a two car garage, loft, and office...located on a seven-thousand, five-hundred square foot, cul-de-sac lot.

Does that sound correct?"

"Ughhh...Yep, I...I guess."

I really hadn't been knowledgeable enough to know to take inventory of so many particular details and other points of finery when we'd only stood around, wide-eyed, and mesmerized, for the most part, as the overly intrusive expressions of the agents had shot clearly over our heads definitively when we were back at the office.

All I knew was were suppose to be getting a home, payments were supposed to start the first of the month of October, and we were scheduled to move in—in August.

But, of course, this didn't phase her or even start to slow her down.

"You'll be needing to furnish me with W-2's, executed tax documentation, the form, 1040, 1041, or whatever you used to file, for the years 99' through 2002 will do. Pay stubs and employment verifications, dating back (To when your parents were babies), bank statements detailing each of the accounts you hold current, and...Oh...*my!* What I mean is; yesss...Written explanations for any and all lates you have..." She took a break. I knew she was flipping through, going over the atrocity that had become *our* credit bureau report from the big three, Equifax, Experian and Trans Union.

Didn't matter...It all came out to being about the same thing—no matter how you looked at it No reason to lie.

-Dismal.

"Hmmm.... I see, that is...Any lates you've had spanning thirty, sixty, or hundred and twenty day periods.

"We've really got to move fast on this Mr. Penn. Your closing's just right around the corner."

She didn't know half the truth.

Our CLOSING—of that application to purchase could be coming, faster than she realized, if I had to gather all those records and stuff, before we moved in.

I mean...Who keeps all that stuff? Ain't it all so unimportant?

I was fixin' my lips to bid her good-bye, after trying to calmly cool the plethora of terms and explanations she'd gone over as each syllable seemed to get stuck, back up, then reverberate around again in a swirling mess, swimming around uselessly inside my head. I felt strangely out of my element and frustrated. But I really did try to take in and recall at least some of the items she'd said she was gonna' be needing.

I thought we were finished when she caught me, dead in my hang-up tracks, and stunning me further.

"And...Mr. Penn?

I'll be needing to receive a faxed copy of your cleared, fifteen hundred dollar check to the builder—for your deposit, and, oh! Dear me...Almost forgot, proof of money to close—to cover closing costs, down-payment, and pre-paids, which appears it comes to...

FIFTEEN THOUSAND, SEVEN-HUNDRED FIFTY dollars...And Thirty-TWO cents..."

Suddenly, I felt myself becoming sick.

"Can you ahhh...assure me that you can meet each of these conditions prior to, let's say, this Thursday or Friday?"

I never even remembered paying her a greeting before hanging up by merely letting the length of the telephone cord slide from my fingers, down my leg, and come to rest at my feet, on the floor.

She'd completely lost me with that horrendous dollar amount and I believe I'd totally blanked everything else out, after *cents*, inside my head, as the throes of not having the fortitude to have lived my life personally, professionally, and financially, preparing for this moment caught up with me.

Instead, it appeared mine and "NETTIE's" dreams had been snuffed out indefinitely, to suddenly, as quickly as they had come, materialize just as fast to nothing more than another *CHOCOLATE CHICKEN* nightmare—all in the huff of a telephone call which wielded the awestricken power of a mighty blow.

Some would have said, "Fate was a *mother,* as it came by, time-and-time again to lay waste to endeavors of haughty ideas, sweet feelings of hope—all because of sacrifices never made.

Some would have felt we were haunted.

Who knows...

We weren't.

Just, that being true to myself, a faint sense of character weakness had been allowed to smolder and ignite within, for far too long. Fueled by a disparaging, on again, off again harmony, and what should have been previously classified as an almost criminal historical precedent of never respecting and guarding our credit status, we'd simply permitted irresponsibility to seep in as we walk around, for years, headlong, seeking and expecting, without the work, to achieve something miraculous. All the while, we were striding through life, merely existing, kidding ourselves as our eventual returns proved ultimately to rightfully produce and have us receive—nothing. We'd become content to become shadowy figures of who we could've been. So much so, that through the scant results of our complacently driven experiences, paying negligible attention to those things most important, we were continually twisted by our own fate and winding up in the earth-shattering numbness of uselessly, irresponsible dazes.

That's *RIGHT!* The two of us, and our family, were going nowhere fast, our paths bogged down, seemingly for a frustrating lifetime of forever and we had nobody to blame, except ourselves.

But man! Come on; fifteen thousand dollars?

I don't know what I'd thought. That you could buy a house with strictly nothing down, not having to come up with any money?

Sure…It can be done.

But not after showing that you couldn't responsibly handle your affairs.

No way.

I didn't know ten, five, or even three people who could be counted among my inner circles of influences that could've come up with that amount of money, without proper preparation and planning.

It was totally out of the question.

When I finally got up the nerve to tell "NETTIE", she just looked at me, with that far off gaze of seeing through and leering past me that overtakes her frequently when she's most disappointed and it's entirely(She feels) my fault.

Upon hearing the news, she just dropped her purse beside our worn and tattered sofa, slumped into a flaccid podge of defeat atop it, and plopped her thumb in her mouth and she began her familiar rocking, back and forth rhythmically, as an indication to me that she had all but given up.

Feeling convicted, I slid slowly away from her not wanting to stair the injured party of my allegation any more directly in the eye.

When I returned to the ship on Monday, there was no work going to be completed by me that day. Instead, I strode around the ship becoming a veritable plague to anyone whose opinion I valued and respected.

The wardroom of any ship is an assortment of extremely intelligent, oftentimes kooky, but always congenial and stark—ravenly serious characters. Most of the men and women inhabiting such a place, steeped richly as they are in echoing hallows of years and years of esteemed and divine convention, had either already *made-it* or were well on their ways to developing *meaningful successes,* both inside the skin of the ship, as well as personally, financially, and professionally, in the outside world; where functional Mothers and Fathers had provided leadership, Love, discipline, trust accounts and reputation, all abounded by solid foundations of centuries old parental lineage, respect and most important, home training.

Then there were some of us…

Don't get me wrong, there were always a handful of us as well—Who, through hard work, dedication and instead of lineage, possessed a dogged, fortunate perseverance, who had made their ways through to be offered opportunities at achieving and excelling on identically the same basis. It's just sometimes, it seems some many have gotten' caught up in attempting to run too far a distance, playing catch up, from behind in this lifetime, too fast, to display patience enough to see a full realization of the spoils the ardent natures of their resilient labors could be, only because a long time ago, they substituted acceptance for the steeling, impenetrable walls of the plain and simple truth.

Man…

Fifteen thousand dollars.

I didn't have one acquaintance, friend or family member who could legally place their hands on such an impossible sum. And if I did, I had no means of successfully convincing them, to loan it to me—Simply for reasons that, *I was good for it*, and would pay them back accordingly, with interest.

But I did learn a thing of something or other while in the Navy.

That, was the power and worthiness of possessing the supportive ability—To *NETWORK* at my best.

First, I hit up the *SUPPO* (Supply Officer). She passed me off, as an errant bugaboo pest, to the *DISBO* (Disbursing Officer), the paymaster extraordinaire, who seamlessly managed thousands of intricate payroll accounts for every breathing member aboard, including the ship's most senior inhabitant, *The Captain.*

After taking in all that he'd told me, I next had an in-passing conversation with the ship's Exec. He was overall, second-in-command, and was routinely charged with the duties of running the daily operations of the entire crew, and therefore highly respected for his sometimes life-changing decision making too.

The Exec's position stood, "Lieutenant…If it's legal, above board, and we can make it all fit and pass the test of common sense, I don't see any reason for denying what you have intended. Go see the *DISBO* again. Tell him I'll consider it, if he can verify for me that there is a supporting statute already precedented and clearly outlined in the BUPERS manual of pay and disbursement annals. "

It was on!

Between the period of about twenty minutes it had taken me to get to work that morning, while thundering through traffic, not even really paying much attention to my driving, the formulation of a *what-if* plan had seeded the interest of there being something I could do and bring off to mend the gaping tenderness of the widening hole I'd caused to penetrate my wonderful "NETTIE's heart.

I was due to transfer from the USS CORONADO (AGF-11) to the aircraft carrier, CONSTELLATION (CV64) in just three months. What if I was able to draw an advance of pay pursuant to me PCS'ing (Making a permanent change of station)?

That would be all I needed to get my now postponed dreams of home ownership securely off the ground.

It was akin to taking a tax-free loan.

Payable in a single lump sum, minus twenty-eight percent in taxes. Plus, I would incur a monthly payback, for a period of twelve, twenty-four, or thirty-six months, I would make the choice.

As the *DISBO* handed me off to his disbursing clerk, I was immediately excited about being able to joyously return home that evening to tell "NETTIE" that I'd worked everything out, not to worry…that I'd found a way to fix the catastrophe that had developed as our latest problem.

This lasted about ten minutes of at first cordial and respectful conversation

with the clerk. Then things began to slide south increasingly. Turns out, that I wasn't eligible to draw such an advance upon *PCS'ing*. All because, I was transferring to a ship located in the same geographical location as the vessel from where I would be checking out.

I became instantly deflated. Good thing I hadn't called "NETTIE" from the ship, info'ing her in on what I'd been thinking. I would've hated to have extended her disappointment and frustration any further.

Still, I just couldn't let it go at that and give up.

The conversation between me and the disbursing clerk quickly became extremely heated. Almost to the point of him raving about how I didn't know or rather didn't want to know, or respect, the accuracy of professional authority evident in his words. That I had somehow brought into question whether or not he knew his job. He stood across from me, panting excitedly now himself, stealing preemptive glances, back and forth between our purely verbal battle ground and the *DISBO's* desk where the man didn't even look up to offer us the slightest concern. Peering across to me, with vengeful eyes, I watched him closely. It wouldn't be the first, or last time, that a highly decorated, sixteen year, salty, enlisted veteran, had had enough with an all assuming, privileged superior and simply tossed all caution to the wind as he washed away a day's frustrations, by very culpably sucker punching a know-it-all Officer in the mouth. For a minute there, I could actually visualize him possibly coming over the counter separating us as I'd just happen to be that one guy that pushed him over the edge of his service best plight.

He stood pat for a second. Then, abruptly, he wheeled about on his haunches, leaving me standing there at the half-counter to worry about myself. He ducked behind an opened door of a safe large enough to take up most of the room in the already crowded space.

I had no clue what he was doing.

But when he reappeared, he came bearing the ten-inch thick volume of the fully updated, BUPERS pay manual. This he thrust at me without muttering the choking semblance of a single, solitary word.

"O.K. SMART GUY, here it is, you read through all twenty billion pages, come back, and then, you tell me how to do my fucc'n job—you cock!"

That's exactly what he was thinking, I knew. Couldn't rightfully blame him. Had the shoe been on the other foot, I'm certain I would've been thinking exactly the same.

The bountiful volume hefted completely under my hand, I prepared to make my own *about-face* as I immediately turned heading for the scuttle, meaning to head for my stateroom, to begin a most desperate read, one which would take me through the entire manuscript cover to bloody *fucc'n* cover.

Just then, the *DISBO*, (Still without raising his head out of the over-read edition of *THE NAVY TIMES* which had previously maintained his interest completely) spoke up.

"Make certain you have it back by day's end, Blu...My only copy. Hate to have ta' *bend ya' over* in front of *the ole' man* tellin' him it's you's the reason MISSUS CAPTAIN gets caught short of funds at the bridge table with the other respectable ladies this weekend, cause *HE* hasn't been paid, cause' you still got hold of my book."

I simply tsk'd and grunted at him, matching his own negativity with my own, before leaving.

FUCC-a'...

Carting the precious index of my accomplice back to the isolated solitude of my stateroom, I sat down in a chair, right in front of my tiny sink, and I flipped through it, start to finish, being sure to touch, peruse or go over every page wrapped in a definitive anxiety of persistence.

After more than six hours of reading, re-reading, and of flipping through page upon page upon page of chalky, dry, meaningless material, I'd all but given in to the sobering fact—that the prideful Disbursing clerk had been right all along.

I'd reached a period of *booty-tingle*, the highly familiar result of being unceremoniously twisted into the same position atop an entirely uncomfortable seat for far too long. I took the opportunity to finally give in to my epiphany of misfortune and failure, and I stood to stretch, and make peace with the veracity of my efforts, when my roommate, Kevin Upland, turned his key in the door and walked in.

Looking at me, with his usual humorous tenor, he threw his cover atop his bed over me and clumped exhaustively into a chair beside me.

"What's up Blu, my man? How's the communications world treatin' ya'?"

"Fiiiine," I slumbered back.

Cocking his head slightly to one side, looking at me stupidly, I could tell he was awkwardly tuning in to what it was that obviously plagued me so utterly.

I didn't offer him much, and remained silent...At first.

Squiggling about, while waiting me out, with the care and kind effort of an attentive, senior counselor, he waited for me to make the first move in leaning forward to spill the intensity of intrepidating frustration locked deeply inside my guts.

When I just sat there appearing ready to offer him nothing, he continued to look at me with an airy, inclusive excitement of increasingly meddling progression locked wantonly on his face. His expression told me I wasn't getting away with remaining pent-up and frustrated, when it came to him, in silence. And I turned to meet his expression with an exasperated sigh as I only offered him, for the most part, nothing

..."W*haaat!"* Hoping that that was enough to ward him off and perhaps clue him in substantially—that I was caught up in some really stiff shit that I felt there was no way I was getting out of, and at that particular juncture, as I found myself, caught up in the moment, I really didn't want to be bothered.

"*WHA'SSSUP* wit' chew-*BLU*?"

Shrugging my shoulders aimlessly at him, I still didn't offer him any reply.

"Come on fool...Spill it! Dish dat' shit out"

I was in no mood for sharing with him right about then.

"*WHAT*? Tha' man got you down again, *HOMEY?* Somebody piss on yo' parade and tell you it's raining chocolate sprinkle drops?"

Kevin was a real trip. It was times like these that I could always count on him as my most trusted friend, roommate and confidante aboard the ship, to say something exactly like that—Just so superiorly and utterly stupid. He had a way of comfortably assisting me without reaching inside to dig too far. More times than I could count, no matter the situation, he'd extended his helping hand out to me, during times when I was gracelessly struggling with complex and difficult situations.

Moreover; and explicitly for reasons having to deal mostly with my upbringing, the absence of a cherishing, positive, paternal experience tended to have me shying away from welcoming wholesome friendships as they were presented to me from the likes of caring and genuinely concerned men. I didn't, and still don't have any very close, trusted male friends. For me, Kevin, was the closest I could ever call a friend of identical gender. And for me, I knew, that was just because we were roommates and we had no other option but to count on one another in situations just like this.

He was sure good for it. He always presented me with positive reinforcement after listening perceptively to everything I felt was a personally intended grind. I liked him immensely, cause' although he did this, he was an honest critic and always told me truthfully—just how it was I was *fucc'n* up.

For me, that was extremely healthy. My conversations with him, about life, our women and our kids, and about Navy, always lifted me up, tending to soften the scourge of the military blow and somehow make my days just a smidgen of a bit better.

All too reluctantly, I turned about and began to miserably fill him in on the details of my depressing home-buying woes.

Completely true to form, he didn't mutter a word, till' I was completely finished with the telling.

When I was done, he just looked at me intently for too long a time, then lifted a hand to smooth out fantasy dust from an imaginary goatee he could never have while aboard ship, and he stood abruptly.

Reaching up to his bunk to grab his cover, and swiftly toss it at a lopsided angle atop his head, he reached for the door handle once again and simply said, "Come—on…".

I had no clue about where we were going. But, the entire time that I knew him, Kevin had always seemed a consummate, if goofy, and sometimes maniacal genius.

The ship's Information and Intelligence Officer, he had a knack for peering with insight into compound, multifarious computations. And his respected opinion was cherished in many professional circles extending even to many academia of our time, not to mention, he was one of the very few young officers aboard who held a *walk-into-his-stateroom* ear of the ship's commanding officer without prior arrangement of having scheduled with the ship's secretary, seeking to be placed on his schedule.

Taking only enough time to reach for and grab my own cover, I followed his lead and took up steps behind him as he and I headed in the direction of the offices of the cantankerously occupied disbursing area.

Once we'd arrived there, Kevin maintained the lead by addressing first, the clerk, then inquiring about the whereabouts of the soulless, exceptionally uncooperative *DISBO.*

Right about then, Mr. maliciously unpleasant strode right in.

He greeted Kevin almost warmly. Then took a solitary look at me and the breadth of his smile dissipated turning dreadfully to an unwelcoming frown.

I understood completely what was going on. I hadn't exactly conducted myself with the full brunt of the most gentlemanly imminence of professional courtesy the last time he'd seen me come around. I guess I deserved it.

But for Kevin, his accommodating nature was abounding with a breathable pleasure of sense-proctoring agreeable reception.

"Hey Kev..." He greeted him lightly, while offering me still the ignorantly maintained expression of faded impoliteness.

"What can I do for you?"

Turning slightly about to me, Keving indicated, "Oh...Blu, and I were wondering if you might confirm a thing or two about PCS'ing that we found—in your bible?"

Just then, the impression of feinted shock and returned apprehension spread to take over and cover his previously good-humored intuition.

"What is it you'd like me to comment on?"

Kevin hefted the mighty book up onto the counter. Reaching for it with a precise sagacity, bearing knowledgeable dexterity, he flipped through a few pages and shuffled about a bunch more, till he'd arrived at a seemingly previously registered mark. Looking up at *DISBO,* with an incredulously mocking fascination, he began.

"You see, Walden, what Blu and I've been researching for—We've found."

He thrust the volume forward, entreating the man to come-onboard with him to take in the logical formation of thought he had obviously, before this, already mastered.

Not even looking in Walden, the *DISBO's* direction, he began to spout what lay there, page, paragraph, verse and chapter, precisely what it had taken me more than six hours of wavering stress—not to find.

"It's all right here in documented prose and print."

The *DISBO* began to recite out loud while Kevin followed him, just moving his lips in identical fashion, completely covering exactly the same information but without uttering another solitary word.

"Should the service member be executing subsequent Permanent Change of Station orders—and those said orders be—within the same geographical location as the transferring command, BUT! Be to a unit, designation or contemporary command possessing the distinction of being classified as "ARDUOUS SEA DUTY as is so faithfully carried out aboard the propensity of any sea going vessel, service member is therefore fully entitled to all advancements of pay, circumstances, and household goods transmissions as would otherwise be afforded commission to standard observation of normal Permanent Change of Station orders carried out to accompanying travel and transfer within geographical locations not deemed extemporaneously evident to be co-located in outwardly geographical and overseas adjoining vicinities. Advise disbursing entities to refer to table 30143.000G for extending identification of all terms detailing explanations of constituent "ARDUOUS" commands."

The idiot had read it all. I'm certain seeking an evident, reversion of the loop hole Kevin had already found.

Kevin was a genius!

We, I mean, *HE* had known or had found the precise paragraph which would suit the culmination of shortening my needs on short order, and there wasn't a single thing the conspicuously, indolent man could do, cept' make preparations for *cuttin' my check.*

Wait a minute…

I looked at Kevin intently.

"Did that say…Something about—household goods transmissions?"

He looked at me, while producing a tattered looking, *ABC* tooth pick from his pocket. Plopping it knowingly inside his mouth, he patted me on the back with a, "happy to help-out" salute, and he wheeled about and departed the space, off perhaps to resolving some other theory of relativity maneuver.

Painstakingly, the *DISBO* indicated that he would have his clerk cut me a check—minus twenty-eight percent in taxes, for three months advanced pay, an amount which came close to equalling seventeen-thousand dollars, by Friday.

All I had to do, was get my Department head, and the Exec to O.K. it.

Butter...I'd already had both of those skids infinitely informed and well-greased.

I was ecstatic. Nothing could have taken place on that ship during the remaining hours of that day which would have dislodged me from the tier of feeling greatly enamored and over-infinitely astute in my blessings.

Because, I had a true friend in Kevin. One I'd been able to count on for positively producing results created through networking, and I had good news too.

When I got off duty that day, I was on my way, straight to seeing the builder's lender lady, Lisa. She and I were going to have a lock-down discuss about me buying my "NETTIE" a house...

It's been three years since we moved in.

Sure, there's been some problems.

STANKAWANK (AshLe') moved out, at seventeen, following the departure of her sister, Britty, for a brief while—Both of them seeking to exercise a freedom we had taught them, and thinking they were experienced and expertly ready, at nineteen and seventeen, to take on and tackle the world's profusely handed out distractions.

"NETTIE" was at first heart-broken to see the both of them go.

Me, I merely continued trudging on. They both knew where home was at...

No reason to get myself all riled up and thinking the world was all falling apart, bent on its end, bout' to blow up.

Besides, I keep strict, very stifling tabs on them. Don't know how much of that they'd admit to knowing...Almost approaching the fete of becoming a parental stalker.For a time, they lived together, in a very nice apartment they shared with one of Britty's co-workers, another wayward child, named Shelly.

That's right! Jobs...

Each of them began working, after fate-filling outings with their *DAD*, on very particular Sundays, where we'd *some how* find ourselves inside malls and shopping centers and ice cream parlors, buying nothing, only there to grab applications, and on-the-spot, filling them out, turning them in and waiting for positive responses, which if waited upon patiently enough, I taught them... Always came... With the proper preparation—sans all the usual head-aches of being forced to excitedly *HAVE TO GET-A-JOB* upon being unceremoniously kicked out.

Britty's entering her second year at attempting to remain afloat in college. Ash, is waiting in the gate, scheduled to graduate in January, a full year early, from high school, as she anxiously awaits her turn at the gate.

Ohhh! Get this. February of this year brought Britty Reggie. August of this year held Reggie showing up bearing Britty a ring.

GAAAAWWWD!

We're talking long... Very long—ENGAGEMENT!

I'm too young to see myself stumbling over my tears leading my golden-haired beloved completely down the path of a wholesome bridal path channel.

BOOMER is *BOOMER*. If I ever go to another basketball game, football game, tennis match, or boxing promotion to watch him skillfully *strut his stuff,* no matter what it is he's out there excelling at and about to do, that fool betta' get me box tickets and V.I.P. seats, way up high, just off of the owner's purvue in his priviledged sky box features. My feet hurt too bad and I'm getting' too old to have ta' keep climbing all those stairs leading me up into—tha' cheap seats to continue getting kicked out of youth arenas—cause' my mouth done got me into the hot mess of a box of chocolates with refs—all on its own... Simply because I told the sucker, "That he couldn't see his way-worth a pair of blank, stolen glasses—*oughtta' be shamed of himself for even thinking bout' making such a twisted, bootied-up call against MY' BIG-DOG.*

MAMA 'N got herself a hefty settlement. We're still arguing with a janky judge in Texas over its disbursement.

"NETTIE" and me...

We're still—holdin' on... TIGHT!

She's a billing specialist for a major outfit situated close to Palm Springs.

I retired from the Navy, after twenty-two years, as the limelight of the refreshing spring in my service began to flicker for me and the border of all that I'd sought in my original reasons for joining began to become tedious and utterly mundane.

Ohhh...Almost forgot...I sold and closed fifty-nine houses, in just over the past six months with a nationally recognized builder, in a planned community located outside of Beaumont, Califrornia.

...Just got a follow-on position with another, one of my current employer's competitors. This time around, I'm being presented an opportunity to take the full community through its paces, from ground-breaking ceremony, model construction and grand opening, to handing out keys, pleasingly when the first of many units close. It'll probably be more than a year and a half from now, when I deliver the final home to my last happy family of buyers.

And I'll move on to the next challenge reaching forward toward success. My woman, most of the time happy, my babies by my side, or off doing things they know they've got every business being about—GOD willing.

...And,—until that moment, when I'm selected to draw on my last breath,

I'll continue putting off that vicious cycle of negativity which originally had me pegged from the start, for at least an early death.

I've learned an awful lot on this journey.

Not the very least of which is:

That it's not all about racism, as a whole. It's not about *THA' MAN*—beatin' you down.

It's not yo' Mamma's fault, yo' Pappy's fault, yo' Aunt Agness's, or your boy, Pookey-Poo's. It's yours!

Yours, mine, his, hers, and their's...

Conscientiously—*TAKING RESPONSIBILITY FOR YOUR ACTIONS*—Holding yourself accountable and accepting qualified criticisms maturely, is the only way to empower yourself and those inside *our* and *your* communities, to think ahead, towards working together and for producing great things—TOGETHER, as a nation; whereby we can support our families and our friends—ourselves, without the withering hand of the iniquitously unfilling scourges of relying on government hand-outs. In seeking or accepting complacency, only for the sake of taking time to become outwardly educated, marketing yourselves diversely within the multiplicity of hopes of quite possibly, waiting your future out, through making varying submissions of investments, which if waited upon patiently, pay out handsome sums of sage sustainability—to carry you, your children, and their children's children's children—safely through to bounce off into a sunset of having done your unequivocal best...At preparing your lives for the unimaginable contingencies of perhaps futuristic capors filled with wonder. If only...

We'd all stop being so doggonned CHICKENSHIT!

Printed in the United States
47981LVS00003B/22-54

9 781424 115150